I0667222

BURN ENGLISH

BURN ENGLISH

A WESTERN STORY

WILLIAM A. LUCKEY

FIVE STAR
A part of Gale, Cengage Learning

GALE
CENGAGE Learning™

Detroit • New York • San Francisco • New Haven, Conn • Waterville, Maine • London

GALE
CENGAGE Learning

Set in 11 pt. Plantin
Printed on permanent paper.

LIBRARY OF CONGRESS CATALOGING-IN-PUBLICATION DATA

Luckey, William A.
    Burn English : a western story / by William A. Luckey. — 1st ed.
        p. cm.
    ISBN-13: 978-1-59414-503-2 (hardcover : alk. paper)
    ISBN-10: 1-59414-503-2 (hardcover : alk. paper)
    1. Wild horses—Fiction. 2. Horse breeders—Fiction. I. Title.
PS3612.U265B887 2008
813'.6—dc22   2007047609

First Edition. First Printing: May 2008.

Published in 2008 in conjunction with Golden West Literary Agency.

Printed in the United States of America
1 2 3 4 5 6 7 12 11 10 09 08

For Margaret MacGregor Full Perry Luckey
1903–2007

PROLOGUE

The sound was clear and strong, moving with him, underneath him. A horse in full gallop, Burn lying close to the sweaty neck, urging on the horse with hands and voice, asking for longer strides—faster, even faster. The dark colt responded with a leap that almost unseated Burn, and he grabbed the black mane, fought for air.

Then it was the gray horse laboring and exhausted short-strided. Time to quit. But there were other horses in a green clearing . . . horses dying . . . bloody . . . tangled. He had to save them.

He woke from the dream, the familiar panic slow to leave, the taste of old copper in his mouth. He spat to one side, saw the reddish stain, knew he'd bitten the inside of his mouth, or had been coughing, that deep cough bent on destroying him.

The dark colt was now an aging, lamed stallion way past his prime; the gray had died twenty years ago—a rogue outlaw that had given everything he had had to Burn, but it hadn't been enough. Burn couldn't save the horses then, couldn't save himself, either.

He shook his hands, warily stood from the narrow bed, and forced himself outside to the shaded sun, the valley spread out in full view of the cabin. Then he understood why he'd dreamed his repeated dream in midday. Hoof beats of a horse pulling a buggy.

The driver waved. Burn barely raised his hand. Davey Hildahl, off on an errand to Springerville, cattle sales or new breeding stock or some fool chore the ranch owner thought only the foreman could handle.

After a quick breakfast, he would make a ride to the Hildahl homestead, knowing Davey was gone for two days. He saddled the bay mare, slowly smoothing out the blanket, setting the gear straight and balanced on her back, doing up the cincha real easy. She wasn't skittish or spoiled, but she was sensitive, thin-skinned, and Burn was always careful with this particular mare. In his mind she was the best of the lot, much like her daddy but with a lady's sweetness of temper and generosity that made her satisfying simply to look at from a horseman's point of view. Riding her was his only true pleasure.

It took him an easy hour's ride to the Meiklejon Ranch headquarters. The older folks in the area, they still called it the Littlefield spread, the owner that Meiklejon had bought the land from, the man who'd carved out a ranch against Indians and wild animals. Littlefield had died quickly after selling out. Burn had heard that the payments went to some relative back East. Some niece, a sister's child.

The Littlefield place appeared on a rise, now the grand home of Gordon Meiklejon, its stone front shadowed by a wide ramada, or verandah as the gentleman himself called it. Burn had been inside only once because there had been a longstanding coolness between him and Meiklejon. A distrust of the other born of a harsh accident, an understanding about what Meiklejon's decision to put up wire had cost Burn. They nodded politely to each other when meeting for celebrations at the Hildahl place. That was room enough for each man, and the distance they kept from one another was honored by those who surrounded them.

She would be in the kitchen, so he put up the mare in an empty side corral, then stood on the bottom step to the back door of the old house. He remembered his trip here that one summer when his blood had soaked into the railing, the top step, even on the doorframe itself. Twenty years of weather and scrubbing had not erased that awful time.

When he knocked, she laughed and told him to come in, that he wasn't a formal visitor. He belonged here, she said. The words stunned him, as they did each time she spoke them. He had learned she did not understand his feelings, would not allow herself to remember how it felt when she had washed his body, fed him, tended to him that summer. The bond such intimacy created had not gone from him even when she had made her choice, and the choice had been Davey.

Katherine Donald Hildahl might be twenty years older now, but she was still beautiful to Burn—tall and straight, her brown hair now lightened by strands of gray, and her eyes fine and watchful. Laughter showed at her mouth, and in those eyes there was an ease and pleasure as he presented himself to her, offering his hand, which she took and used to pull him closer, to give him that soft kiss on the cheek. To her it was a gesture; to him it was agony.

She had carried five children, one of them dying at birth, and still she was slender and graceful, and each move, as she worked at her chores, drew him closer inside the kitchen walls. It was a familiar room, safe, a place he'd once wanted for himself.

"You look sorrowful, Burn. Anything Davey and I can do?"

There it was—the cause of his sorrow. She didn't realize the pain caused by her own words. He forced a grin, knowing it would look terrible, but he wasn't given to easy smiles and careless chatter. He took a chair from the worn table, pulled it to where he could sit and watch her, lean on the back of the chair, and say nothing. She would eventually smile at him absently, as if barely acknowledging him as her hands shaped a loaf of bread or fashioned a pie crust.

Burn English was his usual self, quiet and too thoughtful, holding doggedly to his out-dated way of life. A quality Katherine had once admired in him, she now knew it was no longer useful, not when the world around them was changing so quickly. Not when his reliance on himself and the horses he bred and raised were no longer productive. This single-minded determination would destroy him. Not like the barbed wire had those years past, when the destruction had been physical, a bleeding death he barely escaped.

Time had brought about changes having to do with motion and possibilities—telephones that let you speak to distant neighbors without the effort of a buggy trip, motorcars that terrified the horses and delighted the men and children. Burn saw none of these changes, refused to see, and for that Katherine mourned him.

She knew that he loved her still, had never stopped loving her. But the decision had come from her heart when she had waited in this very kitchen years ago, standing between Burn and Davey, steadied by their physical presence as she had learned of her father's death. It was Davey she had turned to, instinct telling her this was the man who could offer protection and comfort.

Burn's face, as she had moved from him to Davey, had been one of the most terrible things she had ever witnessed. That pain going deeper than any bullet or cutting wire, a pain to the soul, impossible to heal. All these years and he had never pressed her, always had held back from that small kiss she gave him each visit. She needed that contact, the smell of him, that breathing in his heart, reminding her that she had made the right choice. Davey could be difficult; any man worth his salt was hard-headed and determined. But Davey cared for the children he had given her, and, when she studied Burn, she could not see him as a father. All these years and Katherine still wished for Burn the pleasure and contentment she had created with Davey.

Looking straight at Burn now, she saw his head tilt, the black hair filled with gray, the green eyes tight at the corners, the harsh face drawn with wrinkles but no loose flesh on his body, no small belly like her Davey carried. There was no one to care for Burn and make certain he was eating well, to wash his clothes, and to keep his bed. Only loneliness—and the horses for company.

She turned, smiling. "Here, Burn. Warm bread and fresh butter. There's jam on the table."

He stood and accepted the treat. His eyes caught hers, thanking her without speaking.

When she looked back a few minutes later, he was gone.

She rubbed her face at the hairline, knowing white flour would mark the gesture. Burn English hadn't changed at all.

Chapter One

The old horse lowered his head as Burn spoke to him. His fingers found the base of the ears, rubbing gently, and the stallion groaned, sighed, then nipped at Burn's arm, telling him that was enough. Burn laughed. A rare sound that sent birds flying up, and one old coyote, limping across a distant fence line, stopped and howled in answer.

"It's time, old man," Burn murmured.

The horse sighed, lower lip flapping. Burn touched the gray over the eyes, then stroked the muzzle that was almost white, where once it had been a dark brown. He slid the rope around the thick neck and fashioned a loop over the nose, in the same way he had first led the horse twenty years ago. Lamed then, a three-year-old attacked by his own sire, dying from an infected wound. Now it was age and hard use and three years of drought killing the old horse. Burn would place the shot, pull the trigger, but it was the times, the place, that confirmed the stallion's end.

Burn tugged on the rope. The stallion raised his head, looked out over the valley. They both watched the coyote slink away. The horse rubbed his head on Burn's arm and they took a step, then another, until the old horse walked with Burn, laboring over the slow rise to the hill top and the single tree waiting for them.

It took a half hour to climb the hill. Burn allowed the old horse to stop, to breathe slowly, even to nibble at the few bushes clinging in vain to the sandy soil. At the top Burn could see for miles—bright sun and clear sky, dry air. And there was nothing to ruin his view—no travelers on the roads to raise dust, no cattle being moved, no train whistling or sending its coal smoke into his world.

The stallion rubbed his head on Burn's shoulder as he loosened the nose loop. Burn let the rope slide, took it off the horse's neck, stood there silently with the animal who'd been a big part of his life for too long.

He had worried, years ago when he had first caught up the colt, that the easy temper that had allowed him to ride the youngster then would breed horses of uncertain heart. But those offspring, many of a similar quality to the bay mare, had been good using horses, quick on cattle, with plenty of endurance and easy to start, even for an old man who had broken as many bones as Burn had.

Now he laid an arm over the stallion's crest, took note of the swayed back, looked down to study the buckling knees barely able to carry the animal's expanding girth. He'd like to sit one more time on the stallion; it had been years since he had raced the horse except in his dreams. But he'd keep his promise to the end, knowing that the once sturdy body and long legs could no longer handle even his own slight weight.

Burn walked away from the hillside edge to the single tree, and, with some grumbling and complaining, the old horse followed reluctantly. When they stood in the shade, Burn went to the horse's head, brushed aside that thinning forelock, and studied the broad plane of bone with its glaring white hairs, the cavities above both eyes almost pure white, the long lashes also turned white. One finger drew a line from the base of the right ear to the top edge of the left eye; the finger's path left behind a mark of disrupted hair. He repeated the gesture from the left ear to the right eye, creating the necessary center target.

He'd buckled on a holster and belt earlier, and had been too aware of the extra, one-sided weight as he'd climbed the hill. Now he retrieved the pistol, an ancient Navy Colt that he'd earned as a kid down in Texas. He'd killed two men with it, and a panicked roan gelding. Now it would kill one more time.

The pistol was heavy. He raised it, placed it on the X made by his finger tracings, and pulled the trigger, exhaling. As the huge body fell, he shot one more time into the top of the ruined skull. Then he turned away, went to his knees, and vomited his crude breakfast of cold coffee and stale biscuits.

The stallion's bowels had loosened. The air was foul. Burn stayed only a moment to be sure the horse was dead. Kneeling at the shattered head, he bent down, waited, held his own breath. There was nothing, no flutter of the clamped nostrils, no small puffs of dust. A trickle of blood through the clamped teeth slowed, pooling on the hard sand. No life.

He staggered down the hillside, throwing the pistol and watching it rise. It shone against the sun, then fell among the rocks and shattered, stock and metal chipping. Burn continued on, caught his boot heel, almost went down, jamming his hand into a cactus when trying to break his fall. Behind him the ravens went to work, squabbling over the excess of flesh and blood.

He was sick again when he got back to the small cabin and ended up on his knees in the paddock where the stallion had lived these past few weeks. He'd been brought in from his mares, fed extra hay. Burn had even brought home a bag of oats, but the stallion would not eat them.

Finally Burn lay on his bed, worn out, feverish, hating himself while knowing he'd done the right thing. Death was a certainty—for the stallion, and for himself.

His head jerked up and his heart began to race. He woke from the same nightmare to the sound of an approaching rider. Sitting forward, listening closely, fretful as to who would be riding up to the cabin. In his mind he could still feel the dream, but he forced himself up, went out to the porch, settled back in a chair, and watched the rider approach.

It was one of the Hildahls' kids on the bay pony, one from his old stallion crossed with a stunted mare. A good size horse and a companion for the boy; horse and rider were both from good stock, well suited to each other.

The boy's name was Henry and he came with a folded piece of paper in one hand, held out to the side as if it were on fire. Burn waited. The pony stopped at the tie rail and Henry stayed mounted, offering delivery in small movements, the paper *crackling* slightly. The bay pony cocked his head and turned one ear back but didn't shy or spook. Burn found himself smiling for the first time since his visit to Henry's mother. Here was his proof—that bay mustang sired good stock no matter what he had been bred to.

He studied Henry as if he'd never seen him before. About fifteen, tall like Davey and plain-looking, but smart, that could be seen in his eyes and his carriage. Katherine had bragged about Henry, saying he knew who he was, knew how to work hard, was good on a horse, had an instinct about where cattle hid, and, despite having grown up on a ranch, he was curious and excited about the few motorcars he'd seen. Burn guessed that when this child went from his family into the world, he'd not come back.

When Burn was the boy's age, maybe a bit older, he'd already killed two men. It made a man think how the world was changing. Burn didn't take to the new ways, not like this boy or his younger brother, Gordon. They were children of a new century, while Burn might as well be stuffed and mounted in the back room of a dusty saloon, where the doors would soon close because the patrons had gone home to their families.

Now here was Henry on that pony, holding a paper, his parents obviously asking one more thing of Burn. Good people, Katherine and Davey Hildahl, but still a demand on Burn. He leaned forward in the crude chair, put his hands on his knees, staring at the two appendages, noting the softening of the terrible scars that bound him to the Hildahls. Without their care, he would have died those years back, wrapped in the damnable barbed wire and leaking life and blood into the ground.

He could close his eyes and still see Davey's face that day. His skin pure white even though he spent most of his time under the sun, his blue eyes wet, staring at Burn who could barely feel any part of himself. His own blood mingled with that of the gray horse that bled out heavily on top of him. The pain hadn't started yet, but Davey's eyes, looking down at him, had told what was coming.

Burn shook and pushed his hands between his clamped knees and the bay pony took one step back, finally unnerved. "What you want, boy?" Burn's voice cracked, a thin quiver telling of his inner wounds, but Henry wouldn't notice. He'd known Burn all his short life, Henry had. It had been Burn who had ridden for the doctor when Henry decided to be born. Katherine had come visiting to Burn's cabin, and there she'd chosen to start labor. The old man, Gayle Souter, had been visiting, too—more company than Burn had ever wanted, even though he had liked both of the folks taking up time and space in his small cabin.

Souter had birthed out his own children and Burn could ride, so there had been no discussion. The doctor was known to be at the Meiklejon house and that made Burn's ride short and sweet. He'd come back with Davey and the doctor, and had been there, walking on the porch with Davey when his wife produced their son. The hurt in Burn had grown with each gulping cry from the little one, each smile on the new papa's face, and the sweet glow from the new mother, Katherine Donald Hildahl.

He'd missed his chance, knew his loss, would have gone right then, but he owed the newborn, owed his life to the parents, and couldn't break himself away from wanting at least to see Katherine once in a while, never for long since it grew the hurt inside, but enough to know that she was content.

He hated the Hildahls' happiness, hated the closeness between husband and wife—Burn's only real friend and the first woman, the only woman, he'd ever loved.

So he stayed for Henry, and those who had come after, even the little one who had died never having drawn a breath. He had watched Katherine's suffering, had known it wasn't for him to offer comfort, but once, in the old Meiklejon ranch house where she and Davey and their growing family lived, Katherine had put her hand on Burn's arm, had pressed down enough so he could feel each finger against the old wire scarring, and he had known what she was telling him. *We need you.* Spoken by touch, words formed but not sounded. He had nodded, keeping his own silence, and given her a brief grin, foolish on his ugly face but enough that Katherine had released him with a short laugh.

That had been ten years ago. Now it was time. He wasn't needed; he wasn't part of any life here. It had been the old horse who'd held Burn this long. He couldn't abandon the youngster deep inside the graying, tired flesh. The colt that had come to Burn when both were injured and in need.

Burn had kept his word and after that first year he never rode the colt again. The awkward youngster matured into a fine herd stallion, siring babies that looked like him and had his temperament. Burn made a good living during those years, training and selling off the four-year-olds and trading for new mares when he could.

An English-bred horse came to mean something in the southwest part of the state and even on up to Santa Fé and into Colorado where folks with too much money liked an English horse for its speed.

Now he was done. The stallion dead, his bones stripped even at this moment, coyotes howling all night as they gorged themselves, and each cry drilling Burn as his bullet had drilled through the stallion's skull. He could add that death to his legacy. His memories were filled with death, blood, gore, wounds so horrific that Burn still could not look at his own body without seeing in the rough, ridged skin across his belly and thigh what had almost killed him then, was killing him again. All those mustanging years had made him an old man at forty-five, hard-moving, slow, aching so much in the morning that getting up was a chore.

"Mister English?" Henry was being polite, asking Burn to come take the paper.

He stood finally, feeling that ancient pull across his belly from the lost battles. "Sorry, boy . . . got to thinking." He took the two steps sideways, less pain in the knees that way, and grinned to himself, probably scaring the hell out of Henry at the sight. He took the piece of paper. "Thanks, boy." Saying the boy's given name was another wound; no reason other than he was Katherine's son, born of Davey Hildahl. He wadded the paper up in his fist, knowing what it was, unable to handle the words. An invitation from the Hildahl clan to celebrate with them—a birthday, a holiday? Hell, he didn't even know what day of the week it was, never could get to a celebration on the right day. It was a standing joke that he'd shown up for Christmas a week late, one time, so they had made it a tradition to tease him as they blew whistles and brought in the New Year.

"Ain't . . . aren't you comin', Mister English? Elizabeth . . . she really wants you to be at her party . . . she's turning six this year." The child smiled and patted his bay on the shoulder. "I think she wants you to bring her a pony. I guess Mama told her about the pinto you been working with. And Elizabeth . . . she thinks it belongs to her."

Then before Burn could put the boy straight, the child kicked the bay as he reined him around, and the pony leaped into an easy lope from a spinning standstill, leaving Burn once again to regret the stallion's death.

Burn had kept a couple of the bay's sons for a while but had had offers on them too high to ignore. So he'd taken the money and put it in a bank in Socorro where it had the names of the Hildahl children on it, shared out to each as they came into the world. He hadn't told their parents yet, knowing Davey and Katherine would refuse his gift. Money wasn't much for Burn. He could always ride a horse and get a meal, a barn for the night. $5,000 was more than he could understand.

But a child, or three, four maybe, they could use that to go to college back East where all education was fancy and important, or, now, maybe to the coast of California where cities were growing back after that awful earthquake, and all kinds of knowledge could be learned. It would have to be paid for, and Burn knew the earnings of a ranch foreman didn't allow for the proper education of four children.

The dust of the bay pony's departure settled. Burn eased back into the chair, rested those outsize and wounded hands on his knees, and worked at thinking, seeing ahead of him a new road promised across his land, poles and wires going up so folks could talk to each other without going outside the door, saddling or harnessing a horse, and making an effort to visit.

Burn didn't want talking most of the time. Once in a while he'd spoken of his feelings with Davey, after that terrible wire accident, and then the facedown with an outlaw gone bad, but, since then, well, Davey'd married Katherine and there was no time for easy talk between friends.

He stood up, tired of thinking back, needing to do what had been tormenting him for months. The stallion's destruction finally would get him moving.

In the corral he had a draft team, steady monsters that could pull anything a man wanted moved. He'd used their mama and a sorrel gelding, borrowed from Meiklejon, to pull the cabin from its old spot to where it was now so that he could look out and see the valley and nothing else. That team was long gone to bone and dust, and the valley was crowded so that a man saw houses and wagons and once in a while one of those motorcars, honking and belching and scaring the chickens.

But he still had his draft team and he'd use them one more time. Burn was slow and deliberate hitching them—Bill on the left, Jake always on the right. They worked better that way. Matched sorrels they were—their sire a big old boy from up in Albuquerque that the owner said was a Belgian. Fancy papers or home-grown, Burn didn't care. The two geldings did their work and more, and occasionally Burn and the team hired out to work for other folks, doing their clearing, plowing, or skidding rafter logs from a distant stand of straight pine.

The first pull on the corral gatepost sent the sorrel geldings to their knees. The damned thing was in deep, but it still was only wood, and the team leaned their considerable weight and stubborn tempers into the task. With a low sigh the gatepost twitched, shivered, and then split apart, tumbling the attached rails that brought down more posts and then railings until the whole prison rolled violently apart like broken tree limbs. Burn laughed as he slapped the team into a brisk trot to get them out of any possible danger.

This time when he reined them around and asked them to back up, it was to the pitch of the cabin. With the chain hooked inside the front door, the team barely had to jerk forward to bring down the loosened boards, old and dried out. The roof quickly collapsed, dust rolling over Burn and Bill and Jake. The house was gone, old history buried. That done, he unhitched the team, letting the harness lay where it fell once stripped from the sweaty bodies as if the animals wearing that leather and metal had disappeared, leaving behind only the outline of their working lives.

He had his shoeing tools away from the barn, nested with his saddle, bridle, saddle blanket, and all the gear he would need. He had put them there this morning, after feeding the three remaining horses. The others had been turned out last night. Now there was only the dark bay mare that looked a lot like her daddy. He'd deliberated about keeping the mule for packing, but he'd changed his mind this morning, so he'd already turned the mule loose. Left the mare alone, set her up for being fretful.

It took him just moments to pull the team's shoes that were shod only on the front hoofs to prevent against bruising from stones in their work. He rasped the hoofs even, set each one down—a job well done, and for the last time. He pulled off the bridles, those damned blinkers stirring up dust where he dropped them. The team stood quietly, close to each other, waiting to be told what to do. It took Burn slapping Bill on the hindquarters to get the big son moving, with Jake trailing along a half stride from his teammate.

He watched the simple thought process go through the team's mind. Nothing held them, nothing on their head, no fence around them, nothing to stop them. Finally Bill lumbered into his heavy trot and Jake followed. Bill reached over and nipped at his buddy. Jake squealed and half bucked, and then the two horses broke into a gallop that shook the ground.

Burn was still laughing as the air slowly settled. In the distance was a long trail of high dust, one sharp whinny, and then the team was gone. Burn turned his attention to the rest of the plan.

The older brood mares, he'd let them go with their foals. They'd either drift into the wild life or be caught, branded with another rancher's mark. He had no geldings—all sold and gone, the money in that bank account, a few dollars in his back pocket. No stud colts, none of them could replace their sire.

Word would get out quickly, hurried along by Henry's visit and the rejected invitation, and the appearance of the well-known English brand on hides throughout Datil and Red Hill and over to the plains of San Agustin. The wandering horses would come up against barbed wire and know to follow the fence line instead of fighting it.

It was more than Burn had known—that damned wire had nearly killed him.

Chapter Two

Alone, the bay mare was nervous in the small, side pen—head up, eyes too white, sweating along her neck and at her loins. She paced the fence, muzzle skimming the top rail. She stopped several times to whinny for Bill . . . Jake.

Burn went in the pen and the mare ran from him, head still high, eyes still showing too much white. He decided that maybe he'd kept the wrong horse, or that he should have thought to hold Bill and Jake until the mare was saddled and ready. When he finally caught her, using soft words and a light rope laid over her neck, he spent a few moments soothing her—a soft brush, his hands on her hide—gently rubbing her muzzle until the tight hold of her lips softened and she finally yawned, dropped her head, and rubbed against him.

He called her Beauty despite an old reluctance to name his horses. Her sire had been nameless except in the beginning, when Burn had called him Jester because he was sure the colt was always playing tricks on him. That name had slipped away as he rode the dark bay hard the long summer of being chased, herding a few mares, ducking the law and angry ranchers. The colt had saved his life over and over, so the name was buried, given away to the wind, and the stallion had nothing to bind him to human need or Nature except to reproduce himself as often as possible.

As Burn slipped the simple jointed bit into the mare's mouth, he braided a long strand of black hair across the brow band carefully as the mare tossed her head before quieting. It was all that remained of her father's physical presence. Too sentimental, too foolish for Burn, but he had taken the strand while the stallion was alive, receiving a peculiar look from the dark bay as he had lifted the black tail and used his knife to cut out the shank of hair. He had needed something more than the legacy of the bay's offspring.

He had everything ready—saddlebags and a bedroll, a good sheepskin coat, a thick black hat and gloves, even a scarf. He was riding north this time, out of the New Mexico Territory. It was going to be a state soon if the politicos up in Santa Fé had their way—a state defined with roads and poles and electricity—and Burn was going north to where maybe he could find a place no one else wanted to be.

He guided the mare through a series of small cañons and valleys, places he knew were free of wire. In the saddlebags were wire cutters and short pieces of wire, and to carry them was illegal, but he didn't care. If he came up against the damned wire—and he would—a quick cut, a wrap he'd done many times, and he'd go through on to the next wire fence that needed cutting. He would make the repairs tight, not wanting to stir up trouble because of his passing.

Word would travel quickly that his place was gone, corral and house destroyed, and eventually the bank in Socorro would let Davey know about the college money and that he now owned the rough 4,000 acres Burn had earned through the horses. An easy transfer, with the banker sworn to remain silent, but Burn had faith in the man's soft conscience, and, when enough time had passed, when word got spread around down into Gutierrezville and Alma and even down the Río Grande Valley to Hot Springs and up to Belen—all in the territory of New Mexico— the banker would be glad to talk, to tell the few curious folks what he'd known all along, and here was what he knew.

Katherine might take a moment to think of him, maybe even to cry, and then Davey would hold her and they'd be with each other again without Burn to watch and be hurt over their constant affection. He valued their place in his life, but being near them kept him wounded and it was a damned fool thing for an old *mesteñero* to accept as his only life.

He hoped most of the horses, even the sorrel team of Bill and Jake, would escape capture, would travel as they chose and eat the sweet grasses, stand in the deep shade, head to tail, to swish away pestering flies, trusting each other for comfort and safety.

He let the mare shift into her easy lope. She came up light in the bridle, used her hindquarters, and it felt more natural to him than sitting on the porch in that damned rocker that the fat old man from his past had left him. The old man had died under the name of Eager Briggs, but Burn had remembered his real name. Riding a good horse was better than any soft-padded chair or thick mattress. It was a lope carrying him out of a life he had never wanted, except for that one woman.

Burn judged the line he chose as straight north, always staying west of the Río Grande Valley. There were times when he and Beauty topped a rise and he could follow the river's dry course by the richness of the yellowed cottonwood leaves. First thing a man learns in dry country—to judge water by the luxury of the trees.

He stayed close to the old fence line Meikeljon had put up, the first fence in the area, eighteen years ago. He still hadn't run into much of the wire yet, except for the railroad tracks coming from Socorro into Magdalena. He'd keep west of there, to avoid getting tangled in the right of way and all that damned wire. Four miles, straight north, to his first fence. Once there, he climbed down, dropped the reins. The mare insisted on rubbing her face on his back while he snipped the five strands of wire. This time it was easy. A lazy ranch hand had left coiled wire nearby, so Burn didn't need to use any of the strands he had brought along. He'd counted on this sloppy habit to make repairs.

He led the mare through the opening, the cut wire carefully dragged to one side. But when a strand *rattled,* the mare cocked her head and turned skittish, and only then did he remember that she and her mama'd been caught in wire once. Beauty had been maybe two months old, so the scar had slowly disappeared, but not the fear. He rubbed between her eyes, laid an arm over her neck, and she walked past the wire, trembling but without further trouble.

It took him a good half hour to rewire, and he knew why. He felt the mare's fear in his own wrist and fingers, deep in his gut, and he almost was sick from the chore. Damned fools, both of them, him and the mare. As he mounted and Beauty tried to bolt, Burn figured he'd chosen the right horse for his leaving. She had his fears and for the same reasons.

Beneath him, under hide and behind bone and ligament, a heart beat too fast, mimicking his own reaction, so Burn let the mare pick her pace. This time it was a run, hard on Burn, so he stood in the stirrups, held to the saddle swell, and let her go. As she slowed, Burn rode down into the saddle seat and felt the years poke and prod him. Pain was a familiar constant. This time, though, heading out to whatever would become his end, he found agony rode inside him, more intense than the simple morning pain he usually felt.

Finally he had to stop the mare and climb down and lean over. He coughed up blood, thin mucus, some liquid. Mostly blood. He'd felt it more than six months ago when he rode his last bronco, a deep palomino stallion left too long unbroken. It had been a hard ride. He'd come off twice, and each time the

owner and his men had laughed as if the bucking son-of-a-bitch
was a toy any child could handle. He had reminded them later,
when the stallion was walking and trotting on command, coming to a good stop, even backing a step or two, that they'd
brought the horse to him because they couldn't do their own
dirty work at home.

The rancher had nodded thoughtfully and offered Burn an
extra $10. He'd refused, taking the $20 they'd bargained on,
saying it was enough.

He'd known the truth then, and nothing had healed since,
nothing had gotten better, and he had had to shoot an old horse,
and now he couldn't let a smooth-gaited mare have a run
without cutting himself more inside. He was tired of the whole
mess, including the mess he'd made of his life. God damn.

He let the mare drift while keeping the valley to his right, not
a line but a boundary he would not cross. The shadows drew
away from the mare's hoofs, leaving spindly marks and exaggerated strides. He laughed. The mare cranked one ear back and
Burn lightly touched her neck. Colors startled him as he passed
one of the looming hills—a vivid red sky, a richer color than
what he'd seen on an apple or the sweaters Katherine had knit-
ted for her blonde daughters. Finally the colors faded to the
softness of Katherine's skin when she blushed, or stood near
her husband. Then the blue came, starting out thin under the
clouds, changing, then thickening to a dark layer that was black.
Burn slapped his thigh and knew the feel of his hand on cured
hide. He wore his old mustanger chaps, the second pair he'd
made and worn through in that year of chasing down the wild
herd that had become the foundation for his time as a breeder
of horses.

He counted them, totaled up the years. Seventeen it had
taken him to leave since their wedding ceremony where he'd
stood up next to Davey and made a jackass of himself, blushing

and stammering. He'd never been in any one place in his life that long; now he was a man with no skills, no money, and nothing holding him down.

There was a soothing rhythm to constant movement, a release from responsibility, owing no one and free to ride on. It came back to him—the day not that long ago when he had left Katherine for the last time, carrying a slice of her fresh bread mounded with butter and jam, made from berries the children had picked high up in the mountains. He'd almost forgotten, with all the civilizing forces around him—children and a home—the horses that depended on him.

Now he understood that Katherine had made the right choice. He'd have been no companion for such a woman. The knowing had freed him and he had put together his plan. Now he was gone.

When he realized the sky was dark gray and no more shadows slipped under the mare's tracks, it registered that he needed to make camp. The careful habits came back easily—strip and hobble the mare, feed her a handful of oats from the saddlebags, tie his gear up into a stunted juniper, and camp close to it so no critter would come around, hunting salt. A dry camp tonight. He'd share water from the canteen with the mare, knowing tomorrow there would be a spring or stream. He'd been headed in the right direction, but hadn't paid much attention to how far out he still was.

Hunger got taken care of by a fry pan of beans, thirst went before an airtight of peaches, the juice sticking to his fingers as he knived through the tin top, a skill he'd once possessed, now lost but coming back, as he let his fingers feel the raw edge, knowing how to use the blade. The juice was perfect and he licked the inside of the airtight, careful not to cut his tongue. He could easily eat another one of these treats, but food would become a problem quick enough and Burn knew he didn't have the edge left to go for days on water and biscuits and a cold camp. Soft now, a long time living with human comforts—an outhouse and water pump, a wood stove, a mattress set over a rope-strung frame. Comforts he couldn't bring with him, didn't want any more.

He knew he was lying to himself. He wanted those and more, but she had never come to him, never left her husband and family, only smiled at him and sent over peach preserves or a salted ham and invited him for the holidays he had forgotten.

Sad affair for him. No choice now but to ride out and find something, almost anything, to keep himself alive, or ride on into the distance where life and death merged. He didn't much care. It wasn't a wish or a hope, but simply the reality that came smacking him on the nose with that birthday invitation and a child wanting a paint pony that wasn't ever going to do for her. He couldn't have looked into that pretty face, so much like her ma's, and told the child no. Never.

He had run from a six-year-old and a growing hatred of the life he had come to accept, and the ache put in his gut from the last bucking horse he'd rode, and years filled with too many of them, with all the bucking horses. He was torn apart, both in his belly and his heart, and it had been time to get free of those wounds.

He was headed north, by God, and he needed sleep. Even the bay mare was dozing maybe ten feet away, head down, tail barely moving, eyes half closed. She'd keep watch. Burn could sleep now, knowing he was safe.

The ground was hard, the sky too bright. He rolled over and a rock dug into his hip. He groaned, and the mare whinnied at him, which made him laugh. At least something was funny.

He'd kept his old rifle cleaned and oiled. Now he lay on the ground, counting the coyote howls and thinking about struggling to get up and maybe firing into the empty night, scaring the sons-of-bitches who would ruin his first free sleep. They kept howling, but finally he went to sleep flat on his back, half out of the bedroll, boots near his head, the rifle just out of reach.

He could tell by the stars. How much they'd moved. Something had awoken him. He grabbed for the weapon, sat up, and spooked the mare that was standing over him. It was more, though, not her presence, but an extra sound. A growl, a metal *rattle*. He scrambled upright, and, bent over with the rifle, he headed toward the sound.

He found a varmint with its head in the airtight. Peaches, just the scent of them, would do that to a varmint, and a starving man, too. Burn managed to straighten up, and, even while he was laughing, he caught the long tail—a raccoon—which was reasonable, and he held onto the tail while trying to pull the can loose. The raccoon wasn't too pleased with getting his butt kicked while he couldn't see. Burn was of the opinion that if the varmint would hold still for only a moment, he could get that damned can off, and they could part in a friendly manner.

But it wasn't going to happen, so Burn stepped on the raccoon's neck just behind the ears pinned inside the can and that stopped the thrashing somewhat but not the squalling echo from inside the can. Then the damned varmint pissed on one of Burn's bare feet, spread wide to balance as he pulled and yanked and swore. Exactly what he'd feared, of course, happened. The raccoon's head slid free and Burn fell backward, foot covered in raccoon piss, and the varmint sat up, paws waving, that black-masked face grinning in the clear early morning sky, and Burn got a good scolding for his wayward treatment of a poor animal just trying to keep on living.

Burn stood up and the raccoon sauntered away, ringed tail trailing behind him, leaving Burn with a stink and a belly aching with laughter.

After he'd rubbed sand on his foot to rid himself of the raccoon smell, he crawled into his blankets. The hobbled mare was some distance from him and she kept watching his struggle to slide in, rest the rifle nearby, draw the blankets to his chin. The night air was chilly. Then Burn was asleep.

The mare snorted and squealed as something kicked Burn in the side. He rolled away, tangled for a moment in his blanket, then, scrambling free, grabbed the rifle and came up rifle in hand, hammer cocked. No point in waiting. Whatever had kicked him needed to know he was ready.

"What the hell you doing in our pasture?" The voice was huge, but Burn didn't look up at it. There were other shapes drifting between him and the mare, and, when she kicked one of them and it cursed, Burn grinned.

"Sleeping, you damned fool! Can't you tell when a man's sleeping?" A different voice, and coming from the same direction.

Burn got his bearings, kept the hammer back, the rifle pointed to the ground. He was surprised they'd given him the chance. It was his warning to the bastards, and the circle of men seemed to read what he was telling them. He could feel his gut turn, tasting bitter blood, and he was getting mad enough to shoot any one of these rannies who tried moving toward him.

They seemed to know that, also. It was in their eyes. Hell, Burn thought, he wasn't far enough from his old grounds that these boys didn't know his reputation. One of the old ones, the fool *mesteñero* folks talked about.

He could see clearly now. His eyes focused on one or two of the intruders—the big one who stood back, and the smaller, younger son-of-a-bitch who had to have been the kicker. It showed in his face, that eagerness to stir trouble.

Burn circled the rifle barrel until it was aimed at the boy's middle—the easiest shot guaranteed to bring a man down. The boy knew that, and so did the men standing nearby. Slowly, hands held wide, they drifted so it was only the boy facing Burn and his rifle. The weapon might be old and out of date, not fancy or engraved, but in Burn's hands, shaky maybe with anger and fear, its threatening message was clear.

The rifle was heavy in Burn's hand. He hadn't fired a shot in years except for killing the stallion. There was *that* leftover taste in him, of powder and death that he hadn't outrun yet. This kid, kicking him for no damned good reason, made him downright ornery.

The big man spoke and the boy eased back.

The rifle was getting heavier, but Burn wasn't ready to lower it, to give the boy any peace of mind.

"Name's Warren Hardesty, Mister English. We surely didn't know it was you. . . . Thought you'd head south this time a year."

Burn wanted to wipe his sweating face but the kid had a mean eye.

"We've been having troubles on this land," Hardesty explained. "Some folks down by the river . . . well, they think this is their private hunting preserve. Ray here, he's been taking care of chasing them off the land. He gets a mite pushy at times, but we sure as hell didn't mean to interrupt your sleep. Just didn't know who you were."

Something caught Burn's eye and he began to laugh. "You boys're riding my stock. All o' you."

"Yes, sir, Mister English. And the boss wants to know what we'll do now you seem bent on leaving."

Burn was just curious enough to ask: "Who's your boss?"

"Ron Platten of the Cross B."

Burn nodded. Platten had bought a lot of his best horses over the years. Burn said: "Tell him Frank Wainright, over to Spring-erville, has a son of the old stallion. He's been coming up with some nice colts."

Even with all the friendly talk, Burn kept the old rifle pointed at the boy's gut.

Finally the big man, Hardesty, asked for a truce. Burn agreed, but only if the kid stepped back to hold the horses and stayed in Burn's line of sight. He wanted to keep an eye on him but didn't want him part of any more talk.

The boy moved back with Hardesty's thick forearm helping him along. "You say Frank's got some of your bloodstock?" Hardesty said, trying to keep Burn's attention. When Burn nodded, Hardesty asked: "You have any say in the mares?"

That was a surprising question. Most ranchers figured it was all from the stallion.

"Yeah," Burn answered. "I sent along a few I thought he could use. We talked a bit. I told him my thinking on the type of mare needed. Guess he's got a good strain going." It was more than Burn usually said to a stranger, but it was about horses, his horses, his only legacy. He turned his back to Hardesty, speaking quickly as he went to the bay mare who was trying to hop away. "You all said what you needed to say. Got me up too god-damn' early, and now my horse's trying to leave without me. Gentlemen, that's enough."

Polite for him, but too wordy. He walked away, rifle still in his hand. At one point he raised the rifle over his head as a reminder. Mutterings behind him, a sharp word, a saddle *jingle*, horses farting, and then it was quiet and he had his hands on the mare, who sighed and rubbed her head on his shoulder. Burn had to take her mane and just above her nostrils and lead her forcibly back to the camp. Then he bridled the mare, loosened her hobbles, watered her from his punched hat, and tied her to the juniper.

The riders were gone except for their dust and a few piles of fresh manure, boot prints, and a present in his blankets—balls of wet manure kicked there. The boy's parting shot.

He wished he had had the *cojones* to pull the trigger, fire at their retreating backs, but he couldn't afford wasting a bullet.

CHAPTER THREE

Burn was three hours in the saddle and it was getting hot out on the flatlands. Dusty, empty, no fences, no nothing until he saw that lick of yellow flame that told him the trees he'd seen yesterday were showing off their water. He and the mare were dry, so he didn't have to lay the rein lightly on her neck, just simply look at the distant trees. Four of them he counted, a good sign, and the mare lit into that easy lope headed straight to the spot Burn was thinking about.

It had been more than twenty-four hours with only one canteen between them. Burn slid off the mare as she slowed to a hard stop and let himself fall into the water, burying his head, blowing water from his mouth, then rolling over and resting his head in the water, looking up at the close sky, listening to the mare snorting and blowing and doing her own wallowing. He spat out one last dribble of water, then rolled himself up and squatted. He washed his hands, ducked his head under again, laughing as he swallowed and coughed and swallowed again. Then he remembered last night and shucked off his right boot, pulled the sock free, ducked his foot in the water, using sand to scrub the flesh. There was no more stink now, nothing but the memory of that miserable raccoon and his opinion of Burn's efforts at rescue.

The bay mare lifted her head and whinnied. Burn scrambled to his feet, hobbling on his naked foot as he reached for the rifle stuck in its scabbard. One hand touching the grip, he settled, listened, heard what the mare already had sensed. More horses. Hell, a man couldn't ride even a half day without meeting up with the whole damned territory.

Burn let go of the rifle butt, loosened the rope from the other side of the horn, and started swinging it lightly. The mare winced, ducked her head, but kept her ears pricked while Burn watched in the direction from where the sound came.

It was nothing more than a band of horses coming up quickly. The singing rope had slowed them considerably, but one dark colt came on ahead.

Burn threw out the rope, intending to miss, but, instead of bolting, the colt struck out at it. Burn laughed as he read the brand. He remembered this one, bold and aggressive with the bad eye of his mama. He'd not wanted to breed the mare, or keep her, but Davey had asked, as a favor, and Burn had given in reluctantly. Then he had tried to get Davey to geld the colt, but Davy had sold it as a weanling, telling the buyer to geld him. The man hadn't yet, most likely wouldn't, and he'd be getting fractious offspring and blaming Burn for not having told the truth. A man didn't want to see that eye and that lean gut. Not meant for a stallion, and he wouldn't hardly be worth the cost of a worn-out livery bronco.

This colt had his mama's fire. She had been an old mare Davey had bought out of pity. This was her last colt, and he was a hell raiser. Temperament ran in families, just as athletic ability and even spookiness. He'd known when he sold the colt, it had been a bad bargain.

It was obvious what was pushing the young stallion. He arched his neck and whickered low, prancing now, his flaccid organ swinging, but his intent clear. Burn was being challenged by the colt for rights to Beauty.

Burn laughed, coiled in the rope, and threw it, hitting the colt's nose and stopping the charge. He quickly coiled the rope again and slapped it against his chaps, yelling. The horses scattered in a slow trot, taking the colt reluctantly with them.

Then Burns was ready to sit down and pull on the damp sock and the boot, once it was shaken free of dust and pebbles. His foot didn't feel like some animal's main dumping ground any more. He actually laughed as he checked the mare's *cincha* and mounted up, easing the mare into her smooth walk, heading north.

He rode a week or more, skirting around any of the larger towns like Albuquerque, barely seeing the smoke from the village of Santa Fé. He managed a high trail alongside the Río Grande but had to cross over when the gorge narrowed and the land got serious. He'd taken a silent oath on the remains of the cabin that he would ride the west side of the river only, but he'd never been this far north and the river water got narrow and rough. In several places the mare balked, being more level-headed than Burn, so he turned her back around and followed a simple path that took him to a wide place in the river where the tracks told him it was safe to cross.

That was a long day. Burn ate a lot of humble pie. The mare proved smarter than her rider, and he found admitting to that flaw a sour experience. What he did realize after that long week was a lessening of the blood he was spitting up. So he guessed that leaving home at his age had been the right thing for his health.

Along the river he stopped at small villages, where he became a cause for excitement. The crowds unnerved Burn, but the mare seemed to delight in the small hands patting her and offering delights such as crystal sugar and sometimes fresh grass pulled from a farmer's pasture. A hot meal, pasture for the mare, a nest in the barn were offered and accepted. He couldn't figure out what these folks got out of their generosity; he had no talents or skills, or money, to share with them.

Mostly the village men seemed to tend sheep or grow a few crops. The women worked the homes. The children ran and played. It was a good life, simple and clean and enticing to a lonesome man with no place to go. But then he would encounter one of those motorcars, sputtering through the narrowed roads, scraping at the walls in places where fences grew close to the track, where neighbors spoke to each other over the adobe walls, and there wasn't room for the width and stink of a motorcar. But still they came, their drivers delighting in honking and scattering everything around them.

With each kindness provided him, Burn knew well enough to say his thank you. After all these years his mama's voice still came to him, clearly directing his manners. It would be said first to the woman of the house who had kindly fed him, then to the husband whose generosity had kept him safe through the night. Finally a touch to the heads of the younger children, a nod to the older boys, barely a glance at the older girls, and he was gone, to be met at the next village with the same kindnesses.

He guessed he was an outdated oddity, a *gringo* on horseback, looking scruffy and old, riding a fine young mare that the men in these villages talked about as if she were magic. He knew her perfection—the glossy mane and tail, the smallest of white on her face between her nostrils, an anklet of white around both her hind coronet bands. Her steps were strong and even. She rarely stumbled through the worst of rock-strewn areas or fallen trees, and the small woods animals, the prairie creatures did not upset her with their quick intrusions. It was only right that the men in these villages appreciated her worth. It made a man feel proud to ride such a fine animal, even if she was a mare.

On several occasions he saw motorcars out in the open. He'd seen them on the road across his land a number of times, and he'd run into one in Socorro that scared the young buckskin he was riding. The bronco had had a pitching fit. Burn had managed to stay aboard, but once again had a feeling deep in his belly that he couldn't take this any more.

He was running from the picture he had seen in his nightmares of doing an old man's work, struggling just to survive. It wasn't for him, that decline of strength, skill, even the ability to see being marred by a film across old eyes. He'd ridden at death too often to let it slowly creep into his belly and spread outward.

Along the river above Santa Fé, he was letting the mare graze as she walked. He wrapped one leg around the saddle horn and was half sleeping, feeling the warmth along the back of his neck, hearing the river's flow. Enjoying the day. Suddenly the mare lurched to a stop. Burn quickly went for the rifle as he stuck his boot back in the off stirrup. Then he heard it, a growling, joined by other threatening sounds, and a high voice, cries, then more growling. He drove the mare toward the sound, jamming his hat down, loosening the rifle to be ready.

It was two children—small boys—circled by a pack of dogs. Yellow and red dogs, tails shivering, growling, creeping closer to the children. The bigger boy threw a stone and hit one of the dogs. It howled and whined as the others drew near it, then all began stalking the children again.

Burn slid off the mare as one of the boys cried to him: "Help us! They will not go away!" Then, just as Burn saw the blood: "One bit my sister . . . she's bleeding."

Burn barely needed to aim the rifle before he shot, lifting the rifle just high enough to hit ribs, spines. The curs howled, snapping at their wounds. One went down and lay still. The others ran as Burn kept firing. Then the children screamed and he felt a tear at his left arm. He looked sideways to find one of the dogs biting down on bone, holding fast, and growling. He used his right arm to slam the rifle butt against the cur's jaw—hard enough that he heard bone break as the animal fell off, struggling to run away. Burn aimed the rifle and fired. The animal dropped, its hind legs frozen. Then it laid its head down in the sand and coughed once before dying.

The children ran toward him. Burn knelt, catching them as they hit his chest. He held them, feeling their thin bodies. Then he pushed them back, turned to the girl—it was a girl, no doubt—whose face was bleeding below the eye. Her wails hurt him. He touched her face and the cries increased.

The boy spoke then, defending his sister. "You will take us home. Mama will take care of her." The boy was a man then, only a child of eight or nine, but a man taking care of his sister. Until he, too, began to cry again, pleading: "Take us home!"

There was a shirt in Burn's saddlebags and he gave it to the little girl, wadding it in her hand and suggesting she hold it to her face. She did not look at Burn, but stared at her brother until he nodded and told her to do what the strange man said.

He lifted them onto the mare's back, both of them fitting into the saddle seat, and instructed the boy to hold his sister with one hand and the saddle horn with the other.

The boy was insulted. "I have my own pony and I can ride alone."

Burn tried a grin. "I know, but your sister needs help staying in that saddle. It's bigger'n she is."

The boy seemed to understand the good sense and immediately grabbed onto his sister.

The mare walked very carefully, and the little girl's cries slowed, then stopped. Burn looked up to study the children's faces. They were Anglo, with blond hair and blue eyes, unusual in this part of New Mexico.

The boy needed no prodding, giving Beauty directions, right and left, until they entered the yard of a small ranch, more of a farm, There were crops near the edge of a ditch and a few cattle and one mule grazing in the high grass.

A woman ran from the house, calling out a man's name—"Ed! Ed!"—and then crying for her children. Her voice was shrill yet it brought some life into the girl, who dropped the soaked cloth and held out her arms to her mama. The woman shoved her way past Burn and grabbed the child down from the saddle, holding her close until she realized the wound was bleeding again. Her face was vivid as she glared at Burn. "What did you do to my child?"

Burn had no answer. Mouth open, he tried to get out a few words, but the woman went on about her precious daughter until the boy tugged on her arm and said: "It was Ulrich's dogs, Mama. The she-dog and her puppies . . . only they grew up and they hurt Missy and wanted to eat me. This man . . . he shot them, and now Ulrich's going to kill us."

The woman grunted a few words and dragged her children into the house.

Burn waited with the mare.

Several minutes passed, and then the woman stuck her head outside again. "You, mister, get in here. My husband's coming up from the field."

Burn slowly wrapped the mare's reins around a tie rail at the front of the yard. He spent a moment touching the mare's neck, loosening her *cincha,* not wanting to be in the house until the husband had made it up from the fields.

Only when he knocked at the door and was told to enter did he begin to feel the effect of the dog bite. His arm throbbed and he could feel blood dripping onto his pants, off the ends of his fingers. His hand was numb, but the bite hurt like hell. He banged up against a wall, cursing.

The husband arrived at that moment, speaking out harshly. "We do not talk so in this house. You will not curse in front of our children!" When his wife explained the situation, he said:

"We have you to thank for our children not being further mangled. We are in your debt, sir."

It was a peculiar family, Burn decided. There he stood bleeding onto their carefully swept wood floor and he was getting lectured on his speech. He was his own man, and he figured he could say what he wanted. Then he saw the big eyes of the girl child, the one he'd first thought was a boy. Her hair was cut short, and she was dressed in britches and a loose shirt, but her face was female all right, pouting mouth and tears filling the huge blue eyes. She was held by her mother, while the bite was washed, a cloth now pressed against the wound so that it would begin to clot.

Burn figured he should keep his mouth shut for the time being. The little girl was brave, and he'd better be able to do the same. He turned toward the father, Ed. The man was tall, heavy through the chest and shoulder. His head butted forward as if looking for a fight. Burn sighed. He'd stepped into a place he didn't want to be. But then he couldn't have left the children to that pack of dogs.

"Your son said the dogs belonged to a man name of Ulrich," Burn said. "He gonna give you trouble? I can go tell him I done the shooting . . . but those dogs. . . ."

Ed raised a large hand. "We will not speak of the transgressions of Mister Ulrich. He has harmed our family. I will take Providence's urging and deal with the matter with my own hand." Ed held himself steady, hardly blinking.

The man was a believer, a Bible-spouter, and Burn's general reaction to such men was to turn around and run like hell. He almost stated these sentiments out loud, except he glanced at the child's eyes, which stared at him as if expecting retribution. Instead, he smiled at the child, half raised his arm. The little girl began wailing even though her mama was holding her.

It took a moment but the words she cried out became clear to Burn.

"He's bleeding like me. Mama help him!" The child struggled in her mother's arms, determined to be put down. Her movements reopened her wound and a thin trickle of blood ran down her face, mixing with her tears, and creating a pale pink streak down the front of her shirt.

Then shyly she went to Burn, holding out one hand to touch his wounded arm. He knelt, letting her small fingers stroke the bloody sleeve. Then there was a feather touch, a bare grazing of open skin. He winced. He couldn't stop his body from reacting, and the little girl withdrew her touch.

"Sir, I will bathe that wound," said the woman. "I might have to take a few stitches, for the dog appears to have opened quite a gap in the muscle." She hesitated, and her husband took over the conversation.

"When my wife has seen to your injuries, I expect you will wish to ride on. We have little enough, but we will provide you with victuals for your journey, and perhaps a handful of grain for that mare you ride. It is the best we can do."

Somehow in all the speechifying Burn perceived an echo of dislike, almost anger that he had appeared to rescue their children. He was obviously not of the quality of folk they preferred to have enter through their door.

Burn grinned, figuring it was the one silent gesture that would irritate the sour husband and father. It wasn't easy for Burn— being rough on a man protecting his own, but the fancy manner, kind of like Gordon Meiklejon at his worst, rubbed wrong against Burn. He opened his mouth, but then shut it, only nodding to the man.

The wife directed him to sit down in a hard-slatted chair near the table. She picked up the pan and poured out the water used for her daughter and splashed in fresh hot water, asking the boy to gather up new cloths. Then she proceeded to tear the sleeve off Burn's shirt before he could protest, and began the painful course of cleaning the wound, pouring on more hot water until the wound pulsed and Burn would have preferred to lie down.

The faces of the two children gave him strength, and, when he smiled at the little girl, she giggled and put two fingers into her mouth. The cut beneath her eye glistened with white skin, a few droplets of blood.

The woman spoke directly into Burn's ear, as if hiding the words from her husband, who tended to the fire in the cook stove. "I would give you whiskey for this, but Edvard does not allow spirits in the house, not even for medicinal purposes."

They were a pair, he thought, as she stitched through his flesh, wincing herself with each pull of the needle as if she could take away the pain. They wanted purity and perfection as they worked the land. Taking pleasure in the marriage bed would be a sin for them, he decided, and found himself feeling sorry for the woman, remembering Katherine's delighted smile whenever Davey came close.

The arm ached and pinched, but Burn held himself tightly, refusing to give in to the pain. The woman quickly wrapped a long white cloth around the wound, and he was able, by lifting his arm, to see the neatly tucked end.

"There, mister. . . ." It showed in her face—dismay and fear. It was her husband's shadow over her, his bulk seeming to push her down. The big voice rumbled from his chest, and Burn had to fight another grin, knowing it would make it harder on the woman after he left.

"You never told us your name." Almost an accusation, as if Burn were the trouble here, not a distant neighbor and a pack of unruly dogs.

He managed to stand, despite feeling light-headed. "My name

is Burn English, but I don't know your name, mister. Or the names of your children . . . and wife." That seemed to confuse the man, for he stammered his answer.

"My name is Edvard Robey. This is my wife Ardith, and our children are Edvard and Henrietta." He hesitated. "We call her Missy."

Ardith had known only Edvard, had been bound to him when she was fifteen by her parents. Their family farm in Illinois could not carry the seven daughters and four sons born to them, so the daughters were given to any man showing an interest. Ardith had been scared of Edvard, until they finally came together in their marriage bed, where she found him to be fearful and shy. Having grown up on the farm with brothers and animals had helped her guide her husband through a natural process, which had produced five children. The three oldest were married and gone; the younger two had come when Ardith was turning into an old woman of forty, and they were her delight even as they exhausted her. But for the rare occasion, Edvard had since foresworn the marriage bed and turned to his Bible, his nightly readings often ending in a sermon delivered to Ardith as they lay side-by-side in bed.

Now he stood towering over the compact man who had delivered their children safely home. Edvard's face showed his inward battle between the rage always within easy reach of his tongue and fists, and the Christian sense of duty to a stranger. It was a swift battle, Ardith already knowing Edvard's response. The husband set out his hand, shook Burn's, which was almost the size of Edvard's fist, and then slammed out the back door to go to the barn to continue the never ending chore of cleaning out manure that vexed him even as it gave a outlet for his excessive energy and strength.

Words of thanks were never uttered. Tonight, Ardith knew,

would be a monument to her husband's torment. He would take her, after much prayer and sermonizing, and she would find delight in the roughness of his skin, the closeness of his flesh. He may have given away his right to their union, but she had not made that promise. It took the internal rage of such happenings as the wound to Henrietta's face to force Edvard into a need great enough that he would foreswear his oath and use his wife as their God intended.

Burn had no idea why the woman smiled as her husband bolted from their home. The handshake had been a quick contest—one Burn had not lost or won. He was betting the man had run because Burn had not been the weaker of the two. It made a man that size plumb ornery to be stood up to by runt like Burn. He'd known that reaction most of his life. At first it had led to fights, but now he was able to laugh at anyone thinking he would be the weaker. Some folks sure were set on their judgments; this big man had a case of hate and Burn was ready to be gone.

Ardith's smile dimmed as she busied herself with picking up foodstuffs and shoving them into a burlap sack. Burn made no attempt to stop her, especially when she put a whole loaf of bread into a second sack. He could taste it, with fresh butter and jam, and it was the memory of the last time he had seen Katherine and not what this woman was doing that flooded over him, and for now he'd accept that fantasy.

"Here." Ardith handed him two bags, a good size load for a woman of her age and tiredness.

"Thank you, ma'am . . . Miz Robey. Ma'am, you got a shirt some smaller than what your husband might wear . . . an old one, or something needs patching. I ain't got much to my saddlebags. A shirt to replace this one would be a kindness."

She nodded and disappeared behind a hanging cloth.

Burn took the two sacks and headed out the front door, met

immediately by the brightness of the noon sun and a whicker from the bay mare. As he approached her, he became aware of two things—his arm was going to give him hell, and the two children had followed him.

The girl, Henrietta—damned fool name, best call her Missy—she reached up and patted Beauty's nose. "What's her name, mister?"

"Beauty."

Then the boy spoke: "Don't go fooling with my sister . . . she just wants to know the horse's name."

Burn laughed, then hung the two bags from the saddle horn.

"Her name is Beauty. Her papa was a friend of mine." He thought on the peculiarity of those words, but they were a kind of truth. It shut the boy up, too.

The two children eyed Burn, then very gently the girl went back to patting wherever she could reach of the mare's shiny hide.

Beauty lowered her head and rubbed her muzzle in the child's hair and the girl laughed as she played with Beauty's whiskers.

Then Ardith Robey called from the doorway, and, without looking back, both children ran to her.

Burn hesitated, then turned, and the woman was holding out a light-colored bundle. "Here," she said. "Keep them . . . they belonged to our eldest son."

Chapter Four

He rode two hours by his reckoning, followed by a beating sun that spoiled his disposition. The cheer left in him by that child's touch on Beauty's muzzle was lost to a gathering fever and throbbing pain. He knew he was in for a day or two of pure misery.

There was a hillside that went down to a small inlet of river water shaded by a big cottonwood. A small meadow spread out at the back of the tree, displaying evidence of a rich spring. Grasses, water, shade, the river close by—the perfect setting for what was about to lay him low.

Beauty was content to be hobbled and turned loose. Burn arranged a soft bed on the river sand, hung his gear from the lowest cottonwood branch, drank a lot of clean spring water, then washed his face, hands, and neck, not having the energy to get out of his clothes despite a growing rankness from riding and the heat. He knew to keep the bandage dry.

Among the various delights, given him by Mrs. Ardith Robey, were a stew, bacon, some coffee beans, a loaf of bread, and a jar of pickles. He figured to eat the stew first, then work on the bacon, probably from their own pig, and a few cans of beans, one jar of peach preserves. If it weren't for the rising fever, he'd be in cowboy heaven. Then again, if the dog had been rabid, he'd be approaching heaven soon, or at least some place other than where he sat right now. It seemed a morbid thought to have when all this food sat in front of him, so Burn started a fire, boiled coffee, and heated up the stew in his fry pan. The smell started out sweet until he forked in a mouthful and his belly quit on him. He lay back, exhausted and sliding in and out consciousness.

He woke to birds yakking at him, and, once he got his eyes open, he saw two ravens standing in the middle of his fry pen, pecking each other, then reaching down to drag up the black and shiny remains of the burned stew. Next to the fry pan lay a glass jar on its side and he could see where gravy had soaked into the sand. There wasn't a bite left of the meal the woman had shared with him.

When he sat up, he was seeing double. Damn those four ravens setting in his fry pan! He wondered what *they* would taste like, slow roasted, but who would remove the damned feathers?

He lay down again, having decided that thinking and looking weren't worth the bother, and he went back to sleep quickly, while the ravens continued their argument.

This time he woke slowly, rubbing his jaw and feeling his whiskers, a good growth. Sitting up merely strained his tired muscles, but no head spin, no ache. He was alive, the ravens were gone, and the fry pan was pecked clean. He itched in a few places, mostly around the bandaged arm. He felt pretty good about the itch; it meant he was healing.

The river water was calm, sun sparkling off its surface, and it was simple to get quickly out of his half shirt, wool pants, and socks that were falling to pieces. Finally shucking out of his combinations, he walked into the water, wounded arm held high as he untied and unwrapped the soiled cloth.

The air felt good on the puckered skin, so he thought to hell with it and threw himself out into the current, bucking against the water's pull, going under, then pushing through and up, sputtering and smiling until he heard a whinny. Sure enough, Beauty was at the edge of the river, still hobbled, not daring to come in.

He half swam to her, standing slowly, letting the water run off him. Damn he felt good, even if hungry and weak, but damned good. He was back to the living.

Beauty stuck out her nose and Burn held up his hand. She licked his fingers, then butted him on the chest with her head and he fell into the water, laughing out loud. The poor horse tried to jump backward away from his splashing while Burn sat in the water, choking and wet and pleased with himself.

A week of riding north. It was cold up beyond Taos, most likely into Colorado now, and too cold when he got up in the mornings. His own stink was getting to him again, and even the mare shook her head and raised her upper lip, mimicking her sire when he got wind of a scent. Burn's whole body itched. Remnants of the fever, days riding chilled, then sweaty. He couldn't blame the mare when she turned her head away as he tried to bridle her.

It had to be almost winter now, pure cold, and the trees had shed all their dried leaves. In the morning, frost covered his blankets, which made the mare hump her back when he saddled her. Still he rode north. No reason other than that's where he was headed and wouldn't quit now.

Midday, of course, he had to shuck his sheepskin and sometimes hang his hat on the saddle horn and let the warm air bathe him. It was surely a pleasure, that soft easy touch on his upturned face. The blaze of sun against his closed eyelids supplied a peace.

However, the thought of one more night of being cold to the bone needled Burn. He was tiring of frozen hard ground, and the cold wind blowing hard into every corner of his bedroll. So this night Burn dug in under a juniper, scaring out small varmints, but he didn't care, the cold had gotten to him. Even that damned dog bite had begun to ache again when he woke in the early morning.

It hurt to move. He was bent over, lamed like those old men he'd watched and made fun of long ago. He'd never be that old, not him. He walked a bit, stomping his feet, blowing on his hands, hoping for a miracle. Getting the mare saddled and packed, even shucking into the sheepskin, was a hard task slowed by soreness in his hands, jelly in both knees.

The miracle came later, when he and the mare crested a hill and looked down into the prettiest valley Burn had ever seen. Like the valley where he had trapped the wild horses, but with knee-high grass and clusters of trees and in the far distance the glitter of a spring. Pooled water ringed with saplings, a few holding onto faded gold leaves. A big old cottonwood lording over everything—biggest damned tree Burn had ever seen.

The rest of the miracle—no fences, that and the water and only small trails for varmints and deer. No cattle sign, no platters of manure and trampled grasses. No horses, either, only a few dried piles from sometime in the past. A place he might rest for a time, give the mare a vacation. She was losing weight. The grain sack was long empty, his own few stores down to a moldy slab of bacon and one airtight of peaches. The burlaps of grub doled out by a grateful Mrs. Rodey were long gone. He'd gotten a meal or two out of the bread loaf even though there had been mold on the crust. Luckily he'd been lying on the burlap bag, using it as a pillow, which had saved the bread from any four legged thieves. He had one shirt that fit well, but the other two were rags now, good for keeping in his short store of clothing. A man never knew when he might be in need of another bandage. This time, though, it wasn't going to be from any damned dog bite.

Originally Burn had decided he would ride into a village, stay a day, find a job if he could, a place to winter. Now that he had found this spot, well, this was heaven, and, if he froze out here, death suited him just fine.

Taking care of Beauty came first. He curried her back, picked out her hoofs, tested the tightness of her shoes. She'd hang here until the grass got chewed down. His hands on her ribs felt bone. He wasn't worried she'd leave. So he turned her loose, free, unfettered, and she ran a few strides, then quickly settled to the good eating.

Next, out of old habit, he hung the gear, saddle, bridle, rope, and emptied saddlebags high in the branches of the old cottonwood. He walked its circle and looked up into the high branches, marveling that something could grow to such a size. It was a big one all right.

He had too many choices for the campsite—flat thick grasses for a mattress, the cottonwood for shelter, and lower saplings that could be drawn down and pulled together to make a windbreak when he needed it.

Taking time to study the land, Burn lay back with his head on the cottonwood trunk, arms locked behind his head as a pillow. When the wind blew, he could smell himself which made him wrinkle his nose.

He stood and shucked out of his clothes, kicked them into a small pile, then thought better of it, and picked them up, carrying them into the water. God, they smelled. He walked into the water without stopping, and, although he could freeze half to death in no time, it was clean water, clear enough that he could see his toes, the grains of sand, a few critters skittering away.

First he stuck the clothes under water, splashing them around some, rubbing the hard wool pants against the softer cotton shirt. Bits of twigs, grass, small leaves, horse hair, all floated to the surface in memory of his recent travels.

Overhead a few birds chided him for his nakedness, but the cold water felt good. He sat down, hard, and laughed as he leaned forward and ducked his head, came up sputtering. My God, the water was cold on his butt and belly. Taking fists of sand, he started scrubbing, carefully around the scars, but confident because he'd had years of washing around them. Still it made him shudder to touch them—ugly raised welts, some wider than his thumb, criss-crossing his belly, thigh, and ribs stretching around to his back. One at his throat. The few on his arms and hands weren't too bad, but the one on his belly. He winced, kept scrubbing, especially under his arms and his privates. He was extra cautious around the dog bite. It still itched, but there was a small pocket of red under one of the stitches. He needed to dig it out, but not now, not while he was enjoying himself.

When he stood, a bird shrieked and several flew up from reeds across from the cottonwood. Burn shook his head, felt water fly off his hair, his beard, and thought he might take the time now to heat some water and shave, maybe even take a knife to his hair. Too much gray in it. He could see the silver strands pass his eyes. It had been almost black just a few years ago.

The sun was hot enough to dry him. He stood naked, allowing air and sun and the world to see his wounds. The mare raised her head and whinnied at him, birds settled in the nearby trees, and Burn let out a sigh that turned into a belch. He grinned, wiped at his damp hair, and for once felt a well-being. No gut ache, no fretting. Gone with the place where his dreams had died.

CHAPTER FIVE

Ruthie Heber knew what men looked like. She had two older brothers still at home—three had moved away. Ruthie was the baby girl, at least that's what her ma called her even though she was twelve and could take care of herself. In addition to her brothers, her ma had a new man that didn't button up when he needed to, like he was advertising something no other man had. Ruthie knew this latest man, Cal, wouldn't be staying long. While Ma liked her men, she didn't take to rudeness or such displays as Cal was offering up to the family. This one, down by the cottonwood, though . . . he was ugly and skinny and too short, and, when he took off those torn clothes, he got uglier.

But the mare that the mister down there rode, she was a beauty. Good legs and a fine head, an eye able to see and know the world around her. She was a rich dark red color with that black mane and tail—Ruthie liked the colors together. She herself had nothing to ride but a speckled Appaloosa, with white around his eye and striped feet, and even his thing was speckled. This mare, though, she was sleek and pretty to watch, and Ruthie thought she would like to ride a mare like her. It would be something special to sit up there and have the world see her and know that she, Ruthie Heber, knew a good horse and deserved to ride one.

The man was bent over searching through a bedroll by Ruthie's reckoning, and she got so embarrassed that she slid back down the hill to her old roan Appaloosa that was chewing at grass and half sleeping. She startled the roan and he raised his head and started to whicker. Ruthie grabbed his nose. She didn't want any sound telling that scrawny naked man he was being watched.

She jumped for the stirrup and found it with the wrong foot, so she pulled herself up, and then switched feet and threw the other leg over the battered old-time saddle. The roan was used to her peculiar way of mounting. He was a tall skinny bronco and it wasn't easy for Ruthie to get on. Another thing she liked about the bay mare down by the pond was that she wasn't as big as this monster horse. And she sure was a whole lot prettier.

Ruthie had been coming everyday for a week now. She had made herself a soft place nestled near a rock, where she could lie flat and then raise her head, peer over the rim, and watch him. He didn't do much usually, just laid around. He seemed to sleep a lot in the beginning. He spent time neatening up his camp. Once she caught him out in the middle of the pond, his skin-white rump pushed out of the water, his head up, his hands grabbing something and pulling him forward. He didn't sink, he didn't fight, he scooped and kicked and made his way across the pond and back. She wanted someone to teach her how to do that.

Sometimes he caught up the bay mare that always nuzzled him, and he would cup her nose and seem to talk into her ear as the two of them stood side by side. Ruthie'd never seen a man talk to a horse like that. She wondered if the horse talked back.

His nakedness scared her even as she was curious. There had been glimpses before, and she'd quickly run away or cover her eyes. But he had to get naked, she guessed, when he went in the water to do that wind-milling around. She had asked her ma what you called that wind-milling, and she had said it was swimming, and then wanted to know why Ruthie had asked. She had

had to make up a lie quickly. " 'Cause I want to learn how to paddle in the water when it's hot and I figured there was a word for what I couldn't do." That had seemed to satisfy her ma, who knew, once Ruthie got started, it could be tough getting her to shut down with the talking. It was useful, knowing this much about yourself.

He was a skinny thing, and scarred—most of them were old, faded, white like his skin, but ridged and raised up so she couldn't help but see them. Except there was a red wound on his left arm, above the elbow, that he sometimes rubbed at, never quite touching the wound itself. It had to be recent, she thought.

Then one day she witnessed him take a knife, burn its tip in a low fire, and dig into the wound. He seemed to be picking out small things that flew through the air. Then she heard him groan as blood dripped out. But he was quiet as he laid the heated knife tip on the bleeding. It made her sick to her stomach, and she had to lead her Roany, which is what she called her horse, for a few minutes before she felt steady enough to climb up into the saddle. The man might be a scrawny thing, but he had courage, she'd give him that.

Cal, Ma's man, had got himself a splinter stuck under a fingernail once, a ratty little bit of wood, and, by the Lord above—she'd heard her Ma say that once—you'd've thought Cal had been scalped. Ma had pulled the darned thing out, and Cal held his hand like it was broken. Ma had shoved him outside, telling him to get away till he could act like a man. That, too, had let Ruthie know Cal wasn't long in their life.

Sometimes her mister, as she now thought of the man with the mare, would take out a brush he had stuffed into a pair of saddlebags that looked as old as forever, but soft, loose as if they had been oiled and taken care of. Not like the way her brothers left things lying on the ground where she fell over them, or hung somewhere until they got covered in dusty webs and made her sneeze when she pushed by them. Harness bridles with those blinkers, and that heavy old collar, the wooden shaped sticks she'd heard called hames—they were all rotting because the boys didn't care.

Her mister, he'd take that brush to the mare, one hand following the brush's path, probably feeling for bumps and cuts Ruthie decided. He sure could make that pretty mare shine, and, when he was done, putting the brush away after scraping it on his boot so dust would fly up, the mare would nuzzle against him. Sometimes he'd lean on her, the two of them motionless, bound together.

He was funny to watch, whistling, even fishing out of the pond. He didn't catch much, but she took note of a few rabbit skins hung out to dry. She figured the man was just making do.

Then one day that no-good Cal left the pen gate open and Lady, the brindle cow, disappeared. Her calf had been partially weaned and was in a separate pen, so the family could share in the milk. Ruthie liked the cheese Ma made, and the taste of fresh butter on the bread pulled from the bake oven to the back of the old fireplace. The plan was to slaughter the calf soon for the winter.

Well, her ma was so mad when the cow escaped that Ruthie was happy to go looking for it, even if she couldn't go and see her mister. Her ma was fearful Lady had gotten onto Haydock Carpenter's land and that they'd have to fight for her return. Old man Carpenter was cranky; even Ruthie knew that from her ma's talking. That was probably why Ma was so mad, thinking about having to deal with the old man and that new wife of his.

So Ruthie saddled Roany, and climbed onto the saddle. She checked the yard first. There were tracks around the side of the barn, where they kept the bull calf in an open stall. She found some dirt dug up, a middle rail from the pen shoved free, but no mama cow around.

A few tracks went up over the rise, wandered sideways some, and then made a straight line toward Carpenters' place. Ruthie kicked the roan, and he threw up his head and sort of stumbled into a slow jog. Not fast enough to catch Lady, but the best she could get out of Roany. It was only her imagination, but she could almost feel the smooth trot, the easy lope of the bay mare back at the pond. It would be like riding the best horse ever in the world; she could tell from the mare's eye and the way her mister cared for her.

CHAPTER SIX

Burn woke to a peaceful, almost warm morning, no frost, no wind, a real pleasure. He had the coffee boiling quickly, and he sat back to enjoy a quiet moment. The mare was lying down, knees folded beneath her belly, nose resting on the ground, as peaceful as the morning itself. Then he noticed a deer entering at the far edge of the pond, alert but not yet aware of Burn or the mare. Burn set his cup down, stood slowly, and reached for his rifle. He had his fingers on the chilled metal when the deer raised its head, perhaps having seen him grab the rifle, and bounded off through the high grass.

The mare woke at the deer's escape. Burn stumbled in his hurry to shoot and the mare came up from her sleep into a panic. She spun around and kicked out, then took off, tail high over her back, kicking, feeling good again. She was a joy to watch until Burn realized the mare was leaving their small valley.

Burn's hand folded over the rifle stock, pulled it to him, and swung it around to fire. The damned deer was gone, and so was the mare. He rested the rifle butt on the ground, wiped his face, and felt a complete fool. From peace to nothing in maybe two minutes.

He walked maybe a half hour before finding the mare. She was pulling at stalky grass, and barely turned her head at his approach. When he got too close, she moved away, not bothering to raise her head from the grass. When she stopped so quickly,

Burn knew what was wrong. Holding out his hand, palm up, fingers wiggling, he crooned to the mare and moved in closer. This time she raised her head and he watched her eye real closely. She took one step and that placid dark eye suddenly showed white. Burn tried to reach her, but she leaned away and shook one front leg. He heard the sound, and called to her over the pounding in his throat, his head—good God damn.

The wire snaked up through the tan grasses and thin soil as the mare set back and pulled, the front leg drawn away from her, haunches set close to the ground. Her other front hoof dug in, but nothing gave except the band of hide around her cannon bone. He saw the blood, could taste it in his mouth, and he spat to the side.

"Hey, Beauty . . . it's me. It's OK, girl. Settle down. I'll take care of you. Won't hurt none at all." He was lying, but any words would do.

She quit pulling, that one leg stretched out, her body weight leaning on the tender skin. Burn wanted to throw up, but he stepped to her shoulder. She tried to hop away from him, but the pain stopped her. She shook, whickered, dug in with her hind legs, and then fell to her side, leg bleeding badly now, damp and hot where Burn grabbed hide and bone above the wire and tried to touch the mare's neck. She threw him off, so he sat on her, on the flat of her jowl, and she trembled under him but had to be still.

He had nothing, no knife or wire cutters, no rope, bridle— nothing. Anything that might be useful was back at camp. He shucked out of his shirt and tore it, wrapped his hands, and bent the wire back, pulling hide with it, but there was no other way. The mare screamed under Burn as he fought to keep her head down as her hindquarters rose, her legs kicked out.

He got it, bending and spreading the wire, so he could open a hole and slide the mare's leg out. It caught for a moment on the rise of the hoof near the coronet band and left a pinprick of blood as it scraped down the horn, leaving a white line. The wire band slipped free, and Burn's hands held only the bleeding leg. He quickly unwrapped his shirt padding and tied one sleeve across the wound, another one above it, and then tore strips from the body of the shirt and knotted them before slipping them around the mare's neck. He felt her skin shudder against his touch.

It was rough, but he stood quickly and stepped back while the mare struggled, got her legs under her, and tossed her head and neck, bringing herself up to a sitting position before standing. When she shook to free herself of the sand, the injured leg buckled. She grunted, went down in front, and came up to strike out at Burn.

He tugged on the noose around her neck, and she looked at him, ears pinned back. "Beauty, it's all right now." At his voice, her ears went forward and she pushed out her muzzle, touching his bare arm.

At first Beauty walked fine on the leg, and that gave Burn hope. By the time they reached camp, the blood had stopped and it looked like, maybe, the cut was not much more than a bad scratch.

Burn was shivering, conscious of his own white skin with those angry scars across his belly. Even the one on his arm, that damned dog bite, seemed raw and open, and there was pain in his gut again. He found another shirt, one that Ardith Robey had given him to ease her conscience. He put it on, buttoned a few buttons, and then bridled the mare, led her to the pond, but she wouldn't walk in with him. He had figured that might be, so he slipped up on her back and rode her in a small circle, then into the cold water. Her whole body shuddered again, splashing up cold drops that chilled Burn, but she was standing in over her knees and he made her stand there for what felt like forever.

When he let her come out, she was shaking. So was he. Burn slipped down, untied the drenched cotton bandage, and saw pink flesh over white bone, clean flesh, bloodless now, no pumping, no red flow. It was bad, though, worse than he had thought. Bone showed through hide, no cut tendons, but close. He shuddered, stood up slowly, and touched Beauty's neck to hide his own fear. He wrapped the leg again, glad he'd kept those shirt pieces.

He couldn't hobble her, so, with a pounding heart, he turned her loose. She took one bobbing step, stopped, put her head down, and closed her eyes. She was exhausted. He was, too.

Burn spent the next four days working on the leg. He had the mare stand in the small pond, until he thought his own feet would turn blue. He spent hours pulling grass for her, making sure she had enough to eat, and, when she did try to graze, he tied her so she wouldn't tear open the wound.

It came to him too frequently that without the mare he was lost, alone in country he didn't know. Tracks led in many directions, but he knew one trail could lead a half mile to a house while another could lead thirty miles to nothing. The mare's leg quit bleeding through the tight wrap of his torn shirt, but Burn didn't like the heat under his fingers when he gently, barely touched the broken skin.

Without her, he was a dead man—a death of little consequence, except perhaps to himself. He imagined himself a pile of whitened bones, maybe tripped over by a kid going down to fish, knocked apart, and carried off until a single bone, resting in a mound of sand, meant nothing to those passing through.

A half hour by the sun, on Ruthie's first attempt to try to find

Lady, and she was home, telling Ma that, no, she hadn't seen the brindle cow. She'd followed the tracks to a creekbed but couldn't figure out which tracks, coming out, belonged to their cow. Tracks didn't have color, she told her ma. The tracks of a single cow, even one with the strange markings that Lady had—a white face and those funny stripes running through her tan hide—weren't any easier to read. She'd go out again later, Ruthie said, maybe try to the west or up against Mr. Carpenter's fence line. The boys sometimes cut that fence and didn't mend it properly; a cow might get in by mistake.

Ma seemed angry at Ruthie's report, so she went out and tended to the roan Appaloosa, and fed hay to the lonesome bull calf. She tried to remember exactly what she'd said that could have made her ma so riled. Probably had to do with that Cal still hanging around.

Days later Ruthie still hadn't found the cow, so she went into the cabin and straight to her mama, leaning against her warmth, distressed that she'd been useless in the hunt. Out in back, she could hear the bull calf bellowing for his mouthful of warm milk.

The mother touched the top of her daughter's head, not really thinking about the child but wanting instinctively to re-assure her. "You'll find her. We need that milk for her calf. He's still penned up, ain't he?" Her worn fingers felt the child's head nod vigorously, up and down—silence being Ruthie's preferred method of communication until she got on a talking streak, and then it was nothing but noise and thoughts and words all caught up in each other.

Margaret Lewis Heber—actually there were more names to go with the husbands but she had given up after a while and had stuck with Ruthie's father's name, finding it easier that way on the children. It wasn't that she was particular or fickle, it was that the men had died, or walked away, gone hunting with a friend and never had come back. Margaret didn't bother with a divorce when these disappearances occurred; she just moved to another place where there would always be another man.

This one—Cal—was about to go. He was pretty enough—tall and strong, taller than her, just the way she liked them. Also handsome in a smooth, slick manner, with thick blond hair and light blue eyes. She didn't always want to look into those eyes, in which meanness showed sometimes. And recently he had been acting irresponsible around Ruthie, who, at twelve, had no figure yet and had her older brothers' bad mouth at times, but, still, she was a girl and Cal needed to mind his manners. And it was Cal who had turned out the cow without her calf and yet couldn't be bothered to go hunting for it. So Margaret—Maggie was what everyone called her—had had to send out a child to deal with the problem resulting from his laziness. Damn the man, and she would tell him so to his face as soon as he showed up at her cabin. *Her* cabin. She'd remind him of that fact, see what came up into those hard blue eyes.

Of course, Ruthie could track and ride better than most men, and, if the child said the cow went through Carpenter's cut fence, then it was true, and there would be trouble. Carpenter wasn't bad, but his wife was a harridan who doubted Maggie's marriage stories and spoke to the folks in the towns of Bayfield and Durango as if Maggie were a whore and not a properly married woman.

Maggie moved her hand from Ruthie's head to her shoulder and felt the thinness of bone in the child. It marveled her that this little thing, with no male muscle and no female body yet, could have such a mouth and such courage.

"You want some switchell, Ruthie? I made up a new batch even though it's coming winter. You doing chores, and the boys, too . . . well, I thought you might like the switchell." It was an old recipe from her mother's folks, out of Vermont they were.

Water and cider vinegar and some molasses, a handful of oatmeal. Made for a head-clearing drink on a hot day, and some folks, mostly children like Ruthie, would chew the oatmeal set up with the molasses like a sweet.

She got the child settled in a chair and was holding a glass in one hand, reaching for the pitcher, when Cal stomped through the door, scaring both of them. Maggie's hand missed in grabbing for the pitcher, bumping it instead and causing it to rock on the table. She almost caught it, but didn't, only felt its slick surface as it tilted, and then poured out the amber liquid, splashing all over Cal's boots and jeans.

Ruthie caught the pitcher before it fell, and there was a moment's suspicion in Maggie that her daughter had figured out just when she could save the pitcher and still get Cal wet. It was how Ruthie's mind worked, quickly, so quickly so that she didn't think about the consequences of her actions.

Cal slapped Ruthie, sending the child reeling. The pitcher broke against the stone fireplace, sending crystal pieces all over the girl and the floor. Maggie went to her daughter, holding her down, and all the while yelling at Cal to get out, get out of their house, how dare he hurt a child, how dare he slap her Ruthie. Cal stood in the doorway, frowning.

One hand on her daughter's back, Maggie realized the child was crying, something Ruthie rarely did. If she was cut or hurt, oh, Lordy, that man would feel the edge of a fry pan or a stick of wood. Ruthie rolled over, mindful of her mother picking out glass from her hair, her shirt, on the floor where she had fallen.

"It's all right, Ma. I ain't cut. He just scared me is all."

Ever true Ruthie, looking out for her mama, instead of worrying about herself. Maggie kissed the child's hair above her closed eyes, and tasted the sharp prick of the smallest sliver of glass on her lip. She picked Ruthie up, plucking at her clothes, seeing all those shiny bits sticking in her shirt.

She brushed through Ruthie's hair, paying no attention to Cal's blaming and mumbling. A man that had no better sense than to hit a child deserved a lot more than Cal was getting from Maggie's mouth. She intended to let the son-of-a . . . well, she never said those things out loud, even if she thought them too often. She could be too hot-tempered just like her first husband had said—hot-tempered the way he had liked her and taken her to him, laughing as she struggled and swore.

Now he was gone, the best of the lot. He'd been taken by a fever that had sickened her three oldest boys, too, but they had been young and had survived. Their pa hadn't made it. Then there was the youngest boy's pa, and he'd sired Ruthie, too, which was why she had kept his name. She'd never bothered to tell Tad his father was someone else. It would be too confusing, so no need to bother. They were all her children, every one of them.

She helped Ruthie out of her shirt, saying: "Careful now." Then she handed her the shirt. "Don't shake it. Wait till you get outside . . . but don't go near the pens."

Then Maggie looked for Cal, but he, too, was gone, and about time. *Good,* she thought, *no need to bother with him any more.* About all that he had offered Maggie was that he was good in the bed, and she appreciated a man who knew what he was doing, but that was all he could do well and it wasn't enough to keep him around. She had children to raise, and Cal only got in the way.

The sound of retreating hoof beats sounded purely good to Maggie. She glanced through the door and saw the back end of Cal's fine horse headed west. *Best place for them,* she thought, although she had to admit she would miss the occasional opportunity she had had to ride his horse. Now all they had was the roan Appaloosa Ruthie said belonged only to her.

Maggie called out for Ruthie, and jumped when the child

spoke almost at her elbow.

"Glad the son-of-a-bitch's gone."

"Ruthie!" Maggie had to act tough with the girl, but the child was right; they were both glad Cal was gone. "You don't say such things."

"Ah, Ma, you know it's the truth."

Maggie knelt down to face her daughter and patted the brushed strands of her brown hair. Then her fingers combed through the thickness, finding no more glass shards to prick her skin. When she heard another commotion outside the door, Maggie looked up in time to see the brindle cow lumber across the yard, her huge udder slapping from side to side, milk being squeezed out by her hind legs.

Ruthie heard the bull calf's bellow and she pushed away from her mama, knowing it was her responsibility to take care of the family cow.

The bossy cow wouldn't let the boys touch her; their hands were just too rough. Lady would stick out her head and bellow whenever they tugged at her teats and made their crude jokes. So it fell to Ruthie to do the milking, resting her head against Lady's warm flank, sitting on the end of her stained tail, talking to the miserable cow as she pulled and pulled. The bucket was full by the time the bull calf started bellowing for some of that sweet foamy milk.

The next day, Maggie let Ruthie go off on her own without comment. She rode west, then slightly south, not having to look for Lady, wanting to see her mister and the pretty mare.

This time she stayed on Roany as she peered down in the valley. There he was, her mister, sitting on the mare, who was limping as she came out of the water. On land, the man slid down off the mare's shiny back. He wore boots and pants, but his shirt was barely buttoned, and, across his belly, those scars flashed at Ruthie, raised and angry, and they made her stomach queasy again.

She forgot she was spying, and yelled at him: "Hey, mister, what'd you do to that pretty mare?"

On his knees, Burn froze, his hands clenching the mare's leg. Beauty reached down, nipped at his shoulder. Burn let go, stood slowly, holding hard to the bridle reins, uncertain and surprised.

The voice hollered again, something Burn couldn't make out. Then a small nubbin on a lanky red Appaloosa came sliding down the hill. The child, he thought it was a girl, stopped the tall horse so quickly she almost bounced out of the saddle. When the mare kicked out and fell to her knees, the Appaloosa slid sideways and lost his rider. Only Burn remained still, bridle reins held so loosely in his hand that they pulled through until, at the last moment, he remembered and closed his fist, holding up the mare's head. She stood next to him, shaken almost as badly as he was.

The red roan trotted to the mare. They touched noses, whickered at each other, and, when the mare rubbed her head on Burn's arm, the roan settled.

It came to Burn that the rider was slow to move, so he let go of the mare, who stayed with the roan as he walked up the sandy hill. The child was sitting up now, blowing dirt from her mouth, and rubbing the side of her head, but Burn didn't see any blood, so he figured she hadn't been hurt too badly.

"What's wrong with the mare?" she asked again.

Burn shook his head, opened his mouth, and thought better of it. Instead, Burn grinned, wiped his face, then felt the swing of his shirt tails, and remembered he was half dressed, and in front of a girl child. He quickly turned his back, buttoned up, and tucked in his shirt before turning around again.

" 'S all right, mister. I been watching you is all. Even seen you get out into the water and not drown. How'd you do that? I tried and went under, and my older brother . . . he had to come get me."

She sure could talk, Burn thought to himself, and. . . . She'd watched him in the water! Burn blushed, feeling the heat flush his whole body as he walked back to the grazing horses. They were nose to nose, seeking out the best blades and snipping gently. Occasionally the bay mare would rub against the roan's leg or shoulder and the taller horse would brace himself, nickering softly and arching his neck.

That child had seen him naked. It was wrong. She was a child, but to hell with her. It sounded to Burn as though she'd been watching him on several occasions and that told him how badly he was slipping, losing the abilities needed to survive. Another instinct he had lost, gone from his younger self, which annoyed him more than knowing a child had seen him naked. It even frightened him a little. This knowledge about himself confirmed what age and sitting on a front porch had done to his life.

He caught up her horse, had to drag it, but finally the roan followed him, and the bay mare came limping along. He needed a new bandage for the wound, and some sulphur tar, anything to keep out infection. At least now he had a chance to find a home nearby. The child owed him that much for her spying.

"Girl, you live close?"

She took the reins to her horse, fished out something from her mouth, and tried standing. " 'Bout a half hour's ride."

"How long leading a sore mare? And while it ain't none of your business . . . she got herself caught in some god-damn' wire." He couldn't stop the cursing, didn't want to. Damned wire always got him so mad.

She glared at him. "I ain't taking you home with me."

"You got no choice. I may be slow, but I can follow your tracks. Don't matter how far out you ride to confuse me, I'll find your home. The mare needs more tending and medicines than I got on me."

That spooked her. Those shiny blue eyes got wet, and the girl took one step toward the mare. "She's right pretty. You think I could ride her?"

"Not on that leg. Nothing rides her till she heals. You got salve and bandages to your house?"

The child got mad, and Burn might have grinned but he knew well enough that it would hurt her pride.

"My ma can take care of 'most anything, mister," Ruthie said, looking somewhat defensive. Then: "How'd she get cut again? I was more mad than listening."

This conversation was getting peculiar for Burn, talking to this bit of a thing as if they were equals. His hands twitched, his mouth got tight, and he looked away from the girl. "Wire."

She came back: "That what cut you up, mister?" He turned to look at her, and she pulled back a step, saying: "I was just asking."

He packed up the bedroll, his rank sheepskin coat, fry pan, and coffee pot, stuffing everything randomly into the saddlebags. The saddle and blankets went on the mare, then he tied everything to its strings, prompting the girl to question him again.

"You said she wasn't going to be ridden . . . what's that saddle weigh? More'n me I bet."

"The saddle stays quiet on her, you'll wiggle 'round and throw her off balance. Besides, I can't leave my stuff here, unless you think that App you're riding'll carry the saddle and my gear."

She dismissed the suggestion without bothering to answer, saying: "Well, you ain't staying at our house."

"I'm trading your family some chores for some bandages and salve."

The girl came right back at him, face turning red around her freckles. "She ain't gonna like it."

Burn studied the child, saying what he was thinking out loud, and surprising them both. "Your ma's anything like you, child, she'll take pity on the mare. No one with a heart wants such a beautiful thing to suffer."

He finished tying the last string, patted the mare's neck, and wished he'd shaved and groomed this morning before he'd gotten himself into this mess. Watching the kid try to climb on the ugly roan almost prompted him to offer help, but he'd learned this much already—stay out of the way of anything having to do with pride, and she was prideful for such a scrawny thing.

He shook his head and bent down to rearrange the sleeve of his shirt on the mare's leg. He didn't want dirt and such getting into the open wound while traveling. This kid, he thought again to himself, barely a grown child, had seen him naked. Since he'd been a baby, there were only two people that had known him that way: the Hildahls—Katherine, while nursing him back to health, and Davey, who had helped her. The few women, well . . . his face caught on fire again. Burn had never been much with the ladies, even in his youth. He couldn't bear the questions, the talking too much, when all he wanted was what they were selling.

He thought about letting the kid ride out, and just staying at the pond and the cottonwood and the good grass. He could work on the mare himself until the leg healed. He was finding it hard to look in the girl's eyes, knowing she'd seen more of him than anyone was meant to. He could feel each scar throb, and the new one itched, and it was wrong to know what she knew.

It wasn't right, but for now he had no choice. There was heat in the mare's leg and he had nothing in those damned saddlebags to treat such a vicious wound. He had left his old life in a hurry, forgetting to bring along some of the necessities.

He could visualize the tin of salve back at the cabin, a stinking tar that took care of many problems. Buried now, along with the shelf it sat on, under the weight of the torn-down roof, the destroyed corral poles. Still it wasn't right, what the girl had seen.

It took more than an hour to get wherever they were headed. Burn walked, cursing his heeled boots, but not wanting to ask the girl for a lift. Besides, the hindquarters to that old roan didn't look too comfortable—a high bony spine and sloping croup. Walking was the better choice, but he stopped frequently, telling the girl he was letting the mare rest. It was the truth. The leg did hurt Beauty now. He could see it. She'd hold it off the ground, and, when he touched her foreleg, she flinched, which meant fluid was swelling up the tissues.

He damned the wire, damned the fool that had pulled down a fence and left coils scattered and hidden in the grasses to bring down a good mare. He might as well damn the entire world for the unfeeling act of a fool. Too many folks were that way, not considerate about who else might have to walk along the path they had used.

By the time they started on a well-trod track with other narrowed tracks slicing in at angles, Burn was footsore and the mare limping badly. The girl wanted them both to hurry. He told the girl to go ahead, and she kicked at the Appaloosa gelding but the ugly roan had no intention of leaving the mare, so the lamed group struggled up a hill slowly, before a small cabin appeared.

The cabin was well built and sturdy, with a good-size barn, and corrals at the back. A calf bellowed and the Appaloosa gelding raised his head, whinnied a high-pitched, foolish response.

Chapter Seven

His given name was Haydock Carpenter. At times, his wife, new to him still, took pleasure from calling him Doc, as if that were his profession. Particularly when they were bedding each other. Women weren't supposed to like those things, but she surely gave him pleasure in their times, and, by God, it was an improvement on his first and second wives, who had babies willingly enough, but didn't seem to like the process of creating them.

This old gal, Rose, she was good in some ways and terrible in others, a real whirlwind to live with. She couldn't cook and she kept after him to make the ranch bigger—big enough to take in the whole damned country. He thought the land he owned now, the sections and grants and rights, was more than any one man could use, especially now that towns were growing and cattle being shipped by rail cars close by, and there wasn't any open range.

She wanted a fancy new house built in town, and a smaller one out by the pond in Salt Valley. Haydock was inclined to neither venture. It meant spending money on something they didn't need. He already had a good house, with a stone fireplace and windows looking out to the distance that she didn't have to wash, no, sir. He had the ranch women do that job, along with many of the other chores. These women lived with their husbands in the old adobes their parents had built, comfortable with work on the Rafter JX and keeping to the way of life they preferred.

Haydock Carpenter, he wasn't so much in love with the woman to want to please her that way. He'd keep what was his, making sure no man took from him, but he didn't want more. All his children had died, none of them reaching more than a few years of life. He grieved still, knowing it was no longer possible to have a family. Not with this woman. Besides, he wouldn't wish her as a mama to any babe of his. Still she pleased him in bed and was a face smiling back at him, most of the time.

He went outside, carrying a tin cup of the thick coffee he liked and she didn't. She preferred to have him sit at a table and use fancy cups with saucers. He accommodated her most of the time, but this morning he wanted peace and quiet and no fool woman serving him. He'd always been his own keeper, almost seventy-five years now, even when growing up and living with his mother and then later with his previous wives. He took care of himself, didn't plan to let this one change a lifelong habit.

The sun was up behind him, glancing light onto the hills to the west. Dark shadows moved down and then up as the light grew. He'd had news almost a week now, news he didn't like. Those Heber boys had cut his fence again, and this time their milch cow had gotten into his good alfalfa. What those fool boys couldn't be made to understand was that it wasn't safe for the cow, but neither seemed to understand or care. She'd die from the gas in a while—frozen alfalfa turned to poison and they had had a frost two nights ago. He'd sent a hand to chouse out the cow, but the boy had come back, saying the tracks showed the cow had gone back through the fence on her own. He'd put the fence back together. "Was that enough, *señor?*"

Haydock had grinned at the boy's cleverness and told him

that most milch cows had their own secret ways, and, if the fence was mended, nothing else needed doing.

The more troubling news had come from Raul Garcia, a tough hand, but loyal, and Haydock had no reason to doubt him. Some ranny had set himself up with a camp inside Salt Valley and that had stirred Haydock. A day or two was one thing, but Raul said he'd checked back, and the man was still there.

Haydock drained the rest of the coffee, tipped the cup over, and watched the sludge of fine grounds slide out, drip onto the grass. The lawn she called it, a fancied-up term for grass. And, by God and dammit, Haydock wasn't having no lawn to his ranch house getting in the way of him dumping out coffee grounds.

He decided he'd ride over to the Heber place, speak to that woman again about her boys. She was a pretty thing, tall and lean with a good shape under those loose-fitting dresses and dark hair that made a man think of other things while he was looking into those blue eyes. She tried keeping herself plain, but it wasn't any use. She was a looker all right.

One advantage that came with being the boss was that as he lazed along toward the corral, Rogelio caught sight of him and came bursting out of the cook shack, wiping breakfast off his face and nodding. Rogelio had been with him from the beginning.

"Which horse you want today, *Señor* Carpenter?"

Haydock liked this small show of respect, of knowing who he was.

"The black colt," he said. "He's been good enough since we cut him, and it ain't a far piece I'm riding. . . ." He added: "Thanks, Rogelio. You roping out that son'll make the day go easy for me." He'd learned to say that word thanks more lately. Of course, *gracias* would be more popular with most of his hands, but he always thought of it too late. He didn't speak Spanish, but at least he was learning manners in his old age.

Carpenter was a tall man with the years underlined by the seams in his face, a belly hanging over his belt. His hands were mottled. Two of the fingers were missing tips and he walked half sideways from a badly set leg. Getting on the black colt was difficult for him, and Rogelio had to hold the young colt while Haydock struggled with the stirrup and pushed off, grabbing hard to the horn. It used to be he could mount up without even thinking about it, but those days were gone, like most of his hair.

Only his eyes showed the man fully; hazel eyes ringed with a darker green, vivid eyes with a slow growing film that dimmed their color. He had a reputation as a man who knew how to size up man or beast, land, a situation, with just a quick assessment. But those day were few and far between now, for Carpenter was having trouble with his vision. He could see shapes and sizes, but not features, and distance confused him. Bright light made distinguishing things even harder. The doctor in Denver had told him he was suffering from cataracts, but they weren't bad yet. He hated the thought of what the future would be like if this was just the beginning.

It usually took him two tries to judge the distance between his boot and the oxbow stirrup. It made him mad enough to curse, but he could count on Rogelio to remain quiet about the problems he was having. The man was nearly as old as Haydock.

Settled in the old Frazier he'd ridden for thirty years, Haydock felt a feathery touch on his leg.

"You be careful, *señor,* this colt is still not to be trusted," Rogelio cautioned.

Two old men, who both knew the truth about aging but wouldn't let on to those younger. Rogelio would not speak of the coming blindness, but he had seen the signs. Once, recently, he had come up to Haydock and said quietly that when one becomes older, "as you and I have, parts of the body give up long before the spirit." Carpenter had nodded at the truth, and they had never spoken of it again.

Until now, when Rogelio was subtly questioning his boss' choice of mounts. Haydock had a reason for wanting the black saddled: he wanted to ride in on the prancing colt and impress the pretty lady, Maggie Heber. An old man's vanity, yes, but worth the risk, with so little joy left in life except for bedding his new wife, and riding a good horse.

Hell, he thought, *I'll get tossed on my head, and the wife and the horses'll never notice the difference.* He nodded down to Rogelio and reined the black towards the west, and then somewhat south.

At first he snugged up on the reins and that kept the black to an uneasy jog. Haydock stood in the stirrups with one hand coiled under the saddle swell above the horse's withers. The damned trot felt like it was jarring his teeth loose and it made his vision swim. *That's right,* he thought to himself, *blame the horse. It's easier than accepting the results of a long hard life, and now old age.*

Finally he gave up and let the son-of-a-bitch run. Speed couldn't undo what was happening to him, but it felt good, like living again, and the colt didn't mind the shallow ditches or deep gullies. He bellied down and jumped, and Haydock got rocketed around, but the high cantle saved him and he even pulled leather once or twice since no one was looking.

Eventually the colt tired and Haydock drew him to a walk in time to take a few deep gulps of air and wipe sweat and dust from his face. It wouldn't do to ride in damp and dirty to visit with that Heber woman.

He came over the slight rise where the cabin was set at the

edge of a shallow bowl. Good cabin. Her last husband had built it some years past for his first wife. He'd died; the wife herself was long gone. Mrs. Heber had right of title by the act of establishing her home there and so far no one had come forward to challenge her.

Mrs. Rose Carpenter watched her husband and that old Mexican chew over the black colt as Haydock's boot slipped from the stirrup. He got it with a second try. *Damned old fool showing off again. Any excuse to ride over to that woman's cabin and prance himself around on a fancy-stepping horse, thinking that he's still a young man.*

As a husband he was moderate to good enough; decent to her when she demanded things and not too active in bed, wanting her to do most of the work and then tell him how great he was. She was familiar with this behavior, had been paid for her acting skills more than anything else in her life. A woman with few morals could make a good living on such lies.

Thirty-five had been the age—when she had hit that number it all gone to hell. A stronger corset, heavy stockings to hide the veins, more powder, a darker rinse in her hair. The lies had made no difference. The men had turned to younger women, and all her efforts, her touches, and teasing hadn't returned them to her.

Her mother had named her Mabel, but, later, she had become Rose, thinking it a better choice. When Haydock Carpenter had asked her to marry, she was glad for the chance, and she kept her name, Rose. She felt it suited her now, with her yellow hair and fleshy mouth, her extra flesh that she let slide inside a softer girdling, and her stubby legs rooted to the ground by sensible shoes. No more wearing those fancy heeled boots that killed her back, no more cinching up her loosening figure. She only had to be with the old man who didn't care she was getting fat. He liked grabbing her belly and pulling her down on him. He liked holding his woman, so he told her, and she wanted to believe him. It was easier than smiling at the boys and pushing herself on them when they wanted younger flesh and she just wanted another helping of potatoes.

This time when Haydock rode off, looking high and mighty, she stayed at the house, and worried. It wasn't just that he had married her; it was that she was getting used to the old coot.

And the old man liked what she said, most of the time, so she was beginning to find that she wanted him around. She certainly hoped he wasn't riding off to that woman's cabin, to talk about that stupid cow or spend time with the children. He couldn't have children, not with her, not with all the times she'd had the pox and kept on working. Nothing inside her was right. She couldn't bear his child even if she was young enough and he wanted to try again. He'd told her that much in his short speech about what marriage would be between them. He didn't want another family, just wanted a woman in his bed.

Tad Heber smacked his younger brother, hard, across the back of the head, then yelped and sucked on his bent finger. Tad was seventeen, dark like his mother, where Jonas was blond, more like someone that nobody but Tad remembered. Jonas hadn't known his pa that well. The man had died when thrown from a horse before Ruthie was born.

Earlier today, Tad and Jonas had gone hunting pronghorn, and they hadn't had any luck, missing every one. It didn't matter how closely or quietly they stalked, or how well they'd hidden, keeping upwind and doing what they'd been taught; the pronghorn caught their scent and bolted. And now both boys were hungry.

Jonas was acting the fool again, doing a war dance and raising his rifle like it was a spear. Tad didn't want to be shot by his own brother, so he slapped Jonas. Jonas abruptly stopped and looked at Tad like he'd committed some terrible crime.

Tad reminded Jonas that they hadn't been able to shoot one damned animal. It meant they had to tell Ma that truth, which meant she wouldn't be happy. So they walked, rifles getting too heavy to carry. One of the things that annoyed Jonas was that Ruthie had the luxury of a horse while he and Tad had to hike their way around the land.

The boys came to the house from the south and east, walking slowly, just about ready to drag the rifles, butt-end down, but not giving in to the urge, knowing it was wrong and one of them might shoot the other. Sometimes they threatened to, but they knew the importance of kin, even if they didn't share a father. Their mother thought the boys didn't know, but they weren't dumb. They could see the differences, and they knew their mother and her liking of men well enough that it made sense.

Two visitors arriving at their cabin at the same time! It was more people than had come to their cabin over the last three months. One of them was a stranger, walking with her daughter, which concerned Maggie more than the arrival of Haydock Carpenter, riding in too fast on a fancy black horse. She didn't turn to her boys as they approached the yard. Hearing them was enough, but who was with Ruthie and why was he walking, leading his horse? Three more strides and she knew—a bloody cloth around the mare's leg, a head bob at each step. It probably had gotten caught in some of that loose wire.

Haydock Carpenter made out the shapes—a man walking, a limping horse, that ugly Appaloosa the girl rode, the little thing perched up high. The black smelled something Haydock hadn't figured on—a lamed horse. As the black picked up a scent and spun toward the group, Haydock realized the bay was a mare. God damn.

Burn saw the wreck coming straight at him. An old man was pulling like a farmer on the open mouth of a young colt. Beauty was pulling the lead out of Burn's hand and spinning around on one foreleg, kicking hard at the colt, catching him in the jaw. The colt was staggering sideways as the Appaloosa, with the child yelling and yanking on him, pushed between the mare and the black and bit down hard on the black's neck, sending the colt backwards. The mare got in another kick and the colt went down, rolled over, then stood, trembling, shaking, riderless.

Ruthie slipped off the shaking roan. The old horse's ears were pinned back, his stub of a tail lifted, thrashing. With neck arched, the Appaloosa stomped a front hoof, clearly protecting the mare that stood close to him. Finding herself on her feet and safe, Ruthie ran for her mother.

Tad and Jonas roared into Burn, Tad swinging his rifle and connecting with Burn's raised arm. He grunted, grabbed the barrel, and pulled the kid to him, then slammed him in the ribs with his own rifle. The second wild boy poked Burn in the gut, and he countered with a slam at the barrel with the other boy's weapon. The boy stepped back, his face turning white as Burn easily picked the rifle out of his hands. He dropped both weapons and stood on them, digging the barrel ends into the dirt. He rubbed at his forearm and cursed the two fool kids.

It was a groan that made him turn. An old man was trying to sit up, grunting at each move. One leg was doubled back un-naturally under him and Burn saw, even as he walked over to the man, that the leg was broken. His head had been hit, blood dripping down. Burn knelt and spoke to the man, who stared up at him, and Burn understood.

Maggie Heber grabbed Ruthie and held her, watching the

situation unfold. She grew furious that the boys had attacked the man, yet, in a way, glad that they had tried. What worried her was that they had been disarmed so quickly. She wanted to ask Ruthie who the man was that she had brought to the cabin, but her daughter, her beloved brave child, was crying. It was so unexpected that Maggie knelt down and just held Ruthie, holding the thin flesh, a heart beating too fast. Tears were wetting her dress, chilling her breast, and she held on tighter.

"You two, get over here," Burn snapped at the two boys.

Maggie wanted to stand at the stranger's words, but Ruthie pulled on her and said—"No, no."—into her ear, so that Maggie hugged her closer and Ruthie cried harder.

Then from the stranger: "You pick him up . . . under his butt . . . and hold each other's arms at the elbow and wrist . . . make a chair, and don't you drop him. Watch the leg, it's broke."

"Where we taking him?" Jonas asked Burn.

"To the house. Do you think you're going to put him back on the horse? What do you mean, where?" Both boys looked at him blankly, as Burn pointed to the house. "You do know where you live, don't you?"

The boys managed to stagger up the two steps to the open front door and to maneuver Carpenter through the doorway without hitting the dangling leg on anything. The old man's head was resting on one boy's shoulder. Then the mother—at least she looked to be the mother of the two boys and the girl—got up, went inside, and started giving them directions, filled with warnings.

Burn let them disappear inside the house. He caught up the black colt, now nickering at the mare but wisely afraid to approach her. Blood dripped from his cut mouth, and, when the colt shook his head, droplets splattered his saddle and sweaty hide. The colt was cut between the hind legs, but the wounds were raw, too recent for instinct to have drained away. The colt whinnied at the mare, needing a warning or two from Burn's hand on the bridle to remember his poor excuse for manners.

Burn bent to pick up the old man's hat, then steered the black colt toward the barn. The mare took one step, her head bobbing, and she stopped. The Appaloosa remained close to her, Beauty's brave protector. Burn called out to the girl, who was watching from the doorway, to help by holding on to the mare, patting her, and speaking to her until she was calm.

Good, Burn thought, *the child seems wise enough,* as she headed toward the mare. He didn't want the mare near the colt again.

Once they got out of the mare's reach, the black colt again snorted and pranced a few steps sideways toward Burn. Burn pulled quickly on the bridle reins and spoke to the colt, drawing his head around to one side, then pushing on the colt's neck until he lowered his head like a spanked child.

The little girl came up to Burn, face streaked with mud, eyes reddened. She explained she'd tied the mare to a fence rail so she could show him where he could put the colt. Her voice was thin, nothing like when she had yelled at him earlier.

"In here, we got a stall," she said, guiding him.

Burn unsaddled the black, hung up the gear, and couldn't help noticing the age of the Frazier rig, the fine quality of the woven blanket, and the beads of silver along the curb edge of the bit. Too bad that bit hadn't had more effect on the rank colt. He shoved an armful of hay into the one box stall.

"There a place I can put up the mare out a sight of this boy?" He immediately regretted his tone of voice, like the girl was a baby. He recognized the girl's look from those given by Elizabeth Hildahl, when her brothers teased her, or her sister Fanny when her mother wouldn't let her go to a dance.

"We got another corral out back . . . where we been keeping the cow."

"Show me," Burn said.

He followed her, and immediately started shaking his head. The corral was knee-deep in loose manure and urine pools. The stench was overwhelming. "Don't those boys know to keep the pens cleaned?" The child only looked at him so he tried to make it clear. "I can't put the mare in that mess, she'll infect the leg." He shook his head and turned back to the barn. When he got to the stall, he realized the girl had followed him.

"What're you gonna do?" she asked.

It would take thought and patience with this one, Burn realized, but he figured he had scared this child enough the past week or so. "My name's Burn English, child." He waited, looking at her.

"That don't answer my question."

Burn laughed. "You tell me your name, and then I'll answer."

"Oh."

Burn waited, knowing kids figured things out, mostly, if you let them have enough time.

"My name's Ruthie Heber, and this here's my home. You took my brothers' rifles away from them, and they're awful mad, but Ma won't let them hurt you."

They stared at each other, each holding onto something new.

Burn rubbed his face. "I'm going to put the colt in that pen. He'll be going home as soon as we can get word to his people. The mare'll go in here . . . least till we can get a clean pen for her. That answer what you wanted to know?"

He made the switch, giving the mare as much time as she needed to hobble inside the barn. He got her unsaddled and in the stall, and spread out more hay as bedding. She immediately laid down, and lipped at the hay with little interest. Burn found a pail, got some water, and went in the stall. He knelt down and offered Beauty water, which she played with, taking delicate sips and holding her mouth closed, swallowing and eventually pushing her muzzle deep into the bucket so that the water level was just below her eyes. Her actions meant she felt safe and that he could leave her alone now.

Then Ruthie started in with the questions. "Why don't you leave the bucket with her? Ma wants me at the house now. You wanna come along?"

He held up the bucket, loosening the bail so it rang against the metal side. "You see this?" Burn asked. "You leave it in with a horse, on the floor, he gets a leg between this handle and the bucket and you got worse than that damned wire cut on the mare."

Her eyes were huge. "I better go."

She left Burn in the peace and quiet, the mare dozing at his feet, the colt outside squealing and doing nothing but getting himself filthy.

Burn got to the task of sorting out his own gear, making a nest for himself near the mare. He'd go to the house in a bit, when they had the old man settled, and find out what needed doing.

CHAPTER EIGHT

Maggie worked on Carpenter's head wound first after the boys had laid him out on her bed, not being too careful of his leg, but they were doing their best. She saw her sons' faces and tried to understand why they were so pale, their eyes fearful, their voices dimmed. She reckoned it was fear over the old man and what folks would say about the accident. Then she shook her head. Her reputation around here had been spoiled already by the bad-mouthing talk of the old man's wife. Nothing was going to change in a hurry.

Ruthie brought in the hot water she had put on the banked stove, having gotten the fire started and the kettle boiling, all without being asked. Maggie set a pan down next to the old man, who hadn't said much so far. He was in pain, that was obvious to anyone—his mouth was pulled tight, the muscles along his jaw twitched, but the biggest giveaway was the crooked leg, bent at a angle below the knee that just looked wrong.

She shook her head. Splints and wrappings were needed, but not quite yet. Her concern was the blood on his face, dripping onto his shirtfront and, if she didn't get him cleaned up, about to make a mess on her wedding ring quilt. Besides, he'd be more comfortable if the blood didn't dry on his skin. The simple task gave her time to prepare herself for what was to come next—his pain when the leg bone was straightened out. She couldn't count on the boys' help. It would fall to the man who had come in with Ruthie. Maggie wondered briefly who he was and where he'd gone? Ruthie would know.

As she washed the old skin, she was awed by the thin feel to it, by the blood vessels so close to the surface, by the papery scent that came from him stronger than the sweat from fear—the scent of blood. She'd never been this close to old age. Her own folks had sent her off to be married, and she'd never seen them again. They were taken by a fever while she was struggling with her first husband on the eastern plains of Colorado. Fool place to try and farm, but he had insisted, since the government promised him free land if he homesteaded. So, by God, they would build a cabin and dig up the land for crops. Of course, there hadn't been any rain and the land had blown away and he had died of a fever after giving her the older of the boys—the ones who were gone now. She often thought of him, the best of her men, certainly better than Cal ever thought to be. And at least the boys wrote home to their ma once every year or so. Sometimes they even sent her a little money.

She felt the old man's hand reach around her fingers and she started, coming back to what she was doing, stopping her thinking about a past that wouldn't ever return. Sort of like the land that had blown away wouldn't ever return.

The bed on which they had laid the old man, Maggie's bed, was in a corner of the cabin, behind a layer of quilts hung from the beams to give her some privacy from Jonas and Tad. They slept close to the wood stove, for, in the winter, they were meant to keep it going even though they usually slept through the chore.

Ruthie had herself a loft in another corner, where she could read and hide and keep herself away from the roughhousing of her brothers. They knew never to go up into the loft. It was Ruthie's only refuge in their unconsciously brutal world.

The old man groaned, and Maggie laid her hand on his shoulder. He shrank away from her touch.

"Missus, you gotta help me," he muttered.

She patted the side of his face gently and felt only the slightest push against her hand. Briefly she had kind thoughts about the rancher. Then practicality got the best of her and she removed her hand, and left in search of rags to wipe up the blood. When she was back, she pressed very softly on the scrapes and the cut by his eyes. The old man shivered, but he did not complain.

Finally cleaned up and the simple wounds dressed, Carpenter opened his eyes. "Thank you, ma'am. I knew you were a good woman."

She smiled at the compliment even as her mind drifted. Pity his new wife didn't think the same way. Maggie looked away from him as she answered. "Mister Carpenter, now we got to set that leg. The man who come in with my daughter, she tells me he's kind." Maggie hesitated, fearing the pain she was about to cause. "I'll be needing his help."

Carpenter nodded, put his hand briefly on her wrist. "It's a bad 'un, missus. I knowed that since I tried to sit up out there. Damned colt . . . excuse me. I know . . . so you do what needs doing."

It was Ruthie who came for Burn, not saying anything but— "Ma. . . ." He nodded, then walked ahead of her to the log house. The woman opened the door. Burn recalled his manners—"Ma'am."—as he entered. The woman stepped aside for him and was behind him as they headed to the room's far corner and the brightly quilted bed. The old man was propped up with pillows and looking pretty spry, save for the busted leg.

The old man studied Burn, and then said: "Well, hell, you ain't much for causing all that ruckus."

Burn set him right. "It was you and the foolish colt you was riding. You cut him too late, rode him too soon."

The two men glared at each other.

Maggie thought she might have to get between them, like she did with her boys sometimes.

Finally the old-timer grinned, saying: "Hell, boy, you're right on that. Plumb foolish thing for me to do, but that colt . . . he's got fire and flash."

Burn disagreed. "Mister, you got a broke leg from the looks of it. Any colt'll be a fool and you know that. Didn't bother you much when you chose to ride him, but you're going to pay now." He remembered the bay colt he'd ridden almost to death one year and how that colt had kept his manners even near a female in heat. Youth wasn't any excuse.

Burn felt the woman beside him draw in a deep breath before she spoke. "Who are you, mister, and what got you with Ruthie? My daughter won't say nothing 'bout you but she keeps talking about your pretty horse."

Burn didn't like the way Carpenter looked so interested, but the woman deserved an answer. After all, he was in her house, set up in her barn. "The name's Burn English. I don't know 'bout your daughter 'cepting she's been watching me for days without my knowing it, which makes me feel plumb foolish." He paused. "The mare got caught in wire, dammit, and I 'pologise, ma'am, but that wire's terrible stuff. Now I got me a lamed. . . ."

Carpenter spoke right over Burn's words. "So you're that son bred all those sorry bronc's down to New Mexico."

Burn took a deep breath, sensing the old man held a grudge against him. He took a gamble, but, from experience, he knew it was a safe bet. "Maybe you lost yourself a wager on one of my English horses, old man."

That got the rancher grinning. "Haydock Carpenter is the name, Burn English. You're smarter than you look to be. Yup . . . lost a thousand bucks and a good racing thoroughbred . . . bred in England, mind you, but he couldn't catch a dark colt out of your stallion. Learned my lesson that day. Ain't owned a racehorse since. Kept one stud for my use and bought me a couple of your good ranch horses, though, branded with your mark. And your training." The old man nodded his head. "Yeah, your training. Way you are, sonny, you'll recognize each one when my men coming riding in here, looking for me." Then Carpenter seemed to grow smaller and his face went pale and one hand drifted toward his chest before settling. The old man closed his eyes.

Burn pushed against the woman. "Best get to his leg, ma'am, before we wear him out."

She snapped at him: "You're the ones doing all the talking."

The woman had gathered sturdy poles and plenty of padding. Burn laid the sticks the length of the old man's leg, then broke off a few inches, rubbing the fresh cut against his pants to smooth the edges. The woman nodded at the old man's chest and between them they slid his body down the bed until he lay flat. The leg was twisted from the knee, no bone through the skin, but close, a bulge on the shin.

Burn slid a wide leather strap under the foot, pushed it up the calf to just below the bulge, then looked at the woman. She nodded her head once, her hands gripping the cloths. He raised the leg quickly, she slid the wrappings under the leather, and the old man bit down hard on his lip but didn't open his eyes.

Letting the leg come down, Burn snugged the poles, one on each side of the break, then raised the leg again while Maggie wrapped and pulled until the break eased into place with a grinding sound. Burn looked at the old man's face. It was white, sweaty. His eyes were shut, his breath hard, short. No complaints, though, no groan or cry.

Burn glanced at the woman. She, too, was white-faced, chewing at her lip, but, when she looked at Burn, her gaze was steady.

"It's in place now. You hold the foot and I'll tie off. Here. . . ." Maggie said, waiting.

Burn raised the leg, and Carpenter groaned out: "Son-of-a-bitch." Maggie tied a square knot with no further response from the injured man. There was blood on his mouth, caught in the cracked lip, at the corners, but still he made no sound.

Burn sat with Carpenter, who was sleeping now, head restless on the flattened pillow, his body rigid, knowing, even in sleep, that to move would bring agony. Behind him, Burn was conscious of the woman moving through her house and its chores with ease and a grace. He found that pleasing. Ruthie helped her mama, getting down pans and going out to what Burn figured was a root cellar. He grinned to himself as the child returned with a armful of orange carrots and a few potatoes.

The mother must have sensed his paying attention for she spun around. "You all suddenly dumping yourselves on us means we got to feed you and take from our winter stores. No one seems to have thought of what we're having to give up!"

He heard desperation above the raw anger and bitter tone. Then he realized it was an insult, and he thought to respond, but, thinking over her words, he reasoned she was right. He stood, careful not to wake the old man.

"You're right," Burn said. "Neither one of us thought to your provisions." He hesitated, scolding himself. "Ma'am." It came to him then. Her boys had come back with heavy rifles, but no food. If she was depending on her two sons, they'd all go hungry tonight.

A few strides and he was through the door, around the corner of the house and on to the barn. There he caught and cleaned up the old man's black colt and saddled the youngster with his own gear. He took the rifle from the old man's fancy rig and checked it for ammunition. There was enough, and the rifle felt better in his hands than had the battered old Winchester he'd been using for too many years. Then he went to climb up on the ungainly colt. The black threatened to buck out, but Burn was quick to feel the colt's mouth and put his legs to the shivering hide. Finally, after small arguments about direction and speed, the colt stepped forward into a stiff-jointed trot that would probably cause trouble with what had been healing in Burn's gut.

He settled the colt into a lope and headed north, over the rise at the back of the cabin where grasses grew knee-high and a few trees offered decent hiding. He slowed the colt after a half hour, noting that he now was willing to listen to Burn's commands. He eased the black to a halt by a stunted juniper and climbed down, tying the colt closely, while hoping he wasn't a talker.

It was pretty clear the boys hadn't gotten this far; their tracks had quit maybe twenty minutes back in a circle of flattened grasses where most likely they'd laid down and napped while thinking they were hunting game.

Burn walked through the grass to a distant setting of rocks and trees, holding himself quiet inside, easing his breath out in small puffs as he placed each step in the loose grass. The rifle rested easily in his hand, tucked under one arm, barrel down— not safe but when hunting he had to be ready.

Each step moved him closer to the rocks. Each time he stopped, a light wind touched his face as he listened to small *clucks* and *twitters*. Burn smiled; supper was waiting. Finally, so close it was almost sinful, the birds flew up, and he raised the barrel, following ahead of their panicky flight, firing quickly, and again, taking down one, two, even a third bird. He focused on where they landed, conscious of the rifle's new heat, the bending grass holding three small corpses.

Then the colt whinnied, twice, three times, as he pulled back on the reins, kicking out, tossing his head. *Not rifle-broke,* Burn decided, as he kept his eyes on where the birds lay waiting. He collected the birds.

Burn struggled getting on the colt, the youngster circling, still kicking out, eyes rolling at the sight and smell of the supper. *To hell with it,* Burn thought, and let the colt have his panicked gallop. At the top of the rise he hauled in the black, saw two young men running at him, one carrying a rusted shotgun. Her boys, a day late and a dollar short, on hearing distant rifle fire and a horse running at them.

Burn circled the anxious black as he held up the trio of birds, motioning for the boys to go back, which they did slowly, coming to a walk, then shaking their heads as they turned around. Burn watched them go to the cabin; the shotgun held in the one boy's grasp was unbroken, but still a potent weapon.

Maggie noted the birds with only the weakest of smiles, a slow headshake, no apologies, no thanks—just what Burn expected. "Outside" was all she said. He did his duty, gutting over a waste pit, then plucking the carcasses clean, removing the heads and feet, feeling the thin heat spread from their sticky blood into his hands. Warm, then cooling, plump breast meat, rounded thighs. Burn laughed, realizing he could be describing the woman inside that cabin, instead of a gutted meal.

Inside, he laid the birds in the iron skillet she had placed on the table. The tallow shone against the black metal. Herbs in a shallow wood bowl were bright green against the scoured grain. He hesitated as she kept her back to him, busy with something else. Burn sprinkled out the herbs, found a touch of salt near the stove, placed the fry pan on a hot empty place, and heard that satisfying *hiss* of heat against fat. He smiled, knowing she could hear yet would not give him the satisfaction of a response.

Sliced carrots, roasted potatoes, and three birds were divided among the six of them. Carpenter took a few sips of the broth water she'd boiled the carrots in before lightly toasting them in the greasy pan.

No one said a word. Heads bent, they all ate quickly, noisily, except for the woman, who leaned back at one point and released a huge sigh. The boys didn't react. The girl child's head jerked, and she leaned into her mother's side. The woman rested her hand on the child's head for a brief moment, then went back to her meal.

Burn hadn't tasted anything so good in a while. The herbs had worked magic, making each bite salty and sweet along with a tang from the bird tallow. The crisped skin of the birds was clean and sharp. Even the carrots, sweetened with molasses and lightly scorched, were a treat.

"Thank you, ma'am," Burn said. "That's a meal for a king you gave us."

Finally she looked at him, directly, her bitter eyes softened only a moment. "You hunt like that for us, mister, and you are welcome for a while. Only for a while, though. That clear?"

He nodded. "Yes, ma'am. It's a deal."

The next morning, when he came in, not too early, carrying a double brace of prairie chickens, the woman was seated at the stained table, both hands holding a tin cup. He could smell the coffee, and only had to glance at the stove where the pot stood, steaming, tempting, and she nodded, no words. An empty cup waited by the stove. He poured out the thick brew. She pushed an airtight of condensed milk across the table near a chair and Burn took the seat, accepting her gesture as an invitation.

He took a swallow, nodded in appreciation—thick, deep, bitter, and barely sweetened. Just the way he liked it. He took a long deep drink and wiped his mouth, put the cup down, careful not to make a sound.

"Mister, you're a rare one," Maggie said.

Burn raised his head just enough to glance briefly at her. She was smiling, and he grinned back. "I'll take that as a compliment, ma'am. Most folks call me something else and it ain't rare at all. More'n likely it's overdone, 'cause my mama was a good woman."

Her head jerked sideways, the slightest smile, opening her face, and for the first time her beauty was offered to him. But then that darkness returned. Her clear eyes clouded and the full mouth tightened to a bitter, too-knowing line. "What did you do to my daughter? Ruthie ain't stopped talking about you, and I don't trust a man 'round any female, especially my Ruthie, and you're one strange man. I don't want to be accusing too soon, so you can tell the truth or get the hell out of my house. Never mind your lamed mare and your hunting for breakfast."

His gut tightened and he would have walked out but for the child whose ma needed some comforting. "I rode north about a month ago. Not going no place in particular. I found that meadow, and the pond, and figured, since it weren't fenced, I could let the mare rest."

He shook his head, planted both hands flat on the table with a crack, forcing the woman to look at what he laid there for her to see. The backs of his hands told a story. Hard ridges of old flesh where wire had torn and healed.

"I hate wire," he said, hesitating, then: "Guess your child was watching me some . . . I never knew, though. Getting old . . . my senses ain't skilled or quick now. She was up there with that old Appy she rides, watching me. Doesn't make me feel any too smart, but that's all there is." He waited again, noting the woman's mouth loosening, but her eyes remained hard. He clenched his hands into fists, which whitened and lifted the terrible scars. There was more he needed to say, an apology of sorts. "Don't want your child thinking most men look like me."

The woman snorted which he knew was a poor attempt at not laughing. He pushed on, wanting his say. "It ain't my height or size . . . it's the scarring. My hide's in a bad way, and most folks, well, they don't keep living cut up this way. You need to tell her I ain't the usual sort of man." That hadn't come out the way he meant it to, sounding more like bragging, and his face got warm. He wanted to start all over again, try to get her to understand what was bothering him.

Instead, her hand came out and one finger traced the ugliest of the scars on his hand.

Burn flinched, almost pulled back, but the touch didn't hurt this time. Even if he touched that scar, he felt a twist in his gut that made him dizzy. Her touch was gentle. It was the same way he handled a skittish horse.

She spoke, surprising him. "Wire?"

He pulled back his hand, hesitated. "Yes."

"So what scared my Ruthie is true. The rest of you . . . ?"

Burn dropped his head, found his mouth dry. He barely nodded.

"Oh." Then a blank space where no thoughts or words would fit. "I'll tell her when she gets talking 'bout you and that mare again. I promise." Her voice had gone soft, and to Burn it felt like forgiveness. "Damn." Her final word, his choice, too, but he couldn't speak it, not deliberately in front of her.

The woman stood, pushed away from the table. "Let's get them birds gutted and plucked. You did a fine job last night." She returned the stiffening bodies to him, saying—"Here."—and Burn was glad for the excuse to get away from her and the cabin walls.

One of the boys approached him as he yanked viciously at the stubborn feathers. His first reaction was to throw the carcass at the kid's head. Attacking him with a rifle—hell, this whole family was crazy, and dangerous.

The kid grunted. Burn kept plucking.

"Mister." As if one word would cause Burn to leave off his chore to listen.

"Mister!"

"The name is English, sonny." He thought a moment. "Then again your sister and probably your ma already told you that. You don't know much about behaving with your elders, now do you, boy." He made it a statement, not a question, but the skinny kid was rough and readied to fight, having learned his early manners from his ma, and the rest from his brother. The rudeness was a choice.

"You been taught better, boy," Burn stated. "Mind what your ma tells you or you'll get a lot more than a fight."

The boy stepped in, too close, and Burn reached out, slapped the beardless face, and sent the boy spinning. He dropped one of the birds. "No threats to me, boy. You got no rifle and you can see this knife I'm holding. Don't go for a fight when the opponent's already better armed."

Burn picked up the dirtied carcass, wiped off most of the dirt specks, and finished pulling out the last of the feathers. He paid no attention to the kid who stayed flat on the earth for a few moments, watching Burn closely. Then he stood, backed himself up a few steps, coughed, and wiped his mouth.

"Mister English, my ma says can you bring her the birds. She's got the pan hot."

Burn pulled out the last feather, then stared straight at the boy. He wasn't bad-looking, rough in the face right now, and the lank hair in his eyes didn't improve what looks he did have, but the size was there in the broad hands, shoulders to match, a length of leg that Burn purely admired. He'd been a runt so long, from that fever that had taken his whole family, that he still got a twinge when he saw promise in a kid like this. And anger when the kid acted a fool.

"Here." He handed off the birds with forced politeness, feeling their stickiness on his fingers and arms. Gutting was an unpleasant chore he hated but did without thought or feeling. It was about survival, either his or the birds', and that made it not much of a choice.

"Thanks, Mister . . . ah . . . English."

Burn had to grin as the kid loped off toward the house, birds hanging from his big hands, bouncing against his thigh and ribs. *Baby boy filled with wanting to be a man,* thought Burn.

He went to the well pump, ducking his head under the faucet as he worked the handle. Couldn't get clean enough this way, but it was better than walking back to the pond. He gasped, drew in the icy water, and spat it out, trying to get the bird taste washed from him.

The everyday act of killing never had gotten easy for him, and that last remembered shot, shattering the stallion's head, driving life and years from the horse's lungs and heart, had almost made him willing to eat grasses and leaves rather than kill one more time. But life didn't work that way. Nothing in life was directed toward saving another. It was about eating or getting bit in two for some bear's dinner. Burn shook his head, felt wet hair slap him, and tried to laugh to mock the foolishness of his turning soft in old age. Instead, he stood up, shuddered, and felt his heart pounding too hard inside his chest. *Too old* was a chant he heard in his sleep. *Too late* a challenge he couldn't face.

She had the birds sliced and frying when he knocked. She didn't turn, merely flipped over a side of white meat and spoke her piece. "You come in, Mister English. Could you see if Carpenter will eat a few bites?" Then there was a hesitation, a softening of her voice. "Thank you again for the birds." She handed him a plate.

If she could know the turmoil going on inside him over the act of providing for her, she'd laugh, call him a fool, send him on his way. He would best keep his mouth shut.

Carpenter was awake, so Burn sat in the nursing chair, speaking gently. "Mister Carpenter, she cooked this up just for you."

There was no movement except for a flutter of the heart visible in his chest, a slow unregulated pounding that echoed what Burn felt. He let the moment drift by, holding the plate with three small bits of soft chicken, warm and moist, their scent rising to tempt even Burn.

Then: "Fine." A whisper that made Burn's head jerk. This was a task he'd never undertaken. He'd been hand-fed himself before, could still see Katherine's hand holding a spoon, trying desperately to tempt him. The image faded when Burn saw the old man looking at the spoon, then at Burn's marked hand.

The words were barely audible as Carpenter's voice croaked: "Ain't never had chicken fed to me for breakfast 'fore this. Prefer coffee and eggs . . . fresh tortillas."

Burn laughed, then steadied himself and offered a chicken bite on the front edge of a broad spoon. The old man opened his mouth, a maw empty of half its teeth. Gingerly, trying to avoid the white spines of the front jaw, Burn slipped in the piece. He watched the jaw close and heard the cautious chewing. Then it stopped, then more chewing, then nothing. Finally a deep sigh. Carpenter closed his eyes. Too much work to eat. Burn knew because he'd felt those small pains take hold. It was hard on a man to admit he couldn't do for himself.

"That's right, Mister Carpenter. Gotta eat when you can. Food ain't always right in front of us. Living hard taught us both that same lesson, if nothing more." He thought there was a nod, a slight dip of the bony skull, a glint to the half-closed eyes as the mouth opened. Bits of chewed flesh stuck to the lower lip.

"More?"

Again almost a nod. The spoon slipped under the chicken bite, slid into the maw easily, and Burn tipped the utensil, felt the tongue gather in that small morsel, and both men sighed. It was an unnatural act for them, a dependency and delicacy neither liked to admit in themselves. One more bite and the jaw hung loosely. The eyes were closed, and that pounding, lifting heart seemed eased, soothed by nourishment into a quiet sleep.

Burn's back ached when he stood and left the bedside. The woman turned to him, smiling now, a true and breathtaking smile. He handed her the small plate, the spoon, and still she smiled.

"Mister English, that was one of the kindest things I've seen a man do. The two of you . . . like you'd known each other for years."

Burn couldn't quite get his breath. He shrugged, looked out the door. "He's gotta eat, ma'am. Pride makes it tough on him . . . being laid up and all." She cocked her head. He shrugged again. "I know . . . that's all."

He scrambled from her smile, her face, the sweetness in her eyes. He needed to check on the mare, wash out that wound, and re-bandage it, rinse out the old shirt rags, see if the wound's heat was still bad. Maybe, somehow, he could soak the leg in cold water—a bucket from the well pump, a hand rag, anything to keep him busy for an hour or so.

CHAPTER NINE

The face came in and out of view. A rough face. A scruffy beard. A damned fool who needed to shave, and get that hair shortened so a good man could trust him. Looks like some kind of a horse thief . . . that's what it was. The black colt . . . a mare . . . and then he couldn't remember any more. But it was about horses. Always about horses. Or women. Damn the both of them for being in a man's life.

The face wasn't familiar, though. He couldn't register the who and why. His leg hurt. By God, it was on fire most of the time. So he slept. Delirious more than likely, but it was an escape he could manage. Still couldn't place the face, and it bothered him some.

He ate the chicken. It tasted like sawdust and some sweet herb— wild fowl, hard, stringy, but salted well. The unfamiliar man fed him, his hand shaking almost as much as Haydock's chest pounded. But he got the food in. Wasn't really chicken even though Haydock swore that's what the man had called it. But it was flavored enough to keep him interested.

The woman was damned pretty. Younger than his wife and had a better figure. Even in a damned plain dress and an apron, her figure filled a man's eye, got him to thinking of better things.

Haydock wished the woman would do the feeding, but he knew why she didn't. The man had the patience. He'd sit his skinny rump in that wood chair and let his head droop, waiting, hands still on the plate, spoon never moving until he was ready. Nervy son-of-a-bitch, but he was careful with that spoon, could take out one of the few teeth left in his mouth if he didn't pay attention. Haydock watched the hand come closer to him, so close that he could no longer see it but could feel it touch his lips. The hands were scarred badly, the hands of a man who had lived his life doing hard work.

Scars. Haydock knew what it was to be useless, hurt, down, and in a bad way. And now unable to hold a damned spoon to his own mouth. Horses, ropes, wire, fast horses, and lost bets. Damn.

Later, maybe midday, he grunted and sort of raised his own skinny behind. The man understood, and blushed like a parlor whore as he spoke in murmurs to the woman. She handed him a large shallow bowl. Her voice was loud. It was all she had. It would be the old man's till he left, then they'd scald it clean from his waste. Haydock knew she meant well, but it was reminding him again he was dying. Wouldn't be long.

The skinny horseman, he tried to hush the woman and that was a mistake. She rested both hands on her hips and got wagging at him and he backed up, holding the bowl, bumping into a chair, and came around to stare at Haydock.

No words were said, but there was insult and fury in the dark face, and Haydock admired the man's gumption. Then it was time to remind him of the why for the fussing. His body needed relief, he wanted to tell the skinny man now hunched over him. Embarrassment stunk from the man's skin, his hot breath on Haydock's belly, but they managed the need and it wasn't too bad. Some kind of curtain was pulled around the bed to shield the rest of the family from his act, especially the little girl. Haydock had no trouble with that. It was the man's turned face, his ice-cold hands on Haydock's wilted flesh that brought out a laugh, and he felt the man flinch. He mumbled—"Sorry."—and hoped it was enough.

"I'm the one sorry, Mister Carpenter," the man said. "I ain't usually this stupid or clumsy."

Damned strange time for an apology, helping a dead man piss.

It was in him already, waiting. Deep in a once-strong heart, a hole, widening with each breath. His ribs barely rose and fell. His heart labored to keep living. Haydock held his eyes open, wanting to look into this stranger's face and know who would sit by him when it came.

"Your name?"

"I told. . . ." The voice cut itself off, acknowledging the beginning of complaint.

Haydock grinned. "I can guess, boy. You tole me enough times, but then my head ain't been too clear." He took the risk, curious. "My heart, neither." That hit. The man ducked his head. He knew, and that knowing allowed Haydock to relax. Again: "Your name?"

"Burn English, Mister Carpenter."

He heard the name, remembered having recognized it. "Your bay colt beat my racer," Carpenter said.

Both men grinned. They shared a past even though they stood as strangers. Carpenter got it out—"Damn' good horses."— before drifting off to sleep.

Burn was careful marching out of the cabin—the cracked china bowl filled with red-stained urine—and on to the outhouse where he kicked open the door and caught one of the boys doing to himself what he'd probably just learned felt good. Burn bellowed for the kid to get the hell out of his way. The whole damned place was mad he realized as the kid bolted, pants down to his knees, drawers flapping, wide open.

His errand done, Burn spent a good ten minutes cleaning his

hands, then his face, under the cold pump water. He could breathe again, lick his lips, and taste the good water, take in air and smell the grasses, even the moist dirt around the pump. He was cleansed.

He went to check on the mare, noticing on the way the long shadows and feeling the winter-chilled air blowing close to the ground, stopping the grass, slowing the trees, shutting down the land before the first snow.

Studying the wire wound, he saw the edges had thickened. The open flesh was bright pink. Good, he thought, no infection, not impossible to keep clean. He chilled the leg again, applying cold water with a fistful of clean rags the woman had given him. The mare winced, tried to pull away. She relaxed when she began to feel the effects of the cold. She let her head rest on top of Burn's shoulder and even took hold of his shirt, fabric between her teeth, quiet, eyes half closed. A peace that surprised Burn. He didn't remember wire being this way.

Done, he wrapped the leg, taking extra care as he placed the material on the open flesh. Still the mare was quiet, her head bobbing against his arm, muzzle rubbing on his shoulder. A week at the most and he could leave, leading the mare, maybe, but he could get out of this hell.

Haydock hadn't come home last night, and at midday there was still no sign of the black colt calling down to the pens. Rose Carpenter was disgusted, annoyed, and, if she admitted it to herself, worried some about what fool thing Haydock might have done this time.

They had been married two years now, and all his promises hadn't been kept yet, so he damned well better not be dead, or something else. Better not be with that woman, Maggie Heber, or whatever her last man's name had been. Haydock had said he was riding out to look at the grass damage. Him and his damned grass, worrying on it, instead of staying home and keeping his wife happy.

His old eyes and rough hands found what they wanted in her flesh, and she was willing to give up to him anything he wanted. It wasn't often, or for long, but her willingness made him feel young he said. He had told her she could fancy up the house and buy herself clothes that made her look like a lady and even get a carriage painted in new colors with a team of matched bays—whatever she wanted. It was a fair bargain for them both. Better than what she'd thought would come to her.

Not bad for a woman of her age and disgrace. A man to pay the bills and give her comforts, maybe even leave her a few dollars when he died. The old coot, where was he? He was all she had now, a fattening woman no one else wanted. He was everything to her.

Rose grabbed a shawl and went down to the corrals, sweeping up the useless long full skirt to get where she was going more quickly. It might look pretty, but, by God, all that material got in her way, and, if she fell on her face, she would get nothing but jeers and catcalls. The Rafter JX hands didn't like her. She could tell by their cold gazes and mutterings as she walked by. But, damn them, she'd earned all this; it hadn't been easy letting men pay for her favors.

Rogelio was standing at the empty corral. He nodded to her, saying—"*Buenas días, señora.*"—in that polite deep voice of his. She smiled before remembering why she was standing in horse shit and dried leaves, staring at an empty space.

"He didn't come home." Her voice was flat, no lightness. Plain fact. The Mexican nodded once, then wiped his mouth with his hand, and for that Rose cursed him and all males who thought a woman only good for one thing. Then Rogelio told her what she had come down to the pens to hear.

"I sent Arcy out to follow the tracks, *señora.* He is our best at such things."

He was worried enough about her husband that his voice had a tremble. Rose turned to look at him. His face in profile had an arched nose and heavily lidded eyes, a wide mouth pulled down at the corners. A strong face, with a dignity surprising to Rose. Men like Rogelio had not come into the places she had worked. They were not welcome because of their dark skin, mixed Indian and Mexican blood.

"The *señor*, he is proud, and that black colt helps him remember he is still a man."

She knew Rogelio knew Haydock pretty darned well, guessed they had worked together maybe fifty years. His comment fit with her speculations.

Rose drew in a quick breath, let it out in short puffs. She wanted to tell the man that it was her job to make Haydock feel like the man he used to be, in those intimate moments—that's what she was paid for. To her the horse and all that male bragging only made Haydock seem foolish. Silly that he would need to show off his skills in subduing the colt.

"Do you know where he went?" she asked, all the while brooding over Maggie Heber.

The Mexican shook his head. "I think, *señora*, that he would ride south to where a man has been staying in Salt Valley, the place you like so much. The *señor*, he does not want anything you like to be spoiled by others."

He kept talking, but the words dissolved as she thought of that one fact: Haydock actually listened to her. She wanted a house in that valley. She had never seen such a place before. That Haydock remembered and might want to ride there and check it out. *Ah*, she thought, *he's taking care of me*.

"Well why don't you send a rider to the valley, if that's where you think he went?"

Rogelio shook his head. "*Señora*, if he did not go to the valley

and we ride there, we have lost time. It is a waste. Arcy will find
him by following his tracks. Please have patience."

Rose glared at the man, who had nerve to smile at her—no
civility, not the behavior of a ranch hand to the boss' wife—a
fine open smile proclaiming his range superiority. She raised her
hand, studying him closely. She saw no fear, no worry, and
carefully brushed a strand of hair off her forehead. This man
was certain of the choice he had made and would not bow to
her demands.

"I will tell the boss what you have decided, *Señor* Rogelio,
and how his life depended on the rightness of that choice." She
tried to be formal, direct, perhaps threatening, and still he
smiled as he reminded her: "Arcy will find him."

Haydock was sleeping now, so Maggie returned to her chair
near the fire. Her second husband had made the chair and it
suited her to rock in it, thinking of him, and life in general.

Life was a pickle right now—one man housebound on her
bed, her two boys angry and taking it out on whatever they
touched. This morning Tad had broken two railings on the corral fence and she'd sent him out to cut and bring in replacements, without his noon meal. The boy had responded with a
sullen and miserable attitude so she had had to be firm. She
had stepped close to him, patted his cheek with one hand, and
told him he best do the chore to make up for his foolishness, or
he was gone off the property. Love didn't matter, he had to pull
his weight, and it was no good asking Jonas to do the job, he'd
not broken the rails.

Jonas was down at the corrals, trying to clean the pens the
way Burn English had told him they should be cleaned. She
hadn't been down there in a long time, having depended on the
boys to tell her they'd done the job right. She was downright
disgusted that her boys had let the pens get so filthy, but there it

was. Now Jonas was pitching manure over the fence into a good size pile, complaining all the while.

Burn English. Skinny and not much to him. Hard to figure him out. No posturing or bragging to make himself important. He had a way of knowing that even Maggie recognized, a way of looking at a problem and setting about a solution, like helping her set old man Carpenter's broken leg. She hadn't known to raise the leg and slide in those splints. She would have laid sticks alongside and tried to tie off even if she'd hurt him, not knowing what else could be done except hope that he passed out and suffered the doctoring unconscious.

A lot of gray was in Burn's wild black hair. And his pale green eyes spooked her when he swung around and was so close she could look straight into them. His skin was dark from the sun, she figured, for she'd seen his pale chest and the marked line at his neck. The darkness made those pale eyes glow. His white skin looked smooth going down into his tattered shirt. Except, of course, for the scars, which she'd glimpsed on his forearm and those others that Ruthie had told her about with eyes wide and fearful, already knowing that such marks meant suffering. She still needed to keep her promise to him, and tell Ruthie that not all men were so scarred. She liked that about him, his wanting to make sure her child wasn't scared.

When she stood next to him, Maggie realized she had to look down at him—shorter than her by a good two inches—yet he didn't try to make up for that lack by any nonsense most men would, posing and wearing a tall-crowned hat, those thicker boot heels. Nothing like that in him at all.

He was pure, unlike the men who usually came sniffing around, making comments and asking if she had a man and did she want one for a while in her bed. She'd never met a man who hadn't tried something with her. And she didn't want to understand the why, not now, not at her used-up age.

Looking in the tin mirror, the boys used for occasional shaving, she saw lines and wrinkles and gray strands in her own dark hair, a neck beginning to wrinkle. She knew too well the flesh under her plain dresses was marked from bearing each child. But the men still came around, like Mr. Carpenter riding up to show off, and then breaking his leg, maybe even bringing about his own death. Maggie wasn't going to take on that burden. Still, she was saddened by his pain, hearing him curse in the night, bathing him as best she could, even with him watching her, sometimes touching her hand when she washed his face.

Mr. Carpenter, he was a full-length man. His fingers were long and blunt, his nails ragged. Creases and wrinkles told of a hard life. Work hard, make do. But he had gotten lucky and rich, hawking cattle to the railroads, the cities, and now he had bedded a younger woman, fleshy and foul-mouthed. And still he came around Maggie.

His touch was gentle, not tense with desire, an old man's hand on hers, rough skin thanking her—a thumb on her wrist, fingers against her forearm, the tips missing on two of them. And when she smiled, his mouth lifted in the smallest of gestures. Once, without thinking, Maggie had leaned over and kissed the stubbled cheek, and the old man had grinned. She had felt the effort under her mouth and it gave her a sense of wonder. His smell had stayed on her lips—heat, sour, and something terribly wrong. She knew it wasn't just the break, that it was something else.

This morning she had sent Ruthie on the old roan to the Rafter JX to tell someone there what had happened, hoping it wouldn't end up being the harridan wife. Perhaps she could tell Rogelio Vigil, or one of the other hands, that their boss was banged up and over at the Heber place. She would let them figure out how and when to move him, or send for a doctor in

Mancos, or even up in Pueblo or Cañon City. Maybe the old man's life could be saved.

She feared her place was going to get crowded soon, with too many voices and opinions, and Maggie wanted only to step back and let the others fight it out. It was the old man's choice, his life, but Maggie guessed the wife would have her own ideas.

It would be simple enough to cart him home in a wagon bed and mourn him when the ugly leg break erupted and took his life. The wife could blame Maggie, the ranch hand who would drive the wagon, the team of horses. She would blame everyone except herself.

The rocker slowed and Maggie leaned forward, looking out the window where she caught sight of Burn English walking from the barn. He stopped at the pump, put his head under the icy flow, and came up blowing out, hands pulling through his hair trying to comb through the tangles. She might offer a haircut; it would be an easy enough chore for her to do. Those birds he'd been shooting, well, they had tasted right good with the seared carrots and potatoes, and she wanted to find a proper way to thank him.

CHAPTER TEN

The rider was young, not a whole lot older than Ruthie, but she didn't like him telling her what she should do. If she was riding to the Carpenter place, no man had the right to stop her. She challenged him with that fact and he tried to explain, but Ruthie had her orders and pulled Roany around the pretty-looking spotted sorrel the man rode and kicked her bronco into a staggering trot.

He called out after her, but Ruthie chose not to listen. The child could have told him about Carpenter—what had happened, where he was—except for her stubbornness. Her ma's words stayed with her: *You get to that ranch house and don't let no one stop you. You tell that woman where her man is.* Exactly what Ruthie would do.

She was a child, pretty enough, but a baby really, too young for Arcy's interest, but she could ride and had a temper. He admired her ability with a horse, but she didn't appear to be a good listener. When he was excited or confused, English did not always make sense to Arcy. He tried to tell her that he was back-tracking *Señor* Carpenter and following the black colt's trail. But she just rode off in silence.

Arcy stood in the stirrups, letting loose on the rein, and the paint stepped into an easy lope, then a slow gallop, ears pricked, moving quickly without fear of the holes hidden by high grasses, ignoring the wandering trail of cattle hoofs and slow broodmares.

Arcy reined in at the low ridge, looking down on the cabin. As he slowly approached the house, he could make out a series of tracks that told him a bad story. A confrontation between a number of horses, including the small girl's roan—one of the horses had gone down—footprints of a number of people, including some small ones, more than likely those of the girl. Some marks indicated that someone had been carried toward the house, and Arcy's gut told him it had been the old man.

He hesitated, letting the sorrel paint spin a tight circle. A loud shout made him look to the right where he saw a boy running at him, a rifle held at his waist, yelling words Arcy could not make out. Then, stumbling, the boy went down and rolled over, and the rifle fired once. Arcy's paint half reared against the tight rein, and Arcy had the humiliation of grabbing for the saddle horn. As he let the paint settle, he studied what was before him. The fallen boy now stood, rifle pointed to the ground, and even at this distance his face showed to be pale, which made Arcy grin. This was another young one who thought he could take on anything, especially with that rifle.

A second boy, he looked to be the older of the two because of his stride, came to the side of the other. Next a woman was at the cabin door, hand above her eyes to shade them against the sun. Her voice was pitched high, but he could not make out the words. From the way the boys abruptly turned, Arcy decided they were being scolded. The boy who had fallen pointed toward Arcy.

Then the child charged, dragging the rifle as he bolted toward the Rafter JX hand The woman screamed something, and the boy slowed. It was then that Arcy decided he, too, was being childish and let the paint pick his way to the cabin. The woman stepped out to meet him.

Arcy slid gracefully off the paint and took one step toward the woman, half bowing as he removed his hat. This was why the old man's tracks led to cabin with its filthy pens, the cow and its slobbering calf.

Even though the *señora,* for the girl was her child, as were the two hulking boys who ran up beside her, was twice Arcy's age, her eyes were wide and knowing, and her face quite beautiful. Her body . . . such a body cried out for man to stroke it. In the boys, who looked so much like her, the facial features showed a lack of depth and appeared all too feminine. The mouths were too wide, the lips too red, too full—on her they were alluring, on the male children they appeared as a flaw.

Arcy realized she was speaking to him over the pounding of his heart and he nodded as if understanding. Slowly the words began to make sense.

"You scared us," the woman said. "My boys were only trying to protect me. Don't be hard on them." Then she smiled and he knew he would do whatever she asked of him. "Don't blame the boys, *señor.* Their hearts are good if their aim is god-awful."

He laughed, unsure if she really meant the words for she seemed to be apologizing for the fact that they had not shot him. Once again he politely bowed and heard one of the boys laugh, but Arcy did not care. The woman's smile was enough reward. But he must attend to the business that had sent him on this miserable errand.

"*Señora.*" He made the polite address, even though he knew she had had several men living with her. "I have come seeking *Señor* Carpenter. He is here?"

Her face sobered but still she was lovely, although her age became more obvious and he revised his guess to be more than twice his age. He was eighteen, almost nineteen, and she had to be over forty.

Her sigh told him what he wanted to know before she began to speak. "Yes. That black colt of his stampeded and fell. Mister Carpenter has broken his leg. He's inside, if you would like to visit him."

Then a man appeared. A horseman, this one. It was easy to tell by his walk and the breadth of his hands, the worn boots. Older, too, like the woman, but his eyes held a different fire. As he approached, the sorrel paint turned snorty, and Arcy had to tug on the bridle to quiet the gelding.

The man walked to Arcy without a word and put his hand on the paint's neck. The horse bowed his head to an open hand, snuffling and then licking the fingers, the exposed palm. Arcy went to jerk on the reins but felt the man's hand hold against his movement. They stared at each other. Arcy's attention was drawn away from the woman to what he assumed would be a more difficult challenge.

The man's voice was pitched low when he spoke, and the sorrel paint nickered. "He's done nothing wrong, son. You can let up on his mouth . . . now."

It was a command, given softly but without mistake. Those eyes held danger, and Arcy felt his face turn red as his hand opened quickly and the reins slid through, falling to the ground. The paint took a small step and leaned his head on the man's outstretched arm.

"I raised this one," the man said. "His ma was a prettily marked mustang. He don't need yanking on his mouth 'less you already ruined him with your riding, *señor.*"

It was an insult but the truth. Arcy had been told by Rogelio and the *señor* himself that his hands were too strong, too harsh with the horses. Bit and reins were used only for asking, and always with kindness, never as punishment. He looked down and away, not wanting to see the man's hand, the strong wrist, the terrible marks that Arcy recognized. His father had had similar scars, and Arcy remembered his painful journey through life and a long lingering death.

He picked up the reins and offered them to the man, careful not to look into those eyes. But the gift was rejected, left hanging, so Arcy dropped the leather, and the sorrel snorted, shied back a step. But the man's soft voice came as a command—"Whoa."—and the sorrel planted his feet, raising a cloud of dust. Arcy sneezed, then apologized. It was becoming clear he had much to learn.

The women stepped forward, as if the man was not there, saying: "You come in and talk to your boss, iffen he's not sleeping. Won't have you wake him . . . sleep's the best thing for him right now. Sleep and some quiet." Here she glared at her two sons, who were keeping their distance, their faces uniformly displaying anger and fear. "Shooting at strangers ain't quiet," she reminded them.

The cabin was clean, that was his first observation as he followed the woman inside. Her body moved precisely, telling any full-blooded man that she knew what he was seeing and appreciating. The table was scoured almost white, ridges of hard grain rising above softer surfaces. Arcy let his hand rest on the surface, feeling each bump, knowing how this family lived. He inhaled deeply, tasted something salty-sweet in the air, and he had to swallow.

Then she said to him: "Over here."

Arcy drew in a new smell, his mouth puckering, and he breathed heavily. She pulled back a thin curtain.

Carpenter did not stir.

Gone a day, and he looked old, ancient to Arcy's young eyes. Mouth drawn down, white stubble sagging in his wrinkles. His eyelids were bluish and so thin Arcy felt he could see the eyes beneath them. His eyes trailed to a broken leg, bound in filthy rags against two sticks. He'd done such wrapping with an amigo who never walked or rode again. *Would have been better if he had died* was the thought that flashed through his mind, which he knew was wrong to think.

He spoke quietly, not knowing if his boss would hear or not. "*¿Señor?*" Once, then a second time as his hand touched the stained quilt. A third time and Carpenter's eyelids slid back, revealing the depths of his soul it seemed to Arcy.

"Boy." Low, wavering much like a bird's song. A tremble rarely heard in such a strong *hombre*.

Arcy felt his throat close, his eyes sting. He struggled to find the words. "*Señor*, Rogelio, he asked me to come find you . . . the colt. These people are caring well for you." He gestured stupidly at the wrapped leg, and the old man grunted. "Your wife, the *señora*, worries . . . but now I can tell her you are resting." Not all of his words were true but rather the kinds of things one must say to keep the old man from knowing the truth. Death was already in this house, the ghost who came for the spirit.

Carpenter made the effort to roll his head and look straight at Arcy, and it was a wonder of will and strength. The old man could feel it in his chest, but mostly in his heart—a flutter that he had occasionally felt before but which was now constant and, in his tired mind, a welcoming sign.

Arcy realized the *señora* soon would have what she wanted, and the ranch hands, too, would get their portion of cash as the old man had promised. This kindness would buy the *señor* some peace.

The man who knew horses stood behind Arcy, his eyes glittering as he studied Carpenter. He cocked his head at the old man.

The old man understood that look, nodded as if saying, yeah, he wanted the visitor gone. Let him sleep, he had nothing more to prove.

Burn let his hand rest lightly on Arcy's shoulder, and the youngster turned to him. The young man's dark eyes were wide open, his face pale. Even with a gentle touch Burn could feel him shiver. He tugged and the boy followed Burn away from his sleeping boss.

"He is going to die?" It was a question, but Arcy already knew the answer.

Burn nodded, and Arcy's torso bunched as he turned his head. *"Ahhh."*

Burn looked at the cabin floor, kicked at a clump of manure, most likely dragged in on his own boots. He, too, was restless, wanting to bolt from the cabin. It wasn't his place. He didn't know the people—the old man, the scared *vaquero*, the ill-tempered sons, and the girl child. But he knew the truth. He stayed because the woman had looked at him with her clear eyes and half smiled and sighed when he had taken over dealing with Carpenter's rider. He nodded at her, seated in her chair. Now her head tilted and Burn lost his breath. No one looked at him like that, not since he first had met Katherine Donald before she married Davey Hildahl.

The woman was too pretty, too sure of herself not to know the effect of her smile, so he scolded himself, tried to hold back his interest. She had three children, maybe more, so there were husbands—or just men. He was being unkind in his thoughts about her in an effort to remind himself of what he was. Old, set in his ways, on the losing end of his life, not at the beginning when a smile from a woman made one an instant fool. Katherine had done that to him, staggered his heart with a look, and he would not let it happen again.

He wrapped his arm around the young *vaquero's* shoulders and walked him outside into the fresh air and the brightness that belied what hovered inside the cabin walls. "Boy, you ride back and try to explain to his wife. It was an accident, pure and

118

simple. That black colt did for the old man . . . trying to mount an unwilling mare. That colt's fresh cut, an' the desire is still there." Burn saw understanding come over the boy's face and decided to give him some direction. "He needs manners taught to him, boy. Not through a harsh bit and spurs, but through lots of work . . . long rides checking fence, and then resting, tied and hobbled. Keep him sweaty and tired, and he'll make a decent mount." The boy nodded, so Burn continued. "Circle him when he gets stiff in the jaw. Ain't no good putting in a hard bit, he'll brace on you and the son can bolt."

A lot of words. Why was it that people always needed something from him—help or advice he wasn't fit to give. As for children. Well, a kindness to a child had always been hard for him. Even Katherine's children had known he wasn't one for niceties, but they had come to him with horse questions and school problems, which he had found an odd pleasure when they weren't pestering him to death. He was hip-deep in the same mess again and only gone a few weeks. It was almost funny. Now this kid was confused, but it was only about horses.

Burn sort of pushed Arcy toward the paint. "Think on it, son. Horses ain't the enemy. We are."

The words rode with Arcy as he headed the sorrel paint back toward the Rafter JX. He had not understood all of the man's instructions, for that was what it had been, a lesson. He had heard it before from others, and now it had come from the man who had created this wonderful horse Arcy was allowed to ride. The horse he had tried to buy from *Señor* Carpenter.

This time, perhaps, he would listen, and try to feel, rather than just yanking and grabbing. But when he felt a weight in the reins and the horse bowed his neck and chewed at the bit, Arcy's fists got hard and that delicate feel went away until he let the strength in his elbow release and the paint chewed again.

It was most peculiar. He wasn't sure of what use this gesture had been, until he turned to look at the rump end of a disappearing pronghorn, and, at the same time, the paint turned underneath Arcy, and seemed to be waiting for him. He could feel the paint's hindquarters bunch with power, and briefly he thought of chasing the pronghorn. At that second the paint leaped forward. So Arcy let the horse run for a half mile, and he threw back his head, letting the hat slip off and hang from its leather strand. He laughed as the paint dodged trees and cactus and seemed to be catching up with the little pronghorn buck. Next he thought about slowing down and the paint eased into a lope. The touch on the reins weighed almost nothing and yet the paint came to a walk and then stretched out his neck, and Arcy let him take the reins until his walk was long and even.

When the ranch house was in sight, Arcy felt both pleasure because of the lesson he had just learned about the paint and disappointment because of the information he must give to the *señora.*

CHAPTER ELEVEN

For the first time Ruthie really understood the ugliness of the roan Appaloosa. His ears were too long—his face looked silly because of the white surrounding both blue eyes—his mane stood straight up, and his tail was thin and straggly so that, once when she had tried to braid it, the hairs wouldn't hold a ribbon. Even his color was wrong—sort of three or four colors all mixed together, making him look like a mistake.

She patted his neck nervously as he swung his big head around, almost knocking over Mrs. Carpenter, who had come out to meet her. She was fancied up, her face painted. Ruthie hadn't ever seen that kind of woman. Her ma didn't use such things, didn't need color plastered to her face to make her beautiful, at least not to Ruthie's eyes.

The woman yelled at Ruthie, telling her to hurry and get on with the story because she had things to do.

"Ma'am." It was a hard word that stuck in her throat, but Ruthie needed to be polite, so she tried again. "You got a husband and a horse missing?" There was no other way but to ask a question, because the woman was fiddling with the roan's bridle reins and it was making Ruthie nervous.

The question caused the woman to jerk on a single rein, and the Appaloosa threw his head, almost knocking her down. Ruthie wanted to laugh but she knew the errand was too serious for foolishness.

"We got your mister at our cabin, I think, and that black

horse . . . he got knocked down, so your mister, he broke his leg and wants you to come to him." She was making up some of what she was saying. Old man Carpenter had never asked to see his wife, but Ruthie knew from listening to her ma that women wanted to know they were useful. Although, looking at the woman—all painted and dressed up in fancy clothes—she couldn't see how a man would need her for much except the bed part. Ruthie knew about the bed part, not what they did exactly, but that her ma and a man seemed to like rolling over each other. She guessed if her ma had married to have these rolling matches, well, then Mr. Carpenter, he could do the same, except why with a woman so bound up she could hardly walk, never mind ride a horse. It would take a wagon and team to get her to the cabin. And Ruthie told the woman just that. "You'll be needing a team and wagon to get you there. The Heber cabin. Best ask one of the ranch men to help." Then she nodded at the woman whose mouth hung open so that Ruthie could see black places between the teeth. She knew the woman's breath would smell.

Roany was happy to leave, swinging his big head back and sideways so that the woman had to step back and didn't have time to tell Ruthie off, or talk about her plans. If she was coming to the cabin, Ruthie thought, well, then let the ranch hands harness the team and show her the way.

Brat! How dare the child, sitting up there on a bone-yard horse, tell the wife of a man who bred only the finest stock what to do with his animals. Nasty child, but, then again, her mother was too loose and free with her affections. Rose Carpenter had worked saloons and such, but she had never considered herself a street whore.

Now she knew where Haydock was—laid up, and taking rest in that Heber woman's home. Rose would not allow her husband to remain in a filthy cabin where manners weren't taught, which was how she envisioned any home run by the likes of Maggie Heber. It was necessary to get Haydock home. She would demand that Rogelio carry out her wishes. She would see to it the wagon was drawn by their best team, the bed lined with blankets and quilts from the house, and the best brandy available to help Haydock deal with whatever pain might come from the journey.

She expected a refusal from Rogelio, and, when he said no, she quite literally stamped her foot and told the man in the most colorful language—words she did not use lightly—that his no wasn't worth a pile of shit, that he was indeed the bastard son of a Chihuahua whore and worth less than what his mother had gotten paid.

His few words were spoken between her outbursts.

"You would know, *Señora* Carpenter, exactly the value of a *peso* or a silver dollar paid for a woman's flesh."

Then Arcy appeared, his horse sweated, the boy himself dusty and scared. He did not ride to Rose, the *señora* of the great ranch, but to Rogelio, who turned his head away from the boss' wife, and then walked to the boy's horse. Arcy leaned down, speaking quickly in that infernal tongue that Rose hated and couldn't understand.

When Rogelio returned to his interrupted discussion with the *señora*, he was brief. "Arcy has seen your husband, *señora*. He is the Heber place as the child told you. Arcy did not say so, but I feel that your husband is injured more seriously than the child understood. We must see to him, and quickly."

Rose retreated to the house, where she changed to clothing more suitable for her errand of mercy. When she came back to the corrals, she and Rogelio had another confrontation. He had harnessed two draft mules to the wagon, not at all suitable for

Haydock's removal from that woman's house—awkward ungainly creatures, one brown with a straggly black tail and an unruly mane, the other a reddish color with a white belly and freckles along its neck.

"They don't match, Rogelio . . . what are you thinking? He needs a good team, not this collection of misfits."

The man was not bothered by her tone of voice or the implied stupidity in his choice of animals. Rogelio's voice was slow, deliberate, and the tone, this time, truly offended Rose. "They *are* his best team, *señora*. Perhaps not in color, but they work together and their pull is easy, smooth. No stops and jerks like the blacks you prefer. They will bring *Señor* Haydock home in some comfort. He would choose this team if it was up to him."

She studied his face, gauging how far she could push. There was steel in the returned gaze, a refusal ready on the thinned mouth beneath its mustached covering.

"I want the team of blacks. Haydock likes their fancy stepping. He needn't feel like a beggar or a plowman coming home."

Rose stood in some discomfort as he unhitched the poor team while speaking in his language to the men who caught up the blacks and readied them. It took a half hour to make the exchange, and Rose knew she would make her complaint well known to Haydock after they got him home. This delay was unreasonable and she was suitably furious.

"Help me into the wagon," she commanded. "Now."

Rogelio offered his arm and she pushed herself up into the wagon seat. Then, as she reached for the lines, Rogelio's hands were faster. The team stepped up into their collars unevenly, and the wagon lurched forward, all the while Rogelio talking softly to the handsome blacks. Rose watched Rogelio's hands and fingers as they guided the blacks into a working team. She decided to be quiet and let a man do his work.

Go on faith, she told herself. *Haydock trusts this man, so it would be his wish.*

Maggie's voice was powerful when she was challenged, so Burn found it necessary to go down to the barn as she lectured her sons, giving them no mercy, caring nothing about their pride.

"You boys have been out hunting these past few days and haven't found us nothing to eat. So stop your hollering and learn to hunt . . . move slow . . . don't scare half the game in the territory by your foolishness. Bring home supper. I'm tired of either Mister English doing your work for you, or just eating roasted potatoes and greens. Now get! And don't shoot at any more strangers that ain't done nothing to you . . . yet."

Burn wouldn't want to be one of her sons, or her man for that matter, if she took it to scold him. In the barn, he made a great show of studying the mare, and, when the boys stomped past, he didn't look at them, but their curses were meant to be heard.

"God damn' smart-mouth son-of-a-bitch getting our own ma turned on us 'cause he shot a measly god-damn' bird or two!"

It came to Burn to remind them that all he had done was to have shot and actually hit something, but he knew any words from him would only make the boys angrier. He could remember being their age, although it took some hard thinking to go back that far. He had had no family then. He had been a feisty, angry seventeen-year-old wanting no man to tell him what to do. In retrospect, he was amazed that he had survived—some luck, some good sense, mostly pure stubbornness, and hunger had gotten him through those bad days.

If a man didn't have a woman to grow a garden and cook for him, he grew used to being quiet, learning how to wait, to hold his breath, to see what barely moved, to feel a soft wind, to hear a step, to watch grass bend against itself. Then he would know, without knowing, that what moved ahead was his to kill.

He'd killed too early, men who'd tormented him, shot him, stolen his horses. They thought he was a child without ever having taken a good look. One of the best lessons of his life had been learning not to judge by looks, to wait and feel the heart of any man, or woman, and not to see something pretty or weaker or smaller and figure it was easy pickings.

Those boys, Tad and Jonas, they'd not heard her words, nor would they listen if he put in his piece. They had their ma to take care of them, to make their mistakes right, to direct them when they got off course. Doing would impress these boys, doing and not lecturing on it, telling them with and without words they weren't men yet.

He watched them climb the ridge at a diagonal, pushing and shoving at each other, their laughter clear on the slow-moving air. Burn shook his head and the mare nipped at him through the rails. He had other things to tend to.

Tugging, Burn wrapped the end of the bandage around the mare's leg. Beauty snipped at his hair, pulled back. Burn grinned. It was her way of saying the leg was healing and that she wanted to get going. Beauty had had enough of the stall or getting turned out into the poorly cleaned pen. She was her sire's daughter, ready to go and keep going, wanting to find out what lay on the other side of any mountain, hill, stream, or distant flat plain. But she was wrong. A horse couldn't know the truth. The hide was delicate still, flesh slowly moving in to fill gaps, no blood though, just a tenderness that couldn't take much running, or the burden of a rider and gear.

Burn stood, rubbed the mare's muzzle, and saw the girl coming toward the pens on that Appaloosa monster. *Ah, hell,* he thought, *I can't answer no more questions.* Then came the memory of Katherine's voice, clear and soft, telling him to pay attention to how he spoke with the children. That he should know better than to dismiss them because they were curious. She had often chastised him for pretending to talk as if he had had no schooling. Sometimes he would grin at her and she would flare up even more, saying—"No nonsense . . . no fooling with the children's ability to learn." The lesson had never stuck. Her fury couldn't hold, and she'd laugh.

The child was coming toward him, grinning and climbing down from the Appaloosa whose lower lip flapped and long ears swiveled. Katherine receded in his memory. Another family, another woman—the wrong woman—but then again he was the wrong man.

"Ma says to come to the house," Ruthie announced.

Burn shook his head. "Little girl, don't you speak to a man like that."

She stopped. The Appaloosa bumped into her. "It's what Ma says . . . I'm just repeating the words."

He got into a staring contest with the girl until the Appaloosa gelding pushed her forward and she stumbled, losing the reins. The big Appaloosa carefully picked up his feet and stepped over her fallen body and walked sedately past Burn to stand next to the mare, its ungainly head turning to avoid stepping on the trailing reins.

Burn walked over to the girl, in no hurry, and, with one hand, picked her up and set her on the ground. "Your ma said that . . . well, now, to keep you out of trouble, I'll go on your word, but just this once."

She spoke right up. "Ma asked for you. Me, I'm going to put up Roany, make sure he's got a clean pen and water, and some of that hay."

He could feel her anger as he walked toward the house. He didn't blame the mite. She was big enough to ride by herself, smart enough to see what went on inside the house with the old man, even with her brothers, and Burn had no cause to tease her. He knew being told what to do always rankled. It was like riding a colt. You didn't demand, you asked and suggested and waited while the colt figured out that doing was usually easier than arguing with a lump of muscle sitting on his back.

He looked back once and saw Ruthie standing, arms crossed, face set. When she realized he was in turn watching her, she picked up the reins to the Appaloosa and marched toward the pen. Burn grinned, went on about his errand heading to the cabin.

Ruthie's cry surprised him. Burn bolted toward the sound.

From the cabin came Maggie's high-pitched voice. "What's happened? Ruthie!"

The child kept yelling: "He's dead! He's dead!"

Behind the barn, near the last pen, Ruthie's eyes sought out Burn. He couldn't see any blood on her and the Appaloosa looked all right. Burn continued toward her, trying to see what she was pointing at.

Then he saw that the black colt lay flat, gut shot, the dirt around him a darker red, flies *buzzing* about even though the air was chilly. Its teeth were bared, its tongue hanging out, and signs of thrashing showed in the churned dirt.

Burn came closer to inspect the colt. One bullet. A bad-luck shot. Then he remembered Tad's rifle having gone off unexpectedly. Everyone had breathed a sigh of relief when no one had been hit. Except there had been. The young black colt, that was now nothing but meat and hide.

The death frightened Burn because he'd been working near the corpse, and none of his senses had picked up on what had happened. Another instinct lost. God dammit.

Standing there, Burn heard the *squeal* of a dried axle, a harness *jingle,* a whip *crack* followed by a "Whoa!" He shook his head, fearing what would greet him as he turned. Ruthie flew past him, heading toward the cabin and her mother's arms.

Sure enough, a fancy, painted wagon, but its wheel *squealed* just the same. The noise bothered the off black who kept shaking his head, putting an extra half-kick step into his poor attempt at pulling. The near black was sturdier and must have been deaf, for he pulled, head held tightly against the fool overcheck. It was a sorry team even if they matched in color, right down to their hind socks and a half star between the eyes.

A *vaquero* was driving, his dark face set, his eyes straight ahead. Burn watched his hands, saw the slightest movement soothe the skittery black while trying to encourage the soured near horse. It was a masterpiece of driving and Burn appreciated it.

The team was brought to a steady, even halt, no lurching forward, no extra step. The man knew his horses, could feel what wasn't right through the reins and make adjustments. Burn was surely impressed. He stepped up to the wagon, where he could directly view the man, and then he nodded. The driver's answer was a brief smile, a similar nod.

The woman next to him in the wagon, however, began snapping as soon as Maggie appeared at the cabin door. A rough voice, using words no decent woman should know or ever use. Maggie took one step back, and Burn could see her push Ruthie inside, whispering something to the child.

As the team stood squarely, the woman gathered up her skirts, glaring at Burn, expecting him to offer his hand. Standing only a few feet from her, he refused, shaking his head. He would not be part of this woman's world. She might be Haydock Carpenter's wife, but she wasn't a lady.

The woman settled back onto the carriage seat. "You get Haydock out here right now! I don't want him staying with her a minute longer! You have no right to keep my husband when he needs me to take care of him!"

At the cabin door, Maggie's skin was red, her eyes wide. Burn glanced at her, then moved a step toward the carriage and the raging woman and slammed his hand on the side of the fancy wood. "Ma'am, you don't talk that way 'round here," he said. He caught the look on the driver's face—a smug set to the mouth, another hint of that peculiar nod. The woman shut up, which surprised Burn.

It was the *vaquero* who spoke next, using a voice that made listening a pleasure compared to the woman. "*Señor,* we are here to inquire as to the health and whereabouts of *Señor* Carpenter. You are the one to ask?" The driver had asked Burn, man to man, which made Burn smile.

"The lady of the house knows best about Mister Carpenter," Burn responded. "She's been tending him. He has a broken leg, and there seems to be more troubling him that I don't understand. . . ."

Rose Carpenter said nothing, but she glared first at her husband's long-time hand, and then at Burn. Both men ignored her, and Maggie had quickly removed herself inside the house where, among the shadows, she could not be seen but could hear.

"My name is Rogelio Vigil, *señor,*" the driver said.

"Burn English."

Rogelio's eyes looked puzzled, then widened.

"Yes, English," Burn said.

They grinned at each other.

"I lost much money, *señor,*" Carpenter's man said. "Who could know a local horse would run with such heart."

"*Senor,*" Burn said, "you know horses. Why didn't you take a long look at that bay colt, instead of believing what you were told in a book or on a piece of paper? It was there for you to see . . . in his lines, his eyes, his eagerness. A horseman such as you. . . ."

Rogelio laughed. "Yes, it was a mistake. I trusted the *señor* when he said his imported stallion was unbeatable. He has a way with him . . . to make you believe."

At this point, Mrs. Carpenter began again. "I don't know what the hell you're talking about, but I want it to stop. I want my husband now! We've got blankets and straw in the wagon, so he can come home with me."

Both men stared at the woman. In the quiet, Maggie stepped out of the cabin and approached the rig. "Missus Carpenter"— her voice carried all the worries and stress of the last day— "your husband is resting quietly. I'm sure you understand a journey to your home might. . . ." She paused, and Burn sensed how difficult this was for her. "Such a trip would kill him," Maggie finally got out.

The level of Rose Carpenter's voice went up a notch: "He is my husband and I know best!"

"Missus Carpenter," Maggie began again, "please step down and come in." Her few words were gracious, hiding how she felt and what she really wanted to add: "And see for yourself."

With the smallest of pleading looks from Maggie, Burn stepped to the wagon and offered his arm. The woman shot him a dark look, but with her wide skirts and tight corset she could not manage to climb from the vehicle on her own. He caught her weight, was surprised by her bulk, the stiffness of her body under her clothing. She pushed at him as he backed away as if he had touched her in an offensive manner.

"That's enough," she said.

Burn was amused as she went to the cabin, knowing that beneath all the geegaws and fluff was a will of iron. He wasn't looking forward to the battle that would be waged once inside. He looked at Rogelio, observing the same concern in his eyes. He couldn't help but grin as the driver nodded his head. They both knew.

Chapter Twelve

Mrs. Carpenter sat there, having swept past Maggie, saying nothing and plunking herself down in the straight-backed chair where usually either Maggie or Burn sat to tend the injured man.

What is wrong with her? Can't she see how poorly her husband is doing? Maggie thought, anticipating disaster. The chair groaned under the weight of the woman and Maggie feared it would give way. If it did break, Maggie knew Mrs. Carpenter would take it as a great insult and have something more to complain about.

The woman's voice was heavy as molasses now as she talked nonsense to a man who most likely couldn't hear her. "Now, darlin' we'll have you home in no time where I can take care of you in much finer conditions. We'll set up a bed in the front parlor. You'll love looking out the window to see the mountains. Just think, though, if you'd already built that house in Salt Valley . . . why the view would be spectacular."

Maggie shook her head, wanting to slap some fool sense into the woman. Old man Carpenter rolled his head on the mound of pillows and Maggie could read the words his mouth formed, plain as day: "Stayin' right here."

His wife didn't see him, just talked on. Nothing from Carpenter but his wrinkled mouth forming and reforming the silent words. "Stayin' right here."

Finally Mrs. Carpenter turned, calling to Maggie: "Miss . . . I need the help of those men out there to get my husband into the wagon! Tell them to come in here now."

That was it. Maggie moved closer until she stood directly behind Mrs. Carpenter. "I am Missus Heber, if you don't mind using my correct name in my own house, Missus Carpenter. And there ain't no way you're taking this man out of here. If you move him to the wagon, he'll suffer terribly." She glanced briefly at Carpenter's face. He nodded as if giving her permission to continue. "That trip'll be hell on him and for no reason. He's in enough pain. So leave him be." She could see a stiffness travel through the woman's flesh—anger, hatred, maybe even fear.

Rose Carpenter's voice rose to a higher pitch. "He needs to be in his own home!" She stared at her husband while speaking, not turning to look at her opponent or acknowledging what Maggie had just said.

Maggie stayed where she could not be seen unless Mrs. Carpenter made the effort to turn around. " 'Less you intend to drag him yourself, he stays here. Ain't nothing to your house can help him now. He needs quiet, good food, and no fussing."

Haydock Carpenter's drawn face attempted a grin, the corners raising just the slightest. Then his eyes closed and he was sleeping again. Sad when a simple grin wore out a man. If his wife had been paying attention, she'd see what was real and right there in front of her. Instead, the woman turned around very slowly. "You will have those men outside your place put Mister Carpenter in the wagon."

"No."

Outside, the rising pitch of Mrs. Carpenter's voice caught Burn and the driver off guard. The team stepped forward quickly, wanting to bolt from the sound. Rogelio was quick to pick up the lines, his fingers moving, his shoulders setting to halt the team. Sweat appeared on the team's necks but they were obedient to their driver.

Burn ran to the house, and bumped into Maggie who was on her way outside. They stood closer than they'd ever been, his eyes almost even with hers, seeing in their blue light a center of green and gold flecks. He saw the pleading in her gaze. He inhaled deeply, knowing that their position was too intimate, but she felt right against him and he wanted all of her.

The shrieking started again, and Burn put a hand on Maggie's forearms and moved around her, taking the few steps to the old man's bed. The woman had Carpenter by the shoulders and was screaming at him to sit up. Carpenter's face was white, his mouth hung open, his eyes were rolling back.

"You're killing him! You're killing him! My husband . . . you're killing him!" Rose Carpenter screamed.

Burn pushed his shoulder between the woman and the old man, leaned in, and felt a small puffing against his neck as he laid the frail body back. In his ear, endless and relentless, the woman's voice became louder. He slid one hand under the old man's head and slowly rested it on the pillows. Then he turned and slapped the woman, pulling back at the last moment so most of the anger he felt was in his head, not in the power of his hand.

For one blessed moment, there was no sound. Nothing. Even Ruthie, who had come over to stand near her mother, was silent. Maggie's stare held on Burn. He didn't know what to expect from either of the two woman, but then he heard a voice. Soft, small, clear.

"Thanks, son. She was hurting me," said Haydock Carpenter.

Then Rose Carpenter's hand went to her mouth and stayed there. And Maggie actually smiled.

Burn nodded and spoke to Mrs. Carpenter as if nothing unusual had just happened. "You best go home now, ma'am. Come back to visit when you can be calm. He may be yours by law, but he's here now . . . and safe . . . and we ain't letting you take him."

It finally sank in. The flounced and curled woman moved rapidly through the small cabin, what remained of her dignity pushing her through the situation.

"English." A whisper from Carpenter. "She means well, but. . . ." Then nothing more but a deep sigh.

Burn felt his heart jump, and, when he knelt down and put his ear to the old man's mouth, he could hear life holding on. He then sat in the chair.

Perhaps a half hour later, when he felt Maggie's hand on his back, he pulled away from her, the old man, the child's wide eyes as she stared at him, still quiet, terrified by the scene that had taken place in her house and that she couldn't really understand. Burn understood. He shook off the Hebers' obvious need for comforting, and went outside, drawing in the sun, the cold air, the emptiness of the yard. No horses or wagon, no driver, no harridan pretending grandness and compassion.

The mare whinnied from the corral, where only the roan Appaloosa kept her company. Burn went to her, conscious, as he walked, of the bone, the muscle, and blood holding him together, keeping him alive. His flesh remembered almost dying. And, when he looked at Carpenter, he could feel that dying, and he understood exactly what Katherine and Davey had done for him. Trying to make another human hold onto life was a rare and terrible responsibility, a difficult thing for the human soul to accept.

Mrs. Carpenter's carrying on, her pretense, her wanting her husband home as if he were suffering from a minor cut or a broken wrist was the woman's only way of dealing with the weakening body she saw lying on Maggie Heber's bed.

Burn entered the mare's pen, and went down on one knee,

inhaling the warm sweet manure, the sweat, the smells of everyday life. The mare approached him and he could see the top edge of the wire cut, smooth and shiny above the dirtied bandage. The flesh was growing together so that soon enough the edges would meet and form a stronger bond. The mare lowered her head and snorted at him. Burn looked up into the opened curled edges of her nostrils, widened to take in his scent. Beauty nickered and nudged the front of his hat, pulling it off so that it dropped in a fresh pile of manure. Burn laughed. The mare stepped back, and then pushed her muzzle against his naked face. Her whiskers brushed into Burn's eyes, his mouth, and he could taste horse. Salt. Sweet. Dirt. Life.

"It won't last you know," Maggie's voice said behind him. "She has to bring him home now. She has to show everyone that she's in command . . . not him, and especially not me. Or you."

Burn shifted the bandage, pretending preoccupation, unwilling to share his fear at what he'd felt when holding the old man or hitting the woman. It had been a crude need to shut the woman's mouth. He still felt all those sensations: human flesh under the bone of his hand, the pain, the crack on solid skin. If he raised his hand, he could smell Rose Carpenter's peculiar female odor even through the manure now coating his fingers. He studied those trembling fingers. They'd hit a woman.

"I don't know what she's thinking," Maggie began again. "One look at Mister Carpenter and the truth is easy to see. He's. . . ." She stopped, unwilling to speak the word she associated in her mind with Carpenter when she looked at him. Death.

Burn rose, using the mare's neck and withers for support. Beauty rubbed her head along his ribs, almost pushing him over.

"Ma'am," he began, "she'll be back with more of Carpenter's men, all primed to rescue their boss on the missus' say-so."

Maggie stared at him briefly before responding. "She can't do that. She's seen him . . . even touched him. How could she . . . ?"

Burn wanted to tell her what she already knew. What he'd felt from the old man. What those tired reddened eyes held. What Ruthie was so scared of. What made Mrs. Carpenter so downright terrified and terrifying to others. It was one thing. A death coming to them, not wanted, not prepared for, not part of what Haydock Carpenter had planned for this end of his living, but visible, nonetheless. That padded and corseted and painted woman was his, by God, and he wanted more of her, on his terms, until he was too old to climb the mountain, and then he could die. Not because some sour-headed bronco had had plans of his own.

"She will come back, ma'am," he told her again. Then he took a leap, adding: "Maggie."

She had turned away from him, looking along the thin wagon road as if the wagon was already returning. But, at the sound of her name, she turned on her boot heel and faced him. Her eyes seemed to glow and Burn knew, if she asked him anything right now, he would become the fool he felt he'd always been.

"Burn. I've been waiting. Am I wrong?" She stepped in closer.

He swallowed hard. "Maggie. . . . No, you're right, even though I tried not to . . . but back there, when she was trying to make him sit up . . . you showed me."

Maggie stepped back, and again Burn remembered slapping Mrs. Carpenter. He knew that it didn't sit right with Maggie and that she needed to understand the why. "He had to be protected," Burn began. "She had to be stopped. No other way . . . and I saw you."

Then Maggie was speaking. "I saw you hold back. In that last moment, when I thought you wanted to kill her . . . and you slapped her . . . I saw you dig in and hold onto your strength.

You even bit yourself in the doing." She reached out one finger and touched a cut on his lip that he hadn't even realized was there.

Neither said anything for several seconds, but then from a distance came a yell: "Ma! Ma!"

Burn put his hand on Maggie's arm. "Your boys. Be damned glad they weren't here a few minutes ago."

She looked at him. "How will I get them to go if the Carpenter men come back? Oh, Lord, Burn, I can't lose them."

He was out of his mind, but he kissed her on the mouth gently, and she kissed him back just as gently. When they pulled apart, she licked her lips. "Your blood . . . you." She headed for the cabin as Burn went to the pen that housed the dead black colt.

The boys were running toward the house. Jonas held a brace of prairie chickens high overhead. Below him, high on the ridge, he could see wheel ridges and prints of horses that made him wonder. He knew they didn't use the old wagon, didn't have a team, and they sure didn't have visitors much.

He hoped the folks, whoever they were, weren't staying on, because the brace of prairie chickens he'd got, and the one goose Tad had managed to hit, wouldn't go far with too many people. He knew he'd have to pick shot out of the birds, which didn't leave much flesh, but he was glad he hadn't come home empty-handed. Supper would be punctuated by the *ping* of folks spitting out lead shot into the pewter bowl Ma liked so much. It had belonged to her own grandma she had told the children, as well as: "Don't you two boys take it outside for target practice or nothing like that."

Tad came up alongside Jonas. "What's going on over there? Hell, it looks like that black colt's dead. A waste o' good horse flesh. Who the hell killed him?"

They skidded sideways down the ridge, noting exactly where that English fellow was fussing around the dead colt. They crossed behind the cabin and went in the front door from the far side, not wanting to get caught up in whatever that devil-hearted man had in mind.

Burn needed a horse stronger than Ruthie's Appaloosa to get the carcass out of the corral and down to an arroyo that ran south of the cabin. The corpse needed to be far enough away to keep the coyotes and the stink away from the cabin. He figured the task would have to fall to the mare, having quickly dismissed a fleeting notion of using the cow. She wouldn't pull, not like a good ox or mule. Burn didn't like the idea of using Beauty, but already, hiding in the air, was that smell of death, and the day was warming up. He knew the smell would get stronger. He had to get the corpse moved.

As he headed toward the barn, it occurred to him he needed to tell the old man since it was his horse. So Burn went to the pump and washed his hands, feeling the water's chill work an ache deep into his bones. Then he stuck his head under the flow of water and scrubbed his face and hands.

At the cabin, he knocked before entering. On the table were a pile of feathers and three plump bird carcasses. Burn grinned. These he wouldn't have to pluck and gut. There was no one in the house. It made him curious, but it gave him time to tell the old man privately.

He stopped near the bed, cleared his throat, and heard a grunt from behind the curtain. Pulling it back, he rehearsed what he would say, but found there was no easy way to tell Carpenter. The empty chair sat in a line of sun. Dust whirled in small circles from the shifting of the curtain. He noticed for the first time that the wood on which it hung was dried out and the pegs were coming loose at the back. He'd have to fix that he thought to himself as he shifted the chair.

The old man still had life. He grinned, not much, but enough. "She's hell on wheels," he said a little above a whisper.

Burn grunted, uncertain which woman Carpenter was insulting—or complimenting.

Carpenter rolled his head. "Both of them going at each other." He stopped, his hands bunched up on the quilt, his face greasy. "Don't like seeing fight in a woman, but there's times. . . . Rose, now, she don't always use much sense. Can't blame her. Her life's not been an easy ride."

Burn sat down, swiping at the agitated dust, still looking out the grimed window to see light and air and freedom. Death was on his mind, inside his whole body now—too much death and no words to tell it.

"Boy." Short breaths. A clawed hand scratching on the quilt. "You got something to tell me. I can see it."

Burn continued to stare out the window, determined not to look at the old man. "In the dust-up this morning, one of your hands, a boy, come in to see you. To find you." His gaze wavered, then he quickly glanced again at Carpenter, who was licking his lips, eyes closed, head turned blindly toward Burn on the pillows. "Maggie's boys," Burn began again, realizing it wasn't right to be speaking her name so casually. "Tad and Jonas, they got excited. They meant to shoot at your man to scare him. No one got hurt."

"But?" Carpenter said.

Burn thought the old man was stronger than he was himself. Carpenter already knew somehow and he was being kind, letting Burn stumble through. "Shot killed your black," he managed to get out. He waited, then heard those short breaths again before saying: "Sorry. They didn't mean to . . . had the rifle loaded and it got dropped."

"Weren't much of a horse. Pretty color, though, that the missus liked." More labored breathing.

Burn watched a chicken hurry across the yard, chased by an overhead shadow. *Another thing to do,* he thought. *Need to build her a better coop or the hawks'll be eating chicken for breakfast.*

"Bet Rogelio got roped into driving them damned blacks," Carpenter said. "She . . . she thinks they're smart. My weakness, boy. Kept that colt uncut too long." A shaky pause. Then: "Vanity does strange things, a man gets older."

Burn spoke, wanting to give the old man a rest. "I'll drag out the body. Need to get it from the pens . . . but I thought, well . . . you needed to know first. Maybe you got something else in mind for the colt."

"Hide'd make a good rug," Carpenter said. "Pretty . . . that black color, but the sun'll hit it inside the house and it'll go green." A grin passed over his face.

Burn laughed and asked: "Pair of chaps, then?"

"Don't think Rose'll be using chaps. She prefers them fancy steppers of hers. But you can make yourself a pair, you have the mind to." Then a pause and a wicked smile. "Can't see that behind of hers in black chaps against them wide-ended britches she'd have to wear."

Burn laughed at the image, and put his hand over his mouth, feeling his face turn red.

"You got it, boy. Ain't a real pretty picture," Carpenter said, then was quiet. His face looked frail, his eyes grew smaller, and his hands spread across the quilt, no longer moving. Burn touched the back of one hand, felt the cool skin, but the old man's chest still rose and fell. Burn hadn't been left alone.

Maggie was back in the room now, near the table, hands on her hips, staring at the three birds. Flies *buzzed* around them, hungry now that winter had disturbed their usual outdoor feasts.

"I told him 'bout the colt," Burn informed her, getting up and walking toward her. He kept the table between them. Yet even this close she was temptation.

"The boys brought in supper," she said.

"Saw them. They went 'way around me to get into the house."

She smiled, her eyes sparkling, her mouth wide, and he wanted to leap over the table. Instead, he planted his ugly hands on its surface.

She touched the back of one hand, where the worst of the scarring began. "They're terrified of you, Burn, but they listen. I don't like them taking the shotgun. We'll be spitting out lead at dinner, but at least they were able to get something this time."

"Ma'am."

She frowned.

"Maggie," he began instead, "they need to learn to shoot straight and to stalk. And they're trying." He left before he had to fight off the desire to kiss her. It wasn't the time or place. An old man dying . . . the colt's bloating flesh needing to be moved.

The mare wasn't much interested when he approached the corral with a harness, and the Appaloosa simply turned his butt toward Burn at the sound of the laying of leather and metal over the top rail.

Burn harnessed the Appaloosa first, and noted ancient gall marks on the bony shoulder and withers. At least one half of the team knew how to work in harness. When he slid the collar and hames over the mare's head and neck, she threw herself back, the white of her eyes showing. Burn talked to her, ran his hand along her neck to the flat jowl, and then to her muzzle. She lowered her head. He used her bridle, not the stiff, moldy one with blinkers, and snapped the reins onto the snaffle rings. The mare sighed and relaxed. At least the bridling was familiar, and she was safe next to the Appaloosa that took the blinkered bridle the way he accepted everything—a shake of his rat-tail, a fart, and a deep exhalation of breath.

Burn had already wrapped a well-used and dusty rope around

the colt's swollen girth. It took a few tries to get the mare in step with the Appaloosa as he guided them together around the outside of the opened corral, careful to keep the mare away from the corpse of the dead colt so she wouldn't spook.

Then it was time to try halting and backing the team. The mare froze when he asked through his hands. She threw up her head and braced her front legs. It had been with his body, his legs against her side, his weight set quietly on her back, then the slightest of touch against her mouth to ask for that backward step. Now it could only be through his hands.

The Appaloosa understood and stepped back, jerking the singletree separating him from the mare. The mare shied sideways, then went back with the Appaloosa, head turned to the outside but finally in step with her teammate. He got them in between the gateposts, and slid the reins through his hands as he stepped back to hook the singletree chain onto the black's rope. It was going to get wild and woolly, but there wasn't any choice besides butchering out the colt where he lay, and for that he didn't have the stomach.

There must have been a shift in the singletree for the mare cocked her head, then jumped sideways, placing herself up against a gatepost where Burn didn't want her. The Appaloosa held his ground, guided by Burn's hand on the lines holding him steady. The mare started to fret, trotting in place, looking for an out now that she felt trapped by the Appaloosa and the post and the thing *jingling* beside her.

When she shifted away from the post and was almost in a straight line with the Appaloosa, Burn urged them both forward, loosening his hold, clucking, calling the mare's name. She jumped at the chance of freedom. The singletree chain *rattled* and tightened. The Appaloosa knew what he was being asked to do, but the mare threw her head wildly, tearing the lines from Burn's right hand and jerking herself against the Appaloosa's slow forward pull.

There was a moment when the Appaloosa pulled, then stopped, and the mare sulled, jerked forward, her body shifting, sliding a foot or two. The mare was panicking, kicking back, just missing Burn as he bent down to reach the line. He called her name, slapped the lines on the Appaloosa's bony rump. The Appaloosa went forward, with ears pinned, insulted at the scolding. The mare found her buddy in step with her and then she, too, began to pull.

As Burn hoped, the corpse turned at a sideways angle and was jerked, bouncing through the gate and out into the yard. The mare wanted to head west. The Appaloosa tried to listen to Burn. The arroyo was south of the cabin, a good half mile or more. Once he convinced the mare she could not take off on her own but was tied to the Appaloosa, they proceeded with jerks, then a breather, then more jerks and tugs until they hit a downhill slope and Burn had to hurry the team so the body didn't roll over them.

When they got to the edge of the arroyo, Burn tried to maneuver the team to the edge without the colt rolling over the lip. He was depending on the Appaloosa to hold steady as the mare fidgeted, kicking out, even whinnying a few times. At that moment he made a promise to her, like he'd promised her sire, he'd never put her in harness again.

The Appaloosa held quiet long enough so that Burn could back the team, loosening the chain and taking the risk of sliding his hand under the rope, which was pulled tight, to release the colt. A jerk now and he'd panic the mare and lose his hand or at least a finger. He was cautious, since he had gotten this far in life with all his fingers and toes and wanted to go out with all his pieces still strung together.

The *jangling* chain spooked the mare and the singletree slammed against her knee and hock and she kicked out, catching the Appaloosa in the flank, who then turned and took a good bite at her neck. Burn hurried to their heads and took both of them at the bit, tugging down, releasing, and tugging again. The two horses finally eased up and the mare even rubbed against him.

He left the rope on the colt while he pushed and kicked until the body rolled down into the arroyo. Coyotes would feast tonight. Then he unhooked the singletree, removed the hames and both collars, and had two bridle horses with leftover reins. So he swung up on the mare's back, talking to her, telling her the humiliation was over, forever forgotten, never to be repeated. She didn't believe him, and, as soon as his butt touched her back, she bogged her head, squealed, and bucked like crazy. All he could think was—*Oh, hell!*—as the third buck sent him flying. He found out then that the extra length of rein was useful, for the mare ran up against the leather's end held tightly in Burn's fist, a reflex from all those years ago, and she turned to the pull, remembering what she'd once been taught.

Through all the bucking, the Appaloosa simply cocked a hind leg and took a short nap.

Chapter Thirteen

Burn walked back leading both horses, footsore by the time he got to the cabin but rump-sore enough from the buck Beauty had given him that he'd chosen the lesser pain. Either way his pride had taken its usual beating. He was getting too old.

The boys were at the cabin door, cleaning their shotgun and squabbling. They were laughing by the time Burn finished un-harnessing the unlikely team. He moved slowly, feeling a rub across his hip when he moved. *Damn.* He took extra time with the mare, being slow and careful in removing the bridle while keeping one rein tied around her neck. She needed his attention now to remind her that their partnership hadn't fallen apart.

He brushed her, scrubbed her neck, especially where the heavy collar and hames had scuffed the hair. She seemed to forgive him, once again rubbing her head on his arm and taking a bite of his coat, holding the thick canvas in her mouth.

He left her alone in the pen and tended to the Appaloosa, who needed the same cleaning up but not the affection. He fed out hay even though it was still light, not suppertime, and then he limped up to the cabin, figuring to make a stop at the pump and remove the muck and filth he'd gotten into. It was the sounds that haunted him more than any of the afternoon's actual efforts—the thickness of heavy flesh slamming, rolling, dragging. Flesh become meat, without soul or heart.

He took off his coat, glanced at the sleeve, and saw the wet uneven circle where the mare had taken hold of the canvas. He was grinning even as he pumped the chilled water over his hands.

The boys were seated on the front steps, watching, silent now. The shotgun lay across their laps, barrel resting on one set of thighs, stock on the other. Burn shrugged back into his coat, shook his head, ran fingers through the mat of his hair, and slammed his hat back on. He walked to within two feet of the boys, who would not look up at him but studied the shotgun. Whether a threat or a distraction, Burn didn't care.

He said: "You killed that colt and I took care of the body. Now you go get the collars and hames, the singletree, and bring 'em home. Clean up that harness and store it decent, in the barn. You might not have a team, but there's no call to let equipment go to hell for want of hard work and some oil."

Jonas stood up, grabbing the butt end of the shotgun. There wasn't enough room to swing the barrel around, which was how Burn had planned it.

"Careful now. That's how you killed Mister Carpenter's fine black horse only you had a rifle then," Burn said as he shoved the barrel away from its position close to his belly. "You boys, clean up your mess. I done the worse part of the dirty work for you."

Maggie was at the door, and she sealed the deal, telling the boys: "You do what Burn tells you . . . *now*. He knows, and you don't."

Burn's hand didn't quiver as he slid the shotgun out of the boys' hands and moved toward the cabin door. He turned back toward the boys. "I drug that colt south to the wash. You can't miss those tracks. Gear got left waiting right there. I didn't want to burden the mare with more work. She ain't ready for it." He couldn't help blaming the boys for their idiotic behavior that had caused the death. "You go get that harness and such. Then hang it right in the barn like I told you."

He was aware that Maggie's head was nodding so the boys couldn't dare object. It was probably more than he needed to say, but the boys were young enough that they needed instructions to be repeated several times to sink in.

A howl drew the attention of all four, followed by another.

Burn looked at Maggie. "They already got to the colt," she said.

Ruthie came outside, stepping in close to her mother and grabbing onto her skirt. She looked up into Maggie's face. "Are they going to hurt Roany," she asked, "and the mare, too? What about our chickens, Mama? How can they be safe?"

The boys returned in about a half hour. It seemed to Burn that the entire day had been taken up with that one chore. Now here were the boys, laughing and punching at each other, unaffected by what had had to be done about the colt. He asked them questions, but they didn't answer until Maggie told them to show some respect.

Finally Jonas said: "Yep . . . them coyotes got right to the colt." Then he began a detailed description about what they'd seen. Ruthie was setting the supper table, and it was easy to see that she was listening and taking in everything that her brothers were saying.

Burn laid a hand on the boys' shoulders and pressed down, smiling at them, but deliberately trying to cause pain. The boys stopped their talk, whining and wiggling, but they didn't try to get away from him. "That's enough," he said.

Maggie told them to get more firewood, which was their chore, reminding them they had not been keeping the woodbox filled.

Jonas headed outside. Tad opened his mouth to complain, but Burn grabbed his forearm. The boy said—"Yes, Ma."—and went out.

Burn looked at Maggie, who was smiling. "They ain't bad boys, Mister English."

He winced. "Burn," he reminded her.

They both smiled, kind of foolish and kind of sweet. The boys brought in wood. The *clunk* and *clatter* broke the small moment between them.

There was little conversation at supper. The only sounds were the *ring* as any piece of shot found by the diners was spit into the bowl set in the middle of the table, and the occasional coyote howl. With each howl everyone would stop chewing as their eyes widened and their heads turned toward the distant sound. They all knew what it meant.

Burn was worried about Ruthie, who ate only tiny bits of the tasty game bird, and some of her turnip, a bite of carrot. She kept herself close to her ma and flinched at the sound of every howl. Burn had a glimpse into the world of parent and child, for Maggie's face mirrored her daughter's fear.

The dark was thick on this moonless night when Burn checked on the mare and the roan. He'd bedded them in the barn, and even then the mare was shivering, and it wasn't that cold. Like Ruthie, she seemed to be made nervous by the echoing howls that announced the animals' triumphant find. He fed out extra hay, then returned to the house.

The old man was half sitting up. His face was pale but there was a new spark in his eyes. "They sure do talk, don't they?" he said. "Kinda like them women that come to the house to knit or something. All talk . . . nothing but. . . ." His voice faded but he had given Burn a glimpse of what Carpenter had put up with in his past.

Burn took the broth bowl from the stove and picked up a big-handled spoon carved out of one piece of wood, well-made and easy to hold. He sat in the chair by the bed and held the bowl as the old man managed two or three dips of the soup. He even picked out the few bits of meat and got them into his mouth. He pushed the meat around, drool showing at the corners of his mouth, but then he swallowed and grinned, and unexpectedly Burn was pleased.

"She's a good woman," Carpenter said.

Burn looked at him, puzzled, and the old man grinned.

"Her . . . the one you're set on . . . not Rose. I married her 'cause I was lonesome and she'd put up with me fumbling over her."

Burn jerked, and broth spilled from the mug.

"Don't mean it dirty, boy. Mean it to be the truth."

Burn said nothing as he dabbed at the spill with a rag he'd brought from the table to use as a napkin.

"She's taken with you, boy. Don't know why. You ain't much to look at. Now don't get in a hissy, but I'm sure you heard this before. Can't tell me no man's ever called you on your size."

Burn tried to keep his face blank as he stared at Haydock Carpenter.

"That's what I mean, boy. You know 'xactly who you are and I admire you for it. Hell, your rep' with them horses you bred is all a man really needs in his life. That, and a good woman. I'm betting you been lonesome too long. Most of your life maybe, or you'd see what that woman standing behind you is thinking."

Burn shifted around on the chair and there was Maggie, one hand on her daughter's neck, rubbing and giving comfort, while her eyes smiled at the old man's blunt words and Burn's confusion. When he turned back to Carpenter, wanting to get the feeding over with, the man was still sitting up, but sound asleep. It took a few moments, a bit of gentle handling, before he was able to slide the old man into a prone position, head propped on the pillow, leg raised up on a mound of blankets. Carpenter snored through the repositioning.

Maggie helped Ruthie take the half-empty broth bowl and pour the soup back into the pot. She then rinsed out the bowl with a small amount of water.

Ruthie said: "Mama, he's getting better. He talks more and I can make sense of what he says." Then she studied on the thought; "Most of it anyway."

A coyote howled and the child jerked. Maggie held her, looking over her head at Burn.

He nodded, decided to go outside, hauling a jacket with him and shucking into it as he went to the woodpile. There were rocks scattered near the barn, so he dumped an armful of wood near them and hunkered down. He was careful to fit the rocks in a circle, making sure each was situated firmly. It was easy to fill in with a bit of dried grass, a few thin sticks. A match against the grass flamed out quickly, caught the twigs, and there was a fire to feed.

Tad came out first. He was slow to approach, but Burn asked him to pick up a log and place it carefully on the fire, which the boy did. Then he, too, hunkered down, knees drawn up to his chest. No words. Just a nod and a smile as his hands turned out to the fire's warmth.

Jonas came out then, picking up more wood without being directed and stacking it neatly near Burn, before he squatted next to his brother. "To keep the coyotes out?" Jonas asked.

Burn only nodded.

"For Ruthie?" This was from Tad.

Burn finally smiled.

Much later Maggie came out, carrying her daughter. Burn rolled over a tall thick log so that she had somewhere to sit other than on the ground, while holding the child. Burn studied Tad as he put two fresh logs across the embers. The fire built up and licked the sky. The howls drifted away and Ruthie shifted in her mother's arms.

The fire warmed their fronts while the chilling wind worked in through gaps in their clothing—a low waistband, a thin-collared shirt. Their unbuttoned coats got fastened tightly up to the throat. No one moved other than to feed the fire. Ruthie slept deeply, no longer flinching each time a coyote howled. After a while Burn got up and stood over Maggie and the child, offering his arm to help pull them up.

Burn watched Maggie walk to the cabin, Ruthie's legs dangling almost to the ground. He saw the effort in Maggie's step to keep her child in her arms. *Too big to be carried . . . too young to be left on her own,* he thought to himself. When the cabin door was shut, Burn sat back down and took note that one of the boys had added a new log.

Tad and Burn curled up near the lowering flames, saddle blankets pulled from the barn providing warmth and safety. Jonas kept watch, fed the fire. Two hours later it was Tad's turn, followed by Burn's taking over after another two rounds of the clock. It was 3:00 in the morning by his reckoning as he laid back, watching the stars, letting the boys sleep out the night.

He was yawning and kicking one booted foot through the glowing ash when Maggie came out and handed him a cup of steaming coffee. The sun was just rising as he took the tin cup that was hot to the touch, and welcome. He sipped the brew, staring at her over the cup rim. He saw her quick glance at the sleeping boys, her approval.

"You'll do, Burn English. Ain't much of you, but it's all the good stuff."

He blushed as he took another sip. "Thank you . . . for this." He lifted the cup.

She waved her arm over her two boys, saying: "For this, and for helping Ruthie last night. I don't think she would have slept at all if you hadn't started the fire watch."

He swallowed more of the hot coffee and it burned all the way down. It tasted like pine oil, the best he'd ever had.

Four Rafter JX riders came into the yard first. Their horses were lathered, their faces red from sun and anger. Neither Arcy nor Rogelio, the driver with the hands like velvet on the horses' mouths, were among the four. These were men with skills Burn recognized.

"We will have the *señor*," one announced. "Now!"

Burn looked up at the speaker. He had a broad face, deeply browned, and his dark eyes were hidden under a brimmed hat. A threat, not spoken but present, was alive between them.

"So, you plan on slinging him over the back of one of these nags you're riding and taking him home?" Burn said. "He's a dying man in no shape for that kind of stunt." He was angry at the men's stupidity. His eyes ached. He wanted to rub them, lie down, and sleep, but the horsemen had circled him and he was conscious that he had no weapon in his hand, no knife at his belt. Nothing.

A horse came close, brushed past Burn's shoulder, intending to spin him. Burn used the opportunity to climb the horse's side, grab the horse's mane and the neck of the rider, and hold on. When he fell back, he took the man with him. Both rolled on the ground, but, as they came to a halt, Burn was seated on the man's considerable belly. There was a knife in his hand now, easily taken from the rider's wide *concha* belt, and convenient for Burn's use. He touched the very tip of the knife blade to the throat that was exposed to him.

He found the remnants of his rough Spanish. "You will not take the old man. He will die from your pride." The knife tip pricked skin, drawing one large blood bead. As the man swallowed, mouth flooding with fear, the blood drop rolled in a reddish thread across the man's skin, sticking in the wrinkles, veins, and dark hairs. Burn pulled himself away and up, spinning slowly, the knife loose in his hand, but moving across his body so it could not be taken away from him.

The fallen horseman struggled to his knees. A *compadre* led the riderless horse in close as the man caught a stirrup and slid up into the saddle. That was all. The horses led off in a line, following the remounted spokesman of the group. A whirl of dust and yells followed in their wake, and curses, if Burn's poor Spanish was right. Then the small yard was quiet again.

Burn was wiping his mouth when Maggie came to him, a half-filled bucket of water in one hand. He grinned as she poured the water over his head, leaving just enough for him to have a good, healthy drink. He felt the tang of the metal rim on his lips, but it didn't matter, the water tasted just fine.

"She won't give up, will she?" Maggie asked.

"No, ma'am." Water dripped from his chin, chilling him as it rolled into his shirt and onto his skin. "Don't know what's got into that woman or the men who work for the brand. But moving him would mean pure death for Carpenter and that don't take a doctor to spell out. Any man with an ounce of sense would know that much."

When Maggie didn't say anything, Burn added what he had been thinking during his watch in the night. "There a doc nearby? A town? I'd send your girl. She can ride and has the heart. She can take the bay mare. That Appaloosa would make a two-day trip out of a three-hour journey."

"There's a doc in Mancos," she said. " 'Bout a three-hour ride on a good horse."

Burn thought about that for only a few seconds. "Yeah . . . the mare can make that trip. Besides, your girl don't weigh much and she can use that light child's saddle."

"But the mare," Maggie said, "she's been laid off quite a while now. Won't she be too much for Ruthie?"

"Beauty's hot, that's a truth, but she's. . . ." He couldn't say it, bragging came hard to him.

She understood the source of his discomfort. "You trained her and you trust her."

He nodded, but he had to tell her the truth about Beauty. "She's a mite more horse than your girl's ever ridden. I'll not say I won't worry about her."

Maggie's hand rested briefly on his face and he leaned against the light pressure. "Thank you, Burn. But after those men . . . and their crazy desire to take him . . . we need someone with authority to tell the Carpenter woman how dangerous her idea is."

Burn smiled, feeling the ghost of her fingers still touching him. "Seems like we're maybe risking too much for the old man, who's probably going to die anyway. Maybe it's a bad idea. I'd go myself . . . but if they came back while I was gone. . . ." Maggie's face tightened as Burn kept talking. "But then again, I don't see that we have a choice. Your boys couldn't ride that mare. I don't trust their sticking to a task. I can't leave, and neither can you. And we can't have the old man die by letting him go home in a damned wagon. He deserves some better than that."

Maggie was quiet. Burn took a risk and pulled her to him, her head bowed and rested on his shoulder. He could feel the in and out of her breathing.

"Burn," she whispered into his ear, "we ain't got a choice."

He buried his face in her hair, only for a moment. She pulled him closer to her. He inhaled her—her cooking and her fear and her being a woman. She was smiling against his neck; he could feel the softest movement of her lips just below his ear.

Burn wrapped the mare's leg in a soft cloth, using more of the tar ointment on the wound. He tied off the bandage with a few wraps from an old shirt and hoped it would hold. He spent extra time brushing the mare, then bridled her, and brought her out into the yard.

Oh, hell, he thought, *one more time ain't going to kill me.* He immediately regretted his choice of words as he swung up onto the mare's back. She humped, swished her tail, and pinned back her ears, and he hadn't done anything but sit on her.

Stroking her neck, speaking sweet words under his breath softly, sort of like praying, he pressed his legs against her sides, asking her, not demanding, that she walk forward in a polite manner.

Beauty's response was predictable. She snorted, pulled the reins loose, and bucked. Nice polite forward bucks with no kicking high behind, no sideways leaps. Polite lady-like crow-hops that took them across the yard in a straight line, almost directly into Maggie who'd come out to watch. Maggie's hand was over her mouth, her eyes glowing as Beauty, with Burn still attached, made a slow circle to the left. Then, as Burn drew in lightly on the reins and used his legs against her sides, the bucks transformed into the trot the mare had inherited from her sire. Long even strides, that were so smooth a man could sit, enjoy a cup of coffee, and read the morning paper if he had a mind to.

"Burn, you're out of your mind!" Maggie called out, smiling.

Burn tipped his head and said: "Yes, ma'am, just thought I'd test her out. She's gonna be fine. Your Ruthie, she's got her a light hand and that's all it takes for Beauty to ride real gentle."

He slid down, landed near Beauty's injured leg, and squatted down to check if the bandage had stayed in place. His hands searched, straightening the wrap. Maggie had moved behind him. He didn't need to turn and look; he could smell her, taste her, feel her hand touch his shoulder. Nothing was like how he felt with her close.

"Will it hold?" she asked.

"I'll give Ruthie more wraps to use as bandages in the saddlebags. She'll need to take a rest, check the leg. But it'll be fine," he assured her.

He did not let her know his concerns or that he felt as though he was sacrificing his horse for the cause of the dying old man. Strangely he felt no anger; in fact, he laughed as he stood up. Short and compact, those strong, scarred hands were gentle on Beauty's face as the mare rubbed against his arm. He cupped her muzzle, played his fingers against her lips until the mare opened her mouth and took hold of one knuckle. Horse and man held each other. Maggie was unaccustomed to seeing such a connection, as she observed that the mare did not bite, the man did not shove.

"She's a good one, Maggie. Ruthie'll do just fine."

Whatever had driven Burn English from his past, Maggie knew he was a gift for her and Ruthie. And the boys, if they would accept him.

The child's saddle was weightless as he lifted and placed it on the doubled blankets. The cinch wasn't long enough, so he used his own, which allowed the latigo to be drawn up and tightened. He'd have to show Ruthie how to check from the saddle. Beauty liked to hold her breath in the beginning, and, down the line, a loosened cinch could cause a wreck.

"I know that already, Mister English," Ruthie said when he advised her. "I know horses blow up, and I always check. I've been riding for years."

He didn't laugh at her adult statement, figuring she was telling the truth. He knew she'd ridden the Appaloosa for at least five years. So he watched the child walk up to the side of Beauty, put her hand, palm up, fingers flattened, to the mare's muzzle for a sniff and a rub. She was already tall, close to his height, but still a kid.

"All right then," Burn announced. "Here." He turned the stirrup, held the mare, and Ruthie swung up quickly, landing lightly, and took up the reins.

"It ain't a regular bit, mister. Anything different to it?"

"She neck reins. Just go light on her mouth and she's fine. Sit down, say whoa, and she stops. Rise to the trot. When she's breathing hard, give her a break. And I already told you 'bout checking the wrap."

"Yes, sir."

CHAPTER FOURTEEN

Ma was in heat again. It was that runt who showed up barely able to walk. Tad had to admit that Burn's horse was a beauty and that he wouldn't mind putting his brand on her, but the man . . . hell, Ma'd done better in the past. Big sons-of-bitches who knew how to treat a woman. But not this sorry bowlegged specimen who thought he could teach Ma's two sons how to stalk game and shoot it. Damn, but they'd been feeding their family all right till the s.o.b. showed up.

Jonas shoved Tad in the ribs as Ruthie rode off on the pretty mare, trotting out while she hung onto the saddle swell and let the mare pick her pace. Jonas knew a good run would get her there sooner. What the hell was wrong with the girl? She knew about horses; she knew how to make time.

Tad opened his mouth to call out to Ruthie, but Jonas knocked him sideways so he couldn't get his breath.

"You shut up, damn you, Tad. Ma'll get mad if we tell Ruthie how to ride. After all, it's that man's horse, not ours. Ma won't take to us talking over him."

Tad rubbed his sore ribs and looked at his brother. He saw that something else was in Jonas's eyes. A light that meant he had a plan. Tad shook his head out of habit—nothing Jonas ever planned worked.

"Listen," Jonas began, "we got to take that old man to his home. Ma'll thank us for the doing 'cause he put Ruthie to the risk of riding all that way, and you know the doctor won't be happy."

Tad thought over what Jonas said. He didn't understand all the fuss being made over the old man. Broke his leg, didn't he? That weren't much. Get him home, let him heal. So maybe Jonas had a plan that finally might work.

It was easy hitching up the roan. Since Burn English had arrived, things were clean and neat so the harness wasn't tangled up or stiff. Tad had some trouble separating the two harnesses and figuring out how to set up the hitching of one horse to the singletree, but he had an eye and got it done. The Appaloosa kept flipping his head and whinnying. Tad slapped him good, but the horse turned around and bit Tad's hand. He slapped the horse again until Jonas told him to quit it.

They lined the wagon bed with lots of straw—no sense in bouncing the old man. Again the Appaloosa began to whinny and fuss, so one of the boys had to hold him at the bridle while the other filled the bed. They fought over who would do what now, which was settled once Tad grabbed the bit and jerked on the roan's head. He glared at Jonas as if daring him.

By the time they pulled the wagon up to the cabin door, Jonas was fighting mad. Tad had a firm grip on the bridle so it was Jonas who had to go get the old man.

Before he got in the door, his ma came out, hands on her hips. "What're you boys planning?"

Jonas brushed past her. Hell, he was old enough that no woman could tell him what to do.

"Boy!" A hand grabbed his arm, spun him around.

It's that son-of-a. . . . Jonas stopped his thoughts before he could speak them out loud.

"You ain't taking that old man nowhere . . . ," Burn said as he stepped outside, still holding Jonas's arm. "In that wagon least of all. You got any sense to you, son?"

Jonas wanted to cry out that he wasn't the runt's son. He wanted his ma to tell the man to let go. English's grip hurt, and, when Jonas pulled back, staring into the horseman's face, those fingers clamped down even more. He quit struggling finally, and just stood quietly, his arm hurting like hell. Then he saw the shotgun in the man's arm and went absolutely still. Only then did Jonas realize that horses and riders were filling up the ranch yard. His mouth went dry. He was actually scared.

The noise, the voices, the telltale dust were distracting all of them. The Appaloosa whinnied and pawed and Maggie heard Tad's voice yelling at the stubborn horse.

Burn shoved Jonas back into the cabin and held Maggie back, pushing himself in front of her. He broke open the shotgun over his arm. No man could misunderstand his meaning. He was ready, but he would wait to see what played out.

It was those same four Rafter JX men on lathered, hard-breathing horses. They were followed by Rogelio in the wagon, eyes looking down, away from Mrs. Carpenter, who was perched next to him. Even the boy was there—Arcy—on a different horse this time.

Rose Carpenter's face displayed the same high tone of the brick-red dress she wore. She directed her first words at Burn English.

"There's too many of us now, whoever you are! I want my husband, and a broke shotgun won't stop me. Besides, you ain't man enough to shoot a woman." As she spoke, she climbed down from the wagon, catching her thick skirt on the end of the doubletree. She reached behind her and yanked at the ruffle, which tore. Not one of the men in her husband's employ made any effort to help her. She only stopped at the sound of the *clicking* into place of shotgun barrels.

Burn spoke clearly. "I can draw back on the hammers, ma'am . . . if you need that much encouragement. I ain't shy 'bout shooting fools.'"

Outrageous, thought Rose Carpenter. *Never would a true gentleman speak to a lady in such a manner.* Still she froze, glaring at her husband's defender. It was absurd.

"You don't scare me, sir. You will put that foolish weapon down and stand aside." Then all the questions she had been asking herself came out without hesitation. "Why do you care what happens to my husband? Are you the person who injured him? What makes him so important to you?"

She thought her words would disarm the man, yet, when she took a step, he cocked one hammer. Now it was up to her.

Maggie drew in a quick breath as she studied the side of Burn's face. He was serious, and, if she were in Rose Carpenter's shoes, she would study those eyes, flashing now, a brilliance unfamiliar to her. She saw him watching the woman, without breathing, without moving, nothing indicating his thoughts except those eyes flat on the woman's face. Maggie was close enough to Mrs. Carpenter to see the rise of color, and she knew how the woman felt. She even had sympathy for Rose Carpenter with her fears. She knew what it felt like, that cold sweaty all-over sensation and a racing heart.

Rose shook her head and her mouth thinned out, making her lumpy face even more unpleasant to look at. Her intentions were clear. She took a step, taunting Burn, thinking the a man would never shoot at a woman, not in the wide open with all these witnesses.

The roar set off a number of reactions. The Appaloosa threw up his head and bolted over Tad. Rogelio's team of steady sorrels snorted and trembled, before settling back in place. And Rose Carpenter fell to her knees, hands over her ears, sobbing out indecipherable words.

The second hammer was drawn back. This time that isolated click held more than a threat. Burn's shot had drilled a chunk of cloth from Rose's wide-brimmed hat and sprinkled the arm of a *vaquero* reaching for his own pistol. The *vaquero* put the reins in his teeth and moved his hand over the bleeding wound as his mount spun in circles, came up against the horse of one of his *compadres*.

Everyone listened as Burn spat out his words directly at Mrs. Carpenter. "Your husband is dying . . . and it's bad. Taking him home means nothing to him. He barely knows where he is sometimes. If you want to comfort him, lady, you come sit with him, hold his hand, feed him, and wipe his bottom so Missus Heber and I don't have to do all the caring of him. Sit up through the night with him and tell him that you love him. He's your husband, ma'am. But right now he's Missus Heber's guest."

Maggie knew Carpenter's men, who faced Burn, heard the quiet conviction in his voice. No fear, no worry about what he'd just done. Only the conscience of a strong man who knew one truth. Maggie wanted to walk over and touch the back of Burn's neck. She even began to take a half step, but he shook his head, the smallest of movements, and Maggie, understanding, stood quietly.

"Ma'am." Burn's voice was stronger now. "Missus Carpenter, no one here challenges you about your husband. No one here deliberately hurt him. You want to see him?" He took a short back step and lowered the shotgun. "You go on inside with Missus Heber. You mind your manners, and she'll take you to your husband."

Harsh, Maggie thought, *and humiliating,* but she also knew that the woman was capable of almost anything. Once Mrs. Carpenter had stood up, Maggie guided her toward the house, her fingers on one hand barely touching the woman's elbow.

Burn laid the shotgun down against the firewood splitting stump, breaking it first, butt down, barrels open, harmless, yet still within reach. It was then that he noticed Tad still sitting on the ground. His head was bowed, cupped in both hands. Jonas had wandered back to the barn. *Good,* Burn thought, *that'll keep 'em out of any more trouble.* Watching the two women enter the cabin unlocked his belly, Burn let out a sigh, and just wished he could simply disappear.

Leaving the broken shotgun as a reminder, he approached the man he'd shot.

"My apologies."

The man nodded, his face set as another of the horsemen ripped at his sleeve.

"I saw you reach for your gun," Burn said, "and thought I'd make my point twice . . . with one shot."

The wounded man's face widened into a grin. "I have often thought of trying such a thing, but. . . . Congratulations, *señor,* you are a fine shot."

Burn grinned back. "Believe me, *señor,* when I tell you luck was steadying my hand."

On the wagon, Rogelio laughed. Behind him, Arcy sat on his steady bronco and held the sorrel team quiet, which did not seem to be much of a job.

"I wish to thank you," Rogelio said. "You are brave to face all of us, and to fire so accurately. I am certain Esequiel agrees that it was his actions that got him wounded. He will not hold a grudge . . . this I promise."

As for Esequiel, he looked down at Burn, stared into the worn face, searched the fading green eyes, and finally reached over the wide horn on his saddle and shook Burn's hand. Those who'd been crowding in moved back, and Burn let out a sigh, echoed by the loosening circle of men.

Inside the cabin, Mrs. Carpenter went straight to the curtained-off corner and ripped the fragile sheet back, tearing one ring through the aged fabric. Her husband lay flat, head resting on a pillow. His broken leg was elevated, a thick stack of old saddle blankets underneath. There was stink from the bed—bodily functions and infection, too. Maggie feared removing the wood splints to find out.

The woman immediately held her nose. "Haven't you been bathing him?" she asked. "Haven't you bothered to wash him after . . . well, you know?"

Maggie bit her lip. "Missus, we've been washing and emptying out his thunder mug and wiping his bottom like he's our own babe, and don't you go suggesting no different. He's sick. We keep telling you that, and, for some reason, you seem to think that sick means having a cold or a bellyache. He's got a broke bone and I believe it's pressing through the skin. Every time we move him, you can see the pain on his face. A full bath ain't high on the list right now. Keeping him quiet and comfortable and getting broth into him's been all we can do."

The old man's eyes opened slightly. One hand lifted from the bed. When Mrs. Carpenter bent to take the hand, he waved her away and said: "I'm going to die in peace, god dammit. Now, leave me alone." He shifted his head toward Maggie. "Where's English gone to? I need him."

"You have turned my husband against me," Mrs. Carpenter accused Maggie. "This is why I want him moved. You have done everything you could to keep him here while you pampered him, and more than likely fed him drugs so that his mind is cloudy."

Maggie heard a sound at the door and she saw Burn peek into the cabin, before entering quietly.

"You listen to me," the rancher's wife hissed at Maggie, "and don't go mooning over something that's not yours, you bitch. He's mine and I want him home."

Burn slid past the rancher's wife and stood slightly in front of

Maggie. His voice was remarkably calm. "You don't call Maggie
any such name, ma'am. This's her home and she's been taking
good care of your husband. No call for such talk."

For that he received a slap from Rose Carpenter. A trickle of
blood began to come out his nose. He used his sleeve to wipe it
away. "Ma'am, I believe you best leave the house. You go sit
with your man, Rogelio, outside. He's got good sense, and he
listens to your husband. Perhaps it's time you did the same."

It was a sight to see. All that boning and stitching and padding taking flight out the door. The woman was so angry she hit
the doorjamb with her shoulder.

Burn shook his head. Maggie laughed softly.

"Let's fix that nose bleed, and then we'll see to Mister
Carpenter," Maggie said. "I want him to know she's not going
to take him from here. Not when we've gone this far."

As she stopped Burn's nosebleed, she mustered the courage
finally to ask him what had been on her mind. "Why'd you get
in so deep, Burn? It ain't just me, I know that." If nothing else,
Maggie Heber was practical.

Burn held her hand quietly. "I know Haydock Carpenter . . .
know his truth . . . and he ain't afraid of death. She is. She's
terrified. Hell. . . ." He stopped and looked down. "Sorry, Maggie. I'm acting as bad as her." He took a breath.

She shook her hand loose from his and wiped at a fresh trickle
of blood.

"It ain't the leg killing him," Burn continued. "I think it's
new times and ideas that he don't like. And marrying that
woman was a wrong choice, and he knows it. She'll talk him to
death if he gets taken back to their home. He's safe here . . . at
home in what he knows, what he remembers from his past . . . a
rough, but clean and honest place. You're a good woman who
cares. He trusts that. Trusts me . . . that I'll bury him right. No
fancied-up coffin or procession. A pine box and a dirt hole

under a tree. She'll want the big hoopla . . . a procession and a preacher and a black hearse. Hell, she's already got the matching black horses." He used his sleeve again to wipe at his nose. It was sore, but, being so close to Maggie, the pain seemed more a pleasure.

"That doesn't answer my question," Maggie said.

Then a low voice came from the bed, and they both turned to Carpenter. "My question, too, boy. Why?"

There was no escape from the question for Burn. He sat down on the chair so hard that the back slats *creaked*.

"My whole family died when I was maybe thirteen. Same illness got me, too, but I didn't die." He laughed at the foolishness of his statement—of course, he hadn't died. He began again. "I went to work mustanging." He was aware of how much he was leaving out, but those details were only important to him. Maybe later, with her, sometime in the future. . . . He shook his head.

Maggie shifted closer to him, put her hand on his shoulder, but he shrugged it off. There was no helping him through this. "Stayed clear of folks, caught my horses, and trained 'em, sold 'em, made me a good life alone, like I wanted."

Now it was getting even tougher and he felt a tightening in his belly. The old wounds began to ache as if new. His mouth felt dried out as he realized the long confession was more for Maggie than the old man—to give her a chance to get out if she wanted.

"Got run into barbed wire . . . nearly killed me. Good folks took me in, foul temper and all, and they nursed me close to four months' time." He swallowed as saliva built up his mouth now. "Took another try at dying to teach me 'bout living, allowing folks to love me . . . to love them. I stayed to that place a long time, longer'n any other place in my whole life. Nineteen years and more." He couldn't look at Maggie. "No, I wasn't married or father to a family. Uncle, I guess, to four kids and a good friend . . . a woman I once loved."

Then his mind seemed to go empty. The Hildahls were gone, their faces barely remembered, and he'd known this woman in front of him only a few days, but they'd lived through a year's worth of learning.

Then: "There's love in this cabin. You and your children, ma'am."

The old man grunted his agreement, while Maggie seemed embarrassed, rubbing her hands together, looking at the floor.

Burn swallowed hard just as a racket came from the yard outside. Loud voices, cursing, a *clunking* explosion that sent Burn to his feet and running out the door, wishing he had a pistol rather than that broken-open, useless shotgun he'd liked to have killed the woman with.

Riding the mare was the closest thing to perfection that Ruthie had ever experienced in her young life. She loved horses, loved sharing their freedom, and, while old Roany did his best and carried her to places she could never reach on her own, Beauty . . . well, she floated and danced and Ruthie wasn't aware of being a rider so much as being part of Beauty's existence.

Ruthie would breathe and the mare would stop. She would look to the right, and Beauty would follow her eyes' direction. She'd stand at the smallest voice, wait while Ruthie made up her mind.

Mostly, though, Beauty trotted, just like she'd been told she would do by her mister. She knew the trot could cover distance and not tire horse or rider. Ruthie recognized the importance of her errand, knew that a doctor was needed to take care of Mr. Carpenter and settle the feud that seemed to be taking place in their lives. Adults were peculiar and Ruthie didn't think much of the Carpenter woman who couldn't see her husband's distress or understand it.

Even though a kid, Ruthie knew things. Like that her two brothers at home were fools. She never listened to their plans or accepted their word as truth. And she knew that her ma liked men, but Ruthie thought that this one had something different to him. None of that loafing around. Her ma looked at him like . . . well, sometimes it made Ruthie blush and she was too young to feel these things.

Mr. Carpenter wasn't hard to understand at all and it puzzled Ruthie why his ugly wife was making such a fuss. The man was purely ill. You only had to look at his hands, pale even though they'd been worked their whole life. But no color was there, only blued veins on the back, like thick worms. He was dying, she knew that. Her riding for the doctor . . . well, there was no hope. But her ma, she wouldn't give up, and Burn English, he tended to the old rancher like a son or good friend.

Ruthie heard them talking together those few times the old man was awake and alert. The subject was usually horses, and something about the mare's pappy, her sire they called it, and what a great horse he'd been. This surprised Ruthie since she was certain sure that the two men didn't know each other. But they sure liked talking horses together, the old man gasping between his words, Beauty's owner patient, letting the old man talk and remember.

The track widened out through a series of small grassy hills, taking the low and easy way through for the carriages she knew traveled this way. Soft dirt, few rocks, no hills. Ruthie had been saving up, walking Beauty until the mare's neck was no longer damp. She'd been puzzling over how to ask. On Roany, she had to use a stick or the end of the reins and kick as hard and often as possible to achieve that slow even lope that Roany had in him once in a great while.

Although no instructions had been given by English as to how to gallop Beauty, Ruthie was pretty sure that kicking the mare would get her bucked off, so she leaned forward and drew her legs against the mare's sides and whispered about how fast she wanted to go. In response Beauty gave a leap, and, if Ruthie hadn't grabbed the horn, she would have tumbled over the mare's rump as the mare shook her head and took huge strides, her whole body seeming to crouch lower to the ground.

The wind took Ruthie's breath, her eyes watered, and she didn't dare let go of the saddle or the reins to wipe them. Briefly she could hear the lightest *thump* as each hoof hit the powdered dirt, but then it was all wind and nothing in the world could catch her.

A wide turn between two hills, and then out onto plains of rolling grass with the trail heading down the middle. In the distance Ruthie could see a black shape coming at her and Beauty. It was fast and quick. But there were no horses in harness, just a black carriage traveling on its own.

Beauty seemed to have her own thoughts about the oncoming monster for she skidded to a stop as the thing got closer, and Ruthie ended up on Beauty's neck, holding to her mane and one ear while she struggled to regain the saddle behind her. The black carriage stopped itself a good distance away, just as Ruthie found the saddle. While she rearranged herself, Beauty, unexpectedly walked forward, almost close enough to touch the steaming, rumbling machine. Ruthie could just hear the mare's snorting over her own pounding heart.

"You all right, young lady?" the man in the machine said.

Ruthie heard the words and found them an insult. " 'Course, I'm all right. It's that thing you're in causing all the trouble."

The rider, or whatever he was called, must have been used to people feeling that way, for he smiled as Ruthie let herself relax in the saddle. Beauty reached out very carefully and rubbed the shiny black front of the thing with her nose, snorting, pawing once, then standing quietly at Ruthie's command.

"My name is Doctor Oliphant, miss. And you are . . . ?"

He knew his manners, this doctor.

Ruthie beat him to the question. "You going to the Heber cabin to see about old man Carpenter?"

Why, yes, but . . . how did you know?"

"I was sent to fetch you."

He shook his head. "Young lady . . . for you have yet to introduce yourself."

She interrupted even though her ma had taught her not to do so with adults, saying that they didn't like it. It didn't matter if you were a kid and got interrupted, though, but that was a talk she should have with her ma, and not this man.

"My name is Ruth Mary Heber . . . and that Mister Carpenter . . . he's at our house and his wife wants to take him home. We got a man staying with us. He owns this mare." Here she patted Beauty, who seemed to bow her head in receiving the attention. "He keeps telling her . . . the wife, that is . . . the old man is too sick to travel, but that mean Missus Carpenter, she keeps coming over and causing trouble." She took a deep breath. "Who told you, anyhow?"

The doctor wiped his face, and then smiled politely. "A young man from the Carpenter ranch . . . name of Arcy . . . rode to my office late last night and gave me the information. I had other patients and only now was able to make the journey to see him . . . Mister Carpenter that is."

It took a moment's thought to gather the courage to ask the question, but then she just blurted out what was on her mind. "What is that thing you're in and how does it move?"

His smile came again, making him look almost nice. "It is a horseless carriage, or automobile, and it runs by an engine underneath where your lovely mare touched her muzzle."

Ruthie patted Beauty's neck. "Ain't she something?"

Despite his riding in a machine, the doctor seemed to appreciate a good horse. "You must run a fine ranch to have a horse like her."

"Ah, I told you she belongs to this man staying at the place. She got hurt and he wouldn't leave until she was sound enough."

"From watching you run her," Dr. Oliphant commented, "I would say the wound has healed quite sufficiently."

There was a moment of silence. Only the mare's slow breathing and a funny ticking from the machine interrupted the sounds of the birds and the wind.

Then finally the doctor bowed his head. "I must be getting to Mister Carpenter, Ruthie. You might want to move the mare some distance while I restart the engine." With that he climbed out of the carriage and stuck a black handle into the front end and yanked on it while something inside started to sputter.

It was easy to move Beauty upslope to stand away from the noise as the doctor got in and moved the machine forward and up to a speed almost as fast as Beauty had been going before coming to a stop.

With a deep sigh Ruthie reined the mare back onto the trail toward home. No more of that wonderful speed, only some trotting and walking to get her there. If she brought Beauty in hot and tired, her master might give her rightful hell.

CHAPTER FIFTEEN

Burn had seen a number of the riding machines before. One had been near his old cabin once. The confounded thing had created quite the commotion when it appeared suddenly into his silent world. On the trip north he had kept running in to the noisy, smelly contraptions. Now here was another one. Smoke streaming out of its nose, bouncing along on those rubber tires, and a heavy-set man sitting inside it, wearing a duster, one like outlaws often wore to hide their guns. Then the man was climbing out of the thing, carrying a black bag. That bag told Burn it was the doctor Ruthie had been sent to fetch. A doctor, over from Mancos, in a motor car. A nasty thing, but it got him here right quickly.

But where were Ruthie and Beauty?

Burn was the first to reach the doctor, who was spending too much time brushing off dust and looking at the rodeo-like scene he'd created with his entrance. Cow ponies and *vaqueros* and the team trying to scatter from each other, anywhere to get away from the monster that had come into their midst.

Burn laughed and the doctor turned.

"Sir, you have seen one of these before?" the man of medicine asked.

"Yep . . . and luckily I ain't on a horse this time." Burn paused before asking: "You seen a girl on a pretty bay mare? She all right? The girl?"

"Your daughter is fine, sir, and on her way back to your home.

That mare must have also seen an automobile before, for she did not spook. She walked right up to the automobile and sniffed it. Your daughter is quite an accomplished horsewoman. I watched her come across the valley. She and that mare were flying and it was a pleasure to watch." The pleasantries being over, he said: "I'm Doctor Oliphant. Would you be so kind as to show me to the invalid."

Burn had to think on that one, but then the Carpenter woman approached and he understood. He took hold of the doctor by the arm and spun him around, directing him inside the cabin, closing the door firmly in Mrs. Carpenter's angry face.

It came to him then that the doctor had assumed Ruthie was his child. A warmth settled in him.

Maggie was there to pull back the torn curtain. Even taking a short breath, you could smell the infection. Burn opened his mouth to defend Maggie and what they'd been doing for Carpenter. But the doctor just held up his hand, settled into the chair next to the bed, and studied Carpenter.

Carpenter studied the man right back. The doctor was a youngster, not what he'd expected. When he had heard the commotion caused by his arrival, he figured either the town of Mancos had grown some recently or the doctor himself was a wealthy man. Owning one of those vehicles out here was risky, even if it made sense. Time could save a life.

The doctor nodded and lifted up Haydock's hand, holding it carefully, thumb and first finger together right where a bone had been broken years back when a steer had horned his bay gelding and brought them both down. Maybe thirty years ago. Damn, it had hurt. He still missed that horse, too. He had been gutted so bad that Haydock had had to shoot the sorry beast. Shot the steer, too, out of rage. Had steak for a week and grinned over every bite. That bay was one of the best horses he had ever raised.

The doctor's face wasn't looking very promising. Haydock tried a grin, but the doctor only shook his head.

"Mister Carpenter. . . ." It was an old voice in a young face. The man had seen too much already. "Your pulse is quite weak. I fear there has been damage to your heart over the years."

At least the young sawbones wasn't a coward. He told the truth to his patient instead of hiding it or confiding it only to the family.

"Hell, doc, I know that. Been lying here feeling that flutter. Don't matter much. I had me a good life, and getting sent out by a horse suits me just fine."

Dr. Oliphant shook his head. Such candid talk from a patient wasn't usual in his practice.

Good-looking youngster, Carpenter thought. *Late thirties . . . dark hair . . . blue eyes, sturdy but not fat, not like most o' the men who ride in them vehicles, instead of working for their living.* Haydock had a feeling the doctor was doing the same thing he was—looking him over, checking out the scars and wrinkles, and making his own judgment.

"Let me look at the leg, Mister Carpenter," the doctor said, and turned his head to address Maggie. "Ma'am, would you boil me some water on the stove and bring fresh linens?"

Where else did he think she'd boil water? Maggie wondered. But it was a request being made by an educated man, even if it didn't seem that getting an education made sense to her. Surely the man could see there was a cook stove with a kettle on it, shoved to the back. But Maggie was quick to do the chore, not wanting anything to make Mr. Carpenter suffer more than he had to.

Thoughts were circling, making Haydock dizzy. He flinched when the doctor cut open the bindings over the wood splints Mrs. Heber and English had used. The doctor's quick intake of breath, plus the stench told Haydock what he already knew. He tried to push his upper body up off the bed, but the doctor placed a small, almost feminine hand on his chest and Haydock couldn't push against it.

"Mister Carpenter, there's no need to tell you, but I will in any case. These people did exactly the right thing. Only . . . it's a shame I was not sent for immediately. The man sent last night by your wife said the accident occurred three days ago. Is that right?"

Haydock nodded, even though he had no idea how long he'd been with the Hebers. It was all he could do. The weight of the hand still pushed against his lungs making breathing difficult.

"Ma'am. . . ." Dr. Oliphant removed his hand to twist about in the chair to speak to Maggie Heber.

Haydock lay back on the bed, thankful for the pillow under his head, holding him up.

"Ma'am . . . this's a good job of splinting. The water . . . ?"

Minutes later, Haydock was feeling good. The air was soothing to the stinking wound, as was the warm water the doctor used to bathe it. Those feminine hands were softer than the callused hands of English, the blunt hands of the woman. His eyes grew heavy as the doctor wiped his face with a strange-smelling ointment. And finally the pain of the broken bone didn't matter.

"Did you move him around much?" Oliphant asked of Maggie and Burn.

"No," Burn said. "We kept him to the bed once we got him inside. I was the one tended mostly to his needs . . . you know, nature calling . . . and I fed him. We tried to keep him still, but there were a couple a times we had a dust-up in the yard and I'd find him trying to sit up. Guess maybe he heard familiar voices."

"Sometime after you put on the splint . . . excellent job by the way . . . the bone finally pushed its way through the flesh.

Couldn't be helped, especially if he moved the leg."

Burn heard the judgment behind the studied praise. He thought of Rose Carpenter's rough treatment on her first visit. He took his frustration out on the doctor. "Mister, we ain't idiots. We knew what we was doing wouldn't be the best of doctoring, but it was all we could do. Don't go trying to act high and mighty 'cause of your learning. If I'd had the sense, I would have opened up that binding, checked everything was all right. Too much going on. So don't sugarcoat what you're saying. He's infected. Hell of a mess. But if the old man's heart were all right, he'd make it through." Here Burn paused, before continuing. "His heart ain't good. I can see it in his breathing, in the color in his face. No matter what we done . . . right or wrong . . . nothing can fix the heart."

Such observations from a rough cowhand were highly unusual, and under the current circumstances Thompson Oliphant, graduate of the prestigious Harvard Medical School and fresh from a practice in Boston, was quite impressed with the man's powers of observation. Whoever or whatever this man was, his life had been of the mind as much as the obvious hard work that had physically taken its toll on him.

Burn felt sheepish now, but had to ask: "How long's he got, Doc?"

It went against all learned medical practice to speak of such details in front of the patient, but he heard a grunt from the bed, and, when he turned to look at Carpenter, he saw a small nod. Then a voice gave consent.

"You tell 'em, Doc. I 'ready know." Carpenter started coughing, before he could continue. Then: "He knows, too. It's that woman outside . . . my wife, you're gonna have trouble convincing."

Dr. Oliphant nodded, and lightly touched the back of the old man's hand.

"You tell us . . . ," Burn said, "then you go out and fight that there dragon. She's been giving her husband fits because she wants to take him home. And she's been cursing Maggie somethin' terrible in her own home . . . in front of her child. I mean Ruthie, the girl who went looking for you." Before Dr. Oliphant could get his thoughts together, the cowboy continued. "Tell her maybe he'll be better in a couple of days. We know the end is going to be soon . . . maybe that way she'll go home and not bother him no more."

An ethical dilemma. One the doctor had never faced before. He looked at the patient, whose bluish eyes were blinking open and closed. Then there was a smile from the man. "Got him a plan, by God," Carpenter said. "And it's a good 'un."

Dr. Oliphant rose carefully from the chair, after having discarded the splint and rebinding the broken limb with fresh medical bandages. The wound was clean, packed with medication so it should not be uncomfortable for the next few hours. "Ma'am." He bowed to Maggie who had remained silent throughout the examination. Abruptly he turned to the small man who seemed to know exactly what the patient wanted. He took his time, studying this odd specimen, staring deeply into his face, seeing compassion, practicality, a sense of humor. And something beyond that when the woman moved close to him. He was dark, well-muscled for such a small man, with quite outsize hands. It was those hands that demanded the doctor's attention, and curiosity overrode manners and decency. Dr. Oliphant reached for one of Burn's scarred hands and oddly enough the man was co-operative. The doctor ran his fingers along the scars, turned the hand over, and pushed back the sleeve. The double ridges disappeared up the forearm.

"This was bad. How long ago?"

"Nineteen years."

"Any more such scars?"

"Yeah, but I ain't showing them to you. They're here . . . and here." The left hand swept across his belly, and then down his thigh with an upward swing across his buttocks.

Oliphant shuddered. "Nineteen years."

"Yeah."

A lot was left unsaid. The doctor turned Burn's wrist over, holding the hand a moment longer, finding it difficult to imagine that someone could survive such violence and brutality.

"How?"

"Ran a horse straight into that bob wire." A pause. "Killed the horse . . . should 'a' killed me."

"What medicines were used?"

"Mostly flour . . . to stop the bleeding." He stopped, as if something was remembered. "Then warm bathing. A lot of prayers from some good people . . . purple coneflower from a *curandera*."

"Unorthodox, but obviously effective." Oliphant let go of Burn's hand.

Burn only shook his head. "Long time in the past."

The doctor head out of the cabin, got to the door, and turned. "That's how you knew?"

"Yeah."

To his surprise, the doctor found it was snowing, very lightly, the softest of flakes. He stood a moment and turned his face up to the sky, delighting at the points of cold caressing his face.

There was a well-endowed woman sitting in the front seat of a wagon. The bed of the wagon was padded with straw and blankets. It looked as though a horse had attempted to make a meal of it. He steeled himself and walked to the wagon.

Her arms folded over her considerable bosom, her eyes straight ahead, Mrs. Carpenter barely glanced at him. She didn't give him a chance to take more than a few steps. "I want my husband home with me this minute," she announced. "The charade has gone on long enough. Those two do not have the right to keep me from tending to my own man."

She was a force of Nature. Thompson Oliphant inhaled, let out a small gust of air, and then rubbed his hands together. He put on his best medical face and, in no uncertain terms, said: "Ma'am, I can understand your concern and your wish to transport your husband to his familiar surroundings." He had a feeling the woman had made what must have been a useable bachelor home into a fanciful showplace of horsehair sofas and carved chairs and no place comfortable for a man to sit. He smiled briefly, not wishing to appear ghoulish. "It appears, ma'am, your husband is resting comfortably, and, perhaps if you and these men would return in the late morning tomorrow, you can visit. And in a few more days . . . who knows. But you really can't move him today." *There,* he thought, *not a lie in anything I've told her.* She would read whatever reality she wanted in the words.

A man of Spanish descent approached. He gave a polite if brief bow, to which Oliphant responded with a tip of his bowler.

"*Señor,* are you saying that our *señor,* he will recover?"

Ah, Oliphant thought to himself, *another man who thinks.* This would be difficult if he was to maintain his no-lies doctrine.

"Sir?"

"Ah, *sí* . . . my name is Rogelio Vigil."

"Doctor Thompson Oliphant."

They exchanged a handshake.

The doctor cleared his throat before beginning. "Mister Carpenter's broken bone, unfortunately, has pushed itself through the skin and become infected. I have cleaned and packed the infection and do not expect it to cause him any more discomfort." *There,* he thought, *that's direct and true even if not responsive to his question.* He could see in Rogelio's eyes disbelief. He thought it best to continue speaking to keep the man from asking any more questions, which would result in having to lie. "Sir, Mister Carpenter is resting well, in no pain for the time being. A good night's sleep is what he needs." Enough, no more, or lies would begin to spill out from his mouth.

Rogelio shook his head and turned, looking at the seated woman, who tried to appear as if she were disinterested in the conversation. It was Rogelio who made the decision. He walked to the wagon and climbed onto the seat, picking up the lines.

"Until tomorrow, *señor,*" he said, and glanced at Mrs. Carpenter.

The crew of riders and their skittish horses fell into a loose formation around the back of the wagon. Several of the horses bucked, but the riders sat their mounts easily. The doctor drove a car because he had never mastered this particular art of horsemanship. So he admired the men's skills, but without any sense of envy.

Jonas kicked his brother. They had settled themselves inside the barn where they could watch and listen. They knew it wasn't their fight, but still. . . .

"We should o' taken a swing at a couple of them . . . *vaqueros* they call themselves," Jonas said. "Don't like them riding in here like they're better'n us."

Tad had a different point of view. "Them's right nice stock they was riding. If we got ourselves work riding for a good brand, hell, Jonas, we could be riding bronc's just like them."

Jonas grumbled: "Still think we needed to beat on some o' them fellas."

Tad shoved his brother, pushing him off the half barrel they were using as a seat. "Jonas don't be stupid. They didn't do nothing to us. Ain't no cause to pound on 'em."

Jonas shoved back at his brother. "I like that machine the

doc's driving. I snuck a look till the horses got calmed. Me, I don't want to ride no horse. That machine looks to be a real good way to travel."

Tad reached down and grabbed Jonas's arm, pulling him back and sprawling him across the barrel seat. Jonas immediately pulled back and tightened his fists, figuring on a brawl with his older brother.

Tad leaned away from him. "I ain't fighting . . . just figuring. We got nothing here. Ma's strong on that new man, and, though I don't take much to him, he's kind to Ruthie."

There wasn't much more that needed saying. The two brothers might fight each other with intent to hurt, but, as close as they were, words didn't need to be spoken. A few minutes later, Jonas stood. "Time to get moving, Tad. We'll tell Ma . . . or wait for Ruthie to get back and tell her, and then she can tell Ma."

Tad looked up at his brother and said: "She's got English and old Carpenter. We don't need to give her more worry. I'll go tell her. You figure out what gear we can take."

Maggie's eyes teared up as she drew Tad close to her. He could smell her tears, her sadness. Smelled something like the medicine they had put on that old man. Tad was embarrassed by being so close. She was so female it hurt right through him. Old enough to know what all that flesh was for, and angry at himself for thinking about that and his ma at the same time.

"I know, Tad. It's time. You and Jonas . . . well, it's time. Jonas likes automobiles. I saw him walking 'round the doc's."

Looking past his shoulder, Tad saw English staring at his ma before he slid behind the curtain where the old man lay. Tad heard the scrape of the wood chair and then the old man's weak voice. Nice of the man to step away from a boy saying good bye to his ma. *Might be this one will stay,* Tad thought.

Maggie helped Tad bundle up their few clothes and put

together a bag of foodstuffs to keep them going for a while. She let him take the rifle, but told him to leave the shotgun, because it wasn't any good for hunting game. They both laughed, then her eyes teared up again. He couldn't stand it, so he lurched in to kiss her cheek, and missed, getting her ear, but it was all he could bear. Then he ran, hauling the burlap bags over his shoulder.

When he heard Maggie crying, Burn held his breath. He half stood until the old man's hand grabbed him and pulled him down, saying: "Let her cry . . . be alone. Time. Then go find her."

Burn listened to her footsteps, the lightness of sound, her particular step, her way of moving. He could imagine her going through the cabin door, standing a moment, staring at the empty yard. If the boys were already gone, she would follow the path they had taken with her wet gaze, study the settling dust, knowing her children had walked that very spot as they left her.

He turned back and stared into the glazed eyes. "You need anything?" Burn kept his voice low, not wanting Maggie to hear him and think she was needed inside. He and the old man, they could take care of almost anything.

It was Ruthie who found her mother crying, huddled in a corner of the barn, nesting in the sweet hay with a white towel on her face. Ruthie was scared at first, for she was standing right next to her ma and she didn't even seem to know that she was there. She was sobbing so hard that it sounded to Ruthie like her ma's heart was broken. Immediately she decided to go kick that English cowboy, give him hell for hurting Ma. Yet it was easy to see that her ma was taken by him, although other than the way he rode a horse, Ruthie didn't see anything special to the man. Just another one hanging around, except that he had a great horse that he might let her ride again, and he worked for his keep.

She sneezed which startled her ma. Maggie pulled the towel away from her wet face and cried out: "Oh, Ruthie!" At this, Ruthie sat down next to her ma and hugged her.

"Tad and Jonas," Maggie began, "they left just now before you got back . . . took their clothes and some food and headed out . . . going the same way that doc rode that machine. Tad told me Jonas was dead set on learning how to ride one of those things."

Ruthie snuggled in closer to her ma, sighing and thinking: *It's about time.* Then she said: "I saw them and I said good bye and good luck. But, Mama . . . I think you drive that beast . . . it ain't alive enough to ride."

Maggie rubbed her hands through Ruthie's hair, catching her fingers in all the tangles. "Not been paying you enough attention, have I? All this . . . fuss . . . it took me away from what's important."

Although she knew the answer, Ruthie asked anyway. "He going to stay with us?"

Her ma's response surprised her. "I don't know, Ruthie. He hasn't asked or said nothing." Then she said what Ruthie wanted to hear. "I hope so."

Good, Ruthie thought, *he stays, I get to ride that mare.*

CHAPTER SIXTEEN

Burn stayed in the chair, letting Carpenter's gnarled hand remain on his arm. There was still life inside those bones and ligaments, a deep breath occasionally, the thin chest rising, falling.

It was getting dark outside, and Maggie had built up a good fire, told the girl to feed out extra hay to the roan and the mare, it was going to be cold tonight. She asked Burn if he wanted supper. He shook his head, but in a few minutes Ruthie brought him a cup filled with a thick soup, anyway. He could identify chunks of soft squash, something green, bits and pieces of the game birds. It tasted good, so he offered the old man a spoonful of broth.

"No point now. It's done," Haydock Carpenter said.

Burn got up once, about midnight. He had to, and the old man smiled, understanding. Maggie took the chair while Burn went to the outhouse. It was damned cold out there, and, coming back in, he appreciated the cabin's tight warmth.

Maybe it was an hour later, maybe three, but he awoke quickly to a twitch from the fingers that were clasped tightly on his wrist. Then the grasp loosened. Harsh breathing gone, eyes motionless, empty. No one else was there to witness. Maggie had wrapped herself in blankets near the fire where the boys usually slept. Ruthie was dreaming up in her loft.

Burn carefully arranged Carpenter's hands across his chest,

shut his eyes, drew up the light quilt to cover the gaunt face. He faced going to the barn to his own nest of blankets and the horses' poor shared warmth, the thin winds that found every crack in the wood framing and crawled into bed with him. But, instead, he took one thick quilt, laying on a chair near the fire, and used a seat cushion as a pillow to make his own pallet. He set a few small logs on the fire, not enough to throw sparks, but enough to keep the coals burning, building life-giving heat.

It was sunrise. The air in the cabin was chilled. There was no sound but a rustle. Then a nudge against his back. Burn remained still, waiting. A soft voice tickled his ear. "I can keep us warm. You want into my bed now?"

He took a long time answering. "What about Ruthie . . . ?"

"Child knows, don't mind. She said yesterday she hopes you'll stay on."

"He died not long ago."

"I know. Heard you stepping around. Figured as much." She pressed up against him, her loose breasts heavy, warming two spots on his back. "You all right, Burn? It ain't easy sitting with death, but he wanted you with him. You two knew each other." She stopped talking, pressed closer. "I sat with my first husband. . . ." Her voice died out and her body shivered and the effect on Burn wasn't one of grief. He rolled over to face her with all the intention of talk, but she simply kissed him and it was too much.

Burn pulled free from the embrace, feeling eerily like he was looking down on his actions, as if he was watching the two of them from above, noting their positions, curious as to why a man was resisting such a woman. He wasn't a prude. He didn't think he was. But this was too much.

"Burn, I got *five* sons, all growed and gone now. And a daughter who means more to me than my own life. But I'm also alive, and a man was meant to have a good woman. You're telling me by pulling away, I ain't a good woman . . . least not good enough for you?"

She amazed him. Her tone wasn't bitter, not hurt, not sad. Just facts—clear as any woman could speak to a man. He owed her an honest response.

So he rolled away from her, conscious of his body's arousal, embarrassed by his flesh even as he fought to keep from touching her. "I ain't much to look at, Maggie. Me, not my face so much as my body . . . what you see and feel when . . . well. . . ."

"You told the doc while I was standing there. I can imagine."

"No, you can't. I have to force my own self to look at the scarring. No woman wants a man cut up the way I am."

She pulled back so she could see his face better in the fire light.

"You trying to tell me something's been cut off?" she asked. "Don't seem that way to me."

As a log flamed up, he could see she was smiling as she spoke, and Burn hoped she couldn't see his face redden.

"Everything's where it needs to be, but I was cut up something terrible. Makes me want to vomit when I have to touch the scars. Been almost twenty years and I still can't deal with them, and I can't ask you or anyone to take me this way."

She was stubborn. "Now that doc," Maggie pressed, "he grabbed onto the scarred hand and arm and wanted to see more. It didn't bother him none at all."

Burn tried to look away from her, but she put one hand on the side of his face and held him steady while she talked. "It weren't that he was a doc. . . . It's that you're a good man, nothing more. He saw it for all his fancy airs . . . and my daughter knows. Even your mare, she knows." She put her hand over her mouth, then grinned and that gesture pleased Burn. Something came to her then. Her face went still, her eyes looked sad. "You telling me it's been that long since you've been with a woman?"

A question no one had ever asked. A subject he'd never shared. Her face was close to his and he could feel her breathing. Her eyes were closed now, as if willing him to talk and giving him room.

"No." He took a big gulp. His face was flushed, his hands sweating. "Whores don't care. It's money to them . . . nothing more. Flesh means dollars. They never noticed the scars. Don't know if they even saw them."

She rested her hand on his mouth. "Enough. I don't want to hear this."

It was a struggle for him. "You asked."

"Yes, and I needed to know, but it's too sad. A good man like you. So alone."

He moved to hold her, and she rested her head on his chest. His body calmed, his skin eased, the flush disappeared. She didn't care.

"Let me see your belly," she said a few minutes later. "Just what's under the shirt. Ruthie told me what you looked like. Imagine, my own daughter spying on a naked man." She shook her head, barely able to keep from laughing. " 'Course, we all figured you was kinda crazy for swimming in that pond this time a year." She was laughing now as her fingers slowly unbuttoned his shirt, then the top of the long johns he wore. True to her word she did not push below the waist of his jeans, unbuttoned so he could sleep in some comfort. She rolled him onto his back and pushed the covers away so he lay exposed.

A small chill brushed across the hairs on his chest. He shivered. His fists tightened, and his throat was so dry he couldn't swallow. She kissed his mouth, then his neck. She said nothing, only kissed him again on his chest, let her fingers touch the side of his mouth, then stroke his jaw, his cheek, until he felt his own tears torn free and he wanted to wipe them away, but she used the lightest touch to do it for him. No one had ever touched him with such gentleness, such intimacy. Not even when he'd been injured.

"Burn, I want to give this to you. To a good man who will be constant." She sighed, tucked her head near his chin, spoke into his naked chest. "I'm faithful to my man, I just ain't shown good sense up till now."

They both fell asleep.

Burn woke, wrapped in the quilt, with her hand against his belly, right on the deepest scarring. He slid free of her, rolling himself out of the quilt. He looked at Maggie and saw her lick her lips as she slept. Worn out by the past few days, he figured. He didn't blame her.

He left the house, bootless, cursing the cold ground till he found a place to sit, pull on his boots, and shuck into his coat. At least the light dusting of snow had melted. He didn't mind that he'd have to leave behind a few things that were still in the house. He needed thinking time, a clear head, his body not wanting her so badly it made it impossible to think. Those kisses on his exposed past, her gentle acceptance challenged his knowledge of himself.

Beauty was still chewing on wisps of last night's hay so he felt no conscience in saddling her without a morning feed. He tied on the few items he could find. Hell and damn, he had to get out, find a place to think.

The ugly Appaloosa gelding nickered sadly when Burn led Beauty from the barn. Burn was grinning despite himself, running his hands over the mare before he saddled up. He found no swelling, no heat in the hard legs, no ill effects from yesterday's gallop. He was careful to check the edge of pink skin still remaining from the wire cut. There was no flinching when he tightened his hand around the bone. The mare leaned down and lipped the top of his head where his black hair was too long, flying loose, in need of a good shearing.

If he stayed, Maggie would offer to cut his hair, like she had done with the boys. Burn couldn't imagine bearing even that small intimacy without the need for more. He barely had the willpower to leave.

He wasn't much and had no illusions about what he could give her. When she woke up, he didn't want to be there to have her see him in full daylight. He didn't want to see what would cross her face—relief, disgust, a certain distance? It was time he was gone. Those had been pity kisses. They had to have come from her sudden loneliness, her recent losses. He couldn't fill the holes in her life. Sitting with that old man had taken all he had had.

He was bent on heading north, knowing full well a big storm with drifts and a howling wind would freeze him solid. His fingers raked the mare's coat, noting the long winter hairs under which the skin was warm and dry. She'd do fine. It would be Burn himself who would come to grief. Deep inside was a knowledge of choosing death. He'd been its witness last night. It was close, waiting on his decision.

The mare wanted to buck when he stepped into the saddle. Burn grinned, let out a bit of rein, and Beauty crow-hopped across the yard. Without looking back, he waved his arm, and pushed the mare into a run. They were gone in a hurry, pounding up dust.

The mare was sensible enough to come to her easy jog. Burn patted her warmed neck, smelled the thick taste of salt through the winter hair. No more galloping for them. She'd be chilled come evening and he'd have to hand walk her and rub her down. It would be damned stupid to mistreat a good horse in such a manner.

A few trees, long yellowed grasses, a narrow game trail where Beauty let each hoof fall in her easy rhythm, taking them both some place else, some place where no one would get into Burn's heart.

The mare stuttered to a halt. Burn got thrown forward, then back. The mare shook violently as if he'd startled her. He apologized by stroking her neck and she shook again until he was loose in the saddle. She had stopped in Salt Valley where only a short time ago he'd found a private heaven. But it had been interrupted, destroyed, complicated by humans and their idiocy. He wanted to rein the mare around and gallop up the slanted ridge and across the edge of the valley where the old man's house sat watching, empty now, even with the unknowing widow living there.

He thought about Maggie's cabin nestled against the north winds, protected by the long-running ridge, facing south for warmth, shaded by the open-weave ramada in the summer. Soft winds that blew out the human scent, doors to be closed tight, a fireplace that drew well enough for good heat, special stews, pies made with fresh apples or cherries picked and dried, sweetened with town molasses.

The mare shook again. Burn climbed down, feeling every tired bone, every old break or wound. He walked toward the familiar cottonwood, leafless now, a cloak of dried leaves rustling, some lifting and then falling back as he had stepped across them to reach the tree's comfort. Then he sat, his back against the trunk of the tree.

Beauty grazed, stepping carefully around the trailing reins. Burn watched her, knowing he needed to get up and go to her, remove the bridle and hang it on the horn, put on her hobbles so she wouldn't take a notion to bolt again and get caught in wire, or return to the cabin and the old Appaloosa and the familiar home corral.

He sat and studied the mare. So much like her papa. A lean neck tied into a good shoulder, defined withers smoothing into a short back. The hindquarters were different than her sire's had been, higher up at the groin, leaner through the stifle like most mares. He figured it was to give room for growing a baby. Like a woman was narrow in the waist, wide in the hip, to support life. He pushed his mind back into judging the mare. Nice gaskin tied into a clean hock. Strong bones and good hoofs. He wished he could breed her to a racing stallion. It would be a good start for another herd.

Burn eased himself lower against the cottonwood trunk, finding just the right spot where his spine fitted into old grooves. He leaned his head back, letting his hat push forward and then slide down to rest between his legs. He needed to move on, ride north, keep Beauty at an even trot, jog a few miles, then walk again, not letting her get sweaty while putting miles between himself and the cabin, the girl child . . . Maggie.

There wasn't long before he turned restless. His back itched. His butt was cold from the freezing ground. Haydock Carpenter was dead, lying behind a tattered curtain. Maggie would have to clean the flesh and see again what the loss of life meant to a man. Nothing there.

Wasn't that much left for Burn now. A year maybe, or a month, even just days, depending on the northern storms, his own despair, the mare's recovered energy. Hiding behind the scattered thoughts was the knowledge that he'd left Maggie with Haydock Carpenter's lifeless body.

Beauty lifted her head and whinnied, her ears pricked, winter grass hanging from her mouth. Burn sat up. It was time, she was telling him. He stood. Then, hearing that particular sound, he turned and looked up at the ridge. An ugly Appaloosa head appeared, long skull and loose ears, those damned blue eyes.

The Appaloosa stepped into his ugly lope when he saw the mare.

Maggie was bouncing with the roan's gait, grabbing mane, white legs showing above gray lisle stockings, thighs gripping the mottled hide. She had the horse steered toward Burn, but, when she saw him waiting, she smiled at him and her concentration was lost and she came off, landing in the matted grasses, laughing even as Burn went to her.

He rolled down beside her, barely touching her leg and shoulder as she twisted around until her face was above his and again she was smiling. He strained upward and caught at her mouth, kissed her until falling back brought her down on top of him and they both were laughing.

Her mouth fitted perfectly over his, and then she spoke the words right into his mouth. "Yes, Burn English, I will marry you."

The next days were focused on getting Carpenter's body to the grieving widow and then, after that task was completed, watching her performance as they lowered the fancy coffin into the ground. Burn learned from the *vaquero,* Rogelio, that as soon as Mrs. Carpenter got back home after her first visit to the cabin, she had ordered the finest coffin she could find in Denver. She was having it delivered and had cleared out a spare bedroom to make space for it.

Most of the Rafter JX hands were going to quit the Widow Carpenter, staying on only to attend the old man's services. Then they would be gone, mounted on their private horses, beholden to no widow who had bought a coffin before her husband had up and died.

Burn knew it wasn't what the old man wanted, not this fuss and money thrown into the ground after a bunch of old bones that were going to rot and roll back into the land. But it was the widow's choice, and, this time, no one was going to tell her different.

At the funeral Maggie stood next to Burn as dirt and rocks were thrown on the ornate golden box by the *vaqueros*. She squeezed Burn's arm, looked sideways at him, and saw signs of tearing, which she would never mention to him. She recalled how he'd sat by the old man's bed, wiped his bottom, held his hand, spoon-fed him like a baby. There had never been any sense of either one being better than the other.

Standing there, Burn regretted not having been a grown man when he lost his father. Regretted having missed all of those long years together, working alongside his pa. Regretted having had the fever himself and not having been there to watch as his father had died, to have held his hand, too, at the end.

Maggie had taken Burn to her bed the day she brought him back from Salt Valley. She told Ruthie they would be marrying in a while, but for now Burn was sleeping with her ma and that was how it would be.

Ruthie grinned up at Burn and said she had figured on that when he had first come to the cabin. Took him long enough, she said. At those words, Maggie took a swipe at her child, who skipped back and said she was going to the pens to brush *her* mare.

Ruthie barely glanced at Burn. He, too, was grinning. Since the girl had ridden Beauty, there had been no way to separate them. He was looking to buy himself a new horse, and maybe find a good stallion to put to the mare. If Ruthie agreed with the idea.

Maybe Haydock's widow would need to sell a few of her horses when she realized what losing just about the whole crew meant. The old man had a papered stallion, a thoroughbred with a fine pedigree. Might be a good enough match for Beauty,

Burn reasoned.

It took Burn two weeks to realize that Maggie had never mentioned marrying again. They'd slipped into a routine of hard work, building better corrals, butchering out the bull calf, and readying for winter. The boys were gone, so it fell to Burn, and sometimes Ruthie, to do the hard work.

One thing that worried him was firewood. The boys had cut down trees, but had left them lying there, rotting on the ground. That made for punky wood, but still it was better than nothing. The first week he saddled up Ruthie's old roan, with her permission, and rode out to the trees with a saw stuck in the rifle scabbard. He felt naked, but he needed the saw, and hoped he wouldn't need the rifle.

He cut the downed trees in chunks, letting the roan graze and put back on some of the weight he had lost, before winter arrived. Much as he disliked the idea, he figured on maybe doing some chores for the Carpenter woman which would help pay for extra feed over the bad months. Grass, here, turned brown and dried up in the cold.

With Ruthie's help, Burn pounded together a sledge of sorts on which he could put the wood chunks and let the roan pull them home. Once they got all the downed trees back to the cabin, he split the wood and Ruthie would stack.

One night in bed, with Maggie up close to him and her hands wandering under the covers, she sat up, surprising him. "Burn," she said, "I ain't never had a man work so hard. We got to feed you better or you're going to up and disappear." He rested his hand on her warm belly as she continued. "Now that I got you here, you ain't escaping. If I make a stew, I want you eating two bowls . . . hear me?"

It took him another week or so, but finally he decided to ask her pointblank if she ever intended to marry him. After all, she'd done the asking, sort of. He asked over that second bowl of stew. "You still planning on getting married?" She looked at him blankly, as he took a big spoon of stew and held it in mid-air. "Thought maybe this week-end, you'd have a mind to marry up with me." He swallowed and dropped the spoon back into the bowl. When he looked at her, she was smiling. He rose, leaned over the table, and kissed her. Tasted of stew and felt like a smile. He persisted. "This Saturday's a good day. You know a preacher?" She looked down, sort of away from him, and sighed, rubbing her hands together. "I thought you might let Ruthie take Beauty and go into Mancos . . . ask the preacher there. That is, if it's all right with you, and if Ruthie wants to make the ride."

They both laughed. It was set. Saturday was five days away. Burn wasn't sure he could wait.

CHAPTER SEVENTEEN

Ruthie came back in the early evening with a fool grin on her face, saying the parson would arrive early in the morning on Saturday and would be wanting breakfast before he spoke the words over the wedding pair. Maggie brushed the top of her child's head and said to run along, and that tomorrow she would have to get herself bathed. They were all taking baths tomorrow night, even if it was Friday.

Ruthie had run across her brothers in Mancos. Jonas had found what he wanted, was working with automobiles, taking bits and pieces off what made them run without horses and putting them back together. Ruthie had stayed to watch him, confused and fascinated at the same time. Grinning through a mask of grease and soot, the boss had told her that her brother was some kind of genius with the pieces of iron formed into strange shapes. Jonas had grinned up at his sister, his face and hands just as filthy as those of his boss', and said to go find Tad. He was down at the livery, Jonas thought. He'd gotten a job there.

And, yes, they were coming in for the marrying, along with the parson.

Ruthie had found Tad sweeping out a filthy aisle packed with damped hay. A harsh stench came from a half-empty line of straight-sided horse stalls. He didn't have that same light in his eyes that Jonas had and wasn't likely, he said, to give up sweeping to come home and watch Ma marry another man. Ruthie reminded her brother that this time it was a good man and a real marriage.

Tad had grunted and said that, if the damned livery boss gave him the time, he'd come. Ruthie told him Jonas's plans to travel in the buggy with the parson. She picked at her brother long enough so that he said he would do the same, God dammit.

Ruthie had stared at him, then laughed. Her brother's face got red. He knew better than to swear in front of her. Ma would have a fit, if Ruthie told.

Burn told Maggie he wanted to go down to the pond in Salt Valley and take his pre-wedding bath there. She could come with him, or stay here and take a warm bath. But it all had begun there at the pond and he wanted to stand in those waters. Felt like he needed to, he said, kind of like a ritual to make himself good enough for her.

She looked at him strangely. He tried to tell her he wasn't crazy but she said it didn't matter, if this was important, then he best go freeze his scrawny behind in the cold water, for in two day's time there would be sparks and fires enough to toast both of them.

Despite her two-day journey under Ruthie's guidance, Beauty was eager to move out after Burn saddled her. She took him straight to the pond, the same way she'd headed when he had tried to run away from Maggie and the girl. Beauty seemed to sense Burn's fear.

He didn't bother to hobble her, but stripped off the gear and watched her graze. She was comfortable here. She knew this place well. She tore into the browned grasses as if she were starving. To his experienced eye, even with all the traveling, the mare looked good, nice weight on her going into the winter. Maybe she even had had a little too much of the barn hay, for she was getting a belly, but she looked fit and ready to go.

Burn smiled to himself. Now that he had a good traveling horse, he was planning to settle down. Wasn't that the way a man's life went? He looked around, feeling a need to tell Maggie what he was thinking. She'd like the foolishness. She'd see the peculiar sadness as well as the joy of a drifter finding one place to settle.

He put his back up to the cottonwood trunk, in that fold that fitted him just right. He laid his head against the rough bark and tried to sort out his feelings.

There was nothing to him that a good woman would want. He was no better now than he had been all those years ago when Katherine had made the sensible choice. Maggie wasn't like Katherine, though. She was more direct, less afraid, which made him wonder. He shook his head, hit it against the tree trunk, and that made him laugh, which brought a whinny from Beauty. Burn himself sure wasn't any beauty, but he worked hard and they were good together in bed. That had surprised him. Women had always been terrifying to him, and those he'd known mostly were store-bought, a fact he had tried to explain to Maggie but she had put a hand over his mouth.

"I ain't asking," she had said. "And I ain't telling you 'bout my husbands. It's a natural fact, Burn English, that men and women do this. How else can there be so many of us? Don't go looking at some old woman bent double with age and forget that she had herself a lover or a husband when she was young. That shocks you? Well, tell me how men can have all the women they want and still expect us to be pure and unsoiled for them. Don't make sense at all."

There it was. Her courage and sense rolled together. He was no match for whatever Maggie Heber decided to want. And she wanted him. That was more than reason enough to marry her.

Finally it was pitch dark and the stars glittered as the winds died down and Burn was freezing, but he'd told Maggie he would bathe here in the pond, so he better, by God, do what he said he would.

It felt like his feet were freezing solid to the sand under the water with his first step in, but no one could call him a coward, so he ran in yelling, then plunged down into the cold, and came up gasping and yelling louder. Paddling and ducking under, he made a small circle of the pond and finally thought he'd suffered enough, had washed off enough of the dirt from the past few weeks. He came out of the water, pushed back his hair, wondering if she would give him a haircut or even if there was time.

Again that question. Why would she want him, a has-been *mesteñero*, broken up and scrawny, no skills that the world needed.

Then he saw the image of her face, clear as if she'd been standing in front of him, and the night wind carried her scent. He could feel her hands on him and that was reason enough to offer her his life.

She was awake, waiting for him. Their bed had new sheets and a fancy quilt, which she shyly told him she'd been working on every time he was out cutting the winter's wood. It was easy to slip in between the sheets, his body still chilled from the cleansing. The heat from her, the tender kissing, warmed him, helped him know this was right between them.

But, she told him, they could hold each other, even if that was all. After the service, with its parson and witnesses, well, they needed to be pure until then.

He would have laughed, remembering all of what they'd done together, but those pictures made his face and body heat up until he thought he understood her reserve. It wasn't right now, not when it would be legal Saturday.

On Saturday, Maggie rose early to prepare the breakfast Ruthie had promised to the parson. The last several days had been much warmer and the sun promised another unseasonably warm day. First thing, though, she wanted Burn up and out of her bed, in the barn doing chores when the parson appeared. Burn agreed to go along with her play-acting.

It wasn't long before a horse and wagon arrived, the driver in a dusty black suit. Maggie's two boys were in the back of the buggy, a two-seater befitting the parson's community position.

Ruthie was there to hold the horse, not trusting the good sense lacking in her brothers, as the man climbed out, heavy-footed and graceless, but he managed. Burn stayed at the barn where he could watch and listen even if he could not make out any distinct words. Still it seemed Ruthie was offering to see to his horse, and the man was agreeing with much head-bobbing and a wide smile. Burn already didn't like the man.

The boys shied away from their sister, wouldn't even go to the house to see their ma all prettied up to receive another man. They headed to the barn, walking some distance from each other, aware in the short time they'd been gone that this was no longer their home.

The barn was dark and smelled good. It was clean, feeling kind of like a place where they wanted to be. Jonas was the first to see English seated on an upturned barrel. He grabbed his brother's arm, tried to yank Tad around so they could escape, but the horse trainer spoke directly to them.

"Jonas, Tad. It's man-to-man time. Here it is. I'm marrying your ma. For some reason she loves me."

Then English stopped, wiped his mouth, and it occurred to Jonas that the mustanger, who had so scared him earlier with his hard edge of action and knowing, was terrified. The thought made Jonas feel more grownup and oddly inclined to sympathy.

Tad wasn't so generous. "What if I told you we don't want Ma with you. Ain't right . . . hell, she's even taller'n you. Don't suit us at all, Mister English."

Jonas shook his head, watched English closely, knowing that his decision would rest on what the man said to his older brother.

English wiped his mouth again. "You're protecting your ma, and I value that. Family is what keeps us safe, and you boys will always be her family."

At these words, Tad kind of relaxed, as if he'd been given something.

English wasn't done, though, and his next words, they shocked Jonas, must have spiked into Tad, also.

"A woman like your ma, she's a true beauty, in her heart as her flesh. She ain't meant to be alone just because her boys want her undivided among them. She's got more life to live, and I'm the one she chose. You boys, you still need to learn, 'bout loving and love, and wanting that one person close to you." He laughed then, still nervous, but something in his mind pleased him and he grunted, grinned even. "We're thinking 'bout our own young 'uns."

That was a scary enough idea that both boys grunted and wiped their mouths in unconscious mimicry of English's nerves.

His next words almost knocked them over. "Might have already started one. Don't know yet, but it's certain possible."

Outside the barn, a commotion and the high pitch of Ruthie's voice caught the attention of the three and they got up quickly to go outside, away from the words and the forced closeness. Each of them had a lot to think about.

Jonas shook his head. "Hell, Tad, this is tough. I can't think on Ma as a woman!"

Burn went out into daylight, exposed and scared. He was getting married soon. Ruthie yelled at him, and he was laughing finally as he came to her rescue. She'd been trying to unharness the parson's horse and had gotten a few of the straps undone wrong, leaving bits and pieces hanging off a very nervous gelding.

Burn steadied the horse with a few pats on the neck, quietly explaining to the listening animal what was about to happen and why Ruthie had gotten her buckles wrong. Next he directed Ruthie on how to unhitch the animal correctly—a lesson the child needed to learn. He spent so much time going over the horse that the animal turned around to bite him just as Ruthie tugged on his arm to tell him that there were folks driving up.

"What folks?" he asked. In response, she turned him around. He witnessed the arrival of several buggies carrying families with fathers driving, mamas cradling small children. And horses with *vaqueros* from the Carpenter ranch. No sign of the widow, which let Burn sigh in relief. But he recognized Arcy and the paint he had started maybe five years ago. Just behind him came Rogelio at the reins of a steady team, a woman beside him, three growing sons in the back. From the other direction, the doctor from Mancos was pulling up in his motorcar. Surprisingly this time the horses barely bothered to turn and look at the metal and rubber that moved on its own.

Burn slapped the horse lightly on the shoulder, then tied it to a post. He told Ruthie to throw down some good hay to keep the horse quiet. Before leaving her, he promised her that, come summer, he would teach her how to swim in Salt Valley pond where they had first become friends. That brought a big smile to her shining face.

And then his wife-to-be stepped out of the cabin and stood on the porch. Her hair was shiny and pinned up, she wore a new printed dress, so low in front that Burn blushed. It was fitted to her waist, then swept into a loose-flowing skirt, tight boots laced above her ankles. Lord, she was a pretty sight.

Maggie laughed at the sight of him. He was a mess—hay and horsehair everywhere, slobber on his shirt, but his face was cleanly shaven, and his pants and boots had been wiped, even polished. He wasn't any knight in shining armor as she'd heard of in stories, but he was hers, about to make that promise in front of a lot of folks. And she loved him.

Burn went toward her, up the few steps to the house to stand close but not touching. Not yet. She took a deep breath and watched his eyes shift to her bosom, and she smiled then, wanting so badly to touch him. His scent, of horses and a light sweat, dirt on his hands, was enough to make her almost dizzy. She directed him into the house, where a clean shirt was waiting on the wood chair where he'd sat so long with a dying old man. There was no sadness in the memory, only a sweet reminder of how they'd come to meet.

Burn did as he was told, passing by the parson who was eating. After drawing the curtain closed around the bed, he found the fresh white shirt and his fingers looked dark and clumsy against the fine material as he picked it up. Soft, each stitch made carefully. Her hands had worked these bits of thread to make his wedding shirt. Burn shivered as he changed out of his old shirt. He ran his fingers through his hair, and said dammit as he looked at his own refection in the tin mirror propped on the windowsill. It was then that he heard Maggie and their guests entering the cabin. When he was ready, he pulled back the curtain.

The preacher rose awkwardly and pulled on his coat. When Burn walked up to him, the man said: "Do you have any questions, son," he asked, "about the state of marriage?"

Son, huh? The man was younger than Burn by a good ten years. "No, sir, parson. I got me a damned . . . a good idea 'bout marriage and what happens next." Guess he had been direct enough since the parson blushed and went silent.

Burn walked to Maggie, and then was standing next to her. The parson got to talking at some length until the gathering became impatient. The parson, his name was Elijah Goodwin, finally got the idea and found his way to the heart of the ceremony.

When he finally asked Burn if he took "this woman to be his wife," Burn said his "I do" before the man was halfway through the question. At that all the men in the gathering laughed before their wives hushed them. At the last words, the witnesses cheered. The sound of a guitar, a singer telling a tale of marriage in high-note Spanish came next.

Maggie stepped in close to her man, her legal husband, and spoke gently into his ear. As she knew it would, the sound of Maggie English startled him. Then he, too, laughed, and in front of friends and neighbors, a few strangers, he kissed her as if they were alone in their own bed.

Epilogue

In early March, Burn started his day as he usually did, with a kiss to Maggie and a trip to the barn to feed out hay and check on the horses. Ruthie's roan Appaloosa was showing his age and Burn figured the girl was wanting something fancier, given all her hints about Beauty, but he wasn't ready to give up the mare yet.

Beauty didn't nicker at him first thing as he walked into the barn, but that old roan, he talked and fussed and even kicked at the stall boards. Burn went to the mare and froze in shock.

Next to the mare's belly, a small tail twisting with pleasure, was a buckskin filly nursing. And he'd missed the signs—the growing belly, that change to the muscles on the hindquarters, even the teats growing full, bagging up. Beauty had managed to find herself a suitor, back down near Springerville, and had herself a fine baby. The filly sure wasn't from the old stallion. He'd never throw that color out of a bay mare.

He'd been wondering all winter how they were going to live the next thirty years or so. Scrabbling for food on the dry land was one thing, making a comfortable life together was different. And he wasn't any cowpuncher, had had to say no to the Widow Carpenter when she asked him to come work the old man's ranch.

And those automobiles, they were more and more what people wanted, not good horses, just tin and iron and tires that rolled. There wasn't much left for a mustanger. It'd kept him up nights, worrying on how he would take care of his family. Maggie thought she was expecting, too, maybe in the fall, if she was. Their life had to change.

The boys had come home for Christmas. Jonas had been the one to put the idea in his mind. The boy was working on those automobiles and had overheard two men talking about a game called polo, played on horseback. The Army up in Fort Robinson and folks around Rayado and Miami in New Mexico, they were chasing a ball and swinging long sticks and they needed good horses to play the game.

Staring at the buckskin filly nursing on her ma, it came to Burn that he could start all over again. He knew of a good stallion that Rogelio owned, and now he had two mares that could be bred. It would take a while, but the English name might have a chance, with these folks playing their polo and wanting as many good horses as a man like Burn English could train.

ABOUT THE AUTHOR

William A. Luckey was born in Providence, Rhode Island, but later went West to work with horses. "I've spent the past forty years dealing with rogue horses using my own methods to retrain and make them useful—I've evented, shown dressage, fox-hunted for twenty seasons, worked cattle, gone on five-day trail rides. I've owned over 150 horses personally, going back to when I was seven. I've actually been riding now for almost sixty years, and have taught riding for over forty years." *High Line Rider* appeared in 1985, the first of eleven Western novels published to date. William A. Luckey's next Five Star Western will be *Bitter Cañon*.

99

Vietnam

Vietnam

Spencer C. Tucker

THE UNIVERSITY PRESS OF KENTUCKY

Published 1999 by The University Press of Kentucky
Scholarly publisher for the Commonwealth,
serving Bellarmine College, Berea College, Centre
College of Kentucky, Eastern Kentucky University,
The Filson Club Historical Society, Georgetown College,
Kentucky Historical Society, Kentucky State University,
Morehead State University, Murray State University,
Northern Kentucky University, Transylvania University,
University of Kentucky, University of Louisville,
and Western Kentucky University.

Editorial and Sales Offices: The University Press of Kentucky
663 South Limestone Street, Lexington, Kentucky 40508-4008

02 01 00 99 98 5 4 3 2 1

Library of Congress Cataloging-in-Publication Data

Tucker, Spencer, 1937-
Vietnam / Spencer C. Tucker.
p. cm.
Includes bibliographical references (p.) and index.
ISBN 0-8131-2121-3 (cloth : alk. paper). —
ISBN 0-8131-0966-3 (pbk : alk. paper)
1. Vietnam—History, Military. 2. Vietnam—20th century—
History. I. Title.
D3556.54.T83 1999   98-37521
959.704—dc21

Contents

List of maps

Preface

In studying the Vietnam War, first as an Army captain in charge of preparing daily intelligence summaries on North Vietnam and Laos for the chief of staff of the Army and later as a college professor offering a course on the war, I learned that it was impossible to look at it in isolation, as so many Americans were wont to do at the time. One could not learn the truth about the Vietnam War without first studying the Indo-China War, which in turn could not be understood without probing Vietnamese nationalist attitudes during the period of French rule. That in turn was conditioned by long Vietnamese opposition to China. All of this reveals the truism that history cannot be understood in isolation. If any war in modern history demonstrates the need to study history, it is the Vietnam conflict.

Although this book is a survey of all of Vietnamese military history, its emphasis is on the twentieth century and the Vietnam War. A traumatic event for the United States in terms of lives and treasure as well as in domestic upheaval, it also taught Americans an important lesson about the limits of power. But what Americans know as the Vietnam War is regarded by Vietnamese as merely one in a long series of struggles against foreign domination. The Vietnamese have in fact done much better at putting that war into perspective than have Americans. In a 410-page "official history" of Vietnam (*Vietnam. A Long History*, Hanoi, 1993), Nguyên Khăc Viên devotes one chapter of only 51 pages ("Building the Foundations of Socialism and the Struggle Against U.S. Neo-Colonialism") to the entire period of 1954–73. Americans would not do as well, in part because the United States lost the Vietnam War. Nor have I; the Vietnam War dominates this book. I have, however, included discussion of the important earlier battles in Vietnamese history, which are not generally known to Westerners.

Chapter 1 treats early Vietnam, dominated by the struggle for independence from China. Chapter 2 treats the coming of the Europeans and the French occupation through World War II; it includes the Black Flag and Tonkin Wars as well as a little-known war between France and Thailand. Chapter 3 deals with the Indo-China War of 1946–54. Chapter 4 treats the beginning of the Vietnam War through the introduction of US combat troops in March 1965. Chapter 5 traces the period 1965–8, when the war was Americanized and the United States sought to win a military victory. It closes with the 1968 Têt Offensive. Chapter 6 discusses the US search for a way out, ending with the Paris Peace Accords of January 1973. Chapter 7 treats the "Third Vietnam War", in which North Vietnam conquered the South. Chapter 8 discusses the post-Vietnam War conflicts: the Socialist Republic of Vietnam's invasion of Cambodia and the 1979 war with China.

Because much of what happened in South Vietnam was determined by decisions in Washington and because SRV archives are unavailable, I have included much on Washington's policies and the factors influencing them; but I have tried throughout to keep the focus on events in Vietnam and place the American connection in perspective.

Throughout I have used Vietnamese spellings for places, with one exception. For ease of reading by the Americans and the British, for whom this volume is largely intended, I have throughout Americanized Viêt Nam to Vietnam. As far as Vietnamese proper names are concerned, I have used the Vietnamese system of family name first, middle name, then given name. Subsequent references are to the given name only. Thus, in the case of Ngô Ðình Diêm, Ngô is the family name, Ðình the middle name, and Diêm the given name. After the first reference I refer to him only as Diêm. This follows the common Vietnamese practice of using the first name with the title, no matter how exalted the individual. The two exceptions to this among Vietnamese are Hô Chí Minh and Ton Duc Thang, both of whom are known as "Uncle" before their last name.

I want to thank Mike Nichols and David Coffey, two graduate students at Texas Christian University who helped with research and bibliographic work. David Coffey, Cecil Currey, Arthur Dommen, Bruce Elleman, James Willbanks, Sandy Wittman, and David Zabecki all read the manuscript and made many helpful suggestions. Cecil Currey, who has written three fine books on Vietnam, was particularly generous with his time and expertise. I am also very grateful to Hô Diêu Anh and Nguyên Công Luân for their close reading of the manuscript, assistance with diacritical marks, and calling many points to my attention. Nguyên was especially valuable as a consequence of his service as a Republic of Vietnam Army officer during the Vietnam War. And as always I greatly appreciate the keen eye and awesome editing skills of my colleague Donald Worcester. TCU History Department Office Manager Barbara Pierce was a great help; former student/now colleague Don Frazier of McMurry University produced the excellent computer-generated maps. Aisling Ryan, administrative assistant of University College of London Press, helped answer my questions and provided helpful suggestions and encouragement. I especially want to thank Beverly for not only reading the manuscript and making thoughtful comments but for her patience and understanding in the process. And, of course, I am grateful to Jeremy Black, editor of this series, and to Steven Gerrard, former editor of University College of London Press, for the opportunity to write a second volume in this series.

Chapter One

The background

Vietnamese history is characterized by two major themes. The first is the effort to preseve the national identity against foreigners. This meant a thousand-year-long struggle against Chinese control (111BCC–AAD938), followed by a long effort to preserve that independence and territorial unity against the Portuguese, Dutch, French, and then the Americans. The second theme is territorial expansionism, most notably the march to the south as far as the Cà Mau Peninsula. Wars, both international and civil, have long been a part of a tumultuous Vietnamese history. The scholar Pham Quynh noted the repeated divisions that wars have caused his country: "We Vietnamese are a people in search of a country and we do not find it."[1]

Geography

Vietnam is part of Indo-China. The term is attributed to Danish carto-grapher Konrad Malte-Brun (1775–1826) and applies collectively to Burma, Thailand, Tonkin, Annam, Cochin-China, Laos, and Cambodia. Through the centuries Indo-China has been a crossroads with India to the west, China to the north, and, through an archipelagic extension into the South China Sea, the southeast.[2] The political entity of Indo-China was a late nineteenth-century French creation and included Laos, Cambodia, and Vietnam.

Vietnam, the easternmost portion of Indo-China, extends east from Laos and Cambodia to the Gulf of Tonkin and South China Sea. As a crossroads of Asia it was destined for a stormy history. It encompasses some 127,300 square miles of territory. Put in the context of the United States, it is approximately one-half the size of the state of Texas. Its coastline is shaped like an "S". Some 1,200 miles from north to south, Vietnam has extremes in climate. North Vietnam has a noticeable winter season; South Vietnam has warm temperatures year around. The country varies in depth from as little as 33 miles to as much as 300 miles, and its shape had led to Vietnam being called "the starving sea horse". Its extensive coastline, which has caused Vietnam to be known as the "balcony on the Pacific", has left it vulnerable to seaborne invasion but has also provided a ready source of food. Additionally, transportation by sea and river encouraged national unity for, throughout most of Vietnamese history, water transportation has been faster and easier than that over land.[3]

Mountain chains running principally north–south from China provide river valleys that have been used by migratory groups entering Vietnam from the north. The most important of these is the Trúóng Són Range, with peaks as high as 10,000 feet near the Chinese border, dropping off to a steep cliff near the sea in central Vietnam. Its watershed forms the western boundary with Laos and Cambodia. There is also the high ground of the Thái Hill area in the northwest and another mountainous area in the northeast. The North Vietnamese Midlands feature terraced hills and rounded mountains north of the Red River Delta. Another important geographical region is the Southern Mountain Plateau known as the PMS (*Plateaux Montagnards du Sud*) to the French and the Central Highlands to the Americans. This vast plateau covers some two-thirds of all Vietnam south of the 17th parallel. These topographical divisions rule out geographical unity.

About three-quarters of Vietnam is covered by trees or brush and close to half of this is high-stand tree cover or dense jungle. The remainder of Vietnam consists of open plains or deltas. Precipitation and summer temperatures are ideal for the cultivation of rice, the region's primary agricultural crop. Vietnam has two large rice-producing areas, the Red River Delta in the northern part of the country and the Mekong River Delta in the South, connected by narrow plains. This has led Vietnamese to describe their country as two rice baskets carried on a pole. In addition to rice, Vietnam produces a variety of other products, both agricultural and industrial.[4]

Economically, Vietnam does form something of a unit. The North possesses the bulk of the raw materials while the South boasts most of the food-producing areas. The 1954 division of Vietnam thus brought an economic burden for each half that forced them to depend on outside economic assistance.[5]

North Vietnam, named Tonkin by the French, is the centre of Vietnamese civilization and contains the 250-mile-wide Red River Delta. Bracketed by inland hills and mountains, this region is blessed with fertile alluvium produced by its numerous rivers. The agricultural heartland contains Hà Nôi, the national capital and centre of Vietnamese culture. Extremes in rainfall forced the creation there of an extensive system of dikes, canals, and dams for water control. Drawing on coal and mineral deposits in the north, Hà Nôi is also a major manufacturing centre and transportation hub. The capital is served by the port of Hai Phòng at the mouth of the Red River Delta on the Gulf of Tonkin.

Central Vietnam, known by the French as Annam (Chinese for "Pacified South"), is interspersed by rivers and mountains, a few touching the shoreline, which have served to inhibit north–south communication. The narrow strip of Annam yields rice, salt, and fish, and has the excellent harbors at Đà Nẵng (Tourane) and Cam Ranh Bay. It also contains the one-time imperial capital of Huê.

The South, called Cochin China by the French, with the wide and fertile Mekong Delta interlaced by streams and canals, is a major rice producing area despite its extensive forests, swamps, and jungle, known to Vietnamese as the land of "bad water". Hô Chí Minh City, the former Sài Gòn, is today Vietnam's most important urban area.[6]

Ethnology

By official count there are at least 58 distinct national groupings in Vietnam, but some 85 per cent of the total population is ethnic Kinh. Vietnam is therefore largely homogeneous ethnically and culturally. Another salient fact about the Vietnamese population, at least in modern times, is its rapid growth. The country has one of the world's highest birth-rates; the two Vietnams numbered about 30.5 million people in 1962, but the reunited country had more than 70 million by 1996. Thus half of the national population has been born since the Vietnam War.

From earliest times Vietnam's population has been concentrated in the coastal lowlands to cultivate rice. Even today there are striking variations in population density, from crowded coastal areas to the sparcely populated interior. Some 90 per cent of the population lives in 20 per cent of the national area.

When they settled the rich farming areas, the Kinh pushed the earlier aboriginal inhabitants into the interior. The French collectively identified these peoples, principally the Thái, Muong, and Meo, as the *Montagnards* (mountain people). The Kinh found the Montagnards useful as a buffer for the Siamese and Cambodians to the west, and largely left them alone. These

3

minorities retained their separate identities into modern times, which created problems for a succession of governments.

Other important ethnic minorities, the vast majority of whom lived in the South, are the Khmers, known as the Khmer Krom, or Southern Khmer, by Cambodians, and the Chinese. In the 1960s ethnic Chinese made up some 10 per cent of Sài Gòn's population and were influential as merchants and bankers.[7]

Traditional Vietnam

Archaeological digs in the 1920s and 1930s identified Stone Age sites in Hoa Bình and Bắc Són in North Vietnam and a Bronze Age site in Đông Són, Thanh Hóa Province. In the 1960s and 1980s several new sites were also excavated.[8]

The first peoples in Indo-China were Austro-Indonesians. These aboriginal inhabitants were pushed to the interior by Mongolian and Thai invaders from the north and Indians who came by sea from the west. Indonesian and Mongolian elements survive today in the Vietnamese spoken language. The Thais arrived about 2000 BC. The Indian migration culminated in the Khmer empire that still survives in present-day Cambodia. In Vietnam it found expression in the Kingdom of Champa, established in AD 192 and subsequently destroyed by the Vietnamese.

Vietnamese consider the founder of their nation to be Hung Vúóng or King Hung, the first of a line of hereditary kings of the Hồng Bàng dynasty (2879–258 BC). Much of this early period is shrouded in legend, and it is unclear whether the country known as Văn Lang actually existed. Legend has it that this kingdom was quite large and included a large portion of south China inhabited by the Nan Yüeh (South Yüeh), as well as North Vietnam and part of central Vietnam. The word Viêt is in fact derived from the Vietnamese pronunciation of Yüeh, the Chinese term to designate the barbarian peoples living south of the Yangtze River. Nam Viêt (Vietnam) is Vietnamese for the southern Yüeh.

In 258 BC King Thuc Phán of neighbouring Tay Au invaded and annexed Văn Lang, setting up a new kingdom, Âu Lac, with himself as ruler. Cô Loa (about a dozen miles from present-day Hà Nôi) became the new capital, and soon a citadel was under construction there. This vast and very sophisticated defensive work is the most important historical ruin of ancient Vietnam.[9]

NAM–VIET
254 BC–111 BC

1890

1831–1893
Temporarily
annexed

938

Gulf of Tonkin

Mekong River

1100

Laos

Thailand

1400

1890

Cambodia

1500

1818–1863
Temporarily annexed

1698

1714

Southern expansion
of
Imperial Vietnam

1757

South China Sea

In 207 BC Triêu Đà (Chao To), a Chinese warlord who had broken with the Ch'in emperor, conquered Âu Lac. He combined it with his previously held territory to form the new kingdom of Nam Việt (Nan Yüeh) or "southern country of the Viet". Its capital was Phiên Ngu (later known as Canton and today as Guangzhou).

Meanwhile the Han dynasty was unifying China, a task it accomplished in the third century BC. In the second century the Han pushed south and in 111 BC they sent an expeditionary corps into Nam Việt and added it to their empire. For the next thousand years present-day northern Vietnam was, save for a few brief periods, a Chinese province.[10]

Chinese rule (111 BC–AD 938)

Geography has forced Vietnam into a close political relationship with China, and Chinese and French historians have tended to treat Vietnamese history during this period as a branch of Chinese history. They see Vietnam as little more than a frontier province, blessed with Chinese civilization but always struggling to be independent. Vietnamese historians, on the other hand, have looked on their country as endeavouring to preserve its own identity; they have taken great pride in its ability both to resist Chinese imperialism and to survive Sinicization.

Chinese rule bred in the Vietnamese a resistance and hatred of all foreign political interference. Vietnamese could admire Chinese philosophy and civilization while at the same time resisting the presence of Chinese soldiers in their midst. As historian Keith Taylor has noted,

> Over the past one thousand years, the Vietnamese have no less than seven times defeated attempts by China to assert its influence by armed force. No theme is more consistent in Vietnamese history than the theme of resistance to foreign aggression.[11]

During the first hundred years Chinese rule was loose and indirect with almost no change in indigenous policies. The Chinese organized their new conquest into the two provinces of Giao Chi (northern Tonkin) and Cúu Chân (southern Tonkin) but they continued the practice of native Vietnamese lords governing at the local level. But gradually Chinese functionaries replaced the indigenous local officials and many settled in Vietnam on a permanent basis. The Vietnamese had both to pay imperial taxes and to maintain the local administration and the military.[12]

The Chinese tried to assimilate Vietnam culturally, for the Han sought a unified empire in all respects. They regarded their great Celestial Empire as the centre of the universe, and they assumed that all people could aspire to nothing better than to become thoroughly Chinese. Their "civilizing mission" was not unlike that of the French in the nineteenth century.

Sinicization included veneration of the emperor, the use of Chinese ideographic writing, and Confucianism. The latter taught a hierarchical social structure with a tightly woven system of obligations that bound subject to ruler, son to father, and wife to husband. The key element was absolute loyalty to the emperor. Buddhism and Taoism also made major inroads in Vietnam.[13]

At the same time Chinese officials seized land from local nobles for Chinese immigrants. This, and the sense that they were losing their national identiy, led Vietnamese nobles to revolt.

The Trúng Sisters

In AD 39 Thi Sách, a Vietnamese nobleman, and his wife Trúng Trắc, daughter of another noble, led a revolt against the Chinese. In the spring of 40 their armed forces carried out a series of successful sieges and defeated one Chinese garrison after another. Much to their surprise, the Vietnamese found themselves free of Chinese control for the first time in 150 years. Trúng Trắc established a court at Mê-linh, northwest of present-day Hà Nôi, and many of the Vietnamese nobles recognized her as queen.

Trúng Trắc and her sister Trúng Nhi, apparently her constant companion, are revered in Vietnamese history as Hai Bà Trúng (the Two Trúng Ladies or the Trúng Sisters). Although Vietnamese tradition has it that Chinese authorities provoked the rebellion by executing Thi Sách, there is no evidence of this. One historian of this period speculates that this came from "the patriarchal bias of later centuries, which could not countenance a woman leading a rebellion and being recognized as queen as long as her husband still lived". Chinese sources indicate that Thi Sách merely followed his wife's leadership; indeed, many Vietnamese women were leaders in the rebellion.[14]

The Han Court was slow to react, but in 41 it appointed one of its best generals, Ma Yüan, to command an invasion army. He invaded with 8,000 regular troops and some 12,000 militiamen gathered from south China. The Chinese did not encounter resistance until they reached the region of present-day Hà Nôi. In the spring of 42 the Vietnamese stopped the Chinese advance and Ma Yüan withdrew his forces eastward to Láng Bac, overlooking the southern shore of Lake Láng Ba.

The rainy season had begun and Ma Yüan apparently decided to wait for dry weather before resuming the offensive. But with her supporters losing heart and fearful that waiting would only encourage further disaffection, Trúng Trắc ordered an attack.

In the subsequent Battle of Láng Bac the Chinese easily defeated the poorly disciplined Vietnamese. Some 10,000 Vietnamese surrendered and thousands more were beheaded. Later Trúng Trắc and her sister were captured. According to Chinese sources the sisters were subsequently executed and their heads sent to the Han court. Vietnamese tradition holds, however, that they committed suicide after the battle by leaping into the Đáy (Hát) River.[15]

General Ma Yüan spent most of 43 establishing direct Han rule in the Red River Delta. Near the end of that year he led a sizeable force in some two thousand ships to attack the south, where he successfully reestablished Chinese control. In the spring of 44 he returned to a hero's welcome at the Han court.[16]

The Han now tightened their control over Vietnam. They deprived the Vietnamese of their traditional ruling class and removed other barriers to their direct rule. They also gradually extended their control southward to include the area of Nhât Nam. At the same time India was spreading its influence in Southeast Asia north toward Nhât Nam. Other outside powers were also establishing contact with Vietnam.[17]

The Chinese and Indian civilizations now confronted one another in southernmost Nhât Nam, the vicinity of modern day Huê. Here, around the year 192, the Cham kingdom of Lin-i came into being; aligned with the Indians, it lasted into the seventeenth century. In this period there were numerous rebellions and considerable fighting along the frontier between Nhât Nam and the new Cham kingdom.[18]

Direct Chinese rule also led to continued Vietnamese rebellions and an expanding list of national heroes, among them Bà Triêu, or Lady Triêu, in 248. Identified only in Vietnamese sources, she is honoured as a Vietnamese Joan of Arc who went into battle on an elephant and died at age 23.[19]

Lý Bôn and the Battle of Điên Triêt Lake (546)

In 542 Lý Bôn led a sizeable rebellion. His forces swept away the Chinese administration and the next year defeated a counterattacking Chinese army. At the beginning of 544 Lý Bôn proclaimed himself emperor of Nam Viêt. His chief preoccupations during his short rule were to keep peace at home and prevent foreign invasion. This included depredations by mountain tribes, called Lào by the Chinese and Vietnamese of that time.

Lý Bôn's luck ran out in 545 when his forces came up against an invading Chinese army that likely came by sea. Defeated in a series of battles, he escaped to rally what was left of his army. By autumn 546 he had assembled 20,000 men on the shores of Điên Triêt Lake and put them to work building boats, with the plan of using them to attack the Chinese camped at the other end of the lake. Chinese General Pa-hsien, aware of the precarious situation of his army deep in enemy territory, staged a preemptive attack and utterly defeated Lý Bôn.

Resistance continued for a time under Triêu Quang Phuc, who waged extensive guerrilla warfare in the Red River plain from an island in the midst of a swamp. Foreshadowing warfare against the French and Americans, his men would strike at night, kill and capture Chinese soldiers and take their supplies, then retreat into the swamps. When a power struggle within China led to the withdrawal of most Chinese forces, Triêu Quang Phuc secured control of the Red River plain and held it until around 570.[20]

With the rise of the strong T'ang dynasty (618–917) in China, rebellion in Vietnam became more difficult. Nonetheless nationalist revolts occurred in 687, 722, 766–91, and 819.[21] By this time the region was known to the outside world by the Chinese term of Annam (the "Pacified South").

With the decline of the T'ang dynasty in the tenth century Vietnamese hopes of shaking off Chinese rule again rose. Dúóng Đình Nghê, who ruled in the southern area of present-day Hà Trung and Thanh Hóa provinces, was determined to drive the Chinese out. In 931, after putting together and training a small army, he routed the Chinese and won recognition from them as military governnor. Although later revered by Vietnamese for his example, he was assassinated in 937 by Kiêu Công Tiên, a subordinate who then attempted to institute a pro-Chinese policy.

Kiêu Công Tiên soon was under attack by Dúóng Đình Nghê's son-in-law Ngô Quyên, and he called on the Chinese for aid. Southern Han ruler Liu Kung, who wanted the area for himself, promptly assembled an army under his son Liu Hung-ts'ao.[22]

Battle of the Bach Đăng River (938)

The Chinese came by sea, but by the time they arrived in Vietnamese waters Ngô Quyên had already defeated and executed Kiêu Công Tiên and had time to prepare for the Chinese attack. The Chinese planned to use the Bach Đăng River, the main water route into the Red River plain, to advance well inland before disembarking to fight ashore. Ngô Quyên guessed their plan, and in the autumn of 938 he assembled his army at the mouth of the river and had his men plant iron-tipped stakes in the water. These were only so high as to be below water at high tide. When the Chinese appeared Ngô Quyên sent out a small naval force to engage them. His ships then withdrew up river, drawing the Chinese fleet after them. When the tide fell the Chinese ships were trapped on the stakes in the river and were easily destroyed. Reportedly more than half the Chinese, including Liu Hung-ts'ao, drowned. This great Vietnamese victory ended the long Chinese rule over Vietnam.

After more than a thousand years of Chinese control the Vietnamese were again independent. Nonetheless the Chinese imprint proved permanent. Vietnam is unique among countries of Southeast Asia in having adopted Chinese cultural patterns; even Vietnamese myths were influenced by the long contact with China. The Vietnamese continued to use Chinese characters in writing and Chinese traditions and customs, although over time a synthesis emerged combining native and Chinese elements.

Although China continued to enjoy nominal suzerainty over Vietnam until the 1885 Treaty of Tientsin, the Vietnamese in fact now controlled all the territory from the foothills of Yunnan to the 17th parallel. During the next nine centuries (938–1884) the Vietnamese built a new country – to use their own term, a Southern nation (Núóc Nam or Nam Quôc) – facing China, the Northern nation (Băc Quôc).

At the same time the Vietnamese expanded their territory from south of Đèo Ngang (Ngang Pass) to Cà Mau at the expense of the Chams and the Khmers. "Resisting the North" (Băc cú) and "Conquering the South" (Nam chinh) became major themes of Vietnamese history, as did development of an original culture and civilization.

In 980 Lê Hoàn, founder of the Tiên Lê (Early Lê) dynasty (980–1009), defeated another Chinese invasion; two years later he launched a victorious southern expedition against the Kingdom of Champa.

The following dynasties succeeded the Tiên Lê: the Lý (1010–1325); the Trân (1225–1400); the Hô (1400–7); the Hâu (Posterior) Trân (1407–13) and the period of Ming domination (1407–27); the Hâu (Posterior) Lê (1428–1788); the Mac (1527–92); the Nguyên Tây Són (1788–1802); and the Nguyên (1802–1945).

Preservation of independence

The Sung invasion of 980 was not the only Chinese effort to regain control of their former southern colony, but each time they met defeat and the

Vietnamese added more names to an already lengthy list of national heroes. In 1285 Trân Húng Ða'o defeated an invading Mongul army of up to 500,000 men led by Thoát Hoan, a son of Kublai Khan, which had occupied much of the north of the country. In 1287 Thoát Hoan returned with another army of some 300,000 men accompanied by 500 warships to attack the coast. Again Trân Húng Ða'o crushed them in April 1288 in the Battle of the Bach Ðang River. Trâ Húng Ða'o is considered one of the most important figures in Vietnamese history and his answer to King Trân Nhân Tông is known to every Vietnamese. When the king asked whether it would be better to surrender to end the people's suffering, Ða'o replied. "Your Majesty, if you want to surrender, please first cut my head off." Trân Húng Ða'o's *Essentials of Military Art* is regarded as a classic of thirteenth-century Vietnamese literature. All subsequent Chinese attempts to reconquer Vietnam failed, except in 1407 for 20 years during the Ming dynasty.[23]

In February 1418 Lê Lói or Lê Thái Tô, a landowner in Thanh Hóa province, proclaimed himself king and led an insurrection against the occupying Minh. At first Lê Lói mounted guerrilla operations in Thanh Hóa. Insurrections against the Ming in other parts of the country kept the Chinese from concentrating on him. By the end of 1425 he had liberated all of the southern part of the country, with the exception of the Nghê An and Tay Ðô (Thanh Hóa) citadels.

The Ming then sent out 50,000 reinforcements commanded by Vúong Thông. But before they arrived, in September Lê Lói began a campaign to conquer the Red River Delta. He sent three armies north: two to intercept Ming reinforcements coming from Yunnan and Lang Son and the third to take the capital of Thanh Hóa. Despite this, in November, Ming troops reached the capital, bringing Chinese strength there to some 100,000 men. But they were soon defeated at Tôt Ðông west of Thanh Hóa and withdrew back into the citadel.

In October 1427 other Ming reinforcements arrived. One column of 100,000 men came by means of Lang Son; another 50,000 arrived via the Red River valley. The Vietnamese decided to attack the more powerful army first, ambushing and destroying it at Chi Lang Pass, where some 30,000 Chinese surrendered. On learning of the defeat the other Ming column fled. With hope of reinforcements now gone, on 29 December 1427 Vúong Thông surrendered and Lê Lói granted his request for provisions so that the Chinese might return home.[24]

Despite having defeated the Chinese, successive Vietnamese rulers of the Lý, Trân, Lê, and Nguyên dynasties never thought of giving up governmental institutions inherited from the Chinese empire, and indeed they modelled their institutions after Chinese examples. The Vietnamese state also continued

Confucianism as the major influence in the education of the country's elite and the use of competitive examinations to recruit mandarins for state government and administration. Chinese characters continued to be used as the country's official writing system at the expense of Nôm, the demotic writing system combining Chinese characters with Vietnamese, until the early twentieth century.[25]

When Vietnam became independent from China in the mid-tenth century its southern boundaries did not extend past Ngang Pass. Nam Tiên, or the effort to expand the national territory to the south, was a constant for much of Vietnamese history. It was advanced at the expense first of the Chams and then the Khmers.

The Indianized Kingdom of Champa had been founded in 192. Its beautiful capital of Indrapura was located near present-day Hôi An on the central Vietnamese coast at about 16 degrees latitude. Champa was a seaborne trading state supported by powerful battle fleets reminiscent of ancient Carthage. One Cham raid even reached up the Mekong to cross the Great Lake (Tonlé Sap) of Cambodia and capture and sack the city of Angkor in 1177.

As with their European contemporaries the Norsemen, the Chams were raiders who lived off plunder but failed to build up their economic base at home by agricultural settlement. As a result they fell prey to slow but steady encroachments by Vietnamese settlers, who were often invited by the Chams to settle vacant agricultural lands. Once they had settled a particular area, however, the Vietnamese state undertook to protect its citizens there. Thus bit by bit the Vietnamese whittled away at the Cham state.

In 1069, after a successful military campaign, Lý Thánh Tông seized the Cham capital and imprisoned the Cham king. The latter won his freedom only by ceding three Cham districts that became the Vietnamese provinces of Quang Bình and Quang Tri.

In the early fourteenth century the Chams ceded two more districts, and in the fifteenth century they had to give up all their territory north of the present province of Quang Nam. These fourteenth- and fifteenth-century additions became the future Thúa Thiên Province with its imperial capital of Huê. Finally in 1471 the Vietnamese took the second Cham capital of Vijaya. This was critical because once the Vietnamese had secured a permanent foothold south of Hai Vân Pass the remaining Cham country was quickly subdued. In the seventeenth century the remnants of the old Kingdom of Champa were definitively absorbed, although a petty Cham king retained nominal independence in the Phan Rang region until 1822.[26]

The Vietnamese Nam Tiên or March to the South did not end with the elimination of Champa. In 1481 the government created the Đồn Điền agricultural settlements, by which it granted lands to Vietnamese settlers, usually ex-soldiers, on the condition that they defend it. It did not matter to the government that these grants were usually in territory belonging to the crumbling Khmer empire. Repeated border incidents brought Vietnamese armed intervention and additional territorial acquisitions.

This process brought the Vietnamese into the Mekong River Delta. By 1658 the Vietnamese had taken all of South Vietnam north of Sài Gòn (then the sleepy fishing village of Prey Kor). Sài Gòn itself fell to the Vietnamese in 1672. By the last decades of the eighteenth century Vietnam had expanded to the full extent of its present shoreline.[27]

Both Vietnam and Siam intervened in Cambodia, which had the misfortune of being caught between two powerful neighbours. In 1623 a Cambodian king called in Vietnamese troops to dislodge the Siamese. In return Vietnam insisted on sending settlers along with troops to protect them. In 1658 Vietnam again sent troops into Cambodia to settle a succession struggle, and in 1660 Cambodia began paying regular tribute to Vietnam.[28]

Soon Cambodia was in complete collapse. Another successionist struggle led to civil war and Vietnamese intervention (1714–16). In 1717 two large Siamese forces invaded Cambodia. The southern invaders were badly defeated in the Battle of Bantea Meas, apparently the result of a panic among the Siamese troops when they learned that their supporting naval forces had been destroyed by a storm at sea. But the northern force was successful and in a series of battles defeated the Cambodians and their Vietnamese allies. It eventually reached the Cambodian capital of Oudong, where the Vietnamese-supported ruler switched his allegiance to Siam.

Meanwhile the Vietnamese had seized control of several Cambodian border provinces in the Mekong River region. When in 1739 a Cambodian army attempted to regain control of these provinces a war with Vietnam ensued (1739–49), in which the Cambodians were not only defeated but lost additional territory to Vietnam. During 1755–60 the Vietnamese continued their expansion into Cambodia. Siam, preoccupied by a war with Burma, was unable to intervene.

During 1769–73 Vietnam fought another war with Siam over Cambodia, but Siam regained control. Since the sixteenth century a condominium (joint rule) policy between Siam and Vietnam over Laos had brought the important Tran Ninh Plateau, known to the French as the *Plaine des Jarres*, under intermittent Vietnamese control.[29]

The Division of Vietnam into two states

Meanwhile Vietnam itself was falling apart. In the North, Mac Dăng Dung, governor of Thăng Long (present-day Hà Nôi), overthrew the Lê dynasty, and by 1527 was king in all but name. This prompted southern feudal lord Nguyên Kim to set up a government in exile in Laos that supported a Lê descendant. In 1545 supporters of the Mac murdered Nguyên Kim and Vietnam dissolved into a long civil war that lasted for the next two centuries.

In the 1630s the Nguyên rulers built a wooden wall across the narrow waist of Vietnam at Dông Hoi, ironically not far from the 17th parallel division of 1954. Reportedly the wall was 20 feet high and six miles long. For the next 150 years the country was divided along that fortified line. The Trinh lords, successors to the Mac, ruled the North while the Nguyên family controlled the South. Each claimed to rule in the name of the powerless Lê king at Thăng Long.

The more powerful Trinh, who controlled four-fifths of the population of Vietnam, never succeeded in conquering the South, despite the fact that the Nguyên were almost constantly at war with Siam and Cambodia over territorial expansion at the expense of the Khmers. Since neither side attempted to conquer the other by taking to the interior jungles or utilizing the sea, stalemate resulted.

In another parallel with the twentieth-century Vietnam War, both sides in this long civil war received some foreign assistance; the Dutch aided the Trinh and the Portuguese the Nguyên, each providing artillery and military advisers. The Nguyên had a smaller land force – only about 50,000 infantry to the Trinh's 100,000 – but it was better trained and equipped. They also had a powerful navy, reportedly 500 galleys, each with 25 rowers and armed with one cannon forward and two aft.[30]

The Tây Són Rebellion

Widespread corruption led to increased financial exactions on the population and to peasant uprisings, the most important of which was the Tây Són Rebellion in the South. Three brothers – Nguyên Nhac, Nguyên Lú, and Nguyên Huê – from the village of Tây Són in present-day Bình Đinh province exploited popular resentment.

The Tây Són brothers urged the seizure of property from the rich and its distribution to the poor. They also attracted the support of powerful Chinese merchants who opposed restrictive Nguyên trade practices. The Tây Són

14

Rebellion thus began as a social revolution with peasants and merchants opposing mandarins and large landowners.

In the An Khe Highlands near Bình Đinh the Tây Són brothers built an army. In this strategically important area they could draw support from disaffected minorities. The brothers were also greatly aided by the fact that the youngest of them, Nguyên Huê, turned out to be a military genius.[31]

In 1773, following two years of careful preparations, a Tây Són army of some 10,000 men took the field against the Nguyên rulers. Soon it had seized the fort of Qui Nhon; the Tây Són next took the provinces of Quang Ngai and Quãng Nam.[32]

By the end of the year the Tây Són were on the verge of overthrowing the Nguyên rulers altogether, when they found themselves caught between their two enemies. In 1775 a Trinh army moved south and took Phú Xuân (present-day Huê). The Trinh then announced they would stay in the South to put down the Tây Són, who lost one military encounter with the Trinh; meanwhile the Nguyên also took back some land lost to the Tây Són earlier. The Tây Són survived by reaching accommodation with the Trinh until they tired of their southern involvement and withdrew.[33]

It took the Tây Són ten more years to defeat the Nguyên. In 1776 they attacked the Nguyên stronghold of Gia Đinh Province and took Sài Gòn. Only one prince, Nguyên Ánh, escaped; he and some supporters fled into the swamps of the western Mekong Delta. In 1778 Nguyên Nhac proclaimed himself king, with his capital at Đô Bàn in Bình Đinh Province.

Later Nguyên Ánh mounted a counter-attack and recaptured Gia Đinh and Bình Thuân Provinces. In 1783 Tây Són troops led by Nguyên Huê again defeated Nguyên Ánh, forcing him into refuge on Phú Quôc Island. Nguyên Ánh then called in the Siamese, who in 1784 sent a force of between 20,000 and 50,000 men with 300 ships into the western Mekong Delta. The invaders treated the Vietnamese badly, however, driving many to support the Tây Són.

In meeting the Siamese invasion Nguyên Huê avoided an attack on the enemy stronghold at Sa Đéc. Rather he sought battle in circumstances that would be favourable to him. In January 1785 he lured the Siamese into an ambush on the Mekong River in the Rach Gâm-Xoài Mút area of present-day Tiên Giang Province.

Nguyên Huê positioned his infantry and artillery along a five-mile stretch of the river between the Gâm and Xoài Mút arroyos that ran at right angles to, and north of, the Mekong. He also placed some of his troops on islands in the river. His ships were in the arroyos behind islands on the other side of the main river channel and at My Tho.

On 18 January Nguyên Huê sent ships west to provoke the Siamese. Feigning flight, they led the Siamese eastward on 19 January toward My Tho and a trap. Nguyên Huê's ships then came out of the two arroyos and cut off the Siamese from advance or retreat. At the same time his land artillery opened fire on the enemy vessels. According to Vietnamese sources all 300 Siamese junks were destroyed and only 2,000–3,000 Siamese escaped to flee westward across Cambodia to Siam by land. The remaining Nguyên family members also fled to Siam.

Vietnamese regard this battle as one of the most important in their history because it halted Siamese expansion into southern Vietnam. It also greatly benefited Nguyên Huê, who became a national hero.[34]

The Trinh were unable to capitalize on the situation in the South because of trouble in their own domain. Bad harvests beginning in 1776 led to disorders, and the Trinh were also embroiled in a succession struggle.[35]

It is not surprising that Nguyên Huê took advantage of the disarray in the North. He marched an army there with the stated purpose of rescuing the Lê kings from Trinh control and won considerable popular support by promising food. In a brilliant May–June 1786 campaign he captured first Phú Xuân then Quang Tri and Quang Bình provinces. By July his troops had reached the Red River Delta and defeated the Trinh.[36] King Lê Hiên Tông reached accommodation with him by ceding territory and giving him his daughter in marriage. Lê Hiên Tông died the next year in 1787 and his grandson, Lê Chiêu Thông, succeeded him.[37]

Nguyên Huê now dominated the North from Thuân Hóa; Nguyên Nhac held the centre with his capital at Quy Nhón; and Nguyên Lú controlled the South, ruling from Gia Đinh near present-day Sài Gòn.

After his northern victory Nguyên Huê returned to the South to assist his brothers in dealing with the surviving Nguyên lord, Nguyên Ánh, whose troops continued to harass Gia Đinh Province. He left behind Nguyên Húu Chinh, who had deserted the king and joined the Tây Són cause, to defend Thăng Long.[38]

Nguyên Húu Chinh took advantage of Nguyên Huê's absence to advance his own interests. He and King Lê Chiêu Thông now joined forces against, Nguyên Huê, who sent General Vũ Văn Nhâm north with an army to attack Thăng Long. Nguyên Húu Chinh was killed in the subsequent fighting and the king fled.

Having secured the capital, General Vũ Văn Nhâm then took power himself and Nguyên Huê was forced to send two other generals to defeat him in turn. The Lê king, meanwhile, refused Nguyên Huê's invitations to return.[39]

16

Nguyên Huê was again forced to shift attention to the South to deal with Nguyên Ánh. To hold the North, Nguyên Huê left behind a garrison of 3,000 men in Thăng Long.[40]

King Lê Chiêu Thông was then in far northern Vietnam, and he sent his mother and son to China to ask for help in reclaiming his throne. The Chinese viceroy in the south, Sun Shi-yi, supported military intervention in Vietnam. He believed it would be an easy matter for China to establish a protectorate over an area weakened by a long civil war. The Emperor Quian-long (1736–96) agreed, but publicly stressed that the Lê had always recognized Chinese hegemony in sending tribute, and that China was merely intervening to restore the Lê to power.[41]

In November 1788 a Chinese expeditionary force commanded by Viceroy Sun Shi-yi and assisted by General Xu Shi-heng crossed the frontier at Cao Băng, Tuyên Quang, and Lang Són. The Chinese columns, totalling up to 200,000 men, converged on Thăng Long.[42]

The advance went well and the Chinese attracted little Vietnamese hostility *en route* to the capital. Indeed, Chinese and Lê edicts to the effect that the intervention was merely to put down Tây Són usurpers garnered Vietnamese support. At the same time, by establishing 70 military storehouses along the way to Thăng Long the Chinese indicated they were in Vietnam to stay.[43]

Most Tây Són troops manning outposts fled, and the Chinese easily won a series of small battles in early and mid-December. Faced with overwhelming force, the fact that their own troops were dispirited, and a lack of public support, Nguyên Huê's commander in the north abandoned the capital to march south and fortify a line at Thanh Hóa from the Tam Điêp mountains to the sea. The Chinese threw a pontoon bridge across the Red River and on 17 December entered Thăng Long with little resistance.[44]

The Chinese believed it would be an easy matter to defeat the Tây Són and bring Vietnam under their control. Sun Shi-yi planned to renew the offensive against the Tây Són after the lunar new year celebrations; in the meantime he kept the bulk of his forces in the vicinity of Thăng Long.[45]

Events worked to undermine the Chinese position. For one thing the Chinese treated Vietnam as if it were captured territory. Although they recognized Lê Chiêu Thông as king of Annam, he had to issue his pronouncements in the name of the Chinese Emperor and report to Sun Shi-yi. The king also punished Vietnamese officials who had rallied to the Tây Són and seemed oblivious to Chinese exactions. Even his supporters were upset with him.[46] And a series of typhoons and disastrous harvests led northerners to believe that the king had lost his "Mandate of Heaven". With few resources available themselves, the Vietnamese in the North were hard pressed to feed the Chinese. Thus the psychological climate in the North came to favour the Tây Són.

Nguyên Huê learned of the Chinese invasion on 24 November and immediately undertook military preparations at Phú Xuân (Huê). At the time he had some 6,000 men in his army. Spies in the North had kept him informed of Chinese intentions, but he faced a difficult decision. Nguyên Ánh was again causing problems in the South. Although Nguyên Huê decided he had to move first against the Chinese, he sent a trusted general south to deal with Nguyên Ánh should he seek to take advantage of the situation.[47]

On 22 December 1788, Nguyên Huê proclaimed himself king, in effect abolishing the Lê dynasty, something he had not attempted before. He took the name of Quang Trung.[48]

Quang Trung then left for Nghê An to recruit for his army. He made strong appeals to Vietnamese nationalism and many men joined, bringing his force to a reported 100,000 men with several hundred elephants. At the same time Nguyên Huê deceived his opponent by an appeal to Sun Shi-yi for negotiations. This threw the Chinese off guard and caused them to neglect military preparations. On 15 January 1789, Quang Trung put his forces in motion northward.[49]

Quang Trung learned from spies that the Chinese planned to leave Thăng Long on the sixth day of the new year to attack Phú Xuân. In order to strike first, he ordered his soldiers to celebrate the lunar new year of Têt early, promising that they would properly celebrate it in Thăng Long on the seventh day of the new year. On 25 January the Tây Són left Tam Điêp to take the offensive.[50]

The Battle of Ngoc Hôi-Đông Đa (1789)

Nearly half the Chinese army was in the vicinity of the capital. Sun Shi-yi's remaining troops were deployed on a north–south line along the major road connecting Thăng Long to the approaches to the Tam Điêp mountains. This line was protected by the natural defences of the Red River and three other rivers. The line was flanked to the west and to the east by posts at Són Tây and at Hai Dúóng. This forced the Tây Són to attack the main Chinese line at some distance from the capital and to reduce in turn a succession of forts.

Sun Shi-yi believed his disposition of forces would allow Chinese reserves sufficient time to intervene. It also ensured that he could maintain contact between all three major elements of his army and protect lines of communication to southern China. But it emphasized offensive rather than defensive operations.

Sun Shi-yi was not expecting a Tây Són attack. When it was obvious that the Tây Són troops would take the offensive he belatedly reinforced key posts and sent his best general to command the southern defensive line.

Quang Trung divided his force into five columns to converge on Thăng Long. He commanded the main force of infantry, cavalry, and elephants with the army's heavy artillery for an assault on Ngoc Hôi, the principal Chinese position south of the capital and headquarters of the Chinese general commanding in that area.

To force the Chinese to disperse their forces Quang Trung sent part of his fleet to the port of Hai Dúong to destroy the small Lê force there, attack the Chinese east of the Red River, and stand ready to assist his drive on Thăng Long. Another part of the fleet sailed north to the border provinces of Yên Thê and Lang Giang to harass Chinese lines of communication. A fourth element with horse cavalry and elephants as well as infantry followed a different route from the main body but was to join it in the assault on Ngoc Hôi. The fifth Tây Són column, also including horsemen and elephants, was to make a sudden attack on Thăng Long to demoralize the Chinese. After destroying Chinese forces southwest of the capital, it was to move directly against the Chinese headquarters east of the capital and attack troops withdrawing from other directions.[51]

Once launched, Quang Trung's offensive had proceeded without let-up day and night over five days. Attacks were usually at night to create maximum confusion for the enemy; days were spent on preparations. Each assault was rapidly mounted to prevent the enemy from bringing up reserves. The simultaneous nature of the attacks added to Chinese confusion and prevented them from shifting resources.

In the middle of the night of 25 January Quang Trung's force took the outpost at Són Nam, whose defenders had been celebrating Têt. It then rapidly seized one after another of the forts defending access to the capital. On 28 January, the Tây Són surrounded the important post of Hà Hôi some 13 miles southwest of the capital. Caught off guard, the Chinese surrendered with all their arms and supplies.

On 29 January Tây Són forces reached Ngoc Hôi, nine miles south of, and the last fort before, the capital. The strongest Chinese defensive position, it was reportedly manned by some 30,000 well-trained troops and well protected by trenches, minefields, pit traps, and bamboo stakes.

Quang Trung waited a day for one of his supporting columns to arrive from the southwest. At dawn the next day his men attacked from two directions; the elephants led and easily defeated the Chinese horsemen, whereupon the Chinese withdrew into their fort. Elite Tây Són commandos then attacked in groups of 20 men, protected by wooden planks covered by straw soaked in water. They immediately came under heavy Chinese cannon and arrow fire. The Tây Són infantry employed *hoa hồ*, small rockets that set fires when they exploded. Mounted on an elephant, Quang Trung directed operations. Vietnamese historians say that his armour was black from the powder smoke. As soon as the assault force reached the walls and ramparts, the troops threw down their shields and fought hand-to-hand. The fighting was intense but the Tây Són emerged victorious and many Chinese were killed.

The other Tây Són columns were also victorious and the Chinese defensive line south of the capital was completely shattered. The Đông Đa post (now within the city of Hà Nôi) was taken after a day of fierce fighting, the Chinese commander there hanging himself.[52]

Sun Shi-yi learned of the defeats at Ngoc Hôi and Khúong Thúong in the middle of the night of 29 January, about the time the Tây Són entered the capital's suburbs. Sun Shi-yi did not bother either to put on his armour or saddle his horse, but fled on it over the Red River, followed by others on horseback. Infantry soon joined in but the bridge collapsed under their weight. According to Vietnamese accounts the Red River was filled with thousands of Chinese bodies. Lê Chiêu Thông also fled with his family into China, ending the 300-year-old dynasty. Quang Trung's troops then entered Thăng Long and as promised celebrated Têt there on the seventh day of the new year.

Quang Trung ordered his generals to pursue the enemy in the hope of causing the Chinese to give up forever any plans of conquering Vietnam. Many Chinese fled in a panic and Vietnamese historians claim that all along the Chinese border "no human voice could be heard". Quang Trung promised to treat humanely all Chinese who surrendered and many did so.[53]

The Vietnamese know this series of victories as the Victory of Ngoc Hôi-Đông Đa, the Emperor Quang Trung's Victory over the Manchu, or the Victory of Spring 1789. It is still celebrated in Vietnam as the greatest military achievement in their modern history. It should have been a lesson that Têt had not always been observed peacefully in Vietnam.[54]

The key to Quang Trung's success was careful preparation. As historian Lê Thành Khôi noted, he devoted 35 out of 40 days of the campaign to preparations and only five to battle.[55] Other factors in the victory were his lieutenant's wise decision not to fight for the capital, keeping that force intact; and the support of the civilian population, which rallied to the Tây Són during their march north, providing food, material support, and tens of thousands of soldiers. Quang Trung had also preserved military secrecy until the moment of his attack, and being on the offensive also helped offset his numerical inferiority. His attack during Têt was a brilliant stroke because it caught his enemy off guard, as would be the case in 1968.

Quang Trung's offensive covered some 54 miles and took six forts, a rate of ten miles and more than a fort a day. Counting the retreat from Thăng Long, this meant that his troops covered 400 miles in just 40 days. Considering the state of Vietnamese roads at the time, this was an astonishing achievement. Victory came from the lightning offensive, concentration of force, excellent training, effective use of combined arms, and rapid mobility. Numbers were less important than morale; the attackers wanted to free their country from foreign domination.

Quang Trung had won two of the most important military victories in all Vietnamese history. He had reunited the realm, repelled the Siamese, and saved Vietnam from Chinese domination. Because of these achievements contemporary Western missionaries compared him to Alexander the Great.[56]

But Quang Trung was more than a military hero; he was also one of Vietnam's greatest kings. Recognizing the need for peace and accommodation with China, he immediately sought normalization of trade relations and pledged fealty to the emperor. He also requested permission to travel to Beijing (Peking), a trip he made in 1790. Meanwhile in December 1789 an imperial emissary presented him with confirmation as king of An Nam.[57]

Domestically Quang Trung did much for Vietnam. He was willing to work with capable individuals regardless of their past loyalties, and this attracted the best men to his service. He reorganized the army and carried out fiscal reforms. He also redistributed unused lands, mainly to peasants. He promoted crafts and trade, and he promoted education, stating that "to build a country, nothing is more important than educating the people".[58]

Quang Trung wanted to open trade with the West, and Western missionaries in the country at the time noted the fact that they were able to carry out their religious activities with more freedom than before. He was also the first Vietnamese leader to stress the importance of science, insisting that it be added to the Mandarinate examinations. He introduced a Vietnamese currency and insisted that *Nôm* be used exclusively rather than Chinese in court documents.

Unfortunately Quang Trung's reign was short. He died of an unknown illness in March or April 1792. Many Vietnamese believe that had he lived a decade longer their history would have developed quite differently. His son, Quang Toan, ascended the throne, but he was only ten years old. With the central power again weak, Vietnam again relapsed into civil war. In 1802 the surviving Nguyên lord, Nguyên Ánh, took power and established the Nguyên dynasty.[59]

Chapter Two

French Indo-China

Contacts between Vietnam and the West date from the second century. An archaeological site along the Mekong River has yielded Roman coins, some of them from the reign of Antonius Pius (138–61), and Chinese records note the arrival in 166 by sea in Giao Chi of merchants claiming to be emissaries of Emperor Marcus Aurelius on their way to the Han court.[1]

Later Europeans were attracted to Vietnam by the desire to secure trade, naval facilities, and religious converts. The first lasting contact between Vietnam and Europe resulted from the arrival in 1535 of Portuguese explorer and sea captain Antônio da Faria. His attempt to establish a major trading centre at the port village of Faifo (now Hôi An), about 15 miles south of present Đà Nẵng, floundered. The Portuguese labelled the area Caucichina, "Cauci" apparently derived from "Giao Chi", and for several centuries the West knew Vietnam as "Cochin China". Later the French used the term Cochin China to describe only the southern part of Vietnam in order to perpetuate the notion of a divided country.[2]

The Dutch established a rival trading post in Vietnam at Thăng Long (Hà Nôi) in 1636. The French established their first regular trading post in Vietnam in 1680 at Phô Hiên. The date for the first Catholic missionaries in Vietnam is uncertain, but the first permanent Catholic mission was established at Tourane (present-day Đà Nẵng) in 1615. Catholicism was soon flourishing.[3]

French priest Alexandre de Rhodes made Catholicism a cultural as well as a religious force. De Rhodes, who arrived in Vietnam in 1626, is generally credited with the creation of Quôc Ngú, the written Vietnamese language that uses the Latin alphabet and diacritical marks. Previously the Vietnamese wrote in the arcane Chinese ideographs. The French used Quôc Ngú in part

Gulf of Tonkin

1893

1883

1863

1858–1862

French conquest of Indo-China

1867

South China Sea

to eliminate the political and cultural influence of Vietnamese Confucian officials, whose power rested in their scholarship. But Quôc Ngú boomeranged against the French, for it eventually brought Western ideas of freedom and democracy.[4]

Gradually Indo-China attracted more French attention. French business interests supported Catholic missionary activity around the world, seeing in it a means of opening trade. Another French Catholic priest, Pierre Pigneau Béhaine (who subsequently enobled himself by adding "de" to Béhaine), played a key role in Vietnamese history in the late eighteenth century. Pigneau was appointed to Vietnam in 1767, but his stay there did not begin well, as his attempt to establish a seminary ended in failure. He was then appointed a bishop in the Middle East, but in 1775 he was back in Vietnam on Phú Quôc Island, where he allied himself with the surviving Nguyên lord Nguyên Phúc Ánh (Nguyên Ánh).

Pigneau experienced a serious setback when Nguyên Ánh was driven into exile in Siam following the 1785 Battle of Rach Gâm-Xoài Mút, but he vowed his support. Pigneau returned to France in 1787 and took with him Nguyên Ánh's seven-year-old son Nguyên Canh. The young boy, clad in exotic dress, caught the fancy of the French court at Versailles. But France was then in the midst of the great financial crisis that triggered the French Revolution of 1789 and, although Louis XVI promised support, no government aid was forthcoming for Pigneau's cause. On his return to Vietnam Pigneau stopped in India and there secured sufficient financial backing from French merchants to raise a force of 300–400 European mercenaries equipped with modern weapons, including field artillery.

Nguyên Ánh had, meanwhile, returned to Sài Gòn. No fool, he offered the mercenaries land in the Mekong Delta area that lay largely in Cambodia. Tây Són power had begun to crumble and many officers defected from them. In July 1789, as France began its Revolution, Nguyên Ánh's forces, trained and bolstered by the mercenaries, marched north. The two ships belonging to the mercenaries formed the basis of his navy and gave him control of the coast. At least one writer claims that the European military advisory group was the reason for the Nguyên victory.[5] Nguyên Ánh was also aided by disenchantment with the long and now oppressive Tây Són rule.

Pigneau did not live to see the victory. In poor health, he died in 1799 during the siege of Qui Nhón and was granted a hero's funeral. Nguyên Ánh attended and delivered a eulogy in which he asserted that the Vietnamese owed Pigneau an "eternal debt". His tomb near Sài Gòn has since disappeared.[6]

Siege of Qui Nhón

A Tây Són relief column was late in arriving there and Qui Nhón surrendered. In 1800 Tây Són general Trân Quang Diêu tried to retake the city,
establishing a naval blockade at the mouth of the Thi Nai River while his
infantry laid siege to the fortress. But Nguyên Ánh's ships destroyed the Tây
Són fleet. Instead of testing the Tây Són land forces at Qui Nhón, which he
judged too strong, Nguyên Ánh moved by land against the Tây Són capital of
Phú Xuân. It fell in 1801. Trân Quang Diêu meanwhile intensified his own
efforts to take Qui Nhón, which fell in 1802. From there he sent a relief
column to Phú Xuân, but it ran out of supplies and was unable to reach its
destination. At Tran Ninh Nguyên Ánh also defeated a force from the North.
He now controlled the three Tây Són capitals and all Vietnam from the Linh
Giang River to Gia Dinh.[7]

Having reunited Vietnam, in 1802 Nguyên Ánh crowned himself emperor
with the name of Gia Long at Phú Xuân, establishing the Nguyên dynasty.
The name Vietnam dates from 1803 when Nguyên envoys went to Peking to
establish diplomatic relations. They claimed the name of Nam Viêt (Nan
Yüeh). Reportedly the Chinese objected to the historical association with a
rebellious area of their empire and changed it to Viêt Nam. Although resented
at the time by the Vietnamese, the name of Vietnam ultimately gained
acceptance.[8]

Gia Long ruled until 1820. Vietnamese have criticized him for both
introducing foreigners into the country and mistreating those who had
brought him to power.[9] Although most of the European mercenaries were
already gone by his death they had introduced Western technological
advances in engineering and metallurgy. They also built a series of star-shaped
forts patterned after those designed by the great Vauban in France. The
imperial palace at Phú Xuân (Huê) is located inside one such large fort,
the sturdiness of which US troops would test in 1968. The influence of the
European mercenaries was short-lived, however; few settled on land grants,
and by the time of Gia Long's death in 1820 only two remained at Huê.[10]

Vietnamese–Siamese wars over Cambodia

Vietnam was also embroiled in Cambodia, where, as already noted, it had
long waged a struggle for predominance with Siam. By the end of the
eighteenth century, Vietnam had gained control of much of the Khmer state.
That struggle was renewed in the nineteenth century, during 1831–4. In

1831 a Siamese army under General P'ya Bodin invaded the country and defeated the Khmer in the Battle of Kompong Chang. Cambodian King Ang Chan fled to Vietnam, whereupon 15,000 Vietnamese troops, supported by a general Khmer uprising, forced the Siamese out. This left Vietnam in virtual control of Cambodia.[11]

The Vietnamese then divided Cambodia into three "residences" under the overall control of a Vietnamese chief resident at Oudong. The Vietnamese adopted the same sort of acculturation process that had been so successful against the Chams. This included the destruction of Cambodian temples, forced adoption of Vietnamese dress, and Vietnamese names for Cambodian cities and provinces. Finally Cambodian monarchs even lost their royal titles. Queen Ang Mey (1834–41) became virtually a prisoner in the Oudong palace and was known officially as "chief of the territory of My Lam".[12]

In 1841 the Cambodians, with encouragement from Siam, rebelled against Vietnam. This led to a savage war between Vietnam and Siam during 1841–5 in which the Siamese dominated. Finally both sides agreed to a compromise peace at the expense of the Cambodians. Vietnam and Siam then exercised joint rule over Cambodia, which continued until the establishment of a French protectorate there in 1863.[13]

Europeans were a more formidable danger to Vietnam than Siam. While Gia Long had welcomed Western military and technological assistance, he was not interested in advancing Christianity. His successors, Minh Mang (1820–41), Thiêu Tri (1841–7), and Tú Đúc (1848–83) shared Gia Long's attitude towards Catholicism, but they lacked his flexibility and understanding of Western strengths and weaknesses. Certainly they were much less successful than he in resisting pressure from the Western powers.

Having cut themselves off from contact with the West, the Vietnamese were unaware of substantial advances in Western military technology that had occurred while their own military remained fixed at late eighteenth-century levels. In fairness to the Vietnamese rulers, it should be pointed out that during Gia Long's reign the European powers were too embroiled in the Napoleonic Wars to pay much attention to Vietnam. It fell to his successors to confront reawakened European imperialism; Gia Long himself would probably have been little more successful in resisting it.[14]

Vietnamese rulers attacked Catholicism because they saw it as a threat to the Confucian concept of order and harmony. Royal concubines were a powerful source of opposition; they regarded Christian opposition to polygamy as a direct threat to their own position. Vietnamese official persecution, at least of foreign missionaries, was fairly mild and was designed to force the missionaries to quit the country. But these were passionate men committed to their cause. As a result, a number of them died and many more were exiled. Thousands of Vietnamese Christians also perished, with their overall number reduced by perhaps half. Catholics were not singled out, for the imperial court also persecuted Buddhists and Taoists, although perehaps not with the same intensity.

This attempt by the nineteenth-century Vietnamese emperors to root out Christianity provided an excuse for French intervention. France was in the midst of a considerable religious resurgence following the French Revolution and Napoleon's defeat, and Catholic missionaries who went to Asia in the 1820s aggressively pursued their proselytizing knowing that the French strongly supported it. Indeed, persecution of French missionaries in Vietnam during the reign of Emperor Minh Mang (1820–41) aroused considerable French popular outcry. Under French King Louis Philippe (1830–48) the government even granted the *Société des Missions Etrangères* a modest subsidy and free passage on French naval vessels.[15]

Of course missionary fervour was not the only factor pushing the French to intervene in Vietnam. French business interests hoped to challenge the British for the vast China trade. In 1842 Britain had obtained trading concessions in China and the port of Hong Kong; the French feared being left out. As a result, although he was more interested in restoring French prestige in Europe, in 1843 Premier François Guizot sent a sizeable squadron to the Far East under Admiral Cécille. Paris saw Vietnam chiefly as a means of accessing the China trade and hoped that France might be able to penetrate the Chinese interior by means of the Mekong River into Tibet and the Red River into Yunnan.

Alleged mistreatment of Catholic missionaries, however, provided the excuse for French intervention in Vietnam. This was encouraged by the activities of Catholic priest and missionary Dominique Lefèbvre, who had arrived in Vietnam in 1835, learned the language, and started converting Vietnamese. He and other French missionaries had also been intriguing on behalf of the Lê pretender to the throne. In 1845 Lefèbvre was arrested and sentenced to death, but from his prison at Huê he managed to smuggle out a message to Captain John Percival of the United States frigate *Constitution* at Tourane.

Percival informed Admiral Cécille of Lefèbvre's plight, and Cécille immediately sent a French warship to the rescue. On the arrival of Captain Fornier-Duplan and his warship the *Alcmène* at Tourane, Emperor Thiêu Tri not only released Lefèbvre but presented gifts to Fornier-Duplan. Thiêu Tri's intention, after all, was not to persecute foreign missionaries, but to pressure them and French warships to leave Vietnam.

For the Vietnamese court the matter did not end there, however. Lefèbvre once again provided the excuse for French armed intervention when in May

1846 he and another priest, Duclos, tried to re-enter Vietnam by bribing border guards. Promptly apprehended by the authorities, Lefèbvre was again sentenced to death. Historian John Cody contends that he died in prison the next month, but this view seems to be in the minority. In any case Cécille dispatched two warships, the *Gloire* and the *Victorieuse*, to Tourane, there to demand not only the release of the two priests but freedom of worship for Catholics in Vietnam. Captains Lapierre and Charles Rigault de Genouilly arrived at Tourane in the early spring of 1847.

Stages of French conquest

As a precaution, the two French captains demanded that Vietnamese vessels at Tourane be stripped of their sails. After several weeks of waiting for a reply, the French became impatient. On 15 April 1847, four Vietnamese vessels approached the French warships, shots were fired, and within about an hour three of the Vietnamese ships were sunk. The French then sailed away without ever finding out what had become of Lefèbvre. Admiral Cécille later admonished that in the future France should talk to Vietnam "only with guns".[16]

During Napoleon III's Second Empire (1852–70) Paris adopted a more militant policy towards furthering its interests in Asia. Defence of the Catholic Church was one of the pillars of Napoleon III's regime, especially because of the exhortations of his pious wife Eugenie. At Biarritz in the summer of 1857 she is alleged to have remarked regarding the persecution of Catholic missionaries in Vietnam: "Our martyrs must be avenged; this will be my war."[17] Louis Veuillot's Parisian daily *L'Univers* also championed intervention.[18] An entente with Great Britain made it possible.

In 1856 Leheur de Ville-sur-Arc arrived at Tourane with a protest from Paris over the executions of Catholics. When the court refused him any explanations, the French warship *Catinat* bombarded Tourane in retaliation.[19]

In mid-July 1857 Napoleon III decided to intervene in Indo-China. At the same time Admiral Rigault de Genouilly, who had distinguished himself at Sevastopol during the Crimean War, received command of French naval forces in Chinese waters. In a December 1857 joint operation the British and French took the port of Canton. They then attacked Tientsin, at which point the Chinese government agreed to open six ports to international trade under European control (formally conferred in the Treaty of Tientsin, 27 June 1858).

The success of operations in China freed the French squadron for employment in Indo-Chinese waters. Both Spain and France sought redress from Vietnam for the execution of missionaries, and Emperor Napoleon III hoped to secure a port there based on the model of Hong Kong.

It was no accident that the French chose to penetrate southern Vietnam first; it was the newest part of the country and its inhabitants were not as wedded to Vietnamese institutions. Indeed, the French conquest proved more difficult the farther it moved north.

In January 1858 instructions issued in Paris the previous November finally reached Rigault de Genouilly. Paris instructed him that while operations in Indo-China were to be only an appendix and entirely subordinate to those in China, he was to halt persecution and assure toleration of Catholics there. Paris thought this could best be achieved by occupying Tourane, mistakenly considered the key to the entire kingdom. Future Indo-China operations would be entirely at his discretion.[20]

On 31 August 1858, Rigault de Genouilly's squadron of 14 vessels carrying 3,000 men anchored off Tourane. He believed that decisive military action would bring fruitful negotiations with the Vietnamese; on 1 September he landed his men, including 300 Filipino troops sent by Spain. The invaders stormed Tourane's forts after only perfunctory Vietnamese resistance, taking them and the port. This inaugurated the first phase of the French conquest of Indo-China.

Within a few months heat, disease, and a lack of supplies forced the French from Tourane. Rigault de Genouilly shifted his attentions southward to the fishing village of Sài Gòn, selected because of its proximity, its promise as a deep-water port, and the fact that it could be important in controlling the southern rice trade. Sài Gòn fell to the French after a brief struggle on 17 February 1859. The French government subsequently criticized this attack, and Rigault de Genouilly then asked to be relieved of his command; Admiral Page replaced him in November 1859. Paris instructed Page not to seek territorial concessions but to sign a treaty that would guarantee religious liberties and French consuls in the major Vietnamese ports.[21]

Regardless, France continued to add to its holdings in southern Vietnam. Before Page could carry out his instructions he was ordered to China with his squadron. He left behind in Sài Gòn a garrison of 1,000 men. Almost immediately a Vietnamese force of 12,000 men besieged the French there. The siege lasted from March 1860 to January 1861, during which time the garrison was completely cut off from outside contact. With fighting in China concluded by the end of 1860, France was free to concentrate its Far Eastern resources in Indo-China. Admiral Charner and 3,000 troops soon arrived and, thanks to superior weaponry, relieved Sài Gòn in February 1861.

In 1862 Emperor Tú Đức, deprived of rice from the French-controlled South and facing a rebellion in the North under the leadership of a remote Lê dynasty descendant, was obliged to sign a treaty with France that provided for a 20 million-franc indemnity, three treaty ports in Annam and Tonkin, and French possession of the eastern provinces of Cochin China, including Sài Gòn. But Tú Đức had been successful in stirring up resistance to the French and, despite the treaty, guerrilla activity continued for some time.[22]

France's holdings in Indo-China expanded by fits and starts, often with little or no initiative on the part of Paris. By 1867 the French had conquered all of Cochin China, but they had also learned that the Mekong was not navigable to the interior of China.

The Franco–German War of 1870–71 temporarily put a stop to French imperialism in the Far East, but soon the process began anew, propelled by the French desire to recoup overseas the power and prestige they had lost in Europe. In the 1870s the French turned their attention to northern Vietnam, where Emperor Tú Đức's hold was weak. The French hoped that, unlike the Mekong, the Red River might offer a viable commercial route to the Chinese interior.

The 1873 seizure of Hà Nôi by Francis Garnier is indicative of French imperialist activity. As a Navy lieutenant Garnier had led one of imperialism's high adventures, the 1866–7 expedition up the Mekong that had determined the river was not navigable past the waterfalls at the Lao–Cambodian border. He then returned to France, taking a credible role in the Siege of Paris and the Commune. In 1872 he resigned from the service and went to Paris as a businessman. In 1873 Governor of Cochin China Admiral M. J. Dupré recruited him to lead a small force to Hà Nôi in order to extricate French arms dealer and merchant Jean Dupuis and to negotiate freedom of navigation on the Red River.[23]

With the British making inroads into Burma, the French feared that they would beat them to the Chinese province of Yunnan from that direction. Dupuis had, in fact, discovered that the Red River was navigable all the way from the Tonkin Gulf to Yunnan and that salt in the latter location sold for 30 times its price in Hà Nôi. Indeed, he had gotten into trouble with Vietnamese authorities by endeavouring to ship salt from Vietnam to China; its export was forbidden by Vietnamese law. When the authorities tried to put a stop to this, Dupuis and his Chinese mercenaries seized a portion of Hà Nôi and appealed to Admiral Dupré for assistance.

Although he was under orders from Paris not to intervene in Tonkin, Dupré hoped that resolving the crisis by sending Garnier to evict Dupuis might bring concessions from Tú Đức. Garnier set out for Hà Nôi with perhaps 180 men in three small ships. But once he reached Hà Nôi he joined forces with Dupuis.

Convinced of Tú Đúc's weakness there, Garnier dropped all pretence of negotiation and on 15 November 1873, simply declared the Red River open for international trade. He also ordered that all Vietnamese customs tariffs be replaced by more favourable rates. On 20 November, after receiving some reinforcements from Sài Gòn, Garnier and his men stormed the Hà Nôi citadel. He then resolved to take all Tonkin, attacking the major forts in the Red River Delta between Hà Nôi and the coast. At the end of three weeks he had captured Nam Đinh. His adventure ended, however, when he was killed on 21 December 1873, in an engagement near Hà Nôi. Although the French government soon repudiated Garnier's actions, Tú Đúc's prestige suffered irreparably, and in March 1874 Dupré secured a treaty with Hué that recognized French control of Cochin China and secured concessions in Hà Nôi and Hai Phòng.[24]

French operations against China

French gains in Tonkin alarmed China. Vietnam was, after all, still its tributary state, and the Chinese were concerned about the increasing French presence along their southwestern frontier. When Tú Đúc appealed to the emperor to intervene, the Chinese proceeded to contest French control of Vietnam. This led to the Black Flag or Tonkin Wars.[25]

Following the great 1864 Taiping rebellion in China many Chinese armed bands had sought refuge in Tonkin. The French called them "pirates", which they certainly were. They were known as the White, Yellow, and Black Flags for the colours flown by each section and officer, but only the Black Flags submitted to the authority of the Huê court. The Vietnamese extended recognition to the Black Flags because the latter helped control the Montagnards to the northeast of the Red River Delta. In 1865 Liu Yung-fu, self-proclaimed leader of the Black Flags, established a base at the strategically located town of Son Tay on the Red River.[26] Although illiterate, Liu Yung-fu was a capable leader and his Black Flags enjoyed support from the Chinese armed forces in Guangxi and Yunnan.[27]

When some 1,500 Chinese regular troops reinforced the 3,000 Black Flags at Són Tây the French grew concerned about their own small garrisons in Hà Nôi and Hai Phòng. In March 1882 French authorities in Sài Gòn dispatched 233 French marines and Vietnamese auxiliaries under Navy Captain Henri Rivière to Tonkin. Despite orders to the contrary, Rivière

31

proceeded to repeat Garnier's action and storm the Hà Nôi citadel. The French then sent reinforcements to Hai Phòng; Rivière, meanwhile, was killed in a Black Flag ambush outside Hà Nôi.

As news of these events reached Paris the Third Republic voted 5.5 million francs to support operations in Tonkin and despatched 3,000 reinforcements. The French sent a naval force up the Perfume River, seized forts guarding access to Huê, and forced the court there to sign a treaty establishing a French protectorate over Vietnam. In December 1883 600 French troops, including a Foreign Legion battalion, attacked and took the Black Flag base at Són Tây. As a result the Chinese reinforced Băc Ninh, which they believed to be the next French target. On 12 March 1884, however, they abandoned it to the French after only minimal resistance. Two months later the Chinese agreed to withdraw entirely from Tonkin.[28]

The fighting should have ended at this point, but in June 1884 the French sent troops to occupy Lang Són, the closest major Tonkinese town to the Chinese frontier. At Băc Lê, 30 miles short of their goal, the French ran into Chinese troops. Accounts differ on the reason for the clash, but the French were repulsed at the cost of 22 dead and 60 wounded.[29]

French Premier Jules Ferry (1883–5) was still determined to see France victorious in Tonkin. Ferry, who became known as "Le Tonkinois" for his support of imperialism in Indo-China, reportedly hoped that France might one day exchange part of an expanded overseas empire for Alsace and Lorraine, lost to Germany in the Franco–German War. Unfortunately for the French, they divided their forces between China and Vietnam and so weakened their impact. They made their main military effort in Tonkin, where in the spring of 1884 they had 9,000 men. By the summer of 1885 this force had grown to 40,000. Under the aggressive Generals Louis-Alexandre Brière de l'Isle and François de Négrier the French spent most of the spring and summer of 1884 clearing the Red River Delta. In relatively easy fighting they managed to push deep into the northwest highlands.

The Black Flags and Chinese regulars, on the other hand, enjoyed a number of advantages in fighting the French – they were far more numerous and for the most part much better armed. They had Remington, Spencer, Martini-Henry, and Winchester repeating rifles, whereas the French carried only the single-shot 1874 model Gras rifle. The Black Flags also excelled at building defensive works.

Vietnam's Chinese allies preferred to fight defensively and built excellent fortifications, although these tended to be badly sited. While courageous and well disciplined, the Chinese were often badly led. They had artillery but they seldom used it, and they were very poor marksmen, preferring not to fire their rifles from the shoulder in aimed fire. In the end the Black Flag/

Chinese predeliction for taking the defence gave the initiative to the attacking French.

Led by aggressive officers, the French used light artillery or dynamite to blast holes in their enemies' bamboo palisades and, although outnumbered by four or even five to one, they employed bayonet charges to rout the defenders. But because the French lacked sufficient manpower to surround the fortresses, most surviving defenders escaped to fight again.

Both sides gave little quarter. The Chinese dug up French corpses to cut off the heads and place them on lances or flag poles. This led the French to slaughter their prisoners. In spite of all this the French won a series of relatively easy victories, which led to a false sense of confidence, an under-estimation of their enemy, and an overextension of their assets.[30]

In early autumn 1884 Chinese regulars from Yunnan reinforced Liu Yung-fu's Black Flags. Liu Yung-fu then positioned much of his force around the town of Tuyên Quang on the Clear River northwest of Hà Nôi. That November Lieutenant Colonel Duchesne led some 700 legionnaires and marines supported by gunboats up the river to Tuyên Quang. Forced to fight their way through a Chinese position, they made it to the town safely. The column departed on 23 November, leaving behind a garrison of 619 men commanded by Major Marc Edmond Dominé. The Chinese then closed in.[31] The French had, meanwhile, pushed the Chinese from Bac Ninh to Bac Le. They might have gone on to take Lang Són to the north had it not been for the necessity of relieving Tuyên Quang, a shortage of manpower, and the insistence of Paris that operations be restricted to the Red River Delta. Things changed in January 1885 with a new French minister of war and the arrival in Tonkin of French reinforcements, including two battalions of legionnaires. French commander General Brière de l'Isle struck north to clear the "Mandarin Road" to Lang Són.

On 3 February 1885, 12 battalions totalling some 9,000 men set out. The French soon encountered a succession of Chinese fortifications. Following an initial headlong encounter they discovered that flanking manoeuvres forced the Chinese from their positions and proved much less costly. On 12 February a desperate fight occurred at Bac Viay, the last defensive position before Lang Són, that cost 200 French casualties. With only their rifles and cartridges, most of the Chinese managed to escape the French soldiers, who were encumbered with heavy packs.

On 13 February the French raised the tricolour over Lang Són. Its square-walled citadel fell without a fight. On the 23rd the French marched out of Lang Són to force the Chinese from Đông Đăng, a settlement ten miles to the north, next to the Chinese border. There the French again prevailed as the Chinese fled through the narrow "Gate of China" across the border.[32]

General Brière de l'Isle left General de Négrier in command at Lang Són while he marched south to deal with Tuyên Quang. In the history of the French Foreign Legion, the three-month siege there is as important as the 1863 Battle of Camerone, Mexico. Militarily Tuyên Quang was of dubious importance, but politically it could be immense and the Chinese regulars and Black Flags who invested that place in December 1884 probably saw it as an opportunity to inflict a great psychological defeat on the French. Virtually indefensible, the town was dominated by wooded hills; its square citadel on the banks of the Clear River was barely 300 yards on a side. Major Dominé's garrison numbered just 13 officers and 619 men, nearly two-thirds of whom were legionnaires, the remainder being *tirailleurs tonkinois* (Tonkin riflemen).

On 16 January the Chinese began digging lines around Tuyên Quang, which were completed four days later. On the night of 26–7 January the Chinese launched a massive assault but were beaten back, losing perhaps 100 soldiers. The attackers then opted for more conventional siege tactics of snaking trenches towards the French lines. During the day they built fascines – bundles of sticks used to shore up parapets – and sniped at the French positions. At night they advanced their saps forward while firing at the French.

On 3 February a Vietnamese escaped from Tuyên Quang to take word of the situation to the French authorities at Hà Nôi. Five days later the Chinese employed artillery for the first time; soon they also used heavy mortars. On the 12th the Chinese blew a large mine beneath the French lines and attempted to exploit the breech, only to be beaten back. A French sortie the next day destroyed some of the Chinese advance works, but on the 22nd the Chinese again detonated a series of mines under the French lines. The next day the Chinese launched another futile assault. On the 25th the process was repeated: a mine explosion followed by an infantry assault.

By 1 March the French had only 180 working rifles to defend a perimeter of 1,200 yards. That day the French heard firing in the distance and assumed it to be a relief force, but they were too exhausted to break out. On the 2nd the Chinese fire increased, causing the garrison to fear it would be overwhelmed before relief could arrive. But on the 3rd the French awoke to find the Chinese gone. The reason was soon apparent: General Brière de l'Isle's relief column had arrived. Leaving Lang Són on 16 February, it defeated a Chinese force at Hoa Mac in what turned out to be the bloodiest battle for the French in Tonkin since their 1883 invasion.[33]

A series of French reversals followed. In late March, seemingly on the brink of defeat a month earlier, the Chinese attacked. Apparently convinced that the

French were going to invade Quangxi, they struck in force. On the 29th the Chinese retook Lang Són and began to organize thousands of Vietnamese volunteers. Already the Tonkin campaign of 1884–5 was one of the more controversial episodes in the history of the Third Republic, and Premier Ferry's opponents used the defeat at Lang Són to drive him from office. Georges Clemenceau, later premier himself during a most difficult military test for France, accused Ferry of "treason" for bogging France down in Vietnam.[34]

An armistice was declared in April before Chinese forces could capitalize on their success at Lang Són. This was largely as a consequence of French naval operations against China proper. In 1884, at the start of fighting, Paris had ordered Admiral Amédée Anatole Courbet to threaten the Chinese naval base at Fuzhou (Foo Chow) and to occupy the coal-mining port of Keelung in Formosa. Courbet complied and in October 1884 French warships bombarded Keelung. The French troops were also sent but these soon had to be re-embarked.

Courbet then moved against Foo Chow on the Min River. Passage to the base was protected by two strongly fortified narrows and Courbet was unable to use his two armoured cruisers because of their draught, leaving him with five unarmoured cruisers, three gunboats, and two small torpedo craft. The Chinese had 11 ships (two cruisers) as well as junks and fireships, but these were sharply inferior to the French, whose strongest vessels were ironclads. Within an hour all Chinese ships were either sunk or on fire and drifting. Courbet estimated Chinese casualties at 2,000–3,000 men and put his own "cruel losses" at 10 dead and 48 wounded.

After blowing up the docks and shelling the arsenal, the French steamed for the open sea. In a three-day progression they methodically destroyed the Chinese barrier forts. Courbet then took his squadron to Keelung to avenge the earlier repulse there. The French Formosa campaign of 1884–5 was largely unsuccessful and a waste of meagre resources. At Keelung the French sank a Chinese frigate. They also sent ashore 1,800 men to occupy the port and a neighbouring harbour; but even with reinforcements this landing force was completely inadequate.

It was not the French military presence on Formosa but rather their naval interdiction of the seaborne rice trade between Formosa and the mainland that caused China to seek peace. On 9 June 1885, France and China signed the Treaty of Tientsin. Under its terms China renounced its suzerainty over Vietnam and recognized the French protectorate there. Both Chinese regular troops and Black Flags retired behind the Chinese border.[35]

French Indo-China

In 1887 Paris formed its conquests into French Indo-China. Laos was added in 1893, after the Siamese had been bluffed into withdrawing their outposts on the left bank of the Mekong and the French had offered protection to the king of Luang Prabang.[36] Technically only Cochin China was an outright colony; the others were merely protectorates. The French left the emperor as a symbol at Huê, although those emperors who proved difficult were removed. The reality was that French officials made all the key decisions. In overall control was a governor-general, responsible to the minister of colonies in Paris.

Guerrilla warfare continued for a time. In July 1885 Vietnamese nationalists acting in the name of Emperor Hàm Nghi led a brief rebellion, launching a major attack on the French at the fort of Mang Cá near the capital. This failed, whereupon Hàm Nghi fled to Quang Tri Province and called for a national uprising against the French. Many responded, beginning what is known to Vietnamese as the Phong Trào Cân Vúóng (Supporting the King Movement). However, Hàm Nghi was betrayed to the French and captured in 1888. He was sent into exile in Algeria, where he died in 1947.[37]

Đê Thám led another another long uprising against the French. Initially centring his activities in Băc Giang province, from 1886 Đê Thám expanded his activities into Thái Nguyên and Húng Hóa Provinces. In 1896 the French sent Colonel Joseph Galliéni against him, with only partial success. The next year the French agreed to create an autonomous zone containing 22 villages in the Phôn Xúóng area in return for the disarmament of Thám's group. But Đê Thám did not disarm, and in 1905 he expanded his activities and established the Nghia Húng Party.

During the next eight years his forces battled the French and inflicted serious losses on them. But in March 1913 Đê Thám was assassinated by one of his associates, a Vietnamese working for the French. Although his followers tried to continue the struggle, the movement soon collapsed. Đê Thám remained a revered figure to Vietnamese nationalists, and during the Indo-China War Viêt Minh offensives in the first half of 1951 were named for him.[38]

The period of French rule in Indo-China was very influential in Vietnamese history, as fateful for the country as the 1,000 years of Chinese domination. French policy was quixotic, however, vacillating between "assimilation" and "association". Assimilation built on the principles of the French Revolution of 1789 that professed the universality of French civilization. It attempted to bridge the gap between humanitarianism and the actualities of French colonial rule. It was bound up in the French term *mission civilisatrice* (civilizing mission), a kind of generous cultural imperialism that suggested the French government should undertake to make the colonies a carbon-copy of France in institutions and in culture. Its influence was strongest in the late nineteenth century when, as Joseph Buttinger has noted, many Frenchmen regarded their country's overseas possessions as "distant suburbs of Paris".[39] But many anthropologists and sociologists came to the conclusion that, desirable or not, assimilation was in fact impossible. It also failed in practice.

By 1905 the policy of association held sway. It held that France should work with native leaders and concentrate on economic policies (economic exploitation), leaving cultural patterns largely untouched. Among its proponents were Pierre Paul Leroy-Beaulieu, editor of *L'Economiste française*, and Jules Ferry. Associationists held that what really mattered was the volume of trade. They were also convinced that Franco–native co-operation was possible. After the Russo–Japanese War (1904–5) the idea of association also gained the support of some military men, who believed that Japan was bent on controlling South Asia. This group included such French Army officers as Joseph Gallieni and Louis Hubert Lyautey. Some even proposed using natives in colonial armies.[40]

French administration in Indo-China was haphazard. Third Republic France saw frequent cabinet changes, governments lasting on the average only about six months. Ministers of colonies in Paris and governors-general came and went at an alarming rate, and with each change came subtly different policies. Many governors-general had little or no Indo-China experience and their policies were often blocked by career functionaries who better understood the system. Also, Indo-China did not attract the most capable civil servants, and many of those assigned there never bothered to learn the local language.

The French believed in government from the top down. They installed their officials at all levels and their personal salaries ate up the relatively small colonial budget. Little was left for education or public works.

The justice system was poorly run. French judges tried to administer the law but, not knowing the language, they often relied on Vietnamese interpreters, many of whom were all too easily corrupted. In education even after World War I only some 10 per cent of Vietnamese of school age were attending Franco–Vietnamese schools and as late as 1940 there were only 14 secondary schools in all of Vietnam and a single university at Hà Nôi. This produced a talented but very small native elite cut off from their roots and aspiring to positions of influence that were closed to them by the colonial regime. Frustration ultimately drove many of them against France.

The small French community of 40,000 to 50,000 people dominated the economy of what was France's richest colony. Europeans controlled metallurgial extraction, as well as textile and rubber production. The Chinese tended to be active in retailing, banking, and the rice trade. Native Vietnamese aspirations were largely restricted to landowning, where 3 to 5 per cent of the population owned about half of the land. The French had large land holdings, particularly in the South. Renters had to pay sums equivalent to half the crop yields.

Even by 1940 peasants still constitued some 90 per cent of the population. Their lot was particularly hard and at best little affected under the French, who failed to introduce new farming techniques. High rents worked against the peasantry and produced a cycle of poverty. Chronically in debt, the peasants were barely able to satisfy their own immediate needs, and this only in good harvest years. Many could find only part-time work.

Conditions on the rubber plantations reflected the horrible conditions in which millions of Vietnamese laboured. Watched by their French colonial masters, workers toiled from dawn until after sunset, lived in squalor, and were frequently beaten, even killed, by sadistic overseers. This hardly mattered to those in charge; replacements were readily availiable.[41]

All of this, of course, provided grist for the nationalist mill. At the turn of the century nationalist hopes were raised by the Russo–Japanese War of 1904–5, when for the first time in modern history an Asian power defeated a European power, and by the Allied victory in World War I, when President Woodrow Wilson of the United States called for the self-determination of peoples. But at the Paris Peace Conference following the war Vietnamese patriots and other Third World nationalists, including the Chinese in the case of Shantung (Shandong), soon learned that "self determination of peoples" did not apply to them. Rejected by the West in their quest for a peaceful transition to self-rule, Vietnamese nationalists turned to force.

Moderate Vietnamese nationalists after World War I took as their model the Chinese Nationalists. Their organization, the Viêt Nam Quôc Dân Đang (Vietnam National Party, or VNQDD), sought an end to French rule and the establishment of a republican form of government. The VNQDD led premature uprisings in 1930–31, notably at Yên Bái. The French easily crushed these revolts, but they had the long-term effect of opening the way for the more militant Indo-Chinese Communist Party (ICP). A number of small Communist parties had sprung into being in Vietnam after World War I.

Hô Chí Minh became the foremost nationalist figure of modern Vietnam. Born Nguyên Sinh Cung in 1890 at Kim Lien in Nghê An Province in northern Annam and later renamed Nguyên Tât Thành, he attended Vietnam's best high school, the Lycée Quôc Hoc at Huê, but he left Vietnam at age 19 as a cook on a merchant ship. He lived in London for a time and in 1917 was in Paris, where he took the name of Nguyên Ai Quôc (Nguyên the Patriot). Later he was known as Hô Chí Minh ("He who enlightens"). He became active in the Vietnamese community in Paris, which had grown during the war, and in 1919 appealed to the leaders of the great powers at the Paris Peace Conference for the extension of self-determination to the peoples of Indo-China. As a member of the French Socialist Party, Hô voted with the majority at the 1920 party conference at Tours to form the French Communist Party. He became its expert on colonial affairs and spent the remainder of the 1920s in the Soviet Union and China. At Hong Kong in 1930 Hô helped carry out a fusion of three Vietnamese Communist parties into what became the Indo-Chinese Communist Party (ICP). By World War II the ICP was the dominant nationalist force in Vietnam.[42]

The impact of World War II

World War II brought the Japanese to Vietnam. Japan had already been at war with China since 1937 and was anxious to take advantage of Germany's victory over France to secure bases in Indo-China from which to strike the Burma Road and prevent supplies from reaching the Chinese. Governor General of Indo-China General Georges Catroux, who came to be one of the outstanding advocates of a liberal policy towards nationalism in the colonies, had virtually no bargaining power in dealing with the Japanese.

In the summer of 1940 Tokyo demanded the closing of the Sino–Vietnamese border and an end to transportation of war materials from Indo-China to the Chinese government at Chungking. Catroux tried to stall for time, but Japanese demands coincided with the French military defeat and replacement of the Third Republic with the Vichy government. With the British and US governments unwilling to help, Catroux had to accept Tokyo's demand for the right to move troops across Tonkin to south China and to organize a control commission to oversee French compliance. Catroux hoped to use the rainy season to strengthen his forces with US assistance, then deal with the Japanese.

Catroux's protest against the armistice between the French government and the Germans and his independence of action in dealing with the Japanese led the Vichy government to replace him with commander of naval forces in the Far East Vice Admiral Jean Decoux. No more able to resist Tokyo than his predecessor, Decoux on 24 September 1940 granted Japan the right to build three airfields and to station 6,000 men in Tonkin. Despite an agreement that their first troops would come by sea, the Japanese moved the 5th Division of the Twenty-Second Army in by land. On the morning of 24 September French and Japanese units clashed in northern Tonkin at Lang Són, Đông Đăng, and other forts. Lang Són surrendered after two days of fighting, and a day later all French resistance ended.[43]

Thailand took advantage of this situation to wage an undeclared war with France. The Thais began the conflict, which lasted from November 1940 to January 1941, to regain the three rich rice-growing provinces of Battambang, Siemréap, and Sisophon, which had been annexed in 1862 from Cambodia but were lost when the French had forced the Thais to restore them to Cambodia in 1907. Thailand also claimed territory in Laos, the return of which the French had secured in 1904. Although in early June 1940 Thailand concluded a non-aggression pact with France, after Germany defeated France the Thais lost interest in ratifying it. The pro-Japanese military government of Marshal Pibul Songgram (which had renamed the country Thailand) believed there was no better time to reassert its claims.

In 1939 the Thai Army numbered some 27,000 men. The Air Force and Navy had some 400 planes, including 93 delivered by Japan in December 1940, but many were not combat types. The Navy had a British-built World War I destroyer, two small gunboats, eight motor torpedo boats (MTB), and several royal yachts. Italy supplied nine small torpedo boats, two mine-sweepers, and nine minelayers. In addition, Japan delivered two armoured coast defence anti-aircraft vessels, four small submarines, two escort/training ships, and three small torpedo boats. The older ships were of limited fighting value, the modern Italian torpedo boats were too flimsy for service in rough seas, and the submarines could not dive. Also, most sailors were poorly trained.

The French Army in Indo-China numbered 50,000 men, but 38,000 of these were native troops of questionable loyalty. The heart of the French military presence was the 5,000-man 5th Foreign Legion Regiment. The French had 30 World War I vintage tanks and most of their artillery was equally outdated; they were also short of artillery ammunition. Their Air Force had fewer than 100 planes and the French Navy had in Indo-Chinese waters only a light cruiser (*La Motte-Picquet*), two gunboats, two sloops, two auxiliary patrol craft, and several non-combatant types. Most of the warships were old, poorly armed, and suffered from mechanical problems.

In mid-November 1940 the Thais sent military units across the Mekong River into eastern Cambodia. These incursions led to skirmishes with the French, who were temporarily sidetracked by an ICP uprising in Cochin China on 23 November that the French crushed in the first week of December. French High Commissioner Admiral Jean Decoux decided to answer the Thais on both land and sea. The French land offensive began on 16 January 1941, when a mixed French brigade attacked Thai positions at Yang Dom Koum. This effort failed for lack of manpower and heavy weapons. The Thais, who had planned an attack for the same day, then counter-attacked. Their offensive, supported by tanks, was beaten back by legionnaires with grenades. Although Bangkok claimed a major victory, both sides withdrew from the immediate area.

The French Navy planned attacks on the Thai Navy detachment at Koh Chang and their principal navy base at Sattahib. The initial strike was carried out by virtually the entire French flotilla: the cruiser, two gunboats, and two sloops. On 16 January this force sailed for the Gulf of Siam to attack Koh Chang, which guarded the passage to Sattahib. The French surprised the Thais early on the morning of 17 January and in the ensuing 90-minute action sank two Thai torpedo boats and a coast defence vessel and mortally damaged another. The French task force escaped with no direct hits or losses and returned to Sài Gòn on the 19th.

There was little air action during the war, although the Thais did use their Curtiss Hawk III biplanes in a dive-bombing role. The French had a plan, not implemented, to fire-bomb Bangkok from the air.

As it turned out, the French triumph at Koh Chang was short-lived. The Japanese applied diplomatic pressure and threatened to intervene on the Thai side. On 31 January they forced the French to sign an armistice at Sài Gòn aboard their cruiser the *Natori*. Also under pressure from Germany, the Vichy government in March accepted Japanese mediation. Negotiations were held in Japan, and on 9 May 1941, in Tokyo, France and Thailand signed a peace treaty whereby France transferred to Thailand three Cambodian and two Laotian provinces on the right bank of the Mekong, in all some 42,000 square miles of territory.

The Franco–Thai War had little lasting effect. In September 1945, when the French reintroduced their forces into Indo-China, the Thais agreed to return the territories and accept the Mekong River as the boundary between their country and Laos and Cambodia. That the issue remained unsettled was evidenced by border skirmishes along the Mekong River (1946), and in clashes between Thailand and Laos (May 1987 through February 1988).[44]

Events in Vietnam worked to help bring about US entry into World War II. In July 1941 Japan expanded its presence in the region by moving into southern Indo-China. This placed her long-range bombers within striking distance of Malaya, the Dutch East Indies, and the Philippines. Alarmed by this development and endeavouring to force Japan to withdraw, the United States, Great Britain, and the Netherlands imposed an embargo on scrap iron and oil on Japan. At this, Tokyo opted for war against the United States.[45]

Soon Japan had 35,000 troops in Indo-China, although the Japanese left local administration in French hands and made no concessions to the Vietnamese nationalists. But the French had suffered a devastating loss of face. It was clear to the Vietnamese that an Asian power had humilated their European masters.

During World War II the Communists opposed both the French and Japanese. In November 1940 the ICP had staged a revolt in southern Vietnam that was crushed by the French military. In May 1941 Hô and his leading lieutenants met at Pǎc Bó in far north Tonkin and formed the Viêt Nam Ðôc Lâp Ðông Minh Hôi (League for Independence of Vietnam), commonly known as the Viêt Minh. According to Hô this national front was to organize the masses to resist both French colonial rule and the occupying Japanese. The ICP provided the bulk of the Viêt Minh leadership, but in a deliberate tactical move its founders played down class revolution in favour of national liberation in order to involve as many Vietnamese as possible, regardless of class, in the national struggle. Anti-colonialism, patriotism, and nationalism were the only prerequisites for membership.[46]

Chinese Nationalist support for the Viêt Minh vacillated, but the latter established base areas along the border with Tonkin in Nationalist-controlled Kwangsi Province. Led by Võ Nguyên Giáp, small numbers of Viêt Minh commandos established themselves in Tonkin, and by 1942 the Viêt Minh had numerous bases there. At the end of 1944 larger Viêt Minh units arrived from south China.

During World War II the US Office of Strategic Services (OSS) provided support. It gave the Viêt Minh small arms, communications equipment, and medical supplies. Eventually it provided instructors to train the Viêt Minh for warfare against the Japanese. US personnel, one of whom probably saved Hô's life during a serious illness, did not conceal their admiration for the Viêt Minh and assured them of Washington's support for their plans for independence from France. After all, President Franklin Roosevelt's Atlantic Charter emphasized self-determination for all peoples. The Viêt Minh, for its part, provided intelligence on the Japanese and helped rescue downed Allied pilots.[47]

By 1943 the French came to view the Viêt Minh as a serious threat to the colonial government. The Viêt Minh had gained control of much of the three northernmost provinces of Cao Bǎng, Bǎc Can, and Lang Són. The French did what they could to disrupt Viêt Minh activities, including the destruction of weapons and food caches, but by early 1945 the Viêt Minh controlled much of northern Tonkin.[48]

Allied victory in World War II now appeared imminent, and the French in Indo-China grew accordingly restive, determined to liberate themselves. Although Japanese forces at the time were slightly outnumbered by those of France, some 55,000 to 60,000 men, they had more combat troops: 35,000 as opposed to 30,000 men. Also with French plans an open secret, partly because of the antipathy between Vichy and Gaullist factions, the Japanese struck first. In a well-planned action on 9 March 1945, they arrested virtually all French administrators and military personnel in Indo-China. Only those troops on manoeuvre and a few who eluded the carefully prepared Japanese attack escaped. Eventually 5,000 of them under Lieutenant General Gabriel Sabattier managed to make their way 600 miles to south China and refuge. Tokyo exacerbated the situation by granting Vietnam its independence, which was proclaimed on 11 March by Bao Đai, who for the previous decade had been the French-controlled emperor of Annam and had spent the war years at Huê.[49]

When Japan surrendered Hô Chí Minh stepped into the vacuum. On 16 August at Hà Nôi he declared himself president of the provisional government of a "free Vietnam". On the 19th the Viêt Minh seized power in Hà Nôi. Bao Đai abdicated, and on the 24th in Sài Gòn Trân Văn Giàu declared the insurrection underway in the South. Hô convened his first cabinet meeting at Hà Nôi on 27 August, at which time it was decided to fix 2 September as National Independence Day. On that day Hô publicly announced the formation of a "Provisional Government of the Democratic Republic of Vietnam" (DRV) with its capital at Hà Nôi. In a clear bid to widen his base at home and win Western support abroad, on 11 November Hô dissolved the ICP.

World War II marked the end of European colonialism. French leaders, however, ignored this historic cue. Although before the end of the war the French government had declared its intention to make concessions and grant more freedom to Indo-China, Paris would still retain ultimate authority. The result was a missed opportunity for an orderly transition to self-rule and a close relationship between France and Vietnam. The war itself was the principal reason why Paris refused to compromise. Weakened by the war, France relied on her empire to allow her to be counted among the great powers in the post-war era.

At the end of the war there were perhaps 70,000 Japanese troops in Indo-China. According to the July 1945 Potsdam agreements the British were to take their surrender south of the 16th parallel, while Chinese Nationalist troops did the same north of that line. The French were to have no role in these operations. The British sent 5,000 troops of the 20th Indian Division. On his own initiative General Douglas Gracey, British commander in the South who detested the Viêt Minh, rearmed some 1,400 French soldiers who had been imprisoned by the Japanese. Clashes soon occurred as French, British and Japanese troops crushed Việt Minh resistance in Sài Gòn. Paris, meanwhile, sent out reinforcements to re-establish its control over southern Vietnam, Cambodia and Laos.

The Chinese sent 150,000 to 200,000 men into the North. These proceeded to bleed the region of its resources. During 16–22 September 1945, the DRV government organized *Tuần Lễ Vàng* (Gold Week), appealing to the people to turn in gold and other valuables so that the government might purchase arms from the Chinese. In fact much of the money went to bribe the Chinese commander in Hà Nôi General Lu Han and his staff to assist Hô and his supporters.[50]

Meanwhile in the Franco–Chinese Accords of 28 February 1946, the French finally secured a Chinese withdrawal from the North in return for yielding certain concessions in China. The Chinese departed in March 1946.[51]

The French military build-up in Indo-China was relatively slow. In June 1945 Provisional President of the French Republic Charles de Gaulle had appointed General Jacques Philippe de Hauteclocque Leclerc to command the French Expeditionary Corps to restore French sovereignty there.[52]

Leclerc was a wise appointment; another was not. On 15 August de Gaulle replaced General Sabattier with monk-turned-admiral Georges Thierry d'Argenlieu as high commissioner for Indo-China. In the first months after the war virtually the entire French political spectrum supported the effort to re-establish French sovereignty in Indo-China.[53]

After representing France in the formal Japanese surrender, Leclerc arrived in Sài Gòn on 5 October. He soon reached an agreement with the British that preserved France's position in southern Vietnam and on 25 October he began the reconquest of Indo-China for France, predicting that it would take about a month for "mopping-up operations". Leclerc's highly mobile mechanized forces quickly established French authority over southern Vietnam and Cambodia. In October French troops marched into Phnom Penh, where the Cambodian premier had declared the independence of his country a month earlier. He was shipped off to France as an "enemy collaborator". French control over Laos was not re-established until April and May 1946, when Vietniane and Luang Prabang respectively were re-occupied.

But with only 40,000 men the French controlled little beyond the cities and main routes of communication; even by March 1946 Leclerc had only 50,000 men. Unlike most of his compatriots, he was aware of the great difficulties of jungle warfare and favoured negotiations for a political rather than military solution. This would mean abandoning the attempt to create an independent Cochin China. Convinced that the Việt Minh was a nationalist movement that France could not subdue militarily, Leclerc pressed the French representative in the North, Jean Sainteny, to secure an agreement with Hô, whose government controlled Hà Nôi and Hai Phòng. In a secret report to Paris on 27 March Leclerc said there would be no solution through force in Indo-China.[54]

On 6 January 1946, Hô carried out elections in the northern part of the country. Although these were not free, there could be no doubt that Hô had won. The government was Communist-dominated but included anti-Communist nationalists because Hô still hoped for US recognition and aid. The country was devastated by the war; in the North the dikes were in poor repair from neglect and Allied bombing, and much of the population there was starving. US support was not forthcoming, however; and Hô was forced to deal with France.[55]

On 6 March 1946, Hô signed an agreement with French representative Sainteny to set the future relationship between the DRV and France. Ignored by the United States, far from the Soviet Union, and under pressure from China, the DRV leadership agreed to a French military presence in the North. France was allowed to introduce 15,000 French and 10,000 Vietnamese troops under unified French command to protect French lives and property, but Paris promised to withdraw 3,000 of its troops each year. All were to be withdrawn by the end of 1951, with the possible exception of those guarding bases.

In return France recognized the DRV as a "free state with its own government, parliament, army and finances, forming part of the Indo-Chinese Federation of the French Union".[56] In a key provision France also agreed to the holding of a referendum in the South to see if it wanted to join the DRV in a unified state, but no date for the vote was specified. France also agreed to train and equip units of the new Vietnamese Army. In April general staff accords were signed by General Võ Nguyên Giáp for the DRV and General Raoul Salan for France. These set the location and size of troop garrisons. After the agreement was signed Hô told Sainteny, "I am not happy about it, for basically it is you who have won. You know very well that I wanted more than that. But I understand that you cannot have everything in a day."[57] The Hô–Sainteny Agreement, although much less than the Viêt Minh desired, was a framework that might have led to a working and positive relationship between France and the DRV had it been allowed to stand.

On 6 March French troops landed at Hai Phòng. Leclerc and the French military returned to Hà Nôi on the 16th to a delirious French reception. In order to negotiate implementation of the Sainteny agreement, Hô now led a delegation to France. By the time it arrived, however, the French government had fallen and it was weeks before a new one was formed. Meanwhile on 1

June, just after Hô Chí Minh's departure for Paris, French High Commissioner d'Argenlieu torpedoed Sainteny's work. He proclaimed at Sài Gòn the establishmnent of the "Republic of Cochin China". He had broached the idea in Paris in February but took the decision on his own initiative. With an "independent" Republic of Cochin China there would be no need of a plebiscite in the South. Hô was furious and told Salan, who accompanied him to France, "You are creating a new Alsace-Lorraine and we will embark on a Hundred Years War."[58]

The DRV delegation sustained another blow when French Socialists lost seats in the June elections; in addition the Communists who were in the government and were trying to demonstrate their patriotism. As a result, at the July–September Fontainebleau Conference, Paris made no concessions to the Vietnamese nationalists. Pham Văn Đông, chief of the DRV delegation and later premier of the Democratic Republic of Vietnam, related that Max André, the chief of the French delegation, told him, "We only need an ordinary police action of eight days to clear out all of you." The sum of the conference's work was a draft accord that reinforced France's economic rights in northern Vietnam without solving the problem of Cochin China. Hô sent the DRV delegation home.[59]

Although there is disagreement on this point, Hô Chí Minh was probably a nationalist before he was a Communist. Writer David Halberstam described him as "part Gandhi, part Lenin, all Vietnamese".[60] Given Vietnam's long antagonistic relationship with China, he might have become an Asian Tito, but in September Hô left Paris empty-handed and forecast an early start of war.[61]

Tensions were already high in Vietnam when, in November 1946, the French sent a war crimes commission to Lang Són to investigate a mass grave in which a number of French soldiers killed by the Japanese in March 1945 had been buried. On 20 November an armed clash occurred between French troops escorting the commission and Vietnamese. The French lost six men and each side accused the other of responsibility.

This was overshadowed by another and more ominous event the same day. The French Navy had virtually blockaded Tonkin's principal port of Hai Phòng, and a French patrol vessel seized a Chinese junk attempting to smuggle contraband. Vietnamese soldiers on the shore fired on the French vessel. Shooting also broke out in the city itself. A subsequent meeting between French and Vietnamese officials resulted in a French promise to respect Vietnamese sovereignty and both sides agreed to separate their troops within the port city. By the afternoon of the 22nd fighting had ended.

At the time High Commissioner d'Argenlieu was in Paris reporting to the French Government. He proposed using the Hai Phòng clash to teach the

Vietnamese a lesson and this suggestion was approved. "Even going so far as the use of cannon?" he asked. "Even that", Premier Georges Bidault replied, although he probably did not realize that there was a likelihood of immediate action.[62]

D'Argenlieu then cabled General Jean-Etienne Valluy, his deputy in Sài Gòn, who ordered General Morlière, commander in the North, to use force against the Vietnamese. Morlière pointed out that the situation in Hai Phòng had been stabilized and that any imprudent act might lead to general hostilities. Unsatisfied with this reply, Valluy telegraphed directly to Colonel Pierre-Louis Debès, commander of French troops at Hai Phòng, and ordered him to "give a severe lesson to those who have treacherously attacked you. Use all the means at your disposal to make yourself complete master of Haiphong and so bring the Vietnamese army around to a better understanding of the situation".[63]

On 23 November Debès delivered an ultimatum to the Vietnamese at Hai Phòng, ordering them to withdraw from the French section of the city, the Chinese quarter, and the port. He gave them only two hours to reply. When that time was up the French subjected the Vietnamese positions to air, land, and sea bombardment, the bulk of the firepower coming from the three- and eight-inch guns of the French Navy cruiser *Suffren*. Only military targets were destroyed and not the Vietnamese quarter as some have claimed. Estimates of the number killed in the shelling and ensuing panic vary widely. Casualties up to 20,000 have been cited. French Admiral Battet later said that no more than 6,000 Vietnamese had died; but in 1981 Vũ Quôc Uy, then chairman of the Hai Phòng municipal committee, told Stanley Karnow that the figure was only 500 to 1,000 dead. Others have put the figure as low as 200.[64]

Fighting in Hai Phòng halted on 28 November, but Franco–Vietnamese relations steadily deteriorated thereafter. Whatever hopes remained on both sides had been irretrievably shattered. On 19 December General Morlière demanded the disarmament of the Tú Vê, the Viêt Minh militia that had been sniping at French troops in Hà Nôi. That night fear and mistrust, fuelled by bloodshed and broken promises, finally erupted into all-out war.

Chapter Three

The Indo-China War (1946–54)

The Indo-China War lasted eight years, from 1946 to 1954. It was the first phase of what might come to be known as the "Second Thirty Years War".[1] In 1946 in Paris Hô Chí Minh predicted to American correspondent David Schoenbrun how the war would be fought and how it would end. It would be, he said, "a war between an elephant and a tiger". If the tiger were to stand still the elephant would crush him with his tusks, but the tiger would not stand still. It would hide in the jungle and at night drop on the elephant and tear huge hunks from its hide; eventually the elephant would bleed to death. "That", Hô confidently predicted, "will be the war of Indochina."[2] Indeed, it played out very much along those lines.

The French did not fight the Indo-China War so much for economic reasons; indeed, by 1950 French military expenditures surpassed the total value of all French investments there. Political and psychological factors provided the chief reasons. Perhaps only with her empire could France be counted a great power, and colonial advocates argued that concessions in Indo-China would have an impact on the rest of France's overseas possessions and that further losses would soon follow. One author has noted that for leading French politicians the fear of disturbing the status quo in Morocco and Tunisia discouraged changes in Indo-China. French leaders also launched the "domino theory". As General Jean de Lattre de Tassigny phrased it in condensed form in Washington in September 1951, "Once Tongking [*sic*] is lost, there is no barrier until Suez." During the Vietnam War the United States employed a version of this same "domino theory".[3]

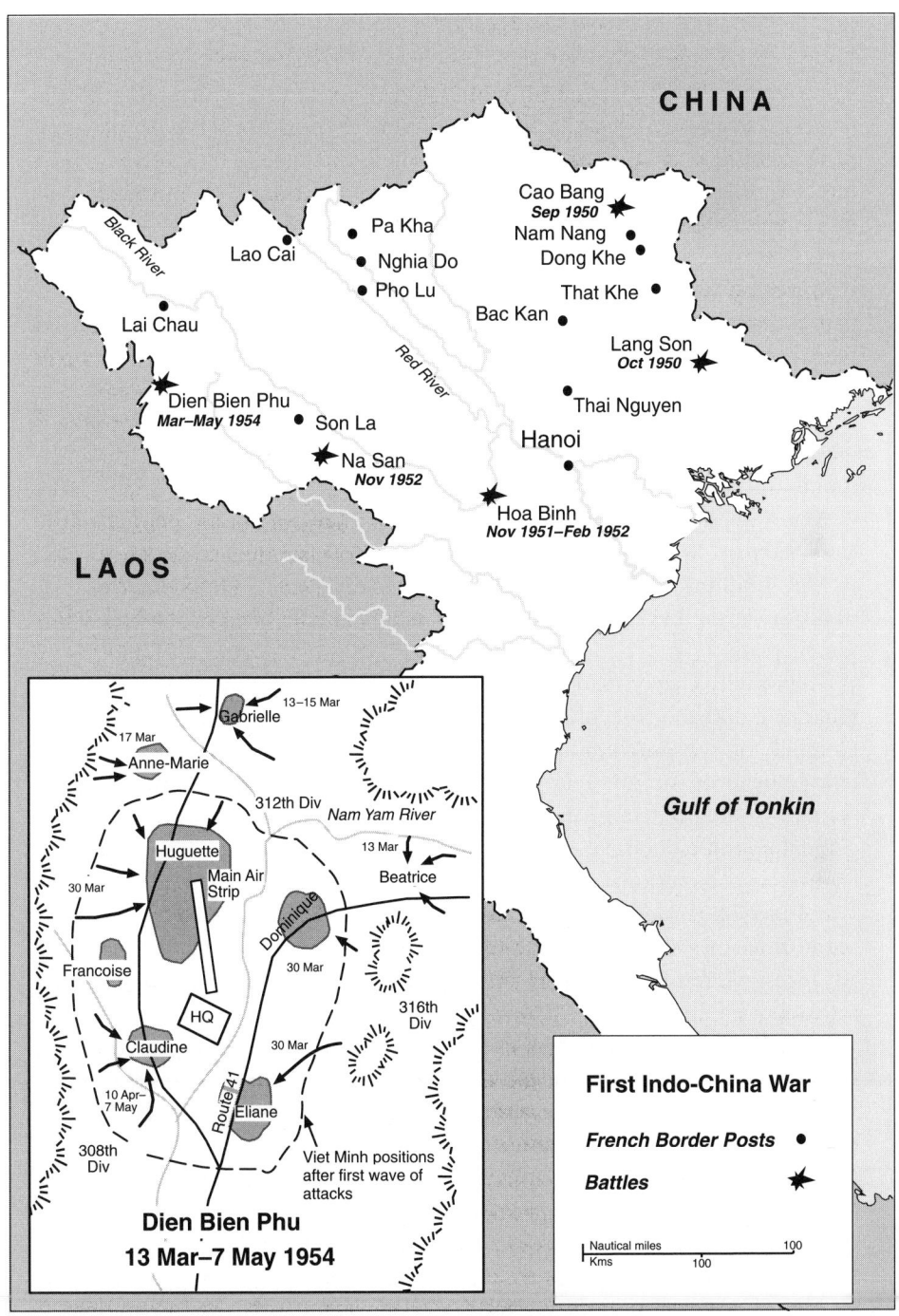

CHINA

Black River

Pa Kha

Lao Cai

Cao Bang
Sep 1950

Nam Nang

Dong Khe

Nghia Do

That Khe

Pho Lu

Bac Kan

Lai Chau

Red River

Lang Son
Oct 1950

Thai Nguyen

Dien Bien Phu
Mar–May 1954

Son La

Hanoi

Na San
Nov 1952

LAOS

Hoa Binh
Nov 1951–Feb 1952

Gulf of Tonkin

13–15 Mar

Gabrielle

17 Mar

Anne-Marie

312th Div

Nam Yam River

Huguette

13 Mar

30 Mar

Main Air Strip

Beatrice

Dominique

Francoise

30 Mar

316th Div

HQ

Claudine

30 Mar

10 Apr–7 May

Route 41

Eliane

308th Div

Viet Minh positions after first wave of attacks

**Dien Bien Phu
13 Mar–7 May 1954**

First Indo-China War

French Border Posts •

Battles ✸

Nautical miles — 100

Kms — 100

49

Giáp and the Viêt Minh

The DRV leadership planned for a long war. Central to their strategy was *đấu tranh* or "struggle": a joint military and political effort using the people as an instrument of war. It involved first controlling the people, then forging them into a weapon, and finally hurling them against the enemy.[4] The Viêt Minh's chief appeal was its stated goal of ridding the country of foreigners. Beginning with its formation, Hô and Võ Nguyên Giáp wanted the Viêt Minh to appeal to as many Vietnamese as possible. They imposed strict rules, including a ten-part oath containing a pledge to respect, help and protect the people. Soldiers were always to be on their best behaviour. For example, they were not to spend the night in villages and thus risk subjecting the inhabitants to French reprisals. Giáp believed that successful warfare grew out of correct political views, and he wanted the Viêt Minh always to appear to take the high moral ground.[5]

Major decisions were made by committee, a process continued during the later Vietnam War. Giáp had command of the DRV's military forces, formed in May 1945 into the People's Army of Vietnam (PAVN). This former teacher of history at the Lycée Thăng Long, self-taught in war, commanded the PAVN for 30 years.

Reportedly Giáp visited Mao Zedong (Mao Tse-tung) in 1941 and learned what he could about revolutionary war from the Chinese Communist leader. Certainly he was much influenced by Mao's writings.[6] Giáp's rival and Secretary General of the ICP Trúóng Chinh adapted Mao's notion of three-stage warfare: strategic defensive, a period of equilibrium, and a final victorious general counter-offensive (guerrilla actions, small-unit encounters, and then large-scale conventional engagements). He defined these in a 1947 pamphlet, *Our Victory is Certain*. Giáp's *People's War, People's Army* is largely a restatement of Maoist ideas with these fighting principles added on: "If the enemy advances, we retreat; if he halts, we harass; if he avoids battle, we attack; if he retreats, we follow."[7]

Giáp's brand of war was, however, eclectic, borrowing from many different streams. If it worked, he utilized it. His chief contribution to revolutionary warfare came in his assessment of political and psychological difficulties that confront a democracy in waging a protracted and inconclusive war. Public opinion would at some point demand an end to the bloodshed and political leaders would find themselves promising an early end to the fighting. As Giáp explained to political commissars of the 316th Division:

> The enemy will pass slowly from the offensive to the defensive. The blitzkrieg will transform itself into a war of long duration. Thus, the

enemy will be caught in a dilemma: He has to drag out the war in order to win it and does not possess, on the other hand, the psychological and political means to fight a long-drawn-out war.[8]

In actual fighting, Giáp sought to take advantage of terrain. In the populous rice-producing areas, where it would be difficult to hide and the French could utilize their superior mobility, the Viêt Minh would employ guerrilla tactics and ambushes. In the difficult-to-penetrate and less populated mountain and jungle regions the Viêt Minh would engage in large-scale operations, hoping thereby to exact a heavy price from their enemy in men and equipment.[9]

Giáp made mistakes, chiefly in going over to the third phase of warfare too soon, but he also showed the capacity to learn from his mistakes and not repeat them. His greatest leadership qualities were his depth of strategic vision, judicious employment of resources, and mastery of guerrilla warfare. Certainly Giáp proved adroit in logistics, timing, surprise, camouflage, and deception.

Giáp had no shortage of recruits. Weapons were another matter. Through 1949 the Viêt Minh had only about 83,000 of all types: about a third were homemade; another third were World War II-vintage Japanese or OSS-supplied; and the other third were purchased abroad, in Thailand or Hong Kong. The DRV purchased communications equipment from the Chinese Nationalists before their departure from Vietnam.

In 1946 the DRV established training schools for officers and NCOs. By the end of 1946 these had turned out some 1,500 NCOs but only a few hundred officers. Perhaps suprisingly, given the Viêt Minh's strong ideological base, at the beginning officer selection was based on ability rather than ideological fervour.[10]

French conduct of the war

Meanwhile the war continued. Despite shortages in numbers and firepower, General Leclerc's troops, augmented by the 2nd Tank Division, soon controlled the major lines of communication and population centres, but little else. The Viêt Minh, who had taken to the hills and jungles, dominated the countryside. The war soon settled into a low-scale affair of ambushes, patrols, and small-unit actions.

One French tactical innovation was the riverine division composed of naval and army forces, *divisions navales d'assaut*, abbreviated in French as *dinassaut*. By 1950 the French had six permanent *dinassauts* in Indo-China. Beginning in 1952 the French also developed commando formations, the

Groupement des Commandos Mixtes Aéroportés (GCMA for composite airborne commando groups). In December 1953 their name was changed to *Groupement Mixte d'Intervention* (GMI), whether they were airborne or not. Essentially guerrilla formations of about 400 men each, these operated permanently behind enemy lines, sometimes in conjunction with friendly Montagnards or Vietnamese. By mid-1954 the French had 15,000 men in such formations; but they required 300 tons of airborne supplies per month, a further strain on the scarce French airlift capacity.[11]

Changing French government policies were another concern. The Fourth Republic was marked by frequent changes in cabinets. With each change came subtle shifts in Indo-China policy and rapid turnover in the leadership there. During 1945–54 the post of high commissioner was held by eight different individuals: d'Argenlieu, Émile Bolleart, Léon Pignon, General de Lattre de Tassigny, Jean Letourneau, Maurice Dejean, and General Paul Henri Ély. The military leadership also underwent frequent changes. General Leclerc was followed in succession by Generals Jean-Étienne Valluy, Roger Blaizot, Marcel Carpentier, Jean de Lattre de Tassigny, Raoul Salan, Henri Navarre, and Ely. This frequent turnover undoubtedly affected the overall efficiency and morale of the Expeditionary Force.

Most French leaders assumed that the conflict in Indo-China would be little more than a classic colonial reconquest, securing the population centres and then expanding outward in the classic *tache d'huile* ("oil slick") pacification method that the French had practised so effectively in Morocco and Algeria.

French pacification efforts were limited largely to what became known as *quadrillage* and *ratissage*. These were key elements in the *tache d'huile* pacification method. They involved splitting up the territory to be pacified into grids or squares. Once this gridding (*quadrillage*) had been accomplished each square was then "raked" (*ratissage*) by pacification forces familiar with the area. If carried out on a regular basis by a sufficient number of troops, it could be successful, but French forces in Indo-China never had the men necessary to make this effective and certainly not in 1945 when Leclerc had only 40,000 troops.[12]

Jacques Dalloz has summed up the French dilemma:

> More generally the generals of the expeditionary corps always had to decide between two options – either to concentrate their forces at the risk of abandoning a large part of the country to "Viet" control, or to disperse their strength so as to hold as much terrain as possible, with the danger of exposing themselves to the attacks of their adversaries.[13]

French efforts were primarily military, to eradicate the Viêt Minh. There was no real attention to "winning the hearts and minds" of the civilian population. The French held much of Cochin China in part because French influence was stronger there, but mainly because the Buddhists and powerful religious sects of the Cao Đài and Hòa Hao opposed the Việt Minh. The French also controlled the Red River Delta and the capital of Hà Nôi. It is true that after they regained control of them during the winter of 1946–7 the French never lost the major population centres; but at the same time the Việt Minh steadily grew in strength and ruled more and more of the countryside.

The fighting, which began at low intensity, was not at first a major concern in France. Public opinion was preoccupied with domestic developments and was hardly disturbed by the little press coverage of places and events 8,000 miles away of which few people had even heard. There were no great battles and it was very much a non-war for most of the French public. By 1950, however, a sense of pessimism towards the war took hold. Less than 30 per cent of those then polled thought it possible to restore the situation, while more than 40 per cent supported stopping the war unilaterally or negotiating with the Việt Minh. A large part of the French population remained indifferent; in all polls between 1948 and 1954, 20 to 30 per cent had no opinion on the war at all.[14]

Despite its determination to hold on to Indo-China, the French government never made the commitment in manpower necessary to have a chance to win. As Paris never allowed draftees to be sent to Indo-China, the war was essentially fought by only a small minority of the French population – its professional soldiers – the officers and non-commissioned officers of the Expeditionary Corps. No more than 100,000 Frenchmen served in Indo-China during the war and the government consistently rebuffed calls by successive Indo-China commanders-in-chief for substantial reinforcements. This was simply inadequate to defeat an ever growing number of Việt Minh. Experience in Malaya and the Philippines had shown that a ratio of 10 to 1 in favour of pacification forces was necessary to defeat guerrillas.[15]

Farther down the chain of command fewer Frenchmen were found. In January 1950, when the French Army as a whole numbered 700,000 men, the Expeditionary Corps had only 68,000 Europeans (including the Foreign Legion), 54,000 Africans (principally Moroccans, Algerians, and Senegalese), and 45,000 Indo-Chinese (not counting some 40,000 auxiliaries). According to official French Army statistics, total French forces went from 67,106 men in 1946 to 183,945 in 1954. The high point in French strength came in 1952 when the Expeditionary Corps totalled 192,069 men (not counting 50,000 auxiliaries).[16]

The Expeditionary Corps had a rigid military hierarchy. At the top were the elite red-bereted paratroopers (paras) and the legionnaires, who were called upon in the most difficult circumstances. Cohesion in the

Expeditionary Corps rested on the personal allegiance of the men to their officers, a serious weakness in confronting those solidly behind a cause.[17]

The small number of effectives available to French commanders left them few options as far as strategy was concerned. Whatever advantage the French might have enjoyed in manpower at the beginning of the war was negated by the need to protect the population centres, garrison the many posts throughout Indo-China, and guard roads and convoys. These requirements consumed some 90 per cent of military resources and precluded large-scale operations against enemy base areas. Shortages of officers and non-commissioned officers, a lack of trained intelligence officers and interpreters, and little interest in or knowledge of the mechanics of pacification, all hampered the French military effort, as did geography, climate, conditions of jungle warfare and lack of airlift capacity.[18]

All this seems to suggest that a diplomatic solution was the only way out. The French Socialist Party showed interest in ending the war through peace talks, but the steady drift of the French coalition government to the right and increasing bloodshed prevented this. French High Commissioner to Indo-China Admiral d'Argenlieu and other French colonial administrators opposed meaningful concessions to the nationalists, and on 25 December 1946, Leclerc departed Indo-China in frustration.

In May 1947 the French did make a stab at settling the war peacefully when Paul Mus travelled from Hà Nôi to meet with Hô Chí Minh in the latter's jungle headquarters. Mus was an Asian scholar sympathetic to the Vietnamese nationalist point of view and a personal adviser to Émile Bolleart, who had replaced d'Argenlieu as high commissioner earlier in 1947. Mus carried a plan drawn up by General Valluy and approved by Socialist Premier Paul Ramadier that called on the Viêt Minh to refrain from hostilities, lay down some arms, permit French troops freedom of movement, and return prisoners, deserters and hostages. Hô rejected this offer as tantamount to surrender. On 15 May Bolleart declared, "France will remain in Indo-China."[19]

In order to increase available manpower, attract Vietnamese nationalist support, and quiet critics at home and in the United States, Paris sought at least the façade of an indigenous Vietnamese regime as a competitor to the Viêt Minh. After years of negotiations, in March 1949 the French government concluded the Élysée Agreements with former Emperor Bao Ðai. These created the State of Vietnam (SVN), with Paris conceding that Vietnam was in fact one country.[20]

The SVN allowed Paris to cast the war as a conflict between a free Vietnam and the Communists, and thus not a colonial war at all. In July 1951 General de Lattre stated, "Not since the Crusades has France undertaken such disinterested action. This war is the war of Vietnam for Vietnam."[21]

The problem for Vietnamese nationalists was that the SVN never had any power. The French continued to control all of its institutions, and its promised army was late in materializing. France simply took the recruited soldiers and added them to its own Expeditionary Corps, where they were commanded by French officers. There were only two choices for the Vietnamese – the Việt Minh or the French. In effect the French pushed most nationalists into the Việt Minh camp.

The Việt Minh successfully wrapped itself in the mantle of nationalism and downplayed Communism. In the first years of the war its leadership judged that winning the support of the people was more important than the military effort. Towards that end the Việt Minh moved slowly regarding social changes and worked to build a broad-based political consensus.[22] The Việt Minh withdrew into the jungle to indoctrinate and train their troops. The French scenario for the war had the Việt Minh eventually tiring of their cause and giving up. It never happened.

On 7 October 1947, the French began Operation Léa. Directed by General Raoul Salan, Léa involved some 12,000 men, about half the number Salan believed necessary, during a three-week period over some 80,000 square miles of nearly impenetrable terrain in the northeast Việt Bắc region. Léa's goals were to capture Hồ Chí Minh and the Việt Minh leadership and to destroy their main battle units.

Seventeen French battalions would move in a pincer movement. One column, supported by a river flotilla, was to move up the Red and Clear Rivers. Another would depart Lang Són, occupy Cao Bang, and then march to the south. The two were to meet near Bac Kan, deep in Việt Minh territory. Léa was followed on 20 November by Operation Ceinture ("Belt"), designed to crush enemy forces in a quadrangle northwest of Hà Nội.

The French did take Thái Nguyên, 50 miles north of Hà Nội, and several other Việt Minh-controlled population centres, and they claimed to have killed 7,200 Việt Minh and taken 1,000 prisoners. They also rescued 200 French and Vietnamese hostages. But they failed to capture the Việt Minh leadership. Hồ and Giáp escaped.

These two operations did destroy significant Việt Minh supply caches and arms production facilities, but not the main Communist units; they also revealed limitations imposed by the lack of resources. French forces were insufficient to hold on to the areas they had taken and were badly needed elsewhere. Indeed, much of the countryside was now opened to Việt Minh penetration. With the onset of the rainy season, on 22 December French troops withdrew to their bases. One Vietnamese source has called the operation the "first major victory for the resistance" and a failure for "France's blitzkrieg strategy".[23]

In September General Carpentier replaced Blaizot as commander of French forces. Largely ignorant of conditions in Indo-China, Carpentier turned over field command to Major General Marcel Alessandri, who had wide experience there. Alessandri's chief accomplishment was the pacification of the Red River Delta. Despite Giáp's guerrilla tactics, Alessandri's own "clear and hold" and "mopping-up" operations were highly effective and he accomplished them with only 20 battalions. Bit by bit the French extended their hold, but the Viêt Minh had already neutralized most of their nationalist rivals and the French found little assistance from this quarter. Alessandri also mounted a major effort to deny rice to the Viêt Minh.[24] The French pacification failed to take hold, however, precisely because the French had nothing to offer the bulk of the Vietnamese. The chief base of French support was the one million Catholics living in Tonkin, perhaps a fifth of the population in the delta area.

People's Republic of China and the war

At the end of 1949 Viêt Minh prospects changed dramatically when the Communists won control in China. In effect the war was lost for the French then and there. The long Chinese–Vietnam border allowed the People's Republic of China (PRC) to supply the Viêt Minh with arms and equipment and to provide advisers and technicians as well as sanctuaries where the Viêt Minh could train and replenish its troops. On 18 January 1950, the PRC formally recognized the DRV and agreed to furnish it with military assistance. On 30 January the Soviet Union also extended diplomatic recognition.[25]

By the end of 1952 more than 40,000 PAVN enlisted men and 10,000 officers had trained in China. Arms were also available from the substantial stocks of weapons, including artillery that the US had supplied to the Chinese Nationalists. PRC support of the DRV grew steadily. In 1951 it provided fewer than 20 tons of military assistance per month; in 1952, 250 tons; in 1953, 600 tons; and in 1954, 4,000 tons per month.[26]

This triggered a change in US policy. To this point Washington had been largely ambivalent towards the war. President Harry S. Truman certainly opposed it.[27] But he did not follow the advice of Asian experts in the State Department who urged him to recognize the DRV and encourage the ultimate independence of the region from French rule; the Europeanists, preoccupied by the Soviet military threat to Western Europe, ultimately won the day. Germany was still disarmed, and in these circumstances France was the only Continental power capable of providing the resources to resist the USSR. In order to keep French support against the Soviet Union in Europe, the United States tacitly supported French policy in Indo-China. This grew to active support as the Cold War intensified with the 1948 Communist takeover of Czechoslovakia and the 1948–9 Berlin Blockade.

PRC support of the DRV was the final straw. On 7 February 1950, the United States recognized the SVN. Few Americans had even heard of Vietnam and, if they had, at this point they were hardly alarmed. In May Washington agreed to furnish forthwith between $20 million and $30 million in direct aid, with more the next fiscal year.[28] The United States also funded the war indirectly. Massive amounts of Marshall Plan aid freed up other French resources for Indo-China.

The Korean War, which began in June 1950, solidified the Truman Administration's position towards Indo-China. Containing the spread of Communism took priority over anti-colonialism. Both Washington and Paris came to see Korea and Vietnam as mutually dependent theatres in a common Western struggle against Communism. The United States also changed its policy of providing only indirect aid to the war in Indo-China. On 27 June 1950, in his statement on Korea, President Truman also announced:

> The attack upon Korea makes it plain beyond all doubt that communism had pushed beyond the use of subversion to conquer independent nations and will now use armed invasion and war. . . . I have similarly directed acceleration in the furnishing of military assistance to the forces of France and the associated states in Indo-China and the dispatch of a military mission to provide close working relations with those forces.[29]

On 30 June eight C–47 transports arrived in Sài Gòn with the first direct shipment of US military equipment. American support for the French effort in Indo-China grew steadily. With the establishment of a Military Assistance Advisory Group (MAAG), US military aid rose from $100 million in 1950 to $300 million in 1952, and over $1 billion in 1954, when it was financing some 80 per cent of the French effort. Overall US military assistance amounted to nearly $3 billion, or nearly 60 per cent of the war's cost.[30]

The French insisted that all US military assistance be channelled directly to them rather than through the SVN. Although a Vietnamese National Army was established in 1951, it remained effectively under French control. General Carpentier welcomed the expanded military support but insisted it remain in French hands. US Major General Graves B. Erskine reported that Carpentier told him that Vietnamese troops were unreliable, would not make good soldiers and were not to be trusted on their own. Erskine said that he replied, "General Carpentier, who in hell are you fighting but Vietnamese?"[31]

France continued to dominate the SVN down to the end of the war. Despite this, the Truman and Eisenhower administrations assured the American people that real authority in Vietnam had been handed over to the Vietnamese. Washington was caught in something of a dilemma, for if Paris were to hand over real authority to the Vietnamese the French would probably lose the incentive to continue the war. But because Paris refused to concede real authority to the SVN, Vietnamese nationalists had no other recourse but the Viêt Minh; in the end the Communists usurped Vietnamese nationalism.

Certain of Chinese support, on 21 February 1950, Hô Chí Minh declared a general mobilization. He had already instituted conscription on 4 November 1949, for all adult males between the ages of 16 and 55. Initially applied only to Tonkin and Annam, by mid-1952 it had been extended to Cochin China.

With arms from China the PAVN shifted rapidly to conventional forces. In April 1949 Giáp commanded 32 regular battalions and 137 regional battalions. Two years later the PAVN included 117 regular battalions – progressively formed into regiments – and 37 regional battalions. Giáp's next step was to bring the regiments together into brigades and then into divisions of some 10,000 men each. By mid-1952 the PAVN fielded five infantry divisions: the 304th, 308th (Iron Division), 312th, and the 316th, all in the Viêt Bắc; and the 320th in cental Vietnam. They were soon joined by the 351st heavy division of 12 infantry and eight engineer regiments. It provided heavy weapons' support to the other divisions as needed. Giáp now had a real army.

PAVN forces were both well-equipped and well-trained. The troops were also highly motivated, the consequence of intense political indoctrination. Both officers and men wore a simple green uniform without rank identification, a practice continued until 1958.[32]

The PAVN had artillery, mortars, and machine guns but no vehicles. Its logistics needs were met by vast numbers of porters (*dân công*), some 50,000 per division. Giáp and his staff carefully worked out what each porter was to carry: 55 pounds of rice or 33 to 45 pounds of arms and ammunition for 15.5 miles a day or 12.4 miles at night, and 9 miles and 7.5 miles for mountainous terrain.[33]

Operations during 1950

In early 1950 Viêt Minh forces penetrated deeply into the French-controlled Red River Delta defensive belt and in Operation Lê Hông Phong I they took the key frontier post of Lào Cai. By the end of the offensive the Viêt Minh controlled virtually the entire northeastern corner of Tonkin, save a string of border outposts along the border with China on *Route Coloniale* 4 (RC4) from Cao Bằng via Đông Khê, Thât Khê, and Lang Són to the Gulf of Tonkin.

His army now well trained and equipped, Giáp was ready for a major offensive against French forts along the China border. The 10,000 French troops manning these outposts were in fact in a perilous position. In May 1949 General Georges Revers, chief of the French general staff, had recommended withdrawal from five of these outposts, separated from the main French lines in the delta by 300 miles of Viêt Minh-held jungles. Revers had called them "a drain on French resources" and noted that they "could probably not withstand a serious attack".[34]

High Commissioner Pignon and General Alessandri opposed this course of action. They believed that control of the road was necessary to prevent Chinese supplies from reaching the Viêt Minh. Nonetheless the supply run along RC4 to Cao Bằng from Lang Són became a costly matter. French convoys could get no further than Thât Khê, and from January 1950 Đông Khê and Cao Bằng had to be resupplied by air.

On the morning of 25 May 1950, five PAVN battalions attacked two Moroccan companies holding Đông Khê, about midway between Cao Bằng and Thât Khê. For two days the Viêt Minh fired their five US-made 75 mm howitzers into the town from the surrounding hills, much as they would do four years later at Điên Biên Phu. On 27 May Giáp's crack 308th "Iron Brigade" (soon the "Iron Division") overwhelmed the defenders in human wave assaults. The French surprised the Viêt Minh by immediately dropping a battalion of paratroopers on the town. They killed 300 men of the Iron Brigade before it withdrew into the jungle.

Giáp then launched Operation Lê Hông Phong II, an effort by 15 battalions and an artillery regiment to retake Đông Khê. On the morning of 16 September fierce artillery and mortar fire hit the town. The earlier procedure was repeated, consisting of two days of softening-up followed by a human wave assault. Despite French air strikes by P–63A Kingcobra fighters and Ju–52 bombers, Đông Khê fell. This cut French communications with Cao Bằng and French garrisons to the northwest. The Viêt Minh also attacked other French positions, including those in Laos.[35]

On 24 September, with much time already lost, General Carpentier ordered the evacuation of Cao Bằng. In a later report to the French government he confessed that the transformation of the Viêt Minh into a modern military force in only "three or four months" had caught him by surprise. The misreading of Viêt Minh capabilities continued to hamper the French, as it later would the Americans.[36]

Cao Băng's garrison, commanded by Lieutenant Colonel Charton, consisted of a reinforced battalion of legionnaires and a battalion of Thô partisans as well as the latter's families and several hundred Vietnamese and Chinese merchants. The roads from Cao Băng, RC3 and RC4, ran through difficult Viêt Minh-controlled terrain, so Carpentier ordered Charton to destroy his heavy equipment and motor transport and bring out his 2,600 men and 500 civilians via foot trails. At the same time a relief force of some 3,500 men commanded by Lieutenant Colonel Marcel Le Page was to move from Thât Khê northwest to Đông Khê and retake that post long enough to allow the Cao Băng garrison to join it there on the morning of 2 October.

Another possibility existed: evacuation by air. The runway at Cao Băng was long enough to accommodate Ju–52 and C–47 Dakota aircraft. French air commander in Tonkin Colonel de Maricourt believed that the entire garrison could have been withdrawn in two days, but Carpentier was unwilling to leave the civilians behind. Were they to be included in the air operation it would take more time and be considerably more dangerous.

But Carpentier's decision to retreat on RC4 rather than RC3 led to disaster. While RC3 was a longer route to the main French defensive line it was safer because there were fewer Viêt Minh along the way. RC4, while only 45 miles to Đông Khê and 15 miles further to Thât Khê, ran close to the Chinese border and through difficult terrain. Apparently no one in authority anticipated a Viêt Minh reaction and no intervention force was organized in case the need arose. As it worked out, the Viêt Minh were far more numerous in the area than the French.

Carpentier's plan probably would have worked had Charton followed orders. With a profound disdain for his adversary and convinced that he could bring out his vehicles, he used the road, which was well covered by the Viêt Minh. Progress was very slow and by the time Charton decided to follow the original plan it was too late. Remnants of the two French forces met in the hills around Đông Khê, only to be wiped out there on 7 October 1950. Only 12 officers and 475 men managed to make it to Thât Khê.

Carpentier now panicked. On 17 October he ordered the evacuation of Lang Són, which had not been under attack and whose good airfield and excellent fields of fire would have allowed a protracted defence. Most of its 1,300 tons of supplies fell into Viêt Minh hands.[37]

By the end of October 1950 northeastern Vietnam was for all intents and purposes a Viêt Minh stronghold with the French largely forced back into their Red River Delta bastion. With the exception of a brief paratroop raid on Lang Són in mid-July 1953 the French did not penetrate the area again. The RC4 debacle cost the French 4,800 killed and missing. To make matters worse, the Viêt Minh captured 13 artillery pieces, 112 mortars, 160 machine guns, 1,209 automatic pistols, 380 submachine guns, and 8,222 rifles – enough to arm an entire PAVN division.[38] Bernard Fall believed this was for France the "greatest colonial defeat since Montcalm had died at Quebec", while General Yvres Gras likened it in its influence on the Indo-China War to the 1808 French defeat at Bailen for Napoleon's Peninsular Campaign. The Viêt Minh now had ready access to China. That the war was allowed to drag on past this point offers ample proof of the dearth of political leadership in Paris.[39]

In part to rectify this disaster, in December 1950 Paris sent to Indo-China perhaps its most illustrious soldier, General Jean de Lattre de Tassigny. To bolster his authority he was also made high commissioner, giving him civilian as well as military authority. Imperious (he was known as "*le roi Jean*"), handsome, and stylish, de Lattre immediately set out to restore confidence within the French military. He weeded out incompetents, promising his men only that they would know they had been commanded. De Lattre also cancelled the planned departure of French women and children from Hà Nôi because of the effect this would have on morale ("As long as the women and children are here", he said, "the men won't dare go").[40] His blunt approach, including open admiration for his opponents' skill, injected a new spirit among the French forces.

De Lattre concentrated his efforts in the North, specifically the fortification of the Red River Delta – building his famous *ceinture* (belt). Ultimately 51 million cubic yards of concrete went into 900 forts and 2,200 pillboxes, many of which survive today as mute testimony to a failed policy. But the Viêt Minh ignored these fortified positions, which tied down 20 French infantry battalions.[41]

Although the French government agreed to send reinforcements to de Lattre, they were not as numerous as he wanted. He hoped to make up the shortfall with the Vietnamese National Army (VNA), but in January 1951 the VNA had only 30,000 regulars (65,000 men overall) in 11 infantry battalions and nine national guard regiments. Using US funds, de Lattre planned to create 11 new battalions. He would do this by *jaunissement* ("yellowing" or "Vietnamizing"), creating wholly Vietnamese units commanded by Vietnamese officers and distributing them into two Expeditionary Corps battalions.

In July 1951 de Lattre secured a mobilization declaration by the State of Vietnam government (SVN). By December the Vietnamese National Army (VNA) had doubled to 54,000 regulars in 33 infantry battalions. It remained ineffective, however. Its problem was never numbers but a lack of training, incapable officers, inadequate equipment, and overall ineffectiveness.[42]

Operations during 1951

After five years on the strategic defensive, Giáp now took the offensive. Buoyed by his 1950 victories that wrested northeastern Tonkin from French control and encouraged by his Chinese advisers, Giáp believed the time had come for a "general counter-offensive" by large conventional units against the main French defensive line in the flat lands of the Red River Delta. His goal was to capture Hà Nôi itself by the Lunar New Year celebration of Têt. Talk of this circulated openly, and there was a sense of panic in the capital.[43]

By mid-January 1951 Giáp had assembled 81 battalions, 20 of them support (12 heavy weapons and eight engineers). On the night of 13–14 January he launched Operation Trân Húng Đao when the 308th and 312th divisions attacked two French mobile groups (*Groupes Mobile*, GMs, each equivalent to a US regimental combat team) defending the approaches to Vinh Yên, some 30 miles from Hà Nôi.

The Battle of Vinh Yên initially favoured the Viêt Minh, but General de Lattre took personal charge. Ordering all possible measures to stop the offensive, he flew to Vinh Yên in a small liaison plane. He then ordered the airlift of reserve battalions from the South and requisitioned Air France aircraft to fly in a battalion of paratroopers. The crisis point came on 16 January when the PAVN 308th division mounted human wave assaults. De Lattre ordered all available fighter aircraft to Vinh Yên as well as any transport planes capable of dropping bombs.

In the largest aerial bombardment of the Indo-China War the French dropped large quantities of napalm, which had first arrived at Hai Phòng from the United States only a few days before. On 17 January de Lattre committed his last reserves, and by the end of the day the PAVN divisions withdrew to the Tam Đao Massif at the end of the delta.

Giáp had been outgunned; air power and artillery were the keys to this French defensive victory. Viêt Minh casualties had been heavy. De Lattre reported them as 1,600 dead, 480 prisoners, and 6,000 wounded; French casualties were 43 dead, 545 missing/captured, and 160 wounded.[44]

Giáp was not willing to concede defeat and in Operation Hoàng Hoa Thám he tried again. De Lattre misread Giáp's intentions, believing that he would next strike at Viêt Trì, northwest of Hà Nôi. As a result the bulk of the French heavy forces were to the west of the capital. But Giáp ordered the 308th, 312th, and two regiments of the 316th divisions to cut off the French in Hà Nôi from Hai Phòng, the port that handled virtually all French military sealift in the North. Meanwhile Giáp would use two other divisions, the 304th and 320th, to threaten Hà Nôi from the west.

The attack began on the night of 23–4 March. De Lattre was in France and had left General Salan in charge. Salan immediately sent French reinforcements eastward, including naval units. The deep water of the Đa Bach River allowed supporting fire from the cruiser *Duguay-Trouin*, two destroyers, and two landing ships. One of the most incredible incidents of the entire war occurred during the fight for Mao Khê, the location of a large coal mine, where a company of 95 Thô tribesmen commanded by Vietnamese Lieutenant Nghiêm Xuân Toàn and three French NCOs managed to hold off a Viêt Minh division for an entire day. After eight days of attacks Giáp called off the offensive. The Viêt Minh had lost another 3,000 men, and once more Giáp had failed to pierce the French defensive Red River Delta ring.[45]

Undaunted, Giáp tried again. He sent three PAVN divisions from the South in an effort to secure important rice-producing areas in the southern part of the delta. One important Viêt Minh innovation in this battle was the co-ordination of the frontal attack with the infiltration beforehand of two entire regiments within the French battle line. This offensive, known as Hà Nam Ninh, with its objectives of Hà Nam and Ninh Bình Provinces, resulted in major battles at Ninh Bình and Phát Diêm in the southeastern Red River Delta.

The Viêt Minh offensive began on 29 May and, as usual, achieved surprise. The first day of fighting claimed the life of Lieutenant Bernard de Lattre, General de Lattre's only child; he died defending an important outpost to the city of Ninh Bình. But by 18 June the latest Viêt Minh offensive had ground to a halt largely because the French had thrown reinforcements into the battle and been able to disrupt Viêt Minh supply lines. Despite his expertise in logistics, Giáp had underestimated the requirements for conventional forces in battle. The French also brought superior firepower to bear, especially from the air and from along the Đáy River, where they were able to employ a *dinassaut* to cut Viêt Minh supply lines. In the Hà Nam Ninh Offensive the Viêt Minh suffered another 10,000 dead. Giáp then withdrew his forces into the mountains.

These battles helped restore French confidence and allowed de Lattre to go to Washington and make a case for additional US assistance. But they also revealed French shortcomings in cross-country mobility, lack of air power and the manpower to exploit local victories.

Viêt Minh morale now plummeted and desertions shot up. This forced Giáp to return to his phase two guerrilla strategy. He would accept battle only on his own terms, while seeking out vulnerable French peripheral units and working to undermine French authority. Never again did Giáp seek a pitched battle with the French in the coastal plains. His strategy became one of forcing the French to disperse their forces into remote areas, while tying down the bulk of their strength in static positions. He and the Viêt Minh leadership believed that this combination of factors would ultimately force the French to quit Indo-China.[46]

The Battle of Hòa Bình and Operations during 1952

In November 1951 de Lattre initiated a "meat-grinder" battle outside the important Red River Delta area, a move made possible by increased US military aid. He did so because of the success of "meat-grinder" battles in the Korean War and the need for a victory to influence the French National Assembly debate over the 1952–3 Indo-China budget. Another important consideration for de Lattre was maintaining the support of Múóng Montagnards in the area, who thus far had remained staunchly pro-French.

De Lattre chose as his objective the major Viêt Minh road connecting their northeastern strongholds on the southern edge of the Red River Delta redoubt with their areas north of central Vietnam. The battle's focus was the city of Hòa Bình (ironically "peace" in Vietnamese) on the Black River.

The Battle of Hòa Bình began on 14 November 1951, when three French paratroop battalions dropped on the city, the last operation in which the French used World War II tri-motor Ju–52 transports for their paratroops and resupply operations. The French occupied the city with almost no resistance. At the same time 15 infantry battalions, seven artillery battalions, and two armoured groups supported by two *dinassauts* and engineering forces, worked their way into the Black River valley.

Giáp had avoided battle with the French except under favourable conditions; thus the Viêt Minh at Hòa Bình simply melted away. But the French position there seemed to offer an excellent opportunity for Giáp to repeat his 1950 successes along RC4, and he ordered south the 304th, 308th, and 312th divisions, along with artillery, anti-aircraft, and engineer troops. He also called in regional forces stationed to the west of the Red River Delta and sent the 316th and 320th divisions to infiltrate French lines and disrupt their lines of communication (LOCs) feeding Hòa Bình.

French land access to Hòa Bình was by means of RC6. This track had been in disrepair since 1940 and was now little more than a trail. It wound for 25 miles through difficult terrain flanked by underbrush and high cliffs and was ideal for ambushes. The French now worked to improve RC6. Communication with Hòa Bình by means of the Đáy River was almost three times as long as by RC6 but it was much more secure; the thin-skinned French landing craft were vulnerable to Viêt Minh recoilless rifle and bazooka fire. This led the

French, as in the case of RC6, to develop a string of forts and strong points to secure the river, but at a high cost in manpower and equipment.

Hòa Bình indeed became a meat-grinder battle, but for both sides. De Lattre left Indo-China in December 1951 before the battle was over, the victim of cancer that would kill him early the next year. Before his departure he stripped French outposts as far as Laos and Cambodia of manpower, making these more vulnerable to Viêt Minh attack. The Battle of Hòa Bình clearly showed the limitations imposed by the scant French manpower resources. Although the French held Hòa Bình, it was to no advantage. The Viêt Minh merely built a bypass road around the town; and by the end of the battle, on 24 February 1952, they had penetrated the Red River Delta as never before.

French participants remembered the battle as "the hell of Hòa Bình". They lost 894 killed and missing; the Viêt Minh suffered some 9,000 casualties. Yet all divisions now had first-hand experience in fighting the French and had learned their strengths and weaknesses. This was of immense benefit in the battles to come. Giáp rotated units in and out of the battle and those that were bloodied had merely to withdraw into the jungle free from French pursuit to rest and regroup.[47]

With de Lattre's departure, French military morale plummeted. Lassitude and resignation took hold, brought on by half victories, shortages of personnel and *matériel* in decisive operations, and a lack of tactical innovation. Another factor was the perceived inability of politicians at home to comprehend what was at stake in Indo-China. Among the professional French soldiers there grew out of the Indo-China experience a determination never to allow these conditions to be repeated. This played itself out in the Algeria War, when in 1958 the French Army helped topple the Fourth Republic.[48]

Giáp now undertook the conquest of the Thái Highlands in northwestern Vietnam in what became known as the Northwest Campaign. Giáp decided to attack across the top of the Indo-Chinese peninsula in order to force the French to fight at long range in difficult conditions and to destroy remaining French battalions there. He reasoned that the French would find it difficult, if not impossible, to bring their heavy equipment to bear. On 11 October 1952, three PAVN divisions – the 308th, 312th and 316th – crossed the Red River and within a week had rolled up most of the small French outposts in the region. Major Marcel Bigeard and his 700-man 6th Colonial Paratroop Battalion (BPC) were sent to Tu Lê Pass to win time for other French units to reach the Black River. On 16 October 15 C–47s dropped the battalion in two lifts. During the next week they fought nearly non-stop against the entire 312th Division. Several days after parachuting into Tu Lê, Bigeard and his men were ordered out. After waiting several days in the hopes of evacuating his wounded and so as to not leave behind tribal Thái auxiliaries, Bigeard withdrew on the 20th. In an extraordinary anabasis, almost without sleep and outnumbered ten to one, the 6th BPC fought its way out over nearly 50 miles of mountain and jungle. On 23 October the French troops reached Nà San and safety, having lost 91 killed and missing. Bigeard was soon a legendary figure in the French Army.[49]

The French organized two airheads (*aéroterrestres*) for resupply, one at Lai Châu and the other at Nà San, and rebuffed Giáp's attempt to take Nà San. But by the end of November PAVN units had reached the Lao border. All this was accomplished without the use of roads or motor vehicles. Seemingly in this war without fronts, the Viêt Minh could be, as Giáp put it, "everywhere and nowhere".[50]

General Salan, de Lattre's replacement, tried to halt this offensive by striking at Viêt Minh supply lines. Salan hoped that by striking Giáp's base areas he could compel him to return divisions to their defences and abandon the effort to conquer the Thái Highlands.

Mounted in some haste, Operation Lorraine involved more than 30,000 men, the largest French military operation of the war. Lorraine included four motorized or armoured regimental combat teams, three airborne battalions, five commando formations, two tank-destroyer squadrons, two *Dinassauts*, and assorted support groups.

Begun on 29 October 1952, Lorraine started out well. The French penetrated about 100 miles and took two important Viêt Minh supply centres west of Hà Nôi. Although the French captured large amounts of arms, ammunition, and equipment, including trucks, they never reached the vital Viêt Minh depots at Yên Báy. Had they captured these it might indeed have turned the campaign.

The operation bogged down on its long and precarious supply lines and was soon in reverse. On 14 November Salan halted Lorraine and the French began their withdrawal. Now fully alerted, PAVN units attacked the retreating French. The 36th Regiment ambushed French Mobile Groups 12 and 4 at Chan Múóng. By 1 December the French had returned to their defensive positions along the so-called "De Lattre Line"; Giáp's forces were still on the Laos border.

Operation Lorraine failed because Giáp refused to abandon his strategy of leaving small units to fend for themselves, even if it meant sacrificing some of them, such as his 36th and 176th infantry regiments. He was certain that such French operations would sooner or later come to an end. Indeed, the larger the operation the more likely it would be of short duration, as its component units, which were drafted for the operation at hand, would soon be required elsewhere.[51]

The Viêt Minh, meanwhile, made significant gains in central Vietnam. French control in the plateau area of the Central Highlands (PMS) was confined to a few beachheads around Huê, Đà Năng, and Nha Trang. The only areas where the French enjoyed real success were in Cochin China and in neighbouring Cambodia. French success in Cochin China was due in large part to support from the resolutely anti-Communist religious sects that controlled much of the area; in Cambodia it resulted from traditional Khmer antipathy towards the Vietnamese. Laos had thus far largely avoided the fighting, but that now changed.[52]

Up to this point the Communist presence in Laos had been limited to four PAVN battalions that trained the pro-Communist Pathet Lao headed by Prince Souphanouvong and allied with the Viêt Minh. The prince, later the first president of the Lao People's Democratic Republic (1975–91), had set up his own rival Laotian government.

In the spring of 1953 Giáp assembled a powerful force to invade Laos, which had an army of only 10,000 men supported by 3,000 French regulars. Giáp employed four divisions totalling 40,000 men, assisted by 4,000 Communist Pathet Lao troops. Rather than sacrifice its smaller posts, as it had the year before in the campaign for the Thái Highlands, the French high command withdrew them inland. One Lao battalion commanded by a French captain bought time for the rest in a heroic stand at Muong Khoua. Ordered to hold out for two weeks against most of the PAVN 316th Division, it fought on for 36 days and had only four known survivors. The garrison at Sam Neua, retreating 110 miles west overland, lost all but 180 of its 2,400 men.

Once more the French had to disperse their meagre resources. They established an airhead on the Plaine des Jarres and began ferrying in troops, equipment, and even tanks. Supplying ten battalions there, as well as the 10,000 troops surrounded at Nà San, required all the available French airlift capacity. In late April the French managed to prevent a PAVN attempt to breach their new lines and overrun the Plaine des Jarres. This would have put them in position to take the Laotian capital of Vientiane. The French also defeated a smaller thrust at the royal capital of Luang Prabang. The onset in May of the rainy season forced the PAVN back on its supply bases, saving Laos for another summer.[53]

The Navarre Plan

In July 1953 a new French commander, General Henri Navarre, arrived in Indo-China. That May French military intelligence had estimated enemy strength at 350,000–400,000 men: 125,000 regulars, 75,000 regional forces, and 150,000 guerrillas. Most were mobile. Of the regulars, some 60,000 were in Tonkin, 25,000 in Annam, 40,000 in Cochin China, 6,000 in Laos, and 8,000 in Cambodia. The French Expeditionary Corps and VNA totalled some 500,000 men. The Expeditionary Corps consisted of 175,000 ground forces (54,000 French, 30,000 North Africans, 18,000 Africans, 20,000 Legionnaires, and 53,000 native troops) and 55,000 auxiliaries. The Navy had 5,000 men and the Air Force 10,000. The VNA included 150,000 regulars and 50,000 auxiliaries. The Laotian Army counted 15,000 men and Cambodia another 10,000. But Navarre had no tangible manpower edge. Nine-tenths of his forces were either stationary or of reduced mobility, and most were tied down in static defences. Against nine PAVN divisions the French could muster only the equivalent of three divisions (seven *groupes mobiles* and eight paratroop battalions).[54]

Navarre was buoyed by promises of increased US military aid. In 1951 this averaged about 6,000 tons a month; in 1953 it was 20,000 tons; and in 1954 it rose dramatically to 100,000 tons per month. Despite this increased aid the French were bitter about what they regarded as a breech of faith over the July 1953 cease-fire in Korea. Washington and Paris had agreed that Indo-China and Korea were interdependent military fronts and that neither country would pursue peace without consulting with the other. Indeed Washington had helped squash peace feelers from the Việt Minh in 1952. French writer Jacques Valette believes that throughout the 1953–4 crisis the French were let down by their ally.[55]

The press in both France and the United States gave much attention to the new commander's initiatives, the so-called "Navarre Plan". This included negotiations with the Indo-China states to grant them greater independence in exchange for their support for a wider war. He demanded from Paris both additional manpower and equipment, especially pressing after the armistice in Korea had freed up substantial Chinese resources. Navarre proposed the deployment to Indo-China of an additional 20,000 French troops and the raising of 108 indigenous battalions. He was quoted as telling the Paris press that if he received the requested reinforcements, if independence was granted to the Indo-Chinese states, and if China did not step up aid to the Việt Minh, the war could be ended in 18 months.

Critical to this was increasing the size and effectiveness of the VNA. This would include forming progressively larger units – first mobile groups and then divisions – and giving the VNA operational autonomy and more responsibility. Navarre planned to bring the VNA up to 54 battalions before the end of the year and to double that in 1954. In fact he succeeded in creating 107 new battalions – a total of 95,000 men. But the same problems persisted; the VNA was never well trained or well led. Navarre did turn over large areas of the country to VNA responsiblity, something that many French opposed. Nonetheless, problems in the VNA abounded: low morale; desertions, even among officers; and the difficulty of getting soldiers to serve away from their homes.[56]

While building up the VNA, Navarre planned in 1953–4 to avoid major confrontations with Giáp in the northern theatre, while at the same time increasing his forces and initiating a pacification programme in the Red River Delta. He planned to take the offensive in the Central Highlands to forestall Viêt Minh attacks there and as a prelude to complete French control of the South. These goals accomplished, Navarre hoped to engage the Viêt Minh in a set-piece battle in the North during the 1954–5 campaign season and destroy them.[57]

To keep Giáp off balance and on the defensive Navarre launched a series of small attacks. The first of these, Operation Hirondelle ("Swallow") on 17 July, was a three-battalion (2,000-man) paratroop operation against the important Viêt Minh base of Lang Són. Although it provided more of a psychological lift than anything else, Navarre's offensive spirit injected enthusiasm among the French military. The paras discovered signficant quantities of military equipment, including 1,000 Czech-manufactured submachine guns and six Russian Molotova trucks. They also destroyed 20,000 pairs of socks and 500 cartons of Russian cigarettes! The paras then made their way overland to the coast and were evacuated by the French Navy.[58]

Navarre's next operation, Camarque, was not successful. Begun on 28 July, it was directed along the central Vietnamese coast between Huê and Quang Tri City, with the aim of trapping the PAVN 95th Regiment between Highway 1 and the sea. Camarque missed its target and, after several days, was called off.[59]

More worrisome to the Viêt Minh high command were the mixed airlifted commando groups. The GMI were soon operating throughout the Viêt Minh battle zone in the northwest. In October 1953 one even attacked Lào Cai in conjunction with 600 Mèo auxiliaries. The GMI had their greatest successes the next spring when Viêt Minh units were siphoned off for the Battle of Ðiên Biên Phu. Mèo, Thái, and Mán commandos actually took Lào Cai and Lai Châu and laid siege to Cao Băng.[60]

To secure additional manpower for his offensive operations, Navarre ordered the evacuation of a series of small posts and airheads. The French withdrew six infantry battalions and an artillery group from Nà San by 12 August and also the three battalions from Lai Châu on 6 December. These operations were accomplished with relative ease.[61]

Even though his resources were stretched to the breaking point, Navarre also ordered an operation to the south. Known as Atlante, it showed how little he understood the Viêt Minh concept of war. Although Giáp had not done this in the past, Navarre expected Operation Atlante to cause him to pull back elsewhere. It did not.

Atlante, launched in January 1954, was a 15-battalion mainly VNA land assault along the coast of Annam northward from Nha Trang with an amphibious landing near Tuy Hòa. Giáp had anticipated it and ordered his regular units north, leaving only guerrilla units to harass the attacking French. Also the VNA performed poorly, with whole units deserting. Giáp also launched heavy attacks in the Central Highlands, taking Kontum and threatening Pleiku. Atlante bogged down and simply petered out.[62]

Battle of Ðien Biên Phu

At the same time Giáp prepared for a larger invasion of Laos. Mobilizing five divisions, he hoped to overrun all of Laos and perhaps Cambodia, then join up with Viêt Minh units in the South for an assault on Sài Gòn itself. In the meantime some 60,000 guerrillas and five regular regiments would tie down the French in the North. In December 1953 and January 1954 the Viêt Minh overran much of southern and central Laos against light resistance. The French had granted full independence to the Kingdom of Laos in October 1953, but Laotian forces were under French Union command. On 25 December French Union forces evacuated Thakhek on the Mekong. This halted river traffic to the north. In Paris it seemed that Indo-China was about to be cut in two, and the French government immediately put pressure on its military commander in Indo-China to do something about it.[63]

Navarre's response was the establishment of a new airhead in far northwestern Tonkin between and actually farther west than the posts he had just abandoned at Lai Châu and Nà San. It would be astride the main Viêt Minh invasion route into northern Laos that threatened the royal capital of Luang Prabang. Navarre saw this as either a blocking position to prevent an outright invasion of north Laos from that quarter or as bait to draw Viêt Minh forces into a set-piece conventional battle in which they would be destroyed by French artillery and air power. It would also help the French curtail the opium trade, sales from which were helping to finance Viêt Minh weapons purchases.[64]

The new French airhead would be at the village of Ðiên Biên Phu, which had been held by a small Viêt Minh garrison since April 1953. Located some 200 miles by air from Hà Nôi, it had a small airstrip. Navarre's decision resulted in a set-piece battle that for all intents and purposes ended the Indo-China War. It was the most famous battle of the war and one of the major battles of the twentieth century.

Navarre stated in his memoirs that the French government had not opposed his plan, that no military leader had expressed opposition, that French Army Chief of Staff General Ély had approved it, and that "none of my subordinates, neither from the Army nor the Air Force – least of all the others more directly involved – had raised the least objection".[65]

This is not true. Many well-placed French officers in the North had opposed Operation Castor. These included staff officer Colonel Dominique Bastiani, who pointed out that "In this country a direction cannot be barred. It is a European notion without value here. The Viêt goes everywhere." Objections also came from commander of French airborne forces in Indo-China Brigadier General Jean Giles, and Brigadier Generals Jean Dechaux (commander of the Northern Tactical Air Group) and René Masson (deputy French commander in northern Vietnam).[66] Nevertheless in November 1953 Navarre ordered Operation Castor to proceed. On the 20th, 2,200 paras dropped into the valley north and south of Điên Biên Phu. They easily defeated the small Viêt Minh garrison there and began establishing defensive positions.

With a hubris not unknown to other French military commanders in Indo-China, Navarre expected to use superior French artillery and air power to destroy any Viêt Minh forces attacking Điên Biên Phu, and he assumed that at most Giáp would commit one division to such an effort. Should this belief prove incorrect, he was confident the garrison could be evacuated. Even in retrospect it is hard to believe that, given prior French experience, Navarre could have so seriously underestimated his enemy.

Giáp was not enthusiastic about the possibilities. His forces were on the brink of exhaustion, food was short and morale was low; nonetheless, he accepted the challenge. Certainly there was political pressure to do so. A diplomatic conference involving the great powers was set to begin in April in Geneva. This meeting would discuss a range of Far Eastern diplomatic problems, and Hô Chí Minh sought a concurrent military victory that might bring negotiations to end the war.[67]

Hardly anyone had heard of Điên Biên Phu when the French occupied it. It was an obscure village situated in a valley surrounded by hills on all sides. To leave the enemy the opportunity to control the high ground surrounding the base would be to court disaster, but Navarre did not take this into his calculations.

The Battle of Điên Biên Phu

Colonel (promoted brigadier general during the subsequent battle) Christian Marie Ferdinand de la Croix de Castries commanded French forces at Điên Biên Phu. An aristocrat with a reputation as a playboy, he had wide experience in Indo-China and was regarded as a capable commander.[68]

By the end of the first week the French had 4,500 men in the valley. They were entirely dependent on air supply by a small number of transport aircraft (three groups of transports with 75 C–47 Dakotas). The French also had 48 B–26 and Privateer bombers and 112 Bearcat and Hellcat fighter-bombers. There were also a few helicopters. After the battle Navarre wrote in his memoirs, "The insufficiency of aviation was, for our side, the principal cause of the loss of the battle."[69]

The Viêt Minh, on the other hand, relied as they had in previous battles on the very primitive system of transport by human porters. Giáp's troops later improved Route 41 leading to Điên Biên Phu to enable it to handle trucks and artillery pieces. Thanks to Chinese support, at the end of April Giáp had 14 transport companies with 800 trucks, part of a total of 1,200 to 1,300 vehicles. Supplies moved to the battlefield by truck, sampan, bamboo rafts, and bicycles. Nonethless, coolies (the "People's Porters" as Giáp called them) remained the core of the Viêt Minh supply system and were critical to the battle's outcome. Giáp recalled, "Day and night, hundreds of thousands of porters and young volunteers crossed passes and forded rivers in spite of enemy planes and delayed-action bombs."[70]

The French central command post was in Điên Biên Phu itself. Around it de Castries ordered the construction of a series of strong points, supposedly all named for his mistresses: Beatrice, Gabrielle, Anne-Marie, Dominique, Huguette, Françoise, Elaine, and Isabelle. Unfortunately for the French, Isabelle was separated from the others; some three miles to the south, it was easily cut off and tied down a third of the French forces.

De Castries had originally planned a wider defensive ring, perhaps 30 miles in length, but the problems of bringing everything in by air shrank the perimeter. Fortifications were also woefully inadequate. The French assumed that the lack of roads would preclude the Viêt Minh moving artillery there, and that if they did, air power and counter-battery artillery fire would destroy it before it became a problem.[71] Indeed, the French were contemptuous of Viêt Minh artillery capabilities; artillery commander Colonel Charles Piroth had assured Navarre that no Viêt Minh gun "would be able to fire more than three rounds without being located".[72] The French made no effort to camouflage their own positions and placed their guns in open pits. The Viêt Minh easily observed French work from the hills, but French light observation aircraft failed to detect the Viêt Minh buildup.[73]

Beginning in December the French flew in US-supplied M–24 "Chaffee" tanks. Ultimately there were ten of these, assembled at Điên Biên Phu,[74] but they had little impact on the battle. The French also flew in troop reinforcements. These were negated by the fact that Giáp not only called off his own offensive but decided to commit all available divisions to an attack on Điên Biên Phu. The defenders thus encountered a much larger force than the single division Navarre had anticipated.

While the French buildup continued, Giáp worked to cripple the French airlift capacity. In daring early March 1954 raids Viêt Minh commandos attacked French air bases at Gia Lâm near Hà Nôi and Dô Són and Cát Bì airfields near Hai Phòng, destroying 22 aircraft.[75]

At Điên Biên Phu, meanwhile, the French had started patrols. Ominously these were routinely mauled by the Viêt Minh, and de Castries' own chief of staff was killed in one patrol just a few hundred yards from one of the strongpoints. The French then abandoned such activity as counter-productive.

Giáp now closed the ring on the French fortress, bringing the 304th, 308th, 312th, and 316th divisions to the area. The French responded with air strikes. F–8F Bearcats and B–26 bombers attacked Viêt Minh hill positions with bombs, napalm, and rocket fire, but the positions were well disguised by natural camouflage and difficult to identify.

By mid-February de Castries had sustained almost a thousand casualties. The Viêt Minh, meanwhile, continued to build their strength. Bernard Fall estimates that the Viêt Minh ultimately assembled at Điên Biên Phu some 49,500 combat troops and 31,500 support personnel, mostly porters. An additional 23,000 troops maintained supply lines back to the China border. Porters and troops also dragged artillery pieces by hand, positioning them in the hills around the fortress.

In mid-March the French had only 10,814 men in the valley, of whom about 7,000 were front-line combat troops. Fully a third of the garrison was Vietnamese, although most of these were tribal Thái. The Viêt Minh therefore enjoyed a superiority of some five to one in manpower in addition to greater firepower.[76]

The siege of Điên Biên Phu officially began on 13 March with a heavy Viêt Minh bombardment. Although the French added 4,000 men during the siege, Giáp more than offset this with manpower increases of his own. He also steadily improved both the quantity and quality of his artillery. Ultimately the Viêt Minh deployed 20 to 24 105 mm howitzers, 15 to 20 75 mm howitzers, 20 120 mm mortars, and at least 40 82 mm mortars. They also had some 80

Chinese-crewed 37 mm anti-aircraft guns, 100 anti-aircraft machine guns, and 12 to 16 six-tube Katyusha rocket launchers. During the battle the Việt Minh fired some 103,000 rounds of 75 mm or larger size, most of it by direct fire, simply aiming down their gun tubes from the surrounding heights at the French positions in the valley. Some 75 per cent of French casualties came from artillery fire.

By contrast French artillery assets proved totally inadequate; the French had only four 155 mm howitzers, 24 105 mm howitzers, and four 120 mm mortars. In contrast to the Việt Minh the French fired 93,000 shells during the battle; but, unlike the Việt Minh, they had difficulty identifying their targets.[77]

On the very first night of the siege, 13–14 March, the Việt Minh took Beatrice. Gabrielle fell two days later. Giáp's original plan called for taking the entire French fortress within a few days. His basic tactic consisted of massive artillery fire followed by infantry human wave assaults.

The Việt Minh also brought the airstrip under fire to try to destroy F–8F Bearcat fighters there. One was destroyed on the 13th and two escaped to Vientiane. The next day three more got away to Cát Bì Airport; the remaining six were destroyed on the ground. The control tower was also badly damaged and the radio beacon was knocked out.[78]

Pessimism now spread throughout the French command. At Hà Nội, French commander in the North General René Cogny, never enthusiastic about the operation, began to consider the possibility of losing the fortress. His resources were stretched thin because Giáp had sent the 320th Division, three autonomous regiments, and 14 regional battalions to disrupt the vital transportation link between Hà Nội and Hai Phòng and divert French resources by attacking French outposts in the Red River Delta. The Việt Minh offensive there began on 12 March, the day before the battle began at Điên Biên Phu, forcing Cogny to fight two battles at once. Navarre, who held to the primacy of central Indo-China, refused any reinforcements.[79] Even ammunition was in short supply as Việt Minh sappers blew up French stocks.

On 22 March the French used their last four tanks to counterattack PAVN troops who had cut off Isabelle. This effort met units from Isabelle striking north. It was the first French success of the battle but cost 151 French dead, one missing, and 72 wounded. Việt Minh casualties were heavier, but Giáp had a seemingly inexhaustible supply of manpower.[80]

The arrival of the rainy season made conditions even more hellish for attacker and defender alike, further complicating French resupply problems. C–47 Dakotas still flew in supplies and took out wounded, but at great risk. On 26 March one was shot down; two more were lost on the 27th. Late that same day one managed to land and pick up 19 wounded. It was the last flight in or out of Điên Biên Phu.[81]

On 26 March Major Bigeard, who had parachuted into the fortress only ten days before, commanded a successful attack against Viêt Minh positions. Supported by artillery, fighter aicraft and a tank platoon from Isabelle, the paras sallied from the fortress to assault the Viêt Minh. Bigeard later put Viêt Minh losses at some 350 dead and more than 500 wounded, as well as ten prisoners. The raiders also captured five 20 mm anti-aircraft cannon, 12 .50 calibre machine guns, two bazookas, 14 submachine guns; and they reclaimed ten prisoners.[82]

Having already suffered about 6,600 killed and 12,000 wounded, Giáp's army suffered from low morale – what Giáp later called a "rightist and negative tendency".[83] Discussions led by political cadres about courage, right thinking and dedication helped to restore morale, as did a change in tactics. Giáp abandoned the costly human wave attacks in favour of attrition warfare that resembled World War I. The Viêt Minh dug hundreds of miles of trenches, using them to cut off a particular strongpoint from outside support.[84]

The last stage of the battle was fought without letup in an area of about one square mile around the airstrip. The Viêt Minh attacked on 29 April and by 4 May French senior officers knew that all hope was lost. The last French reinforcements, 165 men of the 1st Colonial Parachute Battalion, jumped into the garrison on 5 and 6 May. They had come at their own insistence to share the fate of their comrades. This brought the cumulative total of the garrison to 16,544 men. By now most of the air drops of supplies were falling into Viêt Minh hands. The final Viêt Minh assault occurred on 6 May, accompanied by the explosion of mines and the firing of Katyusha rockets. The last French troops surrendered on the evening of 7 May.[85] General Yves Gras summed it up in these words: "The fortress of Dien Bien Phu had finally succumbed because it had not been relieved from the outside. . . . Without doubt, it had immobilized the main part of the enemy for six months . . . The fortress ended by falling as, in the course of history, all besieged fortresses fall when left to their fate."[86]

During the siege the French suffered 1,600 killed, 4,800 wounded, and 1,600 missing. The Viêt Minh immediately sent their 8,000 prisoners off on foot on a 500-mile march to prison camps. Less than half returned. Of the Vietnamese taken only 10 per cent were seen again. The Viêt Minh had also shot down 48 French planes and destroyed 16 others on the ground. Viêt Minh casualties amounted to some 7,900 killed and 15,000 wounded.[87]

The French had two plans to rescue the garrison. Operation Condor called for an infantry thrust from Laos to link up with airborne forces from Hà Nôi. Operation Albatross had the garrison attempting to break out on its own. Navarre did not order Cogny to begin planning for this until 3 May. This was because Navarre steadfastly refused to consider Điên Biên Phu the principal battle of the campaign. Not until 7 May did de Castries decide to attempt to execute the plan but it was then too late.

Washington discussed with French Army Chief of Staff General Ély the possibility of US intervention to enable the French to "disengage the garrison" and "resume the initiative".[88] Vice President Richard Nixon was a "hawk" on Vietnam, suggesting in April that the United States might have to "put American boys in".[89] In Operation Vulture Chairman of the Joint Chiefs of Staff Admiral Arthur B. Radford proposed massive B–29 airstrikes from the Philippines and carrier strikes from the Gulf of Tonkin involving up to 350 aircraft. There was even discussion of employing nuclear weapons. A Joint Chiefs of Staff (JCS) study committee concluded that three tactical nuclear bombs would be sufficient to smash the Việt Minh at Điên Biên Phu. President Dwight D. Eisenhower considered American participation but made it contingent on British support – and London was opposed. The British government believed that the battle was too far gone and chose to pin its hopes on the Geneva Conference.[90] As perceptive Foreign Minister Anthony Eden noted prophetically: "I am beginning to think Americans are quite ready to supplant French and see themselves in the role of liberators of Vietnamese patriotism and expulsers or redeemers of Communist insurgency in Indo-China. If so they are in for a painful awakening."[91]

The battle of Điên Biên Phu signalled the death-knell for the French in Asia. In Paris Premier Joseph Laniel, dressed in black, gave the news to the National Assembly. The 8 May headline of *Le Figaro* announced: "After fifty-five days of heroic resistance, the fortress of Dien Bien Phu fell yesterday."[92]

Although the battle had tied down Việt Minh resources, it did not help the French situation elsewhere in Indo-China, except perhaps in the northwest. The Việt Minh increased its presence in the Red River Delta and in the Central Highlands, where in late June 1954 the 108th and 803rd PAVN regiments destroyed *Groupe Mobile* 100 as it headed west along Route 19. After that French control in the Central Highlands was limited to a small area around Ban Mê Thuôt and Đà Lat.[93]

On 8 June General Ély, who had headed a fact-finding mission to Indo-China in May, took command from Navarre. Paris also invested Ély with political power as Commissary General.[94] Navarre never took any responsibility for the debacle. Embittered, he retired to write his memoirs. He blamed the politicans for not having the backbone to tell the nation that there was a war in Indo-China, for failing to enunciate a clear policy and for stabbing the army in the back by not providing the manpower or resources with which to win.[95]

Although much of what Navarre charged was true (and his view was widely shared within the Army), the dramatic French military defeat at Điên

Biên Phu allowed the politicians to shift blame for the Indo-China debacle to the military and extricate the nation from the morass. A new government under Radical Party leader Pierre Mendès-France, a long-time critic of French colonial policy, came to power to carry out that mandate. The vehicle would be the Geneva Conference, which had opened on 26 April before the fall of the French fortress.

The Geneva Conference and Accords

On 17 June Mendès-France became premier and foreign minister. Three days later he imposed a 30-day timetable for an agreement and promised to resign if one was not reached; the Geneva Accords were signed on the last day of the deadline, 20 July (but only because the clocks were stopped; it was actually early on 21 July).

The leading personalities at Geneva were Mendès-France, Zhou Enlai (Chou Enlai, PRC), Vyacheslav Molotov (USSR), Anthony Eden (UK), John Foster Dulles (USA), Phạm Văn Đông (DRV) and Nguyên Quôc Đinh (SVN). Dulles left the conference after only a few days. He saw no likelihood of an agreement on Indo-China that Washington could approve, and he disliked the idea of negotiating with Zhou Enlai (the United States did not then recognize the PRC). Dulles ordered the US delegation not to participate in the discussions and to act only as observers.

The Geneva Conference produced separate armistice agreements for Vietnam, Cambodia, and Laos. But Phạm Văn Đông found himself pressured by Zhou Enlai and Molotov into an agreement that gave the Viêt Minh far less than it had won on the battlefield. Pending unification of Vietnam there was to be a *temporary* dividing line ("provisional demarcation line") at the 17th parallel. A demilitarized zone (DMZ) would extend five kilometres on either side of the line in order to prevent incidents that might lead to a breach of the armistice. The final text provided that "the military demarcation line is provisional and should not in any way be interpreted as constituting a political or territorial boundary". Vietnam's future was to be determined "on the basis of respect for the principles of independence, unity, and territorial integrity" with "national and general elections" to be held in July 1956. Troops on both sides would have up to 300 days to be regrouped north or south; civilians could also move in either direction if they so desired. An international supervisory and control commission (ISCC) composed of representatives of Canada, Poland and India (a Western State, a Communist state and a non-aligned state), would oversee implementation of the agreements.[96] Phạm Văn

Đồng was bitterly disappointed that nationwide elections were put off for two years. The DRV accepted the arrangements because of heavy pressure from the PRC and USSR and because it was confident it could control the South. There is every reason to believe that the Chinese leadership was willing to sabotage their ally in order to prevent the formation of a strong regional power on their southern border.

In the Indo-China War the French and their allies sustained 172,708 casualties: 94,581 dead or missing and 78,127 wounded. These broke down as 140,992 French Union casualties (75,867 dead or missing and 65,125 wounded) with the allied Indo-China states losing 31,716 (18,714 dead or missing and 13,002 wounded). French dead or missing numbered some 20,000; legionnaires, 11,000; Africans, 15,000; and Indo-Chinese, 46,000. The war took a particularly heavy toll among the officers, 1,900 of whom died. Việt Minh losses were probably three times those of the French and their allies. Perhaps 150,000 Vietnamese civilians also perished. The war had cost France a million francs a day.[97]

One major issue throughout the war and for some years afterward was that of prisoners held by the Việt Minh, both military and civilian. Their status was always ambiguous because they were more hostages than prisoners of war, especially as the Việt Minh did not recognize the Geneva Convention. Their prisoners were held in barbarous conditions throughout the war, and beginning in 1950 were subjected to an intensive political re-education effort. As a paratroop priest who spent three years in the camps put it, "The worst wasn't to die, but to see one's soul change."[98]

Only a small percentage of the 36,979 reported missing during the war returned. Depending on the source, the number of confirmed prisoners in the summer of 1954 was between 21,526 and 22,474. Only 10,754 returned home and 6,132 of them required immediate hospitalization. Lengths of captivity varied from between four to five months for those taken at Điện Biên Phu to up to eight years for some civilians. For many of the prisoners the Indo-China War thus continued well past 1954.[99]

The Indo-China War had really been three wars in one. Begun as a conflict between Vietnamese nationalists and France, it became a civil war between Vietnamese – hardly new in Vietnamese history – and it was also part of the larger Cold War. As it turned out, in 1954 the civil war and the East–West conflict were only suspended. Ten years later a new conflict broke out, but by then the French had ceded place to the Americans.

Chapter Four

The Vietnam War: the United States takes over (1954–65)

The 1954 Geneva Conference that ended the Indo-China War temporarily divided Vietnam at the 17th parallel. A Demilitarized Zone (DMZ) separated the two parts and national elections to reunify the country were to be held in 1956. Regroupment of the 120,000-man French Expeditionary Corps from Tonkin and 140,000 PAVN soldiers and guerrillas from the South proceeded without incident. The French had 100 days to withdraw to Hai Phòng and an additional 200 days to re-embark for the South. They evacuated Hà Nôi on 9 October and Hai Phòng on 30 October. At the same time Viêt Minh units in central and southern Vietnam carried out their own regroupment. By 30 October the Viêt Minh had only two bridgeheads in the South, at Quâng Ngãi and at the tip of the Cà Mau peninsula.

A great many Northerners took advantage of Article 14D of the Accords that gave them free passage south during the 300-day regroupment period. The great majority were Roman Catholics from the Red River Delta area who, following their priests, often moved as entire communities. Minorities, such as the Nùng, also left. The US Navy provided sealift support. The Viêt Minh employed a variety of means to try to stem this exodus, but upwards of a million people left the North to resettle in the South – a propaganda bonanza for the State of Vietnam.[1]

Hô Chí Minh's Democratic Republic of Vietnam (DRV) governed the North. The State of Vietnam (SVN), headed by Emperor Bao Đai, then living in France, held sway in the South. In June 1954 Bao Đai appointed Ngô Đình Diêm to head his government.

Demilitarized Zone

Cam Lo
Dong Ha
Quang Tri City
Khe Sanh
Quang Tri
Province
Hue
Phu Bai
A Shau
Valley
Da Nang
An Hoa
Tam Ky
Route 14
Chu Lai
My Lai
Route 1
Dak To
Pleiku
Kontum
Route 19
Pleiku
Qui Nhon
An Khe
Ia Drang
Valley
Tuy Hoa
Route 21
Ban Me Thuot
Nha Trang
Gia Nghia
Cam Rahn
Phuoc
Binh
Da Lat
Nui Ba Den
(Black Virgin Mountain)
Bao Loc
Phan Rhang
Tay Ninh
Lai Khe
Lai Khe
Route 1
Ben Suc
Phan Thiet
Bien Hoa
Sai Gon
Long Binh
Ha tien
My Tho
Rach Gia
Vung Tau
Can Tho
Bac Lieu
Ca Mau
Peninsula

Republic of Vietnam

Miles 200
Kms 200

PEOPLE'S
REPUBLIC OF
CHINA
Hanoi
Laos
Gulf of
Tonkin
Hainan
Demilitarized
Zone (DMZ)
THAILAND
CAMBODIA
Sai Gon
South China Sea

Ngô Đình Diêm

Ngô Đình Diêm was born in a Catholic family in Quang Bình Province in 1901. His father had been an official in the imperial court at Huê before the French removed him. Diêm attended his father's private school and then French Catholic schools in Huê. For a time he considered becoming a priest like his older brother Ngô Đình Thuc, later archbishop of Huê. Instead he attended the School of Law and Public Administration in Hà Nôi, from which he graduated at the top of his class. Afterward he entered government administration as a provincial governor.

A popular administrator, Diêm carried out land reforms and endeavoured to secure justice for all. His 1929 experience in helping to crush a Communist uprising made him an ardent anti-Communist. In 1933 Emperor Bao Đai appointed him minister of the interior for Annam, but Diêm soon discovered that he had no power and resigned. For the next ten years he lived in seclusion in Huê, keeping in touch with Vietnamese nationalists.

In September 1945 the Viêt Minh kidnapped Diêm, and during his captivity he contracted malaria. On his recovery he learned that the Viêt Minh had killed his older brother, Ngô Đình Khói. Six months later Diêm was taken to Hà Nôi where Hô Chí Minh asked him to join the Communists. Diêm refused and, much to his surprise, was released. During the next four years he travelled the country seeking political support, but an attempt on his life in 1950 prompted him to go abroad.

Diêm spent two years in the United States at Catholic seminaries in New Jersey and New York, where he seemed more suited to be a priest than a politician. He also met with prominent Americans such as Justice William O. Douglas, Senators John F. Kennedy and Mike Mansfield, and Francis Cardinal Spellman, his greatest American supporter.[2] Diêm convinced them that, because of his opposition to both the French and the Communists, he was the only viable nationalist alternative.

In May 1953, frustrated by the Eisenhower Administration's support for the French, Diêm went to stay in a Benedictine monastery in Belgium, but regularly visited with members of the large Vietnamese exile community in Paris that included Ngô Đình Luyên, his youngest brother and a prominent engineer.

Diêm needed Emperor Bao Đai to legitimize his rise to power, and Bao Đai needed the support of Diêm's powerful allies, including his brother Ngô Đình Nhu, who had set up in Sài Gòn the Front for National Salvation as an alternative to the Communists. While Diêm's reputation as a nationalist was tarnished by his having been abroad during much of the Indo-China War, his lack of co-operation with the French enhanced it. Because of the time Diêm had spent in the United States and his meetings with American leaders there, Bao Đai believed that Washington backed him. On 18 June 1954, Bao Đai summoned Diêm to his villa in Cannes and appointed him prime minister. Diêm returned to Sài Gòn on 26 June, and on 7 July officially formed his new government, which claimed to embrace all Vietnam.

Although Diêm had been given significant authority by Bao Đai, his initial power base in Vietnam was quite narrow. It consisted of Catholics (especially the nearly one million who had come South), the landed gentry, and fervent anti–Communist nationalists. Many of the rich and powerful as well as Francophiles opposed him, as did most of the nationalist parties and religious sects.

As a leader Diêm was fiercely nationalistic. He was also a micro-manager who insisted on attending to every detail. Distrustful of those beyond his immediate family circle, he was both proud and rigid. Diêm welcomed US financial and military support but not American advice.[3]

Diêm faced staggering tasks, the most pressing of which were organizing a government, absorbing the influx of northern refugees, and restoring economic stability. Beyond that he sought to eradicate French influence and to neutralize both the Cao Đài and Hòa Hao religious sects and his political opposition. Many observers believed that Diêm would not last long in power, but he proved to be an adroit political manipulator. American aid was also crucial in his survival.

The United States supported Diêm, at first cautiously and then without qualification. The Eisenhower Administration, eager to establish a strong anti–Communist regime in South Vietnam, held up Diêm as a model for Asia and supplied increasing amounts of aid to his government.

US military involvement

The United States also sent military personnel to train the South Vietnamese armed forces. The Joint Chiefs of Staff (JCS) believed that creation of an effective Vietnamese National Army was impossible under then-prevailing conditions, but agreed to undertake the task because of political considerations.[4] Assistant Chief of Staff for Operations Lieutenant General James M. Gavin noted, "We in the Army were so relieved that we had blocked the decision to commit ground troops to Vietnam that we were in no mood to quibble."[5] This decision, however, led precisely to what Gavin and others at the Pentagon had sought to prevent.

Diêm, meanwhile, was locked in a test of wills with Army Chief of Staff General Nguyên Văn Hinh. Although honest and a patriot, Hinh had been a regular officer in the French Air Force and a naturalized French citizen with a French wife; many in the Vietnamese Army regarded him as more French than Vietnamese. By late August Hinh openly admitted to US authorities that he was talking to leaders of the religious sects about a coup. When Diêm ordered Hinh to leave the country on a six-week "study tour" in France, Hinh refused.

Talk of a coup ended when Eisenhower sent former Army Chief of Staff General J. Lawton Collins to South Vietnam as special ambassador with authority over all US government agencies in Vietnam. Collins arrived in Sài Gòn on 8 November. Meanwhile Senator Mansfield strongly endorsed Diêm as the only possible leader for a non-Communist South Vietnam and argued that if he was toppled the United States should cut off all aid. Eisenhower also made his support for Diêm public. Upon his arrival Collins stated that Washington would deal only with Diêm, and at the end of November Hinh left Vietnam for exile in France.

Critical to Diêm's survival was Washington's October decision to channel all aid directly to his government; this greatly upset the French, as it undercut their remaining authority in the South. Washington and Paris had seen the struggle between Diêm and Hinh as an effort by the other side to undermine its own interests and prestige in Vietnam. By February 1956 only 15,000 French troops remained in South Vietnam, and on 26 April France officially abolished its high command in Indo-China. The last French troops left Sài Gòn on 14 September.[6]

Internationally the United States supported Diêm by taking the lead in the creation, on 8 September 1954, of a loose-knit regional collective security alliance – the Southeast Asia Treaty Organization (SEATO). Unlike the North Atlantic Treaty Organization (NATO), it had no standing military force and no specific action was required in the event of hostile action. Its members – the United States, France, Britain, New Zealand, Australia, Pakistan, the Philippines and Thailand – pledged themselves only to "act to meet the common danger" in the event of aggression against any signatory state. A separate protocol extended the treaty's security provisions to Laos, Cambodia and the "free territory under the jurisdiction of the State of Vietnam".[7]

President Eisenhower also sought to buttress Diêm's authority by sending high-ranking US officials to Vietnam, including Secretary of State John Foster Dulles in 1955 and Vice President Richard Nixon in 1956. In 1957 Diêm travelled to the United States and spoke to a joint session of Congress.

General Collins, meanwhile, had drawn up a plan for a smaller Vietnamese Army. It called for its reduction by July 1955 from 170,000 to 77,000 men in six divisions: three conventional divisions that could at least delay an invasion from the North and three more mobile and lightly equipped divisions capable of reinforcing the others while providing internal security.[8]

The issue of army reform touched off a confrontation with the various opposition groups in South Vietnam that maintained their own military formations. A number of these, including the Cao Đài and the Hòa Hao, the Dai Viêt Party and the Bình Xuyên, had already united against the government. The Bình Xuyên were Sài Gòn-based gangsters who had their own well-organized militia. Central to the sect leaders' opposition to Diêm was his plan to incorporate only a few of their armed units into the VNA and to disband the rest. In March and April 1955 fighting erupted between Vietnamese Army units loyal to Diêm and the Bình Xuyên.[9] Diêm, meanwhile, managed to splinter his opposition. The liberal use of bribes helped rally to the government portions of the Cao Đài, Hòa Hao and even some Bình Xuyên. By the end of May government troops had driven the remaining Bình Xuyên from the capital. Still Diêm's struggle with the sects led Collins to reconsider his support. He believed Diêm lacked the ability to govern and called on the State Department to replace him with a coalition government.[10]

Bao Đai also tried to topple Diêm. He named General Nguyên Văn Vy, a well-known opponent of Diêm, to replace Hinh as commander of the VNA and summoned Diêm to France for a meeting. Diêm refused to go and turned the tables by calling for a referendum in which the people would choose between himself and Bao Đai. Diêm would easily have won any honest contest, but he ignored US appeals and falsified the results so that it was 98 per cent in his favour. The Sài Gòn announced vote was 605,025, a third more than the 450,000 registered voters there.[11] On 26 October 1955, using the results as justification, Diêm proclaimed the Republic of Vietnam (RVN) with himself as president. Its military forces were identified by the acronym RVNAF. The army was now known as ARVN; its navy, VNN; and its air force, VNAF.

Building the Vietnamese military

Plans to cut the size of ARVN proved illusory, especially as the PAVN continued to increase. In May 1955 Lieutenant General John W. O'Daniel, head of the US Military Assistance Advisory Group (MAAG), recommended to Washington an army of 150,000 men: four field divisions and six light divisions with 13 territorial regiments for regional security that were capable of consolidating into three or more light divisions. O'Daniel and his successor presumed that any PAVN attack would be a conventional invasion across the DMZ in the fashion of Korea, in which case ARVN would fall back and hold at Đà Nẵng. Two field divisions and one light division would then stage an amphibious landing at Vinh and cut off the invaders.

O'Daniel's field divisions were only about half the size of comparable US divisions, but had half again the number of automatic rifles and a third more 81 mm mortars. His light divisions were small mobile strike forces (about a third the size of standard US infantry divisions) with sufficient firepower for close-in fighting. They would have 30 per cent more machine guns than an American division, 10 per cent more Browning automatic rifles, and the same number of 60 mm and 81 mm mortars. But they would have no organic artillery and only a fraction of the transportation alloted to an American division.[12]

In October 1955 the blunt-speaking Lieutenant General Samuel T. Williams succeeded O'Daniel as chief of MAAG, Vietnam. He developed a close relationship with Diêm, which was one reason why he held the post until October 1960. Williams continued to see the primary military threat as a conventional PAVN attack across the DMZ. But while O'Daniel believed that the light forces could perform some security functions, Williams would leave that to specially trained paramilitary organizations. Williams saw guerrillas as drawing off main units, at which point PAVN forces would mount a conventional attack. Neither O'Daniel nor Williams regarded guerrillas as a serious threat. To them guerrillas were essentially a police problem.[13] Bernard Fall called such thinking "utterly disastrous, for it created a road-bound, over-motorized, hard-to-supply battle force totally incapable of besting the *real* enemy (i.e., the elusive guerrilla and not the Viet-Minh divisional regular) on his own ground".[14]

Victorious armies tend to prepare for the next war along the same lines as the last conflict; in the case of the United States this meant World War II and Korea. This ignored counter-insurgency warfare, despite the long American involvement in such operations. Few in the US Army had any practical experience in combating guerrillas, and the conduct of such warfare was itself restricted to the Army Special Forces.[15] The inability to forecast the nature of the military threat was the first great US military mistake in Vietnam.

In 1956 and well afterward the ARVN was largely ineffective. It was very short of officers, especially in the higher ranks. Many of these had fought on the French side in the Indo-China War and some were French citizens, so there were few with nationalist credentials. Diêm placed political reliability over military ability, and his officer corps was rife with favouritism and politicization. Corruption was endemic, particularly at the higher levels where some officers sold goods on the black market and engaged in drug smuggling. Communist agents also heavily infiltrated the RVNAF. Woefully untrained, the

ARVN was also short of equipment and its maintenance was below US minimum standards. Pay was not a problem; by Asian standards it was surprisingly high.

Racial stereotyping (the US military referred to the Vietnamese as "natives" until the term was officially banned in 1957) and lack of American familiarity with the Vietnamese culture and language were barriers to US–RVN military co-operation and efficency. General Cao Văn Viên, later chief of the Joint General Staff, could not recall a single instance "in which a US advisor effectively discussed professional matters with his counterpart in Vietnamese". For too long Williams was unaware of the magnitude of these problems.[16]

Committed as he was to crushing his internal opposition, Diêm was reluctant to begin concentrating scattered battalions so that they might be trained and reorganized into divisions. This process began only in the fall of 1955. ARVN was largely a collection of scattered battalions involved in suppressing sects and dissidents. Guard duty and security operations also impeded this process.[17]

It was not until 1959 that substantial reorganization of the 150,000-man ARVN began, a process not completed until 1960. Both light and field divisions were disbanded and replaced by seven "field divisions" of 10,450 men. Each had three infantry regiments, two artillery battalions (one of 4.2-inch mortars), and combat support and service units. General Williams believed that such units would be better suited to resisting an invasion from the North and carrying out internal security. Building around a single type of combat unit would also facilitate logistics, maintenance, and planning operations.[18]

Although Williams bristled at comparisons between the new divisions and those in the US Army, there were similarities. Perhaps this was inevitable, given logistical requirements. ARVN infantry divisions were lighter, without the artillery, tanks, personnel carriers and helicopters available in their US counterparts. But as with the French Expeditionary Corps, the new divisions were road-bound. The soldiers moved on foot but artillery had to come by road, and increasingly ARVN commanders showed a disinclination to fight where their artillery could not go with them.[19]

Growing US aid to South Vietnam

US aid to the Republic of Vietnam was vital to Diêm's survival, especially as in 1955 his government collected revenues equal to only one-third of expenditures. Such aid enabled Diêm to reject talks with Hà Nôi over the Geneva-mandated elections, which the Viêt Minh, confident of electoral victory, so ardently sought. During the period 1954–63 total US aid came to about $1.7 billion.[20] More than three-quarters of all US assistance went into the military budget, with the remainder supporting the bureaucracy and transportation. Most non-military aid stayed in the cities, with a minority of the population. Of the non-military aid, only modest amounts were set aside for land reform and agricultural improvement, education, health, industrial development and housing and community development. Most of the remainder supported Vietnamese settlements in the Central Highlands and the building of a secondary road system to connect the Highlands with the more populous coast.[21] This US assistance freed Diêm from the necessity of carrying out economic reforms.

Certainly Diêm was out of touch with the countryside and little was done to carry out much-needed land reform, vital in winning the peasants; in 1961 75 per cent of the land was owned by 15 per cent of the population. By 1962, although slightly more than a million acres of land had been transferred to the peasants, this was less than a quarter of the acreage eligible for expropriation and purchase. To 1960 less than 2 per cent of Washington's aid to Sài Gòn went for agrarian reform.

In 1956 Diêm launched his Tô Công (denunciation of Communists) campaign to locate secret Viêt Minh arms caches and to arrest hundreds of their political cadres who had remained in the South to prepare for the planned national elections. The arrest of the cadres was a violation of the Geneva Agreements. Diêm also ordered the imprisonment of many non-Communists and alienated the ethnic minorities. Diêm alienated many Montagnards by his effort to impose Vietnamese culture on them; this also reversed a long-standing French policy. The Montagnards also suffered in Diêm's efforts to relocate rural populations into government-controlled areas. Growing Montagnard discontent led dissidents among them to form the ethnonationalistic FULRO (Le Front Unifié de Lutte des Races Opprimées, or United Struggle Front for Oppressed Races).[22]

Diêm refused to enter into economic talks with the DRV or to hold the elections called for in the Geneva Accords. He declared that his government was not a party to the agreements and thus not bound by them, and Washington supported him in this. Since the State of Vietnam delegation had not signed anything at Geneva, this was strictly speaking true. The crux of the matter was whether Diêm was bound by France's adherence. Both Washington and Sài Gòn also claimed that no elections could be held until there was a democratic government in Hà Nôi. This was not a part of the 1954 agreements.[23]

On 4 March 1956, the South Vietnamese elected a 123-member national legislative assembly; a new constitution, heavily weighted towards control by the executive, came into effect on 26 October. The country was divided into 41 provinces, then subdivided into districts and villages.

These apparent reforms were largely a sham, as Diêm increasingly subjected the South to authoritarian rule. He completely dominated the National Assembly. His government was also highly centralized and the administration appointed officials even at the local level. Most province chiefs were military officers loyal to Diêm. Catholics, many of them Northerners who had only recently come South, received key positions. Political loyalty rather than ability was the test for leadership posts in both the government and the military.

But Diêm proved an adroit practitioner of the divide-and-rule concept. Rarely did he reach out for advice beyond his immediate family circle; his closest adviser was probably his older brother, Bishop Ngô Đình Thuc. Diêm also delegated a great deal of authority to his brother Ngô Đình Nhu, who controlled the secret police and the Personalist Labour Party (Cân Lao Party).

General Williams believed Diêm was generally popular. US State Department personnel, including Ambassador Elbridge Durbrow, had a very different opinion. Perhaps British journalist David Hotham best summed up the situation in South Vietnam in 1957 when he wrote: "Diem holds the fort through the Army and the police force provided by US [money]. It is not that the communists have done nothing because Diem is in power, rather Diem has remained in power because the communists have done nothing."[24] That situation now changed.

Fighting resumes in the South

Diêm's initial difficulties had come not from the Viêt Minh but from the armies of the religious sects, the Bình Xuyên, and the Đai Viêt party. By 1957 Diêm had subdued these, but in doing so destroyed the most powerful non-Communist groups. The Viêt Minh proved more difficult. A number of their political cadres had remained in the South, as provided in the Geneva Accords to prepare for the 1956 national elections. Many had been arrested, but in 1957 others, joined by recruits, began a campaign of terror and subversion against the government, often in conjunction with remnants of the sects. At first the insurgents operated without tangible Northern support.[25]

Although the Diêm government originally enjoyed acceptance, opposition to it steadily grew within South Vietnam. This was occasioned by many factors, including the loss of village autonomy and the appointment of un-familiar officials, activities of Nhu family members, favouritism shown to

Catholics, forced labour on district facilities, and widespread corruption and mismanagement at the local level.[26]

Insurgent activity increased throughout 1957 and into 1958. One large action occurred on the night of 10 August 1958, when 400 raiders attacked the large Michelin rubber plantation north of Sài Gòn, easily defeating a security force and making off with more than 100 weapons and 5 million piasters (some $143,000). Such activities were concentrated in the southern provinces, mainly in inhospitable terrain along the Cambodian border.[27]

Following the Geneva Accords Hà Nôi's leaders, while confidently looking forward to the reunification of Vietnam in 1956, had concentrated on economic rehabilitation. In fact Northern leaders continued to focus on economic problems at the expense of reunification efforts, even after the date for the elections had come and gone.

The North had been rocked economically by the departure south of such a large and productive element of its population. The regime was also hard pressed to feed those who remained because it had a larger population – some 16 million compared to 14 million in the South – and yet it produced only about 40 per cent of Vietnam's rice. Economic hardship, in part caused by the rebuff by the RVN of any economic co-operation, forced the DRV into further economic dependence on the Communist camp.

The DRV leaders instituted land reform, at least partly to rid themselves of a potential opposition. Beginning in 1953 many owners of small plots of land were reclassified as "landlords" and thousands were sentenced to death. The policy ultimately produced wholesale revolt, and in November 1956 the PAVN 325th Division had to be called out to crush rebels in Nghê An province. In all some 6,000 farmers were deported or executed. In the end Hô Chí Minh concluded that it was easier to change the policy than the peasants, and agricultural production was increased to where it was sufficient to sustain Northern requirements. Industrialization also went forward. Thanks to Chinese and Russian assistance, the DRV constructed the first steel plant in Southeast Asia, at Thái Nguyên near Hà Nôi.

Just when the North began to support the southern insurgency materially is uncertain, but it is clear that by late 1958 the insurgents in the South had presented the North with a *fait accompli*. At the end of the year Hô Chí Minh sent his trusted lieutenant Lê Duân to the South on a fact-finding mission. Known as the "Flame of the South" for his leadership there during the Indo-China War, Lê Duân was then *de facto* general secretary of the Lao Đông Party[28] and second in authority only to Hô Chí Minh. He returned with the recommendation that the North assume leadership of the insurgency. In January 1959 the party central committee agreed to support armed insurrection in the South, although it should remain secondary to the "political struggle". This position was formalized at the May Fifteenth Party Plenum.[29]

At the Third Party Congress, held in Hà Nôi in September 1960, the leadership went on public record as supporting the establishment of a United Front and approving a programme of violent overthrow of the Diêm government.[30] There were now two pre-eminent tasks: carrying out a "socialist revolution" in the North and "liberating the South".

In May 1959 General Giáp, a reluctant convert to aggressive action in the South, had formed the 559th Transportation Group (for the fifth month of 1959) to move supplies south through eastern Laos. Group 759, organized that July, was to arrange resupply by sea.[31] Land resupply was by far the most important, however. Vastly expanded and made more sophisticated over the years, the Laotian network became known as the Hô Chí Minh Trail. Infiltrators moved south in groups of up to 500 men, but usually about 50. Initially these were native southerners who had fought against the French and been relocated to the North in 1954. Way-stations along the trail quartered and fed the groups, and local guides assisted them between stations. Infiltrators were usually issued a set of black civilian pyjama-like clothes, two unmarked uniforms, rubber sandals (known later to American GIs as "Hô Chí Minh sandals"), a sweater, a hammock, mosquito netting and a poncho. They also carried a three- to five-day supply of food and some medical supplies.[32]

The old Nam Bô (South Region) Central Committee that had directed the Viêt Minh effort against the French in Cochin China now reappeared as the Central Office for South Vietnam (COSVN). Then on 20 December 1960, Hà Nôi established the National Front for the Liberation of South Vietnam, usually known as the National Liberation Front (NLF). Designed to replicate the Viêt Minh as an umbrella nationalist organization, it reached out to all those disaffected with Diêm. From the beginning the NLF was completely dominated by the Lao Đông Party Central Committee and was the North's shadow government in the South.[33]

Growth of the insurgency

The southern insurgency grew much more quickly than the DRV leadership anticipated. It was fed by the Diêm government's weakness, its inattention to the needs of the peasants, and its unwillingness to acknowledge problems. In addition to promising reform, especially in returning land to the peasants (what the Americans called "winning hearts and minds"), the NLF sought physically to control the villages. In 1957 perhaps some 80 per cent of the

INDO-CHINA
infiltration routes

International boundaries — · — · —

Ho Chi Minh and Sihanouk Trails:
Personnel routes
Logistical routes
Infiltration bases ☆

Miles 200
Kms 200

southern population lived in 17,000 hamlets spread over 8,000 villages. Controlling these would be the key both to supporting existing guerrilla forces and later to expanding them. Towards this end the NLF stepped up its programme of assassinations of Diêm-appointed local officials. During 1957–8 some 700 village-level officials were killed; 1,200 died in 1958–9, 2,500 during 1959–60, and 4,000 died from May 1960 to May 1961. School-teachers, social workers, and medical personnel were also favoured targets for kidnapping and assassination.[34]

NLF main force units increasingly attacked regular ARVN troop formations. On 26 September 1959, the 2nd Liberation Battalion ambushed two compa-nies of the 23rd Division, killing 12 men and capturing most of their weapons. It was from this attack that RVN government and US officials began referring to the rebels as "Viêt Công", a pejorative for "Vietnamese Communist". The term, soon abbreviated to VC, stuck.[35]

The VC also overran district and provincial capitals. Diêm's claim of improved security in the South was dealt a serious blow on 17 January 1960, when insurgents on their own initiative in Bên Tre Province in the Mekong Delta, about 100 miles from Sài Gòn, staged the first "concerted uprising". Led by Madame Nguyên Thi Đinh, later deputy military commander of the NLF, it showed the depth of popular resentment against government policies, especially Diêm's "agroville" programme, a proposed network of protected communities designed to isolate the rural population from the Viêt Công. Peasants armed with machetes, spears and sharpened sticks joined some 162 VC troops with only four rifles and a few home-made mortars to storm guard posts and rout government officials. The insurgents captured enough weapons to arm an entire company and then defeated the initial government counter-attack. It was the first time that popular insurrection had been successful on a provincial scale. Madame Dinh repeated it the next September on a wider scale, and the rebels seized over 1,700 weapons. Not only an example of what effective leadership could accomplish, the Bên Tre uprisings showed the independence of some southern leaders.[36]

On 26 January 1960, four Viêt Công companies totalling about 200 men easily overran an ARVN regimental headquarters at Trang Súp in Tây Ninh Province northeast of Sài Gòn. They inflicted 66 casualties and carried off 350 rifles, 30 automatic rifles, 150 carbines, 40 pistols, 2 machine guns, 2 mortars, and large quantities of ammunition.[37]

The numbers of weapons the VC seized from the government grew rapidly. From mid-January to mid-April 1960 government forces captured only 150 VC weapons; at the same time South Vietnamese forces lost over 1,000; time and again the attackers disappeared before ARVN reaction forces could arrive.[38] Far from changing the military balance in the countryside, new weapons that the US had provided the ARVN merely meant that the VC would now capture newer, better American weapons instead of older French models (as one Việt Công paper put it, "Ngô Đình Diêm will be our supply sergeant").[39] Frustrated US advisers referred to government military posts as "VC PXs" (for post exchange, where US soldiers purchase goods).

VC tactics stressed careful preparation, deception, speed, rapid concentration and dispersal of force, mass and surprise. Their most common large-scale attack was the ambush, carefully laid and concealed, usually along roads or canals. Other attacks were mounted against government outposts, often with the aid of civilian sympathizers. The VC also employed a wide range of mines and booby traps, ranging from trip-wired grenades to devices as simple as the *pungi* stake: a sharpened bamboo stake covered with faeces or poison and placed at the bottom of a pit, under water, or along a trail to be stepped on by troops. They even salvaged unexploded US ordnance, cutting it apart and using the explosive filler to make mines.[40]

Hà Nôi also sent additional manpower down the trail. Initially the infiltration was minimal, but in 1961 increasing numbers of former southerners returned to the South. Even so, US official figures put their number at only 6,200 in all of 1961.

For Sài Gòn reform took a back seat to fighting the insurgency, with the result that it continued to grow. Diêm's response was more oppression. In May 1959 the National Assembly passed an internal security measure. Known as Law 10–59, it empowered the government to try suspected terrorists by roving tribunals that could impose the death penalty.[41]

But Diêm was not alone in misreading the roots of the problem. General Williams also discounted social and economic factors, choosing to blame hard-core VC, abetted by infiltrators from the North. And he discounted South Vietnamese corruption, incompetence, poor morale and inadequate leadership. Williams believed that improved training would solve the problem.[42]

Williams was caught off guard by Diêm's decision on 15 February 1960 to order commanders of divisions and military regions to form ranger companies. Each would have 131 men – an 11-man headquarters unit and three 40-man platoons. Diêm wanted 50 of these companies in place by March. Williams opposed the plan, favouring a well-organized civil guard instead. He believed it was risky to employ units smaller than battalions in counter-insurgency operations. It would also be costly, with Diêm expecting the United States to pick up the tab. Many US observers saw this as an effort by Diêm to raise the previously agreed-to 150,000-man force ceiling.

With Diêm experimenting with counter-insurgency techniques, the Eisenhower Administration agreed to send Army Special Forces, specialists in guerrilla warfare, to provide assistance in counter-insurgency training. The Special Forces were, however, trained for partisan-type guerrilla warfare in the context of World War II or the Korean War rather than counter-insurgency warfare such as in Vietnam.[43]

In May 1960 at Diêm's invitation three training teams of ten men each from the 77th Special Forces Group on Okinawa arrived in Vietnam. They set up training schools at Đà Nẵng, Nha Trang and Sông Mao. But even though the Vietnamese were volunteers, the same pattern repeated itself: inefficiency, corruption, apathy and lack of leadership.[44]

At the same time the ARVN failed to penetrate insurgent-controlled areas. It had little ability in guerrilla warfare and failed to threaten training bases and rest areas. One week was about as long as an ARVN unit could be absent from its own base at any one stretch.[45]

Meanwhile opposition within South Vietnam against Diêm continued to grow, even in the cities that had benefitted most under his regime. In April 1960 18 prominent South Vietnamese issued a manifesto protesting governmental abuses. They were promptly arrested. On 11–12 November 1960, American officials were caught by surprise when three battalions of the ARVN's elite paratroop group surrounded the presidential palace and demanded reforms, a new government and more effective prosecution of the war. Diêm outmanoeuvred them, agreeing to a long list of reforms – including freedom of the press, a coalition government and new elections – until he could bring loyal units to the scene. Diêm refused to see the need for far-reaching political or social reform. The coup attempt merely intensified his distrust of others and caused him to concentrate more authority in his own hands.[46]

On 27 February 1962, Diêm survived another coup attempt when two Vietnamese Air Force pilots tried to kill him and his brother Nhu by bombing and strafing the presidential palace. As a consequence dozens of Diêm's political opponents disappeared and thousands more were sent to prison camps.

The Kennedy Administration and Indo-China

With Washington already having second thoughts about Diêm, there was a change in US administrations. In a closely contested election, in November 1960 Democrat John F. Kennedy defeated Republican Richard M. Nixon. Throughout much of the Kennedy Administration Vietnam yielded place to Laos, the immediate Indo-China problem for the new administration. Dulles had called Laos a "bulwark against communism" and a "bastion of freedom", and Eisenhower told Kennedy that it was the key to Southeast Asia. If Laos fell the Communists would bring "unbelievable pressure" on Thailand, Cambodia and South Vietnam. By the end of 1960 Washington had already provided the Laotian government with $300 million in assistance, of which 85 per cent was military.[47]

Civil war in Laos now flared anew. A military coup occurred against the rightist government and both the DRV and USSR actively intervened, but Kennedy decided not to send US troops. In contrast to the Eisenhower Administration, JFK was not averse to a neutralist solution. After much diplomatic activity, a 14-nation conference convened in Geneva in June 1961, and over the next year it worked on a solution for a tripartite coalition government, which, however, proved short-lived. Certainly the DRV wanted to partition Laos in order to secure the vital trail network that supplied insurgents in the South. The failure of the Communists to live up to the Geneva agreements concerning neutralization of Laos greatly angered Kennedy and influenced his policies regarding Vietnam, precluding a retreat there.[48]

Kennedy continued the previous administration's policy of maintaining the RVN. In 1961 he sent Frederick Nolting as US ambassador. The gentlemanly Nolting was a career diplomat who, however, had had no Asian experience when he was posted to Sài Gòn. Nolting deferred to Diêm, believing that Washington had to get along with the top RVN leadership. This meant not pressuring Diêm to improve the desperate conditions in the countryside. David Halberstam notes that if Diêm could have picked a US ambassador it would have been Nolting. At a reception Diêm remarked to one American reporter, "Your ambassador is the first one who has ever understood us."[49]

At the same time Kennedy escalated US involvement. There were many reasons behind this. One was the now long-standing US commitment to battle Communism as enunciated in the Containment doctrine. Many in Washington saw South Vietnam as part of a larger fabric of Communist expansion. While Kennedy and many of his advisers tended to regard the fighting in Vietnam as a civil war, this position was not shared by Secretary of State Dean Rusk, who was obsessed with the 1938 Munich Conference's sell-out to Hitler and who held to the belief in "aggression from the North" in Vietnam. The "domino theory" also held sway. Its proponents believed that if South Vietnam fell to the Communists, then the rest of Southeast Asia would surely follow. There was also the argument that US prestige as the leader of the "free world" was on trial. If the United States failed in Vietnam, other nations would lose confidence in Washington's willingness to project power. Also at stake was the matter of whether the West could respond to what was regarded as a new Communist strategy of "wars of national liberation".

Domestic political considerations also played a role. Kennedy was sensitive to Republican charges that the Democrats had "lost" China, and the Administration had suffered rebuffs in the "Bay of Pigs" fiasco in Cuba (planning for which had begun under Eisenhower) and the erection of the Berlin Wall. Another "retreat" before Communism could be fatal politically.

In May 1961 Kennedy sent Vice President Lyndon Johnson to Sài Gòn. Although he expressed private reservations about Diêm, Johnson publicly hailed him the "Winston Churchill of Southeast Asia". Less than a week after Johnson's return to Washington, Kennedy agreed to increase ARVN's size from 170,000 to 270,000 men. As with their predecessors, these troops tended to be poorly trained in guerrilla warfare, indifferently led, inadequately provided for and ineffective in combat.

Kennedy then sent two fact-finding missions to Vietnam. Economist Dr Eugene Staley led the first in June and July 1961. His findings, reported to Kennedy in August, stressed that the RVN needed a self-sustaining economy and that military action alone would not work. Only with substantial social and political reform could favourable results be achieved.

Staley's recommendations centred on protection of the civilian population. He advocated substantial increases in the size of ARVN, the Civil Guard and local militias, and he sought improved arms and equipment at the local level. Finally, he called for the construction of a network of strategic hamlets.

The strategic hamlet idea began with the 1959 Diêm-sponsored "agroville program", of which only a small fraction of 80 proposed communities were ever completed. Two years later Sir Robert Thompson, a counter-insurgency expert, advanced the strategic hamlet idea, based on his own experience against Communist insurgents in Malaya. Staley's advocacy, which promised US funding, brought Diêm's acceptance.

Begun with much fanfare, the Strategic Hamlet (*ấp chiến lúớc*) Programme was a belated effort at counter-insurgency. Run by Diêm's brother Nhu, it called for the forced removal of peasants from their ancestral lands with resettlement in new fenced and armed compounds that would provide health and educational advantages as well as protection from the Việt Công. Some 16,000 rural hamlets were to be turned into 14,000 stockaded strategic hamlets, all to be completed early in 1963. By that spring some 8,000 hamlets had been stockaded and partially organized for self-defence. Although VC recruitment fell off, the primitive RVN administrative machinery was unable to cope; many hamlets were poorly sited and there was little co-ordination. Riddled with corruption, the programme turned out to be a vast and expensive failure and alienated much of the peasantry.[50]

Probably most of the peasants simply wanted to be left alone and certainly many found the RVN as much an enemy as the VC. The government moved them off their lands, taxed them unfairly and did not deliver on promises. ARVN soldiers often exacerbated the situation by stealing produce and by other actions against civilians. When the VC came into an area it set up its own administrative system, including tax collection, over that of the RVN. The VC redistributed land in areas it controlled and its taxes were often fairer. Many peasants believed that the VC offered the promise of real improvements in so far as their daily lives were concerned.

Increases in US military assistance

In October 1961 Kennedy's chief military adviser General Maxwell D. Taylor and Special Assistant for National Security Affairs Walt W. Rostow led a second fact-finding trip to Vietnam. They saw the situation primarily in military terms and recommended a change in the US role from advisory to "limited partnership" with the RVN. They urged increased US economic aid and military advisory support to include intensive training of local self-defence forces and a large increase in airplanes, helicopters and support personnel. A secret appendix recommended the deployment of 8,000 American combat troops that might be used to support the ARVN in military operations. To overcome Diêm's sensitivity regarding foreign troops, these were to be called a "flood control team". Taylor concluded that "as an area for the operations of US troops, SVN [South Vietnam] is not an excessively difficult or unpleasant place to operate". He also stressed North Vietnam's vulnerability to air strikes.[51]

Under Secretary of State George W. Ball sensed the seductive nature of the US involvement in Vietnam and was a strong voice against escalation until his resignation from the department in September 1966. He met privately with Kennedy to express his opposition to the Taylor–Rostow findings and predicted that if the United States accepted its recommendations in five years it would have 300,000 men in Vietnam. Kennedy responded, "George, you're just crazier than hell. That isn't going to happen."[52]

Kennedy accepted the Taylor–Rostow recommendations, except for the introduction of US troops, which Diêm, prescient in this at least, opposed as a potential Viêt Công propaganda bonanza. To co-ordinate this increased aid, on 8 February 1962, Washington opened a new military headquarters in Sài Gòn. Known as the Military Assistance Command, Vietnam (MACV), and headed by General Paul D. Harkins, it came to resemble an operational command in a theatre of war. Henceforth MACV directed US military activities in Vietnam.

Table 4.1: American military personnel in South Vietnam

(end of year)	1960	1961	1962	1963	1964
US military personnel	875	3,164	11,326	16,263	23,310
Deaths from hostile action	NA	1	31	77	137
USAF sorties flown	NA	NA	2,334	6,929	5,362
USAF aircraft lost to hostile action:					
Fixed–wing	NA	NA	7	14	30
Helicopters	NA	NA	4	9	22

US helicopter pilots were soon at work supporting the ARVN (the first US helicopter was shot down on 4 February 1962[53]), and from the end of 1961 to the end of 1962 the number of American military personnel in South Vietnam quadrupled.[54]

While this US military infusion may have helped prevent an outright VC victory in 1962, the advantage was only temporary. The DRV now increased its own effort, and while US helicopters provided greatly enhanced mobility for ARVN forces, the VC soon learned the vulnerability of helicopters to ground fire.[55]

The Battle of Ấp Bắc (2 January 1963)

In January 1963 ARVN forces suffered a stinging rebuff in the Battle of Ấp Bắc (for Bắc hamlet, Ấp meaning hamlet in Vietnamese) about 40 miles southwest of Sài Gòn. Most US military personnel held the VC in contempt, hoping that one day they would stand and fight so they might be destroyed. At Ấp Bắc the VC did just that, but with results far different from those the Americans anticipated.

Radio intercepts had revealed the location of a VC transmitter guarded by what was thought to be no more than a reinforced company of 120 men. The unit in question turned out to be the 320-man VC 261st Main Force Battalion augmented by some 30 guerrillas. Lieutenant Colonel John Paul Vann, senior US military adviser to the ARVN 7th Division, planned a converging attack. A battalion of the division would be airlifted to the north, while two battalions of Civil Guards marched up from the south and a company in M–113 armoured personnel carriers also moved north as a reaction force. Additional units were in reserve.

The plan was a good one, but it was appallingly executed by ARVN troops and their commanders, who refused to advance against VC fire. The VC stood and fought from prepared defensive positions in tree lines and along canals. Finally ARVN airborne forces arrived and by nightfall the village was secured. The VC were simply allowed to escape. They suffered 18 killed and 39 wounded. The ARVN had about 80 dead and over 100 wounded in action.

General Harkins characterized the operation as a success because the objective had been secured, but US correspondents on the scene thought otherwise. A major ARVN unit with US military assistance and vastly superior firepower had been defeated by an inferior force. The Battle of Ấp Bắc was symbolic of ARVN's many problems.[56] As one writer noted:

In itself, the battle was of no strategic importance . . . but the psychological repercussions rippled far afield. The army had shown itself to be still timorous and incompetent, as well as ill commanded and undisciplined; the adviser–counterpart relationship had been shown up as a false one; and the superior firepower and tactical mobility in the air available to the defence had laid bare its own inherent superfluity.[57]

Shortly after the battle Senator Mansfield visited Sài Gòn. On his return to Washington he informed Congress that even after eight years and $2 billion, US efforts to set up an independent Vietnam were "not even at the beginning of a beginning".[58]

The war was not the only thing going badly for the Diêm government. In 1963 Buddhist protests and rallies increased in frequency. In Hué on 8 May, Buddha's birthday, thousands demonstrated against a ban imposed on flying the multicoloured flag of the World Fellowship of Buddhists, which had been flown for more than a decade at Buddhist celebrations. A concussion grenade thrown by an ARVN soldier killed eight demonstrators, including some children. This led to Buddhist demonstrations throughout the country, and on 11 June elderly Buddhist monk Thích Quang Đúc publicly burned himself alive.[59] By November six other monks had followed his example. Ngô Đình Nhu's wife, Madame Nhu exacerbated the crisis by referring to the self-immolations as "barbecues".

Madame Nhu, who acted as the first lady of the state (Diêm was celibate) and headed the Women's Solidarity Movement, also embarked on her own bizarre puritanical campaign that outlawed divorce, dancing, beauty contests, gambling, fortune telling, prostitution, adultery and even certain music and hair-dos. Harsh punishments for violations of these new rules antagonized many.

Diêm, who saw only the Communist threat, seemed oblivious to the fact that his regime's oppression was feeding the insurgency. His response was more oppression. Not unlike Chinese Nationalist Party leader Jiang Jieshi (Chiang Kai-shek), Diêm believed that halting the insurgency had to come first and reform only afterward. Increasing numbers of South Vietnamese saw Diêm as isolated and out of touch with the people. Especially after the November 1960 coup attempt, loyalty, rather than military ability, was *the* test for military command. Distrustful of the military leadership, Diêm fragmented the command structure so that he could control it himself. Overly aggressive commanders whose actions led to higher casualties were sacked.

Nhu was particularly embarrassing to Washington. He was responsible for the 22 August 1963 raids on Buddhist pagodas that damaged many of them and led to the arrest of over 1,400 Buddhists. The government also proclaimed a three-week curfew. Washington saw these raids as the last straw.[60]

Overthrow of Diêm

That same month Henry Cabot Lodge replaced Nolting as US ambassador. Lodge was a prominent Republican, for Kennedy wanted bipartisanship in his Vietnam foreign policy. The CIA had already reported that an influential faction of South Vietnamese generals wanted to overthrow Diêm. Lodge's frank views gave this new credence. Washington was initially opposed to a coup, preferring that Diêm purge his entourage, especially the Nhus; but it was clear that to insist on this would alert Nhu and probably bring a bloodbath, since Nhu had troops loyal to him in the capital. At the end of August Washington assured the generals of its support and President Kennedy in a television interview publicly criticized Diêm.

Following further outrages against the Buddhists, on 2 October Washington suspended economic subsidies for RVN commercial imports, froze loans for developmental projects and cut off financial support of Nhu's 2,000-man Vietnamese Special Forces. This action was a clear signal to the dissidents, who were, however, fearful of a double-cross and refused to reveal the timing of their coup attempt. Shortly after midnight on 1 November 1963, Major Generals Dúóng Văn Minh, Tôn Thât Đính, and Trân Văn Đôn began their takeover. The next day both Diêm and Nhu, whom Washington had assumed would be given safe passage out of the country, were murdered.

Diêm's death brought political instability to the RVN. Washington never could find a worthy successor to him. Certainly no subsequent RVN leader had his air of legitimacy or as much respect from the general public. Economically and socially, except for the confusion at the beginning of his rule, life had never been better for South Vietnamese than under Diêm. US leaders, who had seen in him a nationalist alternative to Hô Chí Minh and the means to stop Communist expansion, soon found themselves taking direct control of the war in Vietnam. The United States, which could not win the war with Diêm, apparently could not win the war without him.

Kennedy's position on the war was by now ambiguous. In the spring of 1963 he had decided to use optimistic reports from Harkins and Taylor to justify a complete withdrawal of US forces, something he intended to keep secret until after the 1964 presidential elections. He told Senator Mansfield that he was determined to withdraw US forces from Vietnam, but that any announcement of this before the election would result in a conservative backlash, possibly costing him the election.[61]

Just how far Kennedy had come may be seen in two news conferences two months apart. On 12 September he had listed three objectives of US policy in Vietnam as: win the war, contain the Communists and bring Americans home. But on 12 November he listed them in these words: "Now, that is our object, to bring Americans home, permit the South Vietnamese to maintain themselves as a free and independent country, and permit democratic forces within the country to operate." There was no mention of winning the war. Two days later in Sài Gòn Major General Charles Timnes announced that 1,000 Americans would be returning home by the end of December, this despite reports to Kennedy of a deteriorating battlefield situation. Kennedy's last statement on Vietnam, made in Fort Worth, Texas, on 22 November, reveals the dilemma he faced: "Without the United States, South Vietnam would collapse overnight."[62] That same day he was killed in Dallas by an assassin. While there is simply no way of knowing what Kennedy would have done about Vietnam had he lived, his statements about withdrawal were made when the US was seen to be winning.

President Lyndon Johnson

Vice President Lyndon Baines Johnson became president on Kennedy's death. His presidency was a tragic one. Johnson's legislative skills and his programmes in education, aid to the poor, Medicare and civil rights – all part of what came to be called the Great Society – held promise that he would be remembered as one of the truly great American chief executives. Instead his presidency was eaten away by the cancer of Vietnam.[63]

The deaths of both Diêm and Kennedy offered an opportunity for the new administration to undertake a reassessment of US policy towards Vietnam, but this was not done. While Johnson believed that losing the Great Society programmes would be terrible, nothing would be worse than being the first president to lose a war with the Communists.[64] Johnson also believed that firm commitment to the war was the best way to secure the support of conservatives in Congress for his domestic social programmes. He expressed his dilemma in these words:

> I knew from the start that I was bound to be crucified either way I moved. If I left the woman I really loved – the Great Society – in order to get involved with that bitch of a war on the other side of the world, then I would lose everything at home. All my programs . . . But if I left that war and let the Communists take over South Vietnam, then I would be seen as a coward and my nation would be seen as an appeaser and we would both find it impossible to accomplish anything for anybody anywhere on the entire globe.[65]

Johnson also told a close adviser in 1964 that he was afraid he might be run out of office if he decided to withdraw: "They'd impeach a President, though, that would run out, wouldn't they?" he asked.[66] No doubt this fear was prompted by events of the McCarthy era in the United States following the Communist victory in China. And Johnson assumed America was strong enough to have both guns and butter.[67]

On 21 December Johnson received a sobering report from Secretary of Defense Robert S. McNamara. One of the key policy-makers on Vietnam under Kennedy and Johnson, McNamara supported escalation. Only belatedly did he come to realize his mistake.[68]

McNamara was a micro manager with a fondness for assessing problems in quantitative terms. George Ball well understood his strengths and weaknesses:

> He was a superb Secretary of Defense – brilliantly skilled in planning, budgeting, devising and administering efficient procurement policies, and controlling all aspects of a great sprawling . . . department. But the very quantitative discipline that he used with such effect as Secretary of Defense did not always serve him well as Secretary of War . . . he could not help thinking that because the resources commanded by the United States were greater than those of North Vietnam by a factor of X, we could inevitably prevail if we only applied those resources effectively – which is what our government frantically sought to do for the next ten years.[69]

Blinded by the statistical measurements of US power and a profound ignorance of Vietnam, McNamara failed to measure ideological commitment. It did not matter that North Vietnam was no match for the US and South Vietnam in terms of resources if its people were prepared to fight for their cause and those of the South were not. But even he could sense the deteriorating military situation in the South. In May 1962, on his first of many visits to Vietnam, McNamara had announced "we are winning the war".[70] But on 21 December 1963, he reported to Johnson that the situation in South Vietnam was "very disturbing" and that "current trends, unless reversed in the next 2–3 months, will lead to neutralization at best or more likely to a Communist-controlled state".[71] McNamara chiefly blamed Diêm's successors for their inept leadership and squabbling, but he was also critical of the US mission, especially Ambassador Lodge, for failing to co-operate with Harkins.[72]

Political instability in South Vietnam

In South Vietnam a military junta held power. Led by General Dúóng Văn Minh as chief of state, the new regime was both unresponsive to the people of South Vietnam and politically unstable. Fearful of undercutting its nationalist credentials, the Minh government opposed any US direction of ARVN military operations. It rejected any increase in American personnel and wanted advisers withdrawn from battalions and no US military advisers below regiments.[73]

Members of the new 12-man Military Revolutionary Council soon fell to quarrelling among themselves. Minh had boasted that the collective leadership would insure that no one else would have Diêm's power. But he as nominal leader showed no inclination to govern and preferred to play tennis, tend to his orchids and pursue an interest in exotic birds.

On 30 January 1964, another coup occurred, this time against Minh, led by 37-year-old Major General Nguyên Khánh. US officials, caught by surprise, promptly hailed him as the new saviour because he promised to rule with a strong hand. Although shrewd and energetic, Khánh showed no more aptitude for governing than had Minh, and his own history of frequently changing sides discouraged trust.

Khánh purged some generals, although he allowed Minh to remain on as titular head of state. Militant Buddhists, alarmed that Khánh's victory might lead to a return to power of Catholics and those faithful to Diêm, again became active. To increase their influence, the heads of different Buddhist sects agreed to form a political alliance. Many ARVN officers also turned against Khánh when he attempted to try rival Generals Trân Văn Đôn and Lê Văn Kim on trumped-up charges.

Khánh sought to resurrect the Đai Việt Party and manipulate it to his advantage. He persuaded its leader, Catholic physician Dr Nguyên Tôn Hoan, to return from exile in Paris as premier. When it was clear that the Đai Việt was hopelessly splintered, Khánh named himself as premier with Hoan as his deputy. Hoan then began to conspire with the Buddhists and other opposition groups against Khánh. Political instability in the RVN was now rampant. As governments rose and fell, nothing alarmed the Americans as much as that one of them might enter into accommodation with the Communists. One Johnson aide suggested that the coat of arms of the RVN government should be a turnstile.[74]

Hà Nôi followed these events with rapt interest, and at the end of 1963 the DRV leadership decided that the time was ripe to escalate dramatically its support for the war in the South. In a major shift in policy that required considerable economic sacrifices, Hà Nôi made three important decisions: to send native northerners south to fight, to authorize direct attacks against US personnel in the South and to introduce the latest models of Communist small arms, including the Kalashnikov AK–47 assault rifle. Noted for its reliability, the AK–47 weighed 6.9 lb, had an effective range of 325 yards, rate of fire of ten rounds per second, and a 30-round magazine. It became one of the world's most important and widespread weapons.[75]

The new weaponry gave the Việt Công superiority over the ARVN, then armed with older US weapons such as the M–1 carbine, but this also greatly added to logistics problems. The ARVN too was improving, although not as fast as its enemy. Increasingly there was talk among policy-makers in Washington about expanding the war by directly attacking what they regarded as the source of the problem, North Vietnam.

In January 1964 Chairman of the Joint Chiefs of Staff (JCS) General Maxwell Taylor sent a memorandum to McNamara, endorsed by the chiefs, that urged covert coastal operations against North Vietnam. Such operations, to be conducted by South Vietnamese forces supported by the United States, would gather intelligence and conduct sabotage in order to destabilize the regime. Johnson approved these secret operations on January 16.

The JCS was particularly interested in employing air power against the DRV. A March 1964 JCS planning report recommended mining the port of Hai Phòng and bombing lines of communication (LOCs); petroleum, oil and lubricants (POL) depots; and key industrial areas.

Certainly the easiest way for Washington to expand the war was through air power. In June 1964, in response to a Communist Pathet Lao/PAVN spring offensive in the Plaine des Jarres, the United States began Operation Barrel Roll, a bombing campaign to support the Royal Laotian Army and CIA-trained Hmong irregular forces led by General Vang Pao. Between 1964 and April 1973, when Barrel Roll ended, Laos became the most heavily bombed country in the world. Allied aircraft dropped over 3 million tons of bombs, three times the amount dropped on North Vietnam. US spending there was also ten times that of the Laotian national budget.[76]

In March 1964 Secretary of Defense McNamara visited the RVN and vowed support for Khánh. He barnstormed the country, describing Khánh in memorized Vietnamese as the country's "best possible leader". On his return to Washington McNamara publicly pronounced improvement in the RVN but privately told Johnson that conditions had deteriorated since his last visit there and that 40 per cent of the countryside was now under Việt Công control or influence. Something had to be done if South Vietnam was to be kept from falling to the Communists.

General William C. Westmoreland

On 20 June 1964, General William C. Westmoreland replaced the ever-optimistic Harkins as commander of MACV. West Point graduate of the class of 1936 and corps first captain, Westmoreland's military outlook was set by his World War II and Korean War experiences. Although he brought energy to the task before him, he remained fixed in the "big war" approach of "finding", "fixing" and "finishing" the enemy by means of big-unit manoeuvre, and he never had much interest in the "other war" of pacification/nation building.

Westmoreland's advocacy of attrition warfare was based on the assumption that the Communists could not sustain large-unit fighting because they lacked the logistics capability. He expressly rejected suggestions that US units be broken down into smaller groups to concentrate on pacification.[77]

Both Westmoreland and Ambassador Lodge favoured vigorous action to stiffen Khánh's resolve. Washington agreed to furnish additional aid, but while more than $2 million a day was arriving in the country, little of it went to public works projects or reached the peasants. Despite promises to put the country on "a war footing", Khánh steadfastly refused to do so, fearful of antagonizing wealthy and middle-class city dwellers, whose sons would be inducted into the army.

In the summer of 1964 Westmoreland experimented with a pacification programme in six provinces around Sài Gòn, in which military forces were to drive the VC from the selected provinces. Aggressive patrolling and ambushes would then follow until such time as security could be entrusted to local militia or an expanded police force. Civilian officials could then establish RVN government agencies and provide protection, services and amenities. As Westmoreland put it, "The idea was to provide a standard of living perceptibly higher than the Viet Cong could provide." Three terms coined by Westmoreland's staff expressed the plan's essence: clearing, securing, and search and destroy. As Westmoreland admitted, Operation Hóp Tác (co-operation) incorporated elements of the French "oil slick" pacification method. Westmoreland saw it as "a laboratory experiment in pacification", which if successful, could be duplicated around other large cities "until eventually all might merge".[78]

Hóp Tác also sought to incorporate lessons learned in the Strategic Hamlet Programme. Under Hóp Tác the Vietnamese would carry the brunt of the effort against the VC. To co-ordinate military and political agencies, the RVN government established a Hóp Tác council that included Westmoreland and Khánh as well as local officials and representatives from the ministry of interior, national police and intelligence agencies.

Hóp Tác got off to a slow start in September 1964. Determined at this stage to keep the ARVN at the centre of efforts against the VC, Westmoreland informed the RVN that the US would contribute only advice and commodities. He persuaded ARVN Chief of Staff General Trân Thiên Khiêm to transfer the 25th Division from Quang Ngãi Province in II Corps to join the operation.[79] This proved to be a mistake. Many of the division's soldiers, faced with separation from their families and having to fight the VC, deserted. As Westmoreland admitted, it was three full years before the 25th Division "recovered from the exercise and became fully proficient. We would have done better to have formed an entirely new division".[80]

Political instability in Sài Gòn was another negative factor. Khánh became so involved in political concerns that he was little interested in Hóp Tác. Rather than have them participate in the project, he held marine and airborne brigades in their barracks close to the capital to prevent a possible coup. The RVN police failed to do their job, and the government did not deliver the American supplies that were to be the economic leverage.[81]

Hóp Tác did give the ARVN experience in pacification. It increased the national police by several thousand men and made the capital more secure. But these positives did not outweigh the negatives and the RVN formally ended Hóp Tác in 1965. Even Westmoreland admitted it was a failure. Frances FitzGerald has described Hóp Tác as "trying to stop a brush fire with rotten sticks".[82] Westmoreland claimed that it prevented the Communists from making "critical inroads on government control of the capital area".[83] But it probably removed some illusions Westmoreland may have had about the ARVN and weakened his commitment to pacification. In 1965 he would increasingly rely on US troops to carry the war.

Operations in 1964 and the Tonkin Gulf Incidents

In the summer of 1964 two covert operations were in progress against the DRV. The first, Operations Plan 34A, was part of the Johnson Administration's programme of gradually escalating pressure on the North. It involved South Vietnamese PT boat raids along the North Vietnamese coast with the United States providing logistics support. The second operation was called De Soto. Both were designed to gather electronic intelligence (ELINT). The plan called for US Navy destroyers to run in close to the North Vietnamese coast to locate and evaluate shore radars. These two programmes were not inter-related (MACV ran 34A and the US Navy De Soto), but there was linkage. It was thus not unreasonable for the DRV to assume that the two programmes were one and the same.

On 2 August 1964, North Vietnamese torpedo boats attacked the destroyer *Maddox* while she was on a De Soto patrol in international waters some 28 miles from the DRV coast. This was probably the consequence of two South Vietnamese PT boat attacks on 31 July – a fact unknown to Captain John Herrick of the *Maddox*.

Captain Herrick sought approval of commander of US forces in the Pacific Admiral Ulysses Grant Sharp to terminate his patrol. Sharp thought that this might call into question US resolve to "assert our legitimate rights in these international waters", and he secured permission from the JCS to strengthen the patrol by adding a second destroyer, the *Turner Joy*, to Herrick's command.

On 3 August another 34A raid took place, and on the next night Herrick reported a "possible" torpeodo boat attack on the two destroyers. Almost all of those on the two ships believed that an attack of up to two hours had occurred, but there were no visual sightings of North Vietnamese patrol craft in the area. Only hours after learning of the American claim of a second attack, the DRV issued a public denial, a position it has maintained ever since.[84]

Edwin Moïse, in his study of the Tonkin Gulf incidents, agrees that there was no attack on 4 August. He attributes the reports to stormy weather, evasive manoeuvring and inexperienced and fatigued radar and sonar operators. Moïse also concludes that there is no evidence that the Johnson Administration knowingly faked the incident to escalate the war, although he concedes that from the DRV side the case for deliberate deception by Washington appears convincing. To Moïse it was a genuine mistake rather than a deliberate deception.[85]

In Washington President Johnson and US military leaders did not want the DRV leadership to equate lack of US response with lack of resolve, especially as Johnson was then locked in an election campaign against Republican hawk and air power advocate Senator Barry Goldwater. Secure in his belief that an attack had occurred, Johnson also wanted to be able to announce a US military response on the evening television news. Despite a radio message from Herrick that "review of action makes many reported contacts and torpedoes fired appear doubtful" and a later message to Sharp of "details of action present a confusing picture", on 5 August Johnson ordered Operation Pierce Arrow, a retaliatory US Navy strike against DRV naval facilities along the coast.

As it turned out, Johnson's public announcement came before some of the US aircraft from the carriers *Ticonderoga* and *Constellation* had reached their targets of torpedo boat bases along the coast and a petroleum storage facility at Vinh. US aircraft flew 64 sorties; two were shot down, one pilot was killed and the other captured.[86]

Even before the incidents, Johnson had told congressional leaders of his intention to seek a resolution of support for his Southeast Asia policy. Such a request reached Congress on 5 August. Two days later Congress passed the so-called Tonkin Gulf Resolution by a vote of 416 to 0 in the House and 88 to 2 in the Senate.

The resolution styled DRV attacks on US ships as "part of a deliberate and systematic campaign of aggression . . . against its neighbors and the nations joined with them in the collective defense of their freedom". It authorized the President to take those steps necessary "to repel any armed attack against the forces of the United States and to prevent any further aggression". It also held that the United States regarded the maintenance of peace and security in Southeast Asia as "vital to the national interest and to world peace" and was thus "prepared, as the president determines, to take all necessary steps, including the use of armed force, to assist any member or protocol state of the Southeast Asia Collective Defense Treaty requesting assistance in defense of its freedom". In effect this resolution gave President Johnson blanket authority to wage war without a declaration of war. Contrary to later charges, the implications of the resolution were fully, albeit briefly, aired before the vote.

Political instability in Sài Gòn

In South Vietnam General Khánh sought to derive advantage from the changed US outlook. Military action against the VC was then nearly at a halt and Khánh was in serious political difficulty. He had been pleading for US action against the DRV as a distraction. Following Pierce Arrow, Khánh announced a state of emergency and imposed censorship and other controls. He also hastily issued a new constitution, promoting himself to the presidency and dismissing former figurehead chief of state Dúóng Văn Minh.

Sài Gòn responded with protests. Students took to the streets, soon joined by Buddhists, complaining that too many Diêm supporters still held key positions. Khánh met with Buddhist leaders but revealed his real strength by telling them he would discuss their complaints with Ambassador Maxwell Taylor, who had succeeded Lodge in July. Taylor urged Khánh not to yield. On 25 August, when thousands of demonstrators gathered outside his office to demand his resignation, Khánh appeared and announced that he did not plan to establish a dictatorship; however, that afternoon he resigned. The Military Revolutionary Council met to choose a new head of state.

After lengthy political manoeuvring a triumvirate of Generals Khánh, Minh, and Trân Thiên Khiêm emerged. Khánh retained the premiership but flew off to Đà Lat as chaos swept the capital. Order was restored only after two days of rioting. Khánh named Harvard-educated economist Nguyên Xuân Oanh prime minister in his absence, but turbulence continued as the government was threatened by dissident army units in the Mekong Delta and militant Buddhists from Huê, whose demands had grown to include a veto over government decisions. New riots in Sài Gòn that November protested Khánh's rule, and Ambassador Taylor urged him to leave the country. By now a faction of younger military officers had come to the fore. Known as the "Young Turks", they were headed by Nguyên Cao Kỳ, who had participated in the coup against Diêm and had been promoted to major general and given charge of the Air Force. It also included army Major General Nguyên Văn Thiêu. Disillusioned by the ineffective national government, in mid-December 1964 the Young Turks overthrew the Military Revolutionary Council of older officers.

In late January 1965 a new Armed Forces Council named Khánh as premier, but in February he was in turn replaced by General Lâm Văn Phát. On 17 February Dr Phan Huy Quát became premier with Phan Khắc Súu as chief of state. Quát, a physician with considerable governmental experience, appointed a broadly representative cabinet. The Armed Forces Council also announced the formation of a 20-member National Legislative Council.

Political instability in South Vietnam greatly alarmed Washington. In November 1964 Johnson won the presidential election, defeating Republican opponent Senator Goldwater, who had called for a sharp escalation in the use of force. The margin of victory was unequalled until 1984. During the campaign Johnson had repeatedly taken the tack that the war should be left to the Vietnamese – that American "boys" should not be sent to do the fighting that Asian "boys" with US assistance could do by themselves. Although Johnson was later accused of merely holding back escalation of the war until he had won the election, there is no evidence to support this. Indeed, there is every indication that Johnson insisted on gradual escalation as the least costly means to end the fighting and thus most likely to preserve his Great Society programmes. There was some point, he believed, at which North Vietnam would have to end its support of the fighting in the South. This approach resulted in both a more costly and prolonged conflict.

Air power

For some time many of Johnson's military and civilian advisers, including Ambassador Taylor, had urged air strikes against the North. The JCS had drawn up a list of targets to be struck; Johnson had resisted. But by January 1965 US policy-makers believed that the situation in South Vietnam was critical; most thought that air strikes were necessary if South Vietnam was to be preserved.[87]

Johnson's advisers believed that the DRV was vulnerable to air power. National Security Adviser Walt Rostow stated, "Ho Chi Minh has an industrial complex to protect; he is no longer a guerrilla fighter with nothing to lose."[88] But a committee headed by a Rostow deputy undertook a study of the possible effect of any such bombing and concluded that it would not work, and that unification rather than economic growth was a principal Hà Nôi goal. Bombing would not weaken the regime and might even strengthen it. Rostow ignored these findings.[89] Increasingly, Johnson's chief advisers moved towards a consensus on bombing North Vietnam.

Other reasons also influenced Washington planners towards flexing US military might. The new Soviet and Chinese leaders were making bellicose statements, and President Sukarno of Indonesia was applying pressure on Malaysia.

Johnson held back. It took direct attacks on Americans to force his hand. A 7 February VC attack on the US base at Pleiku killed eight Americans and wounded 126; it also destroyed or damaged 25 aircraft. Johnson authorized a

AIR WAR

LINEBACKER Strikes
Port mining
Main rail line
Main road

retaliatory strike. In Operation Flaming Dart 49 A–4 Skyraiders and F–8 Crusader jets from the carriers *Coral Sea* and *Hancock* struck North Vietnamese barracks and port facilities at Đông Hới just north of the DMZ. On 8 February Air Vice Marshal Nguyên Cao Kỳ led a follow-up raid by the VNAF against the North Vietnamese communications centre of Vinh Linh.[90]

These air attacks occurred while Soviet Premier Alexei Kosygin was in Hà Nôi, the first premier of the USSR to visit the DRV. There is speculation that the DRV leadership timed the Pleiku raid to coincide with Kosygin's visit on the assumption that it would bring US retaliation and force the Soviet Union to commit itself to North Vietnam. In any case, Soviet pleas that the VC not attack the Americans proved in vain.

On 10 February a Soviet United Nations official termed US raids during Kosygin's visit an "unfriendly act". Kosygin himself could not forget this "humiliation". As one scholar has noted,

> The Pleiku incident and US retaliation destroyed what was left of Moscow's hope to avoid internationalization of the conflict in Vietnam. As a result the Soviet Union was forced to set aside its policy of propaganda and noninvolvement and plunge into a war with unpredictable consequences.[91]

Although wary of endangering better ties with the West, the Soviets pledged substantial economic and military assistance and, within several weeks, surface-to-air missiles were arriving in Hai Phòng.[92]

On 10 February the VC blew up a hotel in Qui Nhon on the central coast, killing 23 Americans as they slept. Two VC sappers also died. A day later a third series of air raids occurred against the North. Some 160 US and South Vietnamese land- and carrier-based aircraft struck Chan Hoa and Chap Le, 160 and 40 miles respectively, north of the DMZ. Three US planes were shot down, with one pilot rescued.[93]

In February the State Department released a white paper on Vietnam. Titled *Aggression from the North: The Record of North Viet-Nam's Campaign to Conquer South Viet-Nam*, it began with a 17 February quotation from President Johnson that spelled out the US policy in Vietnam as joining "in the defense and protection of freedom of a brave people who are under attack that is controlled and . . . directed from outside their country". It held Hà Nôi responsible for "aggression" that had "been going on for years" and stated "Above all, the war in Viet-Nam is *not* [emphasis in original] a spontaneous and local rebellion against the established government." It charged that since 1959 Hà Nôi had sent some 37,100 military personnel south. It also stated that three-quarters of 4,400 infiltrators from the North in the first eight months of 1964 were native Northerners. Personnel from the North, it charged, "are now and have always been the backbone of the entire VC operation". The paper also blamed Hà Nôi for arms shipments to the South, including a trawler sunk in shallow waters off Phu Yen Province on 16 February 1965, which had transported more than 100 tons of arms and ammunition, including a recoilless rifle, 17 machine guns, more than 3,600 small arms, a million rounds of small-arms ammunition, and grenades and explosives. The position paper was clearly designed to justify a US military response.[94]

The US response primarily took the form of bombing North Vietnam. This appealed to Johnson for a number of reasons. Certainly it was the least risky and least costly option as far as the loss of American lives was concerned, and it would also perhaps win the support of influential congressional advocates of air power.

Operation Rolling Thunder, the sustained bombing of North Vietnam, began on 24 February. It ignored a DRV response. When former Eisenhower Administration aide and Dulles critic Emmett John Hughes asked Special Assistant to the President for National Security Affairs McGeorge Bundy what the Administration would do if Hà Nôi retaliated by escalating the ground war, he replied, "We can't assume what we don't believe."[95]

Rolling Thunder was both a measured and limited bombing of the North below the 19th parallel. Washington policy-makers intended it to halt the movement of men and supplies south and to cause the North Vietnamese leadership to give up its support for the war. There had to be, Washington reasoned, some point at which DRV policy-makers would break.

Throughout the entire course of the war American leaders consistently underestimated the determination of the DRV leadership to continue the war as well as the support of the North Vietnamese people for reunification. They continued to see the war through American lenses. But what would have been unacceptable to Americans was quite manageable to the Vietnamese.

Johnson also dramatically changed the face of the war by sending the first US ground troops to South Vietnam. By early 1965 three PAVN regiments, the first regular units sent, were in South Vietnam. Beginning in February, some 2,000 South Koreans arrived in the South to assist the RVN. In late February General Westmoreland cabled Washington with a request for two battalions of Marines to protect the US base at Đà Nẵng. Ambassador Taylor disagreed and warned that introducing US ground troops would encourage the Vietnamese to "shuck off greater responsibilities". But the JCS approved Westmoreland's request. Taylor was told to secure RVN approval. On 8 March the US 9th Marine Expeditionary Brigade (MEB) arrived at Đà Nẵng.[96] The war had dramatically escalated in a way that neither side had foreseen or desired.

Chapter Five

The Vietnam War: the quagmire (1965–8)

In the spring of 1965 the war was going badly for the Republic of Vietnam Armed Forces (RVNAF). For the most part the VC left US forces alone and concentrated on ARVN units, apparently in the belief that they could defeat them before the Americans could deploy sufficient ground forces.

ARVN pacification efforts

The RVN's spring 1965 objectives were to defend bases and lines of communication, seek out its enemy in his base areas and support the Chiên Thǎng ("Victory") pacification programme. Begun in 1964, this effort placed priority on securing control of the populated areas by a combination of military actions and social programmes. At its heart was the "New Life" hamlet programme, similar in many ways to the disastrous Strategic Hamlet programme under Diêm. The New Life programme was to have been better planned and called for securing one area before going to another, in the fashion of the classic "oil slick" pacification method. But once again the RVN plan was overly ambitious and poorly run, and by spring 1965 it was in a shambles.[1] One study of pacification programmes in the RVN concludes that governmental instability in Sài Gòn greatly affected prosecution of the war and pacification efforts at both the national and local levels. It held that there was "neither the time nor the inclination on the part of the various governments . . . to deal with anything but the most urgent military threats".[2]

The Marines who had arrived in Vietnam in March 1965 found their mission modified in early April. No longer merely defending air bases, they could now seek out their enemy in offensive operations, at first limited to within 50 miles of US bases. On 7 May the 9th Marine Expeditionary Brigade (MEB) was redesignated the III Marine Amphibious Force (MAF). The Marine force grew in numbers and established itself in three coastal enclaves, Đà Nẵng, Phú Bài, and then Chu Lai. Most contact between them and the VC came at Marine initiative.[3]

With the military situation in South Vietnam rapidly deteriorating, Westmoreland's demands for additional ground troops became irresistible, especially after a car bomb on 30 March virtually destroyed the US Embassy in Sài Gòn, killing 22 people and wounding another 183.[4] On 1 and 2 April President Johnson met with his key advisers and decided to increase US forces there by an additional 18,000–20,000 men, although he still hoped to coax the DRV to the bargaining table.[5]

In a major speech at Johns Hopkins University on 7 April Johnson called on Hà Nội to negotiate a reasonable settlement and promised a vast economic development plan for Southeast Asia, for which he would ask Congress to appropriate $1 billion. "Old Ho can't turn that down", Johnson told an aide.[6] But Hà Nội did just that, rejecting any negotiations while the United States was bombing North Vietnam.[7]

On 20 April Westmoreland met with McNamara and other Johnson Administration officials in Honolulu and secured approval of his March request to add nine battalions to the four (Marine) already in the country. This brought the total to 13 US battalions and four from other countries (one from Australia and three from the Republic of Korea), in all 82,000 Americans and 7,250 from other countries.[8]

In early May the 173rd Airborne Brigade began arriving from Okinawa, the first Army combat unit in South Vietnam.[9] On 8 June the White House outlined the circumstances under which Westmoreland might commit US forces:

> If help is requested by the appropriate Vietnamese commander, General Westmoreland also has authority within the assigned mission to employ these troops in support of Vietnamese forces faced with aggressive attack when other effective reserves are not available and when in his judge-ment, the general military situation urgently requires it.[10]

Westmoreland believed that the South Vietnamese could not contain the VC on their own and demanded authority to assign US forces to offensive operations.[11] On 26 June he received permission to commit American forces in support of the South Vietnamese "in any situation ... when in COMUSMACV's [Westmoreland's] judgment their use is necessary to strengthen the relative position" of ARVN forces. Two days later Westmoreland initiated his first "search and destroy" operation, ordering the 173rd Airborne Brigade (only two of its battalions were then available), an Australian battalion, and two ARVN airborne battalions into the VC stronghold known as War Zone D northwest of Sài Gòn.[12]

ARVN forces were now being chewed up at an alarming rate. On 30 May in northernmost I Corps the VC 1st Regiment ambushed the 1st Battalion of the ARVN 51st Regiment outside the small hamlet of Bà Già, 20 miles south of Chu Lai. Vietnamese Rangers and Marines were then committed to the battle, with US Marine aircraft providing air support. When fighting ended the next day the South Vietnamese had lost 392 killed and missing, along with 446 rifles and carbines and 90 crew-served weapons. They claimed 556 VC killed but captured only 20 weapons.[13]

In July 1965 President Johnson decided to "Americanize" the war. In his reports to Washington Westmoreland had increasingly painted a picture of a deteriorating military situation. Then on 20 July Secretary of Defense McNamara laid a report before the President with three options: 1) cutting American losses and withdraw from Vietnam; 2) continuing US forces at their then approximate level of about 75,000 men (14 manoeuvre battalions and support personnel) and "playing for the breaks", which in McNamara's opinion "almost certainly would confront us later with a choice between withdrawal and an emergency expansion of forces, perhaps too late to do any good"; and 3) to "expand promptly and substantially" the US military presence in Vietnam.[14]

McNamara strongly recommended the third choice, with a tripling of combat strength. Johnson agreed and by 22 July Washington authorized a total of 44 battalions in South Vietnam, exclusive of ARVN. Total US forces were to go from 75,000 to 125,000 men. These would be largely US Army and Marines, apart from South Koreans, Australians, and New Zealanders.[15]

In July more Marines arrived, then the Army's 1st Infantry and the 101st Airborne Divisions. By the end of 1965 nearly 200,000 US military personnel were in South Vietnam, and Westmoreland was projecting troop levels of up to 600,000 men by the end of 1967. Hà Nội, however, matched these escalations by increasing its own manpower commitment in the South.[16]

Strategic options

A number of individuals argued at the time and since that strategic options were open to the United States in 1965 and afterwards that would have brought military victory. Two would have shifted resources towards more conventional warfare: an invasion of North Vietnam or an incursion into Laos to the Thai border to seal the frontier between North and South Vietnam. Two others were an enclave strategy and the demographic frontier.

General Maxwell Taylor, a strong advocate of an invasion of North Vietnam, argued that the United States "should never have put a soldier into South Vietnam". Instead it "should have gone directly to Ha Noi by amphibious/airborne landing".[17] The Johnson Administration strongly opposed this, fearful that it would provoke a direct Chinese military intervention in the fashion of the Korean War. Throughout the Vietnam War the Pentagon brass was preoccupied with monitoring the Chinese military presence in North Vietnam and determining its strength and intentions. At all costs Washington wanted to avoid a military confrontation with China.[18]

The plan would also have required substantial US military resources and there is nothing to indicate that it would have worked out any better than it had for the French, and certainly it would have increased US casualties. Also, even without a direct military intervention in Vietnam, China could have easily supplied PAVN forces in base areas along its southern border.

The invasion of Laos has been the most discussed option in retrospect. Colonel Harry Summers argued in his book *On Strategy, A Critical Analysis of the Vietnam War* that it was the best chance for a US military victory. In 1965 ARVN General Cao Văn Viên suggested fortifying a zone from Đông Hà in Vietnam to Savannakhet on the Lao–Thai border, with a landing to the north at Vinh or Hà Tinh in North Vietnam to cut off PAVN forces to the south. In August 1965 the Joint Chiefs developed a similar DMZ plan. Westmoreland proposed much the same in April 1967, although his plan included Viên's amphibious landing north of the DMZ.[19]

Its advocates argued that the line could easily have been held by eight divisions – five US, two Republic of Korea (ROK), and one ARVN – and that this would have cut the flow of men and supplies to the South, isolated the battlefield and allowed the ARVN to carry the brunt of the war against the VC. But it would also have entailed staggering logistics problems and required large numbers of support personnel (18,000 engineer troops alone). Besides, Communist forces in the South obtained the bulk of their resources within the South, and pulling US troops to the northern barrier would speed up the disintegration of the RVNAF. There was also every likelihood that Communist forces would simply skirt the barrier by going around it to the east through Thailand.

The last two strategies emphasizing counter-insurgency operations offered greater promise. The enclave strategy called for US forces to be concentrated in the population centres and coastal bases, freeing up ARVN to carry the brunt of the fight against the Communists. US forces might also be committed if opportunities for decisive pitched battle occurred. Although this strategy would have ceded the strategic initiative to the Communists and would not have taken advantage of the chief US strengths of firepower and manoeuvreability, in hindsight it probably offered the best hope of buying time to train the ARVN. And, by reducing US casualties, it would have minimized political pressure in the US for a withdrawal.

The final strategic option was proposed in 1968 after three years of US combat involvement. It called for denying the Communists access to the bulk of the population by concentrating US forces in pacification efforts along the coastal plain. This option, which placed greater emphasis on defeating the insurgent threat, had the same advantages as the enclave strategy of buying time for ARVN and reducing US casualties. In the final analysis those policies that increased the effectiveness of the South Vietnamese military and government probably held the best hope of defeating the Communists.[20]

But in 1965 Washington's response was to fall back on "graduated response" or slow escalation as the strategic answer, while within Vietnam Westmoreland placed priority on an attrition strategy of seeking out and destroying PAVN/VC units. Westmoreland had little patience for pacification. His big unit operations meant that US troops were not in any one area long enough to become familiar with it or to develop a close relationship with its people. As Krepinevich has noted, "It was far easier to fall back on the logistical and technological elements of strategy – sensors, ground radars, firepower on call, helicopter gunships, herbicides and defoliants – all of which gave the Army the opportunity to wage counterinsurgency American style."[21]

Rolling Thunder (1965–8)

Meanwhile bombing of the North continued, with only a few pauses, from spring 1965 to the eve of the 1968 US presidential election. During the war the United States and its allies would drop nearly 8 million tons of bombs on Indo-China (6,162,000 tons by the US Air Force). This is more than twice the tonnage dropped by the Allied powers in all of World War II. Most of it fell in Laos and South Vietnam.[22]

The air war against the North was actually separate from the war in the South, in that it was controlled by Washington rather than MACV. Although commander of US forces in the Pacific (CINCPAC) Admiral Ulysses Grant Sharp in Honolulu had operational command, Washington determined the targets to be struck. In the air war, as on the ground, gradual escalation was the operational mode. Ostensibly a military operation, the air war over the North was in reality a political tool, designed to force the DRV to give up its support of the insurgency in the South. Its goals were to halt infiltration and bring North Vietnam to the bargaining table.

Fighter-bombers and interceptor aircraft rather than strategic bombers carried the bulk of the war over the North. Operation Rolling Thunder consisted of some 304,000 sorties, but only 2,380 were by B–52s. The Air Force relied chiefly on the F–105 Thunderchief and F–4 Phantom. The F–105 flew more than 75 per cent of all Rolling Thunder strike sorties. At more than 50,000 pounds fully loaded, the "Thud" had difficulty turning in dogfights but still accounted for more MiG kills than any other US aircraft save the F–4. The F–4 Phantom may have been the best multi-role aircraft ever built, although the tell-tale black smoke from its engine made it an easy target for air defenses. Flown by the Air Force, Navy and Marines, the F–4 shot down 55 MiGs (18 MiG–21s), more than any other aircraft. The A–4 Skyhawk, a small single-seat fighter capable of carrying 4 tons of bombs, flew more bombing missions than any other Navy aircraft in Vietnam. There were also the Navy and Marine all-weather capable A–6 Intruder and the Air Force F–111 (Aardvark).[23]

Rolling Thunder underwent the same gradual escalation as the ground war. At the beginning of the bombing campaign Hà Nôi had no jet aircraft, no missiles, fewer than 20 radar installations and only a few obsolete anti-aircraft guns. But within two years thanks to support from the USSR the DRV boasted the most sophisticated air defense system in the world. Colonel Jack Broughton, Deputy Commander of the 355th Tactical Fighter Wing, described North Vietnam "as the center of hell with Hanoi as its hub".[24]

On 24 July Russian surface-to-air missiles (SAMs) claimed their first victim, an F–4C. By the end of the year there were 60 SAM sites in North Vietnam. Also that year the DRV obtained MiG–15 and MiG–17 aircraft. On 3–5 April 1965, US aircraft struck rail lines to Hà Nôi, the furthest penetration north to that time. Six US aircraft were lost, including one downed by MiGs in the first air-to-air combat of the war.[25]

North Vietnam's air defence system grew dramatically. By the end of 1966 the DRV had some 150 SAM sites and 70 MiG interceptors; over 100 radar sites provided early warning and tracking for some 5,000 anti-aircraft guns. During 1967 SAM sites increased to some 250. That year there were also 7,000 anti-aircraft guns and 80 MiG fighters, ranging from the MiG–15 to the advanced MiG–21. The number of SAM firings illustrate this growth. In 1965 a total of 194 SAMs were fired, but over the next year 990 were launched, followed by 3,484 in 1967.[26]

Against these defences Admiral Sharp committed the most sophisticated aircraft and weaponry in the US inventory. In 1967 the US first used the Walleye "smart bomb", a 1,000lb bomb locked onto a target by a TV eye. US fliers also developed technological countermeasures to deal with MiG and SAM threats. They were slower to develop air tactics for dealing with North Vietnamese pilots, abetted by problems with inaccurate air-to-air missiles. In late 1967, in a stunning turn of events, DRV pilots began shooting down more US aircraft than they were losing. The Air Force largely ignored problems with its tactics, formations and missiles, but the Navy undertook a complete reassessment of its air-to-air operations and in 1969 established its Top Gun training course for pilots. Thereafter it enjoyed a 12-to-1 kill ratio.[27]

Despite SAMs and MiG interceptors, guns remained the most deadly threat to attacking aircraft. Of 3,000 US aircraft lost during the Vietnam War, some 85 per cent were downed by guns. Missiles accounted for only 8 per cent; less than 2 per cent of some 9,000 SAMs fired at US aircraft reached their targets.[28] MiG kills amounted to 7 per cent. In the air war over North Vietnam the United States lost nearly 1,000 aircraft, hundreds of men taken prisoner, and hundreds more killed or missing in action.[29]

Washington steadily escalated the bombing of the North from more than 10,000 sorties a month in 1966 to more than 13,000 a month in 1967. Bombs struck thousands of fixed targets, many more than once, and thousands more moving targets. By the end of Rolling Thunder the US had dropped more than a million tons of bombs on North Vietnam. This cost the DRV more than half its bridges, virtually all of its large petroleum storage facilities, and nearly two-thirds of its power generating plants. It also killed some 52,000 people. US pilots could, and often did, drop more bombs in one day than the French had been able to deliver during the entire siege of Điên Biên Phu, but the bombing did not bring Hà Nôi to the negotiating table. Undoubtedly it strengthened US and South Vietnamese morale and made the war much more costly for the DRV, both in terms of lives lost and *matériel*. It also forced the diversion of labour from farming and other pursuits to repair bomb damage and man air defences.[30]

Throughout Rolling Thunder the Air Force searched for a magic technological bullet to win the war, without success. Earl Tilford has noted:

> Cluster bombs, napalm, herbicide defoliants, sensors dropped along the Ho Chi Minh Trail to monitor traffic and aid in targeting, gunships, and electro-optically guided and laser-guided bombs all promised much, and while some delivered a great deal of destruction, in the end technologically sophisticated weapons proved no substitute for strategy.[31]

Operation Rolling Thunder was a failure. Supplies still reached the South at a level sufficient to sustain DRV/VC military operations, especially as they required only a small fraction of that necessary to sustain US/RVN forces. One estimate held that 10 to 20 truckoads of supplies a week supplemented by porters would maintain the insurgency, and there was no way the bombing could prevent that amount from getting through. Also, despite pauses in the bombing, Hà Nôi showed no inclination to end its support for the war. If anything, the bombing intensified Hà Nôi's determination and solidified popular support in the DRV for the war effort.

While not as dramatic as the air war over North Vietnam nor as costly in terms of casualties as the ground war in the South, the war at sea was important, and the US Navy played a large role in it. The Navy had found itself largely unprepared for Vietnam. Long geared to nuclear war, it had neglected shore bombardment and amphibious assault. After the Tonkin Gulf incidents the Navy instituted frequent gunnery exercises and extended the service life and returned from mothballs several gun cruisers and the battleship *New Jersey*. New aircraft such as the RA–5C and the A–6 Intruder aided reconnaissance and strike capabilities, and Shrike missiles allowed aircraft to hit North Vietnamese anti-aircraft radars.

The most visible US Navy role was in Seventh Fleet carrier operations. Carrier aircraft participated in Rolling Thunder and also provided support to ground forces in South Vietnam, and on occasion in Laos and Cambodia. Surface warships gave fire support to friendly troops ashore. In Operation Sea Dragon the Navy mounted harassment and interdiction raids along the North Vietnamese coastline. Another important mission was halting infiltration by sea from the North. Market Time patrols, begun in 1965, involved long-range aircraft, medium-sized surface ships, and fast patrol craft known as "swift boats".

In the Mekong delta a "brown-water fleet" came into being, consisting of fibreglass patrol boats, shallow-draft landing craft, and fire-support monitors. US Navy unconventional warfare teams known as SEALs (Sea–Air–Land) and Navy helicopter units searched out VC/PAVN troops far from the sea; and Navy river convoys resupplied the Army and Marines inland. On several occasions, the Navy also put Marines ashore in amphibious assaults.[32]

Land/air battle: "the helicopter war"

By May and June 1965 the military situation in the South had sharply deteriorated. During June ARVN lost the equivalent of an infantry battalion a week.[33] In these circumstances General Westmoreland decided to try to hit first, always his preferred strategy during the war. He committed the 1st Cavalry Division (Airmobile), an entirely new military formation that went to war on the wind.

Helicopters came into their own during the Vietnam conflict, which is sometimes known as "the helicopter war". US Army, Marine, Air Force and Navy helicopters flew an astonishing 36,125,000 sorties: 3,932,000 attack; 7,547,000 assault (troop landing); 3,548,000 cargo; and 21,098,000 reconnaissance, SAR (search and rescue), and other missions. The US lost ten helicopters over North Vietnam and 2,066 in South Vietnam to hostile fire, and an additional 2,566 went down to non-hostile causes. Army aviators suffered the highest per capita casualty ratio of any US military contingent in the war.[34]

The US Army embraced the helicopter following the 1947 Key West Agreement that gave the Air Force control of most fixed-wing military aircraft. While very vulnerable to ground fire, helicopters proved invaluable in a variety of roles, including reconnaissance, liaison, troop lift, resupply and medical evacuation (medevac). Utilizing the helicopter, the Army created a new type of division that seemed ideally suited to a war with few roads. The Army experimented with the 11th Air Assault Division (Test), which then became the 1st Cavalry Division (Airmobile). The 1st Air Cavalry Division, as it was known, was entirely airmobile. Although it would take many lifts to move the entire division, all of its 16,000 men and equipment, including artillery, moved in 435 helicopters.[35]

Westmoreland considered breaking up the division into its component brigades and stationing them at various locations around South Vietnam. Division commander Major General Harry W. O. Kinnard strongly objected and Westmoreland assigned the 1st Air Cavalry intact to an area of central Vietnam, just north of Route 19 where it passed through the village of An Khê.[36] The division arrived there in September 1965 and had been in Vietnam only a month when Westmoreland committed it to battle.

US intelligence had identified a PAVN troop concentration in the western Central Highlands, where General Giáp had been assaulting Special Forces camps for some time with the intent of seizing them preparatory to a drive to the sea.[37]

Brigadier General Chu Huy Mân commanded PAVN units on the western plateau. He planned to lay siege to the Special Forces camp at Plei Me, with its 12 Americans and some 400 Montagnards, in the expectation that this would attract a road-bound ARVN relief force, which could then be ambushed. With the relief column destroyed and the Special Forces camp taken, Mân hoped to assault Pleiku City, clearing the way for an advance down Route 19 toward Qui Nhón and the coast. As Lieutenant General Harold G. Moore, who was then a battalion commander and participated in the subsequent fighting, noted, "Whoever controls Route 19 controls the Central Highlands, and whoever controls the Highlands controls Vietnam."[38]

Mân positioned his three regiments around the 2,500-foot-high Chu Pong massif on the Cambodian border, and on 19 October attacked the Plei Mei Special Forces camp. This attack and the ambush of an ARVN relief force failed, thanks in large part to US air support and air-lifted artillery.[39]

Operations in mid-October by units of the 1st Air Cavalry provided intelligence on PAVN dispositions and General Westmoreland decided on a spoiling attack. This resulted in the Battle of the Ia Drang Valley, a forested area just east of the Chu Pong massif, from 23 October to 20 November. It was the first major battle between PAVN and US Army units and one of the war's bloodiest encounters.[40]

On 27 October Westmoreland committed a brigade of the 1st Air Cavalry to search-and-destroy operations. For two weeks there was sporadic but light contact between the opposing sides. This changed on 14 November. Over the next four days savage fighting erupted over landing zones (LZs) X-Ray and Albany. It began when Lieut. Col. Harold Moore's understrength 1st Battalion of the 7th Cavalry Regiment – some 450 men – landed at LZ "X-Ray" almost on top of two PAVN regiments of 2,000 men. Outnumbered and in unfamiliar terrain, the Americans fought desperately. In bitter, sometimes hand-to-hand combat, the Americans drove back the attackers. Beginning the next day, 15 B–52 bombers from Guam began six days of Arc Light strikes on the Chu Pong massif.[41] It was the first time that B–52s were employed in a tactical role in support of ground troops. Moore's battalion was relieved by Lieut. Col. Robert Tully's 2nd Battalion of the 7th Cavalry Regiment, which was then ordered to vacate LZ "X-Ray" and march overland to "Albany" two miles away. Three PAVN battalions ambushed the Americans *en route*, and in the most savage one-day battle of the war 155 Americans were killed and another 124 wounded.[42]

The battle ended when PAVN units withdrew across the border into Cambodia. In a month of fighting the 1st Air Cavalry had lost 305 killed. The Americans estimated PAVN losses at 3,561, less than half of these confirmed. Both sides claimed victory. The PAVN learned they could survive high-tech American weapons and the new helicopter tactics. They also learned to minimize casualties by keeping combat troops close to US positions in what Giáp referred to as his "grab them by the belt" tactic.[43]

The PAVN had inflicted heavy casualties on the Americans, even while suffering horrendously themselves. But the PAVN leadership believed that even lopsided body counts favoured them and would eventually wear down American resolve. The Americans believed they had prevented a decisive PAVN success before the US deployment could be completed. Westmoreland and his chief deputy, General William DePuy, both of whom had learned their trade in the meat-grinder battles of World War II, saw their estimated 12 to 1 kill ratio advantage as proof that the war could be won through attrition, by carrying the conflict to the PAVN in search and destroy operations.[44] Indeed, *Time* magazine selected General Westmoreland as its Man of the Year for 1965. In that year the United States lost 1,275 killed, 5,466 wounded, 16 captured, and 137 missing. RVN forces lost 11,403 killed, 23,296 wounded, and 7,589 missing. The Allies estimated VC/PAVN dead at 35,382 killed and 5,873 captured.[45]

Nguyên Cao Kỳ

Meanwhile the revolving political door continued in Sài Gòn. On 11 June 1965, the RVN government collapsed and the Armed Forces Council chose a military government with Air Vice Marshal Nguyên Cao Kỳ as premier and General Nguyên Văn Thiêu in the relatively powerless position of chief of state.[46] It was the ninth RVN government in less than two years.

Kỳ took steps to strengthen the armed forces. He also instituted needed land reforms, programmes for the construction of schools and hospitals, and price controls. Additionally, his government began a much-touted campaign to remove corrupt officials. At the same time, however, Kỳ instituted a number of unpopular repressive actions, including a ban on newspapers.

The new government was soon embroiled in controversy with the Buddhists and powerful ARVN I Corps commander General Nguyên Chánh Thi, one of the members of the ten-man National Leadership Committee and now a rival to Kỳ. When the other nine members sought to remove Thi from his post, in March 1966 workers in Đà Nẵng began a general strike and Buddhist students in Huê began protests. Soon Thi's removal was no longer the central issue as Buddhist leaders pushed for a complete change of government. With evident growing sympathy for the movement among the civil service and many ARVN units, in early April Kỳ announced his intention to liberate Đà Nẵng, which he claimed had been taken over by the Communists.[47] In fact it is unclear what role, if any, the Communists played.

On 10 April Kỳ appointed General Tôn Thất Đính as the new commander of I Corps, but Đính could not assert his authority with Thi still in Huê. The Americans, desperate to have order restored, lent airlift to Kỳ to transport 4,000 troops to Đà Nẵng in order to suppress the Buddhists and rebel ARVN units. Thi accepted his dismissal on 24 May and went into exile in the United States. Tensions also eased with Buddhist leaders when Kỳ agreed to dissolve the junta and hold elections for an assembly with constituent powers. In June Kỳ's troops put down opposition in Huê. Kỳ's popularity and political clout were enhanced by a February 1966 meeting with President Lyndon Johnson in Hawaii. The two delegations agreed on the need for social and economic reforms as well as national elections in South Vietnam.

The war became an escalating stalemate. By the end of 1966 more than 400,000 US troops were in Vietnam and as many as 60,000 men from other countries. President Johnson had sought the widest possible participation in what became known as the "Many Flags Program". Several allies contributed, but by far the largest military contingent (peak strength of 48,000 men) came from the Republic of Korea, which furnished two divisions. Although well-trained and effective, ROK troops were under orders from Seoul to limit casualties, and for that reason they were reluctant to move without extensive US air and ground support. Australia provided the next largest contingent (peak of 8,000 men), while Thailand, New Zealand and the Philippines also contributed men. With the exception of Australia and New Zealand, all demanded and received remuneration from the United States for their service. Many other nations sent non-combatant aid. In all 44 nations participated.[48]

For the most part VC/PAVN units avoided contact with US forces. The difficulty of conducting effective large-unit sweeps was seen early during Operations Double Eagle I and II, a January–March 1966 attempt by US Army and Marine Corps and ARVN forces to trap VC/PAVN main-force units over a 500 square mile area in Quang Ngãi Province. Most Communist casualties occurred during the first week of the operation, and by the time the Marines and 1st Air Cavalry Division had linked up most PAVN and VC had escaped. As Marine Corps Lieutenant General Victor Krulak, commanding the Fleet Marine Force, Pacific, later noted, the operations failed because the VC/PAVN had been forewarned. He also believed that they taught the people in the area that the Marines "would come in, comb the area and disappear, whereupon the VC would resurface and resume control".[49]

Marines and civic action

The Marines had quite a different strategic view. Krulak and Lieutenant General Lewis W. Walt, commanding general of III MAF, were its chief spokesmen. They saw guerrillas rather than main-force enemy units as the principal threat.[50]

Krulak favoured an enclave strategy that placed emphasis on pacification. His "three cornered strategy" included protecting the South Vietnamese people from the guerrillas; concentrating US air strikes in North Vietnam on rail lines, power, fuel and heavy industry; and placing maximum efforts in

South Vietnam on pacification, in which he believed US forces could be more effective than the RVN government. Krulak saw the Vietnamese people as the key to victory, and if the Communists could be denied access to them the war could be won. He continually admonished his superiors that attrition warfare sapped manpower necessary to protect the villages.[51] As one historian has noted, "In that meat grinder war, those feeding the machine felt they could outlast those grinding it."[52]

For two years the Marines aggressively pursued their pacification strategy in I Corps, engaging in considerable pacification and village welfare work. Each battalion in III MAF was to carry out military civic action programmes in its own tactical area of operation (TAOR). Initially the most common form of this was the MEDCAP, whereby Marine units with Navy corpsmen paid regular visits to villages, offering medical assistance and training local villagers in basic medical practices. For many villagers this was the first time they had received such aid.

Because haphazard civic action programmes proved ineffective in gaining the allegiance of the local population, in August 1965 the Marines developed the Combined Action Company (CAC), whereby RVN Popular Forces (PF) soldiers were integrated into Marine tactical units. By placing these units into Vietnamese hamlets and relying on indigenous PFs, "combined action" operations began to achieve success against the VC. By spring 1966 there were some 40 CACs operating throughout the I Corps area.

By February 1967 the Combined Action Platoon (CAP) became the means to wage what the Marines termed "the other war". Begun in the Phú Bài enclave and then taken up at Đà Nẵng, CAP combined a 14-man Marine rifle squad and one Navy corpsman with three ten-man PF militia squads and a five-man platoon headquarters into a platoon of 50 American and Vietnamese soldiers. They provided security at the local level and initiated civic action programmes as part of the pacification effort. The CAP's mission was to destroy the VC infrastructure within the area of responsibility, provide security for the friendly infrastructure, protect bases and communication within villages and hamlets, organize intelligence nets, participate in civic action and conduct propaganda.[53]

The Marines saw such civic action projects as an integral part of their mission to gain the allegiance of the people. From 1965 to 1971 114 Marine CAPs operated throughout the five I Corps provinces, implementing Marine counter-insurgency strategy.

In the end this effort failed. Neither the RVN government nor General Westmoreland were particularly interested in pacification and they did not provide the requisite support. Also the Marines experienced difficulty in securing effective CAP personnel. With the exception of the Marine Corps

CAPs and Army civil affairs teams, few Americans lived with the Vietnamese long enough to learn their language and culture and win their allegiance to a government that failed to meet their concerns.[54]

New RVN constitution

In September 1966 South Vietnamese elected a 117-member constituent assembly, which completed its work the following March. The new constitution provided for a president with wide powers, a premier and a cabinet responsible to a bicameral legislature with strengthened authority. The judiciary was to be co-equal to the executive and legislative branches. The president would serve a four-year term and could stand for re-election once. He still had command of the armed forces and the ability to promulgate laws and initiate legislation. The two-house legislature was to be chosen by universal suffrage and secret ballot.

Local elections under the new document were held in May 1967 with elections for the lower house in October. The constitution allowed for political parties but prohibited those promoting communism "in any form". Unfortunately, the complex electoral law involved the use of ten-member lists and voters in 1967 had to choose from 48 such slates, a process that favoured well-organized voting blocks.[55]

Tensions were now high between Kỳ and Thiêu. At first the two had gotten on fairly well, but then both vied openly for control of the government. Kỳ was later sharply critical of Thiêu, who he said "wanted power and glory but he did not want to have to do the dirty work".[56] Although the more senior Thiêu had stepped aside in 1965 to allow Kỳ to take the premier's post, his determination to challenge Kỳ for the highest office in the 3 September 1967 elections led the Armed Forces Council to force the two into a joint ticket, giving the presidential nomination to Thiêu and the vice presidential nomination to Kỳ simply on the basis of military seniority. The Thiêu–Kỳ ticket won the election with only 34.8 per cent of the vote; the remaining vote was split among ten other slates.[57]

Meanwhile the war continued. In March 1967 Westmoreland submitted two plans for reinforcements. The first called for a "minimum essential" reinforcement of 80,500 men that would bring US troop strength in Vietnam to 550,500. His second, "optimum" reinforcement, was for 200,000 men, for a total of about 670,000. This would enable him to take the war into Laos and/or Cambodia as well as stage an amphibious landing north of the DMZ. The administration, however, pared Westmoreland's "minimum essential" figure almost in half, deciding on 47,000 reinforcements – the maximum number that could be sent short of calling up the Reserves.[58]

Ground war in South Vietnam

Westmoreland was unwilling to adopt a defensive role in Vietnam. Throughout his tenure as MACV commander he remained committed to large-scale search and destroy operations, the standard US military tactic between 1965 and 1968. He believed that search and destroy operations would best utilize superior American firepower and technology, inflict maximum casualties on VC/PAVN forces and hold down US casualties.

Ground troops, transported in part by Army helicopter units and supported by artillery, were to locate VC/PAVN forces and endeavour to destroy them and their base areas. These tactics emphasized locating and destroying Communist forces rather than acquiring territory. Search and destroy was described by the three Fs: "find, fix and finish". Troops would then withdraw to their bases until ordered out on the next such operation. Westmoreland believed that such tactics would eventually wear down his enemy and force him to sue for peace.

In search and destroy operations, Allied units would enter jungle sanctuaries, search methodically during the day, then occupy strong night defensive positions, daring the Communists to attack. MACV's approach depended on superior intelligence data and sufficient airmobile combat units to exploit an opportunity. Search and destroy operations were also predicated on the assumption that combat had moved from insurgency/guerrilla actions to larger unit actions.

Not everyone agreed with Westmoreland's approach. Air Force Chief of Staff General John P. McConnell and Marine Corps Commandant General David M. Greene both opposed it, as did Marine generals in Vietnam. Retired Army Lieutenant General James Gavin disapproved as well. He called for an "enclave strategy" whereby US troops would be restricted to certain enclaves, which they would then protect. This would free ARVN forces to carry the brunt of the fight. Retired Air Force Major General and counter-insurgency expert Edward Lansdale favoured the concentration of most US manpower resources into pacification and counter-insurgency activities rather than in combat manoeuvre battalions.[59]

Neither Westmoreland nor officials in Washington ever comprehended the degree of sacrifice that the DRV leaders were willing and able to absorb. Hà Nội did not have to answer to public opinion and was absolutely committed to prosecuting the war to a victorious conclusion, even if this meant sacrificing an entire generation. Within the DRV more than 200,000 North Vietnamese males reached draft age every year, and Westmoreland's forces never came close to inflicting that number of casualties in any 12-month period.[60]

Also it was generally the VC/PAVN rather than the US and its allies who held the initiative. They chose to fight on ground favourable to them and broke off contact when they saw fit. This was relatively easy, as guerrillas were lightly armed and might carry only ten pounds of equipment, whereas American soldiers often carried five times that amount. Through it all the VC/PAVN focused on one objective – to crush the Americans' will to continue the war. The American style of war was in fact a risky business that exposed US troops to ambushes, mines and booby traps. Even without these, Americans encountered extremes of climate, tropical diseases, leeches and the ubiquitous "immersion foot".[61]

During 1966 the ARVN and Allied forces mounted 18 major operations, each supposedly resulting in more than 500 VC/PAVN dead. A total of 50,000 VC/PAVN troops were supposedly killed that year. Despite these impressive figures, the operations did not have a major impact on Hà Nôi's ability to conduct the war. For one thing the operations never seemed to realize their full potential. Part of this lay in the difficulty of co-ordinating large operations in secrecy. The more people who were informed, the more likely it was that the very efficient VC intelligence network would get word as well, especially given the need to co-ordinate planning with Vietnamese area commanders. After the war it was learned that VC operatives had infiltrated the highest command levels within the RVNAF. Also, the prepositioning of vast amounts of equipment indicated an impending operation, as did the "prepping" of helicopter landing zones (LZs) from the air or by shelling. All of this usually meant that most enemy troops could escape the dragnet. The larger the operation, the more likely it was to be compromised. The pluses and minuses of this are illustrated in Operations Attleboro, Cedar Falls, and Junction City.

Attleboro (5–25 November 1966) targeted the VC 9th Division in War Zone C, a 30 by 50-mile flat, marshy area along the Cambodian border northwest of Sài Gòn, chequered with rice paddies and thick patches of jungle. Núi Bà Đen (Black Virgin Mountain), a 3,235-foot-high land mass, dominated the surrounding flat countryside. Honey-combed with caves, it was long believed to be the forward headquarters of COSVN. Attleboro was the largest American joint operation of the war to this point. It ultimately involved more than 22,000 US and ARVN troops, supported by B–52 strikes and massive artillery fire. MACV put VC/PAVN losses during Attleboro at 2,130 killed, nearly 900 wounded and more than 200 missing or captured. US and

Allied losses were 155 killed and 494 wounded. Attleboro destroyed the VC 9th Division's extensive base area, including shops and factories, and crippled its effectiveness for about six months. It also showed that VC/PAVN units were no match for the superior manoeuvreability and firepower of large US and ARVN units in pitched battles. Yet Major General William E. DePuy, commander of the 1st Infantry Division, noted that when their casualties became too high the VC simply backed off and waited out the Americans: "They controlled the battle better. They were the ones who decided whether there would be a fight."[62]

Cedar Falls (8–26 January 1967) was the next large Allied search and destroy operation. Directed against the so-called Iron Triangle and headquarters of VC Military Region IV, it was the war's first corps-sized operation. Cedar Falls included two US and one ARVN infantry divisions as well as supporting units. For the first time Westmoreland used all his different combat forces, including paratroopers, and large armour and mechanized units. Extensive efforts were made to preserve security, and the ARVN corps commander was briefed only two days before the operation began.

Cedar Falls was a "hammer and anvil" attack, the anvil being a blocking position along the Sài Gòn River at the southwestern boundary of the Iron Triangle. It was put in place by air assault. The hammer consisted of ground and air assaults into the jungle north of the Iron Triangle. Infantry squads and fire teams then destroyed tunnel systems and military engineers worked heavy Rome ploughs to level villages and clear the jungle. For the most part VC forces avoided battle and escaped. By 26 January engineers had cleared some 2,711 acres of jungle and created 34 landing zones. MACV reported 750 VC/PAVN killed, 280 prisoners and 540 defectors. Allied losses came to 83 killed and 345 wounded. Although a setback for the Việt Công, Cedar Falls was hardly what DePuy characterized as a "turning point . . . and a blow from which the VC in this area may never recover".[63]

A month later Westmoreland launched Junction City (22 February–14 May 1967), another foray into War Zone C. The war's second corps-sized operation, it lasted from late February to mid May 1967, and involved four ARVN and 22 US battalions. Its primary objective was the destruction of the VC 9th Division. In the course of the operation the 173rd Airborne Brigade's 2nd Battalion, 503rd Infantry, parachuted into drop zones only seven miles from Cambodia in the only major US "combat" jump of the war. From 19 March to the 22nd, and again from 31 March to 1 April, heavy fighting occurred.

During Junction City US and ARVN units lost 282 killed and 1,576 wounded. MACV listed Communist losses as 2,728 killed and an undetermined number of wounded. The Allies also seized 490 weapons and significant quantities of supplies, rations and documents. Despite this the operation did not produce long-term gains. The VC 9th Division, although temporarily shattered, was back in force less than a year later; and War Zone C was far from neutralized. When US troops withdrew the VC moved back in. Giáp moved his military headquarters in the South across the border into Cambodia, where PAVN troops were already based.[64]

Operations Attleboro, Cedar Falls and Junction City showed that even a series of successful battles did not translate into strategic advantage. In fact they played into Giáp's hands by taking US forces from the more populous coastal plain to support operations in the remote interior. Once units were removed from pacification duties, it was virtually impossible to reestablish trust within the villages.

The jungle was too thick for US forces to prevent the VC/PAVN from escaping; they returned as soon as the Americans departed. Within two weeks after Cedar Falls the official report on the operation noted that the base area as "literally crawling with what appeared to be Viet Cong".[65]

Westmoreland was in fact playing to the Communist strategy of protracted warfare. As Giáp put it at the time, his objective was to draw the Americans into peripheral battles, inflicting casualties and sapping the US will to continue the war. Certainly the results were minimal for the expenditures of funds, equipment and lives they entailed. Yet in June 1967 some 86 per cent of MACV's battalion operations time was expended in such operations.[66]

Although Westmoreland believed that the war had moved to large-unit conventional warfare, analysis of captured PAVN documents suggested that it was still a small-unit war. By 1967 over 96 per cent of all US engagements with Communist forces were at company strength or less. That is where most US casualties occurred. Ironically, one of the safest places for a US soldier to be in Vietnam was in one of Westmoreland's big battles, since they provided the best opportunity to minimize contact with the enemy.[67]

Throughout the conflict the US Army fought so as to minimize casualties. The dominant idea was to locate its enemy using infantry as a reconnaissance force and then destroy him with artillery and air power. Notoriously wasteful of *matériel* resources, this indiscriminate method meant that innocent civilians often got caught in the crossfire. It also led to "firebase psychosis" whereby US commanders grew reluctant to commit troops beyond the range of firebase support. Firepower was substituted for aggressive small-unit tactics. No more did the infantry use the time-honoured tactic of "fire and manoeuvre". Ground commanders were unwilling to fight on their own at some distance from an artillery support base or a helicopter pad, and airtillery fire and air support became the principal destructive tools.[68]

The US Army in Vietnam was not employed efficiently. Too many men were wasted in non-essential tasks, with only a small minority actually fighting. One officer in the 173rd Airborne Brigade charged that it could on an average day employ only 800 of its 10,000-man complement in field operations. Extra creature comforts, unknown in earlier American wars, proliferated for the support troops; and much equipment, including weapons, was wasted or pilfered.[69]

Another serious problem was the lack of cohesion in combat units, owing to the Johnson Administration's failure to mobilize National Guard and reserve units or declare a state of emergency that would permit the Army to extend the tours of its best-trained soldiers. Moore noted that, because of this, his battalion of the 1st Air Cavalry Division was at little more than half strength when it arrived in Vietnam. The war, he said, was fed "by stripping the Army divisions in Europe and the continental United States of their best personnel and matériel, while a river of new draftees . . . flowed to do the shooting and the dying".[70] Soldiers were fresh out of training camps for the most part and served one-year tours in Vietnam. Replacements came and went constantly. In World War II men remained together for the duration of the conflict, producing a sense of camaraderie and esprit sadly lacking in the US Army in Vietnam. As Napoleon put it, "Soldiers have to eat soup together for a long time before they are ready to fight".[71] It is a truism in war that soldiers fight not for some abstract cause or even for country, but rather for their comrades. And Army personnel policies negated this because often soldiers in the same unit hardly knew one another.

Much of this was self-inflicted. As Andrew Krepinevich has noted, "the Army gave priority to those personnel actions concerning tour lengths and duty assignments that promoted traditional service goals rather than successful counterinsurgency operations". The standard Vietnam officer tour was 12 months, and those in command slots could serve only six months before being transferred. That was hardly sufficient time for an officer to become familiar with his command. It also angered soldiers who served longer combat tours and believed that risks were not equally shared. In a rather amazing statement, Westmoreland justified the policy by saying that the Army had "to look after its long-term interests". The more officers with command experience the better off the army would be in fighting future wars.[72]

In Vietnam control of the ground was judged to be less important than destroying VC/PAVN units. The measure of success became the "body count", one of the more ghoulish terms of the war. MACV's weekly totals of VC/PAVN and Allied killed and wounded grimly measured the war's ups and downs and were regarded as the primary indicator of success or failure. But pressure to secure high counts led to abuses. Kill ratios were very loosely tabulated and usually exaggerated; any dead body tended to be counted as an enemy.

Captured enemy documents indicated that enemy losses were perhaps 30 to 50 per cent less than what MACV claimed.[73] Weapons taken were probably a much more reliable indicator of actual losses.

Hà Nôi's strategy

The VC/PAVN learned that the best way to deal with the Americans was to fight close in, "to cling to their cartridge belts" as they put it. This would nullify US advantages in artillery and air support. If the VC/PAVN fought at any distance they ran the risk of heavy casualties. Still, Giáp was not winning major battles, and it seemed probable that if he prepared to do so the US would launch spoiling attacks. But neither was he close to defeat and PAVN strength had actually risen.

Giáp favoured a continuation of protracted war to outlast the United States. But in April 1967 a majority of the Politburo, including Lê Duân and General Nguyên Chí Thanh, Giáp's military rival and commander in the South, voted to approve party theoretician Trúóng Chinh's proposal for a "spontaneous uprising [in the South] to win the war in the shortest possible time". It seemed far-fetched at the time: a massive military offensive with the goal of achieving a quick victory.[74]

Giáp dutifully prepared a repeat of 1953–4: a "peripheral strategy" to draw US forces away from the main population centres, perhaps in the process isolating a major unit and repeating Điên Biên Phu. He could then launch a massive offensive, which Hà Nôi expected to be accompanied by a popular uprising of the civilian population against the RVN government and the Americans. It was known as TCK–TKN, the abbreviation for Tông Công Kích – Tông Khói Nghia ("General Offensive – General Uprising"). In October Giáp accompanied Party Secretary Lê Duân and Foreign Minister Nguyên Duy Trinh to Moscow and then to Beijing. Pleased at the North Vietnamese commitment to continue the war, the PRC pledged 100,000 logistics troops and 200,000 rail and road maintenance workers. Beijing also promised to supply artillery pieces. Hô Chí Minh accepted part of the offer, although this was not acknowledged officially until 1977.[75]

The first step in Giáp's strategy brought a series of battles, especially in northern I Corps. In the spring of 1966 PAVN forces had begun a build-up in South Vietnam's northernmost Quang Tri Province. This led to a series of bloody fights with the Marines. In Operations Prairie I–IV between early August July 1966 and the end of May 1967, 525 Marines were killed and 3,167 wounded.[76]

The bloodiest fighting occurred in late April and early May 1967 near Khe Sanh. This strategically insignificant base with an air strip was located in western Quang Tri about six miles east of Laos and 14 miles south of the DMZ. It had been established to monitor PAVN infiltration through Laos. Westmoreland hoped that an enlarged base there could block such movements along Route 9 and perhaps serve as a jumping-off point for a future invasion of Laos.[77]

In order to control nearby infiltration routes the Marines were ordered to take three enemy-held hills. Fighting for these was intense, even hand-to-hand; but at the end of these "hill fights" – later known as the First Battle of Khe Sanh (24 April–12 May) – the Marines had suffered 160 killed and 746 wounded. They claimed 570 confirmed VC/PAVN dead and another 589 probables.[78]

The First Battle of Khe Sanh was only one of many in Giáp's "peripheral campaign". In September PAVN forces crossed the DMZ to attack a Marine outpost at Côn Thiên. For the first time in the war PAVN forces used long-range guns and rockets to support an infantry assault. In just nine days they fired 3,000 shells.[79]

Westmoreland supported US operations in I Corps with a bombing campaign planned by Air Force General William Momyer. Dubbed SLAM – for Seek, Locate, Annihilate, and Monitor – the campaign was on a massive scale. At Côn Thiên alone, B–52s dropped 22,000 tons of bombs. This was in addition to ordnance delivered by fighter bombers, naval gunfire and ground artillery. SLAM's success convinced Westmoreland that with adequate bombing and aerial resupply US outposts could survive even when outnumbered. As Westmoreland said of Côn Thiên, "It was Dienbienphu in reverse. . . . massed firepower [is] in itself sufficient to force a besieging enemy to desist."[80]

On 29 October the VC 273rd Regiment attacked the RVN district headquarters and Special Forces camp at Lôc Ninh 70 miles north of Sài Gòn. Both sides rushed in reinforcements; and in a week of fighting the VC lost at least 852 dead before being driven back. The attackers were well armed with new AK–47 assault rifles, flame throwers and grenade launchers. They also had anti-aircraft weapons and 120mm mortars and 122mm rockets. Westmoreland professed to be unworried and declared the fighting at Lôc Ninh (29 October–3 November 1967) to be "one of the most significant and important operations" of the war.[81] It was after this battle that MACV announced that Communist forces had reached the "crossover point" and were now losing more men than they were replacing. Westmoreland reported that the VC/PAVN had lost 60,000 soldiers in the first ten months of 1967 while securing only 20,000 replacements.[82]

Another "peripheral battle" occurred in some 200 square miles of territory around Dak Tô, some 280 miles north of Sài Gòn near the Cambodian border in the 173rd Airborne Brigade's tactical area of responsibility. Four PAVN infantry regiments and an artillery regiment, their largest concentration of the war to date, gathered around the Dak Tô Special Forces camp. Warned by a defector of the impending attack, Westmoreland reinforced the 1,000 men already there with other troops from the 173rd and men from the US 4th Infantry and 1st Cavalry Divisions. Six ARVN battalions also were sent, along with support troops.

On 3 November PAVN forces initiated what would become one of the bloodiest and most sustained battles of the war. Eleven days later PAVN rockets destroyed two C–130 cargo planes on the runway and the main ammunition dump at the fire support base. The battle's climax, during 19–22 November, came in a savage fight for Hill 875, 12 miles southwest of Dak Tô, where PAVN units surrounded a battalion of the 173rd Airborne Brigade. On 19 November an errant 500 lb bomb exploded in the middle of a US aid station, killing 42 men and wounding another 45.

Dak Tô was one of the biggest battles of the war. The Allies lost 347 dead and US losses alone were 287 killed, 985 wounded and 18 MIA. The official count of PAVN dead was 1,200. The American after-action report claimed, "In a classic example of allied superiority in firepower and maneuver, fifteen US and Vietnamese battalions beat the enemy to the punch and sent the survivors limping back to their sanctuaries."[83] Still, given Hô Chí Minh's earlier statements, 4 to 1 would seem a loss ratio readily acceptable to the DRV leadership.

Giáp had forced US/ARVN troops into fighting in terrain and circumstances of his choosing, and his units had gained experience in larger unit combat against the Americans. The PAVN had the advantage of short supply lines into Laos and North Vietnam and could withdraw when it chose, and it had siphoned US forces away from pacification efforts and the defence of populated areas.

By the end of 1967 the first phase of Giáp's plan was complete. US ground strength had been dispersed in the North away from the populated centres. Indeed, in January 1968 Westmoreland deployed two additional 1st Cavalry Division brigades from rice-rich Bình Định Province to Dak Tô.

Westmoreland was pleased with the battlefield progress in 1967. He firmly believed that the Allies now had the initiative. The VC/PAVN had sustained heavy personnel losses and had lost control of large sectors of the country. US casualities, however, had shot up from 2,500 in 1965 to 33,000 in 1966, and to 80,000 in 1967.[84]

At the end of 1967 Westmoreland was even more optimistic. He returned to the United States in mid-November to give a glowing report to President Johnson, who asked him to make his views public. On 21 November Westmoreland appeared before the National Press Club and asserted, "We have reached an important point when the end begins to come into view. I am absolutely certain that, whereas in 1965 the enemy was winning, today he is certainly losing. The enemy's hopes are bankrupt."[85] Westmoreland told a *Time* interviewer, "I hope they try something, because we are looking for a fight."[86]

The Tết Offensive (31 January–24 February 1968)

While US attention was riveted on the peripheral fights, especially at Khe Sanh, VC/PAVN leaders were preparing their most ambitious and costly military venture to date, one that was to change the course of the war, although not as intended. As mentioned, Giáp had planned to draw US forces away from the populated areas and then mount a widespread military offensive that would bring a popular uprising against the RVN government and the Americans.

The DRV leadership selected the Lunar New Year celebrations or Tết as the time for the general offensive. Tết was the most important holiday of the year, when traditionally both sides had observed a cease-fire. South Vietnamese military units would be at low strength with many men at home with their families for the customary celebrations and worship at family shrines. With roads choked with people returning to their childhood homes, guerrillas found it easy to slip undetected among them. Security was also lax at checkpoints. Disguised as ARVN soldiers, many Communist troops even hitched rides on American military vehicles.

The Tết Offensive lasted for 25 days, from 31 January until 24 February. There was precedent for an attack during Tết in Emperor Quang Trung's 1789 victory over the Chinese.

Contrary to popular myth, MACV was not caught completely by surprise. Military intelligence, especially in III Corps, had learned through a variety of sources that VC/PAVN units were on the move from the border areas and were concentrating around the cities. Commander of II Field Force Lieutenant General Frederick C. Weyand, alarmed over increased Communist radio traffic around Sài Gòn and an unusually low number of enemy contacts in the border areas, met with Westmoreland on 10 January and convinced him to pull additional US combat battalions back in around the capital. It was one of

Tet Offensive

Key Battles

Cities and provincial capitals

Military installations

RVN national highway   *QL–1*
Main road
Secondary road

DMZ · Quang Tri
Khe Sanh · Hue
Lang Vei · Phu Loc
Da Nang
Hoi An
Tam Ky · Chu Lai
Quang Ngai
Dak To
Kontum
Pleiku · An Khe · Qui Nhon
Hau Bon
Tuy Hoa
Ban Me Thuot
Ninh Hoa
Nha Trang
Da Lat · Cam Ranh
An Loc · Phan Rang
Tay Ninh
Phu Cuong · South China Sea
Tan Son Nhut · Bien Hoa · Xuan Loc
Chau Phu (Chau Doc) · Moc Hoa · Phan Thiet
Sai Gon · Long Binh · Phuoc Le
My Tho · Vung Tau
Sa Dec · Go Cong
Vinh Long · Ben Tre
Rach Gia · Can Tho
Soc Trang (Khanh Hung) · Phu Vinh
Quan Long (Ca Mau)
Vinh Loi (Bac Lieu)

the critical decisions of the war, because this meant that when the offensive began there were 27 battalions (instead of the planned 14) in the Sài Gòn area.[87]

Where MACV erred was in incorrectly anticipating the timing of the attack and its scale. Westmoreland's chief of intelligence Brigadier General Philip B. Davidson believed that VC/PAVN forces would attack either just before or just after Têt.[88] On 22 January Westmoreland informed General Earle Wheeler in Washington that a major attack might come just before Têt.[89]

MACV's chief error was in underestimating the size of the offensive. As Davidson put it to Westmoreland later, "Even had I known exactly what was to take place, it was so preposterous that I probably would have been unable to sell it to anybody. Why should be enemy give away his major advantage, which was his ability to be elusive and avoid heavy casualties?"[90] Giáp's plans played to Westmoreland's belief that his enemy had been severely wounded during the peripheral battles of the preceding autumn and winter. Westmoreland and Davidson could not conceive that an offensive of such magnitude would be unleashed or that it would be directed against the cities.[91]

With tension mounting, Westmoreland visited with both President Thiêu and ARVN Chief of the Joint General Staff General Cao Văn Viên and tried to convince them to end the cease-fire over Têt altogether or to shorten it from 48 to 24 hours. They refused, but agreed to reduce the cease-fire to 36 hours and to keep at least 50 per cent of ARVN duty troops on full-alert status.[92]

During the early morning hours of 30 January VC/PAVN forces struck Nha Trang, Ban Mê Thuôt, Tân Canh, Hôi An, Đà Năng, Qui Nhón, and Pleiku. Three battalions also hit Kontum in the Central Highlands. Apparently this was because Communist Military Region 5 used the calendar that Hà Nôi had put into effect in August 1967, while the remaining Communist commanders in the South used the Republic of Vietnam calendar.[93]

The bulk of the attacks began the next night, 30–31 January. Communist forces struck 36 of 44 provincial capitals, 5 of 6 autonomous cities, 64 of 242 district capitals and about 50 hamlets.[94] In the vital strategic area around Sài Gòn, roughly a 30-mile zone around the capital known as the "Sài Gòn Circle", the Communists committed the equivalent of more than two divisions. In the capital itself Communist sappers actually penetrated the US Embassy. More importantly the attackers blew up part of the large Long Bình ammo storage dump and captured all of Biên Hòa City, which had to be retaken. Most of the fighting inside the "Sài Gòn Circle" was over in a matter of days, except in Chó Lón, the Chinese district of Sài Gòn, where ARVN forces shouldered most of the effort. Most of Chó Lón was cleared by 7 March, but sporadic fighting erupted in the capital for the remainder of the month.[95]

At Huê the Communists made a large investment of resources during the offensive, probably for the psychological effect that the capture of the former imperial capital would have on the rest of the country. Eight vc/pavn battalions participated in the initial assault there, but this force grew to 20 battalions during the battle.

Aided by heavy ground fog, by the night of the 31st the attackers held most of the city, including part of the Citadel. ARVN and US commanders immediately committed the ARVN 1st Infantry Division and a company of the US 1st Marine Division. Other units were fed into the battle as they became available. Finally, on 12 February Allied leaders called in air power and artillery support. Fighting was house-to-house and reminiscent of street fighting in Europe during World War II. In the 25 days it took to retake Huê, perhaps 50 per cent of the city was destroyed and 116,000 civilians out of a population of some 140,000 were homeless. The US Army suffered 74 dead and 507 wounded; the US Marines lost 142 dead and 857 wounded. ARVN losses totalled 384 dead and 1,830 wounded. vc/pavn losses exceeded 5,000 dead, 89 captured and countless others wounded, but most escaped.[96]

There was heavy fighting elsewhere, but not on the scale of Huê. At Quang Tri City a battalion of the 1st Cavalry Division arrived just in time to break a PAVN assault and kill more than 400 attackers.

Overall the Têt offensive was a major Communist military defeat. North Vietnamese leaders had not realized their goals; there was no crushing defeat of Allied forces in the South, especially the ARVN. The PAVN had paid a horrendous price, suffering losses at a greater rate than those sustained by the Japanese in their fanatical charges in World War II. The US estimated vc/pavn losses during 29 January–11 February at 32,000 killed and 5,800 captured, close to half the force committed. ARVN and Allied killed ran to 2,082 and the US lost 1,001. Civilian deaths reached 12,600. By the end of February, after vc/pavn forces had been completely routed, MACV estimates of their dead grew to 37,000.[97]

There also had been no general rallying of the civilian population to the Communist cause – no "general uprising". A 1 February COSVN directive calling for continuation of the offensive admitted failure: "We failed to seize a number of primary objectives and to completely destroy mobile and defensive units of the enemy. We also failed to hold the occupied areas. In the political field we failed to motivate the people to stage uprisings and break the enemy's oppressive control."[98]

Much to the relief of the Americans the RVNAF had fought well – no ARVN unit broke or defected and as Westmoreland himself noted, "To the ARVN, other members of the South Vietnamese armed forces, the militia, the

National Police – to those belonged the major share of credit for turning back the offensive."[99]

If anything, the Têt Offensive stimulated support for the RVN government, especially with revelations of the butchering of civilians at Huê. During the Communist occupation all those suspected of being "enemies of the people" – government officials, city administrators, teachers, students, soldiers and foreigners – were rounded up. In all 5,000 people disappeared. Later mass graves containing some 3,000 of them were discovered; some people had been buried alive. The remaining 2,000 missing were never found but are presumed to have been executed.[100]

The RVN government took steps to care for the refugees and to bolster the ARVN by drafting 18- and 19-year-olds.[101] But the government faced staggering problems after the offensive, particularly in caring for what official figures admitted to be some 627,000 newly homeless people.[102] As mentioned above, pacification also had suffered a serious blow in the withdrawal of troops from the countryside to defend the cities.

The American public perceived Têt very differently. The early reporting of a smashing Communist victory went largely uncorrected in the media.[103] Many shapers of public opinion now came out forcefully against the war. CBS television anchorman Walter Cronkite, widely regarded as the most trusted man in America, travelled to South Vietnam after Têt. He declared in the course of his 27 February television special:

> To say we are closer to victory today is to believe, in the face of the evidence . . . optimists who have been wrong in the past. To suggest that we are on the verge of defeat is to yield to unreasonable pessimists. To say we are mired in stalemate seems the only realistic yet unsatisfactory conclusion.
>
> It is increasingly clear to this reporter that the only rational way out would be to negotiate . . . as an honorable people who have lived up to their pledge to victory and democracy and did the best they could.[104]

Second Battle of Khe Sanh (January–April 1968)

In January 1968 attention turned again to the Marine base at Khe Sanh, inspiring frequent comparisons to Điên Biên Phu. Although surrounded by hills that could conceal PAVN artillery, Khe Sanh was not in a bowl as was Điên Biên Phu; indeed its location on a plateau gave the defenders the advantage of high ground against an assault.

For 77 days, from late January until early April, some 20,000–40,000 PAVN troops in four divisions besieged the base at Khe Sanh and the high terrain around it. PAVN forces also employed a dozen or so PT–76 tanks, one of only two such instances in which they used tanks prior to 1972.[105]

The defenders were equally split between the base and the hill positions around it. The defence centred on 6,000 Marines, supported by artillery and a small contingent of Army Special Forces. There was also an ARVN Ranger battalion, which Westmoreland had insisted on as a sign of Allied solidarity.[106]

Fighting erupted on 20 January when a reinforced Marine patrol encountered heavy contact. The next day PAVN troops attempted to take the high ground of Hill 861. Alerted by a deserter, the Marines drove back the attackers in hand-to-hand combat. That same day 82 mm mortar rounds and 122 mm rockets rained down on Khe Sanh itself, hitting the main ammunition dump, which blew up in spectacular fashion.

The first major ground attack against the base came on 8 February but was repulsed in heavy fighting at a cost of 150 PAVN and 21 Marine dead. Over the following weeks the attackers concentrated on a relentless artillery barrage from 82 mm and 120 mm mortars, 122 mm rockets, and 130 mm and 152 mm artillery pieces. PAVN forces fired an average of 2,500 rounds a week into an area barely 330 by 600 metres.[107] This artillery fire caused few casualties among the sandbagged and dug-in defenders. The last major land attack occurred over 29 February to 1 March and was directed principally against the ARVN 37th Ranger Battalion. With heavy supporting fire the Rangers turned back three separate PAVN attacks.

Khe Sanh loomed large in American attention. This otherwise obscure fortress became the focus of daily newspaper and television reports and fears of a repetition of Ðiên Biên Phu. President Johnson, obsessed with the battle, even had a terrain model of the base erected in the White House "war room" and insisted that the Joint Chiefs sign a declaration stating their belief that Khe Sanh would hold.

Westmoreland was determined to do just that and saw the battle as a rare opportunity to inflict a major defeat on a massed enemy. Khe Sanh would be his Ðiên Biên Phu rather than Giáp's. He would destroy his enemy with air power. Westmoreland himself came up with the operation's name. As he put it, Niagara was "to invoke an image of cascading shells and bombs".[108] Aided by electronic sensors, Operation Niagara was to destroy PAVN forces and interdict supply lines to the fortress. A wide range of tactical aircraft flew around the clock to provide air support, and the area around the base became one of the most heavily bombed targets in military history. The Seventh Air Force flew 9,961 sorties and dropped 14,233 tons of bombs. The 1st Marine Air Wing flew another 7,078 sorties and dropped 17,015 tons of ordnance, while the Navy flew 5,337 sorties and dropped 7,941 tons of bombs. This totalled one-fifth of all ordnance dropped by the United States in the Pacific theatre in all of World War II.

While tactical aircraft attacked to within 400 yards of the defender's positions, B–52s flying at 30,000 feet, which up to that time had always bombed targets only beyond 3,000 yards of friendly positions, now struck to within 1,000 yards. Some bombs came closer than that. Each B–52 could carry a payload of up to 108 500 lb and 750 lb bombs capable of producing craters up to 40 feet wide and 24 feet deep. The "Buffs" (Big Ugly Fat Fellows) flew 2,548 Arc Light sorties and dropped 59,542 tons of bombs, turning the area around the base into something resembling the surface of the moon. B–52s also devastated PAVN staging areas and depots.[109]

US air power was also vital in supplying the base. C–130 and C–123 aircraft, along with Marine CH–46, Army CH–47 and UH–1E helicopters, ran a gauntlet of anti-aircraft fire to bring in supplies and evacuate wounded. On 10 February a C–130 was destroyed while unloading fuel. After that C–130 landings were suspended, although the planes continued to resupply the base by parachute drops or a hook and line system for extracting pallets in flight (LAPES).

Although PAVN forces withdrew from the vicinity of Khe Sanh beginning on 6 March, the siege officially ended on 8 April when, in Operation Pegasus, Allied units pushed in by land and relieved the Marine defenders. The official MACV casualty count for the Second Battle of Khe Sanh was 205 Marines killed and over 1,600 wounded, although base Chaplain Ray W. Stubbe placed the actual death toll closer to 475. This does not include those killed in collateral actions, ARVN Ranger casualties on the southwest perimeter, 1,000–1,500 Montagnards who died during the fighting, or the 97 US and 33 ARVN killed in relief efforts. MACV's official count of PAVN dead was 1,602, but Westmoreland put the number at between 10,000 and 15,000.[110]

Both sides had seen the battle largely as a test of wills and the opportunity to inflict a major psychological defeat. But the true measure of Khe Sanh's strategic importance may be seen in the fact that US forces abandoned the base in June 1968. John S. Carroll, an Associated Press correspondent who wrote about this, had his press credentials lifted.[111]

Who won at Khe Sanh? Controversy still surrounds the battle and what Giáp intended there. Westmoreland believed that Giáp intended a repeat of Điên Biên Phu and that it had been an "abject failure" for him.[112] As General Davidson noted, if the siege of Khe Sanh was a PAVN diversion, "military history provides few examples of one more expensive".[113] Giáp paid a very heavy human cost in the battle, including a significant number of front-line troops.[114]

Anti-war movement in the United States

Early 1968 was a political watershed in the United States. In February President Johnson asked former Secretary of State Dean Acheson to undertake a study of the Vietnam situation. Much to Johnson's dismay Acheson concluded that the United States could not hope to win without an unlimited commitment of resources, and even with that it might take five years. He also told Johnson that American public opinion had turned against the war.[115]

In the United States disenchantment with Johnson's conduct of the war was in fact widespread, although for many Americans this was because he was not sufficiently aggressive in pursuing it. The heavy casualties of Tết accelerated that trend, abetted by disillusionment over the earlier overly optimistic reports of progress in the war. By now a strong anti-war movement had grown up, which, along with the Civil Rights campaigns of the 1960s, proved to be a most divisive force. It consisted of a number of independent streams, including Students for a Democratic Society (SDS), the Free Speech Movement and "teach-ins" about the war on college campuses across the nation. The anti-war movement had gained national prominence in 1965 with an April march on Washington. Civil Rights leaders, most notably Martin Luther King, Jr, joined the cause and pointed out that the war drained resources that might be used to effect change at home. Although false, the perception that African Americans had disproportionate representation and casualties among US soldiers in Vietnam also fueled anger. After the Tết Offensive fully half the US population opposed further escalation of the war and dissent turned to violence. All of this affected the US political arena.[116]

Chapter Six

The Vietnam War: the US search for a way out (1968–73)

Post-Têt military operations

Thanks to the heavy VC/PAVN casualties of Têt, Allied forces held the initiative in 1968 and made serious inroads into VC/PAVN-controlled areas. Although Communist influence in the rural areas of South Vietnam was seriously weakened and their harsh requisitions of manpower alienated many peasants, the Việt Công infrastructure remained largely intact.

US aircraft flew 281,730 sorties over South Vietnam in 1968, more than in any other year of the war. B–52 strikes tripled.[1] On the ground, Operation Pegasus proceeded (see Chapter five) as the 1st Air Cavalry and ARVN units relieved the Marines at Khe Sanh and US airborne units swept VC/PAVN troops from around Huê. In March and April US and ARVN troops conducted around the capital of Sài Gòn some the largest search and destroy operations of the war to that point, claiming several thousand enemy dead in the process. To the north the 1st Air Cavalry and the 101st Airborne Divisions invaded the Communist A Shau Valley stronghold, last entered by the Allies in 1966. Allied forces also conducted successful operations in the Mekong Delta area. Westmoreland claimed that 120,000 Communist troops had been killed in the first six months of 1968. But during that period the Allies suffered their heaviest losses of the war, including more than 24,000 KIA.[2]

VC/PAVN forces were still strong enough to launch a spring offensive beginning on 5 May. Dubbed by the Americans "Little Têt", it was probably offered to influence talks in Paris. The Communist rallying cry was "Blood in May, Peace in June". Although country-wide, these attacks were nowhere near the level of the Têt Offensive and consisted principally of rocket and mortar attacks against cities, towns and US installations. The most significant action was a thrust against the Khâm Đúc Special Forces camp in Quang Tín province, held by 1,500 men: US and Vietnamese Civilian Irregular Defense Group (CIDG). Westmoreland ordered the camp evacuated by air in the worst possible circumstances; General Creighton Abrams called it "a minor disaster".[3] VC/PAVN attacks in the Central Highlands were aborted owing to pre-emptive attacks by the US 4th Infantry Division, 173rd Airborne Brigade, and B–52 strikes. Although militarily insignificant, the VC also attacked Sài Gòn with rockets and small suicide squads, chiefly in the Chó Lón district.[4] The aim of this offensive was not to win the war but to increase problems for the RVN and the Americans and to keep US casualties high. Certainly the sustained nature of these attacks indicated that the Communists had no intention of giving up the fight.

While General Westmoreland was confident that VC/PAVN forces lacked the capability to inflict a major setback on his forces, Washington was not so certain. Immediately after Tết, President Johnson was eager to provide whatever forces were needed to prevent disaster, and he told General Wheeler that if Westmoreland needed reinforcements beyond the 525,000 ceiling set in mid-1967 he need only ask for them. On 12 February Westmoreland requested an additional Marine regiment and a brigade of the 82nd Airborne Division. These were, he told Wheeler, "not because I fear defeat . . . but because I do not feel that I can fully grasp the initiative from the recently reinforced enemy without them".[5] In Washington Wheeler and the JCS saw the aftermath of Tết as an opportunity to discuss long-shelved options, including calling up the Reserves. Wheeler wanted this because of world-wide US military commitments and the need to rebuild the national strategic manpower reserve.

On 23 February Wheeler arrived in Sài Gòn. Westmoreland found him depressed, but as Wheeler recalled, the newspapers had given the impression that the Tết Offensive was "the worst calamity since Bull Run".[6] Westmoreland saw an opportunity to pursue a more aggressive policy, "the possibility of destroying the enemy's will to continue the war". With reinforcements he could attack PAVN base areas and sanctuaries in Laos and Cambodia and even possibly cut the Hô Chí Minh Trail.[7]

In discussing Vietnam troop reinforcements, the two generals settled on a figure of 206,000 men. Probably by design this represented the total of previous shortfalls in Westmoreland's requests. Such a figure would force mobilization of the Reserves. Wheeler wanted to deploy about half this number to Vietnam by the end of the year and hold the remainder in the US as a strategic reserve.[8]

Wheeler, well aware of Johnson's desire not to expand the war, cautioned Westmoreland not to propose a new military strategy until the troop additions had been approved. He then returned to Washington and gave a pessimistic appraisal of the situation, noting that the Têt Offensive had been "a very near thing" and that the Communists had in many instances been defeated only by the timely arrival of US units. Given the VC/PAVN ability to recover quickly, a renewal of the offensive could soon be expected, and without reinforcements Allied forces would likely have to give ground. Wheeler was never as optimistic about the war as Westmoreland, but his pessimism was likely intended to pressure Johnson into providing the troops for the strategic reserve. In any case this troop request now brought at long last a thorough review of Vietnam policy by a new Secretary of Defense.[9]

By October 1967 Defense Secretary McNamara had changed his position on the war. On 1 November he had given Johnson a memorandum in which he opposed JCS proposals for widening the ground war and expanding the bombing. McNamara urged a bombing halt to bring about negotiations and a review of US ground operations in order to reduce losses and transfer greater responsibility to ARVN.[10]

Clark Clifford

McNamara had previously sounded out Johnson about the presidency of the World Bank and the President now suggested that he take the post. McNamara left Washington in February after eight years as Defense Secretary. Johnson appointed as his successor Clark Clifford, a successful Washington lawyer, Democratic Party power broker, and supporter of his Vietnam policies.[11]

Clifford urged Johnson not to make an immediate decision on the troops request and recommended a full-scale review of Vietnam policy. Johnson said he would not make any immediate decision about the troops and that he wanted "a new pair of eyes and a fresh outlook". He told Clifford, "Give me the lesser of evils."[12]

Clifford undertook a complete review of Vietnam policy, demanding hard answers of the military and asking his civilian advisers to review possible courses of action. In meetings with military leaders Clifford found no assurances that even the full troop request would do the job. They agreed that Hà Nôi could certainly match future escalations, and they had no idea when the South Vietnamese would be ready to carry the burden of the war. Clifford was "appalled" and believed that military leaders offered no "acceptable rationale for the troop increase".[13]

This resulted in a strong indictment of US Vietnam policy. Clifford's advisers noted that in all probability US troop increases would bring the "total

Americanization of the war". They urged a shift from search and destroy operations to pacification, which would allow the Americans to hold major populated areas while the bulk of the fighting would be shifted to the ARVN. They believed the goal should be a negotiated settlement rather than military victory.[14]

Perhaps fearing that the civilian recommendations would be more than Johnson would accept, Clifford did not recommend to the President any major changes in policy and he dropped the idea of a bombing halt. He advocated only an immediate deployment to Vietnam of 22,000 men, some call-up of Reserves to restore the strategic reserve, and a "highly forceful approach" to get South Vietnam to shoulder more of the fighting.[15]

Johnson agreed. He had always opposed further escalation and the military situation in Vietnam had now stabilized. Both Westmoreland and Ambassador Ellsworth Bunker (who had replaced Lodge in Sài Gòn in April 1967) reported that the immediate crisis was over and that US and ARVN forces were about to mount a major counter-offensive. In these circumstances Johnson was unwilling to send additional troops.

Administration officials believed that the South Vietnamese had to do more themselves. One of the strongest arguments against sending additional man-power was that this would discourage the Vietnamese from doing more of the fighting. The ARVN's performance during the Tết Offensive prompted the administration to believe that what was later termed "Vietnamization" might work. Given this, the administration decided that Sài Gòn should be told that the United States would provide only limited reinforcements but much greater material aid. Continued US support would depend on reforms in the RVN and the assumption of more of the fighting load by the RVNAF. This was a return to pre-1965 policy and the start of "Vietnamization", supposedly begun a year later by the Nixon Administration.[16]

The Johnson Administration also began to consider the possibility of curtailing the bombing and the pursuit of a new peace initiative. The impetus for this came when Secretary of State Rusk proposed scaling back the bombing to "those areas which are integrally related to the battlefield" at a time (March, April and early May) when bad weather would in any case impede flights in the North. If the pause did not work, the President could then escalate the war, presumably with expanded public support.[17] Johnson asked only that it be studied and proposals presented to him for a major speech he was to give later that month.

On 10 March the *New York Times* broke the news of the closely guarded Wheeler–Westmoreland request for 206,000 reinforcements and there was an immediate explosion in Congress. Over 11 and 12 March Secretary Rusk was subjected to 11 hours of hearings that revealed sharp congressional disagreement with administration policies. A week later 139 members of the House voted for a resolution that called for a complete review of Vietnam policy. Discontent in Congress mirrored sentiment in the country. In March some 78 per cent of Americans expressed disapproval of Johnson's handling of the war.[18]

Compounding problems for Johnson, 1968 was an election year. On 12 March in New Hampshire, Senator Eugene McCarthy of Minnesota stunned Johnson by winning 42 per cent of the vote in that state's Democratic primary.[19] This prompted Senator Robert Kennedy of New York to join the race. Worried Democratic Party leaders urged the President to do something dramatic to bolster his sagging popularity.

On 22 March Johnson scaled down the 22,000 reinforcements recommended by Clifford, authorizing only 13,500 men, and he decided to bring General Westmoreland home as Army chief of staff. Westmoreland had been much criticized for his predictions of victory and the resultant Têt Offensive, and Johnson may have wanted to save him the embarrassment of having to follow a policy that he did not approve.[20] On 3 July General Creighton Abrams replaced Westmoreland at MACV. Abrams had served a year as Westmoreland's deputy and had worked hard to improve ARVN; its performance during the Têt Offensive owed much to his efforts.

Meanwhile Johnson wrestled with the difficult decision of what to do about the war. By the last week of March, Clifford, thoroughly discouraged by his talks with the military leadership, supported major concessions to bring about a settlement. Administration hawks such as Secretary of State Rusk and National Security Advisor Walt Rostow urged Johnson to stand firm.[21] The President then met with a group of senior civilian and military advisers known as the "Wise Men" who had first convened in July 1965.[22] Shocked to learn about the damage the Têt Offensive had inflicted on RVN security and pacification programmes, the majority of them concluded that the United States could no longer win militarily and warned against further escalation. Disengagement was the only alternative, something Johnson was slow to acknowledge.[23]

Johnson bows out

On 31 March Johnson announced on television that he was restricting bombing of North Vietnam to the area just north of the DMZ. He committed the United States to talk peace at any time and any place, and he named veteran US diplomat W. Averell Harriman as his personal representative to any such talks. Then Johnson dropped a bombshell by announcing that because of the demands of seeking peace, he would not accept renomination for the presidency. Later Johnson said that he had been considering not running for some time, largely because of poor health. He wrote in his memoirs, "I frankly did not believe in 1968 that I could survive another four years."[24] But while Johnson had given up power voluntarily, it was also clear that the President who had won election by the greatest landslide in US history had been driven from office by Vietnam.

Whatever the reasons, Johnson's 31 March speech marked a decisive turning point in the war and a return from graduated response to the pre-1965 policy of trying to deny the Communists victory. More of the burden would be shifted to the South Vietnamese, but just how this would be achieved was not clear.

Both Washington and Hà Nôi rejected numerous sites for peace talks proposed by the other. Finally they agreed on Paris, and talks there opened on 13 May. Onetime foreign minister Xuan Thuy headed the DRV delegation. The talks quickly deadlocked when Hà Nôi insisted that the sole purpose of the meetings was to arrange for "the unconditional cessation of the U.S. bombing raids and all other acts of war so that the talks might start".[25]

Johnson was reluctant to halt the bombing for fear of jeopardizing US troops in South Vietnam. He demanded that Hà Nôi take reciprocal de-escalatory steps, but the DRV leadership refused terms that would limit its ability to fight in the South while allowing the US a free hand there. In June the US delegation headed by Harriman proposed a compromise: the US would halt the bombing on the assumption that the DRV would respect the DMZ and halt rocket attacks on cities. If this were done then "prompt and serious talks" would follow. Hà Nôi did not respond and the talks deadlocked.

Harriman pointed out to Johnson that rocket attacks had eased and that there were indications that some North Vietnamese troops had been withdrawn from the South. Although Hà Nôi had not formally responded to the US offer, these signs, he believed, constituted tacit acceptance. Clifford supported Harriman, but US military leaders warned that the lack of activity was merely a lull before the next offensive. In the end Johnson rejected Harriman's counsel and even threatened that if no breakthrough occurred he might have to re-escalate the war. The peace talks in Paris would drag on another five years, during which time more Americans would be killed than had previously died in the war and the United States would witness bitter internal discord.[26]

Pacification

In South Vietnam General Abrams dramatically changed the military emphasis from search and destroy tactics and body counts to pacification. He believed that population security was the key to winning the war and that all military operations should be built around this goal. He sought to combine combat operations, pacification, and upgrading the RVNAF into a "One War" concept. Abrams cut back on multi-battalion sweep operations and replaced them with multiple small-unit patrols and ambushes that blocked VC/PAVN access to the people. He employed US and ARVN forces in combined operations and urged commanders to reduce drastically H&I (harassment and interdiction) fire, the unobserved artillery fire that did little damage to the Communists and much to innocent civilians.[27] The increasingly small-unit nature of the war under Abrams was reflected in casualty figures. The percentage of US wounded from fragments, including mines and booby traps, as opposed to gunshot wounds from conventional battles, went up substantially.[28]

Pacification ("nation-building") now became the US priority and the chief agency for this was Civil Operations and Revolutionary Development Support (CORDS). Established in May 1967, it brought under the military chain of command all US civilian agencies involved in the pacification effort and united them with comparable military efforts. CORDS activities were primarily directed towards the rural population in an effort to deprive the VC of its traditional population base. Robert Komer, a MACV civilian deputy commander with ambassadorial (three-star) rank, headed CORDS. When he left Vietnam in November 1968 William Colby took over.

One CORDS division had responsibility for the Chiêu Hôi ("Open Arms") programme, which was now intensified. It offered amnesty and "rehabilitation" to Viêt Công and PAVN defectors who surrendered to the RVN as Hôi Chánh ("returnees"). Such individuals would receive job training, welfare services and resettlement assistance; and many were eventually integrated into the ARVN.

The Revolutionary Development division of CORDS worked to provide security and promote economic development at the village level. Its teams trained at the National Training Centre in Vũng Tàu before being assigned to villages throughout the country. Working through the United States Agency for International Development (USAID), a refugee programme assisted in resettling millions of displaced villagers.

Komer and Colby also worked to improve the effectiveness of RF/PF units, important in providing security to the villages, by insuring that their manpower and firepower equalled that of local VC units. By the end of 1969 there were 475,000 men in Ruff-Puff units, and by February 1970 95 per cent of them were equipped with the M–16 rifle.[29]

In addition to pacification efforts, Washington stepped up support for the Phoenix Program. Initiated by Westmoreland, it had as its goal the destruction of the Việt Công Infrastructure (VCI). Over the objections of his own military, Westmoreland had given CORDS responsibility for gathering intelligence on the VCI. Phoenix combined RVN and US civilian and military intelligence collection efforts with the goal of obtaining information and making it available to regular and special police to use against the VCI. Westmoreland approved the concept in July 1967 and it became operational a year later. Colby tried hard to convince President Thiệu to asuume control of Phoenix in order to avoid a US Congressional probe into why Americans were running an operation that should have been led by Vietnamese.[30]

Phoenix did have considerable success against the Communist infrastructure. Between 1968 and 1972 it accounted for the deaths of 26,369 people; another 33,358 were captured and 22,013 surrendered.[31] But many of these were innocent Vietnamese – victims of quota systems and abuses. Phoenix proved so controversial that it is impossible to make a clear assessment of its value.

Vietnamization

Concurrently the Johnson Administration pressed ahead with Vietnamization, developing plans to augment the size and effectiveness of the RVNAF and to give the South Vietnamese more responsibility for fighting the war. ARVN was to grow from 685,000 to 850,000 men, with intensified training programmes so that it could operate and maintain modern US equipment. But such steps would take some time to implement.[32]

Although the ARVN was larger and better equipped, the same problems remained: too few qualified officers, poor leadership, and corruption. Desertions were at an all-time high in 1968 and at the end of that year, of 11 ARVN divisions US advisers rated two as "outright poor", eight as "improving" and only one as "excellent".[33] On 14 July Clifford flew to Sài Gòn to meet with RVN leaders and returned to Washington "depressed". While Ambassador Bunker saw "statesmenlike" qualities in Thiệu, Clifford saw only "a group of squabbling and corrupt generals, selfishly maneuvering for their own advantage". In a meeting with Johnson, Rusk and Rostow, Clifford said he was "more certain than ever that we could not win the war". Corruption in the RVN was endemic, and Clifford recalled that "the South Vietnamese government did not want the war to end – not while they were protected by over 500,000 American troops and a 'golden flow of money'".[34]

US officials tried to persuade President Thiêu to institute meaningful reforms; but he resisted, especially after the start of the Paris talks, which he opposed. Washington pressed Thiêu to bring civilians into the government and give them more power. While Thiêu appointed civilian Trân Văn Húóng premier, he refused to surrender real authority. Increasingly Thiêu turned inward and became distrustful of those around him. Certainly he believed that Washington might leave him and the RVN in the lurch. There were heated and divisive rivalries within the government and the military, especially between Thiêu and Kỳ. Religious groups were also active. Certain Buddhist leaders pushed for peace on the assumption that if the RVN government collapsed they would fill the vacuum.

Meanwhile American servicemen were openly expressing frustration over a war they could not win. Many now regarded the ARVN, indeed all Vietnamese, with open contempt. At the same time they came to think of the VC/PAVN as a resourceful and able foe. Some US servicemen took out their frustrations on the Vietnamese, as was evident in the My Lai Massacre.

On 16 March 1968, the most notorious US military atrocity of the war occurred in My Lai 4, a cluster of hamlets in Són Tinh District in Quang Ngai Province, I Corps Tactical Zone. There soldiers of Charlie Company, 1st Battalion, 20th Infantry, 11th Infantry Brigade (Light) of the 23rd (Americal) Division killed between 200 and 500 Vietnamese civilians. The Army later investigated the affair, but only after congressional pressure. Only one individual, 1st Platoon commander Lieutenant William L. Calley, was convicted for the massacre and President Richard Nixon later pardoned him.[35]

Negotiations in Paris

In the summer of 1968 domestic political pressures increased on President Johnson. Opposition to the war, which had subsided after his March announcement, rose again that summer as the presidential campaign intensified. The August 1968 Democratic Party convention in Chicago was the scene of considerable violence as those opposed to the war clashed with police. Although Democratic Party nominee Vice President Hubert Humphrey endorsed administration policies, he and campaign leaders sought a major breakthrough in order to have a chance to win.

In the polls Humphrey trailed Republican nominee Richard M. Nixon by a wide margin and this helped win Johnson over to a bombing halt. Harriman continued to hold that the relative lull in VC/PAVN attacks was proof of Hà Nôi's interest in serious negotiations. Abrams assured Johnson that a bombing halt would not pose an undue risk for US troops, and the monsoon season over the North in the next few months would in any case limit bombing effectiveness.

Harriman then reached an understanding with his DRV counterparts. The US would halt the bombing unconditionally. Hà Nôi would then cease rocket attacks and shelling of South Vietnamese cities and respect the DMZ. After that "meaningful" talks would begin. Although the DRV representatives at Paris refused to commit themselves to anything, they gave Harriman private assurances that once the bombing was ended they would act accordingly.

The talks still posed problems since the National Liberation Front (NLF) and North Vietnamese refused to negotiate with RVN representatives, who in turn refused to recognize the NLF. Harriman suggested bilateral talks in which each side would determine the composition of its own delegation. Sài Gòn's leaders worried that Washington was about to abandon them. Candidate Nixon warned the Democrats not to sell out Sài Gòn; and Thiêu balked at concessions, certain that he could do better with the Republicans in the White House. Thiêu insisted that South Vietnam was not "a car that can be hitched to a locomotive and taken anywhere the locomotive wants to go".[36]

Thiêu's intransigence presented a problem for Johnson but on 31 October he announced the bombing halt. Johnson did this without Thiêu's approval, although he assured him that the United States would not recognize the Viêt Công or impose a coalition government on the RVN. At the same time, however, Johnson threatened Thiêu with cuts in US aid if he did not join the talks. The North Vietnamese responded to the bombing halt by ending indiscriminate rocket attacks on South Vietnamese cities and respecting the DMZ.[37] One military corollary was that this enabled Abrams to shift two divisions south from I Corps to defend the populated areas.[38]

Johnson's announcement of the bombing halt came only a week before the elections, too late to save Humphrey. The Democratic candidate had already begun to distance himself from the President's policies and had been gaining in public opinion polls. Some believe that if Johnson had acted earlier, Humphrey would have won and the war in Vietnam might have ended sooner. In the 6 November elections Nixon defeated Humphrey by one of the narrowest popular vote margins in US history.

Possibly a peace settlement might have been arranged before the new administration took office, but in Paris the South Vietnamese delegation, determined to delay meaningful talks until after Nixon was inaugurated, raised procedural issues. Prolonged discussions over the shape of the negotiating table (finally resolved by the placement of two square tables separated by a round table) ended only in the last days of the Johnson Administration. It is by no means clear that Hà Nôi would have made concessions on substantive matters. Most likely only a US withdrawal and coalition government in the South would have been satisfactory to the DRV. Although he was angry at Thiêu, Johnson had made it clear that he would not impose a coalition government as a means of bringing about a US military withdrawal, and he urged General Abrams to maintain military pressure on the VC/PAVN to convince them that they could not win the war on the battlefield.[39]

By the end of 1968 there were 536,040 American servicemen in Vietnam, an increase of 50,500 from 1967. The year was the bloodiest of the war. MACV estimated VC/PAVN dead at 181,149, close to half of their operation strength. But Allied deaths were up: 27,915 South Vietnamese, 14,584 Americans (a 56 per cent increase over 1967) and 979 South Koreans, Australians, New Zealanders, and Thais.[40]

Richard Nixon's Vietnam policy

During the campaign, candidate Nixon had been vague about his Vietnam policies, but he had promised to "end the war and win the peace". A journalist reported that Nixon had a "secret plan" to end the war, something Nixon did nothing to dispel; it was also not true. Nixon's central belief regarding Vietnam was that the United States had failed there because it had not used available military force. As with Johnson before him, Nixon saw bombing as a panacea; despite his criticism of third-party (American Independence Party) vice presidential candidate General Curtis LeMay's remarks during the campaign that the United States should "bomb Vietnam back to the Stone Age", Nixon basically agreed with that position.

Nixon's major mistake was that he believed the war could still be won. Even more a prisoner of ideology than Johnson, Nixon had led the acrimonious attack on the Democrats after the 1949 "loss" of China, and in part because of this he feared domestic political upheaval if South Vietnam succumbed to the Communists. Besides, the new world that he and National Security Advisor (later Secretary of State) Henry Kissinger sought to create depended on US power and prestige remaining intact. Nixon believed that time and massive air power could bring "peace with honor", a euphemism for military victory. The key is found in his remark: "For the United States, this first defeat in our nation's history would result in a collapse of confidence in American leadership, not only in Asia but throughout the world." Later, defending his invasion of Cambodia, Nixon said, "If, when the chips are down, the world's most powerful nation . . . acts like a pitiful, helpless giant, the forces of totalitarianism and anarchy will threaten free nations and free institutions throughout the world."[41]

Another Nixon error was to accept uncritically the previous administration's rationale for staying in the war. George Ball noted that both Johnson and Nixon put obsession with their own place in history ahead of the national interest.[42] Nixon repeatedly used Johnson's own phrase about not wanting to be the first US President to lose a war. The irony is that historians have ranked both presidents lower precisely as a result of their Vietnam policies.

Then there was Kissinger. His doctoral dissertation at Harvard, published under the title *A World Restored, 1812–22* (1957), dealt with the balance of power in Europe following the Napoleonic Wars. He now sought to apply its lessons to his own time. Kissinger was not as interested in morality as in creating a new international balance of power to secure lasting world peace. Less doctrinaire than his chief, he exhibited the same hubris that affected most architects of US Vietnam policy by continuing to underestimate the depth of North Vietnamese commitment just as they continued to overestimate US power and its ability to influence the outcome in Vietnam. Despite repeated evidence of the South's lack of cohesion, sense of purpose and motivation, the United States continued to support the RVN.

Although he was a good friend of French diplomat Jean Sainteny, Kissinger rejected as nationalist posturing the Frenchman's characterization of the US presence in Vietnam as a "hopeless enterprise". As with their predecessors, Nixon and Kissinger believed there was nothing to be learned from the French experience. George Ball noted that Kissinger's initial assessment – that the administration could achieve peace in Vietnam in six months – made it appear "that he had been absent on Mars during the preceding three years".[43]

But Kissinger did not shrink from the use of force and remained convinced that air power would carry the day. He refused "to believe that a fourth-rate power like Vietnam doesn't have a breaking point".[44] Nixon and Kissinger's increasing reliance on force, especially bombing, cost the United States in terms of support for its other policies from states around the world. They also forgot the role of public opinion in a democracy.

Nixon sent word to Hà Nôi expressing his hopes for peace based on a mutual withdrawal of forces from South Vietnam and restoration of the DMZ as a boundary between the two Vietnams. Kissinger, meanwhile, assured Moscow that Washington was eager to work with the USSR on a range of issues, including the increased trade so desired by Moscow. The precondition was a Vietnam peace settlement.

Nixon's plan for ending the war was to utilize Eisenhower's 1953 tactic in Korea. Shortly after he had become President, Eisenhower had let it be known that if the Korean stalemate continued he would push to win the war militarily, even if it meant using nuclear weapons. An armistice was concluded three months later. Nixon called this the "Madman Theory". He told an aide,

> I want the North Vietnamese to believe I've reached the point where I might do *anything* to stop the war. We'll just slip the word to them that, "for God's sake, you know Nixon is obsessed about Communism. We can't restrain him when he's angry – and he has his hand on the nuclear button" – and Ho Chi Minh himself will be in Paris in two days begging for peace.[45]

The ploy failed to impress Hà Nôi. Ultimately Nixon fell back on and intensified the same inadequate Johnson policies, especially the use of air power. As Kissinger noted later, "unfortunately, alternatives to bombing the North were hard to come by".[46] During the Nixon years the United States dropped twice the bomb tonnage in Indo-China that fell during the Johnson years, while US casualties on the ground were almost as great.[47]

Nixon's pressure on the DRV took the form of bombing PAVN sanctuaries in "neutral" Cambodia, a step long advocated by General Wheeler and the JCS but rejected by Johnson. On 9 February General Abrams cabled that a deserter had identified COSVN headquarters just across the Cambodian border. Abrams wanted to bomb it and Ambassador Bunker seconded the notion. As Kissinger put it, "these recommendations fell on fertile ground".[48]

The military justification for bombing the Cambodian sanctuaries was to prevent a PAVN thrust against Sài Gòn. But Nixon's real reason for approving it was to take a step that Johnson avoided and thus terrify Hà Nôi into peace on his terms. Beginning on 18 March 1969, for 14 months B–52s flew some 3,600 sorties against suspected Communist base areas in Cambodia. The first phase was known as "Breakfast", followed in succession by "Lunch", "Snack", "Dinner", "Dessert" and "Supper". Taken together the operation was known as Menu.[49] Even Kissinger believed the code names were "tasteless".[50] Menu's hallmark was secrecy; it was kept from the American public and, significantly, from much of the US government.

Both Nixon and Kissinger defended the secrecy as necessary to allow Cambodian chief of state Prince Norodom Sihanouk, who was trying to steer a delicate balance between the DRV and the US, to avoid a protest, and in this at least it succeeded.[51] Although on 26 March the *New York Times* reported the bombing, there was little adverse public reaction. Nonetheless the revelation infuriated Nixon and Kissinger and led to FBI wiretaps and the presidential abuses of authority that would finally drive Nixon from office.[52]

The bombing of Cambodian sanctuaries did not alter Hà Nôi's resolve to replace losses and continue the war. DRV leaders rejected Nixon's peace proposals as essentially the same as Johnson's and tantamount to surrender. Their delegation in Paris continued to insist on the total and unconditional removal of all US forces from the South and a coalition government that would exclude Thiêu.

DRV leaders resolved to outlast the United States regardless of the cost or additional suffering. Hà Nôi now returned to a protracted war strategy with low intensity operations. Giáp used 1969 to regroup and rest his forces for offensive action the next year.[53] In South Vietnam the RVN seemed to have the upper hand; the VCI was weaker than just before Têt in 1968, partially as a result of the Phoenix Program, which eliminated many VC.

The Nixon Administration seized on Vietnamization, realizing the political advantage that would accrue from withdrawing US forces. American combat strength in Vietnam was at its peak in April 1969 with 543,482 men (625,866 counting Navy personnel offshore and forces in Thailand).[54] The Johnson Administration had initiated the process of turning the fighting over to the South Vietnamese, but on 8 June Nixon and Thiêu met on Midway Island and Nixon announced that 25,000 US combat troops would be withdrawn by the end of August to be replaced by ARVN forces.[55] To cover the withdrawal, Nixon again ordered the bombing of the North, although it was masked in the euphemism of "protective reaction strikes" in response to North Vietnamese firing on US reconnaissance aircraft.

In July Nixon sent a private message to Hà Nôi reaffirming his desire for a "just peace", but threatening that unless there was progress towards a settlement by 1 November he would have no choice but to resort to "measures of great consequence and force". At the same time Kissinger warned the Soviet Union through Ambassador to the United States Anatoly Dobrynin of US resolve. Nixon then ordered the National Security Council to formulate plans for what he described as "savage, punishing blows" against North Vietnam, including bombing attacks on major cities and even the possible use of nuclear weapons. News of these initatives were then deliberately leaked to the press.

Again, threats did not work on Hà Nôi. But DRV leaders did agree to secret talks apart from the Paris framework, and Kissinger flew to France on weekends to meet privately with the head of the DRV delegation Xuân Thuy. But the North Vietnamese stood firm on their position that there could be no settlement until the United States agreed to withdraw all of its forces and abandon Thiêu.[56]

Anti-war movement in the United States

As hopes for peace dimmed, the anti-war movement in the United States became more powerful though at the same time less cohesive. Congressional critics also found their voice, reflecting the beliefs of most Americans who opposed escalating the US role in Vietnam. Many supported Clark Clifford's call in the summer 1969 issue of *Foreign Affairs* for all US troops to be out of South Vietnam by the end of 1970.[57] On 15 October 1969, protest rallies drew perhaps a million people nationwide, while a 15 November peace march on Washington drew at least 250,000 participants.[58] But the peace movement seemed to peak at this point, as public opinion polls showed solid support for Nixon's policies.

In April 1970 there were still 429,900 US troops in South Vietnam. That month Nixon announced the unilateral withdrawal of 150,000 men from Vietnam over the next year.[59] This made sense domestically as it helped defuse the peace movement, but it conceded to the DRV the one thing it wanted most in negotiations: the removal of US ground troops. Hà Nôi was confident that with American forces gone it could easily defeat ARVN. Thus Vietnamization meant throwing away Washington's most important bargaining chip. General Abrams opposed the withdrawal, believing that it would leave the RVN vulnerable to VC/PAVN attacks and potentially devastate pacification programmes.

Meanwhile negotiations in Paris remained deadlocked because, at the same time as it was withdrawing forces, Washington insisted that the DRV do the same. But no government in Hà Nôi would ever concede its hard-won gains in the South, which again would be tantamount to surrender. Hà Nôi realized that the American people would never allow Nixon to reverse course; all it had to do was to wait.[60] Furious at this turn of events, Nixon wanted to strike back, but Secretary of State William Rogers and Secretary of Defense Melvin Laird dissuaded him. Kissinger's study group had by this time come to the conclusion that air strikes and even a naval blockade of the port of Hai Phòng would not dissuade Hà Nôi from its support of the war in the South. With little other option Nixon focused on Vietnamization, believing that he could build up the RVNAF to the point where it could stand on its own. Once Hà Nôi realized that he would not abandon Thiêu and that it could not win the war militarily, the DRV would have to negotiate with the United States and he would have "peace with honor".[61]

ARVN's authorized strength was about 850,000 men when Nixon took office. It was now increased to more than 1,000,000 men, and as US troops withdrew they turned their equipment over to the RVNAF. This included 1,000,000 M–16 rifles, 12,000 M–60 machine guns, 40,000 M–79 grenade launchers and 2,000 artillery pieces or heavy mortars, as well as tanks, ships and planes; with more than 500 aircraft, the VNAF became the fourth largest in the world.[62] Washington also augmented its advisory effort.

Cambodian "incursion" (April 1970)

At the same time Nixon was looking for a means to show Hà Nội that the United States was "still serious about our commitment in Vietnam". An early April public opinion poll showed 48 per cent approval for his Vietnam policies, while 41 per cent disapproved – a sizeable drop from his 65 per cent approval rating in January.[63] Cambodia provided Nixon the opportunity to show that he meant business, and the Vietnam War now became a second Indo-China War.

On 18 March 1970, pro-US Premier/Defense Minister Lon Nol led a coup against Cambodian Prince Sihanouk, then abroad.[64] Lon Nol closed the port of Sihanoukville to DRV resupply activities, shutting down the so-called "Sihanouk Trail", and sent his small army, the FANK (National Khmer Armed Forces or Forces Armées Nationale Khmer) against an estimated 40,000–60,000 Vietnamese Communist troops in three Cambodian border provinces. The new Cambodian leaders called for a national mobilization and exacerbated traditional anti-Vietnamese feelings for their own political purposes. Thousands of young Cambodians flocked to recruiting stations to join the crusade.

Nixon sought both to shore up Lon Nol's regime and to strike at the Cambodian sanctuaries, a move long sought by MACV. From 14 to 20 April, although President Thiêu denied the presence of his forces in Cambodia, ARVN mounted a number of multi-battalion operations just across the border that resulted in the seizure of major supply caches; US advisers stayed behind in South Vietnam. Surprised PAVN and VC forces merely withdrew into the Cambodian interior.[65] ARVN authorities claimed 637 VC/PAVN KIA, while losing only 34 men of its own.[66]

With Communist forces seriously threatening the new Cambodian government, General Abrams argued for a full ARVN intervention with US combat support. On 25 April, despite opposition from Secretary of Defense Laird and Secretary of State Rogers, Nixon authorized the use of American ground forces. US forces would be allowed to penetrate up to 30 kilometres into Cambodia while ARVN could move up to 60 kilometres. This "Cambodian incursion" involved 50,000 ARVN and 30,000 US troops and was the largest series of Allied operations since Operation Junction City in 1967.

On 29 April 6,000 ARVN troops crossed into the Parrot's Beak area of Cambodia west of Sài Gòn. It was an ARVN operation with the US providing

DMZ

THAILAND   LAOS   I Corps

Labang Siek   • Pleiku

CAMBODIA
Snuol   II Corps

Kompong Cham

Phnom Penh • Neak Luong   Republic
                            of
                            Vietnam
            III Corps

            •Sai Gon

IV Corps

Cambodian Incursion
April–May 1970

only air support, military advisers and medical evacuation teams. Then on 30 April Nixon informed the American people by television that US troops were invading the Fishhook, a PAVN Cambodian base area northwest of Sài Gòn. Lon Nol had not even been consulted. Nixon said it was "in response to the request of the Government of the Republic of Vietnam". It was not an invasion, he said, but an "incursion", an extension of the war "to protect our men who are in Vietnam and to guarantee the continued success of our withdrawal and the Vietnamization process". Apart from buying time for Vietnamization and additional US troop withdrawals, Nixon hoped it would relieve pressure on FANK, destroy Communist base areas and COSVN (which he seemed to think was a Pentagon-style complex) and break the stalemate in the Paris negotiations by proving that the United States was not a "pitiful, helpless giant". Yet Nixon lied to the American people when he stated that since 1954 the United States had "respected scrupulously the neutrality of the Cambodian people".[67]

The United States also provided small arms and ammunition to Lon Nol's army, which quickly expanded to more than 100,000 men. Utterly untrained, it soon fell prey to the Communists, who drove it into the urban areas and even threatened Phnom Penh. ARVN forces in Cambodia, outraged by FANK murders of hundreds of ethnic Vietnamese, looted several Cambodian towns.[68] Later President Thiêu ordered his troops to evacuate some 20,000 ethnic Vietnamese from Cambodia.[69]

The Cambodian incursion yielded important short-term advantages for the Allies. It captured or destroyed 22,892 individual weapons, 2,509 crew-served weapons, nearly 17 million rounds of small-arms ammunition, some 200,000 anti-aircraft rounds, 69,000 rounds of mortar ammunition, 62,022 hand grenades, some 45,000 rockets, 435 vehicles, six tons of medical supplies and 700 tons of rice. This was ten times the amount captured inside Vietnam during the previous year and in small arms alone was sufficient to supply 55 Communist main force battalions for as much as a year. MACV estimated casualty totals at 11,349 Communists, 638 ARVN and 338 US killed; 4,009 ARVN and 1,525 US wounded; and 35 ARVN and 13 US missing. In addition, 2,328 Communist soldiers defected or were captured.[70]

The incursion did buy additional time for Vietnamization, and forestalled some planned attacks. During 1970 and 1971 ARVN held the initiative on all battlefields in South Vietnam. But the operation exposed ARVN's serious tactical and organizational deficiencies and showed its complete dependence on US air support.

These gains were short-lived. The Communists soon reclaimed their sanctuaries and reestablished control in eastern Cambodia. Giáp compensated for the temporary losses there by concentrating on expanding PAVN control in southern Laos and building up the Hô Chí Minh Trail, which eventually became an all-weather network capable of handling tanks and heavy equipment. And the withdrawal of US combat units from III Corps forced ARVN to redeploy its forces, reducing its strength in the north. Nixon's action also seriously undermined support in Congress for the long-term aid to the RVN that he himself thought necessary if Vietnamization was to succeed.[71]

All US ground forces departed Cambodia by 30 June, but President Thiêu, who considered Lon Nol's survival vital, refused to be bound by the deadline. ARVN units operated inside Cambodia into 1971, creating several hundred thousand new refugees. US long-range artillery, tactical air support and B–52 bombings supported their effort.

The departure of US troops left a void far too great for ARVN or FANK to fill. This 1970 widening of the battlefield in Indo-China eventually left Cambodia the most devastated nation in the region. To avoid massive bombings, Communist forces moved into the Cambodian interior. Meanwhile Lon Nol's army, receiving only minimal US assistance, struggled for the next five years against both the Cambodian Communists, known as the Khmer Rouge (Red Khmer), and the PAVN, which increased its military aid to its Khmer counterparts.[72]

In the United States the Cambodian incursion rejuvenated the anti-war movement. On 4 May National Guardsmen shot to death four students and wounded nine others at Kent State University in Ohio, and later police shot and killed two students and wounded 12 others at Jackson State College in Mississippi. Hundreds of college campuses erupted in protest. Opposition was not limited to students. Nixon's June withdrawal of US troops from Cambodia failed to placate Congress, which enacted a series of legislative initiatives that severely limited presidential war-making powers. The Cooper–Church Amendment of 29 December 1970 prohibited expenditures for US forces operating outside South Vietnam, something Nixon subverted for a time in Cambodia by using the CIA. An angry Congress also repealed the Tonkin Gulf Resolution. In addition, the incursion damaged peace negotiations in Paris as the Communists refused to talk until US troops were withdrawn from Cambodia.

Situation in South Vietnam

In South Vietnam Thiêu continued his authoritarian rule, although he did restore local elections. By 1969 95 per cent of villages under RVN control had elected chiefs and councils. Village chiefs received control over their Popular

Forces (PF) and some central government financial support. Thiêu also secured passage of laws that froze rents and forbade landlords from evicting tenants, and in March 1971 he presented land grants to 20,000 people in accordance with passage of the Land-to-Tiller Act. This gave land to those who worked it and reduced tenancy to only 7 per cent, while the government pledged to compensate landlords for the confiscated property.[73]

Thiêu faced the serious challenge of replacing withdrawing US ground units. In 1970 he mobilized many high school and college students for the war effort. This and increases in taxes brought considerable popular opposition, which in turn led to arrests, trials, and a surge of support for the Communists.

In 1971 Thiêu pushed through a new presidential election law that had the practical effect of disqualifying major opponents Kỳ and Dúóng Văn Minh. The law required that candidates be supported by at least 40 national assembly members or 100 provincial/municipal councillors. Opposition groups claimed that the law was designed to exclude them from political power. Although the Supreme Court ruled that Kỳ, who had charged Thiêu's government with corruption, might run, he chose not to do so, as did Minh. Thiêu's re-election in October 1971 did serious injury to the RVN image abroad.

By the end of 1970 there were increasing signs that the North Vietnamese would not long remain quiescent on the battlefield. Intelligence indicated increased numbers of men and equipment moving down the Hô Chí Minh Trail and a special threat to ARVN forces in northern South Vietnam.

Nixon, meanwhile, continued his Vietnamization policy, but to quiet domestic critics he accelerated the withdrawal of US forces. Over the objections of General Abrams, Nixon ordered the American troop ceiling reduced to only 175,000 men (75,000 of them combat troops) by the end of 1971. At the same time US aircraft bombed PAVN staging areas in Laos and Cambodia, and "protective reaction" strikes targeted lines of communication in North Vietnam. Finally Nixon authorized the ultimate test of Vietnamization, an ARVN invasion of Laos.

Operation Lam Són 719 (8 February–24 March 1971)

President Thiêu had long wanted to demonstrate the ARVN's ability to assume the fighting burden. Lam Són 719 was his effort to reduce the flow of supplies to the South and forestall a PAVN invasion of northern South Vietnam. The operation was named for the fifteenth-century Lam Són Insurrection, while 71 stood for the year and 9 for Route 9, along which it was launched. Its objective was Tchepone, a key transhipment point 25 miles inside Laos. Along the way the ARVN hoped to destroy supply caches in nearby PAVN Base Areas 604 and 611.

Although the Cooper–Church Amendment prohibited US ground forces in Laos, American support was critical. Indeed the operation began with several American deceptions and operations to prevent PAVN units from building up in Laos. Elements of the 101st Airborne went into the A Shau Valley and, in Operation Dewey Canyon II, the 1st Brigade of the 5th Infantry Division returned to Khe Sanh. From there and from surrounding fire support bases (FSBs) inside South Vietnam 9,000 US troops provided the ARVN with logistical and artillery fire support, while 2,600 helicopters ferried ARVN troops into, and later out of, Laos. In all, US helicopters flew 90,000 sorties into Laos while American fighter-bombers and B–52s provided air cover.[74]

General Hoàng Xuân Lãm commanded 17,000 ARVN troops in the operation, which began on 8 February. Its main axis of advance was along Route 9, a single-lane dirt road west to Tchepone. The troops advanced slowly, building FSBs as they went. The FSBs provided locations for artillery support and bases from which patrols and raids could be mounted into the surrounding countryside. Because of the Cooper–Church Amendment no US advisers accompanied the South Vietnamese and the ARVN had no US forward air controllers.

Intelligence estimated PAVN/Pathet Lao strength in the area of operations at some 22,000 personnel, of which perhaps 7,000 were well trained combat troops. The Communists also had 170 to 200 23 mm to 100 mm antiaircraft artillery pieces. In one of the major miscalculations of the war the US and the ARVN believed it would take up to a month for a PAVN division to move from the North Vietnamese panhandle into the area of operations. In fact, within two weeks as many as 40,000 PAVN troops were engaging the invaders.[75]

By the third week of Lam Són 719 the ARVN advance ground to a halt at A Loi, a FSB 12 miles inside Laos. PAVN forces, meanwhile, took one ARVN FSB after another. Their 122 mm and 130 mm guns outranged the ARVN's 105 mm and 155 mm howitzers. Their infantry assaults were supported by PT–76 light tanks and, for the first time in the war, heavier T–34 and T–54 tanks, which were clearly superior to the ARVN light M–41 tanks. This revealed one of the weaknesses of Vietnamization. Too often upgrading of RVNAF came only in reaction to prior PAVN modernization.[76]

ARVN planners assumed that American air power would be critical, but deteriorating weather conditions limited its effectiveness. PAVN leaders understood that the B–52s, which could bomb through the clouds, would not normally be used on targets closer than three kilometres from friendly forces.

Operation Lam Son 719

Accordingly the PAVN "clung to the cartridge belts" of its enemy and partially negated B–52 bombing effectiveness.

When the weather cleared VNAF and US pilots had to contend with a combination of anti-aircraft artillery (AAA) and heavy machine gun fire that covered most potential helicopter landing zones. The North Vietnamese also positioned SAM sites in Ban Raving Pass, threatening B–52s within 17 miles of the pass and fighter-bombers flying above 1,500 feet in the same area. Although B–52s flew 1,358 sorties and dropped 32,000 tons of bombs, most missions were against suspected supply dumps in Base Area 604.[77]

President Thiêu now ordered Lãm to carry out an airborne assault on Tchepone. The PAVN had already abandoned the town, which had little military value, when on 6 March US helicopters flew in two ARVN battalions from Khe Sanh. Two days later two additional ARVN battalions reached Tchepone on foot. The South Vietnamese spent the next two weeks destroying PAVN supply caches.

The capture of Tchepone allowed Thiêu to claim success for the operation, after which he ordered General Lãm to withdraw. Retreats are among the most difficult of military operations; and ARVN units were not sufficiently trained, led, or disciplined to conduct an orderly retreat under sustained attack. Up to 40,000 PAVN troops, including two armoured regiments, struck the outnumbered and increasingly demoralized ARVN. Poor weather, devastating anti-aircraft fire, and the inability of pilots to co-ordinate strikes with friendly ground units diminished air support effectiveness. Much of the retreat became a rout.[78]

Thanks in large part to the bravery of US Army helicopter pilots, most of the original ARVN force returned; but it sustained 1,529 KIA, 5,483 WIA and 625 MIA. American casualties numbered 219 KIA, 1,149 WIA and 38 MIA, many of these when the PAVN counter-attack spilled into South Vietnam and as a result of artillery fire against Khe Sanh. Some 107 helicopters were destroyed; five were lost as a result of accidents. The figure for destroyed helicopters did not include those retrieved from the battlefield even as burned out hulks; 618 were reported as damaged, many so badly that they were scrapped. PAVN anti-aircraft fire shot down seven USAF planes. The operation revealed serious problems in ARVN planning and leadership as well as faulty intelligence that had underestimated the speed and intensity of the PAVN counter-attack.

Nonetheless the Allies declared victory. Including those killed in US air strikes, MACV claimed upwards of 19,360 PAVN KIA and 57 captured. ARVN claimed an impressive tally of weapons taken/destroyed: 5,170 individual weapons, 1,963 crew-served weapons, 106 tanks, 13 artillery pieces, 93 mortars and 170,346 tons of ammunition. ARVN also netted 2,001 trucks and 1,250 tons of rice. Lam Són 719 may indeed have delayed a PAVN offensive into northern South Vietnam by a year. In a televised address on 7 April President Nixon stated, "Tonight I can report Vietnamization has succeeded." President Thiêu dubbed Lam Són 719 "The biggest victory ever." But Radio Hà Nôi proclaimed "The Route 9–Southern Laos Victory" as "the heaviest defeat ever for Nixon and Company."[79]

In the United States congressional disaffection over the war now reached an all-time high, although resolutions calling for a specific timetable for ending US involvement in Southeast Asia were defeated. Throughout 1971 peace negotiations continued in Paris. Sài Gòn's leaders knew that South Vietnam would never be secure unless the VC were eliminated and PAVN forces driven from the South. Thus they could never agree to any arrangement that left the NLF in control of substantial areas of the South. Yet Kissinger no longer tried to please Sài Gòn by insisting on a mutual withdrawal. US forces continued their unilateral withdrawal while Washington reassured its ally with pledges that would not be kept. Washington's policy had become one of expedient escape.[80]

On 13 January 1972, Nixon announced that an additional 70,000 troops would leave Vietnam by 1 May, reducing the total force from the 545,000 when he had entered office to only 64,500.[81] On 25 January Nixon disclosed that for months Kissinger had been flying to France to meet secretly on weekends with Xuân Thuy and/or Politburo member Lê Dúc Tho. These talks ended upon their disclosure, when Nixon also announced his terms for peace: withdrawal from South Vietnam of all US and North Vietnamese troops within six months of an agreement, at which time internationally supervised elections would take place. If President Thiêu wished to run for president, he would have to resign to do so.[82] These terms, with the exception of the last, were essentially those that might have been negotiated in 1969. Meanwhile, Communist forces had been rebuilding.

Nguyên Huê Campaign (Spring or Easter 1972 Offensive)

As early as January 1972 Abrams had warned that a Communist offensive was imminent.[83] Ground action steadily intensified during the spring. On 16 March Communist forces carried out 41 attacks in a 24-hour time period, most of these in Quang Ngai province. On 17 and 18 March ARVN forces killed an estimated 180 PAVN troops between Huê and the A Shau Valley. In heavy fighting west of Huê ARVN claimed 513 PAVN troops KIA over a two-week period compared to their own losses of 86 killed and 186 wounded.[84]

In the Spring of 1972 General Giáp launched the Nguyên Huê Campaign, known to the South Vietnamese and Americans as the Spring or Easter Offensive. This massive, conventional-style invasion of South Vietnam, intended as a decisive blow against the ARVN and the RVN, was the largest offensive ever undertaken by Hà Nôi and precisely the type of attack anticipated by US military advisers in the 1950s.

A number of factors prompted the offensive. Hà Nôi feared the diplomatic isolation threatened by President Nixon's dramatic overtures to Moscow and Beijing. Indeed the offensive began after Nixon's historic February visit to Beijing but before his planned May visit to Moscow. Furthermore, DRV leaders did not believe that the US, with only some 65,000 troops in South Vietnam, would be able to influence the situation. Nor did they believe that the political situation in the United States would allow Nixon to introduce additional troops or combat support. Ultimately Hà Nôi hoped to discredit the Vietnamization and pacification programmes and accelerate the US withdrawal. Perhaps it hoped that a military victory would help topple Nixon in the November presidential elections and bring in a Democratic Party president less disposed to Vietnam involvement.

Throughout 1971 Hà Nôi requested and received large numbers of modern weapons from the Soviet Union and China, including advanced MiG–21 jet fighters, SAM missiles, T–54 tanks, 130 mm guns, 160 mm mortars, 57 mm anti-aircraft guns (some self-propelled), and, for the first time, heat-seeking, highly portable, shoulder-fired SA–7 Strella anti-aircraft missiles, capable of bringing down aircraft at less than 8,000 feet. Spare parts, ammunition, vehicles and fuel all arrived in the DRV in unprecedented quantities. At the same time Hà Nôi launched a massive effort to secure additional manpower. Many of those previously deferred now found themselves in uniform as Hà Nôi assembled 15 divisions. Giáp had two in Laos, tied down there by Hmong guerrillas, and only one in North Vietnam. But there was no risk in this since the South Vietnamese could not invade the North and the United States would not. For the offensive Giáp planned to employ some 150,000 troops in 12 infantry divisions, along with T–54 and T–55 tanks and 122 mm and 130 mm artillery pieces.[85]

On the ground, with the exception of US advisers, the ARVN would be on its own. In 1972 it numbered 429,000 men in 11 divisions of 120 manoeuvre battalions, 19 of which were armoured, and 58 artillery battalions. The Navy had 43,000 men and 1,688 small vessels. The VNAF had 57,000 men with 500 planes and 500 helicopters. The RVN had 250,000 men in the Popular Forces, 300,000 in Regional Forces and 120,700 in the National Police.[86]

Despite his own misgivings that this was the wrong time for an offensive, Giáp loyally prepared to carry out the Politburo's orders. At best Giáp hoped to achieve a knock-out blow against the ARVN. But he believed that even partial success would put the Thiêu government in jeopardy. His plan called for a three-pronged attack. First, a northern multi-divisional attack would push across the DMZ into Quang Tri province while a separate and simultaneous drive from the A Shau Valley moved towards Huê. Giáp hoped to take the northern two RVN provinces and be in position to threaten Đà Nẵng, South Vietnam's second largest city.[87]

Giáp expected Thiêu to commit reserves to protect the northern provinces, whereupon he would launch his second attack, a drive into the Central Highlands to take Kontum. Simultaneous with this he would try to secure the coastal province of Bình Định. Success in these would effectively split South Vietnam in two along Route 19.

The third attack would come on the southern front, where Giáp would employ three Viêt Công divisions (actually consisting of PAVN regulars) in Bình Long province to take Lôc Ninh and the provincial capital of An Lôc, only 65 miles north of Sài Gòn. This thrust would seriously threaten Sài Gòn itself. Another division would attack in the Mekong Delta to seize rice production and tie down ARVN troops that might otherwise be employed elsewhere.[88]

The Nguyên Huê Offensive began on Easter, 30 March 1972, when three PAVN divisions reinforced by T–54 tanks struck south across the DMZ and along Highway 9 out of Laos towards Quang Tri and Huê. Three days later three other divisions attacked from Cambodia into Bình Long province, capturing Lôc Ninh. Additional PAVN forces moved towards Kontum and two other PAVN divisions took control of several districts in Bình Định Province. All of these were massive infantry attacks supported by armour and artillery. The thrusts were at first successful, particularly in Quang Tri Province where they overran the newly formed ARVN 3rd Division. While PAVN troops threatened both Huê and Kontum, ARVN forces were able to halt them before both cities. Meanwhile PAVN forces besieged An Lôc.[89]

As the military situation in the South hung in the balance, President Nixon ordered a resumption of the bombing of North Vietnam. This was something of a gamble, taken on the eve of his trip to Moscow to meet with Soviet leader Leonid Brezhnev. On 8 May Nixon ordered the aerial mining of Hai Phòng, Đông Hói and other North Vietnamese ports. This risked a Soviet–US confrontation at sea. While both Moscow and Beijing denounced the American action, Nixon had gauged correctly; both Communist powers wanted *détente* and agreement with the West on a host of issues, including enhanced technology, more than escalation of the war in Vietnam. The DRV was largely abandoned by its allies.

The US aerial offensive was dubbed Linebacker. Gone were many of the restrictions of Rolling Thunder. Linebacker I (8 May–23 October 1972) was a classic aerial interdiction operation and the most effective use of air power during the war. It was also the first modern air campaign in which precision guided munitions (PGMs or "smart bombs"), laser guided bombs (LGBs) and electro-optically guided bombs (EOGBs) played a key role. These and the long-range electronic navigation (LORAN) bombing system made it possible to strike targets with a precision that minimized collateral damage and civilian casualties. US aircraft sought to isolate the battlefield and cut off supplies moving within the DRV to the PAVN forces, and commanders were given latitude in target selection and in determining the best combination of tactics and weapons.

On 8 May Navy A–6 and A–7 fighter-bombers dropped 2,000-pound mines at the entrance to Hai Phòng Harbour, beginning the isolation of the DRV from seaborne resupply. Two days later 32 Air Force F–4 Phantoms struck Hà Nôi's Long Biên Bridge and the Yên Viên railroad yard, dropping 29 LGBs on the bridge and 84 conventional bombs on the marshalling yard. Over the next few days smart bombs destroyed bridges and tunnels along LOCs from Hà Nôi to the Chinese border. Fighter-bombers attacked supplies that accumulated while awaiting repair of the bridges and tunnels. By the end of June US Air Force and Navy aircraft had destroyed more than 400 bridges and tunnels in North Vietnam, including the Thanh Hóa and Long Biên Bridges.

Planners then directed Linebacker strikes against petroleum storage facilities, power-generating plants, military barracks, training camps and air defence facilities. The new munitions made it possible to attack targets proscribed during Rolling Thunder because of their proximity to civilian structures.[90]

By September it was evident that Linebacker I was having an effect. Overland imports into the DRV dropped from 160,000 tons a month to 30,000 tons a month, while seaborne imports fell from 25,000 tons a month to virtually nothing.[91] The PAVN offensive inside South Vietnam also stalled and the ARVN regained much of the territory lost in the initial PAVN attacks; and US aircraft attacked PAVN units inside South Vietnam while Linebacker missions pounded the North.

Linebacker I prevented North Vietnam from winning the war militarily in 1972, and it forced the DRV to negotiate seriously in Paris. On 23 October, after the two sides concluded an agreement, Nixon ordered bombing halted north of 20 degrees latitude. From 31 March to 23 October 1972, Linebacker had dropped some 155,548 tons of bombs on North Vietnam. It succeeded where Rolling Thunder had failed, but in an entirely different situation where a conventional military force needed massive amounts of munitions, fuel and other supplies to remain in the field. The attacking PAVN divisions required about 1,000 tons of supplies a day to sustain their offensive.[92]

Linebacker I took considerable pressure off the ARVN forces. So too did US air strikes within South Vietnam, including B–52s. These provided close air support to the ARVN and demonstrated the consequences of control of the air in conventional military operations. Nonetheless, intense ground fighting continued throughout the summer all over South Vietnam. But in June ARVN forces began a counter-offensive that eventually recaptured Quang Tri Province. The Easter Offensive had failed.

Although the ARVN's performance had been uneven at best, the Nixon Administration chose to regard this as proof of the success of Vietnamization. Estimates placed VC/PAVN dead in the offensive at more than 83,000; 15,000 ARVN died. The PAVN also lost at least half of its large-calibre artillery pieces and tanks. Despite this, territory controlled by the Communists in South Vietnam rose from 3.7 per cent in February to 9.7 per cent in July. The offensive had also created 970,000 new refugees. Hà Nôi believed it was now in a stronger bargaining position at Paris.[93]

Thiêu scuttles a peace agreement

In July 1972 the Paris peace talks resumed. US troop withdrawals from South Vietnam continued. Finally having achieved Washington's retreat on the issue of withdrawing its remaining forces, on 8 October Tho agreed for the first time that the Thiêu government could remain. After a cease-fire it would negotiate with the Communist Provisional Revolutionary Government of South Vietnam (PRG, the old NLF) for a permanent political settlement. Hà Nôi also agreed to US demands for the return of its prisoners of war. On 26 October Kissinger made a dramatic announcement that "peace was at hand" and flew off to Sài Gòn to secure President Thiêu's signature.

Kissinger was unprepared for his reception. Thiêu announced his opposition to the Paris agreement, seeing it correctly as little more than a "decent interval" before South Vietnam would fall to the Communists. In letters kept secret from the American people, Nixon promised Thiêu that if the DRV did not abide by the cease-fire he would "take swift and severe retaliatory action" and use "full force" against the North.[94]

Nonetheless Thiêu refused to budge. Kissinger urged Nixon to sign the agreement without him but the President refused, blaming Hà Nôi for the impasse. Kissinger has suggested that Nixon rejected implementing the October agreement without Thiêu because he would have found it awkward prior to the elections "to risk his support among conservative groups whom he considered his base".[95] In order to regain Thiêu's co-operation in the peace negotiations, in November the Pentagon turned over massive amounts of equipment to the RVNAF, including some 300 airplanes, 277 helicopters, 200 armoured vehicles, 56 artillery pieces and 2,000 trucks in what was known as Operation Enhance Plus.[96]

On 13 December negotiations in Paris, which had resumed in early November, broke down. Nixon gave Hà Nôi an ultimatum to return to the conference table within 72 hours "or else". When the DRV rejected this, on the 18th Nixon launched new air raids against the North. As George Ball noted, "Squalid politics provides the most charitable explanation for a bloody and otherwise irrational act."[97]

It was then winter in North Vietnam and the only US planes capable of all-weather bombing were Air Force B–52s and F–111 fighter-bombers and Navy A–6 Intruders. A–6s and F–111s could hit most targets with relative precision, but there were not sufficient numbers of them available to inflict the degree of damage desired. As a result B–52s carried the brunt of what airmen dubbed the "Eleven Day War" and peace activists referred to as the "Christmas Bombing". The B–52s would strike "area targets" such as air-fields, petroleum storage facilities, warehouse complexes and railroad marshal-ling yards. On 14 December Nixon ordered the remining of Hai Phòng harbour.

Operation Linebacker II began on the night of 18 December with B–52s from Andersen AFB, Guam, and U-Tapao Air Base, Thailand, striking the Kinh Nô storage complex and the Yên Viên rail yard, in addition to airfields and other targets around Hà Nôi. That first night three B–52s were lost to SAMs. The next night B–52s struck the Thái Nguyên power plant and the Yên Viên rail yard with no planes lost.

On the night of 21 December, when some of the same targets were restruck along with oil and other storage facilities, six B–52s went down. This 6 per cent loss rate was unsustainable given the smaller number of aircraft in the theatre. The problem lay in mission planning whereby the three-plane cells flew at more or less the same altitude, speed, heading and turn points.

Once the Strategic Air Command reworked its planning, B–52 losses dropped dramatically. Bombing was suspended for 36 hours over Christmas, by which point 11 B–52s had been lost. But by that date most legitimate targets in North Vietnam had been destroyed. Linebacker I had already devastated North Vietnam. As historian Earl Tilford notes:[98]

The so-called "Christmas Bombing" mostly just rearranged the rubble. The differences in the two campaigns, however, were in their objectives and in their intensity. During LINEBACKER I the primary objective was to stop a massive, conventional invasion. It was an interdiction campaign that had the strategic effect of compelling the DRV to negotiate seriously for the first time in the war. LINEBACKER II . . . was a strategic bombing campaign aimed at the will of the North Vietnamese leadership. Its sole objective was to force the Hà Nôi government to come to an agreement on a ceasefire quickly . . .

LINEBACKER II was much more focused and time compressed, meaning more bombs fell on North Vietnam in a shorter period of time. The attacks by the B–52s were, therefore, psychologically more devastating if for no other reason than that a three-plane cell of B–52s could drop over 300 bombs into an area the size of a railroad marshalling yard or on an airfield in less than a minute.

Linebacker II resumed the day after Christmas with the objective of rendering North Vietnam defenceless. On that day F–105 and F–4 fighter bombers attacked SAM sites and guidance radars, and USAF F–4 Phantoms struck the main SAM assembly area in Hà Nôi. Air Force F–111s cratered runways so that MiG interceptors could not take off. By the end of the day North Vietnam lay virtually defenceless.

That night 120 B–52s struck ten different targets over a 15-minute period. Attacks over the next nights involved only half as many B–52s but their pilots noticed that few SAMs were fired and that DRV air defences seemed in disarray. On 28 December Hà Nôi agreed to Nixon's conditions for reopening negotiations. The next day Nixon limited the bombing to targets south of the 20th parallel and Linebacker II came to an end.

US bombing continued in North Vietnam's southern panhandle and against targets in South Vietnam until the cease-fire agreement was signed. In all, 739 B–52 sorties dropped 15,237 tons of bombs over North Vietnam, and Air Force and Navy fighter-bombers added another 5,000 tons. North Vietnam launched virtually every SAM in its inventory to shoot down 24 US aircraft, including 15 B–52s.

Air power advocates claimed that Linebacker II showed what might have been accomplished had they been given a chance to win the war earlier. As Tilford notes, "It became an article of faith in the Air Force that LINEBACKER II had 'brought the enemy to their collective knees.'" Although damage to DRV targets was significant, the country was far from devastated. According to Hà Nôi's own figures, only 1,312 people perished in the capital and 300 in Hai Phòng. Linebacker II did have a psychological effect on DRV leaders. With their air defence in a shambles and virtually all military targets destroyed, DRV leaders did not want to risk attacks on neighbourhoods and the vital dike system. Accordingly, they agreed to resume peace talks.[99]

On 23 January 1973, Hà Nôi and Washington concluded a new agreement, which was now imposed on Sài Gòn and for which Kissinger and DRV negotiator Lê Ðúc Tho were later awarded the Nobel Peace Prize. Four parties signed: the US, RVN, DRV and the PRG. Despite a few cosmetic changes, the agreement was for practical purposes identical to that signed the previous October. The Accords opened with the statement that "the United States and all other countries respect the independence, sovereignty, unity and territorial integrity of Vietnam as recognized by the 1954 Geneva Agreements on Vietnam". This was what Hà Nôi had argued for years: that Vietnam was one country and that its effort in the South was not "foreign aggression" but rather a legitimate struggle for national independence and unity. The agreement provided for a cease-fire, withdrawal of all US troops and advisers from South Vietnam, release of prisoners, the formation of a Council of National Reconciliation and Concord that would resolve disagreements between the RVN and DRV and organize new general elections, new supervisory machinery (the International Commission of Control and Supervision, consisting of representatives of Canada, Hungary, Poland and Indonesia), and withdrawal of foreign troops from Laos and Cambodia.[100]

For all practical purposes the United States had abandoned South Vietnam to its fate. Kissinger's subsequent claim that without Watergate and Nixon's departure, the United States could have intervened militarily in Vietnam rings hollow. Congress and the American public would not have allowed the reintroduction of US ground troops, and air power alone would not have prevented a Communist victory in 1975.[101]

George Ball notes that had the United States yielded on the removal of US forces from the South when there were still 500,000 troops in the country, the RVN would still have been defeated by the DRV, but it would have saved 20,000 American and 600,000 Vietnamese lives and pre-empted the invasion of Cambodia that helped bring the Communist Khmer Rouge to power. An earlier exit from Vietnam would have ended much of the social protest in the United States and halted inflation and economic disruption; the war had cost the United States an estimated $150 billion.[102]

Vietnam War casualties

Estimates of Vietnam War casualties vary. Through 1975 the RVN lost at least 110,357 killed in action and 499,026 wounded. The number of civilian deaths

**Cease-fire areas of control
January 1973**

Major land-grab fighting ✶

Areas under
Communist control ▮

Demilitarized Zone

Dong Ha
Quang Tri City
Hue
Phu Bai
Da Nang
An Hoa
Tam Ky
Chu Lai
Mo Duc
Dak To
Sa Huynh
Tan Quan
Kontum
Pleiku
Qui Nhon
An Khe
Duc Co
Tuy Hoa
Ban Me Thuot
Nha Trang
Phuoc Binh
Cam Rahn
Da Lat
Phan Rhang
Than Linh
Tay Ninh
Ben Suc
Route 1
Bien Hoa
Phan Thiet
Sai Gon
Xuan Loc
Ha Tien
Chau Doc
Dat Do
My Tho
Vung Tau
Rach Gia
Can Tho
Ca Mau

Miles 200
Kms 200

Route 1

will never be known with any accuracy, but the lowest estimate is 415,000. In 1995 Hà Nôi announced that 1,100,000 Communist fighters had died and another 600,000 were wounded between 1954 and 1975. This includes both Viêt Công guerrillas in South Vietnam and PAVN personnel. Presumably it also includes some 300,000 MIA, over which Hà Nôi has never made an issue with Washington. Hà Nôi estimated civilian deaths in the war over the same time period at 2,000,000.

US forces lost 47,382 KIA, 10,811 non-combat deaths, 153,303 WIA (some 74,000 survived as quadriplegics or multiple amputees), and 10,173 captured and missing in action (MIA). The majority of the casualties were Army personnel: between 1961 and 1975, 30,868 soldiers died in Vietnam as the result of hostile action and 7,193 from other causes. In April 1995 the US Department of Defense listed 1,621 Americans MIA in Vietnam and 2,207 for all of Southeast Asia. In November 1995 Washington announced that the remains of more than 500 American servicemen missing in Southeast Asia would never be recovered but held out hope for recovering the other 1,500. Among other countries that fought in South Vietnam the Republic of Korea lost 4,407 KIA; Australia 423 KIA and 2,398 WIA; Thailand 351 KIA; and New Zealand 83 KIA.[103]

America was finally out of Vietnam. Successive US governments had ignored nationalism and revolution, choosing to see only the spectre of Communism. Americans paid a high price for such ideological blinders, and they learned a painful lesson in the limitations of power and the high cost of trying to maintain "reputation". It was now time to shrink US commitments to the resources available. The experience marked the end of what George Ball called "an uncritical globalism that reflected our postwar preeminence".[104] The United States could no longer be "the world's policeman". Former Secretary of State Dean Rusk made no apologies. As he put it in April 1975, "Personally, I made two mistakes. I underestimated the tenacity of the North Vietnamese and overestimated the patience of the American people."[105] Nixon claimed that he had secured "peace with honor". But although the United States was no longer at war, South Vietnam's travail continued.

Chapter Seven

The Third Vietnam War (1973–5)

The Paris Peace Agreement was signed on 23 January 1973; a truce went into effect on the 28th. President Thiêu was particularly unhappy with this, especially as it allowed the continued presence in the South of some 300,000 Communist troops. The Provisional Revolutionary Government (PRG) controlled wide swaths of territory in South Vietnam, especially that adjacent to Laos and Cambodia, significant portions of the Central Highlands and parts of the Mekong Delta. The RVN controlled the eastern portion of the country, the cities and most of the Central Highlands. North Vietnamese troops remained in Laos, contrary to an understanding Kissinger thought he had obtained from Tho.[1]

The Allies quickly completed the withdrawal of their military contingents, including 23,000 US troops. The last American ground forces left at the end of March. Some 8,500 US military personnel stayed on in South Vietnam as "civilians", with 5,000 of these on contract to maintain ARVN equipment. Additionally, Washington turned over all of its military bases to RVN government control.[2]

Between February and April 1973 the Communists released 591 US POWs. A total of 106 American POWs, most of them pilots shot down over North Vietnam, had died in captivity.[3] Although the POW issue remained contentious for years to come, Hà Nôi never wavered from its insistence that it had turned over all prisoners in its hands at the time of the agreement.

The governments of Canada, Hungary, Indonesia and Poland furnished contingents for the International Commission of Control and Supervision (ICCS) and for the military commissions charged with supervising the ceasefire. On 13 February Thiêu announced the formation of a "Popular Front" coalition to "fight for peace and the right of self-determination" and to contest the upcoming elections.[4]

The Paris Accords had not delineated territorial boundaries between the warring parties and merely specified a "cease-fire in place". As a result, immediately before the truce took hold, heavy fighting occurred with both sides endeavouring to seize as much territory as possible. Communist forces took advantage of the fact that the bulk of the ARVN forces were tied down in the population centres. They attacked and won control of hundreds of villages and cut major highways, isolating Sài Gòn. The RVN government calculated that 378 engagements occurred in the 24 hours before the cease-fire was to take effect, the largest number for any single day of the war. Fighting continued even after the cease-fire began. President Thiệu was determined that the Communists would not retain these late gains. In the two weeks after the cease-fire was supposed to begin the ARVN recaptured all but 23 of 400 villages seized by the Communists in the pre-cease-fire fighting.[5]

Continued fighting

Both sides circumvented the Paris Accords. Talks held near Paris between the RVN government and the Communist PRG proceeded only in fits and starts. The Council of National Reconciliation and Concord called for by the Paris Accords never came into being and the elections were never held. Nor did the fighting stop. Each side held that military operations, including attacks in its enemy's zone, were justified by the other side's prior violations of the cease-fire. As there had been no agreement on force boundaries, no method existed to restore the lines supposedly frozen by the truce. There was only an endless chain of retaliations. As one member of the international observation force put it, the Accords were "like a dictionary for a language that nobody speaks".[6]

During the whole of 1973 Communist military incidents averaged an all-time high of 2,980 a month. This compared with only 2,072 a month for 1972, the year of the Spring Offensive.[7] In late March the Communists initiated a 13-month siege of Tông Lê Chân, which the ARVN finally evacuated in April 1974. Meanwhile the ARVN conducted sweeps around Sài Gòn and in the Mekong Delta.

Communist military activities throughout 1973 and 1974 were for the most part low-intensity harassing attacks and guerrilla actions designed to wear down the RVNAF as much as possible prior to a final military offensive. Typical of such activities were a rocket attack on 6 November on Biên Hòa Air Base that destroyed three F–5A fighters and a sapper attack on 2 December that destroyed 9 million gallons of fuel at the Nhà Bè petroleum tank farm on the Sài Gòn River.[8]

Where possible, the Communists pushed their control in the lightly defended, isolated rural areas. From September onwards the fighting intensified, especially in the Central Highlands where the PAVN employed tanks in an attack on the Plei Djereng Special Forces camp west of Pleiku.

Hà Nội also worked to strengthen its forces in the South and to improve its ability to supply them. The Hồ Chí Minh Trail was widened and paved much of the way. Soviet 5- to 6-ton capacity ZIL trucks now could travel day and night on all-weather roads that were two lanes in places. An oil pipeline extended south from the A Shau Valley, eventually reaching Lộc Ninh. A trip down the trail that before the cease-fire had taken four months with travel only at night to avoid air attack could now be made in daylight in just three weeks. The North also moved supplies into the South across the DMZ. The PAVN built up its strength with additional manpower, heavy artillery, and anti-aircraft weapons, including SAM missiles.[9]

On 24 October US officials in Sài Gòn announced that since the cease-fire some 70,000 men, 400 tanks and at least 200 artillery pieces had moved into the South.[10] In mid-1973 the DRV had some 176,000 troops in the South in 11 divisions and 24 independent regiments.[11]

Communist forces did indeed wear down the ARVN, which lost an estimated 25,473 killed in battle in 1973; Sài Gòn claimed that 45,057 Communist troops died in the same year.[12] On 4 January 1974, Thiệu announced that while pre-emptive actions by the ARVN had forestalled a Communist offensive, the RVN could not "allow the Communists a situation in which . . . they can launch harassing attacks against US". He then stated, "As far as the armed forces are concerned, I can tell you the war has restarted."[13] ARVN forces then began a counter-offensive against the PAVN 5th Division in the Tri Phap wasteland sanctuary. In six weeks of fighting the ARVN claimed 1,000 Communists killed and 600 weapons and eight tons of ammunition captured. At the end of 20 April ARVN battalions attacked the Parrot's Beak salient of Cambodia in a three-week effort to destroy Communist bases there.[14]

At the same time, the RVN's most ardent champion, President Nixon, was under increasing political attack in the United States. In November 1973 Congress passed the War Powers Act that severely reduced the possibility of further US intervention in Vietnam. On 9 August 1974, under pressure over the Watergate scandal and his handling of the war, Nixon resigned the presidency. Vice President Gerald R. Ford succeeded him.

Both sides stood poised to continue the war. By March 1974 PAVN strength in the South had grown to 185,000 troops supported by 500 to 700 tanks, 350 122mm and 130mm field pieces, and 24 anti-aircraft regiments armed with SAMs.[15] The RVNAF had received massive amounts of military equipment from the United States prior to the peace agreement. The Paris Accords also allowed the ARVN to replace equipment as it was worn out or used up, but the US Congress sharply cut back funding, which severely curtailed the ability of South Vietnamese forces to fight the high-tech war for which they had been trained. As one historian of the war put it, "in 1974, the RVNAF had to fight a rich man's war on a pauper's budget".[16]

The high price of fuel resulting from the Arab oil embargo also had an impact on the situation. Although in 1974 the VNAF had 1,277 aircraft in its inventory, it could deploy only 921 of them. Shortfalls in fuel and ammunition reduced sorties flown in 1974 from the year before by 40 per cent and their firepower by 60 per cent. Whereas in 1972 the ARVN had received 66,500 tons of war materials a month, by July 1974 this was down to only 18,267. The disparity only worsened. By September 1974 the entire ARVN helicopter fleet was restricted to only 2,000 flying hours a month, including medevac missions. One-fifth of VNAF planes were grounded and ARVN artillery was rationed to three rounds per tube per day. Helicopters lost in action were not replaced and the ARVN was forced to operate on one-fifth the ammunition and one-tenth the gasoline as during the high-point of US funding.[17] Such shortages severely lowered ARVN morale.

In October 1973 DRV leaders had decided on a new offensive in the South with a projected final victory in 1976. Command went not to Giáp but to Senior General Văn Tiên Dũng. Giáp had been in poor health and was also under attack for the failure of the 1972 offensive, responsibility for which lay with Party Secretary Lê Duân. Dũng faced formidable problems. The PAVN had suffered serious losses in the 1972 offensive and was short of supplies. The South mirrored this situation. Colonel General (the equivalent of lieutenant general) Trân Văn Trà, commander of the southern B–2 Front, noted later, "In 1973 our cadres and men were fatigued, we had not had time to make up our losses, all units were in disarray, there was a lack of manpower, and there were shortages of food and ammunition."[18]

Trà now recalled PAVN units into the North to be brought up to strength and re-equipped. He also reorganized his command into four corps and strengthened the logistics network through Laos. By the end of 1974 the PAVN was not only in position to fight again, but as historian Cecil Currey notes, "For the first time ever, it could be resupplied fully and in time without depending on prepositioned stockpiles and coolie-borne matériel. It had finally become a modern army."[19]

In 1974 the fighting intensified. Beginning in March PAVN forces carried out a series of "strategic raids" designed to seize the initiative, gain territory and population, secure supply corridors, sap ARVN strength and morale and heighten PAVN combat effectiveness.[20] Heavy fighting in the Central Highlands was followed by attacks that summer in Quang Ngãi, Quang Tín and Quang Nam provinces in northern South Vietnam. From 2 August to 2 September at Plei Me the 410-man 82nd ARVN Ranger Battalion held out against 20 ground assaults and an artillery/mortar onslaught of some 10,000 rounds by the PAVN 320th Division. But ARVN defensive stands were rare and usually the Communist attacks were successful. At the end of the year fighting renewed in the Mekong Delta, and in the second week of December the ARVN lost 706 KIA and 3,758 WIA, the most in any week since the start of the cease-fire. ARVN battle deaths in the entire year ran nearly 31,000; only 1972 was costlier.[21]

In January 1975 ARVN strength on paper came to 465,000 men: 13 divisions (11 infantry, one airborne and one Marine), two independent infantry regiments, 18 armoured squadrons, three motorized squadrons, 43 Ranger battalions and 14 artillery regiments. There were also some 2 million men in paramilitary forces around the country. But the ARVN was characterized by inadequate pay and allowances caused in part by rampant inflation, corruption, a sense of fatalism that the war could not be won and low morale. ARVN's desertion rate shot up to 24,000 men a month. Thiêu also faced daunting political problems as opposition to his rule mounted.[22]

While ARVN was struggling with shortages and manpower losses, PAVN strength was growing. By December 1974 the PAVN had in South Vietnam some 200,000 men, 1,000 armoured vehicles and 600 artillery pieces. PRG/ Việt Công troops numbered only about 60,000 men.[23]

Lê Duẩn, Lê Đức Tho, and other DRV leaders now pushed General Dũng to begin the final offensive. Dũng was cautious, worried that the United States might intervene with a repeat of 1972. At a meeting with the Politburo in late 1974 he predicted that victory in the South might take several more years. Giáp, who still chaired the military committee, told him, "Our planning must provide for the contingency that it [the war] could end in 1975."[24]

Phúóc Long offensive

In order to test whether the United States would intervene with air power, Dũng decided on an offensive to secure a single province, Phúóc Long – which at its closest point was only 40 miles from the RVN capital.[25] On 13 December 1974, General Trân Văn Trà and COSVN head and political commissar for Communist forces in the South Pham Hùng ordered their 7th Division and the newly formed 3rd Division to attack Phúóc Long.

Years of warfare, corruption, and the loss of US support all sapped the South Vietnamese will to resist. Soon the PAVN laid siege to Phúóc Long's capital of Phúóc Bình. They greatly outnumbered ARVN defenders and only a few ARVN reinforcements arrived. Although they fought well, they gave way to heavy PAVN artillery fire followed by infantry and tank assaults. All resistance ended on 6 January 1975; only 850 of 5,400 ARVN defenders made it to friendly lines. Two Ranger companies lost all but 85 men. Twenty VNAF planes were also lost in the battle, many to SAM–7s. The Communist capture of Phúóc Bình was a tremendous psychological boost to them because it was the first provincial capital they had taken since Quang Tri City in 1972, and that had been regained.[26]

Dũng was greatly reassured when the United States did not intervene. On 28 January President Ford requested immediate additional assistance for the RVN and Cambodia but found himself at loggerheads with a Congress that was determined to end US intervention in Southeast Asia. The United States did little more than to defy the Paris Accords by carrying out reconnaissance flights. One other consequence was a sharp increase of political opposition within the RVN to Thiêu.[27]

Lê Đúc Tho, second in the Politburo only to Lê Duân, now ordered Dũng to attack Ban Mê Thuôt, capital of Darlac province.[28] What happened next surprised even the most optimistic in Hà Nôi. The resulting offensive was actually a repeat of the autumn 1965 PAVN attempt to secure the Central Highlands, drive to the sea and cut the country in two. But this time the US 1st Air Cavalry Division and B–52s were not available to defeat the Communist thrust.

The Battle of Ban Mê Thuôt (10–18 March 1975)

Three PAVN divisions – the 316th, 320th and 10th – moved towards Ban Mê Thuôt. Including support units, the force numbered up to 80,000 men with a massive superiority in artillery. ARVN II Corps commander Major General Pham Văn Phú assumed that any major PAVN attack would fall on the traditional Communist targets of Kontum or Pleiku. Ban Mê Thuôt was thus weakly defended by a single regiment of the ARVN 23rd Division, one Ranger group, and some Regional Forces (RF) units. The Battle for Ban Mê Thuôt really began on 1 March with a series of diversionary attacks west of Pleiku, which helped deceive Phú. PAVN troops then isolated Ban Mê Thuôt by cutting its highway access to the coast. Early on 10 March PAVN forces attacked the city itself and its airfield. Ban Mê Thuôt fell on the 12th.[29]

That same day Congress turned down President Ford's request for $300 million in military aid for the RVN.[30] Also on the 12th, President Thiêu ordered General Phú to retake Ban Mê Thuôt. The ARVN counter-attack on 15 March by two regiments of the 23rd Division failed. One factor in the subsequent rapid ARVN collapse, illustrated at Ban Mê Thuôt and repeated elsewhere on a wider scale, was the "family syndrome", the mass desertion of soldiers who wanted to rescue their families.[31] On 12 March Giáp transmitted to Dũng the latest Politburo directive – invest Pleiku.[32]

On 14 March President Thiêu flew to Cam Ranh and made a fateful decision that greatly speeded up the Communist victory. He ordered the withdrawal of ARVN troops from the nine Central Highlands provinces and the two northernmost provinces. Thiêu intended to hold all the territory south of an east–west line from Tuy Hòa on the coast, some of which would have to be retaken, and he hoped to retain such cities in the north as Huê and Đà Năng. His reasoning was that this would shorten the ARVN's lines of communication and concentrate forces to defend the major cities.[33]

Thiêu's precipitous abandonment of the north was a disaster. His rival Nguyên Cao Kỳ later criticized the decision, blaming Thiêu and the Joint General Staff for the subsequent ARVN defeat. As Kỳ put it in his memoirs, "Thiêu's strategic error turned a tactical withdrawal into a rout and [led to] the eventual disintegration of our entire armed forces."[34]

Sensing an imminent ARVN collapse, Hà Nôi poured resources into the South. Between September 1974 and 30 April 1975, the DRV sent 170,000 troops south, 58,000 in April alone.[35] Soon the entire ARVN II Corps was in full retreat from the Highlands. The troops and hordes of civilian refugees sought to escape. The civilian exodus, hastened by PAVN artillery fire, heightened the panic.

With PAVN forces controlling Highway 19, Thiêu ordered General Phú to extract his troops from Kontum and Pleiku south along a single road, Route 7B, that wound to Tuy Hòa and the sea. Jungle had reclaimed much of it, bridges were down and South Korean forces that had operated in the area had mined stretches of 7B. The retreat was a debacle from the very beginning.[36]

Some 1,500 vehicles and hundreds of thousands of civilians now formed a 50-mile-long exodus moving at only two or three miles an hour. On 18 March, as ARVN engineers struggled to bridge the Ba River, the PAVN 320th Division attacked the disorganized "Convoy of Tears" or "Column of Sorrow". ARVN Rangers fought valiantly to keep the road open and protect the convoy's rear. The next day VNAF planes, flying too high, accidently bombed the Rangers, destroying four tanks and nearly wiping out a battalion.

Only some 700 of 7,000 Rangers made it to Tuy Hòa a week later. In all just one-third of the 60,000 men in II Corps reached safety and only 60,000 to 100,000 of 400,000 civilians.[37]

I Corps now experienced a similar disaster, also of Thiêu's making. I Corps commander Lieutenant General Ngô Quang Trúóng had three ARVN divisions, an armour brigade, and four Ranger groups.[38] On 13 March Thiêu called Trúóng to Sài Gòn and ordered him to relinquish most of his area but to hold Đà Nẵng and sufficient territory around it to protect the city. Confronting Trúóng in I Corps, the PAVN had five divisions and 35 separate regiments (9 infantry, 3 armour, 8 artillery, 12 anti-aircraft, and 3 sappers), about double Trúóng's strength.[39]

The removal of the elite Airborne Division from Quang Nam traumatized the people of that province. When the Marine Division moved out of Quang Tri and Thúa Thiên provinces to replace it, this in turn demoralized the people there. Panicked refugees who remembered what had happened in Huê during the 1968 Tết Offensive greatly hampered ARVN movements. Trúóng's forces were now under PAVN attack from the north and the south. By 20 March all of Quang Tri Province was in PAVN hands. On the 22nd PAVN forces cut Route 1 between Huê and Đà Nẵng. Some ARVN forces and civilians were evacuated from Huê and Chu Lai by sea, but for the most part these evacuations were disasters. The old imperial city fell to the Commnunists on 26 March.[40]

Demoralized ARVN defenders now gave way nearly everywhere. One after another towns and bases succumbed to the relentless PAVN advance. The equivalent of six PAVN divisions closed in on Đà Nẵng, which almost overnight had doubled in size to a million people. A frantic sea lift began and by 31 March, when the city fell, some 16,000 troops and 50,000 civilians had managed to flee in overcrowded boats and ships. Some were evacuated by air, but this effort had to be suspended because of the crush of people trying to board the planes. Particularly heinous was the flight of some ARVN commanders. Understandably, when their leaders took off, the soldiers deserted as well. Lost at Đà Nẵng were 180 aircraft and 70,000 troops in four divisions, four Ranger groups, an armoured brigade and an air division.[41]

By 1 April the Communists had taken all of northern I Corps. During the previous three weeks the PAVN had captured 12 of 44 RVN provinces and killed, captured, or isolated some 150,000 ARVN troops. They had also captured military equipment worth about $1 billion, including 400 planes and helicopters. On 1 April Qui Nhón and Nha Trang fell. The following day ARVN forces evacuated Tuy Hòa.[42]

Hồ Chí Minh Campaign (April 1975)

On 25 March the Politburo in Hà Nôi revised its timetable for ending the war, deciding that Sài Gòn should be taken before the beginning of the mid-May rainy season. Dũng asked permission to call this the Hồ Chí Minh Campaign, in the hope of achieving victory before Hồ's 19 May birthday anniversary, and the Politburo agreed.[43]

In early April 200,000 Communist troops in 173 regiments had overrun two-thirds of South Vietnam.[44] Communist forces now greatly outnumbered those of ARVN, and by mid-month nine Communist divisions converged on Sài Gòn. To defend the capital, Thiêu had only the three divisions assigned to III Corps (the 5th, 18th and 25th), a reconstituted division from Military Region II (the 22nd), and what remained of the armour brigade, the Marine division, the Airborne division, and a few Ranger groups.[45]

The only major ARVN stand during the Communist offensive occurred at Xuân Lôc, capital of Long Khánh Province. Located on Route 1 just east of the junction with Route 20 and some 40 miles northeast of Sài Gòn, Xuân Lôc was strategically important to the RVN capital's defence. The city was defended by Brigadier General Lê Minh Đao's 18th Division. On 9 April, following a 4,000-round artillery and rocket barrage, three PAVN divisions (the 6th, 7th and 341st) attacked Xuân Lôc, now isolated because the Communists had cut Route 1.

VNAF A–1 Skyraiders and F–5 fighter-bombers struck the PAVN attackers and ARVN armoured columns attempted to push through PAVN roadblocks on Route 1. A brigade of the 1st Airborne Division arrived by helicopter, but PAVN troops pinned it down at its landing zone east of the city. Meanwhile the PAVN force continued to grow. On 14 April PAVN 130mm heavy guns pounded Biên Hòa Air Base for the first time in the war. On the 15th Communist sappers blew up the base's ammunition dump. The next day PAVN 130mm shells damaged 20 aircraft on the ground, which effectively ended air support for Xuân Lôc. Although they were heavily outnumbered and the outcome of the battle was certain, Đao's troops fought on courageously in what was probably the most heroic stand of any ARVN division of the war. They destroyed 37 PAVN tanks and killed over 5,000 PAVN troops.

At Xuân Lôc the VNAF employed 750-pound CBU–55 cluster bombs and 15,000-pound "Daisy Cutter" bombs. On the 21st a VNAF C–130 dropped a CBU–55 "fuel bomb", the most powerful non-nuclear weapon in the US arsenal. This was the first time the weapon had ever been employed. It consumed the oxygen over a two-acre area and killed more than 250 PAVN troops.

Ho Chi Minh Campaign
April 1975

PAVN advances

Areas under Communist
control since 1973
cease-fire

Communist gains as of
late March 1975

Demilitarized Zone

Dong Ha
Quang Tri City
Hue
Phu Bai
Da Nang
An Hoa
Tam Ky
Chu Lai
My Lai
Route 1
Dak To
Kontum
Pleiku
Qui Nhon
An Khe
Tuy Hoa
Ban Me
Thuot
Nha Trang
Cam Rahn
Phuoc
Binh
Da Lat
Phan Rhang
Tay Ninh
Ben Suc
Bien Hoa
Route 1
Phan Thiet
Sai Gon
Xuan Loc
My Tho
Vung Tau
Can Tho

Miles   200
Kms   200

In the battle more than 7,500 ARVN soldiers died or were wounded. On the 23rd the remaining ARVN defenders and PF and RF elements conducted a well-executed retreat south from Xuân Lôc.[46]

Sài Gòn, meanwhile, was in turmoil. US evacuation flights began removing key Vietnamese officials and dependents. On 8 April VNAF pilot Lieutenant Nguyên Thành Trung dropped two bombs from his F–5 on the presidential palace and then defected. President Thiêu was unhurt, but General Dũng immediately ordered Trung sent to Đà Nẵng to help train North Vietnamese MiG pilots to fly captured VNAF A–37 and F–5 jets.[47]

The US evacuation of Cambodia on 12 April reinforced Hà Nôi's assessment that Washington would not intervene to prevent the collapse of the RVN, although some Sài Gòn officials refused to believe they would be abandoned. Even the loss of Military Regions I and II did not dissuade many US officials in South Vietnam from acting as if the Sài Gòn government could at least bring off a negotiated settlement.[48]

On 21 April President Thiêu resigned in favour of Vice President Trân Văn Húong. In a televised farewell address he lied when he stated, "What happened in the highlands was the decision of leaders in Military Region II". He blamed Washington for forcing Sài Gòn to sign the Paris Accords, for failing to replace military equipment lost after the US withdrawal and for its refusal to honour its pledges to come to the aid of South Vietnam.[49] Despite Thiêu's speech on the 21st, or perhaps because of it, he lingered on in the capital until flying out on the 26th.

Dũng did not halt the PAVN offensive.[50] He assembled 130,000 troops in 18 divisions for the final assault on Sài Gòn, which began on the 26th. Early the next morning four rockets hit the city, killing ten people, injuring 200 and leaving 5,000 homeless. In a fierce tank battle PAVN forces took Long Thành, which was located on Route 15 to Vung Tau on the coast. On 28 April President Húong resigned in favour of Dúóng Văn Minh, who had helped overthrow President Diêm in 1963. Minh called for an immediate cease-fire and the opening of peace negotiations, but the PRG rejected this. That same day five captured A–37 jets led by Lieutenant Trung flew from Phan Rang to attack Tân Són Nhút. The raid destroyed seven planes. It was the only Communist air strike in South Vietnam during the entire war, but it helped bring about the final surrender of Sài Gòn.[51]

At the end of March 7,500 Americans remained in the RVN. On 16 April President Ford had ordered all "unneeded" Americans to leave. The PRG announced it would impose no obstacles to this. A greater issue was some 50,000 "high risk" Vietnamese who had co-operated with the Americans. Many of them now began to depart. On the 27th the RVN stopped issuing exit visas, although this did not prevent many high-ranking RVN officials from departing the next day.[52]

The air attack of the 28th and a rocket barrage on Tân Són Nhút the next day finally convinced US Ambassador Graham Martin to order a full evacuation. Fearing its negative impact on morale, he waited until the 29th. The operation (Frequent Wind) took place in chaotic circumstances as 81 helicopters and a thousand US Marines evacuated 395 Americans and 4,475 Vietnamese. Only a minority of Vietnamese thought to be at risk were evacuated by helicopter or managed to escape by other means. Forty US Navy ships off shore did rescue a large number of refugees fleeing by boat from Vũng Tàu under artillery fire.[53]

ARVN units around the Sài Gòn perimeter came under heavy PAVN attack on 29 April and ceased their resistance the next day when elements of General Dũng's force walked unopposed into the centre of the city. At noon on 30 April a PAVN tank crashed through the gate of the presidential palace. The Republic of Vietnam had come to an end. Some ARVN forces held out in the Central Highlands and Mekong Delta for a time, but for all intents and purposes the Third Vietnam War was over.[54]

Although the United States had extracted its own personnel, it left behind in South Vietnam a vast military stockpile. The PAVN now seized from the RVNAF 467 aircraft, 466 helicopters, 80 self-propelled guns, 1,250 105mm and 155mm howitzers, 3,300 armoured personnel carriers, 400 tanks, 42,000 trucks, 47,000 grenade launchers, 63,000 light anti-tank weapons, 15,000 machine guns, 12,000 mortars, 791,000 M16 rifles and 857 other small arms, 90,000 pistols, 940 ships (mostly landing craft) and 130,000 tons of ammunition. In the years to come the Vietnamese government sold much of this abroad to gain hard currency.[55]

Communist victories in Laos and Cambodia

Communist forces also triumphed in Laos and in Cambodia. In Laos following the Paris Accords the three factions of Communist Pathet Lao, Neutralists and Royalists agreed to a cease-fire in February 1973. US bombing stopped on 22 February. The new coalition government under Souvanna Phouma was not invested until April 1974. Given the large PAVN presence in eastern Laos and the end of US involvement, the Communist victory there of May 1975 was inevitable.

The only major action occurred around Sala Phou Khoun, where after weeks of fighting in April in violation of the cease-fire, Hmong leader

General Vang Pao was forced to retreat before Pathet Lao infantry supported by tanks. Thousands of Hmong were extracted by air from Vang Pao's headquarters at Long Cheng but many more, who had been so loyal to their CIA case officers, were simply abandoned to their fate. Some 40,000 managed to flee to Thailand, where they lived a squalid existence in refugee camps. For years afterwards Hmong guerrillas continued to fight the Communist government. The new Communist rulers of Laos carried out a brutal purge of former Lao elites. All the high command of the Royal Army and perhaps 40,000 other citizens were sent to malaria-infested "re-education camps" where a high percentage died. For years up to 50,000 PAVN occupation troops remained in Laos.[56]

US policy in Cambodia helped bring about in the spring of 1975 the direct opposite of what Washington had intended. Instead of preserving Cambodian neutrality, US intervention helped push the country towards Communist control. Just prior to congressional restrictions on US aid on 31 May 1973, Lon Nol had reversed course and offered to negotiate with Prince Sihanouk, now allied with the Khmer Rouge. Sihanouk, who had earlier favoured negotiations, now rejected them because the Khmer Rouge was doing well on the battlefield, thanks in part to increased military aid from Hà Nôi. US bombing of Cambodia ceased on 15 August, but from 8 March to 15 August 1973, the Air Force had dropped 257,465 tons of bombs on Cambodia. During World War II the United States had dropped only 160,000 tons of conventional ordnance on Japan.[57]

Contrary to expectations, fighting in Cambodia died down for a time. Although Sihanouk was the nominal head of the National Unity Government of Cambodia, he remained in Beijing, and Khmer Rouge leader Khieu Samphan exercised real power. Beginning in November 1973 Khmer Rouge forces blockaded Phnom Penh. At the end of February 1974 Lon Nol's FANK troops pushed the Khmer Rouge back some distance from the capital. In March the Khmer Rouge captured the old royal capital of Oudong, about 24 miles from Phnom Penh. It was the first provincial capital they had taken since 1970. FANK recaptured Oudang in July.[58]

To circumvent the Cooper–Church Amendment President Nixon had authorized the employment of CIA-funded Bird Air Company with planes loaned by the Pentagon. It made reconnaissance flights and damage assessments, and flew in supplies for the Lon Nol government, especially to outlying garrisons.[59]

Throughout the second half of 1974 there was a stalemate in Cambodia. The Khmer Rouge, not as well armed or supplied as its adversary, was, however, better led. It controlled the countryside, but with only about 70,000 men lacked the strength for an offensive against the cities. The much larger

FANK numbered about 200,000 men. It controlled the towns but, plagued by poor leadership, low morale and corruption, was in turn unable to undertake aggressive action in the rural areas. FANK resources were also spread thin. Some 50,000 of its best troops defended Phnom Penh while the remainder were dispersed throughout the rest of the country.

At the end of 1974 US aid to Lon Nol was sharply curtailed. Up to that point Washington had provided him some $1.85 billion. US bombing had cost an additional $7 billion. In December, however, Congress placed strict restrictions on US aid. This had a material effect on FANK's fighting ability and perhaps an even greater psychological impact on the troops themselves.[60]

In January 1975 Khmer Rouge troops received sufficient PAVN assistance to launch a major offensive against FANK forces; soon they controlled Mekong River access to Phnom Penh. Previously some 80 per cent of provisions for the capital had come in by water; now it could only be resupplied by air. Hunger became a major problem in a city of some 600,000 people.

A majority of the Cambodian Assembly called on Lon Nol to resign and he did so on 11 March, leaving the country on 1 April. After the last US personnel left the Cambodian capital on the 12th, airborne provisions no longer arrived in Phomn Penh. On 17 April Khmer Rouge troops simply walked into the city and took control.[61] Five years of war had brought the deaths of some 10 per cent of Cambodia's seven million people. The economy was in ruins; few schools and hospitals were operating and half of the population had been uprooted from their homes. But much worse lay ahead.[62] The new leaders renamed the country Kampuchea, emptied the cities of their populations and tried to take the country back into the Middle Ages, herding the population into agricultural communes and initiating a reign of terror that has few precedents in history.

Chapter Eight

Vietnamese invasion of Cambodia and the war with China

Following the April 1975 Communist capture of Sài Gòn a military administration took charge in the South. In April 1976 general elections took place for a single National Assembly. It met in June and the next month proclaimed the reunified country the Socialist Republic of Vietnam (SRV) with its capital at Hà Nôi; Sài Gòn became Hô Chí Minh City. In September 1977 the SRV was admitted to the United Nations.

The SRV faced staggering problems. These included rebuilding the war-ravaged country, knitting the two halves of the country together after decades of division and war, reconciling markedly different patterns of economic development, and providing for the needs of a burgeoning population that would double in the next 20 years. In December 1976 the Lao Đông Party was renamed the Đang Công San Viêt Nam (Vietnamese Communist Party, VCP), but it retained its monopoly on power. Indeed the constitution guaranteed it as the only force leading the state and society.

Immediately after the war the government conducted a political purge in the South. Some deaths occurred but nothing like the bloodbath feared and so often predicted by Washington. Over a million former RVN officials and military officers were sent to Re-education Camps for varying terms, there to be politically indoctrinated and to undergo varying degrees of physical and mental discomfort, even torture. Many were held for years.

Efforts were made to reduce the population in the cities, especially Hô Chí Minh City, by far the nation's largest metropolitan area. Its population had swelled in the last years of the war and the concentration of population in urban areas of the South meant that perhaps one-third of the arable land lay idle. So-called New Economic Areas were created to develop new agricultural land and to get other areas back into cultivation.

SINO-VIETNAMESE CONFLICT
FEBRUARY 1979

PEOPLE'S REPUBLIC OF CHINA

Ha Giang
Lao Cai
Cao Bang
Black River
Red River
Lang Son
SOCIALIST REPUBLIC OF VIETNAM
Ha Noi

MYANMAR

LAOS

Gulf of Tonkin

Hainan Island

20°

Vientiane
Mekong River

THAILAND

16°

Bangkok

Adaung Pech
Pleiku
Stung Treng

VIETNAMESE INVASION OF CAMBODIA
DECEMBER 1978

Kratie
CAMBODIA
Kompong Cham
Phnom Penh
Tay Ninh
HO CHI MINH CITY
(SAI GON)

12°

INDO-CHINA

Sino–Vietnamese conflict
and
Vietnamese invasion of
Cambodia

Miles 200
Kms 200

Kompong Som
Takeo
Ha Tien

South China Sea

Con Son

100°
104°
106°

Economically Vietnam even in the best of times had been a poor, developing nation. In the immediate aftermath of the war the Vietnamese began quite literally to pick up the pieces. In addition to the ravages of the war, Vietnam inherited vast amounts of scrap metal and more than a $1 billion in unused US military equipment. The broken machines of war fed the scrap-metal furnaces of the country for years afterwards and the SRV exported American military hardware. In another move to gain badly needed foreign currency the government later sent some 200,000 of its people to work in the USSR and Eastern Europe. These workers sent home an estimated $150 million a year.

The government introduced farm collectivization in the South and new regulations that governed business practices, which led to the collapse of light and medium industry. Although the policy was soon abandoned, economic unrest helped fuel an exodus of refugees.

Floods in north and central Vietnam in the summer of 1978 hastened the collapse of agricultural co-operatives and in 1981 the government introduced an incentive system. Peasants paid fixed rents for the use of the land and were able to sell surplus produce on the private market.

Vietnam had no official ties with the United States. Both countries would have benefited economically had such a relationship been established early on, but Hà Nôi insisted on the reconstruction aid promised by the Nixon Administration. Talks collapsed over what Washington saw as Hà Nôi's callous disregard for those fleeing Vietnam ("the boat people"), SRV preparations to invade Cambodia, and its conclusion of a treaty of friendship and co-operation with the USSR that November. The Carter Administration also decided to make normalization of relations with China a priority over Vietnam.

Relations between Vietnam and Cambodia

Meanwhile relations between the SRV and Kampuchea (Cambodia) deteriorated. The reasons for this lay not in ideology, but in the traditional animosity between the two countries. Khmer Rouge leaders, instinctively anti-Vietnamese, were bitter that in the 1960s the Vietnamese Communists had given them little support. On entering into an uneasy alliance with the Vietnamese Communists after Sihanouk's fall, Khmer Rouge leaders believed they had been betrayed a second time when Hà Nôi signed the 1973 Paris Peace Accords. Khmer Rouge leaders ordered the Vietnamese to leave Cambodian territory and endeavoured to eliminate pro-Vietnamese elements within the Khmer Rouge. This purge killed nearly all the "Khmer Việt

Minh" or "Hà Nôi Khmers". These were Cambodians who had fought against the French and then settled in the DRV until 1970, when the government there had ordered them to help lead the Cambodian resistance.[1]

Beginning in the spring of 1973 the Vietnamese Communists no longer played a role in the Khmer Rouge fight against the Lon Nol government. Indeed, from time to time there were armed clashes between Vietnamese forces in Cambodia and the Khmer Rouge.

After the Khmer Rouge defeated the Lon Nol government in April 1975 they ordered the people out of the capital of Phnom Penh and larger towns and put them to work in agricultural labour camps in the countryside. They abolished private property and replaced paper money by ration tickets earned by productive labour. The Khmer Rouge closed schools and destroyed Buddhist temples. Thousands of people died, including many ethnic Vietnamese. Hundreds of thousands of Vietnamese fled Cambodia.[2]

In January 1976 the Khmer Rouge promulgated a new constitution and changed the name of the country to the Democratic Republic of Kampuchea. In April Prince Sihanouk resigned as head of state. Khieu Samphan took his place but Pol Pot, another Khmer Rouge leader, was the dominant figure in the cabinet. Meanwhile the government announced that 800,000 people, roughly 10 per cent of the population, had died in the fighting that brought the Khmer Rouge to power.[3]

There had long been border disputes between Vietnam and Cambodia, and by 1977 there was serious fighting. In September Vietnam claimed that four Kampuchean divisions had invaded its Tây Ninh Province. In September and December Vietnam retaliated. In the December incursion 60,000 troops, supported by tanks and artillery, pushed as far as the outskirts of Svay Rieung and Kompong Cham. This led to the first public disclosure of the conflict and an angry radio broadcast on 31 December from Phnom Penh denouncing the Vietnamese. A week later the Vietnamese withdrew, most probably of their own accord, but the Khmer Rouge declared it had won a "historic victory" and rejected calls for negotiations. The Khmer Rouge proceeded to carry out a violent purge centred on its armed forces in the eastern part of the country that were supposed to defend the regime from the Vietnamese. Up to 100,000 Cambodians were executed. Many Khmer Rouge fled into Vietnam to avoid being arrested and killed. Later they formed the backbone of the Vietnamese-sponsored anti-Khmer Rouge resistance.[4]

Kampuchea also laid claim to much of southernmost Vietnam (Cochin China) with its large Khmer minority, and to small islands in the Gulf of Thailand. In 1960 Sài Gòn had claimed seven of these, including Phú Quôc, the largest, and landed troops. A major clash between Vietnam and Kampuchea over these islands occurred in May 1975, almost certainly prompted by the belief there was oil in the area.[5]

With border conflicts intensifying, Hà Nôi supported an anti-Khmer Rouge resistance. Eastern Cambodia had been an important part of the vc/pavn logistics system during the Vietnam War and ties between the people there and Vietnam were strong. They were strengthened by the fact that many of those opposed to the Khmer Rouge fled to the border area. Hà Nôi now organized those who had fled to Vietnam, including many ex-Khmer Rouge fighters, into anti-Khmer units to fight alongside the Vietnamese Army against Kampuchean forces. Fighting escalated along the border, much of it in the Parrot's Beak area; and beginning in June 1978 both sides used aircraft, with Chinese pilots flying on the Kampuchean side. The Khmer Rouge rebuffed several Hà Nôi offers to negotiate.[6]

Although Kampuchea remained largely cut off from the outside world, stories of mass killings there began to circulate. In October 1978 Hà Nôi claimed the Khmer Rouge had killed two million Kampucheans. At the time this was thought to be propaganda, but clearly something was amiss. Kampuchea, regarded as the rice bowl of Southeast Asia, was close to starvation.[7]

Tensions between Vietnam and Kampuchea were abetted by the fact that the two states became proxies in the developing Sino–Soviet rivalry. Kampuchea was a client state of China and Vietnam of the Soviet Union. Loyalties of the Communist world divided accordingly; most of the Warsaw Pact nations and Cuba, then relying heavily on financial assistance from the Soviet Union, supported Vietnam; North Korea backed Kampuchea.

In early December 1978 several anti-Khmer Rouge factions formed the Kampuchean National Front led by Khmer Rouge defector Heng Samrin, former deputy commander in eastern Cambodia. Hà Nôi gave the Front full support, including military assistance, and it soon fielded a 20,000-man army.[8]

Vietnamese occupation of Cambodia (1978–85)

Finally on 25 December 1978, the Vietnamese Army invaded Cambodia. Initially the srv committed 12 divisions, half its army, to the operation. Ultimately there were 200,000 Vietnamese troops in Cambodia. Pol Pot had only about 60,000 men in four divisions and three independent regiments, armed with a mix of weapons. Heavily outnumbered and outgunned, the Khmer Rouge retreated into the countryside and waged guerrilla warfare. Heng Samrin and his forces took Phnom Penh unopposed and soon controlled all principal Kampuchean cities.[9]

Heng Samrin became president, but only the presence of several Vietnamese divisions enabled him to remain in power. The Soviet Union, Laos, srv, and most other Communist states recognized the new government. In January 1979 the ussr vetoed a un Security Council resolution that demanded the withdrawal of all foreign troops from Kampuchea. Heng Samrin, meanwhile, concluded treaties with the srv and Laos.

Although his army had been reduced to only about 25,000 men, Pol Pot continued guerrilla warfare, concentrating in the thick jungles of northeastern Kampuchea near the Thai border. China, which at least since the 1954 Geneva Accords had championed the principle of a Cambodia free from Vietnamese influence, aided the Khmer Rouge, funnelling assistance through Thailand. Generals in that country profited handsomely from the misery, allowing the transit of military assistance to the Khmer Rouge and securing gems and timber from their areas of control.

In yet another ironic legacy of the Vietnam War the United States also aided the Khmer Rouge. Supposedly Washington sent military assistance only to the non-Khmer Rouge resistance groups, but it was an open secret that much of this aid was used by the Khmer Rouge. Only the Vietnamese occupation prevented the Khmer Rouge from returning to power and continuing its genocidal policies, and it was only thanks to the Vietnamese invasion that the mass killings of Cambodians by the Khmer Rouge were confirmed.

China meanwhile threatened the srv with force to punish Hà Nôi for the invasion of Kampuchea. Indeed, its People's Liberation Army (pla) actually invaded Vietnam briefly during February–March 1979, but this did not force the Vietnamese to quit Cambodia. That came from the sheer expense of the operation and resultant drain on the Vietnamese economy and the srv's attendant isolation in the international community at a time when the leadership understood the need to revitalize the national economy and secure foreign investment.

Finally in May 1988 Hà Nôi announced it would withdraw 50,000 troops, about half of its forces, from Cambodia by the end of that year. In July the Phnom Penh government and rebel coalition met for the first time face-to-face in inconclusive peace talks in Indonesia. On 5 April 1989 Hà Nôi and Phnom Penh announced jointly that all Vietnamese troops would leave Cambodia by the end of September, even if no settlement was reached. On 26 September 1989, Vietnam said that all its troops had departed. Some 25,000 Vietnamese troops had died during the Cambodian occupation.

After prolonged negotiations in late 1990, rival Cambodian factions, including the Vietnamese-installed regime then headed by Hun Sen and the Khmer Rouge, agreed to a supreme national council headed by Prince Sihanouk. The United Nations mounted a vast peacekeeping operation and supervised elections. In the years to follow, Khmer Rouge influence declined.[10]

Sino—Vietnamese war (17 February—5 March 1979)

In February and March 1979 the People's Republic of China and Vietnam fought a brief war, sometimes referred to as the Third Vietnam War and known to the Chinese as the "Punitive War".[11] This 18-day conflict between two former allies seemed to many in the West a strange event indeed. To critics of American involvement in Vietnam, it was proof of the historical animosity between the two powers and the fact that self-interest was more important in relations between states than ideology. The causes of the war were numerous: border disputes between the two states, the SRV's treatment of its Chinese minority, PRC determination to punish Vietnam for its invasion of Cambodia and China's desire to weaken ties between Vietnam and the Soviet Union.[12]

For some time there had been border disputes between the two states over a common 797-mile-long border demarcated in colonial times by the French. Although the actual territory in dispute was quite small, border incidents had multiplied since 1974. According to the SRV there were 21,175 such incidents in 1978. Negotiations over the disputed territory, begun in October 1977, broke off in the summer of 1978.[13] More important economically were quarrels between the two states over the Paracel and Spratly Islands in the South China Sea and territorial waters in the Gulf of Tonkin, both of which were spurred on by the possibility of oil deposits.[14]

The second major cause of the war was Vietnam's treatment of its Chinese minority, the *Hoa*. In the late 1970s some 1.5 million *Hoa* lived in Vietnam. Many had been there for generations. The largest concentration of *Hoa*, some 1.2 million, lived in Chó Lón, the Chinese section of Sài Gòn. The *Hoa* were an important economic element in the country, but many refused to become Vietnamese citizens.[15]

In March 1978 the government abolished private trading, although it allowed many Chinese merchants to continue their enterprises after that date because they were essential to the economy. Once the government established its own state-run shops, however, those in private enterprises were ordered to register for productive work. This meant the confiscation of at least 50,000 Chinese firms and the removal of some 320,000 Chinese into the countryside for agricultural work – part of the government plan to reduce population in Hô Chí Minh City.[16]

Faced with this prospect, many Chinese fled overland into China. In only 13 days (9–21 May) more than 57,000 Chinese left northern Vietnam for China; by early July more than 150,000 had crossed the border.[17] Many more attempted to escape by sea to Hong Kong and other points. This exodus of "boat people" was prompted in part by *provocateurs*, working for either the SVN government in an effort to rid the country of a minority population or Chinese gangsters motivated by greed. These opportunists informed the Chinese community that war with China was inevitable and then extracted money in return for providing escape by sea. There had been a steady flow of refugees from Vietnam after 1975, but by 1978 it reached crisis proportions largely because Southeast Asian countries refused to take in the thousands of refugees arriving on their shores. Many refugees perished on the seas in their flimsy craft or were set upon by pirates. The exodus of the *Hoa* was certainly a serious blow to the Vietnamese economy. China expressed outrage over what it considered a deliberate act by the SRV. In June the PRC reduced aid to Vietnam and recalled its ambassador; the next month it recalled 880 aid specialists and cancelled all Chinese assistance to the SRV.[18] The Chinese exodus slackened off after July 1979, when the DRV announced it would take major steps to prevent illegal departures, but it remained a serious cause of friction between the PRC and SRV.

The third major cause of the war was disagreement between the two states over the Vietnamese invasion of Cambodia. Beijing regarded Kampuchea as part of its sphere of influence. In early January 1979 PRC Deputy Premier and Chief of Staff of the People's Liberation Army Deng Xiao-ping ruled out immediate Chinese military intervention in the Kampuchea–Vietnam conflict, but said that one day China might be forced to take measures contrary to its desire for peace. He considered the Vietnamese invasion part of a greater Soviet expansionist design and the Soviet–Vietnamese threat to China.[19] Chinese leaders certainly hoped that PRC military action against the SRV would relieve pressure on the Khmer Rouge, which it supported militarily.

Historian Bruce Elleman has suggested a fourth cause of the conflict, linking this event to the termination of the 30-year Sino–Soviet friendship treaty. The Chinese leadership used the brief war to expose as worthless

Soviet assurances of military support for Vietnam. The Soviet Union pumped as much as $2.25 billion a year into the SRV economy, more than half of this in military assistance, and it had established a naval base at Cam Ranh Bay.[20]

Whatever the reasons for the war, the PRC appeared to enjoy tremendous advantages over its opponent. Its population numbered nearly a billion people, with some 4.3 million in its military. The regular army, the PLA, contained 3.6 million men in 175 divisions (121 infantry, 11 armoured, 3 airborne, and 40 artillery) and had 9,000–10,000 tanks and 16,000–20,000 artillery pieces and rocket launchers. But the 1979 war with Vietnam revealed Chinese weakness rather than military prowess. With the exception of a month-long clash with India in 1962, the PLA had not fought a major war since the Korean conflict. It was basically an infantry force with antiquated equipment, commanded by old men. The PLA was sadly deficient in motor transport, and logistics proved to be a major problem.

The Chinese navy included some 280,000–300,000 men and 1,050 vessels, 300 in the South Sea Fleet. Its air force numbered about 400,000 men and 5,000 combat aircraft. Many of the latter were obsolete; its 4,100 interceptors were mostly MiG–15s, MiG–17s, and MiG–19s. China had only 80 MiG–21s.[21]

In preparation for war, Beijing evacuated some 300,000 inhabitants from along the border. The government also placed the Northern Front (facing the Soviet Union) on maximum alert to prevent a surprise attack from that quarter. Deng Xiao-ping assumed overall command of Chinese forces for the Punitive War and assembled some 31 divisions (330,000 men) and 1,200 tanks in the Vietnam border area.[22]

Seemingly the SRV was at a serious military disadvantage. Its entire military establishment numbered only about 615,000 men, centred on 25 infantry divisions, plus a number of independent regiments and specialized units. The PAVN was, however, a modern force, relatively well-equipped, well-disciplined and hardened in war. It was also widely dispersed. Six of its divisions were in Laos and 14 in Kampuchea. That left only five divisions in Vietnam, four of which protected Hà Nôi. Guarding the border with China were some 70,000 well-armed members of the Border Security Force; another 50,000 lightly armed militia troops were also available. Vietnam boasted up to 485 combat aircraft, including 70 MiG–19s, a like number of MiG–21s, and some captured US-made F–5s. Also it still maintained a formidable anti-aircraft array, including SAMs. The Vietnamese prepared by placing obstacles and laying mine fields along the border and covering possible invasion approaches with artillery and mortars.[23]

The punitive war

On 17 February 1979, 100,000 Chinese troops led by field commander General Xu Shih-yu attacked simultaneously at some 43 different points along the border, seeking both to spread the Vietnamese defenders and probe for weak spots. The main Chinese attacks came along the half dozen traditional invasion routes to Hà Nôi, with the Chinese intent on securing the key mountain passes as quickly as possible. Chinese attacks were marked by heavy artillery barrages followed by human-wave infantry assaults. They met intense Vietnamese resistance and surprisingly strong border defenses.[24]

After advancing into the SRV an average of ten miles the Chinese halted for two days to replenish ammunition and bring up additional troops, of whom there were soon some 200,000 inside Vietnam. Following fierce battles on 22 February the Chinese captured the important border cities of Lào Cai and Cao Băng. That same day the Chinese first encountered PAVN regular troops. At the same time Deng announced on 19 and 23 February that the Chinese incursion would be of limited duration and that PLA forces would be withdrawn once their objective had been achieved.[25] The Chinese hoped to force the SRV into redeploying units from Kampuchea and Laos.

Although Giáp no longer had charge of the PAVN, now commanded by Senior General Văn Tiên Dũng, he remained defence minister and worked closely with Dũng.[26] The two refused to panic, choosing instead to wait and see where the major Chinese thrust would develop. But as Vietnamese frontier towns continued to fall they had to act. On 3 March Hà Nôi committed the 308th Division to the battle for the key northeastern railhead city of Lang Són, which fell to the PLA soon afterward. A second PAVN division moved north from Đà Năng to support Vietnamese forces fighting around Móng Cái on the coast. Hà Nôi also withdrew a division from Kampuchea, although it did not arrive in time to take part in the fighting. Had the war lasted longer, Hà Nôi would certainly have been forced to shift additional divisions from Kampuchea.[27]

By the beginning of March the Chinese had advanced up to 40 miles into Vietnam. But on 5 March Beijing abruptly announced that it had accomplished its ends and was extracting its forces. A circular from the Central Committee of the Communist Party claimed that the PLA had advanced into Vietnam 30 to 80 miles, taken a number of its provincial capitals, and severely damaged four regular PAVN divisions and ten regiments. As the Chinese withdrew they carried out a scorched-earth policy, destroying what they could not carry away with them. The Vietnamese simply watched the Chinese depart, as Hà Nôi put it on 7 March, to show SRV "good will for peace". The Chinese withdrawal was completed by 16 March.[28]

Casualty figures for the war are in dispute; the Chinese claim to have suffered 20,000 casualties while inflicting 50,000 Vietnamese casualties. Historian King Chen estimated Chinese losses at 26,000 killed and 37,000 wounded with Vietnamese casualties at 30,000 killed and 32,000 wounded. After the war the Chinese exchanged 1,636 Vietnamese prisoners for 260 Chinese.[29]

China obtained only a portion of its objectives. It had not destroyed any of the SRV's regular divisions, it failed to free the border area of armed conflict, it had not forced Vietnam to withdraw from Cambodia and it had not altered Hà Nôi's policies towards its Chinese minority.[30] The war also exposed glaring Chinese weaknesses, especially in communications, for which the Chinese relied largely on bugles and whistles. The Chinese were also deficient in transport and weaponry. One remarkable development was that neither side committed its air forces in the war.

Although the Soviet Union had not intervened militarily on the side of the SRV, beginning on 22 February it had initiated an airlift of supplies to Vietnam. Over the next year the USSR doubled its military advisers in Vietnam (there had been about 3,000 in the SRV at the start of the war); it also increased its naval units in Vietnamese waters. In May 1979 the first Soviet submarines arrived at Cam Ranh Bay.[31] Despite these Soviet moves, one long-term effect of the war was that it exposed shortcomings in Soviet–Vietnam ties.

The SRV continued to maintain an extremely large military establishment. In the mid-1980s it had 1.2 million people under arms – the world's fourth largest armed force. This figure did not include numerous "Public Security" personnel. The downside to this was that the military consumed up to a third of the national budget.

The large military establishment and a bloated government bureaucracy consumed revenues badly needed elsewhere. As a result, the economy remained vastly under mechanized. Many foreign observers believed that Vietnam worked more effectively at war than at peace, perhaps because it had little experience with the latter.

By 1986 the economy was in a shambles. Famine – the result of failed farm collectivization and botched currency reform – and rampant inflation took their toll. An economic growth rate of only 2 per cent a year was outstripped by a 3 per cent per year birthrate, one of the highest in the world. All this led to striking changes in policy and leadership announced at the December 1986 Sixth National Communist Party Congress. These changes were based on material incentives, decentralized decision-making, and limited free enterprise. Much of the old hardline leadership – including Pham Văn Đông, Lê Đúc Tho, and Trúóng Chinh – retired. Two proponents of change, Nguyên Văn Linh and Vo Vân Kiêt, came to the fore. Linh replaced Trúóng Chinh as party secretary and the most powerful figure in the state. He had overseen the tentative steps towards a free market economy that had helped the South remain more prosperous than the North.

Linh's reform programme known as *đối mới* (renovation) produced progress. It introduced a profit incentive for farmers and allowed individuals to set up private businesses. Companies producing for export were granted tax concessions and foreign-owned firms could operate in the country and repatriate their profits (with a guarantee against being nationalized). However, Linh rejected opposition political parties and free elections.

Đối mới registered successes. Inflation dropped dramatically, food production went up and consumerism spread. But reform was uneven, as Party bureaucrats and conservatives inhibited its spread. Most advances came in the cities rather than in the countryside, where 80 per cent of the population lived.

The leadership also attempted to open Vietnam to the West and participated in talks in August 1987 with a US delegation on the MIA issue. The regime also came to terms with former South Vietnamese officials and groups once considered enemies of the SRV. In September 1987 the SRV released more than 6,000 military and political prisoners, including generals and senior officials of the former RVN government.

Hà Nôi realized that the SRV had to join the Southeast Asia development race or be left behind forever. Cambodia was the main problem inhibiting better relations with both the West and China. Leaving Cambodia would end the SRV's diplomatic isolation and lead to Western investment. It would also improve the possibility of the US ending its embargo of the SRV. Driven largely by economic reasons, in July 1988 Vietnam began withdrawing from Cambodia, an operation completed in September 1989. The Vietnamese also reduced their troop strength in Laos. And Foreign Minister Nguyên Có Thach travelled to Washington for talks, the highest-ranking Hà Nôi official to do so.

Meawhile in 1989 Soviet leader Mikhail Gorbachev embarked on reform programmes in the USSR that led to reduced aid to Vietnam. The Soviets also sharply cut back on their military presence, especially at Cam Ranh Bay, which had become the largest Soviet military base outside the USSR. Soviet aid ended altogether in 1991, when the USSR announced that henceforward all trade between the two countries would be in dollars at world market prices. The cutback in Soviet aid was another reason for Vietnam to mend its fences with Beijing, and in September 1990 Deputy Prime Minister Võ Nguyên Giáp travelled to China for talks.

At the same time within Vietnam the battle between conservatives and reformers intensified. The conservatives used the collapse of Communism in Eastern Europe to try to halt any movement towards political pluralism. In

1990, prompted by fears of an upheaval such as that occurring in Eastern Europe, the government ordered the arrests of hundreds of people, most of them in the South, some of them for what was referred to as too much contact with Westerners. There was also a public campaign against reported efforts of "reactionary forces overseas" to sabotage the state and socialism.

In August 1991 a major cabinet shake-up occurred. Đô Múoi became general secretary of the VCP succeeding Linh and Võ Văn Kiêt replaced Đô Múoi as premier. Giáp, who had been removed as minister of defence in 1986 and had been retained only as vice premier in charge of family planning, now lost that post as well. Among other changes, General Bùi Thiên Ngô became minister of the interior and General Đoàn Khuê, army chief of staff, became the new defence minister. At the same time Vietnam announced its intention to patch up relations with China.

Relations with the United States also improved. In February 1991 the SRV allowed the US to set up a "temporary" office in Hà Nôi to co-ordinate efforts to locate American MIAS of the Vietnam War. Hà Nôi also took steps to account for American MIAS in order to end Washington's economic embargo. US businesses seeking to invest in the SRV also applied pressure, and in September 1993 President Bill Clinton allowed American firms to compete for development projects in the SRV funded by international lending institutions. In 1995 Clinton normalized relations with the SRV and in May 1997 former Air Force POW Douglas "Pete" Peterson arrived in Hà Nôi as US ambassador.

PAVN influence remained strong. In 1996 military and internal security forces held six seats on the 19-member Politburo and three of five seats on a new standing committee charged with conducting day-to-day affairs. Clearly the party leadership hoped to protect the country's political and social structure. From the mid-1980s to 1996 the PAVN shrank by 50 per cent to an army of about 550,000 soldiers, navy of 40,000, air force of 15,000 and paramilitary force of 15,000. These figures do not include the Public Security force. The military budget remained high, however, having risen every year since 1992.

Vietnam, with its 75 million population (13th in the world with half born since the Vietnam War), aspires to be one of the "Asian Tigers". Chronic problems must be resolved first before that can happen. These include knitting North and South together and a lack of purchasing power, the consequence of a per capita income of $250 a year, among the world's lowest. The central issue for an aging leadership remains whether Vietnam can modernize using the Chinese model, successful thus far, without the Party relaxing political control. The leaders want continued rapid economic growth, but this has begun to transform the SRV in ways that make many of them uneasy.

Much of Vietnam's history has been forged in war. All warfare is unfortunate, but many of the conflicts that engulfed Vietnam, particularly those in her modern history, seem tragically unnecessary. Part of this was geographical, as Vietnam has been forced into a close relationship with China. But the rest is rooted in ideology, big-power confrontation, and miscalculations of individual leaders, many of them not Vietnamese.

Certainly the Vietnamese experience has much to teach the student of history and world statesmen about the causes of wars. By closely studying the history of warfare in Vietnam we can learn much about how to prevent other such conflicts.

Notes

EVW refers to S. C. Tucker (ed.), *Encyclopedia of the Vietnam War. A political, social, and military history* (Denver, CO, 1998).

Chapter One: The background

1. Quoted in General Y. Gras, *Histoire de La Guerre d'Indochine* (Paris, 1992), p. 584.
2. W. E. Echard (ed.), *Historical dictionary of the French Second Empire, 1852–70* (Westport, CT, 1985), p. 299.
3. R. J. Ross, "Geography of Indo-China and Vietnam", *EVW*.
4. In 1976 the Socialist Republic of Vietnam produced 13.5 million tons of rice; in 1992, 24 million. Other important agricultural products (all 1992 figures) are: peanuts, 223 million tons; coffee, 79.5 million tons; rubber, 74.2 million tons; sedge, 49.8 million tons; tea, 31.9 million tons; and tobacco, 29.7 million tons. Principal industrial products (all 1992 figures) are: crude oil, 5.5 million tons; coal, 4.8 million tons; cement, 3.4 million tons; steel, 175,000 tons; chemical fertilizers, 507,100 tons; and sugar, 303,600 tons. In 1992 Vietnam also produced 275,700,000 metres of cloth and 111,600 tons of paper. Nguyên Khač Viên, *Vietnam. A long history* (Hà Nôi, 1993), pp. 444–5.
5. B. Fall, *The two Viet Nams* (rev. ed., New York, 1964), pp. 4 and 8.
6. Ross, "Geography of Indo-China and Vietnam," *EVW*.
7. Fall, *The two Viet Nams*, pp. 5–6.
8. Such as Tân Van in Lang Són province, Nui (Mount) Do in Thanh Hóa, Quỳnh Vân in Nghê An, and Phung Nguyên in Phu Tho. For a brief survey of early Vietnamese history see Pham Cao Dúóng, "Vietnam: prehistory to 938", *EVW*; Nguyên Khăc Viên, *Vietnam. A long history*, p. 7.
9. It contained three rings of walls, the outer one of which extended some 8,000 metres and was 12 metres thick at the top (25 at the base) and 3 to 4 metres high. Moats protected the walls. In 1959 a cache of several thousand bronze arrowheads was unearthed nearby, and stone and bronze axes have also been discovered there. Nguyên Khăc Viên, *Vietnam. A long history*, p. 17.
10. Pham Cao Dúóng, "Vietnam: prehistory to 938", *EVW*.

11. K. W. Taylor, *The birth of Vietnam* (Berkeley, CA, 1983), pp. xvii–xviii. This is the standard work on the period.

12. Nguyên Khăc Viên, *Vietnam. A long history*, pp. 20–21; Pham Cao Dúóng, "Vietnam: Prehistory to 938", *EVW*.

13. Nguyên Khăc Viên, *Vietnam. A long history*, p. 24; also Pham Cao Dúóng, "Vietnam: prehistory to 938", *EVW*.

14. Taylor, *The birth of Vietnam*, pp. 38–9.

15. *Ibid.*, pp. 38–40.

16. *Ibid.*, p. 41.

17. *Ibid.*, p. 60.

18. *Ibid.*, pp. 60–66.

19. *Ibid.*, p. 90; Nguyên Khăc Viên, *Vietnam. A long history*, p. 26.

20. Taylor, *The birth of Vietnam*, pp. 135–55.

21. Pham Cao Dúóng, "Vietnam: prehistory to 938", *EVW*.

22. Taylor, *The birth of Vietnam*, pp. 264–8.

23. Pham Cao Dúóng, "Trân Húng Đao," in *VWE*; Nguyên Khăc Viên, *Vietnam. A Long History*, pp. 41–9. Other Vietnamese leaders resisting the Chinese include Lý Thúong Kiêt and Tôn Đan of the eleventh century; and Trân Quang Khai, Trân Khánh Dú, and Pham Ngu Lao of the thirteenth century.

24. Nguyên Khăc Viên, *Vietnam. A long history*, pp. 66–9.

25. Pham Cao Dúóng, "Vietnam: from 938 through the French conquest", *EVW*.

26. *Ibid.*; Fall, *The two Viet Nams*, pp. 12–13.

27. *Ibid.*, p. 13.

28. *Ibid.*, p. 14.

29. R. E. Dupuy and T. N. Dupuy, *The Harper encyclopedia of military history. From 3500 BC to the present* (4th ed., New York, 1993), pp. 718 and 768; Fall, *The two Viet Nams*, p. 14.

30. O. Chapuis, *A history of Vietnam from Hong Bang to Tu Duc* (Westport, CT, 1995), p. 155; Fall, *The two Viet Nams*, pp. 17–18.

31. Trúóng Búu Lâm, *Resistance, rebellion, and revolution: popular movements in Vietnamese history* (Singapore, 1984), p. 10; Nguyên Khăc Viên, *Vietnam. A long history*, p. 105.

32. Nguyên Lúóng Bich and Pham Ngoc Phùng, *Tìm Hiêu Thiên Tài Quân Sú cua Nguyên Huê* (Hà Nôi, 1971), p. 34.

33. Trân Trong Kim, *Viêt Nam Sú Lúóc* (Sài Gòn, 1971), pp. 105–6.

34. Nguyên Khăc Viên, *Vietnam. A long history*, pp. 106–7, gives 25 January 1785 as the date. The correct date is 18 January according to Nguyên Lúóng Bích and Phan Ngoc Phùng, *Tìm Hiêu Thiên Tài Quân Sú cua Nguyên Huê*, p. 94, or 19 January according to Uy Ban Khoa Hoc Xa Hôi Viêt Nam, *Lich Sú Viêt Nam* (Hà Nôi, 1971), p. 342. See also Lê Thành Khôi, *Histoire de Viêt Nam des origines à 1858* (Paris, 1981), pp. 316–17. A longer discussion of the battle is in Nguyên Lúóng Bich and Pham Ngoc Phùng, *Tìm Hiêu Thiên Tài Quân Sú cua Nguyên Huê*, pp. 47–103.

35. Trân Trong Kim, *Viêt Nam Sú Lúóc*, p. 113.

36. Nguyên Khăc Viên, *Vietnam. A long history*, pp. 106–7.

37. G. Devéria, *Histoire des relations de la Chine avec L'Annam-Viêtnam du XVIe au XIXe siècle* (Paris, 1880), pp. 16–17.

38. *Ibid.*, p. 17.

39. Trân Trong Kim, *Viêt Nam Sú Lúóc*, pp. 124–5.

40. Devéria, *Histoire des relations*, pp. 17–18.

41. Trân Trong Kim, *Viêt Nam Sú Lúóc*, p. 130; Devéria, *Histoire des relations*, pp. 19 and 24.

42. Devéria, *Histoire des relations*, pp. 23–4 and 30 gives Chinese strength as 10,000 men. Lê Thành Khôi, *Histoire de Viêt Nam*, pp. 323–4 cites 200,000, as does Nguyên Khăc Viên in *Vietnam. A long history*, p. 108.

43. Nguyên Lúóng Bích and Pham Ngoc Phùng, *Tìm Hiêu Thiên Tài Quân Sú Cua Nguyên Huê*, p. 189.

44. Ngô Gia Văn Phái, *Hoàng Lê Nhât Thông Chí*, p. 119; Lê Thành Khôi, *Histoire de Viêt Nam*, pp. 323–4; Devéria, *Histoire des relations*, pp. 27–30. Devéria gives 20 January, the Lunar date.

45. Nguyên Lúóng Bích and Pham Ngoc Phùng, *Tìm Hiêu Thiên Tài Quân Sú Cua Nguyên Huê*, p. 210; Devéria, *Histoire des relations*, pp. 32–3.

46. Trân Trong Kim, *Viêt Nam Su Luoc*, p. 131.

47. Chapuis, *A history of Vietnam from Hong Bang to Tu Duc*, p. 155; Nguyên Lúóng Bích and Pham Ngoc Phùng, *Tìm Hiêu Thiên Tài Quân Sú Cua Nguyên Huê*, p. 217.

48. Trân Trong Kim, *Viêt Nam Sú Lúóc*, p. 131.

49. Lê Thành Khôi, *Histoire de Viêt Nam*, p. 325; Nguyên Lúóng Bích and Pham Ngoc Phùng, *Tìm Hiêu Thiên Tài Quân Sú Cua Nguyên Huê*, pp. 219–20; Ngô Gia Văn Phái, *Hoàng Lê Nhât Thõng Chí*, pp. 356–60; Trân Trong Kim, *Viêt Nam Sú Lúóc*, p. 132.

50. Nguyên Lúóng Bích and Pham Ngoc Phùng, *Tìm Hiêu Thiên Tài Quân Sú Cua Nguyên Huê*, p. 231.

51. *Ibid.*

52. Lê Thành Khôi, *Histoire de Viêt Nam*, p. 326; Nguyên Khăc Viên, *Vietnam. A long history*, p. 109.

53. Lê Thành Khôi, *Histoire de Viêt Nam*, p. 326; Nguyên Lúóng Bích and Pham Ngoc Phùng, *Tìm Hiêu Thiên Tài Quân Sú Cua Nguyên Huê*, p. 246.

54. The victory is given little mention in most Western histories of Vietnam. J. Buttinger, *The smaller dragon: a political history of Vietnam* (New York, 1968), gives it less than a sentence and S. Karnow, *Vietnam, a history* (New York, 1983) and Dupuy and Dupuy, *The Harper encyclopedia of military history* do not mention it at all.

55. Lê Thành Khôi, *Histoire de Viêt Nam*, p. 328.

56. Đô Bang, *Nhúng Khám Phá Vê Quang Trung Hoàng Đê*, p. 202.

57. Devéria, *Histoire des relations*, pp. 35–44; Đô Bang, *Nhúng Khám Phá Vê Quang Trong Hoàng Đê*, p. 246.

58. *Ibid.*, pp. 226–7; Trân Trong Kim, *Viêt Nam Sú Lúóc*, pp. 136.

59. Đô Bang, *Nhúng Khám Phá Vê Quang Trung Hoàng Đê*, pp. 232–4; Nguyên Khăc Viên, *Vietnam. A long history*, pp. 110–12.

Chapter Two: French Indo-China

1. K. W. Taylor, *The birth of Vietnam* (Berkeley, CA, 1983), p. 60.

2. S. Karnow, *Vietnam, a history* (New York, 1983), p. 70; J. Buttinger, *Vietnam: a political history* (New York, 1968), p. 57.

3. Buttinger, *Vietnam: a political history*, pp. 59 and 62.

4. H. McAleavy, *Black Flags in Vietnam. The story of a Chinese intervention* (New York, 1968), p. 34. C. B. Currey, "De Rhodes, Alexandre", *EVW*; Pham Cao Dúóng, "Quôc Ngú," *EVW*.

5. B. Fall, *The two Viet Nams* (rev. ed., New York, 1964), p. 20.

6. A. J. Dommen, "Pigneau de Béhaine, Pierre," *EVW*; McAleavy, *Black Flags in Vietnam*, pp. 36–40; Karnow, *Vietnam*, pp. 75–8.

7. O. Chapuis, *A history of Vietnam from Hong Bang to Tu Duc* (Westport, CT, 1995), pp. 141–2.

8. Taylor, *The birth of Vietnam*, p. 44.

9. Chapuis, *A history of Vietnam from Hong Bang to Tu Duc*, p. 188.

10. McAleavy, *Black Flags in Vietnam*, pp. 39–40; Fall, *The two Viet Nams*, p. 21.

11. R. E. Dupuy and T. N. Dupuy, *The Harper encyclopedia of military history* (New York, 1993), pp. 866–7.

12. Fall, *The two Viet-Nams*, p. 14; M. E. Osborne, *The French presence in Cochinchina & Cambodia. Rule and response (1859–1905)* (Ithaca, NY, 1969), p. 10.

13. Dupuy and Dupuy, *The Harper encyclopedia of military history*, pp. 866–7.

14. Fall, *The two Viet-Nams*, p. 22.

15. W. E. Echard (ed.), *Historical dictionary of the French Second Empire* (Westport, CT, 1985), p. 299.

16. Buttinger, *Vietnam: a political history*, pp. 76–9; Karnow, *Vietnam, a history*, pp. 81–2.

17. G. Taboulet, "Les origines immédiates de l'intervention de la France en Indochine (1857–1958)", *Revue d'histoire des colonies françaises* **344** (1954–5), p. 293.

18. *Ibid.*, p. 294.

19. Chapuis, *A history of Vietnam from Hong Bang to Tu Duc*, p. 195.

20. Taboulet, "Les origines immédiates de l'intervention de la France en Indochine (1857–1958)", p. 299.

21. V. Thompson, *French Indo-China* (New York, 1968), p. 24; D. Porch, *The French Foreign Legion* (New York, 1991), p. 203; Buttinger, *Vietnam: a political history*, pp. 84–5.

22. Osborne, *The French presence in Cochinchina & Cambodia*, pp. 30 and 61; Thompson, *French Indo-China*, pp. 24–5; Nguyên Khăc Viên, *Vietnam. A long history* (Hà Nôi, 1993). pp. 142–3.

23. See F. Garnier, *Voyage d'exploration en Indochine*, ed. J.-P. Gomane (Paris, 1985); M. Osborne, *River road to China: the Mekong River expedition, 1866–73* (New York, 1975).

24. A. Dommen, "Garnier, Francis," *EVW*; Porch, *The French Foreign Legion*, p. 204. See also A. de Pouvourville, *Francis Garnier* (Paris, 1931).

25. On the Tonkin Wars see Porch, *The French Foreign Legion* and McAleavy, *Black Flags in Vietnam*. For the French side see J. Dupuis, *Le Tonkin de 1872 à 1886* (Paris, 1910) and J. F. C. Ferry, *Le Tonkin et la mère patrie* (Paris, 1890).

26. Nguyên Khăc Viên, *Vietnam. A long history*, p. 147.

27. Porch, *The French Foreign Legion*, pp. 207–8.

28. *Ibid.*, pp. 204–5.

29. *Ibid.*, p. 205.

30. *Ibid.*, pp. 207–12.

31. *Ibid.*, pp. 212–13.

32. *Ibid.*, pp. 213–15.

33. *Ibid.*, pp. 215–18.

34. McAleavy, *Black Flags in Vietnam*, pp. 272–5.

35. E. F. Jenkins, *A history of the French Navy* (Annapolis, MD, 1973), p. 306; Porch, *The French Foreign Legion*, pp. 205–6; McAleavy, *Black Flags in Vietnam*, pp. 256 and 276.

36. A. J. Dommen, *Conflict in Laos. The politics of neutralization* (New York, 1965), pp. 9–15.

37. Pham Cao Dúóng, "Hàm Nghi", *EVW*.

38. Ngô Ngoc Trung, "Đê Thám", *EVW*.

39. Buttinger, *Vietnam: a political history*, p. 133.

40. For a discussion of assimilationist theory see Thompson, *French Indo-China*.

41. Nguyên Khăc Viên, *Vietnam. A long history*, pp. 182–8; Thompson, *French Indo-China*, pp. 82, 87, and 145; C. B. Currey, *Victory at any cost. The genius of Viet Nam's Gen. Vo Nguyen Giap* (London, 1996), p. 19.

42. W. J. Duiker, *The rise of nationalism in Vietnam, 1900–1941* (Ithaca, NY, 1976), pp. 213–16.

43. S. Tucker, "Catroux, Georges", *EVW*. See also Général Catroux, *Deux actes du drame Indochinois* (Paris, 1959); Currey, *Victory at any cost*, p. 41; and D. G. Marr, *Vietnam, 1945. The quest for power* (Berkeley, CA, 1996), pp. 14–27.

44. On the war see Admiral J. Decoux, *A la barre de L'Indochine* (Paris, 1949); J. Meisler, "Koh Chang. The unknown battle. Franco–Thai War of 1940–41", *World War II Investigator* (London) **II** (14) (1989), pp. 26–34; J. Mordal, *Marine Indochine* (Paris, 1953); and J. Mordal and G. Auphan, *La marine française pendant la Deuxième Guerre Mondiale* (Paris, 1958).

45. Marr, *Vietnam, 1945*, pp. 24–7.

46. Duiker, *The rise of nationalism in Vietnam*, pp. 275–7.

47. On this see A. L. A. Patti, *Why Viet Nam? Prelude to America's albatross* (Berkeley, CA, 1980), pp. 337–9.

48. Currey, *Victory at any cost*, pp. 67–9.

49. Marr, *Vietnam, 1945*, pp. 51–69; S. Tucker, "Sabattier, Gabriel", *EVW*.

50. Patti, *Why Viet Nam?*, pp. 337–9.

51. *Le Clerc et l'Indochine, 1945–1947. Quand se noua le destin d'un empire* (Paris, 1992), pp. 95 and 182; Currey, *Victory at any cost*, pp. 106–7.

52. On Leclerc see a series of essays by various authors in *Leclerc et l'Indochine, 1945–7* and P. Devillers, *Histoire du Vietnam de 1940 à 1952* (Paris, 1952).

53. C. de Gaulle, *The complete war memoirs of Charles de Gaulle* (New York, 1955), p. 927; E. J. Hammer, *The struggle for Indochina* (Stanford, CA, 1954), p. 112; G. Férier, *Les trois guerres d'Indochine* (Lyon, 1993), pp. 19 and 40–42; *Leclerc et l'Indochine*, passim.

54. *Leclerc et l'Indochine*, pp. 280–81.

55. Férier, *Les trois guerres d'Indochine*, p. 19.

56. J. Sainteny, *Histoire d'une paix manquée, Indochine 1945–7* (Paris, 1953), p. 183.

57. *Ibid.*, pp. 182–5.

58. J. de Folin, *Indochine, 1940–1955. Le fin d'un rêve* (Paris, 1993), pp. 149 and 162.

59. S. Tucker, "Sabattier, Gabriel", *EVW*; Sainteny, *Histoire d'une paix manquée*, pp. 197–211; interview with Pham Van Dong, *Vietnam: a television history*, (wGBH Boston, Central Independent Television/UK and Antenne-2, France, 1985 and 1987), vol. 1.

60. D. Halberstam, *Ho* (New York, 1971), p. 12.

61. D. Schoenbrun, *As France goes* (New York, 1968), pp. 234–5.

62. Hammer, *The struggle for Indochina*, p. 183.

63. *Ibid.*

64. *Ibid.*; Karnow, *Vietnam, a history*, p. 172. De Folin estimates the dead at a maximum of 300; J. de Folin, *Indochine, 1940–55* (Paris, 1993), p. 179.

Chapter Three: The Indo-China War (1946–54)

1. R. E. Dupuy and T. N. Dupuy, *The Harper encyclopedia of military history* (New York, 1993), p. 1321. The authors note that CBS correspondent Eric Sevareid used the phrase "Thirty Years War" in a news broadcast on 22 April 1975.

2. D. Schoenbrun, *As France Goes* (New York, 1968), pp. 234–5.

3. J. de Folin, *Indochine, 1940–55. La fin d'un rêve* (Paris, 1993), p. 192. J. Dalloz, *The war in Indo-China, 1945–54* (trans. J. Bacon; New York, 1990), p. 97.

4. T. R. Carver, *Đấu tranh, EVW.*

5. C. B. Currey, *Victory at any cost* (London, 1996), pp. 80–81, 145, and 150–51.

6. Mao Tse-tung, *Struggle of the Chin Kan Shan Mountains* (1928), which outlined the training of guerrilla units; *Guerrilla warfare* (1937); and *The strategic problems of the Anti-Japanese War* (1938).

7. Currey, *Victory at any cost*, pp. 52–3 and 165; Dalloz, *The war in Indo-China*, p. 97. For Giáp's own writings see *Dien Bien Phu* (Hanoi, 1984), *The military art of people's war, selected writings* (New York, 1971), and *People's war, people's army* (forward by R. Hilsman; New York, 1962).

8. B. Fall, *The two Viet Nams* (rev. ed., New York, 1964), p. 113.

9. Currey, *Victory at any cost*, pp. 52–3; G. Férier, *Les trois guerres d'Indochine* (Lyon, 1993), pp. 52–6; Fall, *The two Viet Nams*, p. 113.

10. P. Macdonald, *Giap. The victor in Vietnam* (New York, 1993), p. 79.

11. B. Fall, *Street without joy* (Garden City, NY, 1967), pp. 268–9. Dalloz gives a figure of a ton of materiel a month for every ten men. Dalloz, *The war in Indo-China*, pp. 147–8.

12. Fall, *The two Viet Nams*, p. 107.

13. Dalloz, *The war in Indo-China*, p. 105.

14. Férier, *Les trois guerres d'Indochine*, p. 49; Dalloz, *The war in Indo-China*, p. 103.

15. US Department of State, *Aggression from the north. The record of North Viet-Nam's campaign to conquer South Viet-Nam* (Washington, DC, 1965), p. 3.

16. *Ibid.*, p. 104. Official French Army figures are slightly different: a total of 144,000 French Union troops, plus 40,000 auxilaries. Férier, *Les trois guerres d'Indochine*, p. 57.

17. L. Bodard, *La Guerre d'Indochine, l'enlissement*, cited by Férier, *Les trois guerres d'Indochine*, p. 56.

18. Férier, *Les trois guerres d'Indochine*, pp. 58–60; H. Navarre, *L'agonie de l'Indochine* (Paris, 1956), p. 48.

19. Dalloz, *The war in Indo-China*, p. 85.

20. E. J. Hammer, *The struggle for Indochina* (Stanford, CA, 1954), pp. 231–6.

21. J. Buttinger, *Vietnam: a political history* (New York, 1968), p. 278.

22. Macdonald, *Giap*, pp. 82 and 88.

23. Dalloz, *The war in Indo-China*, pp. 96–7 and 86; J. Vallette, *La guerre d'Indochine, 1945–1954* (Paris, 1994), pp. 108–10. Nguyên Khăc Viên, *Vietnam. A long history* (Hà Nôi, 1993), p. 264. Fall gives French strength in the operation at 15,000 men. Fall, *Street without joy*, pp. 28–31.

24. Currey, *Victory at any cost*, pp. 162–4.

25. De Folin, *Indochine*, p. 204.

26. R. H. Spector, *Advice and support. The early years. United States Army in Vietnam* (Washington, 1983), p. 125; MacDonald, *Giap*, p. 93.

27. In 1947 this went as far as Truman insisting that US-made propellers not be used on British aircraft supplied to the French in Indo-China. V. Bator, *Vietnam: a diplomatic tragedy* (Dobbs Ferry, NY, 1956), p. 206.

28. Spector, *Advice and support*, p. 110.

29. *New York Times* (28 June 1950).

30. Spector, *Advice and support*, p. 123; Férier, *Les trois guerres d'Indochine*, p. 22; S. Karnow, *Vietnam a history* (New York, 1983), p. 192; de Folin, *Indochine*, pp. 204 and 319–20.

31. Spector, *Advice and support*, p. 131.

32. Currey, *Victory at any cost*, pp. 157 and 93; Spector, *Advice and support*, p. 124.

33. Currey, *Victory at any cost*, p. 161.

34. Ibid., p. 167. On the fighting for RC4 see P. Charton, *Indochine 1950. La tragédie de l'évacuation de Cao Bang* (Paris, 1975); and Đăng Văn Kiêt, *Highway 4, the border campaign (1947–1950)* (Hanoi, 1990).

35. D. Porch, *The French Foreign Legion* (New York, 1991), pp. 520–21.

36. *Ibid.*, p. 521.

37. *Ibid.*, pp. 521–5; Y. Gras, *Histoire de la guerre d'Indochine* (Pasis, 1992), pp. 323–54.

38. Fall, *Street without joy*, p. 33; Gras, *Histoire de la guerre d'Indochine*, p. 354; Valette, *La guerre d'Indochine*, pp. 115–16. The figure of 4,800 killed and missing is from Gras; Fall gives 6,000.

39. Fall, *Street without joy*, p. 33; Gras, *Histoire de la guerre d'Indochine*, p. 354.

40. Currey, *Victory at any cost*, p. 178.

41. *Ibid.*; Valette, *La guerre d'Indochine*, p. 119.

42. Currey, *Victory at any cost*, p. 178; Spector, *Advice and support*, pp. 135–6; Férier, *Les trois guerres d'Indochine*, p. 44; Fall, *The two Viet Nams*, p. 115; Gras, *Histoire de la guerre d'Indochine*, pp. 390 and 443–4.

43. Currey, *Victory at any cost*, p. 131; Valette, *La guerre d'Indochine*, p. 117.

44. Gras, *Histoire de la guerre d'Indochine*, pp. 375–83; Fall, *The two Viet Nams*, p. 116.

45. Gras, *Histoire de la guerre de l'Indochine*, pp. 399–400; Fall, *The two Viet Nams*, p. 116.

46. Fall, *Street without joy*, pp. 43–7; Fall, *The two Viet Nams*, p. 117; Currey, *Victory at any cost*, pp. 173–5; Gras, *Histoire de la guerre d'Indochine*, pp. 404–10.

47. Fall, *Street without joy*, pp. 47–60; Fall, *The two Viet Nams*, pp. 118–19; Gras, *Histoire de la guerre d'Indochine*, pp. 424–37.

48. Férier, *Les trois guerres d'Indochine*, p. 70.

49. M. Bigeard, *Pour une parcelle de gloire* (Paris, 1976), pp. 107–18; Gras, *Histoire de la guerre d'Indochine*, p. 476.

50. Fall, *The two Viet Nams*, p. 119; Currey, *Victory at any cost*, p. 178; M. Bigeard, *De la brousse à la jungle* (Paris, 1994), p. 38.

51. Fall, *Street without joy*, pp. 103–5.

52. *Ibid.*, p. 120.

53. *Ibid.*, pp. 121–2.

54. Navarre, *Agonie de l'Indochine*, pp. 44 and 46–7.

55. Currey, *Victory at any cost*, p. 181; Fall, *The two Viet Nams*, pp. 122–5; Vallete, *La guerre d'Indochine*, p. 400; see also pp. 293–311. De Folin notes that US ambassadors to France Jefferson Caffery and David Bruce rejected out of hand possible peace feelers. De Folin, *Indochine*, p. 192.

56. Navarre, *L'agonie de l'Indochine*, pp. 103–10, 132 and 140–42; Valette, *La guerre d'Indochine*, pp. 183–92; Fall, *The two Viet Nams*, p. 124.

57. Navarre, *L'agonie de l'Indochine*, pp. 62–88.

58. Bigeard, *Pour une parcelle de gloire*, pp. 128–32. Gras gives the number of submachine guns taken at only 500, still enough for ten battalions. He also notes that the destruction of the arms was not complete. Gras, *Histoire de la guerre d'Indochine*, pp. 515–16.

59. P. B. Davidson, *Vietnam at war* (Novato, CA, 1988), pp. 168–9.

60. Gras, *Histoire de la guerre d'Indochine*, p. 516; Dalloz, *The war in Indo-China, 1945–54*, pp. 147–8; H. R. Simpson, *Dien Bien Phu: the epic battle America forgot* (Washington, 1994), p. 170.

61. Gras, *Histoire de la guerre d'Indochine*, pp. 517 and 526.

62. Fall, *The two Viet Nams*, p. 127; Davidson, *Vietnam at war*, pp. 211–12; Currey, *Victory at any cost*, p. 182.

63. Fall, *The two Viet Nams*, pp. 125–6; Valette, *La guerre d'Indochine*, pp. 319–20.

64. On the battle see B. Fall, *Hell in a very small place: the siege of Dien Bien Phu* (Philadelphia, 1967); J. Roy, *The battle of Dienbienphu* (New York, 1965); Simpson, *Dien Bien Phu*; and Võ Nguyên Giáp, *Dien Bien Phu*, 5th ed., revised and supplemented (Hanoi, 1994).

65. Navarre, *L'agonie de l'Indochine*, p. 197.

66. Gras, *La guerre d'Indochine*, p. 521.

67. Currey, *Victory at any cost*, pp. 183–4.

68. *New York Times*, 31 July 1991.

69. Navarre, *L'agonie de l'Indochine*, pp. 107–9. Fall states that until April 1954 the French never had more than ten operational helicopters in Indo-China. Fall, *Street without joy*, p. 242.

70. Valette, *La guerre d'Indochine*, p. 331; Giáp, *The military art of people's war*, p. 159.

71. Roy, *Dien Bien Phu*, p. 138; Currey, *Victory at any cost*, p. 189.

72. Simpson, *Dien Bien Phu*, p. 40.

73. Roy, *Dien Bien Phu*, p. 138; Currey, *Victory at any cost*, p. 189

74. Simpson, *Dien Bien Phu*, p. 36. Delivered in two sections, chassis and turret, they were then assembled with block and tackle rig.

75. Gras, *Histoire de la guerre d'Indochine*, p. 546.

76. For the order of battle see Fall, *Hell in a very small place*, pp. 479–87.

77. Since Giáp has never spelled out precisely PAVN artillery strength in the battle, these are only estimates. Davidson, *Vietnam at war*, pp. 223–4. See also Fall, *Hell in a very small place*, p. 451; Currey, *Victory at any cost*, p. 196.

78. Fall, *Hell in a very small place*, pp. 134–5 and 144.

79. Gras, *Histoire de la guerre d'Indochine*, p. 560.

80. Fall, *Hell in a very small place*, pp. 174–5.

81. *Ibid.*, pp. 183–5.

82. Bigeard, *Pour une paracelle de gloire*, pp. 161–7.

83. Giáp, *Dien Bien Phu*, p. 130.

84. Currey, *Victory at any cost*, pp. 202–3; Giáp, *The military art of people's war*, p. 152.

85. Fall, *Hell in a very small place*, p. 432.

86. Gras, *Histoire de la guerre de l'Indochine*, p. 561.

87. Fall, *Hell in a very small place*, pp. 432 and 483–4; Fall, *Street without joy*, p. 300; A. Teulières, *Les guerres du Viêt-nam* (Paris, 1978), p. 248; Porch, *The French Foreign Legion*, p. 561.

88. Spector, *Advice and support*, p. 194.

89. G. W. Ball, *The past has another pattern* (New York, 1982), p. 360.

90. Gras, *Histoire de la guerre de l'Indochine*, p. 560; De Folin, *Indochine*, pp. 259–60; A. Short, *The origins of the Vietnam War* (New York, 1989), p. 130. See Spector, *Advice and support*, pp. 191–214. See also M. Billings-Yun, *Decision against war: Eisenhower and Dien Bien Phu* (New York, 1988) and J. Prados, *The sky would fall. Operation Vulture: the US bombing mission to Vietnam, 1954* (New York, 1983).

91. Eden to Foreign Office, 26 April 1954, in L. C. Gardner, *Approaching Vietnam. From World War II through Dienbienphu* (New York, 1988), p. 256.

92. Férier, *Les trois guerres d'Indochine*, pp. 61–2.

93. Fall, *The two Viet Nams*, p. 127. On the death of Groupe Mobile 100 see Fall, *Street without joy*, pp. 185–243.

94. P. Ély, *Mémoires. L'Indochine dans la tourmente* (Paris, 1964), pp. 133–62.

95. Navarre, *L'agonie de l'Indochine*, pp. 318–21.

96. The standard work on the conference is R. F. Randle, *Geneva 1954. The settlement of the Indochinese War* (Princeton, NJ, 1969). The full text of the Accords is on pp. 569–610. See especially Document I, Articles 6 and 7, pp. 570–71.

97. Dalloz, *The war in Indo-China*, p. 185; Férier, *Les trois guerres d'Indochine*, pp. 57 and 69; Fall, *The two Viet Nams*, p. 129.

98. Férier, *Les trois guerres d'Indochine*, pp. 62–5; Fall, *Street without joy*, p. 308.

99. Férier, *Les trois guerres d'Indochine*, pp. 62–5; Dalloz, *The war in Indo-China*, p. 186; Valette, *La guerre d'Indochine*, p. 398; Fall, *Street without joy*, p. 300; de Folin, *Indochine*, pp. 290–91.

Chapter Four: The United States takes over

1. Y. Gras, *Histoire de la guerre de l'Indochine* (Paris, 1992), pp. 580–81. Spector gives a figure of 800,000 people "transported to South Vietnam", 311,000 of whom were moved by US Navy Task Force 90. R. H. Spector, *Advice and support* (Washington, DC, 1983), p. 227.

2. C. B. Currey, "Ngô Đình Diêm", *EVW*. On early American support see J. G. Morgan, *The Vietnam lobby. The American friends of Vietnam, 1955–1975* (Chapel Hill, NC, 1997).

3. Currey, "Ngô Đình Diêm", *EVW*. Spector, *Advice and support*, p. 304.

4. Spector, *Advice and support*, pp. 228–30.

5. J. M. Gavin, *Crisis now* (New York, 1968), p. 49.

6. Spector, *Advice and support*, pp. 231–7 and 254; Gras, *Histoire de la guerre de l'Indochine*, p. 582.

7. US Department of State, *American foreign policy, 1950–1955: basic documents*, I, pp. 913 and 916; R. J. Ross, "Southeast Asia Treaty Organization (SEATO)", *EVW*.

8. Spector, *Advice and support*, pp. 237–8.

9. See C. B. Currey, *Edward Lansdale: the unquiet American* (Boston, 1988), p. 174.

10. Spector, *Advice and support*, pp. 243–9. Interview with Collins, *Vietnam, a television history* (WGBH Boston, Central Independent Television/UK and Antenne-2, France, 1985 and 1987), vol. II, part 1.

11. Currey, *Edward Lansdale*, p. 180.

12. Spector, *Advice and support*, pp. 253–68.

13. H. J. Meyer, *Hanging Sam. A military biography of Samuel T. Williams* (Denton, TX, 1990), pp. 137–44; Spector, *Advice and support*, pp. 272–6; J. R. Arnold, *The first domino*.

Eisenhower, the military, and America's intervention in Vietnam (New York, 1991), pp. 306–7.

14. B. B. Fall, *The two Viet Nams* (New York, 1964), p. 325.
15. Spector, *Advice and support*, pp. 272–3.
16. *Ibid.*, pp. 278–86, 300, 344–7.
17. *Ibid.*, pp. 265, 268 and 295.
18. *Ibid.*, pp. 296–7.
19. *Ibid.*, pp. 298–9.
20. D. J. Duncanson, *Government and revolution in Vietnam* (New York, 1968), p. 277.
21. In 1958 US aid paid for 84 per cent of RVN military and 44 per cent of nonmilitary expenditures. Spector, *Advice and support*, p. 306.
22. Spector, *Advice and support*, p. 308; also D. Berman, "FULRO", *EVW*.
23. Eisenhower estimated that if elections had been held at the end of the fighting, Hô Chí Minh would have won 80 per cent of the vote. D. D. Eisenhower, *Mandate for change 1953–1956* (Garden City, NY, 1963), p. 372.
24. D. Hotham, "South Vietnam, shaky bastion", *New Republic* (25 November 1957) quoted in Spector, *Advice and support*, p. 305.
25. See Spector, *Advice and support*, pp. 311–12.
26. E. M. Bergerud, *The dynamics of defeat. The Vietnam War in Hau Nghia Province* (Boulder, CO, 1991), pp. 48–9.
27. *Ibid.*, pp. 313–16.
28. Formed in the DRV in 1951, the Lao Đông Party was in existence until 1986. Its formal name was Dang Lao Đông Viêt Nam. It was in fact synonymous with the Indo-Chinese Communist Party, which underwent a number of metamorphoses.
29. C. B. Currey, *Victory at any cost* (New York, 1996), p. 238. See also W. J. Duiker, *The Communist road to power in Vietnam*, 2nd ed. (Boulder, CO, 1996).
30. *Ibid.*
31. *Ibid.*, p. 233.
32. *Aggression from the North*, p. 5.
33. Nguyên Khăc Viên, *Vietnam. A long history* (Hà Nôi, 1993), p. 305; Currey, *Victory at any cost*, pp. 238–9.
34. Fall, *The two Viet Nams*, pp. 359–61.
35. G. McT. Kahin, *Intervention. How America became involved in Vietnam* (New York, 1986), p. 111.
36. *Ibid.*, p. 112.
37. Arnold, *The first domino*, pp. 354–5; Spector, *Advice and support*, p. 338.
38. Spector, *Advice and support*, pp. 342–3.
39. D. Halbertstam, *The best and the brightest* (New York, 1969), p. 183.
40. Spector, *Advice and support*, pp. 340–41.
41. Nguyên Khăc Viên, *Vietnam. A long history*, p. 304.
42. Spector, *Advice and support*, pp. 335–6 and 353.
43. For US Army doctrinal failure regarding counter-insurgency warfare see A. F. Krepinevich, Jr. *The Army and Vietnam* (Baltimore, MD, 1986), pp. 44–6.
44. *Ibid.*, pp. 349–55; S. L. Stanton, *Green Berets at war. US Army Special Forces in Southeast Asia 1960–1975* (Novato, CA, 1985), pp. 36–7.
45. Duncanson, *Government and revolution in Vietnam*, p. 323.
46. Spector, *Advice and support*, pp. 36–71.
47. Ball, *The past has another pattern*, p. 361–2.

48. See A. J. Dommen, *Conflict in Laos. The politics of neutralization* (New York, 1964).
49. Halberstam, *The best and the brightest*, pp. 132 and 182.
50. D. Coffey, "Staley, Eugene", *EVW*; Duncanson, *Government and revolution in Vietnam*, pp. 316–27.
51. P. Roberts, "Rostow, Walt W.", *EVW*; P. S. Daum, "Taylor, Maxwell D.", *EVW*, pp.; Ball, *The past has another pattern*, pp. 365–6.
52. Ball, *The past has another pattern*, p. 366.
53. J. S. Bowman (ed.), *The world almanac of the Vietnam War* (New York, 1985), p. 55.
54. Office of Assistant Secretary of Defense (Comptroller). In G. Lewy, *America in Vietnam* (New York, 1978), p. 24.
55. Duncanson, *Government and revolution in Vietnam*, p. 323.
56. We have an accurate picture of the VC side of the battle thanks to a report captured two months later. C. J. Gaspar, "Âp Bắc, Battle of", *EVW*; and N. Sheehan, *A bright shining lie. John Paul Vann and America in Vietnam* (New York, 1988), pp. 203–65.
57. Duncanson, *Government and revolution in Vietnam*, pp. 324–5.
58. *Ibid.*, p. 325.
59. *Ibid.*, pp. 228–33.
60. *Ibid.*, pp. 336–7.
61. J. M. Newman, *JFK and Vietnam. Deception, intrigue, and the struggle for power* (New York, 1992), pp. 322–4.
62. *Ibid.*, pp. 324–5.
63. In a recent rating of US Presidents by prominent US historians, Johnson received votes for both "Great" and "Failure". He ended up ranked "Average (High)". Clearly the Vietnam War dragged down his rating. A. M. Schlesinger, Jr., "The ultimate approval rating," *New York Times Magazine*, 16 December 1996, p. 49.
64. G. C. Herring, "The War in Vietnam", in R. A. Divine (ed.), *The Johnson years. Volume One: Foreign policy, the Great Society, and the White House* (Lawrence, Kansas, 1987), p. 337.
65. Quoted in S. Karnow, *Vietnam* (New York, 1983), p. 336.
66. Recorded phone conversation with National Security Adviser McGeorge Bundy, 27 May 1964, reported in the *New York Times*, 15 February 1997.
67. N. Podhoretz, *Why we were in Vietnam* (New York, 1982), p. 80.
68. R. S. McNamara with B. VanDeMark, *In retrospect. The tragedy and lessons of Vietnam* (New York, 1995).
69. Ball, *The past has another pattern*, p. 369.
70. Bowman, *The world almanac of the Vietnam War*, p. 56.
71. McNamara, *In retrospect*, p. 105.
72. A. Short, *The origins of the Vietnam War* (London and New York, 1989), p. 281.
73. Kahin, *Intervention*, p. 189.
74. J. Valenti, in *Vietnam, a television history*, vol. II, part 2.
75. Up to 1997 more than 70 million had been produced and they were used in the armies of 55 nations. M. R. Gordon, "Burst of pride for a staccato executioner: AK–47", *New York Times*, 13 March 1997. The US M–16, however, could fire more rounds without overheating and had a greater effective range; its ammunition was also lighter (hence more could be carried) and it was easier to reload.
76. W. Head, "BARREL ROLL, Operation", *EVW*.
77. Krepinevich, *The Army and Vietnam*, pp. 166–7.
78. W. C. Westmoreland, *A soldier reports* (New York, 1976), pp. 98–9 and 101.

79. MACV divided South Vietnam into four corps zones with I Corps located in the north and IV being the Mekong Delta area.

80. Westmoreland, *A soldier reports*, pp. 99–100.

81. *Ibid.*, p. 101.

82. F. FitzGerald, *Fire in the lake. The Vietnamese and the Americans in Vietnam* (Boston, 1972), p. 271.

83. Westmoreland, *A soldier reports*, p. 102.

84. In February 1968 McNamara testified before the Senate Foreign Relations Committee in closed session that he had "unimpeachable" proof of a second attack. In November 1995 General Giáp met with McNamara in Hà Nôi and discussed the Tonkin Gulf incidents. He confirmed the first attack, which he said was the work of "a local coast guard unit". But he denied there had been any attack on 4 August. He also charged the Johnson Administration with a deliberate "plan of sabotage activities on the sea and in the air in order to seek the approval of Congress". T. Larimer, "Hanoi, ex-foes revisit Vietnam War's turning point", *New York Times*, 10 November 1995.

85. See E. E. Moïse, *Tonkin Gulf and the escalation of the Vietnam War* (Chapel Hill, NC, 1996), especially pp. 106–207.

86. The best study of the Tonkin Gulf incidents is Moïse, *Tonkin Gulf and the escalation of the Vietnam War*.

87. Principal opposition came from Under Secretary of State George W. Ball. See Ball's memoirs.

88. *The Pentagon papers* (New York, 1971), p. 249.

89. J. G. Stoessinger, *Why nations go to war*, 5th ed. (New York, 1990), p. 100.

90. Bowman, *The world almanac of the Vietnam War*, p. 104.

91. I. V. Gaiduk, *The Soviet Union and the Vietnam War* (Chicago, 1996), pp. 27–31.

92. Bowman, *The world almanac of the Vietnam War*, p. 104.

93. *Ibid.*, pp. 104–5.

94. *Aggression from the North*, pp. iii, 3, 11 and 15–19.

95. Halberstam, *The best and the brightest*, p. 528.

96. Bowman, *The world almanac of the Vietnam War*, p. 106. On the Marines' arrival see J. Shulimson and Major C. M. Johnson, USMC, *US Marines in Vietnam, 1965, the landing and the buildup* (Washington, DC, 1978).

Chapter Five: The quagmire

1. J. Shulimson and Major C. M. Johnson, *U.S. Marines in Vietnam, 1965* (Washington, DC, 1978), p. 50.

2. C. L. Cooper *et al.*, *The American experience with pacification in Vietnam* (3 vols, Washington, 1972), vol. I, p. 4.

3. Shulimson and Johnson, *U.S. Marines in Vietnam, 1965*, pp. 35–50.

4. J. S. Bowman (ed.), *The world almanac of the Vietnam War* (New York, 1985), p. 110.

5. *Ibid.*, p. 110; G. W. Ball, *The past has another pattern* (New York, 1982), p. 393.

6. Repeated by Bill Moyers, in *Vietnam, a television history* (WGBH Boston, Central Independent Television/UK and Antenne-2, France, 1985 and 1987), vol. II, part 2.

7. Bowman, *The world almanac of the Vietnam War*, p. 111.

8. W. C. Westmoreland, *A soldier reports* (Garden City, NY, 1976), p. 159.

9. Bowman, *The world almanac of the Vietnam War*, p. 114.

10. Shulimson and Johnson, *U.S. Marines in Vietnam, 1966*, p. 51.

11. Westmoreland, *A soldier reports*, pp. 168 and 170.

12. Bowman, *The world almanac of the Vietnam War*, p. 119.

13. Shulimson and Johnson, *U.S. Marines in Vietnam, 1965*, pp. 51–2.

14. L. Berman, *Lyndon Johnson's war* (New York, 1989), p. 9; Westmoreland, *A soldier reports*, p. 51; "Memorandum for President Lyndon Johnson by Secretary of Defense Robert McNamara", 20 July 1965, Lyndon Baines Johnson Presidential Library.

15. Westmoreland, *A soldier reports*, p. 51; Berman, *Lyndon Johnson's war*, p. 9.

16. J. G. Stoessinger, *Why nations go to war*, 5th ed. (New York, 1990), pp. 102–03.

17. Quoted in A. F. Krepinevich, Jr, *The Army and Vietnam* (Baltimore, MD, 1986), p. 261. For Taylor's views on the war see M. Taylor, *Swords and plowshares* (New York, 1972).

18. Author's personal experience as the desk officer for Laos and the DRV, Special Security Detachment, Assistant Chief of Staff for Intelligence, Army, at the Pentagon, 1966–7.

19. H. G. Summers, Jr, *On strategy, a critical analysis of the Vietnam War* (Novato, CA, 1982), p. 119.

20. Krepinevich, *The Army and Vietnam*, pp. 261–8.

21. *Ibid.*, p. 214.

22. E. H. Tilford, Jr, "Why and how the U.S. Air Force lost in Vietnam", *Armed Forces & Society* **17**(3) (Spring 1991), p. 327. On the air war see M. Clodfelter, *The limits of air power. The American bombing of North Vietnam* (New York, 1989) and E. H. Tilford, Jr, *Setup. What the Air Force did in Vietnam and why* (Maxwell Air Force Base, AL, 1991).

23. W. J. Boyne, "Airplanes, US and DRV", *EVW*; Clodfelter, *The limits of air power*, p. 133.

24. Clodfelter, *The limits of air power*, p. 131.

25. On air-to-air combat during the war see M. Michel, *Clashes. Air combat over North Vietnam 1965–1972* (Annapolis, MD, 1997).

26. Clodfelter, *The limits of air power*, p. 131; P. K. Barker, "Air defense, Democratic Republic of Vietnam (1964–1972)", *EVW*; P. K. Barker, "Surface-to-air missiles (SAMs)", *EVW*. SAM totals are from M. Clodfelter, *Vietnam in military statistics* (Jefferson, NC and London, 1993), pp. 227–8.

27. M. Muir, Jr, "Aircraft carriers", *EVW*.

28. Barker, "Surface-to-air missiles (SAMs)", *EVW*.

29. E. H. Tilford, Jr, "ROLLING THUNDER", *EVW*.

30. *Ibid.*, p..

31. Tilford, "Why and how the U.S. Air Force lost in Vietnam", p. 330. See also Tilford, "ROLLING THUNDER", *EVW*.

32. M. Muir, Jr, "U.S. Navy", *EVW*.

33. Shulimson and Johnson, *US Marines in Vietnam, 1965*, p. 51.

34. S. S. McGowen, "Helicopters, employment of in Vietnam", *EVW*.

35. On its formation see J. D. Coleman, *Pleiku. The dawn of helicopter warfare in Vietnam* (New York, 1988), pp. 1–32; C. B. Currey, *Victory at any cost* (New York, 1996), p. 255.

36. Coleman, *Pleiku*, pp. 46–8.

37. Currey, *Victory at any cost*, p. 253.

38. Lt. Gen. H. G. Moore and J. L. Galloway, *We were soldiers once ... and young* (New York, 1992), p. 12.

39. Coleman, *Pleiku*, pp. 70–90.

40. The best book on the battle is Moore and Galloway, *We were soldiers once … and young*.

41. Arc Light was the code name for B–52 strikes within South Vietnam.

42. J. L. Bell, "Ia Drang, Battle of", *EVW*; Currey, *Victory at any cost*, p. 255.

43. Moore and Galloway, *We were soldiers once … and young*, p. 339; letter from Cecil Curry to the author, 16 May 1997.

44. Moore and Galloway, *We were soldiers once … and young*, p. 339.

45. E. O'Ballance, *The wars in Vietnam, 1954–1980* (rev. ed,) New York, 1981), p. 86.

46. See S. C. Tucker, "Nguyên Cao Kỳ", *EVW*. See also Kỳ's memoir, *Twenty years and twenty days* (New York, 1976).

47. S. Karnow, *Vietnam, a history* (New York, 1983), p. 460.

48. The total far surpassed that of 39,000 Allied troops supporting the Republic of Korea during the Korean War. See J. H. Willbanks, "Australia", *EVW*; F. H. Thompson, "Korea, Republic of", *EVW*. On "Many Flags" see S. R. Larsen and J. L. Collins, Jr, *Allied participation in Vietnam* (Washington, DC, 1975).

49. J. Shulimson, *US Marines in Vietnam, 1966, an expanding war* (Washington, DC, 1982), pp. 19–36.

50. See General L. W. Walt, *Strange war, strange strategy, a general's report on Vietnam* (New York, 1970).

51. W. E. Fahey, Jr, "Krulak, Victor H.", *EVW*; M. E. Peterson, *The combined action platoons; the US Marines' other war in Vietnam* (New York, 1989), p. 22. See also V. H. Krulak, *First to fight* (Annapolis, MD, 1984).

52. D. R. Palmer, *Summons of the trumpet. US–Vietnam in perspective* (San Rafael, CA, 1979), p. 151.

53. Peterson, *The combined action platoons*, pp. 35 and 69.

54. D. M. Berman, "Civic action", *EVW*. On the CAP concept see A. Hemingway, *Our war was different: Marine combined action platoons in Vietnam* (Annapolis, MD, 1994) and Peterson, *The combined action platoons*.

55. P. R. Camacho, "Elections (National), Republic of Vietnam: 1955, 1967, 1971", *EVW*.

56. Nguyên Cao Kỳ, *Twenty years and twenty days*, p. 77.

57. Camacho, "Elections (National), Republic of Vietnam: 1955, 1967, 1971", *EVW*.

58. Westmoreland, *A soldier reports*, pp. 276 and 280.

59. C. B. Currey, "Search and destroy strategy", *EVW*.

60. *Ibid.*

61. *Ibid.*, pp.; J. W. Votaw, "Westmoreland, William C.", *EVW*.

62. J. F. Votaw, "ATTLEBORO, Operation", *EVW*; Krepinevich, *The Army and Vietnam*, p. 190.

63. J. F. Votaw, "CEDAR FALLS, Operation", *EVW*.

64. D. T. Zabecki, "JUNCTION CITY, Operation", *EVW*; Krepinevich, *The Army and Vietnam*, p. 191.

65. P. B. Davidson, *Vietnam at war* (Novato, CA, 1988), p. 428.

66. Krepinevich, *The Army and Vietnam*, pp. 190 and 192.

67. *Ibid.*, p. 192.

68. E. M. Bergerud, *The dynamics of defeat* (Boulder, CO, 1991), p. 132.

69. A. B. Herbert with J. T. Wooten, *Soldier* (New York, 1973), pp. 127–8. The 173rd was a separate brigade and therefore larger than a regular brigade.

70. Moore and Galloway, *We were soldiers once … and young*, p. 24. Moore notes also the rapid turnover of skilled officer personnel. *Ibid.*, p. 24.

71. Quoted in Krepinevich, *The Army and Vietnam*, p. 205.
72. D. T. Zabecki, "United States: Army", *EVW*; Krepinevich, *The Army and Vietnam*, p. 206.
73. Bergerud, *The dynamics of defeat*, pp. 168–9.
74. Currey, *Victory at any cost*, pp. 262–4.
75. *Ibid.*, pp. 264–5.
76. Clodfelter, *Vietnam in military statistics*, pp. 83–4 and 96–8.
77. Westmoreland, *A soldier reports*, p. 240.
78. O'Ballance, *The wars in Vietnam*, p. 106.
79. R. Pisor, *The end of the line. The siege of Khe Sanh* (New York, 1982), p. 69.
80. *Ibid.*, pp. 69–70.
81. *Ibid.*, pp. 70–72.
82. *Ibid.*, p. 72.
83. *Ibid.*, pp. 73–4. Casualties, even those for US forces, vary widely. Those cited here are from Pisor.
84. *Ibid.*, p. 77.
85. *Ibid.*, p. 76.
86. Karnow, *Vietnam, a history*, p. 527.
87. D. T. Zabecki, "Tết Offensive, overall strategy", *EVW*.
88. Davidson, *Vietnam at war*, p. 479.
89. Westmoreland, *A soldier reports*, p. 389.
90. *Ibid.*, p. 390.
91. Davidson, *Vietnam at war*, p. 479.
92. Westmoreland, *A soldier reports*, p. 388.
93. Davidson, *Vietnam at war*, p. 474; letter from former ARVN intelligence officer Nguyên Công Luân.
94. Westmoreland, *A soldier reports*, p. 399.
95. D. T. Zabecki, "Tết Offensive – the Sài Gòn circle (1968)", *EVW*.
96. D. T. Zabecki, "Hué, Battle of (1968 Tết Offensive)", *EVW*.
97. Westmoreland, *A soldier reports*, p. 404.
98. *Ibid.*
99. *Ibid.*, p. 403.
100. Zabecki, "Hué, Battle of (1968 Tết Offensive)", *EVW*.
101. Westmoreland, *A soldier reports*, p. 430.
102. M. Young, *The Vietnam wars, 1945–1990* (New York, 1991), p. 220.
103. For an analysis of press and television coverage of the Tết Offensive, see P. Braestrup, *Big story* (2 vols, Westview, CO, 1977).
104. Quoted in W. M. Hammond, *United States Army in Vietnam. Public affairs: the military and the media, 1962–1968* (Washington, DC, 1968), p. 369.
105. The other was at Ben Het, another outpost on the Laotian border, in 1969. Westmoreland, *A soldier reports*, p. 414. For the PT–76s at Khe Sanh see D. B. Stockwell, *Tanks in the wire. The first use of enemy armor in Vietnam* (Canton, OH, 1989).
106. *Ibid.*, p. 411.
107. C. J. Novak, "Remembering Khe Sanh", *The Retired Officer Magazine* (February 1993), p. 29.
108. Westmoreland, *A soldier reports*, p. 412.
109. *Ibid.*; Novak, "Remembering Khe Sanh", p. 29.

110. Pisor, *The end of the line*, p. 259; Westmoreland, *A soldier reports*, p. 422.
111. Pisor, *The end of the line*, pp. 258–9.
112. Westmoreland, *A soldier reports*, p. 421.
113. Davidson, *Vietnam at war*, p. 552.
114. Novak, "Remembering Khe Sanh", pp. 27–30; W. Head and P. Brush, "Khe Sanh, battles of", *EVW*.
115. Ball, *The past has another pattern*, p. 407.
116. On the impact of the war on US society, see M. MacPherson, *Long time passing, Vietnam & the haunted generation* (Garden City, NY, 1984). For a short survey see M. Barringer, "Anti-war movement", *EVW*. African Americans made up 10.5 per cent of the population, were 13.4 per cent of the draft pool of 18- to 25-year-olds, and sustained 12.5 per cent of the casualties of the war. B. G. Burkett, "Telling it like it is", *Vietnam* (February 1967), p. 31.

Chapter Six: The US search for a wayout

1. M. Clodfelter, *Vietnam in military statistics* (Jefferson, NC and London, 1993), p. 227; G. C. Herring, *America's longest war. The United States and Vietnam, 1950–1975* (New York, 1979), p. 209.
2. Clodfelter, *Vietnam in military statistics*, p. 142.
3. For this battle see R. H. Spector, *After Tet: the bloodiest year in Vietnam* (New York, 1993), pp. 169–76.
4. W. C. Westmoreland, *A soldier reports* (Garden City, NY, 1976), p. 437.
5. *Ibid.*, p. 428.
6. *Ibid.*, pp. 429–30.
7. *Ibid.*, p. 431.
8. *Ibid.*, pp. 431–2.
9. *Ibid.*, p. 433.
10. R. S. McNamara, *In retrospect* (New York, 1995), pp. 307–9.
11. Spector, *After Tet*, pp. 9–10.
12. C. Clifford with R. Holbrooke, *Counsel to the President* (New York, 1991), p. 480.
13. *Ibid.*, pp. 493–4.
14. Herring, *America's longest war*, pp. 192–4.
15. P. B. Davidson, *Vietnam at war* (Novato, CA, 1988), pp. 518–19; Herring, *America's longest war*, p. 195; Clifford, *Counsel to the President*, pp. 494–5.
16. Herring, *America's longest war*, pp. 195–6.
17. Clifford, *Counsel to the President*, pp. 496–7.
18. Herring, *America's longest war*, p. 199.
19. This was taken at the time to be a vote for de-escalation, but the November general election showed that "hawks" far outnumbered "doves" in that state.
20. Herring, *America's longest war*, p. 201.
21. Clifford, *Counsel to the President*, pp. 510–11.
22. Dean Acheson, George W. Ball, McGeorge Bundy, Douglas Dillon, Cyrus Vance, Arthur Dean, John J. McCloy, General Omar Bradley, General Matthew Ridgway, General Maxwell Taylor, Robert Murphy, Henry Cabot Lodge, Jr, Abe Fortas and Arthur Goldberg.
23. Clifford, *Counsel to the President*, pp. 511–18.

24. L. B. Johnson, *The vantage point: Perspectives on the Presidency, 1963–1969* (New York, 1971), pp. 425–6. Johnson had experienced a heart attack in 1955 and there was a family history of heart ailments. Close Johnson advisor Jack Valenti does not mention health and cites instead Johnson's desire for peace and the ugly prospects of the 1968 campaign. J Valenti, *A very human President* (New York, 1975), pp. 367–9.

25. Spector, *After Tet*, pp. 242–4.

26. Herring, *America's longest war*, pp. 206–9.

27. L. Sorley, "Abrams, Creighton", *EVW*.

28. From 49.6 per cent in 1966 to 80 per cent in 1970. Clodfelter, Vietnam in military statistics, p. 153.

29. D. M. Berman, "Civil operations and revolutionary development support (CORDS)", *EVW*. Clodfelter, *Vietnam in military statistics*, p. 152.

30. Westmoreland, *A soldier reports*, p. 262; letter to the author from Nguyên Công Luân.

31. Clodfelter, *Vietnam in military statistics*, p. 152.

32. Herring, *America's longest war*, p. 210.

33. *Ibid.*

34. Clifford, *Counsel to the President*, pp. 550–52.

35. On the massacre and cover up see S. M. Hersh, *My Lai 4: a report on the massacre and its aftermath* (New York, 1970); and same author, *Cover-up: the Army's secret investigation of the massacre at My Lai 4* (New York, 1972). See also Lieut. General W. R. Peers, *The My Lai inquiry* (New York, 1979).

36. Herring, *America's longest war*, pp. 213–14.

37. *Ibid.*, pp. 215–16.

38. H. Kissinger, *White House years* (Boston, 1979), p. 236.

39. Herring, *America's longest war*, p. 216.

40. Clodfelter, *Vietnam in military statistics*, pp. 149 and 151.

41. G. W. Ball, *The past has another pattern* (New York, 1982), pp. 410–11.

42. *Ibid.*, p. 422.

43. *Ibid.*, pp. 411 and 422.

44. *Ibid.*

45. H. R. Haldeman with J. DiMina, *The ends of power* (New York, 1978), p. 83.

46. Kissinger, *White House years*, p. 239.

47. Ball, *The past has another pattern*, p. 411. US Secretary of Defense figures in Clodfelter, *Vietnam in military statistics*, p. 258.

48. Kissinger, *White House years*, p. 241.

49. W. Shawcross, *Sideshow. Kissinger, Nixon and the destruction of Cambodia* (New York, 1979), p. 28.

50. Kissinger, *White House years*, p. 247.

51. *Ibid.*

52. *Ibid.*, p. 252. Kissinger denied he knew about the wiretaps.

53. C. B. Currey, *Victory at any cost* (New York, 1996), p. 276.

54. *Ibid.*, p. 152.

55. J. S. Bowman (ed.), *The world almanac of the Vietnam War* (New York, 1985), p. 229.

56. Herring, *America's longest war*, pp. 221–2.

57. Clifford, *Counsel to the President*, p. 608.

58. Bowman, *The world almanac of the Vietnam War*, p. 240.

59. *Ibid.*, p. 254; O'Ballance, *The wars in Vietnam*, p. 151.

60. Ball, *The past has another pattern*, pp. 414–15.

61. Herring, *America's longest war*, pp. 224–5.

62. Clodfelter, *Vietnam in military statistics*, p. 152; E. O'Ballance, *The wars in Vietnam* (New York, 1981), p. 204.

63. Bowman, *The world almanac of the Vietnam War*, p. 254.

64. For amplification see D. Kirk, *Wider war* (New York, 1971), pp. 92–102; and D. Chandler, *The tragedy of Cambodian history* (New Haven, CT, 1991), pp. 192–9.

65. Bowman, *The world almanac of the Vietnam War*, p. 254.

66. J. D. Root, "Cambodian incursion", *EVW*.

67. *New York Times*, 1 May 1970; Kissinger, *White House years*, pp. 504–5.

68. On 10 April FANK massacred hundreds of ethnic Vietnamese villagers in Svayrieng province. Bowman, *The world almanac of the Vietnam War*, p. 254.

69. Root, "Cambodian incursion", *EVW*.

70. Clodfelter, *Vietnam in military statistics*, p. 178.

71. Currey, *Victory at any cost*, p. 276; Root, "Cambodian incursion", *EVW*; E. M. Bergerud, *The dynamics of defeat* (Boulder, CO, 1991), p. 287.

72. Root, "Cambodian incursion", *EVW*.

73. C. R. Sasso, "Nguyên Van Thiêu", *EVW*.

74. E. H. Tilford, Jr, "LAM SÓN 719, Operation", *EVW*. J. D. Root, "DEWEY CANYON II, Operation", *EVW*. K. W. Nolan, *Into Laos: the story of Dewey Canyon II/Lam Són 719* (Novato, CA, 1986), pp 33–4 and 125. Nolan's book is the standard study of Lam Són 719.

75. Davidson, *Vietnam at war*, p. 644.

76. *Ibid.*, p. 660.

77. Tilford, "LAM SÓN 719, Operation", *EVW*.

78. Tilford, "LAM SÓN 719, Operation", *EVW*.

79. *Ibid.*, p.; Nolan, *Into Laos*, pp. 357–61.

80. Ball, *The past has another pattern*, p. 415.

81. Kissinger, *White House years*, p. 1101.

82. Bowman, *The world almanac of the Vietnam War*, pp. 297–8.

83. Kissinger, *White House years*, p. 1099.

84. Bowman, *The world almanac of the Vietnam War*, pp. 301–2.

85. J. H. Willbanks, "Easter Offensive", *EVW*; Currey, *Victory at any cost*, p. 285; Clodfelter, *Vietnam in military statistics*, p. 107.

86. Clodfelter, *Vietnam in military statistics*, p. 197.

87. See Currey, *Victory at any cost*, pp. 383–4.

88. *Ibid.*, pp. 284–5.

89. Willbanks, "Easter Offensive", *EVW*. On the Battle of An Lôc see same author, *Thiet Giap! The Battle of An Loc, April 1972* (Fort Leavenworth, KS, 1993).

90. E. H. Tilford, Jr, "LINEBACKER I", *EVW*.

91. Clodfelter, *The limits of air power*, p. 167.

92. Tilford, "LINEBACKER I", *EVW*.

93. Willbanks, "Easter Offensive", *EVW*; Clodfelter, *Vietnam in military statistics*, p. 204.

94. Ball, *The past has another pattern*, pp. 418–19. See also Nguyen Tien Hung and J. L. Schlecter, *The palace file* (New York, 1986).

95. Kissinger, *White House years*, p. 1308.

96. Clodfelter, *Vietnam in military statistics*, p. 205.

97. Ball, *The past has another pattern*, p. 421.
98. E. H. Tilford, Jr, "LINEBACKER II", *EVW*.
99. *Ibid.*
100. A. R. Isaacs, "Paris Peace Accords", *EVW*.
101. Ball, *The past has another pattern*, p. 420. See also S. Hoffmann, *Primacy or world order: American foreign policy since the Cold War* (New York, 1978), p. 29.
102. Ball, *The past has another pattern*, pp. 416–17. The figure on financial cost may be found in Stoessinger, J. G. *Why nations go to war*, 5th ed. (New York, 1990), p. 112.
103. S. C. Tucker, "Casualties", *EVW*.
104. Ball, *The past has another pattern*, p. 433.
105. Stoessinger, *Why nations go to war*, p. 111.

Chapter Seven: The Third Vietnam War

1. H. A. Kissinger, *Years of upheaval* (Boston, 1982), p. 36.
2. E. O'Ballance, *The wars in Vietnam* (New York, 1981), pp. 188–9.
3. H. G. Summers, *Vietnam War almanac* (New York, 1985), p. 287; M. Clodfelter, *Vietnam in military statistics* (Jefferson, NC and London, 1993), p. 225.
4. O'Ballance, *The wars in Vietnam*, p. 189.
5. Clodfelter, *Vietnam in military statistics*, p. 208.
6. A. R. Isaacs, "Paris Peace Accords", *EVW*.
7. Cao Van Vien, *The final collapse* (Washington, 1983), p. 31.
8. Clodfelter, *Vietnam in military statistics*, p. 209.
9. O'Ballance, *The Vietnam wars*, pp. 190–91; Clodfelter, *Vietnam in military statistics*, pp. 208–9; C. B. Currey, *Victory at any cost* (New York, 1996), p. 292.
10. J. S. Bowman (ed.), *The world almanac of the Vietnam War* (New York, 1985), p. 341.
11. Clodfelter, *Vietnam in military statistics*, p. 206.
12. *Ibid.*, p. 209.
13. *New York Times*, 5 January 1974, p. 341.
14. Clodfelter, *Vietnam in military statistics*, p. 209.
15. *Ibid.*, p. 207.
16. P. B. Davidson, *Vietnam at war* (Novato, CA, 1988), p. 747.
17. Clodfelter, *Vietnam in military statistics*, p. 207. See also Cao Van Vien, *The final collapse*, pp. 48–55.
18. Currey, *Victory at any cost*, pp. 293–4.
19. *Ibid.*, p. 294.
20. The DRV military committee coined the term. See Davidson, *Vietnam at war*, pp. 752–5.
21. Clodfelter, *Vietnam in military statistics*, pp. 210–11.
22. *Ibid.*, p. 207; O'Ballance, *The Vietnam wars*, pp. 203–4; Davidson, *Vietnam at war*, pp. 748–51.
23. Clodfelter, *Vietnam in military statistics*, p. 207; O'Ballance, *The Vietnam wars*, pp. 204–5.
24. Currey, *Victory at any cost*, p. 294.
25. *Ibid.*, p. 295.
26. Clodfelter, *Vietnam in military statistics*, pp. 211–12; O'Ballance, *The Vietnam wars*, pp. 204–5; Davidson, *Vietnam at war*, pp. 763–4; Col. W. E. Le Gro, *Vietnam from cease-fire to capitalism* (Washington, 1981), p. 136.
27. O'Ballance, *The Vietnam wars*, pp. 205–6.

28. Currey, *Victory at any cost*, p. 295.

29. Davidson, *Vietnam at war*, pp. 769–72; Le Gro, *Vietnam from ceasefire to capitalism*, pp. 147–51.

30. G. C. Herring, *America's longest war* (New York, 1986), p. 260.

31. Davidson, *Vietnam at war*, p. 773; A. Isaacs, *Without honor: defeat in Vietnam and Cambodia* (Baltimore, MD, 1983), pp. 346–7.

32. Currey, *Victory at any cost*, p. 295.

33. Davidson, *Vietnam at war*, pp. 774–7.

34. Nguyen Cao Ky, *How we lost the Vietnam War* (New York, 1978), p. 210.

35. Clodfelter, *Vietnam in military statistics*, p. 212.

36. Davidson, *Vietnam at war*, p. 777.

37. A. Dawson, *55 days. The fall of South Vietnam* (Englewood Cliffs, NJ, 1977), pp. 7–72; Clodfelter, *Vietnam in military statistics*, p. 213; Davidson, *Vietnam at war*, pp. 778–9.

38. The three divisions were the 1st and 3rd Infantry and the Marines. On 10 March Thiêu had withdrawn the Airborne Division from Trúóng's command and ordered it back to the capital.

39. Davidson, *Vietnam at war*, pp. 779–81.

40. *Ibid.*, pp. 783–4; Clodfelter, *Vietnam in military statistics*, p. 213.

41. Clodfelter, *Vietnam in military statistics*, p. 213.

42. *Ibid.*, pp. 213–14; O'Ballance, *The Vietnam wars*, p. 208.

43. Currey, *Victory at any cost*, p. 295.

44. Clodfelter, *Vietnam in military statistics*, p. 214.

45. Davidson, *Vietnam at war*, p. 788.

46. J. P. Dunn, "Xuân Lôc, Battle of", *EVW*; Clodfelter, *Vietnam in military statistics*, pp. 214–15; Dawson, *55 days*, pp. 300–03; Davidson, *Vietnam at war*, pp. 789–90; General Cao Van Vien, *The final collapse*, p. 132.

47. Dawson, *55 days*, pp. 224–9.

48. J. M. Gates, "Hô Chí Minh Campaign", *EVW*.

49. Dawson, *55 days*, pp. 286–90.

50. O'Ballance, *The Vietnam wars*, p. 210.

51. Clodfelter, *Vietnam in military statistics*, p. 215; O'Ballance, *The Vietnam wars*, p. 210; Dawson, *55 days*, pp. 229, 299–300 and 320–21; and Gates, "Hô Chí Minh Campaign", *EVW*.

52. O'Ballance, *The Vietnam wars*, p. 210.

53. Clodfelter, *Vietnam in military statistics*, pp. 215–16; O'Ballance, *The Vietnam wars*, pp. 210–11.

54. Clodfelter, *Vietnam in military statistics*, p. 216; O'Ballance, *The Vietnam wars*, p. 211.

55. Clodfelter, *Vietnam in military statistics*, p. 216.

56. O'Ballance, *The Vietnam wars*, pp. 194–8 and 226; Isaacs, *Without honor*, p. 181; Clodfelter, *Vietnam in military statistics*, pp. 269–70. See also J. Hamilton-Merritt, *Tragic mountains. The Hmong, the Americans, and the secret wars for Laos, 1942–1992* (Bloomington, IN, 1993). For a short overview see A. Dommen, "Laos", *EVW*.

57. Shawcross, *Sideshow*, p. 297.

58. O'Ballance, *The Vietnam wars*, p. 200.

59. *Ibid.*, pp. 200–01; Shawcross, *Sideshow*, pp. 347–8.

60. W. Shawcross, *Sideshow* (New York, 1979), pp. 350–51.

61. O'Ballance, *The Vietnam wars*, pp. 201–3.

62. A. R. Isaacs, "Cambodia", *EVW*.

Chapter Eight: *Vietnam invasion of Cambodia and the war with China*

1. S. C. Tucker, "Vietnamese invasion and occupation of Cambodia", *EVW*; W. Shawcross, *Sideshow* (New York, 1979), p. 385.
2. Tucker, "Vietnamese invasion and occupation of Cambodia", *EVW*.
3. E. O'Ballance, *The wars in Vietnam, 1954–1980* (New York, 1981), p. 216.
4. Tucker, "Vietnamese invasion and occupation of Cambodia", *EVW*.
5. *Ibid.*
6. *Ibid.*
7. O'Ballance, *The wars in Vietnam*, pp. 217–18.
8. Tucker, "Vietnamese invasion and occupation of Cambodia", *EVW*.
9. *Ibid.*
10. *Ibid.*
11. The best study is K. C. Chen, *China's war with Vietnam, 1979* (Stanford, CA, 1987).
12. See *ibid.*, pp. 39–95.
13. O'Ballance, *The wars in Vietnam*, p. 221; Chen, *China's war with Vietnam, 1979*, p. 39.
14. See Pham Cao Dúóng, "Paracel and Spratly Islands", *EVW*. Also see Chen, *China's war with Vietnam*, pp. 39–50.
15. O'Ballance, *The wars in Vietnam*, p. 221.
16. Chen, *China's war with Vietnam*, p. 64.
17. *Ibid.*, pp. 64–5. Chen takes the position that the Chinese were forced to leave.
18. *Ibid.*, pp. 65–6 and 81.
19. *Ibid.*, p. 37.
20. B. Elleman, "Sino–Soviet relations and the February 1979 Sino–Soviet conflict", paper delivered at the Vietnam War Symposium, Texas Tech University (April 1996).
21. Chen, *China's war with Vietnam*, pp. 100–101.
22. *Ibid.*, p. 102.
23. O'Ballance, *The Vietnam Wars*, pp. 223 and 225; Chen gives srv combat air strength at only 300 planes. Chen, *China's war with Vietnam*, p. 103.
24. Chen, *China's war with Vietnam*, pp. 107–8.
25. *Ibid.*, pp. 108–9.
26. C. B. Currey, *Victory at any cost* (New York, 1996), p. 308.
27. O'Ballance, *The Vietnam Wars*, p. 224; Chen, *China's war with Vietnam*, pp. 110–11.
28. Chen, *China's war with Vietnam*, pp. 110–11 and 113.
29. *Ibid.*, pp. 113–14.
30. *Ibid.*, pp. 115–16.
31. O'Ballance, *The Vietnam Wars*, pp. 225–26.

Select bibliography

Alvarez, E., Jr & A. S. Pitch. *Chained eagle* (New York: Donald I. Fine, 1989).

Anderson, C. B. *The grunts* (San Rafael, CA: Presidio Press, 1976).

Anderson, D. L. (ed.). *Shadows on the White House: Presidents and the Vietnam War, 1945–1975* (Lawrence, KS: University of Kansas Press, 1993).

Anderson, W. C. *Bat–21* (Englewood Cliffs, NJ: Prentice-Hall, 1980).

Andrade, D. *Trial by fire* (New York: Hippocrene Books, 1995).

Appy, C. *Working-class war: American combat soldiers and Vietnam* (Chapel Hill, NC: University of North Carolina Press, 1993).

Arlen, M. *The living room war* (New York: Viking Press, 1969).

Baker, M. *Nam: the Vietnam War in the words of the men and women who fought there* (New York: Morrow, 1981).

Baritz, L. *Backfire: a history of how American culture led us into Vietnam and made us fight the way we did* (New York: Morrow, 1985).

Barrett, D. *Uncertain warriors: Lyndon Johnson and his Vietnam advisors* (Lawrence, KS: University Press of Kansas, 1993).

Bass, T. A. *Vietnamerica: the war comes home* (New York: Soho Press, 1996).

De Benedetti, C. & C. Chatfield. *An American ordeal: the antiwar movements of the Vietnam era* (Syracuse, NY: Syracuse University Press, 1990).

Bergerud, E. M. *The dynamics of defeat. The Vietnam War in Hau Nghia Province* (Boulder, CO: Westview Press, 1991).

Bergerud, E. M. *Red Thunder, Tropic Lightning: the world of a combat division in Vietnam* (Boulder, CO: Westview Press, 1993).

Berman, L. *Lyndon Johnson's war* (New York: Norton, 1989).

Berman, L. *Planning a tragedy: the Americanization of the war in Vietnam* (New York: Norton, 1982).

Bigeard, M. *Pour une parcelle de gloire* (Paris: Plon, 1976).

Billings-Yun, M. *Decision against war: Eisenhower and Dien Bien Phu* (New York: Columbia University Press, 1988).

Bilton, M. & K. Sim. *Four hours in My Lai* (New York: Viking Press, 1992).

Blair, A. E. *Lodge in Vietnam: a patriot abroad* (New Haven, CT: Yale University Press, 1995).

Bodard, L. *The quicksand war: prelude to Vietnam* (Boston: Little, Brown, 1967).

Bowman, J. S. (ed.). *The world almanac of the Vietnam War* (New York: Pharos Books, 1985).

Brace, E. C. *A code to keep: the true story of America's longest-held civilian prisoner of war* (New York: St. Martin's, 1988).

Braestrup, P. *Big story: how the American press and television reported and interpreted the crisis of Tet 1968 in Vietnam and Washington* (Boulder, CO: Westview Press, 1977).

Broughton, J. *Going downtown: the war against Hanoi and Washington* (New York: Orion Books, 1988).

Bryan, C. D. B. *Friendly fire* (New York: Putnam, 1976).

Bui Diem with D. Chanoff. *In the jaws of history* (Boston: Houghton, Mifflin, 1987).

Burchett, W. G. *The furtive war: the United States in Vietnam and Laos* (New York: International Publishers, 1963).

Butler, D. *The fall of Saigon: scenes from the sudden end of a long war* (New York: Simon and Schuster, 1985).

Buttinger, J. *The smaller dragon: a political history of Vietnam* (New York: Frederick A. Praeger, 1968).

Cable, L. E. *Conflict of myths: the development of American counterinsurgency doctrine and the Vietnam War* (New York: New York University Press, 1988).

Cady, J. F. *The roots of French imperialism in eastern Asia* (Ithaca, NY: Cornell University Press, 1954).

Caputo, P. *A rumor of war* (New York: Holt, Rinehart & Winston, 1977).

Chanoff, D. & Doan Van Toai. *Portrait of the enemy* (New York: Random House, 1986).

Chapuis, O. *A history of Vietnam. From Hong Bang to Tu Duc* (Westport, CT: Greenwood Press, 1995).

Charlton, M. & A. Moncrief. *Many reasons why: the American involvement in Vietnam* (New York: Hill & Wang, 1978).

Charton, Colonel. *Albatros* (Paris, 1975).

Charton, P. *Indochine 1950. La tragédie de l'évacuation de Cao Bang* (Paris: Société de production littéraire, 1975).

Chen, K. C. *China's war with Vietnam, 1979: issues, decisions, and implications* (Stanford, CA: Hoover Institute Press, 1987).

Chomsky, N. *Rethinking Camelot: JFK, the Vietnam War, and U.S. political culture* (Boston: South End Press, 1993).

Clayton, A. *Three Marshals of France: leadership after trauma* (London: Brassey's, 1992).

Clifford, C. with R. C. Holbrooke. *Counsel to the President: a memoir* (New York: Random House, 1991).

Clodfelter, M. *Vietnam in military statistics* (Jefferson, NC and London: McFarland & Co., 1993).

Coedès, G. *The making of South East Asia*, trans. H. M. Wright (Berkeley: University of California Press, 1966).

Colby, W. E. *Honorable men: my life in the CIA* (New York: Simon and Schuster, 1978).

Colby, W. E. with J. McCargar. *Lost victory: a firsthand account of America's sixteen year involvement in Vietnam* (Chicago: Contemporary Books, 1989).

Coleman, J. D. *Pleiku: the dawn of helicopter Vietnam* (New York: St. Martin's Press, 1988).

Conboy, K. & J. Morrison. *Shadow war: the CIA's secret war in Laos* (Boulder, CO: Paladin, 1995).

Currey, C. B. *Edward Lansdale, the unquiet American* (Boston: Houghton Mifflin, 1988).

Currey, C. B. *Self-destruction: the disintegration and decay of the United States Army during the Vietnam era* (New York: Norton, 1981).

Currey, C. B. *Victory at any cost: the genius of Viet Nam's General Vo Nguyen Giap* (New York: Brassey's, 1996).

Cutler, T. J. *Brown water, Black Berets: coastal and riverine warfare in Vietnam* (Annapolis, MD: Naval Institute Press, 1988).

Dalloz, J. *The war in Indo-China, 1945–54*, trans. J. Bacon (Savage, MD: Barnes and Noble, 1990).

Đăng Văn Kiêt. *Highway 4, the border campaign, 1947–1950* (Hà Nôi: Foreign Languages Publishing House, 1990).

Dawson, A. *55 days: the fall of South Vietnam* (Englewood Cliffs, NJ: Prentice-Hall, 1977).

Davidson, P. B. *Vietnam at war: the history, 1946–1975* (Novato, CA: Presidio Press, 1988).

Denton, J. A. *When hell was in session* (New York: Reader's Digest Press, 1976).

Van Devanter, L. *Home before morning: the story of an army nurse in Vietnam* (New York: Beaufort Books, 1983).

Devillers, P. *Histoire du Vietnam de 1940 à 1952* (Paris: Editions de Seuil, 1952).

Dommen, A. J. *Conflict in Laos. The politics of neutralization* (New York: Frederick A. Praeger, 1964).

Donovan, D. *Once a warrior king: memories of an officer in Vietnam* (New York: McGraw-Hill, 1985).

Duiker, W. J. *The Communist road to power in Vietnam*, 2nd ed. (Boulder, CO: Westview Press, 1996).

Duiker, W. J. *Historical dictionary of Vietnam* (Metuchen, NJ: The Scarecrow Press, 1989).

Duiker, W. J. *The rise of nationalism in Vietnam, 1900–1911* (Ithaca, NY: Cornell University Press, 1976).

Duiker, W. J. *Vietnam: revolution in transition*, 2nd ed. (Boulder, CO: Westview Press, 1995).

Duncanson, D. J. *Government and revolution in Vietnam* (New York: Oxford University Press, 1968).

Ellsberg, D. *Papers on the war* (New York: Simon and Schuster, 1972).

Emerson, G. *Winners and losers: battles, retreats, gains, losses, and ruins from the Vietnam War* (New York: Random House, 1976).

Fall, B. B. *Hell in a very small place: the Siege of Dien Bien Phu* (Philadelphia: Lippincott, 1967).

Fall, B. B. *Last reflections on a war* (Garden City, NY: Doubleday, 1967).

Fall, B. B. *Street without joy* (Harrisburg, PA: Stackpole, 1961).

Fall, B. B. *The two Viet Nams*, rev. ed. (New York: Praeger, 1964).

Fall, B. B. *Vietnam witness, 1953–66* (New York: Praeger, 1966).

Férier, G. *Les trois guerre d'Indochine* (Lyon: Presses Universitaires de Lyon, 1993).

FitzGerald, F. *Fire in the lake: the Vietnamese and the Americans in Vietnam* (Boston: Little, Brown, 1972).

De Folin, J. *Indochine, 1940–1955: la fin d'un rêve* (Paris: Perrin, 1993).

DeForest, O. & D. Chanoff. *Slow burn: the rise and bitter fall of American intelligence in Vietnam* (New York: Simon and Schuster, 1990).

Franklin, H. B. *M.I.A., or mythmaking in America* (Brooklyn, NY: Lawrence Hill Books, 1992).

Gaiduk, I. *The Soviet Union and the Vietnam War* (Chicago: Ivan Dee, 1996).

De Gaulle, C. *The war memoirs of Charles de Gaulle*, vol. 3 *Salvation, 1944–1946*, trans. R. Howard (New York: Simon and Schuster, 1960).

Gilbert, M. J. & W. Head (eds). *The Tet Offensive* (Westport, CT: Praeger, 1996).

Goff, S. R. Sanders & C. Smith. *Brothers: black soldiers in the Nam* (Novato, CA: Presidio Press, 1982).

Goldman, P. & T. Fuller. *Charlie Company: what Vietnam did to us* (New York: Morrow, 1983).

Gottlieb, S. G. *Hell no, we won't go!: resisting the draft during the Vietnam War* (New York: Viking Press, 1991).

Gould, L. L. *1968: the election that changed America* (Chicago: Ivan R. Dee, 1993).

Grant, Z. *Survivors* (New York: Norton, 1975).

Gras, Y. *Histoire de La Guerre de l'Indochine* (Paris: Editions Denoël, 1992).

Le Gro, Col. W. E. *Vietnam from ceasefire to capitalism* (Washington, DC: U.S. Army Center of Military History, 1981).

Groom, W. & D. Spencer. *Conversations with the enemy: the story of Pfc. Robert Garwood* (New York: Putnam, 1983).

Gruner, E. *Prisoners of culture: representing the Vietnam POW* (New Brunswick, NJ: Rutgers University Press, 1993).

Guilmartin, J. F. *A very short war: the Mayaguez and the Battle of Koh Tang* (College Station, TX: Texas A&M University Press, 1995).

Gustainis, J. J. *American rhetoric and the Vietnam War* (New York: Praeger, 1993).

Hackworth, D. H. & J. Sherman. *About face: the odyssey of an American warrior* (New York: Simon and Schuster, 1989).

Halberstam, D. *The best and the brightest* (New York: Random House, 1972).

Halberstam, D. *Ho* (New York: Random House, 1971).

Halberstam, D. *The making of a quagmire: America and Vietnam during the Kennedy era*, rev. ed. (New York: Knopf, 1988).

Hamilton-Merritt, J. *Tragic mountains: the Hmong, the Americans, and the secret wars for Laos, 1942–1992* (Bloomington, IN: Indiana University Press, 1993).

Hammel, E. *Fire in the streets: the Battle for Hué, Tet, 1968* (Chicago: Contemporary Books, 1991).

Hammel, E. *Khe Sanh: siege in the clouds: an oral history* (New York: Crown, 1989).

Hammer, E. J. *A death in November: America in Vietnam, 1963* (New York: Dutton, 1987).

Hammer, E. J. *The struggle for Indochina* (Stanford, CA: Stanford University Press, 1954).

Hammond, W. M. *Public affairs: the military and the media, 1962–1968* (Washington, DC: U.S. Army Center of Military History, 1988).

Hammond, W. M. *Public affairs: the military and the media, 1968–1973* (Washington, DC: U.S. Army Center of Military History, 1996).

Hayslip, Le Ly & J. Wurts. *When heaven and earth changed places: a Vietnamese woman's journey from war to peace* (New York: Doubleday, 1989).

Head, W. & L. E. Grinter (eds). *Looking back on the Vietnam War: a 1990's perspective on the decisions, combat, and legacies* (Westport, CN: Greenwood Press, 1993).

Hellman, J. *American myth and the legacy of Vietnam* (New York: Columbia University Press, 1986).

Hemingway, A. *Our war was different: Marine combined action platoons in Vietnam* (Annapolis, MD: Naval Institute Press, 1994).

Herr, M. *Dispatches* (New York: Knopf, 1977).

Herring, G. C. *America's longest war: the United States and Vietnam, 1950–1975*, 2nd ed. (New York: Knopf, 1986).

Herring, G. C. *LBJ and Vietnam: a different kind of war* (Austin: University of Texas Press, 1994).

Herrington, S. A. *Silence was a weapon: the Vietnam War in the villages: a personal perspective* (Novato, CA: Presidio Press, 1982).

Hersh, S. *Cover-up: the Army's secret investigation of the massacre at My Lai 4* (New York: Random House, 1972).

Hersh, S. *My Lai 4: a report on the massacre and its aftermath* (New York: Random House, 1970).

Higham, C. *The archaeology of mainland Southeast Asia* (New York: Cambridge University Press, 1989).

Hoffmann, S. *Primacy or world order: American foreign policy since the Cold War* (New York, McGraw-Hill, 1978).

Hooper, E. B., D. C. Allard & O. P. Fitzgerald. *The United States Navy and the Vietnam conflict*, vol. 1 *The setting of the stage to 1959* (Washington, DC: U.S. Navy, Naval History Division, 1976).

Hubbell, J. G. *P.O.W.: a definitive history of the American prisoner-of-war experience in Vietnam, 1964–1973* (New York: Reader's Digest Press, 1976).

Hunt, R. A. *Pacification: the American struggle for Vietnam's hearts and minds* (Boulder, CO: Westview Press, 1995).

Huynh, Jade Ngoc Quang. *South wind changing* (St Paul, MN: Graywolf Press, 1994).

Isaacon, W. *Kissinger: a biography* (New York: Simon and Schuster, 1992).

Jensen-Stevenson, M. & W. Stevenson. *Kiss the boys goodbye: how the United States betrayed its own POWs in Vietnam* (New York: Dutton, 1990).

Johnson, L. B. *The vantage point: perspectives of the presidency, 1963–1969* (New York: Holt, Rinehart & Winston, 1971).

Kahin, G. McT. *Intervention: how America became involved in Vietnam* (New York: Knopf, 1986).

Karnow, S. *Vietnam: a history* (New York: Viking Press, 1983).

Katsiaficas, G. N. (ed.). *Vietnam documents: American and Vietnamese views of the war* (New York: M. E. Sharpe, 1992).

Kimball, J. P. (ed.). *To reason why: the debate about the causes of involvement in the Vietnam War* (Philadelphia: Temple University Press, 1990).

King, P. (ed.). *Australia's Vietnam: Australia in the second Indochina war* (Boston: Allen & Unwin, 1983).

Kissinger, H. *White House years* (Boston: Little, Brown, 1979).

Kissinger, H. *Years of upheaval* (Boston: Little, Brown, 1982).

Kolko, G. *Anatomy of a war: Vietnam, the United States, and the modern historical experience* (New York: Pantheon, 1985).

Krepinevich, A. F., Jr. *The Army and Vietnam* (Baltimore, MD: The Johns Hopkins University Press, 1986).

Krohn, C. A. *The lost battalion: controversy and casualty in the Battle of Hué* (Westport, CN: Praeger, 1993).

Lacouture, J. *Ho Chi Minh: a political biography* (New York: Random House, 1968).

Lane, M. *Conversations with Americans* (New York: Simon and Schuster, 1970).

Lang, D. *Casualties of war* (New York: McGraw-Hill, 1969).

Lansdale, E. G. *In the midst of wars: an American's mission to Southeast Asia* (New York: Harper & Row, 1972).

Larson, S. R. & J. L. Collins, Jr. *Allied participation in Vietnam* (Washington, DC: U.S. Government Printing Office, Department of the Army, Vietnam Studies, 1975).

Le Thanh Khoi. *Histoire du Viet Nam des origines à 1858* (Paris: Sudestasie, 1981).

Ly Qui Chung (ed.). *Between two fires: the unheard voices of Vietnam* (New York: Praeger, 1970).

McConnell, M. *Inside the Hanoi secret archives: solving the MIA mystery* (New York: Simon and Schuster, 1995).

Maclear, M. *The ten thousand day war, Vietnam: 1945–1975* (New York: St. Martin's, 1981).

McNamara, R. S. with B. VanDeMark. *In retrospect, the tragedy and lessons of Vietnam* (New York: Times Books, 1995).

McNeill, I. *To Long Tan: the Australian Army and the Vietnam War, 1950–1966* (St Leonards, NSW, Australia: Allen & Unwin/Australian War Memorial, 1993).

MacPherson, M. *Long time passing: Vietnam and the haunted generation* (Garden City, NY: Doubleday, 1984).

Mangold, T. & J. Penycate. *The tunnels of Cu Chi* (New York: Random House, 1985).

Marolda, E. J. *By sea, air, and land: an illustrated history of the U.S. Navy and the war in Southeast Asia* (Washington, DC: Naval Historical Center, 1994).

Marolda, E. J. & O. P. Fitzgerald. *The United States Navy and the Vietnam conflict*, vol. 2 *From military assistance to combat* (Washington, DC: Naval Historical Center, 1986).

Marr, D. G. *Vietnam 1945: the quest for power* (Berkeley, CA: University of California Press, 1996).

Marshall, K. *In the combat zone: an oral history of American women in Vietnam, 1966–1975* (Boston: Little, Brown, 1987).

Marshall, S. L. A. *Ambush* (New York: Cowles, 1969).

Marshall, S. L. A. *Battles in the monsoon: campaigning in the Central Highlands, Vietnam, summer 1966* (New York: Morrow, 1967).

Marshall, S. L. A. *Bird: the Christmastide battle* (New York: Cowles, 1968).

Marshall, S. L. A. *West to Cambodia* (New York: Cowles, 1968).

Mason, R. *Chickenhawk* (New York: Viking Press, 1983).

Mauer, H. *Strange ground: Americans in Vietnam, 1945–1975, an oral history* (New York: Henry Holt, 1989).

Michel, M. *Clashes. Air combat over North Vietnam 1965–1972* (Annapolis: Naval Institute Press, 1997).

Moïse, E. E. *Tonkin Gulf and the escalation of the Vietnam War* (Chapel Hill, NC: University of North Carolina Press, 1996).

Moore, H. G. & J. L. Galloway. *We were soldiers once … and young* (New York: Random House, 1992).

Morrison, W. H. *The elephant and the tiger: the full story of the Vietnam War* (New York: Hippocrene Books, 1990).

Moss, G. *Vietnam: an American ordeal*, 2nd ed. (Englewood Cliffs, NJ: Prentice-Hall, 1994).

Moyar, M. *Phoenix and the birds of prey. The CIA's secret campaign to destroy the Viet Cong* (Annapolis: Naval Institute Press, 1997).

Murphy, E. F. *Dak To* (Novato, CA: Presidio Press, 1993).

Murphy, J. *Harvest of fear: a history of Australia's Vietnam War* (Boulder, CO: Westview Press, 1994).

Neilands, J. B. *et al. Harvest of death: chemical warfare in Vietnam and Cambodia* (New York: Free Press, 1972).

Newman, J. M. *JFK and Vietnam: deception, intrigue, and the struggle for power* (New York: Warner Books, 1992).

Nguyûn Cao Kỳ. *Twenty years and twenty days* (New York: Stein & Day, 1976).

Nguyûn Khăc Viên. *The long resistance, 1858–1975* (Hà Nôi: Foreign Languages Publishing House, 1975).

Nguyûn Khăc Viên. *Vietnam. A long history* (Hà Nôi: Gioi Publishers, 1993).

Nguyûn Tien Hung & J. L. Schlecter. *The palace file* (New York: Harper and Row, 1986).

Nichols, J. B. & B. Tillman. *On Yankee station: the naval air war over Vietnam* (Annapolis, MD: Naval Institute Press, 1987).

Nixon, R. M. *No more Vietnams* (New York: Arbor House, 1985).

Nixon, R. M. *The real war* (New York: Warner, 1980).

Nixon, R. M. *RN: the memoirs of Richard Nixon* (New York: Grosset & Dunlap, 1978).

Nolan, K. W. *Battle for Hué: Tet, 1968* (Novato, CA: Presidio Press, 1983).

Nolting, F. *From trust to tragedy: the political memoirs of Frederick Nolting, Kennedy's Ambassador to Diem's Vietnam* (New York: Praeger, 1988).

O'Ballance, E. *The wars in Vietnam, 1954–1980*, rev. ed. (New York: Hippocrine Books, 1981).

Oberdorfer, D. *Tet!* (Garden City, NY: Doubleday, 1971).

Olson, J. S. (ed.). *Dictionary of the Vietnam War* (New York: Greenwood Press, 1988).

Olson, J. S. & R. Roberts. *Where the domino fell: America and Vietnam, 1945–1990* (New York: St. Martin's, 1991).

Palmer, B. *The 25-year war: America's military role in Vietnam* (New York: Simon and Schuster, 1984).

Palmer, D. R. *Summons of the trumpet: U.S. Vietnam in perspective* (San Rafael, CA: Presidio Press, 1978).

Patti, A. L. A. *Why Viet Nam? Prelude to America's albatross* (Berkeley, CA: University of California Press, 1980).

Pedroncini, G. & P. Duplay (eds). *Leclerc et l'Indochine* (Paris: Albin Michel, 1992).

Peterson, M. E. *The combined action platoons; the U.S. Marines' other war in Vietnam* (New York: Praeger, 1989).

Pham Cao Dúóng. *Lich Sú Dân Tôc Viêt Nam, Tâp I: Thói Kỳ Lâp Quôc* (*History of the Vietnamese people*, vol. I *The formation of the nation*) (Fountain Valley, CA: Truyên Thông Viêt, 1987).

Phillips, W. R. *Night of the silver stars. The Battle of Lang Vei* (Annapolis, MD: Naval Institute Press, 1997).

Pike, D. *A history of Vietnamese Communism, 1923–1978* (Stanford CA: Hoover Institute Press, 1978).

Pike, D. *Viet Cong: the organization and techniques of the National Liberation Front of South Vietnam* (Cambridge, MA: M.I.T. Press, 1966).

Pisor, R. *The end of the line: the Siege of Khe Sanh* (New York: Norton, 1982).

Porch, D. *The French Foreign Legion: a complete history of the legendary fighting force* (New York: HarperCollins, 1991).

Prados, J. & R. W. Stubbe. *Valley of decision: the Siege of Khe Sanh* (Boston: Houghton, Mifflin, 1991).

Pratt, J. C. (ed.). *Vietnam voices: perspectives on the war years, 1941–1982* (New York: Viking Press, 1984).

Prochnau, W. *Once upon a distant war* (New York: Random House, 1995).

Puller, L. B., Jr. *Fortunate son: the autobiography of Lewis B. Puller, Jr.* (New York: Grove Weidenfeld, 1991).

Race, J. *War comes to Long An. Revolutionary conflict in a Vietnamese province* (Berkeley, CA: University of California Press, 1972).

Randle, R. F. *Geneva 1954: the settlement of the Indochinese War* (Princeton, NJ: Princeton University Press, 1969).

Robbins, C. *Air America* (New York: Putnam, 1979).

Rotter, A. (ed.). *Light at the end of the tunnel: a Vietnam War anthology* (New York: St. Martin's, 1991).

Rowe, J. C. & R. Berg (eds). *The Vietnam War and American culture* (New York: Columbia University Press, 1991).

Roy, J. *The Battle of Dienbienphu* (New York: Harper & Row, 1965).

Rusk, D., R. Rusk & D. S. Papp. *As I saw it* (New York: Norton, 1990).

Sainteny, J. *Histoire d'une paix manquée: Indochine, 1945–1947* (Paris: Amiot-Dumont, 1953).

Sainteny, J. *Ho Chi Minh and his Vietnam: a personal memoir* (Chicago: Cowles, 1972).

Salisbury, H. E. (ed.). *Vietnam reconsidered: lessons from a war* (New York: Harper & Row, 1984).

Santoli, A. (ed.). *Everything we had: an oral history of the Vietnam War by thirty-three American soldiers who fought it* (New York: Random House, 1981).

Santoli, A. (ed.). *To bear any burden: the Vietnam War and its aftermath in the words of Americans and Southeast Asians* (New York: Dutton, 1985).

Schell, J. *The military half* (New York: Knopf, 1968).

Schell, J. *The village of Ben Suc* (New York: Knopf, 1967).

Scholl-Latour, P. *Death in the ricefields: an eyewitness account of Vietnam's three wars, 1945–1979* (New York: St. Martin's Press, 1985).

Schreadley, R. L. *From the rivers to the sea: the United States Navy in Vietnam* (Annapolis, MD: Naval Institute Press, 1992).

Shapley, D. *Promise and power: the life and times of Robert McNamara* (Boston: Little, Brown, 1993).

Shawcross, W. *Sideshow: Kissinger, Nixon, and the destruction of Cambodia* (New York: Simon and Schuster, 1979).

Sheehan, N. *A bright shining lie: John Paul Vann and America in Vietnam* (New York: Random House, 1988).

Sheppard, D. *Riverine: a brown-water sailor in the delta, 1967* (Novato, CA: Presidio Press, 1992).

Showalter, D. E. & J. G. Abert (eds). *An American dilemma: Vietnam, 1964–1973* (Chicago: Imprint Publications, 1993).

Simpson, H. R. *Dien Bien Phu: the epic battle America forgot* (Washington, DC: Brassey's, 1994).

Simpson, H. R. *Tiger in the barbed wire: an American in Vietnam, 1952–1991* (Washington, DC: Brassey's, 1992).

Smith, W. *American daughter gone to war: on the front lines with an army nurse in Vietnam* (New York: Morrow, 1992).

Snepp, F. *Decent interval: an insider's account of Saigon's indecent end* (New York: Random House, 1977).

Spector, R. H. *Advice and support: the early years, 1941–1960* (Washington, DC: U.S. Army Center of Military History, The U.S. Army in Vietnam Series, 1983).

Spector, R. H. *After Tet: the bloodiest year in Vietnam* (New York: Free Press, 1993).

Stanton, S. L. *Green Berets at war* (Novato, CA: Presidio Press, 1985).

Stanton, S. L. *The rise and fall of an American army: U.S. ground forces in Vietnamm, 1965–1973* (Novato, CA: Presido Press, 1985).

Stevens, F. *The trail* (New York: Garland, 1993).

Stockdale, J. B. *A Vietnam experience: ten years of reflection* (Stanford, CA: Hoover Institute Press, 1984).

Summers, H. G. *Historical atlas of the Vietnam War* (Boston: Houghton Mifflin, 1995).

Summers, H. G. *On strategy* (Novato, CA: Presidio Press, 1982).

Taylor, J. M. *General Maxwell Taylor: the sword and the pen* (New York: Doubleday, 1989).

Taylor, K. W. *The birth of Vietnam* (Berkeley, CA: University of California Press, 1983).

Taylor, M. D. *Swords and plowshares* (New York: Norton, 1972).

Terry, W. *Bloods: an oral history of the Vietnam War by black veterans* (New York: Random House, 1984).

Thompson, V. *French Indo-China* (New York: Octagon Books, 1968).

Trúóng Nhu Tang with D. Chanoff & Doan Van Toai. *A Vietcong memoir* (New York: Harcourt, Brace, Jovanovich, 1985).

Tuchman, B. W. *The march of folly: from Troy to Vietnam* (New York: Knopf, 1984).

Tucker, S. C. (ed.). *An encyclopedia of the Vietnam War*, 3 vols (Denver, CO: ABC-Clio, 1998).

Turley, G. H. *The Easter Offensive: Vietnam 1972* (Novato, CA: Presidio Press, 1985).

U.S. Department of State. *Aggression from the north. The record of North Viet-Nam's campaign to conquer South Viet-Nam* (Washington, DC: U.S. Government Printing Office, 1965).

Valentine, D. *The Phoenix Program* (New York: Morrow, 1990).

Valette, J. *La Guerre d'Indochine, 1945–1954* (Paris: Armand Colin, 1994).

VanDeMark, B. *Into the quagmire: Lyndon Johnson and the escalation of the Vietnam War* (New York: Oxford University Press, 1991).

Võ Nguyên Giáp. *"Big victory, great task." North Viet-Nam's Minister of Defense assesses the course of the war*. Introduction by David Schoenbrun (New York: Praeger, 1968).

Võ Nguyên Giáp. *Dien Bien Phu*, 5th ed., revised and supplemented (Hà Nôi: The Gioi Publishers, 1994).

Võ Nguyên Giáp. *The military art of people's war. Selected writings of Vo Nguyen Giap*, edited with an introduction by R. Stetler (New York: Monthly Review Press, 1970).

Võ Nguyên Giáp. *People's war, people's army. The Viet Cong insurrection manual for underdeveloped countries*. Forward by R. Hilsman (New York: Praeger, 1962).

Võ Nguyên Giáp. *Unforgettable months and years* (Ithaca, NY: Cornell University Press, 1975).

Võ Nguyên Giáp. *Viet Nam people's war has defeated U.S. war of destruction* (Hà Nôi: Foreign Languages Publishing House, 1969).

Walt, L. W. *Strange war, strange strategy: a general's report on Vietnam* (New York: Funk & Wagnalls, 1970).

Warr, N. *Phase line green. The Battle for Hue, 1968* (Annapolis, MD: Naval Institute Press, 1997).

Wells, T. *The war within: America's battle over Vietnam* (Berkeley, CA: University of California Press, 1994).

Westmoreland, W. C. *A soldier reports* (Garden City, NY: Doubleday, 1976).

Wexler, S. *The Vietnam War: an eyewitness history* (New York: Facts on File, 1992).

Willbanks, J. H. *Thiet Giap! The Battle of An Loc, April 1972* (Fort Leavenworth, KS: The Combat Studies Institute, 1993).

Williams, W. A. (ed.). *America in Vietnam: a documentary history* (Garden City, NY: Anchor/Doubleday, 1985).

Wirtz, J. J. *The Tet Offensive: intelligence failure in war* (Ithaca, NY: Cornell University Press, 1991).

Young, M. B. *The Vietnam Wars, 1945–1990* (New York: HarperCollins, 1991).

Zaffiri, S. *Hamburger Hill, May 11–20, 1969* (Novato, CA: Presidio Press, 1988).

Zaffiri, S. *Westmoreland: a biography of General William C. Westmoreland* (New York: Morrow, 1994).

Zumwalt, E. III and E. R. Zumwalt, Jr. *My father, my son* (New York: Macmillan, 1986).

Zumwalt, E. R., Jr. *On watch: a memoir* (New York: Quadrangle/Times Books, 1976).

Index